T5-AGU-434

The Tales of
HENRY JAMES

VOLUME ONE
1864–1869

EDITED BY
MAQBOOL AZIZ

CLARENDON PRESS
OXFORD
1973

FERNALD LIBRARY
COLBY-SAWYER COLLEGE
NEW LONDON, N.H. 03

PS
2110
F73
vol. 1

Oxford University Press, Ely House, London W.1

GLASGOW NEW YORK TORONTO MELBOURNE WELLINGTON
CAPE TOWN IBADAN NAIROBI DAR ES SALAAM LUSAKA ADDIS ABABA
DELHI BOMBAY CALCUTTA MADRAS KARACHI LAHORE DACCA
KUALA LUMPUR SINGAPORE HONG KONG TOKYO

© *Oxford University Press 1973*

*All rights reserved. No part of this publication may be reproduced,
stored in a retrieval system or transmitted, in any form or by any means,
electronic, mechanical, photocopying, recording or otherwise, without
the prior permission of Oxford University Press*

88255

*Printed in Great Britain by
Northumberland Press Ltd., Gateshead*

ACKNOWLEDGEMENTS

IN THE COURSE OF MY WORK ON THIS VOLUME, I HAVE received advice, help and encouragement from many friends, colleagues and students, to all of whom I am deeply indebted and grateful.

I am particularly grateful to Mr. J. I. M. Stewart, Sir Rupert Hart-Davis and Mr. W. W. Robson, who oversaw the work in a different form and gave many useful suggestions. I record with pleasure my association with Mr. Simon Nowell-Smith from whose characteristic generosity, in dispensing advice and practical help, I have benefited more than I deserved. I thank Mr. F. W. Bateson for many useful suggestions in the early stages of the work.

It is a pleasure to record my thanks to Mr. Alexander R. James, in charge of the Henry James Estate, and to John Farquharson Ltd., the agents for the Estate in Britain, for permission to reproduce some manuscript material. Also, I am grateful to Dr. William H. Bond, the Librarian of the Houghton Library, for similar permission to use manuscript material in the superb Collection of the James Family Papers in that library. The Manuscript and Archive Division of the New York Public Library, Astor, Lenox and Tilden Foundation, very kindly provided microfilms of Henry James's letters to W. C. Church and F. P. Church, and gave permission to quote from the same. For this I am grateful to the library. For permission to quote from manuscript material in the Macmillan Archive in the British Museum, I owe thanks to the Museum's Keeper of Manuscripts.

Information on some matters was very kindly provided by Mr. Alexander P. Clark, Curator of Manuscripts at the Princeton University Library, and by Mr. Alan Jutzi, Assistant Curator of Literary Manuscripts at the Huntington Library, for which I am grateful to both. To the staff of the Bodleian Library, the British Museum, the Houghton Library, the Cambridge University Library, and the Mills Memorial Library, I owe thanks for their unfailing courtesy and help.

I take this opportunity to thank the Canada Council for two research grants which enabled me to give final touches to the work. I am also grateful for the Summer Stipends that were kindly awarded me by the Arts Division of McMaster University.

To my colleague, Dr. Brian John, I owe thanks for many suggestions which helped to improve my small part in the book, the Introduction.

I wish to thank three of my graduate students, Sister Stephanie Vincec, Mrs. Thomi Duncan and Miss Elizabeth Wood for helping me with the proofs and in many other ways. For preparing the typescript, I wish to acknowledge with thanks the remarkable patience of Miss Sheila Ashmore, Mrs. Carolyn Robinson and Mrs. Audrey Alexander of the Department of English at McMaster.

My special thanks are, of course, to Bushi, Ali, Deena and Maaya, who all not only helped in many ways, but also gave support.

Quotations from *Thomas Sergeant Perry*, by Virginia Harlow, and *Life in Letters of William Dean Howells*, edited by Mildred Howells, are by kind permission, respectively, of the Duke University Press and Russell & Russell.

CONTENTS

LIST OF ILLUSTRATIONS

REFERENCES AND ABBREVIATIONS

A Passionate Pilgrim	Henry James, *A Passionate Pilgrim and Other Tales* (Boston: James R. Osgood and Company, 1875).
Stories by American Authors	*Stories by American Authors*, v (New York: Charles Scribner's Sons, 1884).
Stories Revived	Henry James, *Stories Revived*, 3 volumes (London: Macmillan and Company, 1914).
Notes of a Son and Brother	Henry James, *Notes of a Son and Brother* (London: Macmillan and Company, 1914).
Letters	*The Letters of Henry James*, 2 volumes, ed. Percy Lubbock (New York: Charles Scribner's Sons, 1920).
Life in Letters	*Life in Letters of William Dean Howells*, ed. Mildred Howells (New York: Doubleday, Doran, 1928; reissued, 1968, by Russell and Russell). Quotations are from the edition of 1868.
The Art of the Novel	*The Art of the Novel*, Critical Prefaces by Henry James, with an Introduction by R. P. Blackmur (New York: Charles Scribner's Sons, 1934). Quotations are from the paperback edition of 1962.
Perry	Virginia Harlow, *Thomas Sergeant Perry: A Biography*, and Letters to Perry from William, Henry, and Garth Wilkinson James (Durham: Duke University Press, 1950).
Bibliography	Leon Edel and Dan H. Laurence, *A Bibliography of Henry James* (London: Rupert Hart-Davis, 1957; revised, 1961). References are to the edition of 1961.
Atlantic	The *Atlantic Monthly*.

| *Review* | The *North American Review*. |
| *Continental* | The *Continental Monthly*. |

COLLECTED EDITIONS OF JAMES'S TALES AND NOVELS

	Collective Edition of 1883, 14 volumes (London: Macmillan and Company, 1883). 13 tales were included in their first revised state.
New York Edition	*The Novels and Tales of Henry James*, 'New York Edition', 24 volumes (New York: Charles Scribner's Sons, 1907-1909). 55 tales were included in this 'definitive' edition, for which James heavily revised the tales for the last time.
	The Novels and Stories of Henry James, 35 volumes, ed. Percy Lubbock (London: Macmillan and Company, 1921-1923). 95 tales were included in a variety of textual states.
	The Complete Tales of Henry James, 12 volumes, ed. Leon Edel (London: Rupert Hart-Davis, 1962-1964). The text follows the first book editions.

[With one or two exceptions, published letters not available in any regular collection of letters have been quoted from manuscripts, and reference is made to their sources in manuscript collections.]

THE COMPLETE TALES:
A CHRONOLOGICAL LIST

THE 112 TALES OF HENRY JAMES ARE LISTED BELOW IN order of their first publication. The original form of the titles is mentioned. The place and date of publication for each tale is given against the title. A brief parenthetical note identifies the works James did not serialize in magazines but first published in a collection or a book edition. The starred tales were included in the New York edition.

1. 'A Tragedy of Error'   *The Continental Monthly* (1864)
2. 'The Story of a Year'   *The Atlantic Monthly* (1865)
3. 'A Landscape Painter'   (1866)
4. 'A Day of Days'   *The Galaxy* (1866)
5. 'My Friend Bingham'   *The Atlantic Monthly* (1867)
6. 'Poor Richard'   (1867)
7. 'The Story of a Master-   *The Galaxy* (1868)
   piece'
8. 'The Romance of Certain   *The Atlantic Monthly* (1868)
   Old Clothes'
9. 'A Most Extraordinary   (1868)
   Case'
10. 'A Problem'   *The Galaxy* (1868)
11. 'De Grey: A Romance'   *The Atlantic Monthly* (1868)
12. 'Osborne's Revenge'   *The Galaxy* (1868)
13. 'A Light Man'   (1869)
14. 'Gabrielle De Bergerac'   *The Atlantic Monthly* (1869)
15. 'Travelling Companions'   (1870)
*16. 'A Passionate Pilgrim'   (1871)
17. 'At Isella'   *The Galaxy* (1871)
18. 'Master Eustace'   (1871)
19. 'Guest's Confession'   *The Atlantic Monthly* (1872)
*20. 'The Madonna of the   (1873)
    Future'
21. 'The Sweetheart of M.   *The Galaxy* (1873)
    Briseux'
22. 'The Last of the Valerii'   *The Atlantic Monthly* (1874)

INTRODUCTION

DURING HIS LONG AND RICHLY VARIED CAREER HENRY
James published 112 works of short fiction varying in length between
seven and fifty thousand words. All were called 'tales' by James. It
was with one of these that he launched himself as a writer in 1864;
and it was with a collection of these that, a decade later, he made his
first book, *A Passionate Pilgrim*. More than five decades after his
first published tale, the work which closed his career as a writer of
fiction was also a collection of reprinted short stories, *The Uniform
Tales of Henry James*.[1] The first volume of this work appeared in
1915, less than a year before his death. There are only eight years in
the forty-six years of his story-telling when he did not publish any
tale. More than two dozen of the many volumes of fiction published
by James are selections or collections of tales. The 'shorter form',
then, 'the beautiful and blest *nouvelle*', the 'small circular frame',[2]
was no diversion from novel writing: 'to write a series of good little
tales' was, young James once told C. E. Norton, 'ample work for a
lifetime.'[3]

All but nine of the 112 tales were originally published in thirty-
four different periodicals on both sides of the Atlantic. Most were
given book status by James himself, some receiving the honour more
than once, in the collections which he issued from time to time.
Only fifty-five stories, however, found their way into the 'definitive'
New York Edition. Many—but not all—of the pieces 'rejected' were
resurrected by Percy Lubbock in his edition of *The Novels and
Stories of Henry James*. The tales included there number ninety-
five. The stories first appeared in their entirety in *The Complete*

---

[1] (London: Martin Secker, 1915-20). The New York Edition text of thirteen
and one newly revised tale are reproduced in this collection in fourteen
separate volumes.

[2] These and several other terms are used by James to describe his fictions
which do not qualify as novels. But within 'the shorter form' there are other
finer distinctions; these are explored and stated in the Prefaces to the volumes
of tales in the New York Edition. The Prefaces are also available in a separate
volume, *The Art of the Novel*.

[3] Letter of 16 January, 1871, to C. E. Norton. *Letters*, i, p. 31. In a letter to
R. L. Stevenson, dated 31 July, 1888, James reiterated his faith in the shorter
form. He told Stevenson that after *The Tragic Muse*, which he was then writing for the *Atlantic*, 'with God's help, I propose, for a longish period, to do
nothing but short lengths. I want to leave a multitude of pictures of my time,
projecting my small circular frame upon as many different spots as possible
and going in for number as well as quality, so that the number may constitute
a total having a certain value as observation and testimony.' *Ibid.*, p. 138.

Tales of Henry James, edited by Leon Edel.

It was James's lifelong practice to revise his magazine writings for book publication and, not infrequently, the book texts for subsequent reprintings. As a result, most of the tales, as well as many novels and other prose writings, now exist in multiple versions.[4] This textual multiplicity is an aspect which no serious student of James can afford to ignore.[5] In the existing state of the texts, when the multiple versions are scattered in old periodicals and early collections of the stories, it is not easy to assemble different versions of a work together for comparison and examination. This new edition of the tales is designed to meet this difficulty. Its principal aim is to provide the reader with a chronologically consistent text of the tales, together with a complete record of substantive textual variants for the stories revised.

The copy-text for the present edition is the original, serial text of the tales. For those James did not serialize the edition will reprint *their* original form in the book editions. The decision to reprint the original versions has been influenced by a variety of factors which I shall now try to explain. But I should first like to attempt a brief survey of the present state of the texts, and of the problems that are likely to confront an editor looking for a suitable basic text for a complete, chronological edition.

The texts of James's tales are available in the following forms:

A. Manuscripts and typescripts—only seven tales appear to have survived in this form.[6]

B. The serial versions—all but nine tales are available in this state.

C. Manuscript revisions—one complete manuscript revision of a tale and a half-finished revision appear to have survived.[7]

D. The first authorized book versions—eighty-seven tales are available in this state. Most are revised forms of the serial versions.

E. Revised reprints (excluding the New York Edition) of the first book versions—over two dozen tales are available in this state.

---

[4] It is difficult to decide when a new edition of a text becomes a separate version. For the purpose of his essay, however, any new edition of a tale showing substantive variants introduced by James constitutes a new version.

[5] See 'Henry James Reprints' [by Simon Nowell-Smith], the *Times Literary Supplement*, February 5, 1949, p. 96; and my paper ' "Four Meetings"; A Caveat for James Critics' in *Essays in Criticism*, xviii (July 1968), pp. 258-274.

[6] See the *Bibliography*, pp. 390-393.

[7] The only complete manuscript revision of a tale to have survived is that of 'A Light Man'. The incomplete manuscript revision which has been preserved is that of 'At Isella'. This item is not mentioned in the *Bibliography*, but I found six heavily revised magazine pages of the tale in the Houghton Library. One of the pages is reproduced in this edition as an illustration.

F. The New York Edition—fifty-five tales were included in this definitive edition.

If we disregard categories A and C, which are of no relevance to the present purpose, we are left with four categories to choose from. All carry James's authority. As three of the four (D, E and F) do not represent all the tales, they may be considered only as *possible bases* for a copy-text.

Viewed from the author's own point of view, the question as to which of the four has the greater authority poses no serious difficulty. In the New York Edition James has given us a 'definitive' edition of his fiction: if his own wishes are to be respected then the text of the tales in that edition is the one which the editor is obliged to reprint. In other words, if the New York Edition texts are being used as the basis, a new edition of the tales would reprint fifty-five works in that text and the remaining fifty-seven in *their* final form. On the face of it this seems a perfectly sensible approach. But there is an inherent contradiction in it. If the principle behind such a policy is to respect the author's own final plan, then common sense would demand that it be accepted in full—in all its detail. The New York Edition is what it is because of three closely inter-related factors: its particular thematic design, the exclusions and rejections which are an integral part of that design, and the extensive revisions specially carried out to give the whole an overall unity of style and structure.[8] The editor cannot claim superior authority for the definitive text without also accepting the principles of exclusion and revision which give the definitive text that authority. In practical terms, he cannot, without violating James's intention, give the rejected tales the status the author himself wished to deny them.

It could be argued that James excluded many of his stories not because he thought they were of inferior quality, but because he did not have space for them, or they did not seem to belong in the grand design he had in mind. For some tales not included this might well have been the case. However, we do know that the number of volumes for the edition was decided upon by James himself, and he was quite perturbed when his original choice of twenty-three came to be twenty-four.[9] It is difficult to believe that James was not aware of the implications of the limit he so insistently wanted to impose upon the final edition. The limit was, indeed, partly dictated by the fact that he simply could not reread some of his early works.[10]

[8] See Leon Edel, 'The Architecture of Henry James's "New York Edition"', the *New England Quarterly*, xxiv (June 1951), pp. 169-178.
[9] *Ibid.*, pp. 177-178.
[10] *Ibid.*, p. 172.

Therefore, it cannot be denied that critical judgement—'the whole growth of one's "taste"', as James put it[11]—played a large role in his decision to limit the number of stories to be included to fifty-five.

The selections made, James proceeded to consolidate the exclusive design of his plan by giving the selected works a uniform style. The stories and novels, especially of the early and middle periods, were so drastically revised for the edition that, in matters of detail, their 'definitive' form bears little relation to their original, in which many had first seen the light several decades before the New York Edition. The final revision is thus a case of 'renewals of vision', the 'exploring tread' taking the author, not back over 'the original tracks', but forcing him to 'break the surface in other places'.[12]

In short, the form in which the fifty-five tales have been revised and arranged in the definitive edition places them in a class by itself from which, if the wishes of the designer of the edition are to be respected, they may not be disengaged. In any case, the problem of textual and chronological inconsistency is not resolved if we decide to reprint one tale in the high manner of the final phase, one in the 'middle style', and one in its early unrevised state—which is precisely the form the new edition would take with the definitive texts as its textual basis.

This latter difficulty stays with us when we turn to an alternative possibility: an edition based on the final versions of the revised tales —categories E and D—but excluding the New York Edition. As the number of tales to have undergone two separate revisions prior to the definitive edition is rather small, such an edition would once again end up with a text in three different states. Some stories will appear in their unrevised state, some in their first (and only) revised form and some in their second revised form. The stylistic difference, however, will not be as great now as it might be with the New York Edition joining in. The one advantage of this approach is that it strikes a good compromise: while allowing the definitive edition its special status, it offers the tales in a text which would have been their final had James not embarked upon a definitive edition of his writings. The major drawback of this approach, as we have said, is that it too cannot cope with the chronological problem. Also, like the definitive texts, the second revised versions, as well as the first, of some tales are far removed from their originals.

For a revised copy-text, the first book versions—category D—seem to offer a more satisfactory alternative. The arguments in favour of this text are the obvious ones. Other than the serial form, this is the

[11] *The Art of the Novel*, p. 340.
[12] *Ibid.*, p. 336.

text in which *most* tales are available in a, theoretically, uniform state. And in this state the revised works have had the benefit of a revision. An edition based on the first book versions would, therefore, be a much simpler, and, in a sense, more logical affair. A great many of the tales would appear in it in their first (and only) revised form, and some in their unrevised form—only two different texts. But this apparently simple policy is not without its problems, which begin to crop up when we examine the character of the first revision in particular cases. To take one example, James revised and reprinted 'The Romance of Certain Old Clothes' (1868) in his first collection of tales, *A Passionate Pilgrim* (1875). Some years later he revised the 1875 text and reprinted the story in *Stories Revived* (1885). Now, if our reason for reprinting the text of 1875 is that in that form this tale has had the benefit of revision then we must be using the term in a very restricted sense, to mean 'mild alteration'. For the text of 1875 is far more a case of small alterations in several places than of revision proper; it is the text of 1885 which gives us a revised text in any significant sense of the term. If, however, we argue that 'mild alteration' is precisely the sense in which we are applying the term, then what are we to do with tales like 'A Light Man', or 'Poor Richard', the first revised form of which, appearing more than a decade after first publication, is radically different from their original? So it is only in theory that this textual policy promises to offer the whole corpus in two different textual states. In actual fact, because of the varying scale of the first revisions, the final design of an edition based on the first book versions would not be any different from the possibilities considered above.

We may now turn to the last of the four possibilities—category B —the first published versions. This is the only form in which *all* of James's writings are available in an historically, chronologically, and textually uniform state—in which, that is, the texts of the tales are simply there in their right, original order. From a strictly historical point of view, this is the only entirely satisfactory alternative for a complete edition of the tales. Yet, obviously, if we apply the authorial point of view here, as we did while considering the New York Edition texts, it is not. For we cannot now decide to go against James's wishes and select the original form of a work which has been revised by him.

The moral to be drawn from the foregoing is that, if we are looking for a copy-text which does not present any chronological difficulties, has been revised and re-revised to the author's complete satisfaction, does no violence to any other of his plans and intentions, conveys a sense of development, etc., is, in short, satisfactory on all counts, then we are not likely to find one in the maze of James's texts. James revised some of his tales only once, some twice, some three times, and some never at all. The gaps of time, moreover, between different classes of revision, and between the original and revised form, or forms, of individual works range from a month-or-so to thirty-five years. The result of this process of 'fingering' has been a state of textual multiplicity in James to which order can now be given only by an outside hand.[13]

There are, in the final analysis, three courses open to the editor of James—or, for that matter, of any constantly revising author—who wants to make a single-text edition of the tales. All involve the editor's own judgement, choice and decision. He can either approach the question from the author's point of view and, disregarding the demands of history and chronology, prepare an edition based on the final texts; or he can take a purely critical view and, disregarding not only the historical principle but also James's final revisions, base his edition on the versions he considers (from his particular point of view) the best; or he can take the historical approach and, completely ignoring the revisions, make an edition based on the original texts. There is one other solution—and it seems the ideal possibility. The editor can combine the three approaches in a 'variant edition' of the works: an edition based on any one version but providing, within the single framework, all the other available textual evidence.

It is this last course which I have chosen for this edition. The decision to use the serial versions of the tales as the basic text for the edition is based on the theory that the *first published* form, in manuscript or print, of a multiple-version work is the only one which may be said to have the 'right' authority. The manuscript, when it exists, which is not the case with the tales, cannot claim this authority simply because, essentially, it is the author's message to the printer, and remains a private document until it is translated into print and thus allowed to become public. If, however, the author allows the manuscript to circulate in public in that form then the manuscript would obviously have definite priority.

The revised versions cannot make such a claim for different reasons. The creative activity which originates with the inception of a new idea culminates when, having been realized in the

---

[13] The image comes from James himself. Dencombe, the writer in the tale, 'The Middle Years' (1893), 'was a passionate corrector, a fingerer of style; the last thing he ever arrived at was a form final for himself. His ideal would have been to publish secretly, and then, on the published text, treat himself to the terrified revise, sacrificing always a first edition and beginning for posterity and even for the collectors, poor dears, with a second.'

finished artefact, the idea is given to the public. Any authorial alterations or revisions which may appear in a future version of the artefact, following the original event, cannot be considered as anything
but the author's second thoughts, his comment and gloss upon the
published work. No revision of a published work is ever an integral
part of the chain of events which make up the original creative
sequence. All published versions are therefore afterthoughts and
represent a consciousness other than the one which created the
original work. This last remark is of special significance in a consideration of James's multiple-version works, who carried out his
major revisions years after their first publication.

   In making these observations, it is of course not my intention to
suggest that the revised versions of the tales are in any way inferior
in quality, or are less authoritative and representative. The distinction I am proposing is that, while most instances of revision in
James make for better literary effects, in his case—as well as in that
of any other 'revisionist'—a revised version can be said to possess
representative authority only insofar as it represents a *new phase* of
his developing consciousness—'the growth', as James put it, 'of the
immense array of terms, perceptional and expressional'.[14] The alterations in the third text of 'The Madonna of the Future', for instance,
which came in 1879, small though they are, cannot claim to represent the writer who first issued the tale in 1873. The authority likewise of the text of 1879 is fixed in time. In other words, when an
editor is confronted with a multiple-version work, he cannot afford
to think of textual authority in any absolute terms—even the so-
called final version is a tentative final with a compulsive revisionist.
The only textual authority that he can single out and establish is
the 'right' authority of the first published version.

   In view of all these considerations, and because an historical
principle seems to me to be inherent in the idea of a variant edition,
I have decided to reprint the serial texts of the tales. It is, for this
edition, a happy coincidence that in their original form—the form
in which they were known to contemporary readers[15]—most of the
tales have never been reprinted before.

   The serial text is here reprinted without any major editorial interference. The few misprints found have been slightly corrected.

[14] *The Art of the Novel*, p. 339.
[15] In the first decade of his career, James did not publish any volume and
was known to his contemporaries as a writer of magazine stories and novels.
He continued to reach a wider audience through magazines even after his
work began to be reprinted in book editions, simply because the magazines
had a much larger circulation than any of his collections or book editions.

Similarly, missing punctuation marks—for the most part involving commas, dashes for compound words, quotation marks, etc.,—have been supplied where the text appeared to need them. Words and phrases appearing in different form, and in different spelling, at different places ('down stairs', 'down-stairs', 'downstairs'; 'good by', 'good-bye'; 'gaity', 'gayety', etc.,) have all been normalized according to current English usage. Full stops after the titles and section divisions have been deleted. Spaced contractions—*had n't, could n't*, etc.,—which, incidently, disappear in most first book versions but come back in the New York Edition, have also been normalized. In two cases, 'Poor Richard' and 'The Story of a Masterpiece', the notes about the division of the texts into parts, which may have had James's tacit approval but may not have been a feature of the manuscripts, have been preserved. English spellings have been substituted for American, and single quotation marks for double. The illustrations accompanying the original texts are being reproduced.

The small number of serious printing errors would suggest that James, who was then residing not far from the places where his manuscripts were being translated into print, was able to see a good many of the proofs. This conjecture finds support in the few surviving letters to his editors of the period in which he is already seen to be insisting for these.[16]

Since it is difficult to determine the dates of composition for many of the tales, I have decided to follow throughout the chronology of publication. The fourteen tales in this volume are arranged in the order in which they were first published in magazines. Each tale carries a brief headnote which provides its complete publishing history during James's lifetime. Textual variants for the revised tales in this volume will be found in the textual section. The first volume covers the first five years of James's career: it closes with the last tale to be published before the inauguration of the 'international' theme.

2.

A convenient starting-point for a brief chronology of Henry James's early tales is the well-known episode of the eighteen-fifties when the James family left America (New York) on an 'educational'

---

[16] Here, for instance, is a postscript to a letter of 23 October, 1867, to the editor of the *Galaxy*: 'Let me reiterate my request that I see a proof [of 'The Story of a Masterpiece']. This I should particularly like to do.' MS. letter in the W. C. Church Collection in the New York Public Library.

tour of Europe.[17] They left in the summer of 1855—the novelist-to-be was then twelve years of age—and the first round of their visit, which took them to England, Switzerland and France, lasted for three years. The Jameses returned to America in 1858 and settled in Newport, Rhode Island. But within a year, in the autumn of 1859, they retraced their steps to Europe for another round of the process begun in 1855. The second round was a briefer affair and they were back in Newport in the autumn of 1860. From 1860 to 1869, the years in which James launched himself as a writer of fiction and published, among other things, the tales collected in this volume, the Jamses were in New England, residing first in Newport, from where they moved to Boston in 1864, and eventually to Cambridge in 1866.

The tours of the fifties appear to have been conceived by Henry James Senior, in part at least, as an educational experiment. Their purpose was to provide for the four sons and a daughter opportunities for a broad, liberal education, based on the principles of freedom and spontaneity, for which the New York schools and tutors they had been attending were not suitable. In 1855, the boys were old enough to benefit from the large landscape of European history and civilization. The idea was to expose them, in an atmosphere of almost complete freedom and against the fine backdrop of Europe, to the world of experience, of ideas, of art and literature. Whatever its impact on the other three sons, the long-term effect of the experiment on the budding novelist came to be a very happy one: it could be argued that Henry James would not have been the kind of novelist he became without the rich 'impressional harvest' gathered during these years on the continent.[18]

The first significant intimation of young James's active interest in literature comes to us from a letter of this period. Giving an account of her grandsons' interests and occupations in Europe, Henry James Senior had this to report to his mother about 'Harry': 'Harry is not so fond of study, properly so-called, as of reading. He is a devourer of libraries, and an immense writer of novels and dramas. He has

---

[17] There are three fine studies which deal exclusively with early James. From a strictly literary-critical point of view, the pioneer work by Cornelia Pulsifer Kelley, *The Early Development of Henry James* (Urbana: University of Illinois Press, 1930; revised, 1965) is still the most useful; the first volume of Leon Edel's five-volume, definitive biography contains a lot of useful information on the early years of James; on a smaller scale, but also full of information, is Robert C. LeClair's *Young Henry James, 1843-70* (New York: Bookman Associates, 1955).

[18] *Notes of a Son and Brother*, p. 5.

considerable talent as a writer, but I am at a loss to know whether
he will ever accomplish much.'[19] This was in 1857. James's lifelong
friend of the first Newport years, 1858-59, Thomas Sergeant Perry,
in his recollections of that year, also speaks of young James 'as an
uninterested scholar' at school, but one who read, with the others of
the Newport group, 'the English magazines and reviews and the
Revue des Deux Mondes with rapture.'[20]

The undercurrent of anxiety in the father's remark seems to refer
not so much to the habit of reading as such—which was a way of life
with the Jamses—as to young James's passion for a particular kind
of reading—the reading of novels. On their second visit to Europe,
the reader of novels was sent to, of all places, a technical school in
Switzerland. According to James himself, the reason was 'that my
parents had simply said to themselves, in serious concern, that I
read too many novels, or at least read them too attentively—*that*
was the vice....'[21] But the cure of scientific discipline—as that of
the Harvard Law School some years later—did not work and James
continued to be fascinated by the 'product of the press' and 'the life
of letters'.[22]

However, the fascination was not without a purpose—though the
purpose was not immediately apparent to the parents; nor, for that
matter, was it clear to James himself at the time. Attempting to
recollect the state of his mind in those early years, he speaks of the
purpose, significantly, as a 'want': 'I didn't want anything so much
as I wanted a certain good ...What I "wanted to want" to be was,
all intimately, just literary....'[23] It was, then, in order just to be
'literary' that he had been so passionately engaged in reading and
gathering impressions.

From the fragmentary evidence available, it seems the 'want'
began to take a serious turn about the year 1860, when James was
seventeen years of age and the question of a career for himself was
beginning to loom large. In a letter of 28 May, 1860, his younger
brother, Garth Wilkinson James, reported to their friend, T. S. Perry,
in Newport:

Harry has become an author I believe, for he keeps his door
locked all day long, & a little while ago, I got a peep in his room,

[19] MS. letter in the Collection of the James Family Papers in the Houghton
Library.
[20] *Letters*, i, p.7.
[21] *Notes of a Son and Brother*, p. 4.
[22] *Ibid.*, pp. 22, 23.
[23] *Ibid.*, p. 274.

and saw some poetical looking manuscripts lying on the table, &
himself looking in a most authorlike way ... the only difference
there is between Willy [William James] & Harrys labours is that
the former always shows his productions while the modest little
Henry wouldn't let a soul or even a spirit see his.[24]

James's own letter to Perry of two months later takes a playful view
of

Wilkie's foolhardy imprudence in disclosing, as he did, my secret
employment. You ask upon what style of work I am employed. I
may reply that to no style am I a stranger, there is none which
has not been adorned by the magic of my touch. I shall be most
happy to send you fifty copies of each work, the payment of which
can await my return.[25]

These letters were written a few months before the family returned
to America to make a permanent home in New England. The year
1860, thus, marks the end of the family's European wanderings and,
as a consequence, the beginning of a new manner of life for James.
With no immediate prospect of a major upheaval, he was now able
to concentrate on being literary more single-mindedly than he had
done before and, what is more important, was able to share his
literary plans and confidences with companions outside the domestic
circle. The time had come for him to address himself to the whole
question of the significance of the 'impressions':

To feel a unity, a character and a tone in one's impressions, to
feel them related and all harmoniously coloured, that *was* positively to face the esthetic, the creative, even, quite wondrously, the
critical life and almost on the spot to commence author. They had
begun, the impressions—that was what was the matter with them
—to scratch quite audibly at the door of liberation, of extension,
of projection; what they were *of* one more or less knew, but what
they were *for* was the question that began to stir, though one was
still to be a long time at a loss directly to answer it.[26].

The immediate reference in this recollection is, again, to the period
when James was still in Europe but its general relevance to the three
years of vigorous searching which followed cannot be ignored. The
manner in which he proceeded to find an answer to the question—

[24] *Perry*, pp. 249-250.
[25] *Ibid.*, p. 255.
[26] *Notes of a Son and Brother*, pp. 23-24.

'to commence author', that is,—is best summarized by the eyewitness and confidant, T. S. Perry:

> After his return to America in 1860, the question what he should do with his life became more urgent. Of course it was in literature that he took the greatest interest. One task that he set himself was translating Alfred de Musset's 'Lorenzaccio,' and into this version he introduced some scenes of his own. Exactly what they were I do not recall, though I read them with an even intenser interest than I did the original text. He was continually writing stories, mainly of a romantic kind. The heroes were for the most part villains, but they were white lambs by the side of the sophisticated heroines, who seemed to have read all Balzac in the cradle and to be positively dripping with lurid crimes. He began with these extravagant pictures of course in adoration of the great master whom he always so warmly admired.
>
> H. J. seldom entrusted these early efforts to the criticism of his family—they did not see all he wrote. They were too keen critics, too sharp-witted, to be allowed to handle every essay of this budding talent. . . .[27]

Perry does not tell us whether there were any attempts by the 'budding talent' to see his 'efforts' in print. According to James's own recollections, there were at least two rejections before the publication of his first tale in 1864. The first was a translation of a story by Prosper Mérimée, *La Vénus d'Ille*. James was introduced to Mérimée as well as to Balzac by the second of his two cherished companions of the Newport years, John La Farge, 'an artistic, an esthetic, nature of wondrous homogeneity',[28] a 'Franco-American' painter he had met in the studio of William Morris Hunt with whom William James was supposed to be studying art. (It is interesting to note that the 'devourer of libraries', who was also a cosmopolite, did not discover Balzac through his own habit of reading.) The translation was sent 'off to the New York weekly periodical of that age of crudest categories which was to do me the honour neither of acknowledging nor printing nor, clearly, . . . in the least understanding it.'[29]

James's second attempt—treated in the recollections as the first—'to enrol [himself] in the bright band of the fondly hoping and fearfully doubting who count the days after the despatch of manu-

[27] *Letters*, i, p. 8.
[28] *Notes of a Son and Brother*, pp. 85-86.
[29] *Ibid.*, p. 88.

scripts'[30] was a review of a dramatic performance he had seen in Boston. The rendering of a character by Miss Maggie Mitchell, one of the actresses who took part in the play—it was a bad translation of 'a German original'—was so impressive that James 'sat down' to write about it and went on to submit the notice for publication, thus 'formally' addressing himself 'to the profession of literature, though nothing would induce me now to name the periodical on whose protracted silence I had thus begun to hang with my own treasures of reserve to match it.'[31]

Although there is no evidence of other contributions to magazines during the years 1860 to the end of 1863, it is difficult to believe that a devotee of 'the life of letters' such as young James, who was 'continually writing stories' and critical essays, would try only two rather insignificant pieces with magazine editors. Perhaps there were more, failures as well as successes, of which we have no record. The temptation to speculate along these lines is increased by the fact that, while James acknowledges the two rejections and mentions the first published book review in his autobiography, he says nothing about his early tales, except in very general terms. It appears as if a conscious principle of selection is at work in the recollections dealing with the early writings.

In fact, James's recollection of his first getting into print is somewhat confusing, if not misleading. According to the autobiography, 'the plot began most to thicken' with the family's move, 'early in 1864',[32] to the then centre of literary activity, Boston. It was in Boston that he found himself gathering the assurance 'from one day to another that fortune had in store some response to my deeply reserved but quite unabashed design of becoming as "literary" as might be.'[33] What 'fortune had in store' first appeared as 'the entrancing presumption that I should have but to write with sufficient difficulty and sufficient felicity to get once for all (that was the point)

---

[30] *Ibid.*, p. 333.

[31] *Ibid.*, p. 334. This amusing posture is repeated in the unfinished third volume of the autobiography, in reference to an early review of *Felix Holt*: 'I had rejoiced without reserve in Felix Holt—the illusion of reading which, outstretched on my then too frequently inevitable bed at Swampscott during a couple of very hot days of the summer of 1866, comes back to me, followed by that in sooth of sitting up again, at no great ease, to indite with all promptness a review of the delightful thing, the place of appearance of which [it appeared in the *Nation*] nothing could now induce me to name, shameless about the general fact as I may have been at the hour itself. . . .' *The Middle Years* (London: W. Collins Sons & Co.), pp. 62-63.

[32] *Notes of a Son and Brother*, p. 375.

[33] *Ibid.*, p. 376.

into the incredibility of print.'[34] But a work by James had been printed before he appeared on the Boston scene: 'A Tragedy of Error', written apparently in the closing months of 1863, or before, appeared in the *Continental Monthly* in the first week of February.[35] The unsigned story fits Perry's account of James's 'early efforts' in the manner of Balzac.

In 1864, then, the year Hawthorne died, James 'commenced author', found out the value of 'impressions', became at last 'literary'. The reason for sending his first fiction to the *Continental* may have been that a work by a new writer stood a better chance in an equally young periodical than in one of the more established papers. The *Continental* had begun to appear in 1862; its first issue carried an invitation to prospective contributors: '... Write and publish; the public is listening. Now is the time, if it ever was, to develop an American character ... We hope to make a bold step forward, presenting in our columns contributions characterized by vigour, variety, and originality. ...'[36] Although there was nothing American about James's story, it was accepted by the editor, Mrs. Martha Elizabeth Duncan Walker Cook, and published in the second issue of the year in which the journal breathed its last: the *Continental* ceased publication in 1864.

But with the move to Boston the 'plot' had, indeed, begun 'to thicken', bringing much more illustrious outlets than the *Continental* within James's reach. In terms of James's career the move meant, in the first place, the beginning of a new set of very meaningful relations, 'of new appearances' which

> became such a throbbing affair that my memory of the time from the spring of '64 to the autumn of '66 moves as through an apartment hung with garlands and lights ... I literally, and under whatever felt restriction of my power to knock about, formed independent relations—several. ...[37]

The reference here is to the distinguished intellectual circle of Boston and Cambridge of the time—men like Emerson, Longfellow, James Russell Lowell, Oliver Wendell Holmes, Charles Eliot Norton, Edwin Lawrence Godkin, William Dean Howells and, of course, the then editor of the most respected magazine of the time, the *Atlantic Monthly*, James T. Fields. It was in 'the delightful Fields

---

[34] *Ibid.*, p. 377.
[35] The Jameses moved to Boston late in February.
[36] *The Continental Monthly*, i (January 1862), p. 99.
[37] *Notes of a Son and Brother*, p. 376.

salon' that 'the light of literature' was 'invoked' and 'received' by young James when he attended regular gatherings there of the intellectuals, most of whom were contributors to the *Atlantic*. As for the magazine itself, it 'seemed somehow, while the good season lasted, to live with us....'[38]

James's entry into this circle, moreover, coincided with some significant developments in the field of magazine publishing. In order to save the *North American Review* from rapid decline, Norton and Lowell became its editors in 1863; Godkin launched the *Nation*, with Henry James Senior's support, in 1865; Howells, who had been on the staff of the *Nation*, joined the *Atlantic* in 1866; in order to give New York a major monthly of its own, W. C. Church and F. P. Church launched the *Galaxy* in 1866. For a talented young writer, nothing could have been more fortunate than the climate created by these events and the preoccupations of the men behind them. It was indeed as a result of his being a part of this scene— though, contrary to the impression given by the autobiography and other later writings, he developed real affection only for Howells, and was not very fond of any of the magazines—that James gave all his writings from 1864 to 1870 to these magazines.

James had begun to plan a story for the *Atlantic* about the time of the move and the publication of his first tale. The plan had been discussed with Perry, and a version written, sometime before March 1864. In a letter of March 25 James told Perry that he had failed to answer his letters because he had to 'finish a certain task

> ... to rewrite that modern novel I spoke of to you and get it off my hands within a certain number of days ... I failed; still, it is almost finished and will go in a day or two. I have given it my best pains: bothered over it too much. On the whole, it is a failure, I think, tho' nobody will know this, perhaps, but myself. Do not expect anything: it is a simple story, simply told. As yet it hath no name: and I am hopeless of one. Why use that vile word novelette. It reminds me of chemisette. Why not say *historiette* outright? Or why not call it a bob-tail? I shall take the liberty of asking the *Atlantic* people to send their letter of reject. or accept. to you. I cannot again stand the pressure of avowed authorship (for the present.) and their answer could not come here unobserved. Do not speak to Willie of this.[39]

James heard the news of acceptance from Perry sometime between

[38] *Ibid.*, p. 273.
[39] *Perry*, p. 273.

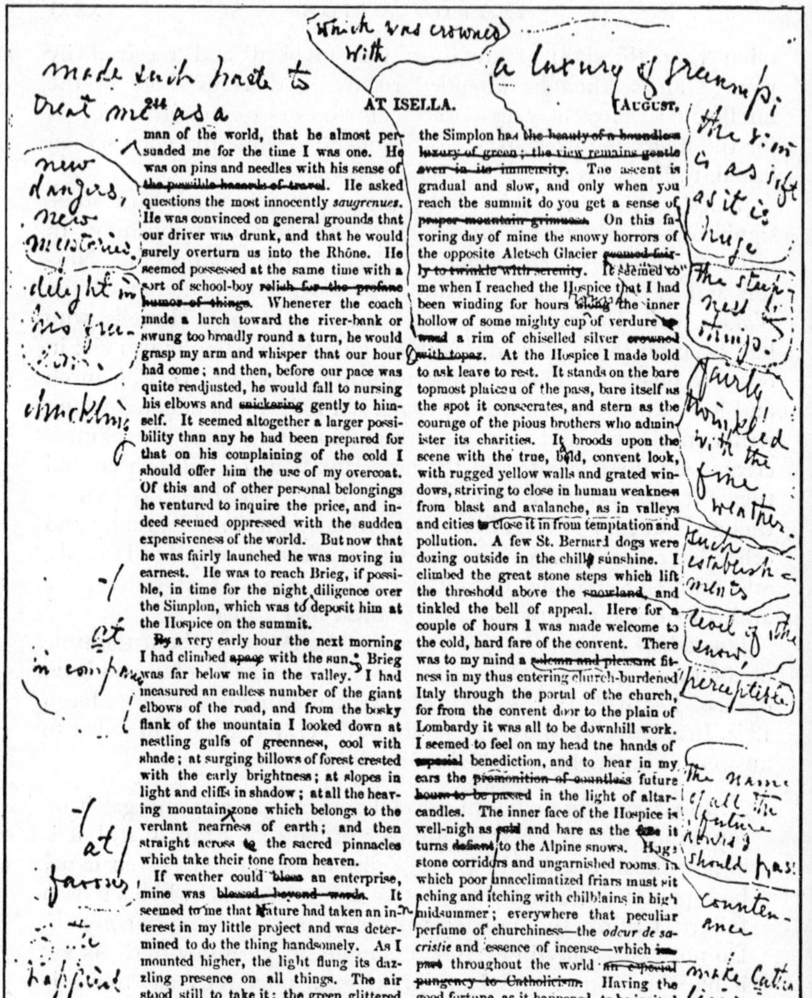

(handwritten above title:) which was crowned with

(handwritten top left:) made such haste to treat me as a

(handwritten top right:) a luxury of greenness

man of the world, that he almost persuaded me for the time I was one. He was on pins and needles with his sense of the possible hazards of travel. He asked questions the most innocently *saugrenues*. He was convinced on general grounds that our driver was drunk, and that he would surely overturn us into the Rhône. He seemed possessed at the same time with a sort of school-boy relish for the profane humor of things. Whenever the coach made a lurch toward the river-bank or swung too broadly round a turn, he would grasp my arm and whisper that our hour had come; and then, before our pace was quite readjusted, he would fall to nursing his elbows and snickering gently to himself. It seemed altogether a larger possibility than any he had been prepared for that on his complaining of the cold I should offer him the use of my overcoat. Of this and of other personal belongings he ventured to inquire the price, and indeed seemed oppressed with the sudden expensiveness of the world. But now that he was fairly launched he was moving in earnest. He was to reach Brieg, if possible, in time for the night diligence over the Simplon, which was to deposit him at the Hospice on the summit.

By a very early hour the next morning I had climbed apace with the sun. Brieg was far below me in the valley. I had measured an endless number of the giant elbows of the road, and from the bosky flank of the mountain I looked down at nestling gulfs of greenness, cool with shade; at surging billows of forest crested with the early brightness; at slopes in light and cliffs in shadow; at all the heaving mountain zone which belongs to the verdant nearness of earth; and then straight across to the sacred pinnacles which take their tone from heaven.

If weather could bless an enterprise, mine was blessed beyond words. It seemed to me that Nature had taken an interest in my little project and was determined to do the thing handsomely. As I mounted higher, the light flung its dazzling presence on all things. The air stood still to take it; the green glittered within the green, the blue burned beyond it; the dew on the forests gathered to dry into massive crystals, and beyond the brilliant void of space the clear snow-fields stood out like planes of marble inserted in a field of lapis-lazuli. The Swiss side of

the Simplon has the beauty of a boundless luxury of green; the view remains gentle even in its immensity. The ascent is gradual and slow, and only when you reach the summit do you get a sense of proper mountain grimness. On this favoring day of mine the snowy horrors of the opposite Aletsch Glacier seemed fairly to twinkle with serenity. It seemed to me when I reached the Hospice that I had been winding for hours along the inner hollow of some mighty cup of verdure crowned a rim of chiselled silver crowned with topaz. At the Hospice I made bold to ask leave to rest. It stands on the bare topmost plateau of the pass, bare itself as the spot it consecrates, and stern as the courage of the pious brothers who administer its charities. It broods upon the scene with the true, bold, convent look, with rugged yellow walls and grated windows, striving to close in human weakness from blast and avalanche, as in valleys and cities to close it in from temptation and pollution. A few St. Bernard dogs were dozing outside in the chilly sunshine. I climbed the great stone steps which lift the threshold above the snowland, and tinkled the bell of appeal. Here for a couple of hours I was made welcome to the cold, hard fare of the convent. There was to my mind a solemn and pleasant fitness in my thus entering church-burdened Italy through the portal of the church, for from the convent door to the plain of Lombardy it was all to be downhill work. I seemed to feel on my head the hands of especial benediction, and to hear in my ears the premonition of countless future hours to be passed in the light of altar-candles. The inner face of the Hospice is well-nigh as cold and bare as the one it turns defiant to the Alpine snows. Huge stone corridors and ungarnished rooms, in which poor unacclimatized friars must sit aching and itching with chilblains in high midsummer; everywhere that peculiar perfume of churchiness—the *odeur de sacristie* and essence of incense—which imparts throughout the world an especial pungency to Catholicism. Having the good fortune, as it happened, to be invited to dine with the Prior, I found myself in fine priestly company. A dozen of us sat about the board in the greasy, brick-paved refectory, lined with sombre cupboards of ponderous crockery, all in stole and cassock but myself. Several of the brothers

(handwritten left margin:) new dangers, new mysteries / delight in his fra... / chuckling / at in company / at farrus / happiest

(handwritten right margin:) the rim is as if as it is huge / the sternness of things / fairly mantled with the fine weather / such establishments / civil of the snow / precipitous / The name of all the future should pass countenance / make Catholicism partly an addr... we chose

(handwritten bottom:) acres of sapphire. / frigid

An example of James's method of revising the serial texts of his writings for book publication. This is a page from the *Galaxy* version of the tale, 'At Isella', with James's revisions in manuscript.

March and October, 1864. His letter to Perry of 28 October begins
with a reference to the news:

> I rec'd. your two letters with great pleasure. The news contained
> in the first was very welcome altho' as you say, 'not unmingled
> with misfortune'. But I suppose I ought to be thankful for so
> much and not grumble that it is so little. One of these days we
> shall have certain persons *on their knees*, imploring for contribu-
> tions.[40]

The passage is followed by a sketch in which a figure representing
the *Atlantic* is seen kneeling before a bearded writer. The exact
nature of the 'misfortune' is not known but it may have had to do
with the fee offered by the magazine; or, perhaps, it had to do with
the absence of enthusiasm on the part of the magazine. It is clear
from the letter, however, that acceptance by the *Atlantic* had a
special value for James. Although no title is mentioned in the letters,
the 'modern novel'—the appearance of the phrase so early is significant—accepted by the *Atlantic* was 'The Story of a Year'. It was
published there in March 1865, more than six months after acceptance.

While 'The Story of a Year' was awaiting publication, James proceeded to try the *North American Review*, with a review of *Essays
on Fiction*, by the distinguished Cambridge economist, Nassau
W. Senior. The letter accompanying the manuscript, dated July 30,
1864, said:

> Gentlemen. I take the liberty of enclosing a brief review of
> Senior's *Essays on Fiction* published in London a few months ago.
> Hoping that you may deem it worthy of a place among your
> Literary Notices, I remain, yours respectfully, HENRY JAMES Jr.[41]

The *Review*'s response was far more encouraging: Norton 'not only
published it in his very next number—the interval for me of breath-
less brevity—but had expressed the liveliest further hospitality, the
gage of which was thus at once his welcome to me at home.'[42]
What the editor said 'at home' was simply that he would be glad to
receive reviews from the young critic. The essay on Senior's book
was published in the October issue of the *Review*. James responded
to Norton's invitation with such enthusiasm—this was the kind of
encouragement he had been waiting for—that for a long time he

---

[40] *Ibid.*, p. 275.
[41] *Selected Letters of Henry James*, ed. Leon Edel (London: Rupert Hart-
Davis, 1956), p. 93.
[42] *Notes of a Son and Brother*, p. 378.

contributed nothing but book reviews, first to the *Review* and later, when Godkin's weekly, the *Nation*, began to appear in July 1865, to that magazine.

By the end of 1864, in short, the 'want' had been fully realized: James had been acknowledged as a literary man by the country's best quarterly of the day and its best monthly. In a letter to William James of February 4, 1865, Perry wrote: '... ask brother Harry to write. If James T. Fields, acting by the advice of C. E. Norton, gives him so much per sheet for everything he writes, let not that restrain him. I will pay him an equal sum if he will only write to me.'[43]

Only one tale by James appeared in 1865—the one he had sent to the *Atlantic* the year before. For almost a year, then, he stayed away from the *Atlantic* and story-telling; when he returned to these, he was already an established critic with no less than fifteen book reviews to his credit. His next tale, 'A Landscape Painter', was published in the *Atlantic* in February, 1866. According to a second-hand report it would appear the story was written some time in the last quarter of 1865 and, probably, had been accepted for publication before the end of the year. The information comes from a casual reference in a letter, of December 1865, by the mother of Steele MacKaye, a Newport friend of Henry and William. Giving news of the James boys to her son in Paris, Mrs. MacKaye wrote: 'We have been to hear Henry James [Senior] lecture on Carlyle. Harry James has written a story for the *Atlantic* called "The Painter's Journal!"'[44] Apparently, Mrs. MacKaye's source of information was the novelist's fond and proud father. It is not known how warmly the new work by James was greeted by 'certain persons' but there is little doubt they were more enthusiastic now than they had been the year before. The *Nation*, however, in the first ever public notice of James, told its readers that its book reviewer had written a 'charming love story'.[45]

Before 'A Landscape Painter' appeared in the *Atlantic*, yet another door seemed to open up for James: invitations to contribute to the *Atlantic*'s new rival, the *Galaxy*, began to go out to distinguished writers in January and February 1866. There is no

[43] *Selections from the Letters of Thomas Sergeant Perry*, ed. Edwin Arlington Robinson (New York: The Macmillan Company, 1929; republished, Michigan: Scholarly Press Inc., 1971), p. 40.

[44] Quoted by Percy MacKaye in the first volume of his two-volume memoir of his father, *Epoch; The Life of Steele MacKaye*, Genius of the Theatre, in Relation to his Times and Contemporaries (New York: Boni and Liveright, 1927), p. 121.

[45] See Appendix ii below.

evidence that James received an invitation, but the fact that his next
fictional bid, 'A Day of Days', was in the hands of the editors before
the appearance of the magazine's first issue on May 1, 1866, would
suggest that, whether he was invited or not, James was quick to
respond to the general call for contributions. The tale was accepted
but the editors suggested some changes before they would print it.
If James had hoped to appear in the first issue of the *Galaxy*, he
must have been disconcerted to find that he was still revising his
tale in the middle of May. 'A Day of Days' was published in the
June issue of the *Galaxy*, after '5 m.s. pages' had been added to the
original manuscript.[46]

Although the editors had some doubts about the original form of
James's first contribution to the *Galaxy*, they wanted him to continue to write for the new magazine. A note to this effect appears to
have followed the acceptance, or publication, of 'A Day of Days'—
and was repeated in the early autumn. James was at Swampscott
(Mass,) at the time, to which 'rural retreat' the family had moved
in May, and was to remain there until November. In his reply to the
second note from W. C. Church, James wrote on October 9, 1866:

> I recd. your letter some days ago; but the accumulation of a num-
> ber of letters upon my hands has prevented my answering it
> earlier. I am surprised that you should be disappointed at not
> hearing from me; insomuch as I have endeavoured to be very
> explicit in my last note—written to you in the beginning of the
> summer—as to my inability to write anything for The Galaxy at
> present. I am compelled, with regret, to repeat the assurance. My
> literary labour at the present moment is almost null and I do not
> hope to add to it for some time to come. I should otherwise be
> very glad to do my best in your service....[47]

While it is true that he contributed nothing to magazines during
the months of May, June and July, the tone of the letter indicates
that he was not very pleased by his first encounter with the magazine and its management. Although he returned to the *Galaxy* with
a story a year and a half later, and continued to write for it, he was
never able to strike a happy relationship with its editors.

But James's relationship with the *Atlantic* was now about to take
a very different, much happier turn. William Dean Howells—'... my
distinguished friend of a virtual lifetime ...'[48]—joined the *Atlantic*

[46] See footnote on page 88 below.
[47] MS. letter in the W. C. Church Collection in the New York Public Library.
[48] *Notes of a Son and Brother*, p. 408.

as its assistant editor in March, 1866. He had accepted the offer in February, the month in which the *Atlantic* carried 'A Landscape Painter' by James. And he must have read 'The Story of a Year' in the same magazine a year before. By the end of February Howells was already in Boston, looking for 'lodgings at Cambridge'.[49] It is about this time that the two are likely to have met each other for the first time; though their close friendship began in November, when the Jameses returned from Swampscott and took up residence in Cambridge. By December, Howells was having lengthy conversations with James on the art of fiction. In a letter of December 5, 1866, he wrote to his friend, the New York poet, Edmund Clarence Stedman:

> Talking of talks: young Henry James and I had a famous one last evening, two or three hours long, in which we settled the true principles of literary art. He is a very earnest fellow, and I think extremely gifted—gifted enough to do better than any one has yet done toward making us a real American novel. We have in reserve from him a story for the *Atlantic*, which I'm sure you'll like.[50]

The occasion referred to in the letter is an important date in James's early development. If Howells spoke to James in terms similar to the ones in the letter, then one can imagine the effect the experience must have had on James. This was the first time he was being received by an editor with discerning praise for his *fiction*—an editor, moreover, who seemed to share his critical and creative preoccupations. The talk led to almost daily conversations between the two men on the art of fiction.[51] Both were cosmopolites, were roughly of the same age, and were passionately interested in fiction and the future of American letters.

---

[49] *Life in Letters*, i, p. 106.

[50] *Ibid.*, p. 116.

[51] The last things Howells wrote before his death in 1920 were two papers on James which he was never able to finish. In the opening paragraph of one of these he tries to recapture the manner of their early meetings and conversations: 'It is not strange that I cannot recall my first meeting with Henry James, or for that matter the second or third or specifically any after meeting. It is so with every acquaintance, I suppose. All I can say is that we seemed presently to be always meeting, at his father's house and at mine, but in the kind Cambridge streets rather than those kind Cambridge houses which it seems to me I frequented more than he. We seem to have been presently always together, and always talking of methods of fiction, whether we walked the streets by day or night, or we sat together reading our stuff to each other; his stuff which we both hoped might make itself into matter for the *Atlantic Monthly*, then mostly left to my editing by my senior editor Mr. Fields.' *Ibid.*, ii, p. 397.

There are two candidates for the tale 'in reserve' mentioned in the letter to Stedman: 'My Friend Bingham', which appeared in March 1867, and 'Poor Richard', which appeared in three instalments in June, July and August. Although first to appear after James's return from Swampscott, 'My Friend Bingham' does not seem to be the work Howells was referring to. For there is another reference to a James tale in a similar state which points fairly definitely to 'Poor Richard'. In a letter of December 25, some two weeks after Howells's letter to Stedman, Mrs. Henry James wrote to Alice James:

> Harry's story has been pushed out, much to Mr. Fields' annoyance, by *Catherine Morne* (Miss Palfrey's story) which was accepted with the understanding that it was to be only in three parts. It now turns out to be thrice that length or more; and as it is very dull Mr. Fields has requested Miss Palfrey to close it at once; but she declines to do so—so Harry has to wait some months longer. He seems very indifferent about it.[52]

Again there is no mention of a title. But the fact that the first instalment of 'Poor Richard' began in June, immediately after the last instalment of *Katherine Morne* (by the 'Author of "Herman"') in May, would suggest that 'Poor Richard' was the tale that had to be placed in reserve because of lack of space. Unlike 'My Friend Bingham', 'Poor Richard needed more than one issue.

In his well-known essay on James of 1882, Howells mentions 'Poor Richard' as the first work by James he saw in manuscript:

> It was during ... three years of his Cambridge life that I became acquainted with his work. He had already printed a tale—'The Story of a Year'—in the *Atlantic Monthly*, when I was asked to be Mr. Field's assistant in the management, and it was my fortune to read Mr. James's second contribution in manuscript. 'Would you take it?' asked my chief. 'Yes, and all the stories you can get from the writer.' ... The story was called 'Poor Richard,'...[53]

This, of course, is not a completely accurate account of James's contributions to the *Atlantic* before Howells was asked to give opinion on 'Poor Richard'. James had published two tales in the *Atlantic* by the time Howells joined the magazine, and had sent one essay, his first full-length paper, 'The Novels of George Eliot', from his sum-

[52] MS. letter in the Collection of the James Family Papers in the Houghton Library.
[53] 'Henry James Jr.,' The *Century Illustrated Monthly Magazine*, iii (November 1882), p. 25.

mer retreat which had appeared in its October issue. In fact, as by August Fields was consulting his assistant on manuscripts, Howells may even have read the essay in manuscript. But there is no doubt 'Poor Richard' was the first *tale* by James he saw in manuscript.

Apparently, James had been working on 'Poor Richard'—his longest, most ambitious and impressive work to date—during the summer, when his 'literary labour' had been otherwise 'almost null'. When he returned from Swampscott in November, he mentioned the work to Howells who invited the manuscript and, after reading it, praised it to Fields and the author. James's own brief account of the matter seems to agree with some such sequence. He speaks of 'having (and, as I seem to remember, at his positive invitation) addressed the most presuming as yet of my fictional bids to my distinguished friend of a virtual lifetime', and of receiving 'his glittering response after perusal'.[54]

Within weeks after the acceptance of 'Poor Richard', James was ready with another work for his new friend. He brought a manuscript to Howells late in December, or early in January, 1867. The work had already been mentioned to Fields. On January 4, 1867, Howells wrote to Fields:

> Mr. James has given me the manuscript of a story about which he has already spoken to you, and I find it entirely acceptable. If you haven't made up the March number entirely yet, wouldn't it be well to get this story into it? I send you the manuscript in order that you may look at it if you like. The title is of course to be changed.[55]

Once again there is no mention of a title. But the fact that there *is* a short tale, 'My Friend Bingham', by James in the March (1867) issue of the *Atlantic* helps to identify the tale. As the letter shows, Howells wanted the tale to appear in March; here was a good opportunity for him to reduce the embarrassment of having to make James wait for the publication of his first major work for seven months. Thus, though written, or completed, after 'Poor Richard', 'My Friend Bingham' preceded that work in print. Whether or not the present title is the one James gave the story could be known only by looking at the manuscript which has not survived. The *Nation* took notice of James's new fiction to appear after a gap of nine

---

[54] *Notes of a Son and Brother*, pp. 407-408.

[55] James C. Austin, *Fields of the Atlantic Monthly*, Letters to an Editor, 1861-1870 (San Marino: The Huntington Library, 1953), p. 148. The date on the letter, January 1866, is obviously a slip: Howells joined the *Atlantic* in the spring of that year. The correct date must be 1867.

months. It praised the tale and described the author as one who could deal with 'complexities of feeling' with 'marked skill'.

But Howells had pinned his hope of securing a reputation for James on 'Poor Richard'. The *Nation* commented on the tale as the instalments began to come out; the first notice was quite favourable, but then the reviewer changed his tune and ended up by attacking the work in rather strong terms. Howells, who rightly felt he had discovered a talent, did not like the criticism. On August 10, 1867, he wrote to Norton:

> Harry James has written us another story, which I think admirable; but I do not feel sure of the public any longer, since the *Nation* could not see the merit of *Poor Richard*. It appeared to me that there was remarkable strength in the last scenes of the story; and I cannot doubt that James has every element of success in fiction. But I suspect that he must in a great degree create his audience. In the meantime I rather despise existing readers.[56]

Although his reaction was exaggerated, Howells once again showed that he had a clear perception of the nature of James's art, and its future.

However, undisturbed by any criticism, and inspired by his frequent dialogues with Howells on the art of fiction, James now began to concentrate his attention on writing tales. He had at least three new tales ready for publication by the end of the year. In fact, eight of the fourteen tales he published in the first five years of his career were written within a period of some eighteen months during the years 1867 and 1868. Six of these were published in 1868.

The new work Howells had received when he wrote the letter to Norton was 'The Romance of Certain Old Clothes'. Like 'Poor Richard', it had to wait for six months before it could be printed, in the February issue of the *Atlantic* in 1868. In the meantime, James had another story completed, 'The Story of a Masterpiece', which he may have wanted to publish in the *Atlantic* but could not simply because the magazine already had one in reserve. The *Galaxy* now seemed an obvious alternative (the *Nation* and the *Review* did not publish fiction); and, as Howells was to say to James on a later date, that it was 'good policy for [him] to send something to the *Galaxy* now and then',[57] he may in fact have encouraged James to send the tale to the *Galaxy*.

The manuscript of 'The Story of a Masterpiece' was despatched

[56] *Life in Letters*, i, pp. 117-118.
[57] *Ibid.*, p. 141.

to the *Galaxy* in September. For two weeks there was no answer. On October 2, 1867, James wrote to F. P. Church:

> I sent you a fortnight ago a letter and a m.s. in different packages. As I have received no answer as yet, I am afraid one or the other has miscarried—if not both. Or perhaps your answer has gone astray. If the m.s. has reached you—a story with my name inscribed—I beg you will let me know at your earliest convenience.[58]

The letter brought a prompt reply, and a cheque. But once again the editors wanted him to make some, this time quite uncalled-for, alterations in the text before they would print the tale. On October 23, James wrote back to say that he was pleased the tale was being printed 'all at once'; but that he thought the story was more dramatic as he had 'left it' than it might be with a 'positive statement' about a marriage at the end. The tale was published, not 'all at once' but in two instalments, in January and February, 1868; and the 'positive statement' did appear in the first published version.

While both 'The Romance of Certain Old Clothes' and 'The Story of a Masterpiece' are quite definitely of 1867, no such claim can be made about the chronology of James's next four tales. As far as I know, there are no useful allusions to these in contemporary documents. Two of the four were published in the *Galaxy* and two in the *Atlantic*, all came out within a short span of four months, between April and July, 1868. The next in order of publication, 'A Most Extraordinary Case', which appeared in the *Atlantic* of April, seems to be the only one which may have been written in the autumn of 1867. The other three—'A Problem' (June, the *Galaxy*), 'De Grey: A Romance' (July, the *Atlantic*), and 'Osborne's Revenge' (July, the *Galaxy*)—are, perhaps, of early 1868. On March 27, 1868, when at least one or two of the four tales, if not all, must have been placed with magazines, James told Perry, who was then in Europe, how he had been spending his time. The letter is of some interest:

> I write little & only tales, which I think it likely I shall continue to manufacture in a hackish manner, for that which is bread. They *cannot* of necessity be very good; but they *shall not* be very bad.[59]

In 1868 James was twenty-five years of age. He had already made a mark on the literary scene of Boston and New York, and had

---

[58] MS. letter in the W. C. Church Collection in the New York Public Library.
[59] *Perry*, p. 288.

derived all the value he could from 'the impressional harvest'. Sometime during the years 1867 and 1868, the need to renew 'the vision
of Europe'—the Europe he had left in 1860 with a host of impressions, hoping they would find him a future in the literary art—began
to be felt all over again. By the end of 1868, James had made definite
plans to revisit the Old World. He left America on his first independent tour of Europe in February, 1869. But before he left he
managed to add two more tales to the output of 1868, 'A Light Man'
and—as if to wind up the cycle begun with a Balzacian narrative
set in France—'Gabrielle De Bergerac', a lengthy romance, also set
in France.

There is evidence to suggest that both tales were written before
the trip. On November 12, 1868, Howells wrote to Norton: 'Harry
James has just been ... here and left the manuscript of a story
which he read me a week ago—the best thing, as I always say, that
he has done yet. He seems in firmer health than ever, and is full of
works and purposes.'[60] James was now regularly reading his new
stories to Howells, as the latter was his to James; and it had become
the assistant editor's practice to procure manuscripts from James of
works, he felt, would 'make matter for the *Atlantic*'. It would appear,
therefore, that the manuscript mentioned in the letter had been
accepted for publication. If so, it must refer to 'Gabrielle De
Bergerac' which appeared in three instalments, July, August and
September, in 1869. There is no other tale by James in the *Atlantic*
between November 1868 and July 1869. If these surmises are right,
then 'Gabrielle De Bergerac' was completed nine months before its
publication.

'A Light Man', too, is mentioned in a letter, of a later date, by
Howells. Howells had heard the tale, if not seen the manuscript,
before its appearance, also in July 1869, but in the *Galaxy*. The
letter this time is to Henry James, then in Europe. Howells began
the letter on June 28, 1869, but could not finish it before July 24,
which is the date on the last instalment. It is in the June part of the
letter that Howells refers to 'A Light Man':

> You see that although you had used me very ill in not writing me
> sooner, my resentment was all melted away by the air of home-
> sickness in your letter, and for a day I really flattered myself that
> there was some reason why you should be so fond of me. But that
> is past now, and the Light Man himself could not address you
> more coldly than this husband and father. I don't know but I've
> got a touch of that diarist's style [the tale is in the form of a

[60] *Life in Letters*, i, p. 137.

diary] I confess the idea of him fascinated me. He's one of your best worst ones; and I'm sorry we hadn't him for the *Atlantic*; though it is good policy for you to send something to the *Galaxy* now and then.[61]

Although the two letters do not help to determine the order in which the two tales may have been composed, it is clear both were written before James left for Europe. If the work mentioned in the letter to Norton is indeed 'Gabrielle De Bergerac', then it is reasonable to assume that 'A Light Man' was written sometime between October 1868 and January 1869. There was, in fact, one more piece which James sent to the *Galaxy* before his departure; it was a short play, his first, called 'Pyramus and Thisbe', which preceded 'A Light Man' in the *Galaxy* of April.

It was 'Gabrielle De Bergerac'—which closes this phase in the sense that it continued to appear for two months after 'A Light Man'—which brought James his first popular success. The tale was universally liked. Even before it came out in print, Howells was telling James, in the first instalment of the letter mentioned above, 'that *Gabrielle De Bergerac* is thought well of by those whose good opinion ought not to be of any consequence, but is.'[62] In the July instalment, he added: 'Your story is universally praised, and is accounted the best thing you've done. There seems at last to be a general waking-up to your merits; but when you've a fame as great as Hawthorne's, you won't forget who was the first, warmest and truest of your admirers, will you?'[63] And when he finally managed to end the letter, he again referred to the story: 'I've read the last proof of your *Gabrielle* and it's really magnificent, as Mrs. Howells, a very difficult critic, declares.'[64] To his chief he reported, before the final instalment of the tale was out, that 'Harry James's story is a great gain upon all that he's done before, in the popular estimation.'[65]

When these tidings reached James on the other side of the Atlantic, his status as a man of letters had already been confirmed. He had been introduced as a writer to such literary celebrities of the day as George Eliot, Ruskin, Tennyson, William Morris, Leslie Stephen and many others. He was author of fourteen tales, fifty-six critical papers and one short play. In his critical papers, he had passed

[61] *Ibid.*, pp. 140-141.
[62] *Ibid.*, p. 141.
[63] *Ibid.*, p. 144.
[64] *Ibid.*, p. 146.
[65] *Ibid.*, p. 149.

judgement on Richardson, Scott, Arnold, Whitman, George Eliot, Mrs. Gaskell, Swinburne, Morris, Anthony Trollope, Goethe, Victor Hugo, George Sand, Sainte-Beuve, and, of course, on many lesser writers.

A Passionate Pilgrim and *Stories Revived*: The Revisions

With two exceptions, the history of James's writings after 1869 is not within the scope of this essay. The exceptions are the publication of his first selection of tales, *A Passionate Pilgrim*, in 1875, and that of a three-volume collection, *Stories Revived*, a decade later. Six of the fourteen tales included in the present volume were revised and reprinted in these two collections.

James returned to America in the spring of 1870 to spend another two years in Cambridge in which he published the first two of his 'international' tales and his first short novel, *Watch and Ward*. He was back in Europe in the spring of 1872, this time on a commission to write a series of papers on European places for the *Nation*. Apparently, he discussed the possibility of bringing out a selection of his tales with Howells and the Boston firm of Osgood and Company while he was still in Cambridge, although no decision appears to have been taken then. The matter was revived in 1873. In a letter of January 14, Henry James Senior wrote to his son saying that Howells was 'clear that you ought to publish a volume under the title of *Romances* ... I told him I would communicate with you at once ... I can help you if you are disposed to publish a selection of your tales. I think it would be a good thing for you to do, and Willy also is clear about it.'[66] And, without waiting to hear from his son, he went ahead and had a talk with Osgood. On March 4, he reported to his son that he had been

> ... to see Osgood about publishing a selection from your Tales. He repeated what he told you: that he would give you fifteen per cent, do all the advertising etc., you paying for the plates: or he would pay everything and give you *ten* per cent on every copy sold after the first thousand. I shall be willing (in case you would like to publish, and I think it is time for you to do so) to bear the expense of stereotyping, and if you will pick out what you would like to be included, we shall set to work at once, and have the book ready by next autumn.[67]

[66] MS. letter in the Collection of the James Family Papers in the Houghton Library.

[67] MS. letter in the Collection of the James Family Papers in the Houghton Library. James did not pay for the plates.

James's answer came in a letter to his mother of March 24. He requested his mother to thank his father

> ... for his trouble in discussing with Osgood the matter of my bringing out a volume. He mentioned it some time since, and it has been on my mind to respond. Briefly, I don't care to do it, just now. I value none of my early tales enough to bring them forth again, and if I did, should absolutely need to give them an amount of verbal retouching which it would be very difficult out here to effect. What I desire is this: to make a volume, a short time hence, of tales on the theme of American adventurers in Europe, leading off with the *Passionate Pilgrim*. I have three or four more to write: one I have lately sent to Howells and have half finished another. They will all have been the work of the last three years and be much better and maturer than their predecessors....[68]

The letter was written from Rome. By the time James returned home, in the autumn of 1874, he had produced enough 'international tales' to make a volume 'on the theme of American adventurers in Europe'. He made a selection and his first book came out in January, 1875. Its publication coincided with the appearance, in the *Atlantic*, of the first instalment of his first full-length novel, *Roderick Hudson*.

The volume contained six tales. Five of these, all dealing with the newly discovered subject of the cultural contrast, were of the early seventies. The one exception was 'The Romance of Certain Old Clothes', of 1867, a tale of the supernatural set in eighteenth-century Massachusetts. Its presence in an otherwise, thematically, uniform collection is difficult to explain as its only qualification as an 'international' story is that a major character in it happens to be an Englishman. However, although there were enough tales about to make a collection of six tales on the international theme, James chose to revive this early romance. In order to do so, he used the serial version to prepare a new text of the tale for the book. The serial version was substantively revised in more than fifty places, and so was the punctuation. Though relatively slight on the whole, the revision is not without interest. Needless to add, James gave the same treatment to all the other tales included in *A Passionate Pilgrim*. From now on the practice of revising was to become a regular habit with him.

The other five tales from the early phase came up for revision a decade later, when they were reprinted, one ('A Light Man') in

[68] MS. letter in the Collection of the James Family Papers in the Houghton Library.

Stories by American Authors, and four in *Stories Revived*. While it could be argued that the re-introduction of 'The Romance of Certain Old Clothes', as well as the *first* reprinting of 'A Light Man' in *Stories by American Authors*, was motivated primarily by James's critical interest in the tales, the same cannot be said of the four pieces first reprinted in *Stories Revived*.

James reprinted 'A Light Man' in response to an invitation from Scribner's to contribute a tale to their series *Stories by American Authors*. Most other writings appearing in the series were not very distinguished; this may have influenced James's decision, who was an acknowledged master by 1884, to select an early favourite to represent him in the series. Once again, James revised the serial text to prepare a new version of the tale for its first book appearance. But this revision was drastic; over five hundred new readings were introduced into the text reprinted in the fifth volume of *Stories by American Authors*, published in the summer of 1884. In most matters of detail the two versions of 'A Light Man' have very little in common.

Some months following the publication of the first revised version of 'A Light Man', there appeared in America a collection of new tales by James. It was called by the name of one of the five tales included in it, the leading piece being 'The Author of Beltraffio'.[69] James wanted the collection to appear in England, and so wrote about the possibility to his principal English publisher, Macmillan and Company. *Stories Revived*—where 'A Landscape Painter', 'A Day of Days', 'Poor Richard', and 'A Most Extraordinary Case' were reprinted for the first time, and where 'The Romance of Certain Old Clothes' and 'A Light Man' made their second book appearance— grew out of this proposal.

In a letter of January 2, 1885, James proposed to Macmillan a two-volume collection of tales based on *The Author of Beltraffio*, etc. He wanted to retain four of the five items in the American edition of this volume, but, as he told his publisher, to 'an English book' he 'should propose to add two other tales'.[70] The proposed additions were the newly revised 'A Light Man' and the equally newly revised, but for a second time, 'A Passionate Pilgrim'.[71] The letter went on to outline a financial arrangement by which James

---

[69] *The Author of Beltraffio, Pandora, Georgina's Reasons, The Path of Duty, Four Meetings* (Boston: James R. Osgood and Company, 1885).

[70] MS. letter in the Macmillan Archive in the British Museum.

[71] The second (1875) text of 'A Passionate Pilgrim' was heavily revised and reprinted in *The Siege of London; The Point of View; A Passionate Pilgrim* (Leipzig: Bernhard Tauchnitz, 1884).

hoped to get a good profit. Before the week was out, he was think-ing in terms of a three-volume collection and had 'material' ready for the third volume: on January 7, he wrote to Macmillan that he could 'without difficulty supply plenty of copy for 3 volumes',[72] and that he was sending the material over. By the end of the month it had been agreed that, instead of the two-volume collection origin-ally proposed by James, in order to issue *The Author of Beltraffio*, etc., in England, Macmillan would publish a three-volume collec-tion of James's tales. It was as a result of this change in plans, largely influenced by financial considerations, that eight more early tales got the chance to be revised and reprinted.

However, the fourteen tales selected had never before appeared in England. All were first serialized in America; seven had already received book status there; the remaining were being reprinted now for the first time. Only four—the ones taken from the American edition of the latest volume—were of recent origin; the others, as the 'Notice' prefixed to the first volume said, were of a 'venerable age'. James gave the collection a title on January 28 when he wrote to Macmillan: '... the best I can think of is "Stories Revived" (not revised) which is a fair general description of them and what I have done to them and does not seem to me amiss. "Stories Late and Early" is the next best, but not, I think, so good and all other titles I have been able to think of are wanting in simplicity ... I recom-mend printing on the title page of each volume (in the French manner) the contents of the same....'[73]

What he had 'done to them' was that he had revised them—re-vised them with the kind of freedom with which he had lately handled 'A Light Man'. In fact, the 'revisionary' impulse was so strong this time that even 'A Light Man', revised only the year before, could not escape further retouching, in some thirty places, on the text of 1884. On the other hand, 'The Romance of Certain Old Clothes', another work with prior revision, was treated differ-ently. Since more time had elapsed between its first revision and the present occasion, the tale underwent, on the text of 1875, a more minute and extensive revision. And for the same reason, 'A Land-scape Painter', 'A Day of Days', 'Poor Richard', and 'A Most Extra-ordinary Case', none of which had been reprinted before, were also revised very extensively. In the case of all these, James used their serial texts as his copy to prepare new versions for book publica-tion.

[72] MS. letter in the Macmillan Archive in the British Museum.
[73] MS. letter in the Macmillan Archive in the British Museum.

No other tale from the first fourteen was reprinted during James's lifetime.

3.

No reader can fail to notice that the tales James produced in the first five years of his career are a gathering of remarkable variety and diversity. The series opens with a tragedy of error and closes with an historical romance set in France. In between, there are two tales about artists, three different versions of the supernatural theme, three pieces of private action set against the turbulence of the American Civil War, one tale dealing with a curious homosexual relationship,[74] and two very different tales which try to explore the effects of chance encounters on human relationships.

The narrative techniques employed to tell the tales are equally various. 'A Tragedy of Error' is told by a controlled first-person narrator; the first-person narrator of 'The Story of a Year' likes to comment on the action in a comic-ironic vein; 'A Landscape Painter' is set in the framework of a diary and has two first-person narrators; 'My Friend Bingham' employs an active first-person narrator; 'A Light Man', clearly and deliberately conceived as a rejoinder to Browning's poem 'A Light Woman', comes in the form of a journal; the narrative mode of 'Gabrielle De Bergerac' is an early experiment in narrative time and perspective; the other tales are carefully executed studies in 'point of view'. In short, the tales amply justify the very precise image James himself used, some five decades later, to describe his early efforts in the shorter form. Before *Roderick Hudson*, he wrote, he 'had but hugged the shore on sundry previous small occasions; bumping about, to acquire skill, in the shallow waters and sandy coves of the "short story"....'[75]

There was, however, a conscious design to James's 'bumping about': his was not the case of the writer who must start from scratch to find his way, often painfully, to his chosen art. In theory at least, most of the fine points of the skill James was in the process of 'acquiring' were already known to him when he began to write fiction. He knew, perhaps a little too well, the limits and possibilities of the art of fiction. The fact is worth emphasising, as in our ability to take a full measure of it lies the essential value of the early tales as tales, and their significance in relation to James's later development.

[74] 'A Light Man'; the homosexual element disappears in the revised version.
[75] *The Art of the Novel*, p. 4.

His aim was to counter, through precept as well as example, the lawlessness, as he tended to see it, of much fiction being produced at the time in English. A glimpse of the nature of his concern can be taken from the opening paragraph of his first published critical paper, the review of Nassau W. Senior's *Essays on Fiction*. The essay was written when the reviewer was author but of one short tale:

> We opened this work with the hope of finding a general survey of the nature and principles of the subject of which it professes to treat. Its title had led us to anticipate some attempt to codify the vague and desultory canons, which cannot, indeed, be said to govern, but which in some measure define, this department of literature. We had long regretted the absence of any critical treatise upon fiction. But our regret was destined to be embittered by disappointment.[76]

In this tone, through a discussion of Senior's ability as a critic and of the relative merits of his 'five authors'—Scott, Bulwer, Thackeray, Mrs. Stowe and Colonel Senior ('We are at a loss to understand this latter gentleman's presence in so august a company ... we believe him to be a relative of the author.')—the reviewer goes on to lament the absence, on the part of readers, writers and critics alike, of any serious view of the art of fiction.

This lament, often appearing as advice, admonition or ridicule, is the keynote of the many reviews of novels which followed the first paper. All of them show that the young critic had, indeed, read 'too many novels, or at least read them too attentively....' In fact, a comprehensive theory of fiction could be assembled from the asides and digressions through which James expresses his own views on the art of the novel. Such a theory would treat the following five as cardinal virtues: a habit of serious thought, a moral sense which is not obtrusive, a sense of form and structure, a sense of style, and a sense of character. Most of the young critic's victims possessed none of these virtues; all, particularly the American lady novelists, miserably failed on the most central of the five: the sense of form and structure. The four who seemed to pass on all counts were Balzac, George Eliot, George Sand and Mrs. Gaskell. Even Dickens failed.

James's own tales of the period are a product of his critical imagination. They are the work of a dedicated reader and critic of fiction, not of a man who has a unique vision of life to communicate. The tales were written by the spirit of Balzac in him, and a part of

[76] *Notes and Reviews* by Henry James, with a Preface by Pierre De Chaignon La Rose (Cambridge, Mass., Dunster House, 1921), p. 1.

their function was to support him in his other capacity—as a budding Sainte-Beuve.[77]

To say this is not to suggest that the tales are laboratory pieces
with no intrinsic merit. The merit is very much there, but it is rooted
in the critical context, the purpose of which is to give the art of
fiction a measure of dignity by showing that a serious concern for
technique and form is as essential to *this* art as it is to the writing
of poetry and drama. Indeed, the variety of technical and formal
interest, which is such an outstanding feature of the tales, and the
subtle manner by which young James is able to draw meaning and
significance out of what are essentially, but deliberately, rather small
occasions, both are virtues which owe their existence to the Sainte-
Beuve in James.

Yet, it is also a source of the tales' principal weakness, and becomes, in the larger context of James's future development, the
characteristic weakness of his art. The preoccupation with 'doing the
thing', especially when it goes with a temperament predisposed to
seeing the turning-world from a still-point, and with subjects which
are imagined rather than lived or observed (as is the case with most
of the tales), tends to reduce the experience narrated to, as one of
the titles has it, 'a most extraordinary case'. The critical imagination seems to keep such a hold on the creative springs that life,
the human aspect in fullness of the situations, is not allowed to
filter through the other, though quite genuine, considerations of the
art. It is interesting to note that in his final phase James tended to do
quite the reverse. Though small, the situations presented in the early
tales are drawn from common human experience, but have been
turned into 'cases'. The situations in some of the late tales and
novels are entirely fanciful—*The Golden Bowl* is a classic example
—but, through an art which has the unique ability to make highly
convincing and profoundly significant mountains out of molehills,
have been infused with meaning and life.

Apparently, young James was aware of his present difficulty and
knew where the problem lay. He had been relying too much on the
windows through which it had become a habit of his mind—and
continued to be so—to observe the world. (He was not only familiar
with 'The Lady of Shalott', but had written his own version of it in

[77] In 1867 James wrote to his friend Perry: 'Deep in the timorous recesses
of my being is a vague desire to do for our dear old English letters and writers
something of what Ste. Beuve & the best French critics have done for theirs.
For one of my calibre it is an arrogant hope. *Aussi* I don't talk about it.'
Perry, p. 284. He had, of course, been doing the Sainte-Beuve for quite some
time.

the tale, 'A Day of Days'.) In 1867, he wrote to his friend Perry:
'... there will be nothing so useful to me as the thought of having
companions and a labourer with whom I may exchange feelings and
ideas. It is by this constant exchange & comparison, by the wear and
tear of living & talking & observing that works of art shape themselves into completeness; and as artists and workers, we owe most to
those who bring to us most of human life.'[78]

James was being his most perceptive and just critic when he told
the same friend, a year later, that he had been writing tales which
cannot of necessity be good; but [which] *shall not* be very bad.'
And he remained as just to the ideals of criticism, and as loyal to
the tales, when, decades later, he spoke of them in the autobiography:

> I am divided between the shame on the one hand of claiming for
> them, these concocted "short stories", that they played so great a
> part, and a downright admiring tenderness to the other for their
> holding up their stiff little heads in such a bustle of life and traffic
> of affairs. I of course really and truly cared for them, as we say,
> more than for aught else whatever—cared for them with that kind
> of care, infatuated though it may seem, that makes it bliss for the
> fond votary never to so much as speak of the loved object, makes
> it a refinement of piety to perform his rites under cover of a
> perfect freedom of mind as to everything *but* them.[79]

[78] *Ibid.*
[79] *Notes and Reviews*, p. 407.

A Tragedy of Error

[First appeared anonymously in the *Continental Monthly*, vol. v (February 1864), pp. 204-16. Documentary evidence attributing the authorship to Henry James was first discovered by Dr. Leon Edel in a letter of February 1864 by Mrs. George De Kay, a friend of the James family. He announced the discovery in the first volume of his biography, *Henry James: The Untried Years, 1843–1870*, London: Rupert Hart-Davis, 1953, pp. 215-18. Three years later, Dr. Edel reprinted the story, 'with a prefatory note', in ' "A Tragedy of Error": James's First Story', *the New England Quarterly*, vol. xxix (September 1956), pp. 291-317.

Not reprinted during James's lifetime.]

I

A LOW ENGLISH PHAETON WAS DRAWN UP BEFORE THE door of the post office of a French seaport town. In it was seated a lady, with her veil down and her parasol held closely over her face. My story begins with a gentleman coming out of the office and handing her a letter.

He stood beside the carriage a moment before getting in. She gave him her parasol to hold, and then lifted her veil, showing a very pretty face. This couple seemed to be full of interest for the passersby, most of whom stared hard and exchanged significant glances. Such persons as were looking on at the moment saw the lady turn very pale as her eyes fell on the direction of the letter. Her companion saw it too, and instantly stepping into the place beside her, took up the reins, and drove rapidly along the main street of the town, past the harbour, to an open road skirting the sea. Here he slackened pace. The lady was leaning back, with her veil down again, and the letter lying open in her lap. Her attitude was almost that of unconsciousness, and he could see that her eyes were closed. Having satisfied himself of this, he hastily possessed himself of the letter, and read as follows:

Southampton, July 16th, 18—.

MY DEAR HORTENSE: You will see by my postmark that I am a thousand leagues nearer home than when I last wrote, but I have hardly time to explain the change. M. P—— has given me a most unlooked-for *congé*. After so many months of separation, we shall be able to spend a few weeks together. God be praised! We got in here from New York this morning, and I have had the good luck to find a vessel, the *Armorique*, which sails straight for H——. The mail leaves directly, but we shall probably be detained a few hours by the tide; so this will reach you a day before I arrive: the master calculates we shall get in early Thursday morning. Ah, Hortense! how the time drags! Three whole days. If I did not write from New York, it is because I was unwilling to torment you with an expectancy which, as it is, I venture to hope, you will find long enough. Farewell. To a warmer greeting!   Your devoted   C. B.

When the gentleman replaced the paper on his companion's lap, his face was almost as pale as hers. For a moment he gazed fixedly and vacantly before him, and a half-suppressed curse escaped his lips. Then his eyes reverted to his neighbour. After some hesitation, during which he allowed the reins to hang so loose that the horse lapsed into a walk, he touched her gently on the shoulder.

'Well, Hortense,' said he, in a very pleasant tone, 'what's the matter; have you fallen asleep?'

Hortense slowly opened her eyes, and, seeing that they had left the town behind them, raised her veil. Her features were stiffened with horror.

'Read that,' said she, holding out the open letter.

The gentleman took it, and pretended to read it again.

'Ah! M. Bernier returns. Delightful!' he exclaimed.

'How, delightful?' asked Hortense; 'we mustn't jest at so serious a crisis, my friend.'

'True,' said the other, 'it will be a solemn meeting. Two years of absence is a great deal.'

'O Heaven! I shall never dare to face him,' cried Hortense, bursting into tears.

Covering her face with one hand, she put out the other toward that of her friend. But he was plunged in so deep a reverie, that he did not perceive the movement. Suddenly he came to, aroused by her sobs.

'Come, come,' said he, in the tone of one who wishes to coax another into mistrust of a danger before which he does not himself feel so secure but that the sight of a companion's indifference will give him relief. 'What if he does come? He need learn nothing. He will stay but a short time, and sail away again as unsuspecting as he came.'

'Learn nothing! You surprise me. Every tongue that greets him, if only to say *bon jour*, will wag to the tune of a certain person's misconduct.'

'Bah! People don't think about us quite as much as you fancy.

You and I, *n'est-ce-pas?* we have little time to concern ourselves about our neighbours' failings. Very well, other people are in the same box, better or worse. When a ship goes to pieces on those rocks out at sea, the poor devils who are pushing their way to land on a floating spar, don't bestow many glances on those who are battling with the waves beside them. Their eyes are fastened to the shore, and all their care is for their own safety. In life we are all afloat on a tumultuous sea; we are all struggling toward some *terra firma* of wealth or love or leisure. The roaring of the waves we kick up about us and the spray we dash into our eyes deafen and blind us to the sayings and doings of our fellows. Provided we climb high and dry, what do we care for them?'

'Ay, but if we don't? When we've lost hope ourselves, we want to make others sink. We hang weights about their necks, and dive down into the dirtiest pools for stones to cast at them. My friend, you don't feel the shots which are not aimed at you. It isn't of you the town talks, but of me: a poor woman throws herself off the pier yonder, and drowns before a kind hand has time to restrain her, and her corpse floats over the water for all the world to look at. When her husband comes up to see what the crowd means, is there any lack of kind friends to give him the good news of his wife's death?'

'As long as a woman is light enough to float, Hortense, she is not counted drowned. It's only when she sinks out of sight that they give her up.'

Hortense was silent a moment, looking at the sea with swollen eyes.

'Louis,' she said at last, 'we were speaking metaphorically: I have half a mind to drown myself literally.'

'Nonsense!' replied Louis; 'an accused pleads "not guilty," and hangs himself in prison. What do the papers say? People talk, do they? Can't you talk as well as they? A woman is in the wrong from the moment she holds her tongue and refuses battle. And that you do too often. That pocket handkerchief is always more or less a flag of truce.'

'I'm sure I don't know,' said Hortense indifferently; 'perhaps it is.'

There are moments of grief in which certain aspects of the subject of our distress seem as irrelevant as matters entirely foreign to it. Her eyes were still fastened on the sea. There was another silence. 'O my poor Charles!' she murmured, at length, 'to what a hearth do you return!'

'Hortense,' said the gentleman, as if he had not heard her, although, to a third person, it would have appeared that it was because he had done so that he spoke: 'I do not need to tell you that it will never happen to me to betray our secret. But I will answer for it that so long as M. Bernier is at home no mortal shall breathe a syllable of it.'

'What of that?' sighed Hortense. 'He will not be with me ten minutes without guessing it.'

'Oh, as for that,' said her companion, dryly, 'that's your own affair.'

'Monsieur de Meyrau!' cried the lady.

'It seems to me,' continued the other, 'that in making such a guarantee, I have done my part of the business.'

'Your part of the business!' sobbed Hortense.

M. de Meyrau made no reply, but with a great cut of the whip sent the horse bounding along the road. Nothing more was said. Hortense lay back in the carriage with her face buried in her handkerchief, moaning. Her companion sat upright, with contracted brows and firmly set teeth, looking straight before him, and by an occasional heavy lash keeping the horse at a furious pace. A wayfarer might have taken him for a ravisher escaping with a victim worn out with resistance. Travellers to whom they were known would perhaps have seen a deep meaning in this accidental analogy. So, by a *détour*, they returned to the town.

When Hortense reached home, she went straight up to a little boudoir on the second floor, and shut herself in. This room was at the back of the house, and her maid, who was at that moment walking in the long garden which stretched down to the water, where there was a landing place for small boats, saw her draw in the window blind and darken the room, still in her bonnet and cloak. She remained alone for a couple of hours. At five o'clock, some time after the hour at which she was usually summoned to dress her mistress for the evening, the maid knocked at Hortense's door, and offered her services. Madame called out, from within, that she had a *migraine*, and would not be dressed.

'Can I get anything for madame?' asked Josephine; 'a *tisane*, a warm drink, something?'

'Nothing, nothing.'

'Will madame dine?'

'No.'

'Madame had better not go wholly without eating.'

'Bring me a bottle of wine—of brandy.'

Josephine obeyed. When she returned, Hortense was standing in the doorway, and as one of the shutters had meanwhile been thrown open, the woman could see that, although her mistress's hat had been tossed upon the sofa, her cloak had not been removed. and that her face was very pale. Josephine felt that she might not offer sympathy nor ask questions.

'Will madame have nothing more?' she ventured to say, as she handed her the tray.

Madame shook her head, and closed and locked the door.

Josephine stood a moment vexed, irresolute, listening. She heard no sound. At last she deliberately stooped down and applied her eye to the keyhole.

This is what she saw:

Her mistress had gone to the open window, and stood with her back to the door, looking out at the sea. She held the bottle by the neck in one hand, which hung listlessly by her side; the other was resting on a glass half filled with water, standing, together with an open letter, on a table beside her. She kept this position until Josephine began to grow tired of waiting. But just as she was about to arise in despair of gratifying her curiosity, madame raised the bottle and glass, and filled the latter full. Josephine looked more eagerly. Hortense held it a moment against the light, and then drained it down.

Josephine could not restrain an involuntary whistle. But her surprise became amazement when she saw her mistress prepare to take a second glass. Hortense put it down, however, before its contents were half gone, as if struck by a sudden thought, and hurried across the room. She stooped down before a cabinet, and took out a small opera glass. With this she returned to the window, put it to her eyes, and again spent some moments in looking seaward. The purpose of this proceeding Josephine could not make out. The only result visible to her was that her mistress suddenly dropped the lorgnette on the table, and sank down on an armchair, covering her face with her hand.

Josephine could contain her wonderment no longer. She hurried down to the kitchen.

'Valentine,' said she to the cook, 'what on earth can be the matter with Madame? She will have no dinner, she is drinking brandy by the glassful, a moment ago she was looking out to sea with a lorgnette, and now she is crying dreadfully with an open letter in her lap.'

The cook looked up from her potato-peeling with a significant wink.

'What can it be,' said she, 'but that monsieur returns?'

II

At six o'clock, Josephine and Valentine were still sitting together, discussing the probable causes and consequences of the event hinted at by the latter. Suddenly Madame Bernier's bell rang. Josephine was only too glad to answer it. She met her mistress descending the stairs, combed, cloaked, and veiled, with no traces of agitation, but a very pale face.

'I am going out,' said Madame Bernier; 'if M. le Vicomte comes, tell him I am at my mother-in-law's, and wish him to wait till I return.'

Josephine opened the door, and let her mistress pass; then stood watching her as she crossed the court.

'Her mother-in-law's,' muttered the maid; 'she has the face!'

When Hortense reached the street, she took her way, not through the town, to the ancient quarter where that ancient lady, her husband's mother, lived, but in a very different direction. She followed the course of the quay, beside the harbour, till she entered a crowded region, chiefly the residence of fishermen and boatmen. Here she raised her veil. Dusk was beginning to fall. She walked as if desirous to attract as little observation as possible, and yet to examine narrowly the population in the midst of which she found herself. Her dress was so plain that there was nothing in her appearance to solicit attention; yet, if for any reason a passer-by had happened to notice her, he could not have helped being struck by the contained intensity with which she scrutinized every figure she met. Her manner was that of a person seeking to recognize a long-lost friend, or perhaps, rather, a long-lost enemy, in a crowd. At last she stopped before a flight of steps, at the foot of which was a landing-place for half a dozen little boats, employed to carry passengers between the two sides of the port, at times when the drawbridge above was closed for the passage of vessels. While she stood she was witness to the following scene:

A man, in a red woollen fisherman's cap, was sitting on the top of the steps, smoking the short stump of a pipe, with his face to the water. Happening to turn about, his eye fell on a little child, hurrying along the quay toward a dingy tenement close at hand, with a jug in its arms.

'Hullo, youngster!' cried the man; 'what have you got there? Come here.'

The little child looked back, but, instead of obeying, only quickened its walk.

'The devil take you, come here!' repeated the man, angrily, 'or I'll wring your beggarly neck. You won't obey your own uncle, eh?'

The child stopped, and ruefully made its way to its relative, looking around several times toward the house, as if to appeal to some counter authority.

'Come, make haste!' pursued the man, 'or I shall go and fetch you. Move!'

The child advanced to within half a dozen paces of the steps, and then stood still, eyeing the man cautiously, and hugging the jug tight.

'Come on, you little beggar, come up close.'

The youngster kept a stolid silence, however, and did not budge. Suddenly its self-styled uncle leaned forward, swept out his arm, clutched hold of its little sunburnt wrist, and dragged it toward him.

'Why didn't you come when you were called?' he asked, running his disengaged hand into the infant's frowsy mop of hair, and shaking its head until it staggered. 'Why didn't you come, you unmannerly little brute, eh?—eh?—eh?' accompanying every interrogation with a renewed shake.

The child made no answer. It simply and vainly endeavoured to twist its neck around under the man's gripe, and transmit some call for succour to the house.

'Come, keep your head straight. Look at me, and answer me. What's in that jug? Don't lie.'

'Milk.'

'Who for?'

'Granny.'

'Granny be hanged.'

The man disengaged his hands, lifted the jug from the child's feeble grasp, tilted it toward the light, surveyed its contents, put it to his lips, and exhausted them. The child, although liberated, did not retreat. It stood watching its uncle drink until he lowered the jug. Then, as he met its eyes, it said:

'It was for the baby.'

For a moment the man was irresolute. But the child seemed to have a foresight of the parental resentment, for it had hardly spoken when it darted backward and scampered off, just in time to elude a blow from the jug, which the man sent clattering at its heels. When it was out of sight, he faced about to the water again, and replaced the pipe between his teeth with a heavy scowl and a murmur that sounded to Madame Bernier very like—'I wish the baby'd choke.'

Hortense was a mute spectator of this little drama. When it was over, she turned around, and retraced her steps twenty yards with her hand to her head. Then she walked straight back, and addressed the man.

'My good man,' she said, in a very pleasant voice, 'are you the master of one of these boats?'

He looked up at her. In a moment the pipe was out of his mouth, and a broad grin in its place. He rose, with his hand to his cap.

'I am, madame, at your service.'

'Will you take me to the other side?'

'You don't need a boat; the bridge is closed,' said one of his comrades at the foot of the steps, looking that way.

'I know it,' said Madame Bernier; 'but I wish to go to the cemetery, and a boat will save me half a mile walking.'

'The cemetery is shut at this hour.'

'*Allons*, leave madame alone,' said the man first spoken to. 'This way, my lady.'

Hortense seated herself in the stern of the boat. The man took the sculls.

'Straight across?' he asked.

Hortense looked around her. 'It's a fine evening,' said she; 'suppose you row me out to the lighthouse, and leave me at the point nearest the cemetery on our way back.'

'Very well,' rejoined the boatman; 'fifteen sous,' and began to pull lustily.

'*Allez*, I'll pay you well,' said Madame.

'Fifteen sous is the fare,' insisted the man.

'Give me a pleasant row, and I'll give you a hundred,' said Hortense.

Her companion said nothing. He evidently wished to appear not to have heard her remark. Silence was probably the most dignified manner of receiving a promise too munificent to be anything but a jest.

For some time this silence was maintained, broken only by the trickling of the oars and the sounds from the neighbouring shores and vessels. Madame Bernier was plunged in a sidelong scrutiny of her ferryman's countenance. He was a man of about thirty-five. His face was dogged, brutal, and sullen. These indications were perhaps exaggerated by the dull monotony of his exercise. The eyes lacked a certain rascally gleam which had appeared in them when he was so *empressé* with the offer of his services. The face was better then —that is, if vice is better than ignorance. We say a countenance is 'lit up' by a smile; and indeed that momentary flicker does the office of a candle in a dark room. It sheds a ray upon the dim upholstery of our souls. The visages of poor men, generally, know few alter-nations. There is a large class of human beings whom fortune restricts to a single change of expression, or, perhaps, rather to a single expression. Ah me! the faces which wear either nakedness or rags; whose repose is stagnation, whose activity vice; ignorant at their worst, infamous at their best!

'Don't pull too hard,' said Hortense at last. 'Hadn't you better take breath a moment?'

'Madame is very good,' said the man, leaning upon his oars. 'But if you had taken me by the hour,' he added, with a return of the vicious grin, 'you wouldn't catch me loitering.'

'I suppose you work very hard,' said Madame Bernier.

The man gave a little toss of his head, as if to intimate the in-adequacy of any supposition to grasp the extent of his labours.

'I've been up since four o'clock this morning, wheeling bales and boxes on the quay, and plying my little boat. Sweating without five minutes' intermission. *C'est comme ça.* Sometimes I tell my mate I think I'll take a plunge in the basin to dry myself. Ha! ha! ha!'

'And of course you gain little,' said Madame Bernier.

'Worse than nothing. Just what will keep me fat enough for starvation to feed on.'

'How? you go without your necessary food?'

'Necessary is a very elastic word, madame. You can narrow it down, so that in the degree above nothing it means luxury. My necessary food is sometimes thin air. If I don't deprive myself of that, it's because I can't.'

'Is it possible to be so unfortunate?'

'Shall I tell you what I have eaten to-day?'

'Do,' said Madame Bernier.

'A piece of black bread and a salt herring are all that have passed my lips for twelve hours.'

'Why don't you get some better work?'

'If I should die to-night,' pursued the boatman, heedless of the question, in the manner of a man whose impetus on the track of self-pity drives him past the signal flags of relief, 'what would there be left to bury me? These clothes I have on might buy me a long box. For the cost of this shabby old suit, that hasn't lasted me a twelve-month, I could get one that I wouldn't wear out in a thousand years. *La bonne idée!*'

'Why don't you get some work that pays better?' repeated Hortense.

The man dipped his oars again.

'Work that pays better? I must work for work. I must earn that

too. Work is wages. I count the promise of the next week's employment the best part of my Saturday night's pocketings. Fifty casks
rolled from the ship to the storehouse mean two things: thirty sous
and fifty more to roll the next day. Just so a crushed hand, or a
dislocated shoulder, mean twenty francs to the apothecary and *bon
jour* to my business.'

'Are you married?' asked Hortense.

'No, I thank you. I'm not cursed with that blessing. But I've an
old mother, a sister, and three nephews, who look to me for support.
The old woman's too old to work; the lass is too lazy, and the little
ones are too young. But they're none of them too old or young to be
hungry, *allez*. I'll be hanged if I'm not a father to them all.'

There was a pause. The man had resumed rowing. Madame
Bernier sat motionless, still examining her neighbour's physiognomy. The sinking sun, striking full upon his face, covered it with
an almost lurid glare. Her own features being darkened against the
western sky, the direction of them was quite indistinguishable to
her companion.

'Why don't you leave the place?' she said at last.

'Leave it! how?' he replied, looking up with the rough avidity
with which people of his class receive proposals touching their
interests, extending to the most philanthropic suggestions that mistrustful eagerness with which experience has taught them to defend
their own side of a bargain—the only form of proposal that she has
made them acquainted with.

'Go somewhere else,' said Hortense.

'Where, for instance!'

'To some new country—America.'

The man burst into a loud laugh. Madame Bernier's face bore
more evidence of interest in the play of his features than of that
discomfiture which generally accompanies the consciousness of
ridicule.

'There's a lady's scheme for you! If you'll write for furnished
apartments, *là-bas*, I don't desire anything better. But no leaps in
the dark for me. America and Algeria are very fine words to cram
into an empty stomach when you're lounging in the sun, out of
work, just as you stuff tobacco into your pipe and let the smoke curl
around your head. But they fade away before a cutlet and a bottle
of wine. When the earth grows so smooth and the air so pure that
you can see the American coast from the pier yonder, then I'll make
up my bundle. Not before.'

'You're afraid, then, to risk anything?'

'I'm afraid of nothing, *moi*. But I am not a fool either. I don't want to kick away my *sabots* till I am certain of a pair of shoes. I can go barefoot here. I don't want to find water where I counted on land. As for America, I've been there already.'

'Ah! you've been there?'

'I've been to Brazil and Mexico and California and the West Indies.'

'Ah!'

'I've been to Asia, too.'

'Ah!'

'*Pardio*, to China and India. Oh, I've seen the world! I've been three times around the Cape.'

'You've been a seaman then?'

'Yes, ma'am; fourteen years.'

'On what ship?'

'Bless your heart, on fifty ships.'

'French?'

'French and English and Spanish; mostly Spanish.'

'Ah?'

'Yes, and the more fool I was.'

'How so?'

'Oh, it was a dog's life. I'd drown any dog that would play half the mean tricks I used to see.'

'And you never had a hand in any yourself?'

'*Pardon*, I gave what I got. I was as good a Spaniard and as great a devil as any. I carried my knife with the best of them, and drew it as quickly, and plunged it as deep. I've got scars, if you weren't a lady. But I'd warrant to find you their mates on a dozen Spanish hides!'

He seemed to pull with renewed vigour at the recollection. There was a short silence.

'Do you suppose,' said Madame Bernier, in a few moments—'do you remember—that is, can you form any idea whether you ever killed a man?'

There was a momentary slackening of the boatman's oars. He gave a sharp glance at his passenger's countenance, which was still so shaded by her position, however, as to be indistinguishable. The tone of her interrogation had betrayed a simple, idle curiosity. He hesitated a moment, and then gave one of those conscious, cautious, dubious smiles, which may cover either a criminal assumption of more than the truth or a guilty repudiation of it.

'*Mon dieu!*' said he, with a great shrug, 'there's a question!.....
I never killed one without a reason.'

'Of course not,' said Hortense.

'Though a reason in South America, *ma foi!*' added the boatman, 'wouldn't be a reason here.'

'I suppose not. What would be a reason there?'

'Well, if I killed a man in Valparaiso—I don't say I did, mind—it's because my knife went in farther than I intended.'

'But why did you use it at all?'

'I didn't. If I had, it would have been because he drew his against me.'

'And why should he have done so?'

'*Ventrebleu!* for as many reasons as there are craft in the harbour.'

'For example?'

'Well, that I should have got a place in a ship's company that he was trying for.'

'Such things as that? is it possible?'

'Oh, for smaller things. That a lass should have given me a dozen oranges she had promised him.'

'How odd!' said Madame Bernier, with a shrill kind of laugh. 'A man who owed you a grudge of this kind would just come up and stab you, I suppose, and think nothing of it?'

'Precisely. Drive a knife up to the hilt into your back, with an oath, and slice open a melon with it, with a song, five minutes after-afterward.'

'And when a person is afraid, or ashamed, or in some way unable to take revenge himself, does he—or it may be a woman—does she, get someone else to do it for her?'

'*Parbleu!* Poor devils on the lookout for such work are as plentiful all along the South American coast as *commissionaires* on the street corners here.' The ferryman was evidently surprised at the fascination possessed by this infamous topic for so lady-like a person; but having, as you see, a very ready tongue, it is probable that his delight in being able to give her information and hear himself talk were still greater. 'And then down there,' he went on, 'they never forget a grudge. If a fellow doesn't serve you one day, he'll do it another. A Spaniard's hatred is like lost sleep—you can put it off for a time, but it will gripe you in the end. The rascals always keep their promises to themselves. .... An enemy on shipboard is jolly fun. It's like bulls tethered in the same field. You can't stand still half a minute except against a wall. Even when he makes friends with you, his favours never taste right. Messing with him is like drinking out of a pewter mug. And so it is everywhere. Let your shadow once flit across a Spaniard's path, and he'll always see it there. If you've never lived in any but these damned clockworky European towns, you can't imagine the state of things in a South

American seaport—one half the population waiting round the corner for the other half. But I don't see that it's so much better here, where every man's a spy on every other. There you meet an assassin at every turn, here a *sergent de ville.* .... At all events, the life *là bas* used to remind me, more than anything else, of sailing in a shallow channel, where you don't know what infernal rock you may ground on. Every man has a standing account with his neighbour, just as madame has at her *fournisseur's*; and, *ma foi*, those are the only accounts they settle. The master of the *Santiago* may pay me one of these days for the pretty names I heaved after him when we parted company, but he'll never pay me my wages.'

A short pause followed this exposition of the virtues of the Spaniard.

'You yourself never put a man out of the world, then?' resumed Hortense.

'Oh, *que si*! .... Are you horrified?'

'Not at all. I know that the thing is often justifiable.'

The man was silent a moment, perhaps with surprise, for the next thing he said was:

'Madame is Spanish?'

'In that, perhaps, I am,' replied Hortense.

Again her companion was silent. The pause was prolonged. Madame Bernier broke it by a question which showed that she had been following the same train of thought.

'What is sufficient ground in this country for killing a man?'

The boatman sent a loud laugh over the water. Hortense drew her cloak closer about her.

'I'm afraid there is none.'

'Isn't there a right of self-defence?'

'To be sure there is—it's one I ought to know something about. But it's one that *ces messieurs* at the Palais make short work with.'

'In South America and those countries, when a man makes life insupportable to you, what do you do?'

'*Mon Dieu!* I suppose you kill him.'

'And in France?'

'I suppose you kill yourself. Ha! ha! ha!'

By this time they had reached the end of the great breakwater, terminating in a lighthouse, the limit, on one side, of the inner harbour. The sun had set.

'Here we are at the lighthouse,' said the man; 'it's growing dark. Shall we turn?'

Hortense rose in her place a few moments, and stood looking out to sea. 'Yes,' she said at last, 'you may go back—slowly.' When the

boat had headed round she resumed her old position, and put one
of her hands over the side, drawing it through the water as they
moved, and gazing into the long ripples.

At last she looked up at her companion. Now that her face caught
some of the lingering light of the west, he could see that it was
deathly pale.

'You find it hard to get along in the world,' said she: 'I shall be
very glad to help you.'

The man started, and stared a moment. Was it because this
remark jarred upon the expression which he was able faintly to
discern in her eyes? The next, he put his hand to his cap.

'Madame is very kind. What will you do?'

Madame Bernier returned his gaze.

'I will trust you.'

'Ah!'

'And reward you.'

'Ah? Madame has a piece of work for me?'

'A piece of work,' Hortense nodded.

The man said nothing, waiting apparently for an explanation. His
face wore the look of lowering irritation which low natures feel at
being puzzled.

'Are you a bold man?'

Light seemed to come in this question. The quick expansion of
his features answered it. You cannot touch upon certain subjects
with an inferior but by the sacrifice of the barrier which separates
you from him. There are thoughts and feelings and glimpses and
foreshadowings of thoughts which level all inequalities of station.

'I'm bold enough,' said the boatman, 'for anything *you* want me
to do.'

'Are you bold enough to commit a crime?'

'Not for nothing.'

'If I ask you to endanger your peace of mind, to risk your personal
safety for me, it is certainly not as a favour. I will give you ten
times the weight in gold of every grain by which your conscience
grows heavier in my service.'

The man gave her a long, hard look through the dim light.

'I know what you want me to do,' he said at last.

'Very well,' said Hortense; 'will you do it?'

He continued to gaze. She met his eyes like a woman who has
nothing more to conceal.

'State your case.'

'Do you know a vessel named the *Armorique*, a steamer?'

'Yes; it runs from Southampton.'

'It will arrive to-morrow morning early. Will it be able to cross the bar?'

'No; not till noon.'

'I thought so. I expect a person by it—a man.'

Madame Bernier appeared unable to continue, as if her voice had given way.

'Well, well?' said her companion.

'He's the person'—she stopped again.

'The person who—?'

'The person whom I wish to get rid of.'

For some moments nothing was said. The boatman was the first to speak again.

'Have you formed a plan?'

Hortense nodded.

'Let's hear it.'

'The person in question,' said Madame Bernier, 'will be impatient to land before noon. The house to which he returns will be in view of the vessel if, as you say, she lies at anchor. If he can get a boat, he will be sure to come ashore. *Eh bien!*—but you understand me.'

'Aha! you mean my boat—*this* boat?'

'O God!'

Madame Bernier sprang up in her seat, threw out her arms, and sank down again, burying her face in her knees. Her companion hastily shipped his oars, and laid his hands on her shoulders.

'*Allons donc*, in the devil's name, don't break down,' said he; 'we'll come to an understanding.'

Kneeling in the bottom of the boat, and supporting her by his grasp, he succeeded in making her raise herself, though her head still drooped.

'You want me to finish him in the boat?'

No answer.

'Is he an old man?'

Hortense shook her head faintly.

'My age?'

She nodded.

'*Sapristi!* it isn't so easy.'

'He can't swim,' said Hortense, without looking up; 'he—he is lame.'

'*Nom de Dieu!*' The boatman dropped his hands. Hortense looked up quickly. Do you read the pantomime?

'Never mind,' added the man at last, 'it will serve as a sign.'

'*Mais oui.* And besides that, he will ask to be taken to the Maison Bernier, the house with its back to the water, on the extension of the great quay. *Tenez*, you can almost see it from here.'

'I know the place,' said the boatman, and was silent, as if asking and answering himself a question.

Hortense was about to interrupt the train of thought which she apprehended he was following, when he forestalled her.

'How am I to be sure of my affair?' asked he.

'Of your reward? I've thought of that. This watch is a pledge of what I shall be able and glad to give you afterward. There are two thousand francs' worth of pearls in the case.'

'*Il faut fixer la somme*,' said the man, leaving the watch untouched.

'That lies with you.'

'Good. You know that I have the right to ask a high price.'

'Certainly. Name it.'

'It's only on the supposition of a large sum that I will so much as consider your proposal. *Songez donc*, that it's a MURDER you ask of me.'

'The price—the price?'

'*Tenez*,' continued the man, 'poached game is always high. The pearls in that watch are costly because it's worth a man's life to get at them. You want me to be your pearl diver. Be it so. You must guarantee me a safe descent,—it's a descent, you know—ha!—you must furnish me the armour of safety; a little gap to breathe through while I'm at my work—the thought of a capful of Napoleons!'

'My good man, I don't wish to talk to you or to listen to your sallies. I wish simply to know your price. I'm not bargaining for a pair of chickens. Propose a sum.'

The boatman had by this time resumed his seat and his oars. He stretched out for a long, slow pull, which brought him closely face to face with his temptress. This position, his body bent forward, his eyes fixed on Madame Bernier's face, he kept for some seconds. It was perhaps fortunate for Hortense's purpose at that moment—it had often aided her purposes before—that she was a pretty woman.[1] A plain face might have emphasized the utterly repulsive nature of the negotiation. Suddenly, with a quick, convulsive movement, the man completed the stroke.

'*Pas si bête!* propose one yourself.'

'Very well,' said Hortense, 'if you wish it. *Voyons:* I'll give you what I can. I have fifteen thousand francs' worth of jewels. I'll give you them, or, if they will get you into trouble, their value. At

---

[1] I am told that there was no resisting her smile; and that she had at her command, in moments of grief, a certain look of despair which filled even the roughest hearts with sympathy, and won over the kindest to the cruel cause.

home, in a box I have a thousand francs in gold. You shall have those. I'll pay your passage and outfit to America. I have friends in New York. I'll write to them to get you work.'

'And you'll give your washing to my mother and sister, *hein*? Ha! ha! Jewels, fifteen thousand francs; one thousand more makes sixteen; passage to America—first class—five hundred francs; out-fit—what does Madame understand by that?'

'Everything needful for your success *là-bas*.'

'A written denial that I am an assassin? *Ma foi*, it were better not to remove the impression. It's served me a good turn, on this side of the water at least. Call it twenty-five thousand francs.'

'Very well; but not a sous more.'

'Shall I trust you?'

'Am I not trusting you? It is well for you that I do not allow myself to think of the venture I am making.'

'Perhaps we're even there. We neither of us can afford to make account of certain possibilities. Still, I'll trust you, too. .... *Tiens!*' added the boatman, 'here we are near the quay.' Then with a mock-solemn touch of his cap, 'Will Madame still visit the ceme-tery?'

'Come, quick, let me land,' said Madame Bernier, impatiently.

'We *have* been among the dead, after a fashion,' persisted the boatman, as he gave her his hand.

III

It was more than eight o'clock when Madame Bernier reached her own house.

'Has M. de Meyrau been here?' she asked of Josephine.

'Yes, ma'am; and on learning that Madame was out, he left a note, *chez monsieur*.'

Hortense found a sealed letter on the table in her husband's old study. It ran as follows:

'I was desolated at finding you out. I had a word to tell you. I have accepted an invitation to sup and pass the night at C——, thinking it would look well. For the same reason I have resolved to take the bull by the horns, and go aboard the steamer on my return, to welcome M. Bernier home—the privilege of an old friend. I am told the *Armorique* will anchor off the bar by day-break. What do you think? But it's too late to let me know.

Applaud my *savoir faire*—you will, at all events, in the end. You will see how it will smoothe matters.'

'Baffled! baffled!' hissed Madame, when she had read the note; 'God deliver me from my friends!' She paced up and down the room several times, and at last began to mutter to herself, as people often do in moments of strong emotion: 'Bah! but he'll never get up by daybreak. He'll oversleep himself, especially after to-night's supper. The other will be before him. .... Oh, my poor head, you've suffered too much to fail in the end!'

Josephine reappeared to offer to remove her mistress's things. The latter, in her desire to reassure herself, asked the first question that occurred to her.

'Was M. le Vicomte alone?'

'No, madame; another gentleman was with him—M. de Saulges, I think. They came in a hack, with two portmanteaus.'

Though I have judged best, hitherto, often from an exaggerated fear of trenching on the ground of fiction, to tell you what this poor lady did and said, rather than what she thought, I may disclose what passed in her mind now:

'Is he a coward? is he going to leave me? or is he simply going to pass these last hours in play and drink? He might have stayed with me. Ah! my friend, you do little for me, who do so much for you; who commit murder, and—Heaven help me!—suicide for you! .... But I suppose he knows best. At all events, he will make a night of it.'

When the cook came in late that evening, Josephine, who had sat up for her, said:

'You've no idea how Madame is looking. She's ten years older since this morning. Holy mother! what a day this has been for her!'

'Wait till to-morrow,' said the oracular Valentine.

Later, when the women went up to bed in the attic, they saw a light under Hortense's door, and during the night Josephine, whose chamber was above Madame's, and who couldn't sleep (for sympathy, let us say), heard movements beneath her, which told that her mistress was even more wakeful than she.

IV

There was considerable bustle around the *Armorique* as she anchored outside the harbour of H——, in the early dawn of the following day. A gentleman, with an overcoat, walking stick, and small valise, came alongside in a little fishing boat, and got leave to go aboard.

'Is M. Bernier here?' he asked of the officers, the first man he met.

'I fancy he's gone ashore, sir. There was a boatman inquiring for him a few minutes ago, and I think he carried him off.'

M. de Meyrau reflected a moment. Then he crossed over to the other side of the vessel, looking landward. Leaning over the bulwarks he saw an empty boat moored to the ladder which ran up the vessel's side.

'That's a town boat, isn't it?' he said to one of the hands standing by.

'Yes, sir.'

'Where's the master?'

'I suppose he'll be here in a moment. I saw him speaking to one of the officers just now.'

De Meyrau descended the ladder, and seated himself at the stern of the boat. As the sailor he had just addressed was handing down his bag, a face with a red cap looked over the bulwarks.

'Hullo, my man!' cried De Meyrau, 'is this your boat?'

'Yes, sir, at your service,' answered the red cap, coming to the top of the ladder, and looking hard at the gentleman's stick and portmanteau.

'Can you take me to town, to Madame Bernier's, at the end of the new quay?'

'Certainly, sir,' said the boatman, scuttling down the ladder, 'you're just the gentleman I want.'

*   *   *   *   *

An hour later Hortense Bernier came out of the house, and began to walk slowly through the garden toward the terrace which overlooked the water. The servants, when they came down at an early hour, had found her up and dressed, or rather, apparently, not undressed, for she wore the same clothes as the evening before.

'*Tiens!*' exclaimed Josephine, after seeing her, 'Madame gained ten years yesterday; she has gained ten more during the night.'

When Madame Bernier reached the middle of the garden she halted, and stood for a moment motionless, listening. The next, she uttered a great cry. For she saw a figure emerge from below the terrace, and come limping toward her with outstretched arms.

The Story of a Year

[First appeared in the *Atlantic Monthly*, vol. xv (March 1965), pp. 257-81. Not reprinted during James's lifetime.]

I

MY STORY BEGINS AS A GREAT MANY STORIES HAVE begun within the last three years, and indeed as a great many have ended; for, when the hero is despatched, does not the romance come to a stop?

In early May, two years ago, a young couple I wot of strolled homeward from an evening walk, a long ramble among the peaceful hills which inclosed their rustic home. Into these peaceful hills the young man had brought, not the rumour (which was an old inhabitant) but some of the reality of war,—a little whiff of gunpowder, the clanking of a sword; for, although Mr. John Ford had his campaign still before him, he wore a certain comely air of camplife which stamped him a very Hector to the steady-going villagers, and a very pretty fellow to Miss Elizabeth Crowe, his companion in this sentimental stroll. And was he not attired in the great brightness of blue and gold which befits a freshly made lieutenant? This was a strange sight for these happy Northern glades; for, although the first Revolution had boomed awhile in their midst, the honest yeomen who defended them were clad in sober homespun, and it is well known that His Majesty's troops wore red.

These young people, I say, had been roaming. It was plain that they had wandered into spots where the brambles were thick and the dews heavy,—nay, into swamps and puddles where the April rains were still undried. Ford's boots and trousers had imbibed a deep foretaste of the Virginia mud; his companion's skirts were fearfully bedraggled. What great enthusiasm had made our friends so unmindful of their steps? What blinding ardour had kindled these strange phenomena: a young lieutenant scornful of his first uniform, a well-bred young lady reckless of her stockings?

Good reader, this narrative is averse to retrospect.

Elizabeth (as I shall not scruple to call her outright) was leaning upon her companion's arm, half moving in concert with him, and half allowing herself to be led, with that instinctive acknowledgment of dependence natural to a young girl who has just received the assurance of lifelong protection. Ford was lounging along with that calm, swinging stride which often bespeaks, when you can read it aright, the answering consciousness of a sudden rush of manhood. A spectator might have thought him at this moment profoundly conceited. The young girl's blue veil was dangling from his pocket; he had shouldered her sun-umbrella after the fashion of a musket on a march: he might carry these trifles. Was there not a vague longing expressed in the strong expansion of his stalwart shoulders, in the fond accommodation of his pace to hers,—her pace so submissive and slow, that, when he tried to match it, they almost came to a delightful standstill,—a silent desire for the whole fair burden?

They made their way up a long swelling mound, whose top commanded the sunset. The dim landscape which had been brightening all day to the green of spring was now darkening to the grey of evening. The lesser hills, the farms, the brooks, the fields, orchards, and woods, made a dusky gulf before the great splendour of the west. As Ford looked at the clouds, it seemed to him that their imagery was all of war, their great uneven masses were marshalled into the semblance of a battle. There were columns charging and columns flying and standards floating,—tatters of the reflected purple; and great captains on colossal horses, and a rolling canopy of cannon-smoke and fire and blood. The background of the clouds, indeed, was like a land on fire, or a battle-ground illuminated by another sunset, a country of blackened villages and crimsoned pastures. The tumult of the clouds increased; it was hard to believe them inanimate. You might have fancied them an army of gigantic souls playing at football with the sun. They seemed to sway in confused splendour; the opposing squadrons bore each other down; and then suddenly they scattered, bowling with equal velocity towards north and south, and gradually fading into the pale evening sky. The purple pennons sailed away and sank out of sight, caught, doubtless, upon the brambles of the intervening plain. Day contracted itself into a fiery ball and vanished.

Ford and Elizabeth had quietly watched this great mystery of the heavens.

'That is an allegory,' said the young man, as the sun went under, looking into his companion's face, where a pink flush seemed still to linger: 'it means the end of the war. The forces on both sides are withdrawn. The blood that has been shed gathers itself into a vast globule and drops into the ocean.'

'I'm afraid it means a shabby compromise,' said Elizabeth. 'Light disappears, too, and the land is in darkness.'

'Only for a season,' answered the other. 'We mourn our dead.

Then light comes again, stronger and brighter than ever. Perhaps you'll be crying for me, Lizzie, at that distant day.'

'Oh, Jack, didn't you promise not to talk about that?' says Lizzie, threatening to anticipate the performance in question.

Jack took this rebuke in silence, gazing soberly at the empty sky. Soon the young girl's eyes stole up to his face. If he had been looking at anything in particular, I think she would have followed the direction of his glance; but as it seemed to be a very vacant one, she let her eyes rest.

'Jack,' said she, after a pause, 'I wonder how you'll look when you get back.'

Ford's soberness gave way to a laugh.

'Uglier than ever. I shall be all incrusted with mud and gore. And then I shall be magnificently sun-burnt, and I shall have a beard.'

'Oh, you're dreadful!' and Lizzie gave a little shout. 'Really, Jack, if you have a beard, you'll not look like a gentleman.'

'Shall I look like a lady, pray?' says Jack.

'Are you serious?' asked Lizzie.

'To be sure. I mean to alter my face as you do your misfitting garments,—take in on one side and let out on the other. Isn't that the process? I shall crop my head and cultivate my chin.'

'You've a very nice chin, my dear, and I think it's a shame to hide it.'

'Yes, I know my chin's handsome; but wait till you see my beard.'

'Oh, the vanity!' cried Lizzie, 'the vanity of men in their faces! Talk of women!' and the silly creature looked up at her lover with most inconsistent satisfaction.

'Oh, the pride of women in their husbands!' said Jack, who of course knew what she was about.

'You're not my husband, Sir. There's many a slip'—— But the young girl stopped short.

' 'Twixt the cup and the lip,' said Jack. 'Go on. I can match your proverb with another. "There's many a true word," and so forth. No, my darling: I'm not your husband. Perhaps I never shall be. But if anything happens to me, you'll take comfort, won't you?'

'Never!' said Lizzie, tremulously.

'Oh, but you must; otherwise, Lizzie, I should think our engagement inexcusable. Stuff! who am I that you should cry for me?'

'You are the best and wisest of men. I don't care; you *are*.'

'Thank you for your great love, my dear. That's a delightful illusion. But I hope Time will kill it, in his own good way, before it hurts anyone. I know so many men who are worth infinitely more than I—men wise, generous, and brave—that I shall not feel as if I were leaving you in an empty world.'

'Oh, my dear friend!' said Lizzie, after a pause, 'I wish you could advise me all my life.'

'Take care, take care,' laughed Jack; 'you don't know what you are bargaining for. But will you let me say a word now? If by chance I'm taken out of the world, I want you to beware of that tawdry sentiment which enjoins you to be "constant to my memory". My memory be hanged! Remember me at my best,—that is, fullest of desire of humility. Don't inflict me on people. There are scme widows and bereaved sweethearts who remind me of the peddler in that horrible murder-story, who carried a corpse in his pack. Really, it's their stock-in-trade. The only justification of a man's personality is his rights. What rights has a dead man?—Let's go down.'

They turned southward and went jolting down the hill.

'Do you mind this talk, Lizzie?' asked Ford.

'No,' said Lizzie, swallowing a sob, unnoticed by her companion in the sublime egotism of protection; 'I like it.'

'Very well,' said the young man, 'I want my memory to help you. When I am down in Virginia, I expect to get a vast deal of good from thinking of you,—to do my work better, and to keep straighter altogether. Like all lovers, I'm horribly selfish. I expect to see a vast deal of shabbiness and baseness and turmoil, and in the midst of it all I'm sure the inspiration of patriotism will sometimes fail. Then I'll think of you. I love you a thousand times better than my country, Liz.—Wicked? So much the worse. It's the truth. But if I find your memory makes a milksop of me, I shall thrust you out of the way without ceremony,—I shall clap you into my box or between the leaves of my Bible, and only look at you on Sunday.'

'I shall be very glad, Sir, if that makes you open your Bible frequently,' says Elizabeth, rather demurely.

'I shall put one of your photographs against every page,' cried Ford; 'and then I think I shall not lack a text for my meditations. Don't you know how Catholics keep little pictures of their adored Lady in their prayer-books?'

'Yes, indeed,' said Lizzie; 'I should think it would be a very soul-stirring picture, when you are marching to the front, the night before a battle,—a poor, stupid girl, knitting stupid socks, in a stupid Yankee village.'

Oh, the craft of artless tongues! Jack strode along in silence a few moments, splashing straight through a puddle; then, ere he was quite clear of it, he stretched out his arm and gave his companion a long embrace.

'And pray what am I to do,' resumed Lizzie, wondering, rather proudly perhaps, at Jack's averted face, 'while you are marching and countermarching in Virginia?'

'Your duty, of course,' said Jack, in a steady voice, which belied a certain little conjecture of Lizzie's. 'I think you will find the sun will rise in the east, my dear, just as it did before you were engaged.'

'I'm sure I didn't suppose it wouldn't,' says Lizzie.

'By duty I don't mean anything disagreeable, Liz,' pursued the young man. 'I hope you'll take your pleasure, too. I wish you might go to Boston, or even to Leatherborough, for a month or two.'

'What for, pray?'

'What for? Why, for the fun of it: to "go out", as they say.'

'Jack, do you think me capable of going to parties while you are in danger?'

'Why not? Why should I have all the fun?'

'Fun? I'm sure you're welcome to it all. As for me, I mean to make a new beginning.'

'Of what?'

'Oh, of everything. In the first place, I shall begin to improve my mind. But don't you think it's horrid for women to be reasonable?'

'Hard, say you?'

'Horrid,—yes, and hard too. But I mean to become so. Oh, girls are such fools, Jack! I mean to learn to like boiled mutton and history and plain sewing, and all that. Yet, when a girl's engaged, she's not expected to do anything in particular.'

Jack laughed, and said nothing; and Lizzie went on.

'I wonder what your mother will say to the news. I think I know.'

'What?'

'She'll say you've been very unwise. No, she won't: she never speaks so to you. She'll say I've been very dishonest or indelicate, or something of that kind. No, she won't either: she doesn't say such things, though I'm sure she thinks them. I don't know what she'll say.'

'No, I think not, Lizzie, if you indulge in such conjectures. My mother never speaks without thinking. Let us hope that she may think favourably of our plan. Even if she doesn't'—

Jack did not finish his sentence, nor did Lizzie urge him. She had a great respect for his hesitations. But in a moment he began again.

'I was going to say this, Lizzie: I think for the present our engagement had better be kept quiet.'

Lizzie's heart sank with a sudden disappointment. Imagine the feelings of the damsel in the fairy-tale, whom the disguised enchan-

tress had just empowered to utter diamonds and pearls, should the
old beldame have straightway added that for the present mademoiselle had better hold her tongue. Yet the disappointment was
brief. I think this enviable young lady would have tripped home
talking very hard to herself, and have been not ill pleased to find
her little mouth turning into a tightly clasped jewel-casket. Nay,
would she not on this occasion have been thankful for a large mouth,
—a mouth huge and unnatural,—stretching from ear to ear? Who
wish to cast their pearls before swine? The young lady of the pearls
was, after all, but a barnyard miss. Lizzie was too proud of Jack to
be vain. It's well enough to wear our own hearts upon our sleeves;
but for those of others, when intrusted to our keeping, I think we
had better find a more secluded lodging.

'You see, I think secrecy would leave us much freer,' said Jack,—
'leave *you* much freer.'

'Oh, Jack, how can you?' cried Lizzie. 'Yes, of course; I shall be
falling in love with someone else. Freer! Thank you, Sir!'

'Nay, Lizzie, what I'm saying is really kinder than it sounds.
Perhaps you *will* thank me one of these days.'

'Doubtless! I've already taken a great fancy to George Mackenzie.'

'Will you let me enlarge on my suggestion?'

'Oh, certainly! You seem to have your mind quite made up.'

'I confess I like to take account of possibilities. Don't you know
mathematics are my hobby? Did you ever study algebra? I always
have an eye on the unknown quantity.'

'No, I never studied algebra. I agree with you, that we had better
not speak of our engagement.'

'That's right, my dear. You're always right. But mind, I don't
want to bind you to secrecy. Hang it, do as you please! Do what
comes easiest to you, and you'll do the best thing. What made me
speak is my dread of the horrible publicity which clings to all this
business. Nowadays, when a girl's engaged, it's no longer, "Ask
mamma," simply; but, "Ask Mrs. Brown, and Mrs. Jones, and my
large circle of acquaintance,—Mrs. Grundy, in short." I say nowadays, but I suppose it's always been so.'

'Very well, we'll keep it all nice and quiet,' said Lizzie, who would
have been ready to celebrate her nuptials according to the rites of
the Esquimaux, had Jack seen fit to suggest it.

'I know it doesn't look well for a lover to be so cautious,' pursued
Jack; 'but you understand me, Lizzie, don't you?'

'I don't entirely understand you, but I quite trust you.'

'God bless you! My prudence, you see, is my best strength. Now,
if ever, I need my strength. When a man's a-wooing, Lizzie, he is

all feeling, or he ought to be; when he's accepted, then he begins to think.'

'And to repent, I suppose you mean.'

'Nay, to devise means to keep his sweetheart from repenting. Let me be frank. Is it the greatest fools only that are the best lovers? There's no telling what may happen, Lizzie. I want you to marry me with your eyes open. I don't want you to feel tied down or taken in. You're very young, you know. You're responsible to yourself of a year hence. You're at an age when no girl can count safely from year's end to year's end.'

'And you, Sir!' cries Lizzie; 'one would think you were a grand-father.'

'Well, I'm on the way to it. I'm a pretty old boy. I mean what I say. I may not be entirely frank, but I think I'm sincere. It seems to me as if I'd been fibbing all my life before I told you that your affection was necessary to my happiness. I mean it out and out. I never loved anyone before, and I never will again. If you had re-fused me half an hour ago, I should have died a bachelor. I have no fear for myself. But I have for you. You said a few minutes ago that you wanted me to be your adviser. Now you know the function of an adviser is to perfect his victim in the art of walking with his eyes shut. I sha'n't be so cruel.'

Lizzie saw fit to view these remarks in a humorous light. 'How disinterested!' quoth she: 'how very self-sacrificing! Bachelor in-deed! For my part, I think I shall become a Mormon!'—I verily believe the poor misinformed creature fancied that in Utah it is the ladies who are guilty of polygamy.

Before many minutes they drew near home. There stood Mrs. Ford at the garden-gate, looking up and down the road, with a letter in her hand.

'Something for you, John,' said his mother, as they approached. 'It looks as if it came from camp.—Why, Elizabeth, look at your skirts!'

'I know it,' says Lizzie, giving the articles in question a shake. 'What is it, Jack?'

'Marching orders!' cried the young man. 'The regiment leaves day after to-morrow. I must leave by the early train in the morning. Hurray!' And he diverted a sudden gleeful kiss into a filial salute.

They went in. The two women were silent, after the manner of women who suffer. But Jack did little else than laugh and talk and circumnavigate the parlour, sitting first here and then there,— close beside Lizzie and on the opposite side of the room. After a while Miss Crowe joined in his laughter, but I think her mirth might have been resolved into articulate heart-beats. After tea she went to bed, to give Jack opportunity for his last filial *épanchements*. How generous a man's intervention makes women! But Lizzie promised to see her lover off in the morning.

'Nonsense!' said Mrs. Ford. 'You'll not be up. John will want to breakfast quietly.'

'I shall see you off, Jack,' repeated the young lady, from the threshold.

Elizabeth went upstairs buoyant with her young love. It had dawned upon her like a new life,—a life positively worth the living. Hereby she would subsist and cost nobody anything. In it she was boundlessly rich. She would make it the hidden spring of a hundred praiseworthy deeds. She would begin the career of duty: she would enjoy boundless equanimity: she would raise her whole being to the level of her sublime passion. She would practise charity, humility, piety,—in fine, all the virtues: together with certain *morceaux* of Beethoven and Chopin. She would walk the earth like one glorified. She would do homage to the best of men by inviolate secrecy. Here, by I know not what gentle transition, as she lay in the quiet darkness, Elizabeth covered her pillow with a flood of tears.

Meanwhile Ford, downstairs, began in this fashion. He was lounging at his manly length on the sofa, in his slippers.

'May I light a pipe, mother?'

'Yes, my love. But please be careful of your ashes. There's a newspaper.'

'Pipes don't make ashes.—Mother, what do you think?' he continued, between the puffs of his smoking; 'I've got a piece of news.'

'Ah?' said Mrs. Ford, fumbling for her scissors; 'I hope it's good news.'

'I hope you'll think it so. I've been engaging myself'—puff,—puff —'to Lizzie Crowe.' A cloud of puffs between his mother's face and his own. When they cleared away, Jack felt his mother's eyes. Her work was in her lap. 'To be married, you know,' he added.

In Mrs. Ford's view, like the king in that of the British Constitution, her only son could do no wrong. Prejudice is a stout bulwark against surprise. Moreover, Mrs. Ford's motherly instinct had not been entirely at fault. Still, it had by no means kept pace with fact. She had been silent, partly from doubt, partly out of respect for her son. As long as John did not doubt of himself, he was right. Should he come to do so, she was sure he would speak. And now, when he told her the matter was settled, she persuaded herself that he was asking her advice.

'I've been expecting it,' she said, at last.

'You have? why didn't you speak?'

'Well, John, I can't say I've been hoping it.'

'Why not?'

'I am not sure of Lizzie's heart,' said Mrs. Ford, who, it may be well to add, was very sure of her own.

Jack began to laugh. 'What's the matter with her heart?'

'I think Lizzie's shallow,' said Mrs. Ford; and there was that in her tone which betokened some satisfaction with this adjective.

'Hang it! she is shallow,' said Jack. 'But when a thing's shallow, you can see to the bottom. Lizzie doesn't pretend to be deep. I want a wife, mother, that I can understand. That's the only wife I can love. Lizzie's the only girl I ever understood, and the first I ever loved. I love her very much,—more than I can explain to you.'

'Yes, I confess it's inexplicable. It seems to me,' she added, with a bad smile, 'like infatuation.'

Jack did not like the smile; he liked it even less than the remark. He smoked steadily for a few moments, and then he said,—

'Well, mother, love is notoriously obstinate, you know. We shall not be able to take the same view of this subject: suppose we drop it.'

'Remember that this is your last evening at home, my son,' said Mrs. Ford.

'I do remember. Therefore I wish to avoid disagreement.'

There was a pause. The young man smoked, and his mother sewed, in silence.

'I think my position, as Lizzie's guardian,' resumed Mrs. Ford, 'entitles me to an interest in the matter.'

'Certainly, I acknowledged your interest by telling you of our engagement.'

Further pause.

'Will you allow me to say,' said Mrs. Ford, after a while, 'that I think this a little selfish?'

'Allow you? Certainly, if you particularly desire it. Though I confess it isn't very pleasant for a man to sit and hear his future wife pitched into,—by his own mother, too.'

'John, I am surprised at your language.'

'I beg your pardon,' and John spoke more gently. 'You mustn't be surprised at anything from an accepted lover.—I'm sure you misconceive her. In fact, mother, I don't believe you know her.'

Mrs. Ford nodded, with an infinite depth of meaning; and from the grimness with which she bit off the end of her thread it might have seemed that she fancied herself to be executing a human vengeance.

'Ah, I know her only too well!'

'And you don't like her?'

Mrs. Ford performed another decapitation of her thread.

'Well, I'm glad Lizzie has one friend in the world,' said Jack.

'Her best friend,' said Mrs. Ford, 'is the one who flatters her least. I see it all, John. Her pretty face has done the business.'

The young man flushed impatiently.

'Mother,' said he, 'you are very much mistaken. I'm not a boy nor a fool. You trust me in a great many things; why not trust me in this?'

'My dear son, you are throwing yourself away. You deserve for your companion in life a higher character than that girl.'

I think Mrs. Ford, who had been an excellent mother, would have liked to give her son a wife fashioned on her own model.

'Oh, come, mother,' said he, 'that's twaddle. I should be thankful, if I were half as good as Lizzie.'

'It's the truth, John, and your conduct—not only the step you've taken, but your talk about it—is a great disappointment to me. If I have cherished any wish of late, it is that my darling boy should get a wife worthy of him. The household governed by Elizabeth Crowe is not the home I should desire for anyone I love.'

'It's one to which you should always be welcome, Ma'am,' said Jack.

'It's not a place I should feel at home in,' replied his mother.

'I'm sorry,' said Jack. And he got up and began to walk about the room. 'Well, well, mother,' he said at last, stopping in front of Mrs. Ford, 'we don't understand each other. One of these days we shall. For the present let us have done with discussion. I'm half sorry I told you.'

'I'm glad of such a proof of your confidence. But if you hadn't, of course Elizabeth would have done so.'

'No, Ma'am, I think not.'

'Then she is even more reckless of her obligations than I thought her.'

'I advised her to say nothing about it.'

Mrs. Ford made no answer. She began slowly to fold up her work.

'I think we had better let the matter stand,' continued her son. 'I'm not afraid of time. But I wish to make a request of you: you won't mention this conversation to Lizzie, will you? nor allow her to suppose that you know of our engagement? I have a particular reason.'

Mrs. Ford went on smoothing out her work. Then she suddenly looked up.

'No, my dear, I'll keep your secret. Give me a kiss.'

II

I have no intention of following Lieutenant Ford to the seat of
war. The exploits of his campaign are recorded in the public
journals of the day, where the curious may still peruse them. My
own taste has always been for unwritten history, and my present
business is with the reverse of the picture.

After Jack went off, the two ladies resumed their old homely life.
But the homeliest life had now ceased to be repulsive to Elizabeth.
Her common duties were no longer wearisome: for the first time,
she experienced the delicious companionship of thought. Her chief
task was still to sit by the window knitting soldiers' socks; but even
Mrs. Ford could not help owning that she worked with a much
greater diligence, yawned, rubbed her eyes, gazed up and down the
road less, and indeed produced a much more comely article. Ah,
me! if half the lovesome fancies that flitted through Lizzie's spirit
in those busy hours could have found their way into the texture of
the dingy yarn, as it was slowly wrought into shape, the eventual
wearer of the socks would have been as light-footed as Mercury. I
am afraid I should make the reader sneer, were I to rehease some of
this little fool's diversions. She passed several hours daily in Jack's
old chamber: it was in this sanctuary, indeed, at the sunny south
window, overlooking the long road, the wood-crowned heights, the
gleaming river, that she worked with most pleasure and profit. Here
she was removed from the untiring glance of the elder lady, from
her jarring questions and commonplaces; here she was alone with
her love,—that greatest commonplace in life. Lizzie felt in Jack's
room a certain impress of his personality. The idle fancies of her
mood were bodied forth in a dozen sacred relics. Some of these
articles Elizabeth carefully cherished. It was rather late in the day
for her to assert a literary taste,—her reading having begun and
ended (naturally enough) with the ancient fiction of the 'Scottish
Chiefs'. So she could hardly help smiling, herself, sometimes, at
her interest in Jack's old college tomes. She carried several of them
to her own apartment, and placed them at the foot of her little bed,
on a book-shelf adorned, besides, with a pot of spring violets, a
portrait of General McClellan, and a likeness of Lieutenant Ford.
She had a vague belief that a loving study of their well-thumbed
verses would remedy, in some degree, her sad intellectual deficiencies. She was sorry she knew so little: as sorry, that is, as she

might be, for we know that she was shallow. Jack's omniscience was one of his most awful attributes. And yet she comforted herself with the thought, that, as he had forgiven her ignorance, she herself might surely forget it. Happy Lizzie, I envy you this easy path to knowledge! The volume she most frequently consulted was an old German 'Faust', over which she used to fumble with a battered lexicon. The secret of this preference was in certain marginal notes in pencil, signed 'J'. I hope they were really of Jack's making.

Lizzie was always a small walker. Until she knew Jack, this had been an unsuspected pleasure. She was afraid, too, of the cows, geese, and sheep,—all the agricultural *spectra* of the feminine imagination. But now her terrors were over. Might she not play the soldier, too, in her own humble way? Often with a beating heart, I fear, but still with resolute, elastic steps, she re-visited Jack's old haunts; she tried to love Nature as he had seemed to love it; she gazed at his old sunsets; she fathomed his old pools with bright plummet glances, as if seeking some lingering trace of his features in their brown depths, stamped there as on a fond human heart; she sought out his dear name, scratched on the rocks and trees,— and when night came on, she studied, in her simple way, the great starlit canopy, under which, perhaps, her warrior lay sleeping; she wandered through the green glades, singing snatches of his old ballads in a clear voice, made tuneful with love,—and as she sang, there mingled with the everlasting murmur of the trees the faint sound of a muffled bass, borne upon the south wind like a distant drum-beat, responsive to a bugle. So she led for some months a very pleasant idyllic life, face to face with a strong, vivid memory, which gave everything and asked nothing. These were doubtless to be (and she half knew it) the happiest days of her life. Has life any bliss so great as this pensive ecstasy? To know that the golden sands are dropping one by one makes servitude freedom, and poverty riches.

In spite of a certain sense of loss, Lizzie passed a very blissful summer. She enjoyed the deep repose which, it is to be hoped, sanctifies all honest betrothals. Possible calamity weighed lightly upon her. We know that when the columns of battle-smoke leave the field, they journey through the heavy air to a thousand quiet homes, and play about the crackling blaze of as many firesides. But Lizzie's vision was never clouded. Mrs. Ford might gaze into the thickening summer dusk and wipe her spectacles; but her companion hummed her old ballad-ends with an unbroken voice. She no more ceased to smile under evil tidings than the brooklet ceases to ripple beneath the projected shadow of the roadside willow. The self-given promises of that tearful night of parting were forgotten.

Vigilance had no place in Lizzie's scheme of heavenly idleness. The idea of moralizing in Elysium!

It must not be supposed that Mrs. Ford was indifferent to Lizzie's mood. She studied it watchfully, and kept note of all its variations. And among the things she learned was, that her companion knew of her scrutiny, and was, on the whole, indifferent to it. Of the full extent of Mrs. Ford's observation, however, I think Lizzie was hardly aware. She was like a reveller in a brilliantly lighted room, with a curtainless window, conscious, and yet heedless, of passers-by. And Mrs. Ford may not inaptly be compared to the chilly spectator on the dark side of the pane. Very few words passed on the topic of their common thoughts. From the first, as we have seen, Lizzie guessed at her guardian's probable view of her engagement: an abasement incurred by John. Lizzie lacked what is called a sense of duty; and, unlike the majority of such temperaments, which contrive to be buoyant on the glistening bubble of Dignity, she had likewise a modest estimate of her dues. Alack, my poor heroine had no pride! Mrs. Ford's silent censure awakened no resentment. It sounded in her ears like a dull, soporific hum. Lizzie was deeply enamoured of what a French book terms her *aises intellectuelles.* Her mental comfort lay in the ignoring of problems. She possessed a certain native insight which revealed many of the horrent inequalities of her pathway; but she found it so cruel and disenchanting a faculty, that blindness was infinitely preferable. She preferred repose to order, and mercy to justice. She was speculative, without being critical. She was continually wondering, but she never inquired. This world was the riddle; the next alone would be the answer.

So she never felt any desire to have an 'understanding' with Mrs. Ford. Did the old lady misconceive her? it was her own business. Mrs. Ford apparently felt no desire to set herself right. You see, Lizzie was ignorant of her friend's promise. There were moments when Mrs. Ford's tongue itched to speak. There were others, it is true, when she dreaded any explanation which would compel her to forfeit her displeasure. Lizzie's happy self-sufficiency was most irritating. She grudged the young girl the dignity of her secret; her own actual knowledge of it rather increased her jealousy, by showing her the importance of the scheme from which she was excluded. Lizzie, being in perfect good-humour with the world and with herself, abated no jot of her personal deference to Mrs. Ford. Of Jack, as a good friend and her guardian's son, she spoke very freely. But Mrs. Ford was mistrustful of this semi-confidence. She would not, she often said to herself, be wheedled against her

principles. Her principles! Oh for some shining blade of purpose to
hew down such stubborn stakes! Lizzie had no thought of flattering
her companion. She never deceived anyone but herself. She could
not bring herself to value Mrs. Ford's good-will. She knew that Jack
often suffered from his mother's obstinacy. So her unbroken
humility shielded no unavowed purpose. She was patient and kindly
from nature, from habit. Yet I think, that, if Mrs. Ford could have
measured her benignity, she would have preferred, on the whole,
the most open defiance. 'Of all things,' she would sometime mutter,
'to be patronized by that little piece!' It was very disagreeable, for
instance, to have to listen to *portions* of her own son's letters.

These letters came week by week, flying out of the South like
white-winged carrier-doves. Many and many a time, for very pride,
Lizzie would have liked a larger audience. Portions of them
certainly deserved publicity. They were far too good for her. Were
they not better than that stupid war-correspondence in the 'Times',
which she so often tried in vain to read? They contained long details
of movements, plans of campaigns, military opinions and conjectures, expressed with the emphasis habitual to young sub-lieutenants.
I doubt whether General Halleck's despatches laid down the law
more absolutely than Lieutenant Ford's. Lizzie answered in her own
fashion. It must be owned that hers was a dull pen. She told her
dearest, dearest Jack how much she loved and honoured him, and
how much she missed him, and how delightful his last letter was,
(with those beautifully drawn diagrams,) and the village gossip,
and how stout and strong his mother continued to be,—and again,
how she loved, etc., etc., and that she remained his loving L. Jack
read these effusions as became one so beloved. I should not wonder
if he thought them very brilliant.

The summer waned to its close, and through myriad silent stages
began to darken into autumn. Who can tell the story of those red
months? I have to chronicle another silent transition. But as I can
find no words delicate and fine enough to describe the multifold
changes of Nature, so, too, I must be content to give you the
spiritual facts in gross.

John Ford became a veteran down by the Potomac. And, to tell
the truth, Lizzie became a veteran at home. That is, her love and
hope grew to be an old story. She gave way, as the strongest must,
as the wisest will, to time. The passion which, in her simple, shallow
way, she had confided to the woods and waters reflected their outward variations; she thought of her lover less, and with less positive
pleasure. The golden sands had run out. Perfect rest was over. Mrs.
Ford's tacit protest began to be annoying. In a rather resentful spirit,

FERNALD LIBRARY
COLBY-SAWYER COLLEGE
NEW LONDON, N.H. 03257

Lizzie forbore to read any more letters aloud. These were as regular as ever. One of them contained a rough camp-photograph of Jack's newly bearded visage. Lizzie declared it was 'too ugly for anything', and thrust it out of sight. She found herself skipping his military dissertations, which were still as long and written in as handsome a hand as ever. The 'too good', which used to be uttered rather proudly, was now rather a wearisome truth. When Lizzie in certain critical moods tried to qualify Jack's temperament, she said to herself that he was too literal. Once he gave her a little scolding for not writing oftener. 'Jack can make no allowances,' murmured Lizzie. 'He can understand no feelings but his own. I remember he used to say that moods were diseases. His mind is too healthy for such things; his heart is too stout for ache or pain. The night before he went off he told me that Reason, as he calls it, was the rule of life. I suppose he thinks it the rule of love, too. But his heart is younger than mine,—younger and better. He has lived through awful scenes of danger and bloodshed and cruelty, yet his heart is purer.' Lizzie had a horrible feeling of being *blasée* of this one affection. 'Oh, God bless him!' she cried. She felt much better for the tears in which this soliloquy ended. I fear she had begun to doubt her ability to cry about Jack.

III

Christmas came. The Army of the Potomac had stacked its muskets and gone into winter-quarters. Miss Crowe received an invitation to pass the second fortnight in February at the great manufacturing town of Leatherborough. Leatherborough is on the railroad, two hours south of Glenham, at the mouth of the great river Tan, where this noble stream expands into its broadest smile, or gapes in too huge a fashion to be disguised by a bridge.

'Mrs. Littlefield kindly invites you for the last of the month,' said Mrs. Ford, reading a letter behind the tea-urn.

It suited Mrs. Ford's purpose—a purpose which I have not space to elaborate—that her young charge should now go forth into society and pick up acquaintances.

Two sparks of pleasure gleamed in Elizabeth's eyes. But, as she had taught herself to do of late with her protectress, she mused before answering.

'It is my desire that you should go,' said Mrs. Ford, taking silence for dissent.

The sparks went out.

'I intend to go,' said Lizzie, rather grimly. 'I am much obliged to Mrs. Littlefield.'

Her companion looked up.

'I intend you shall. You will please to write this morning.'

For the rest of the week the two stitched together over muslins and silks, and were very good friends. Lizzie could scarcely help wondering at Mrs. Ford's zeal on her behalf. Might she not have referred it to her guardian's principles? Her wardrobe, hitherto fashioned on the Glenham notion of elegance, was gradually raised to the Leatherborough standard of fitness. As she took up her bed-room candle the night before she left home, she said,—

'I thank you very much, Mrs. Ford, for having worked so hard for me,—for having taken so much interest in my outfit. If they ask me at Leatherborough who made my things, I shall certainly say it was you.'

Mrs. Littlefield treated her young friend with great kindness. She was a good-natured, childless matron. She found Lizzie very ignorant and very pretty. She was glad to have so great a beauty and so many lions to show.

One evening Lizzie went to her room with one of the maids, carrying half a dozen candles between them. Heaven forbid that I should cross that virgin threshold—for the present! But we will wait. We will allow them two hours. At the end of that time, having gently knocked, we will enter the sanctuary. Glory of glories! The faithful attendant has done her work. Our lady is robed, crowned, ready for worshippers.

I trust I shall not be held to a minute description of our dear Lizzie's person and costume. Who is so great a recluse as never to have beheld young ladyhood in full dress? Many of us have sisters and daughters. Not a few of us, I hope, have female connections of another degree, yet no less dear. Others have looking-glasses. I give you my word for it that Elizabeth made as pretty a show as it is possible to see. She was of course well-dressed. Her skirt was of voluminous white, puffed and trimmed in wondrous sort. Her hair was profusely ornamented with curls and braids of its own rich substance. From her waist depended a ribbon, broad and blue. White with coral ornaments, as she wrote to Jack in the course of the week. Coral ornaments, forsooth! And pray, Miss, what of the other jewels with which your person was decorated,—the rubies, pearls, and sapphires? One by one Lizzie assumes her modest gimcracks: her bracelet, her gloves, her handkerchief, her fan, and then—her smile. Ah, that strange crowning smile!

An hour later, in Mrs. Littlefield's pretty drawing-room, amid music, lights, and talk, Miss Crowe was sweeping a grand curtsy before a tall, sallow man, whose name she caught from her hostess's redundant murmur as Bruce. Five minutes later, when the honest matron gave a glance at her newly started enterprise from the other side of the room, she said to herself that really, for a plain country-girl, Miss Crowe did this kind of thing very well. Her next glimpse of the couple showed them whirling round the room to the crashing thrum of the piano. At eleven o'clock she beheld them linked by their finger-tips in the dazzling mazes of the reel. At half-past eleven she discerned them charging shoulder to shoulder in the serried columns of the Lancers. At midnight she tapped her young friend gently with her fan.

'Your sash is unpinned, my dear.—I think you have danced often enough with Mr. Bruce. If he asks you again, you had better refuse. It's not quite the thing.—Yes, my dear, I know.—Mr. Simpson, will you be so good as to take Miss Crowe down to supper?'

I'm afraid young Simpson had rather a snappish partner.

After the proper interval, Mr. Bruce called to pay his respects to Mrs. Littlefield. He found Miss Crowe also in the drawing-room. Lizzie and he met like old friends. Mrs. Littlefield was a willing listener; but it seemed to her that she had come in at the second act of the play. Bruce went off with Miss Crowe's promise to drive with him in the afternoon. In the afternoon he swept up to the door in a prancing, tinkling sleigh. After some minutes of hoarse jesting and silvery laughter in the keen wintry air, he swept away again with Lizzie curled up in the buffalo-robe beside him, like a kitten in a rug. It was dark when they returned. When Lizzie came in to the sitting-room fire, she was congratulated by her hostess upon having made a 'conquest'.

'I think he's a most gentlemanly man,' says Lizzie.

'So he is, my dear,' said Mrs. Littlefield; 'Mr. Bruce is a perfect gentleman. He's one of the finest young men I know. He's not so young either. He's a little too yellow for my taste; but he's beautifully educated. I wish you could hear his French accent. He was been abroad I don't know how many years. The firm of Bruce and Robertson does an immense business.'

'And I'm so glad,' cries Lizzie, 'he's coming to Glenham in March! He's going to take his sister to the water-cure.'

'Really?—poor thing? She has very good manners.'

'What do you think of his looks?' asked Lizzie, smoothing her feather.

'I was speaking of Jane Bruce. I think Mr. Bruce has fine eyes.'

'I must say I like tall men,' says Miss Crowe.

'Then Robert Bruce is your man,' laughs Mr. Littlefield. 'He's as tall as a bell-tower. And he's got a bell-clapper in his head, too.'

'I believe I will go and take off my things,' remarks Miss Crowe, flinging up her curls.

Of course it behooved Mr. Bruce to call the next day and see how Miss Crowe had stood her drive. He set a veto upon her intended departure, and presented an invitation from his sister for the following week. At Mrs. Littlefield's insistance, Lizzie accepted the invitation, despatched a laconic note to Mrs. Ford, and stayed over for Miss Bruce's party. It was a grand affair. Miss Bruce was a very great lady: she treated Miss Crowe with every attention. Lizzie was thought by some persons to look prettier than ever. The vaporous gauze, the sunny hair, the coral, the sapphires, the smile, were displayed with renewed success. The master of the house was unable to dance; he was summoned to sterner duties. Nor could Miss Crowe be induced to perform, having hurt her foot on the ice. This was of course a disappointment; let us hope that her entertainers made it up to her.

One the second day after the party, Lizzie returned to Glenham. Good Mr. Littlefield took her to the station, stealing a moment from his precious business-hours.

'There are your checks,' said he; 'be sure you don't lose them. Put them in your glove.'

Lizzie gave a little scream of merriment.

'Mr. Littlefield, how can you? I've a reticule, Sir. But I really don't want you to stay.'

'Well, I confess,' said her companion.—'Hullo! there's your Scottish chief! I'll get him to stay with you till the train leaves. He may be going. Bruce!'

'Oh, Mr. Littlefield, don't!' cries Lizzie. 'Perhaps Mr. Bruce is engaged.'

Bruce's tall figure came striding towards them. He was astounded to find that Miss Crowe was going by this train. Delightful! He had come to meet a friend who had not arrived.

'Littlefield,' said he, 'you can't be spared from your business. I will see Miss Crowe off.'

When the elder gentleman had departed, Mr. Bruce conducted his companion into the car, and found her a comfortable seat, equidistant from the torrid stove and the frigid door. Then he stowed away her shawls, umbrella, and reticule. She would keep her muff? She did well. What a pretty fur!'

'It's just like your collar,' said Lizzie. 'I wish I had a muff for my feet,' she pursued, tapping on the floor.

'Why not use some of those shawls?' said Bruce; 'let's see what we can make of them.'

And he stooped down and arranged them as a rug, very neatly and kindly. And then he called himself a fool for not having used the next seat, which was empty; and the wrapping was done over again.

'I'm so afraid you'll be carried off!' said Lizzie. 'What would you do?'

'I think I should make the best of it. And you?'

'I would tell you to sit down *there*'; and she indicated the seat facing her. He took it. 'Now you'll be sure to,' said Elizabeth.

'I'm afraid I shall, unless I put the newspaper between us.' And he took it out of his pocket. 'Have you seen the news?'

'No,' says Lizzie, elongating her bonnet-ribbons. 'What is it? Just look at that party.'

'There's not much news. There's been a scrimmage on the Rappahannock. Two of our regiments engaged,—the Fifteenth and the Twenty-Eighth. Didn't you tell me you had a cousin or something in the Fifteenth?'

'Not a cousin, no relation, but an intimate friend—my guardian's son. What does the paper say, please?' inquires Lizzie, very pale.

Bruce cast his eye over the report. 'It doesn't seem to have amounted to much; we drove back the enemy, and recrossed the river at our ease. Our loss only fifty. There are no names,' he added, catching a glimpse of Lizzie's pallor,—'none in this paper at least.'

In a few moments appeared a newsboy crying the New York journals.

'Do you think the New York papers would have any names?' asked Lizzie.

'We can try,' said Bruce. And he bought a 'Herald', and unfolded it. 'Yes, there *is* a list,' he continued, some time after he had opened out the sheet. 'What's your friend's name?' he asked, from behind the paper.

'Ford—John Ford, second lieutenant,' said Lizzie.

There was a long pause.

At last Bruce lowered the sheet, and showed a face in which Lizzie's pallor seemed faintly reflected.

'There *is* such a name among the wounded,' he said; and, folding the paper down, he held it out, and gently crossed to the seat beside her.

Lizzie took the paper, and held it close to her eyes. But Bruce could not help seeing that her temples had turned from white to crimson.

'Do you see it?' he asked; 'I sincerely hope it's nothing very bad.'

'*Severely*,' whispered Lizzie.

'Yes, but that proves nothing. Those things are most unreliable. *Do* hope for the best.'

Lizzie made no answer. Meanwhile passengers had been brushing in, and the car was full. The engine began to puff, and the conductor to shout. The train gave a jog.

'You'd better go, Sir, or you'll be carried off,' said Lizzie, holding out her hand, with her face still hidden.

'May I go to the next station with you?' said Bruce.

Lizzie gave him a rapid look, with a deepened flush. He had fancied that she was shedding tears. But those eyes were dry; they held fire rather than water.

'No, no, Sir; you must not. I insist. Good-bye.'

Bruce's offer had cost him a blush, too. He had been prepared to back it with the assurance that he had business ahead, and, indeed, to make a little business in order to satisfy his conscience. But Lizzie's answer was final.

'Very well,' said he, '*good* bye. You have my real sympathy, Miss Crowe. Don't despair. We shall meet again.'

The train rattled away. Lizzie caught a glimpse of a tall figure with lifted hat on the platform. But she sat motionless, with her head against the window-frame, her veil down, and her hands idle.

She had enough to do to think, or rather to feel. It is fortunate that the utmost shock of evil tidings often comes first. After that everything is for the better. Jack's name stood printed in that fatal column like a stern signal for despair. Lizzie felt conscious of a crisis which almost arrested her breath. Night had fallen at midday: what was the hour? A tragedy had stepped into her life: was she spectator or actor? She found herself face to face with death: was it not her own soul masquerading in a shroud? She sat in a half-stupor. She had been aroused from a dream into a waking nightmare. It was like hearing a murder-shriek while you turn the page of your novel. But I cannot describe these things. In time the crushing sense of calamity loosened its grasp. Feeling lashed her pinions. Thought struggled to rise. Passion was still, stunned, floored. She had recoiled like a receding wave for a stronger onset. A hundred ghastly fears and fancies strutted a moment, pecking at the young girl's naked heart, like sandpipers on the weltering beach. Then, as with a great murmurous rush, came the meaning of her grief. The flood-gates of emotion were opened.

At last passion exhausted itself, and Lizzie thought. Bruce's parting words rang in her ears. She did her best to hope. She reflected that wounds, even severe wounds, did not necessarily mean death. Death might easily be warded off. She would go to Jack; she would nurse him; she would watch by him; she would cure him. Even if Death had already beckoned, she would strike down his hand: if Life had already obeyed, she would issue the stronger mandate of Love. She would stanch his wounds; she would unseal his eyes with her kisses; she would call till he answered her.

Lizzie reached home and walked up the garden path. Mrs. Ford stood in the parlour as she entered, upright, pale, and rigid. Each read the other's countenance. Lizzie went towards her slowly and giddily. She must of course kiss her patroness. She took her listless hand and bent towards her stern lips. Habitually Mrs. Ford was the most undemonstrative of women. But as Lizzie looked closer into her face, she read the signs of a grief infinitely more potent than her own. The formal kiss gave way: the young girl leaned her head on the old woman's shoulder and burst into sobs. Mrs. Ford acknowledged those tears with a slow inclination of the head, full of a certain grim pathos: she put out her arms and pressed them closer to her heart.

At last Lizzie disengaged herself and sat down.

'I am going to him,' said Mrs. Ford.

Lizzie's dizziness returned. Mrs. Ford was going,—and she, she?

'I am going to nurse him, and with God's help to save him.'

'How did you hear?'

'I have a telegram from the surgeon of the regiment'; and Mrs. Ford held out a paper.

Lizzie took it and read: 'Lieutenant Ford dangerously wounded in the action of yesterday. You had better come on.'

'I should like to go myself,' said Lizzie: 'I think Jack would like to have me.'

'Nonsense! A pretty place for a young girl! I am not going for sentiment; I am going for use.'

Lizzie leaned her head back in her chair, and closed her eyes. From the moment they had fallen upon Mrs. Ford, she had left a certain quiescence. And now it was a relief to have responsibility denied her. Like most weak persons, she was glad to step out of the current of life, now that it had begun to quicken into action. In emergencies, such persons are tacitly counted out; and they as tacitly consent to the arrangement. Even to the sensitive spirit there is a certain meditative rapture in standing on the quiet shore, (beside the ruminating cattle), and watching the hurrying, eddying flood, which makes up for the loss of dignity. Lizzie's heart re-

sumed its peaceful throbs. She sat, almost dreamily, with her eyes
shut.

'I leave in an hour,' said Mrs. Ford. 'I am going to get ready.—
Do you hear?'

The young girl's silence was a deeper consent than her companion supposed.

IV

It was a week before Lizzie heard from Mrs. Ford. The letter,
when it came, was very brief. Jack still lived. The wounds were
three in number, and very serious; he was unconscious; he had not
recognized her; but still the chances either way were thought equal.
They would be much greater for his recovery nearer home; but it
was impossible to move him. 'I write from the midst of horrible
scenes,' said the poor lady. Subjoined was a list of necessary medi-
cines, comforts, and delicacies, to be boxed up and sent.

For a while Lizzie found occupation in writing a letter to Jack,
to be read in his first lucid moment, as she told Mrs. Ford. This
lady's man-of-business came up from the village to superintend
the packing of the boxes. Her directions were strictly followed; and
in no point were they found wanting. Mr. Mackenzie bespoke
Lizzie's admiration for their friend's wonderful clearness of memory and judgment. 'I wish we had that woman at the head of
affairs,' said he. ''Gad, I'd apply for a Brigadier-Generalship.'—'I'd
apply to be sent South,' thought Lizzie. When the boxes and letter
were despatched, she sat down to await more news. Sat down, say
I? Sat down, and rose, and wondered, and sat down again. These
were lonely, weary days. Very different are the idleness of love and
the idleness of grief. Very different is it to be alone with your hope
and alone with your despair. Lizzie failed to rally her musings. I
do not mean to say that her sorrow was very poignant, although she
fancied it was. Habit was a great force in her simple nature; and
her chief trouble now was that habit refused to work. Lizzie had to
grapple with the stern tribulation of a decision to make, a problem
to solve. She felt that there was some spiritual barrier between herself and repose. So she began in her usual fashion to build up a
false repose on the hither side of belief. She might as well have
tried to float on the Dead Sea. Peace eluding her, she tried to resign
herself to tumult. She drank deep at the well of self-pity, but found
its waters brackish. People are apt to think that they may temper
the penalties of misconduct by self-commiseration, just as they

season the long after-taste of beneficence by a little spice of self-applause. But the Power of Good is a more grateful master than the Devil. What bliss to gaze into the smooth gurgling wake of a good deed, while the comely bark sails on with floating pennon! What horror to look into the muddy sediment which floats round the piratic keel! Go, sinner, and dissolve it with your tears! And you, scoffing friend, there is the way out! Or would you prefer the window? I'm an honest man forevermore.

One night Lizzie had a dream,—a rather disagreeable one,—which haunted her during many waking hours. It seemed to her that she was walking in a lonely place, with a tall, dark-eyed man who called her wife. Suddenly, in the shadow of a tree, they came upon an unburied corpse. Lizzie proposed to dig him a grave. They dug a great hole and took hold of the corpse to lift him in; when suddenly he opened his eyes. Then they saw that he was covered with wounds. He looked at them intently for some time, turning his eyes from one to the other. At last he solemnly said, 'Amen'! and closed his eyes. Then she and her companion placed him in the grave, and shovelled the earth over him, and stamped it down with their feet.

He of the dark eyes and he of the wounds were the two constantly recurring figures of Lizzie's reveries. She could never think of John without thinking of the courteous Leatherborough gentleman, too. These were the *data* of her problem. These two figures stood like opposing knights, (the black and the white,) foremost on the great chess-board of fate. Lizzie was the wearied, puzzled player. She would idly finger the other pieces, and shift them carelessly hither and thither; but it was of no avail: the game lay between the two knights. She would shut her eyes and long for some kind hand to come and tamper with the board; she would open them and see the two knights standing immovable, face to face. It was nothing new. A fancy had come in and offered defiance to a fact; they must fight it out. Lizzie generously inclined to the fancy, the unknown champion, with a reputation to make. Call her *blasée*, if you like, this little girl, whose record told of a couple of dances and a single lover, heartless, old before her time. Perhaps she deserves your scorn. I confess she thought herself ill-used. By whom? by what? wherein? These were questions Miss Crowe was not prepared to answer. Her intellect was unequal to the stern logic of human events. She expected two and two to make five: as why should they not for the nonce? She was like an actor who finds himself on the stage with a half-learned part and without sufficient wit to extemporize. Pray, where is the prompter? Alas, Elizabeth, that you had no mother!

Young girls are prone to fancy that when once they have a lover, they have everything they need: a conclusion inconsistent with the belief entertained by many persons, that life begins with love. Lizzie's fortunes became old stories to her before she had half read them through. Jack's wounds and danger were an old story. Do not suppose that she had exhausted the lessons, the suggestions of these awful events, their inspirations, exhortations,—that she had wept as became the horror of the tragedy. No: the curtain had not yet fallen, yet our young lady had begun to yawn. To yawn? Ay, and to long for the afterpiece. Since the tragedy dragged, might she not divert herself with that well-bred man beside her?

Elizabeth was far from owning to herself that she had fallen away from her love. For my own part, I need no better proof of the fact than the dull persistency with which she denied it. What accusing voice broke out of the stillness? Jack's nobleness and magnanimity were the hourly theme of her clogged fancy. Again and again she declared to herself that she was unworthy of them, but that, if he would only recover and come home, she would be his eternal bond-slave. So she passed a very miserable month. Let us hope that her childish spirit was being tempered to some useful purpose. Let us hope so.

She roamed about the empty house with her footsteps tracked by an unlaid ghost. She cried aloud and said that she was very unhappy; she groaned and called herself wicked. Then, sometimes, appalled at her moral perplexities, she declared that she was neither wicked nor unhappy; she was contented, patient, and wise. Other girls had lost their lovers: it was the present way of life. Was she weaker than most women? Nay, but Jack was the best of men. If he would only come back directly, without delay, as he was, senseless, dying even, that she might look at him, touch him, speak to him! Then she would say that she could no longer answer for herself, and wonder (or pretend to wonder) whether she were not going mad. Suppose Mrs. Ford should come back and find her in an unswept room, pallid and insane? or suppose she should die of her troubles? What if she should kill herself?—dismiss the servants, and close the house, and lock herself up with a knife? Then she would cut her arm to escape from dismay at what she had already done; and then her courage would ebb away with her blood, and, having so far pledged herself to despair, her life would ebb away with her courage; and then, alone, in darkness, with none to help her, she would vainly scream, and thrust the knife into her temple, and swoon to death. And Jack would come back, and burst into the house, and wander through the empty rooms, calling her name, and for all answer get a death-scent! These imaginings were the more creditable or discreditable to Lizzie, that she had never read 'Romeo and Juliet'. At any rate, they served to dissipate time,—heavy, weary time,—the more heavy and weary as it bore dark foreshadow-ings of some momentous event. If that event would only come, what-ever it was, and sever this Gordian knot of doubt!

The days passed slowly: the leaden sands dropped one by one. The roads were too bad for walking; so Lizzie was obliged to con-fine her restlessness to the narrow bounds of the empty house, or to an occasional journey to the village, where people sickened her by their dull indifference to her spiritual agony. Still they could not fail to remark how poorly Miss Crowe was looking. This was true, and Lizzie knew it. I think she even took a certain comfort in her pallor and in her failing interest in her dress. There was some satis-faction in displaying her white roses amid the apple-cheeked pros-perity of Main Street. At last Miss Cooper, the Doctor's sister, spoke to her:—

'How is it, Elizabeth, you look so pale, and thin, and worn out? What you been doing with yourself? Falling in love, eh? It isn't right to be so much alone. Come down and stay with us awhile,—till Mrs. Ford and John come back,' added Miss Cooper, who wished to put a cheerful face on the matter.

For Miss Cooper, indeed, any other face would have been diffi-cult. Lizzie agreed to come. Her hostess was a busy, unbeautiful old maid, sister and housekeeper of the village physician. Her occupation here below was to perform the forgotten tasks of her fellow-men,—to pick up their dropped stitches, as she herself de-clared. She was never idle, for her general cleverness was com-mensurate with mortal needs. Her own story was, that she kept moving, so that folks couldn't see how ugly she was. And, in fact, her existence was manifest through her long train of good deeds,—just as the presence of a comet is shown by its tail. It was doubtless on the above principle that her visage was agitated by a perpetual laugh.

Meanwhile more news had been coming from Virginia. 'What an absurdly long letter you sent John,' wrote Mrs. Ford, in acknowl-edging the receipt of the boxes. 'His first lucid moment would be very short, if he were to take upon himself to read your effusions. Pray keep your long stories till he gets well.' For a fortnight the young soldier remained the same,—feverish, conscious only at intervals. Then came a change for the worse, which, for many weary days, however, resulted in nothing decisive. 'If he could only be moved to Glenham, home, and old sights,' said his mother, 'I should have hope. But think of the journey!' By this time Lizzie had stayed out ten days of her visit.

One day Miss Cooper came in from a walk, radiant with tidings. Her face, as I have observed, wore a continual smile, being dimpled and punctured all over with merriment,—so that, when an unusual cheerfulness was super-diffused, it resembled a tempestuous little pool into which a great stone has been cast.

'Guess who's come,' said she, going up to the piano, which Lizzie was carelessly fingering, and putting her hands on the young girl's shoulders. 'Just guess!'

Lizzie looked up.

'Jack,' she half gasped.

'Oh, dear, no, not that! How stupid of me! I mean Mr. Bruce, your Leatherborough admirer.'

'Mr. Bruce! Mr. Bruce!' said Lizzie. 'Really?'

'True as I live. He's come to bring his sister to the Water-Cure. I met them at the post-office.'

Lizzie felt a strange sensation of good news. Her finger-tips were on fire. She was deaf to her companion's rattling chronicle. She broke into the midst of it with a fragment of some triumphant, jubilant melody. The keys rang beneath her flashing hands. And then she suddenly stopped, and Miss Cooper, who was taking off her bonnet at the mirror, saw that her face was covered with a burning flush.

That evening, Mr. Bruce presented himself at Doctor Cooper's, with whom he had a slight acquaintance. To Lizzie he was infinitely courteous and tender. He assured her, in very pretty terms, of his profound sympathy with her in her cousin's danger,—her cousin he still called him,—and it seemed to Lizzie that until that moment no one had begun to be kind. And then he began to rebuke her, playfully and in excellent taste, for her pale cheeks.

'Isn't it dreadful?' said Miss Cooper. 'She looks like a ghost. I guess she's in love.'

'He must be a good-for-nothing lover to make his mistress look so sad. If I were you, I'd give him up, Miss Crowe.'

'I didn't know I looked sad,' said Lizzie.

'You don't now,' said Miss Cooper. 'You're smiling and blushing. A'n't she blushing, Mr. Bruce?'

'I think Miss Crowe has no more than her natural colour,' said Bruce, dropping his eye-glass. What have you been doing all this while since we parted?'

'All this while? it's only six weeks. I don't know. Nothing. What have you?'

'I've been doing nothing, too. It's hard work.'

'Have you been to any more parties?'

'Not one.'

'Any more sleigh-rides?'

'Yes. I took one more dreary drive all alone,—over that same road, you know. And I stopped at the farm-house again, and saw the old woman we had the talk with. She remembered us, and asked me what had become of the young lady who was with me before. I told her you were gone home, but that I hoped soon to go and see you. So she sent you her love'—

'Oh, how nice!' exclaimed Lizzie.

'Wasn't it? And then she made a certain little speech; I won't repeat it, or we shall have Miss Cooper talking about your blushes again.'

'I know,' cried the lady in question: 'she said she was very'—

'Very what?' said Lizzie.

'Very h-a-n-d——what everyone says.'

'Very handy?' asked Lizzie. 'I'm sure no one ever said that.'

'Of course,' said Bruce; 'and I answered what everyone answers.'

'Have you seen Mrs. Littlefield lately?'

'Several times. I called on her the day before I left town, to see if she had any messages for you.'

'Oh, thank you! I hope she's well.'

'Oh, she's as jolly as ever. She sent you her love, and hoped you would come back to Leatherborough very soon again. I told her, that, however it might be with the first message, the second should be a joint one from both of us.'

'You're very kind. I should like very much to go again.—Do you like Mrs. Littlefield?'

'Like her? Yes. Don't you? She's thought a very pleasing woman.'

'Oh, she's very nice.—I don't think she has much conversation.'

'Ah, I'm afraid you mean she doesn't backbite. We've always found plenty to talk about.'

'That's a very significant tone. What, for instance?'

'Well, we *have* talked about Miss Crowe.'

'Oh, you have? Do you call that having plenty to talk about?'

'We *have* talked about Mr. Bruce,—havn't we, Elizabeth?' said Miss Cooper, who had her own notion of being agreeable.

It was not an altogether bad notion, perhaps; but Bruce found her interruptions rather annoying, and insensibly allowed them to shorten his visit. Yet, as it was, he sat till eleven o'clock,—a stay quite unprecedented at Glenham.

When he left the house, he went splashing down the road with a very elastic tread, springing over the starlit puddles, and trolling out some sentimental ditty. He reached the inn, and went up to his sister's sitting-room.

'Why, Robert, where have you been all this while?' said Miss Bruce.

'At Dr. Cooper's.'

'Dr. Cooper's? I should think you had! Who's Dr. Cooper?'

'Where Miss Crowe's staying.'

'Miss Crowe? Ah, Mrs. Littlefield's friend! Is she as pretty as ever?'

'Prettier,—prettier,—prettier. *Tara-ta! tara-ta!*'

'Oh, Robert, do stop that singing! You'll rouse the whole house.'

V

Late one afternoon, at dusk, about three weeks after Mr. Bruce's arrival, Lizzie was sitting alone by the fire, in Miss Cooper's parlour, musing, as became the place and hour. The Doctor and his sister came in, dressed for a lecture.

'I'm sorry you won't go, my dear,' said Miss Cooper. 'It's a most interesting subject: "A Year of the War." All the battles and things described, you know.'

'I'm tired of war,' said Lizzie.

'Well, well, if you're tired of the war, we'll leave you in peace. Kiss me good-bye. What's the matter? You look sick. You are home-sick, a'n't you?'

'No, no,—I'm very well.'

'Would you like me to stay at home with you?'

'Oh, no! pray, don't!'

'Well, we'll tell you all about it. Will they have programmes, James? I'll bring her a programme.—But you really feel as if you were going to be ill. Feel of her skin, James.'

'No, you needn't, Sir,' said Lizzie. How queer of you, Miss Cooper! I'm perfectly well.'

And at last her friends departed. Before long the servant came with the lamp, ushering Mr. Mackenzie.

'Good evening, Miss,' said he. 'Bad news from Mrs. Ford.'

'Bad news?'

'Yes, Miss. I've just got a letter stating that Mr. John is growing worse and worse, and that they look for his death from hour to hour.—It's very sad,' he added, as Elizabeth was silent.

'Yes, it's very sad,' said Lizzie.

'I thought you'd like to hear it.'

'Thank you.'

'He was a very noble young fellow,' pursued Mr. Mackenzie. Lizzie made no response.

'There's the letter,' said Mr. Mackenzie, handing it over to her. Lizzie opened it.

'How long she is reading it!' thought her visitor. 'You can't see so far from the light, can you, Miss?'

'Yes,' said Lizzie.—'His poor mother! Poor woman!'

'Ay, indeed, Miss,—she's the one to be pitied.'

'Yes, she's the one to be pitied,' said Lizzie. 'Well!' and she gave him back the letter.

'I thought you'd like to see it,' said Mackenzie, drawing on his gloves; and then, after a pause,—'I'll call again, Miss, if I hear anything more. Good night!'

Lizzie got up and lowered the light, and then went back to her sofa by the fire.

Half an hour passed; it went slowly; but it passed. Still lying there in the dark room on the sofa, Lizzie heard a ring at the door-bell, a man's voice and a man's tread in the hall. She rose and went to the lamp. As she turned it up, the parlour-door opened. Bruce came in.

'I was sitting in the dark,' said Lizzie; 'but when I heard you coming, I raised the light.'

'Are you afraid of me?' said Bruce.

'Oh, no! I'll put it down again. Sit down.'

'I saw your friends going out,' pursued Bruce; 'so I knew I should find you alone.—What are you doing here in the dark?'

'I've just received very bad news from Mrs. Ford about her son. He's much worse, and will probably not live.'

'Is it possible?'

'I was thinking about that.'

'Dear me! Well that's a sad subject. I'm told he was a very fine young man.'

'He was,—very,' said Lizzie.

Bruce was silent awhile. He was a stranger to the young officer, and felt that he had nothing to offer beyond the commonplace expressions of sympathy and surprise. Nor had he exactly the measure of his companion's interest in him.

'If he dies,' said Lizzie, 'it will be under great injustice.'

'Ah! what do you mean?'

'There wasn't a braver man in the army.'

'I suppose not.'

'And, oh, Mr. Bruce,' continued Lizzie, 'he was so clever and good and generous! I wish you had known him.'

'I wish I had. But what do you mean by injustice? Were these qualities denied him?'

'No indeed! Everyone that looked at him could see that he was perfect.'

'Where's the injustice, then? It ought to be enough for him that you should think so highly of him.'

'Oh, he knew that,' said Lizzie.

Bruce was a little puzzled by his companion's manner. He watched her, as she sat with her cheek on her hand, looking at the fire. There was a long pause. Either they were too friendly or too thoughtful for the silence to be embarrassing. Bruce broke it at last.

'Miss Crowe,' said he, 'on a certain occasion, some time ago, when you first heard of Mr. Ford's wounds, I offered you my company, with the wish to console you as far as I might for what seemed a considerable shock. It was, perhaps, a bold offer for so new a friend; but, nevertheless, in it even then my heart spoke. You turned me off. Will you let me repeat it? Now, with a better right, will you let me speak out all my heart?'

Lizzie heard this speech, which was delivered in a slow and hesitating tone, without looking up or moving her head, except, perhaps, at the words 'turned me off'. After Bruce had ceased, she still kept her position.

'You'll not turn me off now?' added her companion.

She dropped her hand, raised her head, and looked at him a moment: he thought he saw the glow of tears in her eyes. Then she sank back upon the sofa with her face in the shadow of the mantel-piece.

'I don't understand you, Mr. Bruce,' said she.

'Ah, Elizabeth! am I such a poor speaker. How shall I make it plain? When I saw your friends leave home half an hour ago, and reflected that you would probably be alone, I determined to go right in and have a talk with you that I've long been wanting to have. But first I walked half a mile up the road, thinking hard,—thinking how I should say what I had to say. I made up my mind to nothing, but that somehow or other I should say it. I would trust,—I *do* trust to your frankness, kindness, and sympathy, to a feeling corresponding to my own. Do you understand that feeling? Do you know that I love you? I do, I do, I do! You *must* know it. If you don't, I solemnly swear it. I solemnly ask you, Elizabeth, to take me for your husband.'

While Bruce said these words, he rose, with their rising passion, and came and stood before Lizzie. Again she was motionless.

'Does it take you so long to think?' said he, trying to read her indistinct features; and he sat down on the sofa beside her and took her hand.

At last Lizzie spoke.

'Are you sure,' said she, 'that you love me?'

'As sure as that I breathe. Now, Elizabeth, make me as sure that I am loved in return.'

'It seems very strange, Mr. Bruce,' said Lizzie.

'What seems strange? Why should it? For a month I've been trying, in a hundred dumb ways, to make it plain; and now, when I swear it, it only seems strange!'

'What do you love me for?'

'For? For yourself, Elizabeth.'

'Myself? I am nothing.'

'I love you for what you are,—for your deep, kind heart,—for being so perfectly a woman.'

Lizzie drew away her hand, and her lover rose and stood before her again. But now she looked up into his face, questioning when she should have answered, drinking strength from his entreaties for her replies. There he stood before her, in the glow of the firelight, in all his gentlemanhood, for her to accept or reject. She slowly rose and gave him the hand she had withdrawn.

'Mr. Bruce, I shall be very proud to love you,' she said.

And then, as if this effort was beyond her strength, she half staggered back to the sofa again. And still holding her hand, he sat down beside her. And there they were still sitting when they heard the Doctor and his sister come in.

For three days Elizabeth saw nothing of Mr. Mackenzie. At last, on the fourth day, passing his office in the village, she went in and asked for him. He came out of his little back parlour with his mouth full and a beaming face.

'Good-day, Miss Crowe, and good news!'

'*Good* news?' cried Lizzie.

'Capital!' said he, looking hard at her, while he put on his spectacles. 'She writes that Mr. John—won't you take a seat?—has taken a sudden and unexpected turn for the better. Now's the moment to save him; it's an equal risk. They were to start for the North the second day after date. The surgeon comes with them. So they'll be home—of course they'll travel slowly—in four or five days. Yes, Miss, it's a remarkable Providence. And that noble young man will be spared to the country, and to those who love him, as I do.'

'I had better go back to the house and have it got ready,' said Lizzie, for an answer.

'Yes, Miss, I think you had. In fact, Mrs. Ford made that request.'
The request was obeyed. That same day Lizzie went home. For
two days she found it her interest to overlook, assiduously, a general
sweeping, scrubbing, and provisioning. She allowed herself no idle
moment until bed-time. Then—— But I would rather not be the
chamberlain of her agony. It was the easier to work, as Mr. Bruce
had gone to Leatherborough on business.

On the fourth evening, at twilight, John Ford was borne up to
the door on his stretcher, with his mother stalking beside him in
rigid grief, and kind, silent friends pressing about with helping
hands.

> 'Home they brought her warrior dead,
> She nor swooned nor uttered cry.'

It was, indeed, almost a question, whether Jack was not dead.
Death is not thinner, paler, stiller. Lizzie moved about like one in
a dream. Of course, when there are so many sympathetic friends, a
man's family has nothing to do,—except exercise a little self-control.
The women huddled Mrs. Ford to bed; rest was imperative; she was
killing herself. And it was significant of her weakness that she did
not resent this advice. In greeting her, Lizzie felt as if she were
embracing the stone image on the top of a sepulchre. She, too, had
her cares anticipated. Good Doctor Cooper and his sister stationed
themselves at the young man's couch.

The Doctor prophesied wondrous things of the change of climate;
he was certain of a recovery. Lizzie found herself very shortly dealt
with as an obstacle to this consummation. Access to John was pro-
hibited. 'Perfect stillness, you know, my dear,' whispered Miss
Cooper, opening his chamber-door on a crack, in a pair of very
creaking shoes. So for the first evening that her old friend was at
home Lizzie caught but a glimpse of his pale, senseless face, as she
hovered outside the long train of his attendants. If we may suppose
any of these kind people to have had eyes for aught but the sufferer,
we may be sure that they saw another visage equally sad and white.
The sufferer? It was hardly Jack, after all.

When Lizzie was turned from Jack's door, she took a covering
from a heap of draperies that had been hurriedly tossed down in
the hall: it was an old army-blanket. She wrapped it round her, and
went out on the verandah. It was nine o'clock; but the darkness was
filled with light. A great wanton wind—the ghost of the raw blast
which travels by day—had arisen, bearing long, soft gusts of inland
spring. Scattered clouds were hurrying across the white sky. The

bright moon, careering in their midst, seemed to have wandered forth in frantic quest of the hidden stars.

Lizzie nestled her head in the blanket, and sat down on the steps. A strange earthly smell lingered in that faded old rug, and with it a faint perfume of tobacco. Instantly the young girl's senses were transported as they had never been before to those far-off Southern battle-fields. She saw men lying in swamps, puffing their kindly pipes, drawing their blankets closer, canopied with the same luminous dusk that shone down upon her comfortable weakness. Her mind wandered amid these scenes till recalled to the present by the swinging of the garden-gate. She heard a firm, well-known tread crunching the gravel. Mr. Bruce came up the path. As he drew near the steps, Lizzie arose. The blanket fell back from her head, and Bruce started at recognizing her.

'Hullo! You, Elizabeth? What's the matter?'

Lizzie made no answer.

'Are you one of Mr. Ford's watchers?' he continued, coming up the steps; 'how is he?'

Still she was silent. Bruce put out his hands to take hers, and bent forward as if to kiss her. She half shook him off, and retreated toward the door.

'Good heavens!' cried Bruce; 'what's the matter? Are you moon-struck? Can't you speak?'

'No,—no,—not to-night,' said Lizzie, in a choking voice. 'Go away,—go away!'

She stood holding the door-handle and motioning him off. He hesitated a moment, and then advanced. She opened the door rapidly, and went in. He heard her lock it. He stood looking at it stupidly for some time, and then slowly turned round and walked down the steps.

The next morning Lizzie arose with the early dawn, and came downstairs. She went into the room where Jack lay, and gently opened the door. Miss Cooper was dozing in her chair. Lizzie crossed the threshold, and stole up to the bed. Poor Ford lay peacefully sleeping. There was his old face, after all,—his strong, honest features refined, but not weakened, by pain. Lizzie softly drew up a low chair, and sat down beside him. She gazed into his face,—the dear and honoured face into which she had so often gazed in health. It was strangely handsomer: body stood for less. It seemed to Lizzie, that, as the fabric of her lover's soul was more clearly revealed,—the veil of the temple rent wellnigh in twain,—she could read the justification of all her old worship. One of Jack's hands lay outside the sheets,—those strong, supple fingers, once so cunning in workmanship, so frank in friendship, now thinner and whiter than her own. After looking at it for some time, Lizzie gently grasped it. Jack slowly opened his eyes. Lizzie's heart began to throb; it was as if the stillness of the sanctuary had given a sign. At first there was no recognition in the young man's gaze. Then the dull pupils began visibly to brighten. There came to his lips the commencement of that strange moribund smile which seems so ineffably satirical of the things of this world. O imposing spectacle of death! O blessed soul, marked for promotion! What earthly favour is like thine? Lizzie sank down on her knees, and, still clasping John's hand, bent closer over him.

'Jack,—dear, dear Jack,' she whispered, 'do you know me?'

The smile grew more intense. The poor fellow drew out his other hand, and slowly, feebly placed it on Lizzie's head, stroking down her hair with his fingers.

'Yes, yes,' she murmured; 'you know me, don't you? I am Lizzie, Jack. Don't you remember Lizzie?'

Ford moved his lips inaudibly, and went on patting her head.

'This is home, you know,' said Lizzie; 'this is Glenham. You haven't forgotten Glenham? You are with your mother and me and your friends. Dear, darling Jack!'

Still he went on, stroking her head; and his feeble lips tried to emit some sound. Lizzie laid her head down on the pillow beside his own, and still his hand lingered caressingly on her hair.

'Yes, you know me,' she pursued; 'you are with your friends now forever,—with those who will love and take care of you, oh, forever!'

'I'm very badly wounded,' murmured Jack, close to her ear.

'Yes, yes, my dear boy, but your wounds are healing. I will love you and nurse you forever.'

'Yes, Lizzie, our old promise,' said Jack: and his hand fell upon her neck and with its feeble pressure he drew her closer, and she wet his face with her tears.

Then Miss Cooper, awakening, rose and drew Lizzie away.

'I am sure you excite him, my dear. It is best he should have none of his family near him,—persons with whom he has associations, you know.'

Here the Doctor was heard gently tapping on the window, and Lizzie went round to the door to admit him.

She did not see Jack again all day. Two or three times she ventured into the room, but she was banished by a frown, or a finger raised to the lips. She waylaid the Doctor frequently. He was blithe and cheerful, certain of Jack's recovery. This good man used to exhibit as much moral elation at the prospect of a cure as an orthodox believer at that of a new convert: it was one more body gained from the Devil. He assured Lizzie that the change of scene and climate had already begun to tell: the fever was lessening, the worst symptoms disappearing. He answered Lizzie's reiterated desire to do something by directions to keep the house quiet and the sick-room empty.

Soon after breakfast, Miss Dawes, a neighbour, came in to relieve Miss Cooper, and this indefatigable lady transferred her attention to Mrs. Ford. Action was forbidden her. Miss Cooper was delighted for once to be able to lay down the law to her vigorous neighbour, of whose fine judgment she had always stood in awe. Having bullied Mrs. Ford into taking her breakfast in the little sitting-room, she closed the doors, and prepared for 'a good long talk'. Lizzie was careful not to break in upon this interview. She had bidden her patroness good morning, asked after her health, and received one of her temperate osculations. As she passed the invalid's door, Doctor Cooper came out and asked her to go and look for a certain role of bandages, in Mr. John's trunk, which had been carried into another room. Lizzie hastened to perform this task. In fumbling through the contents of the trunk, she came across a packet of letters in a well-known feminine hand-writing. She pocketed it, and, after disposing of the bandages, went to her own room, locked the door, and sat down to examine the letters. Between reading and thinking and sighing and (in spite of herself) smiling, this process took the whole morning. As she came down to dinner, she encountered Mrs. Ford and Miss Cooper, emerging from the sitting-room, the good long talk being only just concluded.

'How do you feel, Ma'am?' she asked of the elder lady,—'rested?'

For all answer Mrs. Ford gave a look—I had almost said a scowl —so hard, so cold, so reproachful, that Lizzie was transfixed. But suddenly its sickening meaning was revealed to her. She turned to Miss Cooper, who stood pale and fluttering beside the mistress, her everlasting smile glazed over with a piteous, deprecating glance; and I fear her eyes flashed out the same message of angry scorn they had just received. These telegraphic operations are very rapid. The ladies hardly halted: the next moment found them seated at the dinner-table with Miss Cooper scrutinizing her napkin-mark and Mrs. Ford saying grace.

Dinner was eaten in silence. When it was over, Lizzie returned to her own room. Miss Cooper went home, and Mrs. Ford went to her son. Lizzie heard the firm low click of the lock as she closed the door. Why did she lock it? There was something fatal in the silence that followed. The plot of her little tragedy thickened. Be it so: she would act her part with the rest. For the second time in her experience, her mind was lightened by the intervention of Mrs. Ford. Before the scorn of her own conscience, (which never came,) before Jack's deepest reproach, she was ready to bow down,—but not before that long-faced Nemesis in black silk. The leaven of resentment began to work. She leaned back in her chair, and folded her arms, brave to await results. But before long she fell asleep. She was aroused by a knock at her chamber-door. The afternoon was far gone. Miss Dawes stood without.

'Elizabeth, Mr. John wants very much to see you, with his love. Come down very gently: his mother is lying down. Will you sit with him while I take my dinner?—Better? Yes, ever so much.

Lizzie betook herself with trembling haste to Jack's bedside.

He was propped up with pillows. His pale cheeks were slightly flushed. His eyes were bright. He raised himself, and, for such feeble arms, gave Lizzie a long, strong embrace.

'I've not seen you all day, Lizzie,' said he. 'Where have you been?'

'Dear Jack, they wouldn't let me come near you. I begged and prayed. And I wanted so to go to you in the army; but I couldn't. I wish, I wish I had!'

'You wouldn't have liked it, Lizzie. I'm glad you didn't. It's a bad, bad place.'

He lay quietly, holding her hands and gazing at her.

'Can I do anything for you, dear?' asked the young girl. 'I would work my life out. I'm so glad you're better!'

It was some time before Jack answered,—

'Lizzie,' said he, at last, 'I sent for you to look at you.—You are more wondrously beautiful than ever. Your hair is brown,—like—like nothing; your eyes are blue; your neck is white. Well, well!'

He lay perfectly motionless, but for his eyes. They wandered over her with a kind of peaceful glee, like sunbeams playing on a statue. Poor Ford lay, indeed, not unlike an old wounded Greek, who at falling dusk has crawled into a temple to die, steeping the last dull interval in idle admiration of sculptured Artemis.

'Ah, Lizzie, this is already heaven!' he murmured.

'It will be heaven when you get well,' whispered Lizzie.

He smiled into her eyes:—

'You say more than you mean. There should be perfect truth between us. Dear Lizzie, I am not going to get well. They are all very much mistaken. I am going to die. I've done my work. Death makes up for everything. My great pain is in leaving you. But you, too, will die on of these days; remember that. In all pain and sorrow, remember that.'

Lizzie was able to reply only by the tightening grasp of her hands. 'But there is something more,' pursued Jack. 'Life *is* as good as death. Your heart has found its true keeper; so we shall all three be happy. Tell him I bless him and honour him. Tell him God, too, blesses him. Shake hands with him for me,' said Jack, feebly moving his pale fingers. 'My mother,' he went on,—'be very kind to her. She will have great grief, but she will not die of it. She'll live to great age. Now, Lizzie, I can't talk any more; I wanted to say farewell. You'll keep me farewell,—you'll stay with me awhile,—won't you? I'll look at you till the last. For a little while you'll be mine, holding my hands—so—until death parts us.'

Jack kept his promise. His eyes were fixed in a firm gaze long after the sense had left them.

In the early dawn of the next day, Elizabeth left her sleepless bed, opened the window, and looked out on the wide prospect, still cool and dim with departing night. It offered freshness and peace to her hot head and restless heart. She dressed herself hastily, crept downstairs, passed the death-chamber, and stole out of the quiet house. She turned away from the still sleeping village and walked towards the open country. She went a long way without knowing it. The sun had risen high when she bethought herself to turn. As she came back along the brightening highway, and drew near home, she saw a tall figure standing beneath the budding trees of the garden, hesitating, apparently, whether to open the gate. Lizzie came upon him almost before he had seen her. Bruce's first movement was to put out his hands, as any lover might; but as Lizzie raised her veil, he dropped them.

'Yes, Mr. Bruce,' said Lizzie, 'I'll give you my hand once more,—in farewell.'

'Elizabeth!' cried Bruce, half stupefied, 'in God's name, what do you mean by these crazy speeches?'

'I mean well. I mean kindly and humanely to you. And I mean justice to my old—old love.'

She went to him, took his listless hand, without looking into his wild, smitten face, shook it passionately, and then, wrenching her own from his grasp, opened the gate and let it swing behind her.

'No! no! no!' she almost shrieked, turning about in the path. 'I forbid you to follow me!'

But for all that, he went in.

A Landscape Painter

[First appeared in the *Atlantic Monthly*, vol. xvii (February 1866), pp. 182-202. The tale was revised and reprinted in volume ii of *Stories Revived* (1885).]

DO YOU REMEMBER HOW, A DOZEN YEARS AGO, A NUMBER of our friends were startled by the report of the rupture of young Locksley's engagement with Miss Leary? This event made some noise in its day. Both parties possessed certain claims to distinction: Locksley in his wealth, which was believed to be enormous, and the young lady in her beauty, which was in truth very great. I used to hear that her lover was fond of comparing her to the Venus of Milo; and, indeed, if you can imagine the mutilated goddess with her full complement of limbs, dressed out by Madame de Crinoline, and engaged in small talk beneath the drawing-room chandelier, you may obtain a vague notion of Miss Josephine Leary. Locksley, you remember, was rather a short man, dark, and not particularly good-looking; and when he walked about with his betrothed, it was half a matter of surprise that he should have ventured to propose to a young lady of such heroic proportions. Miss Leary had the grey eyes and auburn hair which I have always assigned to the famous statue. The one defect in her face, in spite of an expression of great candour and sweetness, was a certain lack of animation. What it was besides her beauty that attracted Locksley I never discovered: perhaps, since his attachment was so short-lived, it was her beauty alone. I say that his attachment was of brief duration, because the rupture was understood to have come from him. Both he and Miss Leary very wisely held their tongues on the matter; but among their friends and enemies it of course received a hundred explanations. That most popular with Locksley's well-wishers was, that he had backed out (these events are discussed, you know, in fashionable circles very much as an expected prize-fight which has miscarried is canvassed in reunions of another kind) only on flagrant evidence of the lady's—what, faithlessness?—on overwhelming proof of the most *mercenary* spirit on the part of Miss Leary. You see, our friend was held capable of doing battle for an 'idea'. It must be owned that this was a novel charge; but, for myself, having long known Mrs. Leary, the mother, who was a widow with four daughters, to be an inveterate old screw, I took the liberty of accrediting the existence of a similar propensity in her eldest born. I suppose that the young lady's family had, on their own side, a very plausible

version of their disappointment. It was, however, soon made up to
them by Josephine's marriage with a gentleman of expectations
very nearly as brilliant as those of her old suitor. And what was *his*
compensation? That is precisely my story.

Locksley disappeared, as you will remember, from public view.
The events above alluded to happened in March. On calling at his
lodgings in April, I was told he had gone to the 'country'. But towards the last of May I met him. He told me that he was on the
look-out for a quiet, unfrequented place on the sea-shore, where he
might rusticate and sketch. He was looking very poorly. I suggested
Newport, and I remember he hardly had the energy to smile at the
simple joke. We parted without my having been able to satisfy him,
and for a very long time I quite lost sight of him. He died seven
years ago, at the age of thirty-five. For five years, accordingly, he
managed to shield his life from the eyes of men. Through circumstances which I need not detail, a large portion of his personal property has come into my hands. You will remember that he was a
man of what are called elegant tastes: that is, he was seriously
interested in arts and letters. He wrote some very bad poetry, but
he produced a number of remarkable paintings. He left a mass of
papers on all subjects, few of which are adapted to be generally
interesting. A portion of them, however, I highly prize,—that which
constitutes his private diary. It extends from his twenty-fifth to his
thirtieth year, at which period it breaks off suddenly. If you will
come to my house, I will show you such of his pictures and sketches
as I possess, and, I trust, convert you to my opinion that he had in
him the stuff of a great painter. Meanwhile I will place before you
the last hundred pages of his diary, as an answer to your inquiry
regarding the ultimate view taken by the great Nemesis of his
treatment of Miss Leary,—his scorn of the magnificent Venus
Victrix. The recent decease of the one person who had a voice paramount to mine in the disposal of Locksley's effects enables me to
act without reserve.

Cragthorpe, June 9th.—I have been sitting some minutes, pen in
hand, pondering whether on this new earth, beneath this new sky,
I had better resume these occasional records of my idleness. I think
I will at all events make the experiment. If we fail, as Lady Macbeth
remarks, we fail. I find my entries have been longest when my life
has been dullest. I doubt not, therefore, that once launched into
the monotony of village life, I shall sit scribbling from morning till
night. If nothing happens—— But my prophetic soul tells me that
something *will* happen. I am determined that something shall,—if

it be nothing else than that I paint a picture.

When I came up to bed half an hour ago, I was deadly sleepy. Now, after looking out of the window a little while, my brain is strong and clear, and I feel as if I could write till morning. But, unfortunately, I have nothing to write about. And then, if I expect to rise early, I must turn in betimes. The whole village is asleep, godless metropolitan that I am! The lamps on the square without flicker in the wind; there is nothing abroad but the blue darkness and the smell of the rising tide. I have spent the whole day on my legs, trudging from one side of the peninsula to the other. What a trump is old Mrs. M——, to have thought of this place! I must write her a letter of passionate thanks. Never before, it seems to me, have I known pure coast-scenery. Never before have I relished the beauties of wave, rock, and cloud. I am filled with a sensuous ecstasy at the unparalleled life, light, and transparency of the air. I am stricken mute with reverent admiration at the stupendous resources posses-sed by the ocean in the way of colour and sound; and as yet, I suppose, I have not seen half of them. I came in to supper hungry, weary, footsore, sunburnt, dirty,—happier, in short, than I have been for a twelvemonth. And now for the victories of the brush!

June 11th.—Another day afoot and also afloat. I resolved this morning to leave this abominable little tavern. I can't stand my feather-bed another night. I determined to find some other prospect than the town-pump and the 'drug-store'. I questioned my host, after breakfast, as to the possibility of getting lodgings in any of the outlying farms and cottages. But my host either did not or would not know anything about the matter. So I resolved to wander forth and seek my fortune,—to roam inquisitive through the neigh-bourhood, and appeal to the indigenous sentiment of hospitality. But never did I see a folk so devoid of this amiable quality. By dinner-time I had given up in despair. After dinner I strolled down to the harbour, which is close at hand. The brightness and breezi-ness of the water tempted me to hire a boat and resume my explor-ations. I procured an old tub, with a short stump of a mast, which, being planted quite in the centre, gave the craft much the appear-ance of an inverted mushroom. I made for what I took to be, and what is, an island, lying long and low, some three or four miles, over against the town. I sailed for half an hour directly before the wind, and at last found myself aground on the shelving beach of a quiet little cove. *Such* a little cove! So bright, so still, so warm, so remote from the town, which lay off in the distance, white and semi-circular! I leaped ashore, and dropped my anchor. Before me rose a steep cliff, crowned with an old ruined fort or tower. I made my way up, and about to the landward entrance. The fort is a hollow old shell. Looking upward from the beach, you see the harmless blue sky through the gaping loopholes. Its interior is choked with rocks and brambles, and masses of fallen masonry. I scrambled up to the parapet, and obtained a noble sea-view. Beyond the broad bay I saw miniature town and country mapped out before me; and on the other hand, I saw the infinite Atlantic,—over which, by the by, all the pretty things are brought from Paris. I spent the whole afternoon in wandering hither and thither over the hills that encircle the little cove in which I had landed, heedless of the minutes and my steps, watching the sailing clouds and the cloudy sails on the horizon, listening to the musical attrition of the tidal pebbles, killing innocuous suckers. The only particular sensation I remember was that of being ten years old again, together with a general impression of Saturday afternoon, of the liberty to go in wading or even swimming, and of the prospect of limping home in the dusk with a wondrous story of having *almost* caught a turtle. When I returned, I found—but I know very well what I found, and I need hardly repeat it here for my mortification. Heaven knows I never was a practical character. What thought I about the tide? There lay the old tub, high and dry, with the rusty anchor protruding from the flat green stones and the shallow puddles left by the receding wave. Moving the boat an inch, much more a dozen yards, was quite beyond my strength. I slowly re-ascended the cliff, to see if from its summit any help was discernible. None was within sight; and I was about to go down again in profound dejection, when I saw a trim little sail-boat shoot out from behind a neighbouring bluff, and advance along the shore. I quickened pace. On reaching the beach, I found the new-comer standing out about a hundred yards. The man at the helm appeared to regard me with some interest. With a mute prayer that his feeling might be akin to compassion, I invited him by voice and gesture to make for a little point of rocks a short distance above us, where I proceeded to join him. I told him my story, and he readily took me aboard. He was a civil old gentleman, of the seafaring sort, who appeared to be cruising about in the evening breeze for his pleasure. On landing, I visited the proprietor of my old tub, related my misadventure, and offered to pay damages, if the boat shall turn out in the morning to have sustained any. Meanwhile, I suppose, it is held secure against the next tidal revolution, however insidious.—But for my old gentleman. I have decidedly picked up an acquaintance, if not made a friend. I gave him a very good cigar; and before we reached home, we had become thoroughly intimate. In exchange for my cigar he gave me his name; and there was that in his tone which seemed to imply that I had by no means the worst of the bargain. His name is Richard Blunt, 'though most people,' he added, 'call me Captain, for short'. He then proceeded to inquire my own titles and pretensions. I told him no lies, but I told him only half the truth; and if he chooses to indulge mentally in any romantic understatements, why, he is welcome, and bless his simple heart! The fact is, that I have broken with the past. I have decided, coolly and calmly, as I believe, that it is necessary to my success, or, at any rate, to my happiness, to abjure for a while my conventional self, and to assume a simple, natural character. How can a man be simple and natural who is known to have a hundred thousand a year? That is the supreme curse. It's bad enough to have it: to be known to have it, to be known only because you have it, is most damnable. I suppose I am too proud to be successfully rich. Let me see how poverty will serve my turn. I have taken a fresh start. I have determined to stand upon my own merits. If they fail me, I shall fall back upon my millions; but with God's help I will test them, and see what kind of stuff I am made of. To be young, to be strong, to be poor,—such, in this blessed nineteenth century, is the great basis of solid success. I have resolved to take at least one brief draught from the pure founts of inspiration of my time. I replied to the Captain with such reservations as a brief survey of these principles dictated. What a luxury to pass in a poor man's mind for his brother! I begin to respect myself. Thus much the Captain knows: that I am an educated man, with a taste for painting; that I have come hither for the purpose of cultivating this taste by the study of coast scenery, and for my health. I have reason to believe, moreover, that he suspects me of limited means and of being a good deal of an economist. Amen! *Vogue la galère!* But the point of my story is in his very hospitable offer of lodgings. I had been telling him of my ill success of the morning in the pursuit of the same. He is an odd union of the gentleman of the old school and the old-fashioned, hot-headed merchant-captain. I suppose that certain traits in these characters are readily convertible.

'Young man,' said he, after taking several meditative puffs of his cigar, 'I don't see the point in your living in a tavern, when there are folks about you with more house-room than they know what to do with. A tavern is only half a house, just as one of these new-fashioned screw-propellers is only half a ship. Suppose you walk round and take a look at my place. I own quite a respectable house over yonder to the left of the town. Do you see that old wharf with the tumble-down warehouses, and the long row of elms behind it?

I live right in the midst of the elms. We have the dearest little
garden in the world, stretching down to the water's edge. It's all as
quiet as anything can be, short of a graveyard. The back windows,
you know, overlook the harbour, and you can see twenty miles up
the bay, and fifty miles out to sea. You can paint to yourself there
the livelong day, with no more fear of intrusion than if you were
out yonder at the light-ship. There's no one but myself and my
daughter, who's a perfect lady, Sir. She teaches music in a young
ladies' school. You see, money's an object, as they say. We have
never taken boarders yet, because none ever came in our track; but
I guess we can learn the ways. I supose you've boarded before; you
can put us up to a thing or two.'

There was something so kindly and honest in the old man's
weather-beaten face, something so friendly in his address, that I
forthwith struck a bargain with him, subject to his daughter's
approval. I am to have her answer to-morrow. This same daughter
strikes me as rather a dark spot in the picture. Teacher in a young
ladies' school,—probably the establishment of which Mrs. M——
spoke to me. I suppose she's over thirty. I think I know the species.

June 12th, A.M.—I have really nothing to do but to scribble. 'Barkis
is willing.' Captain Blunt brought me word this morning that his
daughter smiles propitious. I am to report this evening; but I shall
send my slender baggage in an hour or two.

P.M.—Here I am, housed. The house is less than a mile from the
inn, and reached by a very pleasant road skirting the harbour. At
about six o'clock I presented myself. Captain Blunt had described
the place. A very civil old negress admitted me, and ushered me
into the garden, where I found my friends watering their flowers.
The old man was in his house-coat and slippers. He gave me a
cordial welcome. There is something delightfully easy in his manners,—and in Miss Blunt's, too, for that matter. She received me
very nicely. The late Mrs. Blunt was probably a well-bred woman.
As for Miss Blunt's being thirty, she is about twenty-four. She wore
a fresh white dress, with a violet ribbon at her neck, and a rosebud
in her button-hole,—or whatever corresponds thereto on the feminine
bosom. I thought I discerned in this costume a vague intention of
courtesy, of deference, of celebrating my arrival. I don't believe
Miss Blunt wears white muslin every day. She shook hands with me,
and made me a very frank little speech about her hospitality. 'We
have never had any inmates before,' said she; 'and we are consequently new to the business. I don't know what you expect. I hope
you don't expect a great deal. You must ask for anything you want

If we can give it, we shall be very glad to do so; if we can't, I give you warning that we shall refuse outright.' Bravo, Miss Blunt! The best of it is, that she is decidedly beautiful,—and in the grand manner: tall, and rather plump. What is the orthodox description of a pretty girl?—white and red? Miss Blunt is not a pretty girl, she is a handsome woman. She leaves an impression of black and red; that is, she is a florid brunette. She has a great deal of wavy black hair, which encircles her head like a dusky glory, a smoky halo. Her eyebrows, too, are black, but her eyes themselves are of a rich blue grey, the colour of those slate-cliffs which I saw yesterday, weltering under the tide. Her mouth, however, is her strong point. It is very large, and contains the finest row of teeth in all this weary world. Her smile is eminently intelligent. Her chin is full, and somewhat heavy. All this is a tolerable catalogue, but no picture. I have been tormenting my brain to discover whether it was her colouring or her form that impressed me most. Fruitless speculation! Seriously, I think it was neither; it was her movement. She walks a queen. It was the conscious poise of her head, the unconscious 'hang' of her arms, the careless grace and dignity with which she lingered along the garden-path, smelling a red red rose! She has very little to say, apparently; but when she speaks, it is to the point, and if the point suggests it, with a very sweet smile. Indeed, if she is not talkative, it is not from timidity. Is it from indifference? Time will elucidate this, as well as other matters. I cling to the hypothesis that she is amiable. She is, moreover, intelligent; she is probably quite reserved; and she is possibly very proud. She is, in short, a woman of character. There you are, Miss Blunt, at full length,—emphatically the portrait of a lady. After tea, she gave us some music in the parlour. I confess that I was more taken with the picture of the dusky little room, lighted by the single candle on the piano, and by the *effect* of Miss Blunt's performance, than with its meaning. She appears to possess a very brilliant touch.

June 18th.—I have now been here almost a week. I occupy two very pleasant rooms. My painting-room is a vast and rather bare apartment, with a very good southern light. I have decked it out with a few old prints and sketches, and have already grown very fond of it. When I had disposed my artistic odds and ends in as picturesque a fashion as possible, I called in my hosts. The Captain looked about silently for some moments, and then inquired hopefully if I had ever tried my hand at a ship. On learning that I had not yet got to ships, he relapsed into a deferential silence. His daughter smiled and questioned very graciously, and called everything beautiful and delightful; which rather disappointed me, as I had taken her to be a woman of some originality. She is rather a puzzle;—or is she, indeed, a very commonplace person, and the fault in me, who am forever taking women to mean a great deal more than their Maker intended? Regarding Miss Blunt I have collected a few facts. She is not twenty-four, but twenty-seven years old. She has taught music ever since she was twenty, in a large boarding-school just out of the town, where she originally got her education. Her salary in this establishment, which is, I believe, a tolerably flourishing one, and the proceeds of a few additional lessons, constitute the chief revenues of the household. But Blunt fortunately owns his house, and his needs and habits are of the simplest kind. What does he or his daughter know of the great worldly theory of necessities, the great worldly scale of pleasures? Miss Blunt's only luxuries are a subscription to the circulating library, and an occasional walk on the beach, which, like one of Miss Bronte's heroines, she paces in company with an old New-foundland dog. I am afraid she is sadly ignorant. She reads noth-ing but novels. I am bound to believe, however, that she has derived from the perusal of these works a certain practical science of her own. 'I read all the novels I can get,' she said yesterday; 'but I only like the good ones. I do so like "Zanoni," which I have just finished.' I must set her to work at some of the masters. I should like some of those fretful New-York heiresses to see how this woman lives. I wish, too, that half a dozen of *ces messieurs* of the clubs might take a peep at the present way of life of their humble servant. We breakfast at eight o'clock. Immediately afterwards, Miss Blunt, in a shabby old bonnet and shawl, starts off to school. If the weather is fine, the Captain goes out a-fishing, and I am left to my own devices. Twice I have accompanied the old man. The second time I was lucky enough to catch a big blue-fish, which we had for dinner. The Captain is an excellent specimen of the sturdy navigator, with his loose blue clothes, his ultra-divergent legs, his crisp white hair, and his jolly thick-skinned visage. He comes of a sea-faring English race. There is more or less of the ship's cabin in the general aspect of this antiquated house. I have heard the winds whistle about its walls, on two or three occasions, in true mid-ocean style. And then the illusion is heightened, somehow or other, by the extraordinary intensity of the light. My painting-room is a grand observatory of the clouds. I sit by the half-hour, watching them sail past my high, uncurtained windows. At the back part of the room, something tells you that they belong to an ocean sky; and there, in truth, as you draw nearer, you behold the vast, grey complement of sea. This quarter of the town is perfectly quiet. Human activity seems to have passed over it, never again to return, and to have left a kind of deposit of melancholy resignation. The streets are clean, bright, and airy; but this fact seems only to add to the intense sobriety. It implies that the unobstructed heavens are in the secret of their decline. There is something ghostly in the perpetual stillness. We frequently hear the rattling of the yards and the issuing of orders on the barks and schooners anchored out in the harbour.

June 28th.—My experiment works far better than I had hoped. I am thoroughly at my ease; my peace of mind quite passeth understanding. I work diligently; I have none but pleasant thoughts. The past has almost lost its terrors. For a week now I have been out sketching daily. The Captain carries me to a certain point on the shore of the harbour, I disembark and strike across the fields to a spot where I have established a kind of *rendezvous* with a particular effect of rock and shadow, which has been tolerably faithful to its appointment. Here I set up my easel, and paint till sunset. Then I retrace my steps and meet the boat. I am in every way much encouraged. The horizon of my work grows perceptibly wider. And then I am inexpressibly happy in the conviction that I am not wholly unfit for a life of (moderate) labour and (comparative) privation. I am quite in love with my poverty, if I may call it so. As why should I not? At this rate I don't spend eight hundred a year.

July 12th.—We have been having a week of bad weather: constant rain, night and day. This is certainly at once the brightest and the blackest spot in New England. The skies can smile, assuredly; but how they can frown! I have been painting rather languidly, and at a great disadvantage, at my window. . . . . . Through all this pouring and pattering, Miss Blunt sallies forth to her pupils. She envelops her beautiful head in a great woollen hood, her beautiful figure in a kind of feminine Mackintosh; her feet she puts into heavy clogs, and over the whole she balances a cotton umbrella. When she comes home, with the rain-drops glistening on her red cheeks and her dark lashes, her cloak bespattered with mud, and her hands red with the cool damp, she is a profoundly wholesome spectacle. I never fail to make her a very low bow, for which she repays me with an extraordinary smile. This workingday side of her character is what especially pleases me in Miss Blunt. This holy working-dress of loveliness and dignity sits upon her with the simplicity of an antique drapery. Little use has she for whalebones and furbelows. What a poetry there is, after all, in red hands! I kiss yours, Mademoiselle. I do so because you are self-helpful; because you earn your living; because you are honest, simple, and ignorant (for a sensible woman, that is); because you speak and act to the point; because, in short, you are so unlike— certain of your sisters.

July 16th.—On Monday it cleared up generously. When I went to my window, on rising, I found sky and sea looking, for their brightness and freshness, like a clever English water-colour. The ocean is of a deep purple blue; above it, the pure, bright sky looks pale, though it bends with an infinite depth over the inland horizon. Here and there on the dark breezy water bleams the white cap of a wave, or flaps the white cloak of a fishing-boat. I have been sketching sedulously; I have discovered, within a couple of miles' walk, a large, lonely pond, set in quite a grand landscape of barren rocks and grassy slopes. At one extremity is a broad outlook on the open sea; at the other, deep buried in the foliage of an apple-orchard, stands an old haunted-looking farm-house. To the west of the pond is a wide expanse of rock and grass, of beach and marsh. The sheep browse over it as upon a Highland moor. Except a few stunted firs and cedars, there is not a tree in sight. When I want shade, I seek it in the shelter of one of the great mossy boulders which upheave their scintillating shoulders to the sun, or of the long shadow dells where a tangle of blackberry-bushes hedges about a sky-reflecting pool. I have encamped over against a plain, brown hillside, which, with laborious patience, I am transferring to canvas; and as we have now had the same clear sky for several days, I have almost finished quite a satisfactory little study. I go forth immediately after breakfast. Miss Blunt furnishes me with a napkin full of bread and cold meat, which at the noonday hours, in my sunny solitude, within sight of the slumbering ocean, I voraciously convey to my lips with my discoloured fingers. At seven o'clock I return to tea, at which repast we each tell the story of our day's work. For poor Miss Blunt, it is day after day the same story: a wearisome round of visits to the school, and to the houses of the mayor, the parson, the butcher, the baker, whose young ladies, of course, all receive instruction on the piano. But she doesn't complain, nor, indeed, does she look very weary. When she has put on a fresh calico dress for tea, and arranged her hair anew, and with these improvements flits about with that quiet hither and thither of her gentle footsteps, preparing our evening meal, peeping into the teapot, cutting the solid loaf,—or when, sitting down on the low door-step, she reads out select scraps from the evening paper,—or else, when, tea being over, she folds her arms, (an attitude which becomes her mightily,) and, still sitting on the door-step, gossips away the evening in comfortable idleness, while her father and I indulge in the fragrant pipe, and watch the lights shining out, one by one, in different quarters of the darkling bay: at these moments she is as pretty, as cheerful, as careless as it becomes a sensible woman to be. What a pride the Captain takes in his daughter! And she, in return, how perfect is her devotion to the old man! He is proud of her grace, of her tact, of her good sense, of her wit, such as it is. He thinks her to be the most accomplished of women. He waits upon her as if, instead of his old familiar Esther, she were a newly inducted daughter-in-law. And indeed, if I were his own son, he could not be kinder to me. They are certainly—nay, why should I not say it?—*we* are certainly a very happy little household. Will it last forever? I say *we*, because both father and daughter have given me a hundred assurances—he direct, and she, if I don't flatter myself, after the manner of her sex, indirect—that I am already a valued friend. It is natural enough that I should have gained their goodwill. They have received at my hands inveterate courtesy. The way to the old man's heart is through a studied consideration of his daughter. He knows, I imagine, that I admire Miss Blunt. But if I should at any time fall below the mark of ceremony, I should have an account to settle with him. All this is as it should be. When people have to economize with the dollars and cents, they have a right to be splendid in their feelings. I have prided myself not a little on my good manners towards my hostess. That my bearing has been without reproach is, however, a fact which I do not, in any degree, set down here to my credit; for I would defy the most impertinent of men (whoever he is) to forget himself with this young lady, without leave unmistakably given. Those deep, dark eyes have a strong prohibitory force. I record the circumstance simply because in future years, when my charming friend shall have become a distant shadow, it will be pleasant, in turning over these pages, to find written testimony to a number of points which I shall be apt to charge solely upon my imagination. I wonder whether Miss Blunt, in days to come, referring to the tables of her memory for some trivial matter-of-fact, some prosaic date of half-buried landmark, will also encounter this little secret of ours, as I may call it,—will decipher an old faint note to this effect, overlaid with the memoranda of intervening years. Of course she will. Sentiment aside, she is a woman of an excellent memory.

Whether she forgives or not I know not; but she certainly doesn't forget. Doubtless, virtue is its own reward; but there is a double satisfaction in being polite to a person on whom it *tells*. Another reason for my pleasant relations with the Captain is, that I afford him a chance to rub up his rusty old cosmopolitanism, and trot out his little scraps of old-fashioned reading, some of which are very curious. It is a great treat for him to spin his threadbare yarns over again to a sympathetic listener. These warm July evenings, in the sweet-smelling garden, are just the proper setting for his amiable garrulities. An odd enough relation subsists between us on this point. Like many gentlemen of his calling, the Captain is harassed by an irresistible desire to romance, even on the least promising themes; and it is vastly amusing to observe how he will auscultate, as it were, his auditor's inmost mood, to ascertain whether it is prepared for the absorption of his insidious fibs. Sometimes they perish utterly in the transition: they are very pretty, I conceive, in the deep and briny well of the Captain's fancy; but they won't bear being transplanted into the shallow inland lakes of my land-bred apprehension. At other times, the auditor being in a dreamy, senti- mental, and altogether unprincipled mood, he will drink the old man's salt-water by the bucketful and feel none the worse for it. Which is the worse, wilfully to tell, or wilfully to believe, a pretty little falsehood which will not hurt anyone? I suppose you can't believe wilfully; you only pretend to believe. My part of the game, therefore, is certainly as bad as the Captain's. Perhaps I take kindly to his beautiful perversions of fact, because I am myself engaged in one, because I am sailing under false colours of the deepest dye. I wonder whether my friends have any suspicion of the real state of the case. How should they? I fancy, that, on the whole, I play my part pretty well. I am delighted to find it come so easy. I do not mean that I experience little difficulty in foregoing my hundred petty elegancies and luxuries,—for to these, thank Heaven, I was not so indissolubly wedded that one wholesome shock could not loosen my bonds,—but that I manage more cleverly than I ex- pected to stifle those innumerable tacit allusions which might serve effectually to belie my character.

Sunday, July 20th.—This has been a very pleasant day for me; although in it, of course, I have done no manner of work. I had this morning a delightful *tête-à-tête* with my hostess. She had sprained her ankle, coming downstairs; and so, instead of going forth to Sunday school and to meeting, she was obliged to remain at home on the sofa. The Captain, who is of a very punctilious piety, went off alone. When I came into the parlour, as the church-bells were ringing, Miss Blunt asked me if I never went to meeting.

'Never when there is anything better to do at home,' said I.

'What is better than going to church?' she asked, with charming simplicity.

She was reclining on the sofa, with her foot on a pillow, and her Bible in her lap. She looked by no means afflicted at having to be absent from divine service; and, instead of answering her question, I took the liberty of telling her so.

'I *am* sorry to be absent,' said she. 'You know it's my only festival in the week.'

'So you look upon it as a festival,' said I.

'Isn't it a pleasure to meet one's acquaintance? I confess I am never deeply interested in the sermon, and I very much dislike teaching the children; but I like wearing my best bonnet, and singing in the choir, and walking part of the way home with'—

'With whom?'

'With anyone who offers to walk with me.'

'With Mr. Johnson, for instance,' said I.

Mr. Johnson is a young lawyer in the village, who calls here once a week, and whose attentions to Miss Blunt have been remarked.

'Yes,' she answered, 'Mr. Johnson will do as an instance.'

'How he will miss you!'

'I suppose he will. We sing off the same book. What are you laughing at? He kindly permits me to hold the book, while he stands with his hands in his pockets. Last Sunday I quite lost patience. "Mr. Johnson," said I, "do hold the book! Where are your manners?" He burst out laughing in the midst of the reading. He will certainly have to hold the book to-day.'

'What a "masterful soul" he is! I suppose he will call after the meeting.'

'Perhaps he will. I hope so.'

'I hope he won't,' said I, roundly. 'I am going to sit down here and talk to you, and I wish our *tête-à-tête* not to be interrupted.'

'Have you anything particular to say?'

'Nothing so particular as Mr. Johnson, perhaps.'

Miss Blunt has a very pretty affectation of being more matter-of-fact than she really is.

'His rights, then,' said she, 'are paramount to yours.'

'Ah, you admit that he has rights?'

'Not at all. I simply assert that you have none.'

'I beg your pardon. I have claims which I mean to enforce. I have a claim upon your undivided attention, when I pay you a morning call.'

'Your claim is certainly answered. Have I been uncivil, pray?'

'Not uncivil, perhaps, but inconsiderate. You have been sighing for the company of a third person, which you can't expect me to relish.'

'Why not, pray? If I, a lady, can put up with Mr. Johnson's society, why shouldn't you, one of his own sex?'

'Because he is so outrageously conceited. You, as a lady, or at any rate as a woman, like conceited men.'

'Ah, yes; I have no doubt that I, as a woman, have all kinds of improper tastes. That's an old story.'

'Admit, at any rate, that our friend is conceited.'

'Admit it? Why, I have said so a hundred times. I have told him so.'

'Indeed! It has come to that, then?'

'To what, pray?'

'To that critical point in the friendship of a lady and gentleman, when they bring against each other all kinds of delightful charges of moral obliquity. Take care, Miss Blunt! A couple of intelligent New-Englanders, of opposite sex, young, unmarried, are pretty far gone, when they begin morally to reprobate each other. So you told Mr. Johnson that he is conceited? And I suppose you added, that he was also dreadfully satirical and sceptical? What was his rejoinder? Let me see. Did he ever tell you that you were a little bit affected?'

'No: he left that for you to say, in this very ingenious manner. Thank you, Sir.'

'He left it for me to deny, which is a great deal prettier. Do you think the manner ingenious?'

'I think the matter, considering the day and hour, very profane, Mr. Locksley. Suppose you go away and let me read my Bible.'

'Meanwhile,' I asked, 'what shall I do?'

'Go and read yours, if you have one.'

'I haven't.'

I was nevertheless compelled to retire, with the promise of a second audience in half an hour. Poor Miss Blunt owes it to her conscience to read a certain number of chapters. What a pure and upright soul she is! And what an edifying spectacle is much of our feminine piety! Women find a place for everything in their commodious little minds, just as they do in their wonderfully sub-divided trunks, when they go on a journey. I have no doubt that this young lady stows away her religion in a corner, just as she does her Sunday bonnet,—and, when the proper moment comes, draws it forth, and reflects while she assumes it before the glass, and blows away the strictly imaginary dust: for what worldly impurity can penetrate through half a dozen layers of cambric and tissue-paper? Dear me, what a comfort it is to have a nice, fresh, holiday faith!—When I returned to the parlour, Miss Blunt was still sitting with her Bible in her lap. Somehow or other, I no longer felt in the mood for jesting. So I asked her soberly what she had been reading. Soberly she answered me. She inquired how I had spent my half-hour.

'In thinking good Sabbath thoughts,' I said. 'I have been walking in the garden.' And then I spoke my mind. 'I have been thanking Heaven that it has led me, a poor, friendless wanderer, into so peaceful an anchorage.'

'Are you, then, so poor and friendless?' asked Miss Blunt, quite abruptly.

'Did you ever hear of an art-student under thirty who wasn't poor?' I answered. 'Upon my word, I have yet to sell my first picture. Then, as for being friendless, there are not five people in the world who really care for me.'

'*Really* care? I am afraid you look too close. And then I think five good friends is a very large number. I think myself very well off with a couple. But if you are friendless, it's probably your own fault.'

'Perhaps it is,' said I, sitting down in the rocking-chair; 'and yet, perhaps, it isn't. Have you found me so very repulsive? Haven't you, on the contrary, found me rather sociable?'

She folded her arms, and quietly looked at me for a moment, before answering. I shouldn't wonder if I blushed a little.

'You want a compliment, Mr. Locksley; that's the long and short of it. I have not paid you a compliment since you have been here. How you must have suffered! But it's a pity you couldn't have waited awhile longer, instead of beginning to angle with that very clumsy bait. For an artist, you are very inartistic. Men never know how to wait. "Have I found you repulsive? haven't I found you sociable?" Perhaps, after all, considering what I have in my mind, it is as well that you asked for your compliment. I have found you charming. I say it freely; and yet I say, with equal sincerity, that I fancy very few others would find you so. I can say decidedly that you are not sociable. You are entirely too particular. You are considerate of me, because you know that I know that you are so. There's the rub, you see: I know that you know that I know it. Don't interrupt me; I am going to be eloquent. I want you to

understand why I don't consider you sociable. You call Mr. Johnson conceited; but, really, I don't believe he's nearly as conceited
as yourself. You are too conceited to be sociable; he is not. I am
an obscure, weak-minded woman,—weak-minded, you know, compared with men. I can be patronized,—yes, that's the word. Would
you be equally amiable with a person as strong, as clear-sighted as
yourself, with a person equally averse with yourself to being under
an obligation? I think not. Of course it's delightful to charm people.
Who wouldn't? There is no harm in it, as long as the charmer does
not sit up for a public benefactor. If I were a man, a clever man
like yourself, who had seen the world, who was not to be charmed
and encouraged, but to be convinced and refuted, would you be
equally amiable? It will perhaps seem absurd to you, and it will
certainly seem egotistical, but I consider myself sociable, for all
that I have only a couple of friends,—my father and the principal
of the school. That is, I mingle with women without any second
thought. Not that I wish you to do so: on the contrary, if the
contrary is natural to you. But I don't believe you mingle in the
same way with men. You may ask me what I know about it. Of
course I know nothing: I simply guess. When I have done, indeed,
I mean to beg your pardon for all I have said; but until then, give
me a chance. You are incapable of listening deferentially to stupid,
bigoted persons. I am not. I do it every day. Ah, you have no idea of
what nice manners I have in the exercise of my profession! Every
day I have occasion to pocket my pride and to stifle my precious
sense of the ridiculous,—of which, of course, you think I haven't a
bit. It is, for instance, a constant vexation to me to be poor. It makes
me frequently hate rich women; it makes me despise poor ones. I
don't know whether you suffer acutely from the narrowness of your
own means; but if you do, I dare say you shun rich men. I don't. I
like to go into rich people's houses, and to be very polite to the ladies
of the house, especially if they are very well-dressed and ignorant
and vulgar. All women are like me in this respect; and all men more
or less like you. That is, after all, the text of my sermon. Compared
with us, it has always seemed to me that you are arrant cowards,—
that we alone are brave. To be sociable, you must have a great deal
of pluck. You are too fine a gentleman. Go and teach school, or open
a corner grocery, or sit in a law-office all day, waiting for clients:
then you will be sociable. As yet, you are only agreeable. It *is* your
own fault, if people don't care for you. You don't care for them.
That you should be indifferent to their applause is all very well;
but you don't care for their indifference. You are amiable, you are
very kind, and you are also very lazy. You consider that you are

working now, don't you? Many persons would not call it work.'

It was now certainly my turn to fold my arms.

'And now,' added my companion, as I did so, 'I beg your pardon.'

'This was certainly worth waiting for,' said I. 'I don't know what answer to make. My head swims. I don't know whether you have been attacking me or praising me. So you advise me to open a corner grocery, do you?'

'I advise you to do something that will make you a little less satirical. You had better marry, for instance.'

'*Je ne demande pas mieux*. Will you have me? I can't afford it.'

'Marry a rich woman.'

I shook my head.

'Why not?' asked Miss Blunt. 'Because people would accuse you of being mercenary? What of that? I mean to marry the first rich man who offers. Do you know that I am tired of living alone in this weary old way, teaching little girls their gamut, and turning and patching my dresses? I mean to marry the first man who offers.'

'Even if he is poor?'

'Even if he is poor, ugly, and stupid.'

'I am your man, then. Would you take me, if I were to offer?'

'Try and see.'

'Must I get upon my knees?'

'No, you need not even do that. Am I not on mine? It would be too fine an irony. Remain as you are, lounging back in your chair, with your thumbs in your waistcoat.'

If I were writing a romance now, instead of transcribing facts, I would say that I knew not what might have happened at this juncture, had not the door opened and admitted the Captain and Mr. Johnson. The latter was in the highest spirits.

'How are you, Miss Esther? So you have been breaking your leg, eh? How are you, Mr. Locksley? I wish I were a doctor now. Which is it, right or left?'

In this simple fashion he made himself agreeable to Miss Blunt. He stopped to dinner and talked without ceasing. Whether our hostess had talked herself out in her very animated address to myself an hour before, or whether she preferred to oppose no obstacle to Mr. Johnson's fluency, or whether she was indifferent to him, I know not; but she held her tongue with that easy grace, that charming tacit intimation of 'We could, an we would,' of which she is so perfect a mistress. This very interesting woman has a number of pretty traits in common with her town-bred sisters; only, whereas in these they are laboriously acquired, in her they are severely natural. I am sure, that, if I were to plant her in Madison Square to-morrow, she would, after one quick, all-compassing glance, assume the *nil admirari* in a manner to drive the greatest lady of them all to despair. Johnson is a man of excellent intentions, but no taste. Two or three times I looked at Miss Blunt to see what impression his sallies were making upon her. They seemed to produce none whatever. But I know better, *moi*. Not one of them escaped her. But I suppose she said to herself that her impressions on this point were no business of mine. Perhaps she was right. It is a disagreeable word to use of a woman you admire; but I can't help fancying that she has been a little *soured*. By what? Who shall say? By some old love affair, perhaps.

July 24th.—This evening the Captain and I took a half-hour's turn about the harbour. I asked him frankly, as a friend, whether Johnson wants to marry his daughter.

'I guess he does,' said the old man; 'and yet I hope he don't. You know what he is: he's smart, promising, and already sufficiently well off. But somehow he isn't for a man what my Esther is for a woman.'

'That he isn't!' said I; 'and honestly, Captain Blunt, I don't know who is'—

'Unless it's yourself,' said the Captain.

'Thank you. I know a great many ways in which Mr. Johnson is more worthy of her than I.'

'And I know one in which you are more worthy of her than he,—that is, in being what we used to call a gentleman.'

'Miss Esther made him sufficiently welcome in her quiet way, on Sunday,' I rejoined.

'Oh, she respects him,' said Blunt. 'As she's situated, she might marry him on that. You see, she's weary of hearing little girls drum on the piano. With her ear for music,' added the Captain, 'I wonder she has borne it so long.'

'She is certainly meant for better things,' said I.

'Well,' answered the Captain, who has an honest habit of deprecating your agreement, when it occurs to him that he has obtained it for sentiments which fall somewhat short of the stoical,—'well,' said he, with a very dry expression of mouth, 'she's born to do her duty. We are all of us born for that.'

'Sometimes our duty is rather dreary,' said I.

'So it be; but what's the help for it? I don't want to die without seeing my daughter provided for. What she makes by teaching is a pretty slim subsistence. There was a time when I thought she was going to be fixed for life, but it all blew over. There was a young fellow here from down Boston way, who came about as near to it as you can come, when you actually don't. He and Esther were excellent friends. One day Esther came up to me, and looked me in the face, and told me she was engaged.

'"Who to?" says I, though of course I knew, and Esther told me as much. "When do you expect to marry?" I asked.

'"When John grows rich enough," says she.

'"When will that be?"

'"It may not be for years," said poor Esther.

'A whole year passed, and, as far as I could see, the young man came no nearer to his fortune. He was forever running to and fro between this place and Boston. I asked no questions, because I knew that my poor girl wished it so. But at last, one day, I began to think it was time to take an observation, and see whereabouts we stood.

'"Has John made his fortune yet?" I asked.

'"I don't know, father," said Esther.

'"When are you to be married?"

'"Never!" said my poor little girl, and burst into tears. "Please ask me no questions," said she. "Our engagement is over. Ask me no questions."

'"Tell me one thing,' said I: "where is that d—d scoundrel who has broken my daughter's heart?"

'You should have seen the look she gave me.

'"Broken my heart, Sir? You are very much mistaken. I don't know who you mean."

'"I mean John Banister," said I. That was his name.

'"I believe Mr. Banister is in China," says Esther, as grand as the Queen of Sheba. And there was an end of it. I never learnt the ins and outs of it. I have been told that Banister is accumulating money very fast in the China trade.'

August 7th.—I have made no entry for more than a fortnight. They tell me I have been very ill; and I find no difficulty in believing them. I suppose I took cold, sitting out so late, sketching. At all events, I have had a mild intermittent fever. I have slept so much, however, that the time has seemed rather short. I have been tenderly nursed by this kind old gentleman, his daughter, and his maid-servant. God bless them, one and all! I say his daughter, because old Dorothy informs me that for half an hour one morning, at dawn, after a night during which I had been very feeble, Miss Blunt relieved guard at my bedside, while I lay wrapt in brutal slumber. It is very jolly to see sky and ocean once again. I have got myself into my easy-chair by the open window, with my shutters closed and the lattice open; and here I sit with my book on my knee, scratching away feebly enough. Now and then I peep from my cool, dark sick-chamber out into the world of light. High noon at midsummer! What a spectacle! There are no clouds in the sky, no waves on the ocean. The sun has it all to himself. To look long at the garden makes the eyes water. And we—'Hobbs, Nobbs, Stokes, and Nokes'—propose to paint that kingdom of light. *Allons, donc!*

The loveliest of women has just tapped, and come in with a plate of early peaches. The peaches are of a gorgeous colour and plumpness; but Miss Blunt looks pale and thin. The hot weather doesn't agree with her. She is overworked. Confound it! Of course I thanked her warmly for her attentions during my illness. She disclaims all gratitude, and refers me to her father and Mrs. Dorothy.

'I allude more especially,' said I, 'to that little hour at the end of a weary night, when you stole in like a kind of moral Aurora, and drove away the shadows from my brain. That morning, you know, I began to get better.'

'It was indeed a very little hour,' said Miss Blunt. 'It was about ten minutes.' And then she began to scold me for presuming to touch a pen during my convalescence. She laughs at me, indeed, for keeping a diary at all. 'Of all things,' cried she, 'a sentimental man is the most despicable.'

I confess I was somewhat nettled. The thrust seemed gratuitous.

'Of all things,' I answered, 'a woman without sentiment is the most unlovely.'

'Sentiment and loveliness are all very well, when you have time for them,' said Miss Blunt. 'I haven't. I'm not rich enough. Good morning.'

Speaking of another woman, I would say that she flounced out of the room. But such was the gait of Juno, when she moved stiffly over the grass from where Paris stood with Venus holding the apple, gathering up her divine vestment, and leaving the others to guess at her face—

Juno has just come back to say that she forgot what she came for half an hour ago. What will I be pleased to like for dinner?

'I have just been writing in my diary that you flounced out of the room,' said I.

'Have you, indeed? Now you can write that I have bounced in. There's a nice cold chicken downstairs,' etc., etc.

August 14th.—This afternoon I sent for a light wagon, and

treated Miss Blunt to a drive. We went successively over the three
beaches. What a time we had, coming home! I shall never forget
that hard trot over Weston's Beach. The tide was very low; and
we had the whole glittering, weltering strand to ourselves. There
was a heavy blow yesterday, which had not yet subsided; and the
waves had been lashed into a magnificent fury. Trot, trot, trot, trot,
we trundled over the hard sand. The sounds of the horse's hoofs
rang out sharp against the monotone of the thunderous surf, as we
drew nearer and nearer to the long line of the cliffs. At our left,
almost from the lofty zenith of the pale evening sky to the high
western horizon of the tumultuous dark-green sea, was suspended,
so to speak, one of those gorgeous vertical sunsets that Turner
loved so well. It was a splendid confusion of purple and green and
gold,—the clouds flying and flowing in the wind like the folds of a
mighty banner borne by some triumphal fleet whose prows were
not visible above the long chain of mountainous waves. As we
reached the point where the cliffs plunge down upon the beach, I
pulled up, and we remained for some moments looking out along
the low, brown, obstinate barrier at whose feet the impetuous waters
were rolling themselves into powder.

August 17th.—This evening, as I lighted my bedroom candle, I
saw that the Captain had something to say to me. So I waited
below until the old man and his daughter had performed their
usual picturesque embrace, and the latter had given me that hand-
shake and that smile which I never failed to exact.

'Johnson has got his discharge,' said the old man, when he had
heard his daughter's door close upstairs.

'What do you mean?'

He pointed with his thumb to the room above, where we heard,
through the thin partition, the movement of Miss Blunt's light step.

'You mean that he has proposed to Miss Esther?'

The Captain nodded.

'And has been refused?'

'Flat.'

'Poor fellow!' said I, very honestly. 'Did he tell you himself?'

'Yes, with tears in his eyes. He wanted me to speak for him. I
told him it was no use. Then he began to say hard things of my
poor girl.'

'What kind of things?'

'A pack of falsehoods. He says she has no heart. She has promised
always to regard him as a friend: it's more than I will, hang him!'

'Poor fellow!' said I; and now, as I write, I can only repeat, considering what a hope was here broken, Poor fellow!

August 23rd.—I have been lounging about all day, thinking of
it, dreaming of it, spooning over it, as they say. This is a decided
waste of time. I think, accordingly, the best thing for me to do is,
to sit down and lay the ghost by writing out my story.

On Thursday evening Miss Blunt happened to intimate that she
had a holiday on the morrow, it being the birthday of the lady in
whose establishment she teaches.

'There is to be a tea-party at four o'clock in the afternoon for
the resident pupils and teachers,' said Miss Esther. 'Tea at four!
what do you think of that? And then there is to be a speech-
making by the smartest young lady. As my services are not required, I propose to be absent. Suppose, father, you take us out in
your boat. Will you come, Mr. Locksley? We shall have a nice
little picnic. Let us go over to old Fort Pudding, across the bay. We
will take our dinner with us, and send Dorothy to spend the day
with her sister, and put the house-key in our pocket, and not come
home till we please.'

I warmly espoused the project, and it was accordingly carried
into execution the next morning, when, at about ten o'clock, we
pushed off from our little wharf at the garden-foot. It was a perfect
summer's day: I can say no more for it. We made a quiet run over
to the point of our destination. I shall never forget the wondrous
stillness which brooded over earth and water, as we weighed anchor
in the lee of my old friend,—or old enemy,—the ruined fort. The
deep, translucent water reposed at the base of the warm sunlit cliff
like a great basin of glass, which I half expected to hear shiver and
crack as our keel ploughed through it. And how colour and sound
stood out in the transparent air! How audibly the little ripples on
the beach whispered to the open sky! How our irreverent voices
seemed to jar upon the privacy of the little cove! The mossy rocks
doubled themselves without a flaw in the clear, dark water. The
gleaming white beach lay fringed with its deep deposits of odorous
sea-weed, gleaming black. The steep, straggling sides of the cliffs
raised aloft their rugged angles against the burning blue of the sky.
I remember, when Miss Blunt stepped ashore and stood upon the
beach, relieved against the heavy shadow of a recess in the cliff,
while her father and I busied ourselves with gathering up our
baskets and fastening the anchor—I remember, I say, what a figure
she made. There is a certain purity in this Cragthorpe air which I
have never seen approached,—a lightness, a brilliancy, a *crudity*,
which allows perfect liberty of self-assertion to each individual

object in the landscape. The prospect is ever more or less like a picture which lacks its final process, its reduction to unity. Miss Blunt's figure, as she stood there on the beach, was almost *criarde*; but how lovely it was! Her light muslin dress, gathered up over her short white skirt, her little black mantilla, the blue veil which she had knotted about her neck, the crimson shawl which she had thrown over her arm, the little silken dome which she poised over her head in one gloved hand, while the other retained her crisp draperies, and which cast down upon her face a sharp circle of shade, out of which her cheerful eyes shone darkly and her happy mouth smiled whitely,—these are some of the hastily noted points of the picture.

'Young woman,' I cried out, over the water, 'I do wish you might know how pretty you look!'

'How do you know I don't?' she answered. 'I should think I might. You don't look so badly, yourself. But it's not I; it's the accessories.'

'Hang it! I am going to become profane,' I called out again.

'Swear ahead,' said the Captain.

'I am going to say you are devilish pretty.'

'Dear me! is that all?' cried Miss Blunt, with a little light laugh, which must have made the tutelar sirens of the cove ready to die with jealousy down in their submarine bowers.

By the time the Captain and I had landed our effects, our companion had tripped lightly up the forehead of the cliff—in one place it is very retreating—and disappeared over its crown. She soon reappeared with an intensely white handkerchief added to her other provocations, which she waved to us, as we trudged upward, carrying our baskets. When we stopped to take breath on the summit, and wipe our foreheads, we of course rebuked her who was roaming about idly with her parasol and gloves.

'Do you think I am going to take any trouble or do any work?' cried Miss Esther, in the greatest good-humour. 'Is not this my holiday? I am not going to raise a finger, nor soil these beautiful gloves, for which I paid a dollar at Mr. Dawson's in Cragthorpe. After you have found a shady place for your provisions, I would like you to look for a spring. I am very thirsty.'

'Find the spring yourself, Miss,' said her father. 'Mr. Locksley and I have a spring in this basket. Take a pull, Sir.'

And the Captain drew forth a stout black bottle.

'Give me a cup, and I will look for some water,' said Miss Blunt. 'Only I'm so afraid of the snakes! If you hear a scream, you may know it's a snake.'

'Screaming snakes!' said I; 'that's a new species.'

What nonsense it all sounds like now! As we looked about us, shade seemed scarce, as it generally is, in this region. But Miss Blunt, like the very adroit and practical young person she is, for all that she would have me believe the contrary, soon discovered a capital cool spring in the shelter of a pleasant little dell, beneath a clump of firs. Hither, as one of the young gentlemen who imitate Tennyson would say, we brought our basket, Blunt and I; while Esther dipped the cup, and held it dripping to our thirsty lips, and laid the cloth, and on the grass disposed the platters round. I should have to be a poet, indeed, to describe half the happiness and the silly poetry and purity and beauty of this bright long summer's day. We ate, drank, and talked; we ate occasionally with our fingers, we drank out of the necks of our bottles, and we talked with our mouths full, as befits (and excuses) those who talk wild nonsense. We told stories without the least point. Blunt and I made atrocious puns. I believe, indeed, that Miss Blunt herself made one little punkin, as I called it. If there had been any superfluous representative of humanity present, to register the fact, I should say that we made fools of ourselves. But as there was no fool on hand, I need say nothing about it. I am conscious myself of having said several witty things, which Miss Blunt understood: *in vino veritas*. The dear old Captain twanged the long bow indefatigably. The bright high sun lingered above us the livelong day, and drowned the prospect with light and warmth. One of these days I mean to paint a picture which in future ages, when my dear native land shall boast a national school of art, will hang in the *Salon Carré* of the great central museum, (located, let us say, in Chicago,) and remind folks—or rather make them forget—Giorgione, Bordone, and Veronese: A Rural Festival; three persons feasting under some trees; scene, nowhere in particular; time and hour, problematical. Female figure, a big *brune*; young man reclining on his elbow; old man drinking. An empty sky, with no end of expression. The whole stupendous in colour, drawing, feeling. Artist uncertain; supposed to be Robinson, 1900. That's about the programme.

After dinner the Captain began to look out across the bay, and, noticing the uprising of a little breeze, expressed a wish to cruise about for an hour or two. He proposed to us to walk along the shore to a point a couple of miles northward, and there meet the boat. His daughter having agreed to this proposition, he set off with the lightened pannier, and in less than half an hour we saw him standing out from shore. Miss Blunt and I did not begin our walk for a long, long time. We sat and talked beneath the trees. At our feet, a wide cleft in the hills—almost a glen—stretched down to the silent beach. Beyond lay the familiar ocean-line. But, as many philosophers have observed, there is an end to all things. At last we got up. Miss Blunt said, that, as the air was freshening, she believed she would put on her shawl. I helped her to fold it into the proper shape, and then I placed it on her shoulders, her crimson shawl over her black silk sack. And then she tied her veil once more about her neck, and gave me her hat to hold, while she effected a partial re-distribution of her hair-pins. By way of being humorous, I placed her hat on my own head; at which she was kind enough to smile, as with downcast face and uplifted elbows she fumbled among her braids. And then she shook out the creases of her dress, and drew on her gloves; and finally she said, 'Well!'— that inevitable tribute to time and morality which follows upon even the mildest forms of dissipation. Very slowly it was that we wandered down the little glen. Slowly, too, we followed the course of the narrow and sinuous beach, as it keeps to the foot of the low cliffs. We encountered no sign of human life. Our conversation I need hardly repeat. I think I may trust it to the keeping of my memory: I think I shall be likely to remember it. It was all very sober and sensible,—such talk as it is both easy and pleasant to remember; it was even prosaic,—or, at least, if there was a vein of poetry in it, I should have defied a listener to put his finger on it. There was no exaltation of feeling or utterance on either side; on one side, indeed, there was very little utterance. Am I wrong in conjecturing, however, that there was considerable feeling of a certain quiet kind? Miss Blunt maintained a rich, golden silence. I, on the other hand, was very voluble. What a sweet, womanly listener she is!

September 1st.—I have been working steadily for a week. This is the first day of autumn. Read aloud to Miss Blunt a little Wordsworth.

September 10th. Midnight.—Worked without interruption,—until yesterday, inclusive, that is. But with the day now closing—or opening—begins a new era. My poor vapid old diary, at last you shall hold a *fact*.

For three days past we have been having damp, chilly weather. Dusk has fallen early. This evening, after tea, the Captain went into town,—on business, as he said: I believe, to attend some Poorhouse or Hospital Board. Esther and I went into the parlour. The room seemed cold. She brought in the lamp from the dining-room, and proposed we should have a little fire. I went into the kitchen, procured an armful of wood, and while she drew the curtains and wheeled up the table, I kindled a lively, crackling blaze. A fortnight ago she would not have allowed me to do this without a protest. She would not have offered to do it herself,—not she!—but she would have said that I was not here to serve, but to be served, and would have pretended to call Dorothy. Of course I should have had my own way. But we have changed all that. Esther went to her piano, and I sat down to a book. I read not a word. I sat looking at my mistress, and thinking with a very uneasy heart. For the first time in our friendship, she had put on a dark, warm dress: I think it was of the material called alpaca. The first time I saw her she wore a white dress with a purple neck-ribbon; now she wore a black dress with the same ribbon. That is, I remember wondering, as I sat there eying her, whether it *was* the same ribbon, or merely another like it. My heart was in my throat; and yet I thought of a number of trivialities of the same kind. At last I spoke.

'Miss Blunt,' I said, 'do you remember the first evening I passed beneath your roof, last June?'

'Perfectly,' she replied, without stopping.

'You played this same piece.'

'Yes; I played it very badly, too. I only half knew it. But it is a showy piece, and I wished to produce an effect. I didn't know then how indifferent you are to music.'

'I paid no particular attention to the piece. I was intent upon the performer.'

'So the performer supposed.'

'What reason had you to suppose so?'

'I'm sure I don't know. Did you ever know a woman to be able to give a reason, when she has guessed aright?'

'I think they generally contrive to make up a reason, afterwards. Come, what was yours?'

'Well, you *stared* so hard.'

'Fie! I don't believe it. That's unkind.'

'You said you wished me to invent a reason. If I really had one, I don't remember it.'

'You told me you remembered the occasion in question perfectly.'

'I meant the circumstances. I remembered what we had for tea; I remember what dress I wore. But I don't remember my feelings. They were naturally not very memorable.'

'What did you say, when your father proposed my coming?'

'I asked how much you would be willing to pay?'

'And then?'

'And then, if you looked "respectable".'

'And then?'

'That was all. I told father to do as he pleased.'

She continued to play. Leaning back in my chair, I continued to look at her. There was a considerable pause.

'Miss Esther,' said I, at last.

'Yes.'

'Excuse me for interrupting you so often. But,'—and I got up and went to the piano,—'but I thank Heaven that it has brought you and me together.'

She looked up at me and bowed her head with a little smile, as her hands still wandered over the keys.

'Heaven has certainly been very good to us,' said she.

'How much longer are you going to play?' I asked.

'I'm sure I don't know. As long as you like.'

'If you want to do as I like, you will stop immediately.'

She let her hands rest on the keys a moment, and gave me a rapid, questioning look. Whether she found a sufficient answer in my face I know not; but she slowly rose, and, with a very pretty affectation of obedience, began to close the instrument. I helped her to do so.

'Perhaps you would like to be quite alone,' she said. 'I suppose your own room is too cold.'

'Yes,' I answered, 'you've hit it exactly. I wish to be alone. I wish to monopolize this cheerful blaze. Hadn't you better go into the kitchen and sit with the cook? It takes you women to make such cruel speeches.'

'When we women are cruel, Mr. Locksley, it is without knowing it. We are not wilfully so. When we learn that we have been un-kind, we very humbly ask pardon, without even knowing what our crime has been.' And she made me a very low curtsy.

'I will tell you what your crime has been,' said I. 'Come and sit by the fire. It's rather a long story.'

'A long story? Then let me get my work.'

'Confound your work! Excuse me, but I mean it. I want you to listen to me. Believe me, you will need all your thoughts.'

She looked at me steadily a moment, and I returned her glance. During that moment I was reflecting whether I might silently emphasize my request by laying a lover's hand upon her shoulder. I decided that I might not. She walked over and quietly seated herself in a low chair by the fire. Here she patiently folded her arms. I sat down before her.

'With you, Miss Blunt,' said I, 'one must be very explicit. You are not in the habit of taking things for granted. You have a great deal of imagination, but you rarely exercise it on the behalf of other people.' I stopped a moment.

'Is that my crime?' asked my companion.

'It's not so much a crime as a vice,' said I; 'and perhaps not so much a vice as a virtue. Your crime is, that you are so stone-cold to a poor devil who loves you.'

She burst into a rather shrill laugh. I wonder whether she thought I meant Johnson.

'Who are you speaking for, Mr. Locksley?' she asked.

'Are there so many? For myself.'

'Honestly?'

'Honestly doesn't begin to express it.'

'What is that French phrase that you are forever using? I think I may say, *"Allons, donc!"*'

'Let us speak plain English, Miss Blunt.'

' "Stone-cold" is certainly very plain English. I don't see the relative importance of the two branches of your proposition. Which is the principal, and which the subordinate clause,—that I am stone-cold, as you call it, or that you love me, as you call it?'

'As I call it? What would you have me call it? For God's sake, Miss Blunt, be serious, or I shall call it something else. Yes, I love you. Don't you believe it?'

'I am open to conviction.'

'Thank God!' said I.

And I attempted to take her hand.

'No, no, Mr. Locksley,' said she,—'not just yet, if you please.'

'Action speaks louder than words,' said I.

'There is no need of speaking loud. I hear you perfectly.'

'I certainly sha'n't whisper,' said I; 'although it is the custom, I believe, for lovers to do so. Will you be my wife?'

'I sha'n't whisper, either, Mr. Locksley. Yes, I will.'

And now she put out her hand.—That's my fact.

September 12th.—We are to be married within three weeks.

September 19th.—I have been in New York a week, transacting business. I got back yesterday. I find everyone here talking about our engagement. Esther tells me that it was talked about a month ago, and that there is a very general feeling of disappointment that I am not rich.

'Really, if you don't mind it,' said I, 'I don't see why others should.'

'I don't know whether you are rich or not,' says Esther; 'but I know that I am.'

'Indeed! I was not aware that you had a private fortune,' etc., etc.

This little farce is repeated in some shape every day. I am very idle. I smoke a great deal, and lounge about all day, with my hands in my pockets. I am free from that ineffable weariness of ceaseless *giving* which I experienced six months ago. I was shorn of my hereditary trinkets at that period; and I have resolved that *this* engagement, at all events, shall have no connection with the shops. I was balked of my poetry once; I sha'n't be a second time. I don't think there is much danger of this. Esther deals it out with full hands. She takes a very pretty interest in her simple outfit,—showing me triumphantly certain of her purchases, and making a great mystery about others, which she is pleased to denominate table-cloths and napkins. Last evening I found her sewing buttons on a tablecloth. I had heard a great deal of a certain grey silk dress; and this morning, accordingly, she marched up to me, arrayed in this garment. It is trimmed with velvet, and hath flounces, a train, and all the modern improvements generally.

'There is only one objection to it,' said Esther, parading before the glass in my painting-room: 'I am afraid it is above our station.'

'By Jove! I'll paint your portrait in it,' said I, 'and make our fortune. All the other men who have handsome wives will bring them to be painted.'

'You mean all the women who have handsome dresses,' said Esther, with great humility.

Our wedding is fixed for next Thursday. I tell Esther that it will be as little of a wedding, and as much of a marriage, as possible. Her father and her good friend the schoolmistress alone are to be present.—My secret oppresses me considerably; but I have resolved to keep it for the honeymoon, when it may take care of itself. I am harassed with a dismal apprehension, that, if Esther were to discover it now, the whole thing would be *à refaire*. I have taken rooms at a romantic little watering-place called Clifton, ten miles off. The hotel is already quite free of city-people, and we shall be almost alone.

September 28th.—We have been here two days. The little transaction in the church went off smoothly. I am truly sorry for the Captain. We drove directly over here, and reached the place at dusk. It was a raw, black day. We have a couple of good rooms, close to the savage sea. I am nevertheless afraid I have made a mistake. It would perhaps have been wiser to go inland. These things are not immaterial: we make our own heaven, but we scarcely make our own earth. I am writing at a little table by the window, looking out on the rocks, the gathering dusk, and the rising fog. My wife has wandered down to the rocky platform in front of the house. I can see her from here, bareheaded, in that old crimson shawl, talking to one of the landlord's little boys. She has just given the little fellow a kiss, bless her heart! I remember her telling me once that she was very fond of little boys; and, indeed, I have noticed that they are seldom too dirty for her to take on her knee. I have been reading over these pages for the first time in—I don't know when. They are filled with *her*,—even more in thought than in word. I believe I will show them to her, when she comes in. I will give her the book to read, and sit by her, watching her face,— watching the great secret dawn upon her.

Later.—Somehow or other, I can write this quietly enough; but I hardly think I shall ever write any more. When Esther came in, I handed her this book.

'I want you to read it,' said I.

She turned very pale, and laid it on the table, shaking her head.

'I know it,' she said.

'What do you know?'

'That you have a hundred thousand a year. But believe me, Mr. Locksley, I am none the worse for the knowledge. You intimated in one place in your book that I am born for wealth and splendour. I believe I am. You pretend to hate your money; but you would not have had me without it. If you really love me,—and I think you do,—you will not let this make any difference. I am not such a fool as to attempt to talk here about my sensations. But I remember what I said.'

'What do you expect me to do?' I asked. 'Shall I call you some horrible name and cast you off?'

'I expect you to show the same courage that I am showing. I never said I loved you. I never deceived you in that. I said I would be your wife. So I will, faithfully. I haven't so much heart as you think; and yet, too, I have a great deal more. I am incapable of more than one deception.—Mercy! didn't you see it? didn't you know it? see that I saw it? know that I knew it? It was diamond cut diamond. You deceived me; I deceived you. Now that your deception ceases, mine ceases. *Now* we are free, with our hundred thousand a year! Excuse me, but it sometimes comes across me!

Now we can be good and honest and true. It was all a make-believe virtue before.'

'So you read that thing?' I asked: actually—strange as it may seem—for something to say.

'Yes, while you were ill. It was lying with your pen in it, on the table. I read it because I suspected. Otherwise I shouldn't have done so.'

'It was the act of a false woman,' said I.

'A false woman? No,—simply of a woman. I am a woman, Sir.' And she began to smile. 'Come, *you* be a man!'

A Day of Days*

[First appeared in the *Galaxy*, vol. i (June 1866), pp. 298-312. The tale was revised and reprinted in volume i of *Stories Revived* (1885.)

MR. HERBERT MOORE, A GENTLEMAN OF SOME NOTE IN the scientific world, and a childless widower, finding himself at last unable to reconcile his sedentary habits with the management of a household, had invited his only sister to come and superintend his domestic affairs. Miss Adela Moore had assented the more willingly to his proposal, as by her mother's death she had recently been left without a formal protector. She was twenty-five years of age, and was a very active member of what she and her friends called society. She was almost equally at home in the very best company of three great cities, and she had encountered most of the adventures which await a young girl on the threshold of life. She had become rather hastily and imprudently engaged, but she had eventually succeeded in disengaging herself. She had spent a Summer in Europe, and she had made a voyage to Cuba with a dear friend in the last stage of consumption, who had died at the hotel in Havana. Although by no means beautiful in person she was yet thoroughly pleasing, rejoicing in what young ladies are fond of calling an *air*. That is, she was tall and slender, with a long neck, a low forehead and a handsome nose. Even after six years of 'society', too, she still had excellent manners. She was, moreover, mistress of a very pretty little fortune, and was accounted clever without detriment to her amiability, and amiable without detriment to her wit. These facts, as the reader will allow, might have ensured her the very best prospects; but he has seen that she had

---

* In a letter to one of the editors of the *Galaxy*, dated 21 May, 1866, James wrote: '... I have at your request added 5 m.s. pages (as far as I could) to my story [*A Day of Days*]. I agree with you, on reflection, that it will be better for them and I enclose them herewith.... P.S. Suppose (if it is not too late to make a change) you call the story *Tom Ludlow's Letters* instead of the actual title. Isn't it a better name?...' MS. letter in the W.C. Church Collection in the New York Public Library.

In the absence of the manuscripts, it is impossible to establish the nature of the interposition—if there was one—caused by the addition of '5 m.s. pages'. If the present title was the 'actual title' of the tale, then it would appear that the editors did not pay full attention to the author's request. However, it is interesting to note that, in 1885, when James himself had the opportunity, he did not change the title of the story.

found herself willing to forfeit her prospects and bury herself in the country. It seemed to her that she had seen enough of the world and of human nature, and that a couple of years of seclusion might not be unprofitable. She had begun to suspect that for a girl of her age she was unduly old and wise—and, what is more, to suspect that others suspected as much. A great observer of life and manners, so far as her opportunities went, she conceived that it behooved her to organize the results of her observation into principles of conduct and of belief. She was becoming—so she argued—too impersonal, too critical, too intelligent, too contemplative, too just. A woman had no business to be so just. The society of nature, of the great expansive skies and the primeval woods, would prove severely unpropitious to her excessive intellectual growth. She would spend her time in the fields and live in her feelings, her simple sense, and the perusal of profitable books from Herbert's library.

She found her brother very prettily housed at about a mile's distance from the nearest town, and at about six miles' distance from another town, the seat of a small college, before which he delivered a weekly lecture. She had seen so little of him of late years that his acquaintance was almost to make; but it was very soon made. Herbert Moore was one of the simplest and least aggressive of men, and one of the most patient and delicate of students. He had a vague notion that Adela was a young woman of extravagant pleasures, and that, somehow, on her arrival, his house would be overrun with the train of her attendant revellers. It was not until after they had been six months together that he discovered that his sister was a model of diligence and temperance. By the time six months more had passed, Adela had bought back a delightful sense of youth and *naïveté*. She learned, under her brother's tuition, to walk—nay, to climb, for there were great hills in the neighbourhood—to ride and to botanize. At the end of a year, in the month of August, she received a visit from an old friend, a girl of her own age, who had been spending July at a watering-place, and who was about to be married. Adela had begun to fear that she had lapsed into an almost irreclaimable rusticity, and had suffered a permanent diminution of the social facility for which she had formerly been distinguished; but a week spent in *tête-à-tête* with her friend convinced her not only that she had not forgotten much that she had feared, but also that she had not forgotten much that she had hoped. For this, and other reasons, her friend's departure left her slightly depressed. She felt lonely and even a little elderly. She had lost another illusion. Laura B., for whom a year ago she had entertained a serious regard, now impressed her as a very flimsy little person, who talked about her lover with almost indecent flippancy.

Meanwhile, September was slowly running its course. One morning Mr. Moore took a hasty breakfast and started to catch the train for S., whither a scientific conference called him, which might, he said, release him that afternoon in time for dinner at home, and might on the other hand detain him until the evening. It was almost the first time during Adela's rustication that she had been left alone for several hours. Her brother's quiet presence was inappreciable enough; yet now that he was at a distance she nevertheless felt a singular sense of freedom; a sort of return of those days of early childhood, when, through some domestic catastrophe, she had for an infinite morning been left to her own devices. What should she do? she asked herself, half laughing. It was a fair day for work: but it was a still better one for play. Should she drive into town and pay a long-standing debt of morning calls? Should she go into the kitchen and try her hand at a pudding for dinner? She felt a delicious longing to do something illicit, to play with fire, to discover some Bluebeard's closet. But poor Herbert was no Bluebeard. If she were to burn down his house he would exact no amends. Adela went out to the veranda, and, sitting down on the steps, gazed across the country. It was apparently the last day of Summer. The sky was faintly blue; the woody hills were putting on the morbid colours of Autumn; the great pine grove behind the house seemed to have caught and imprisoned the protesting breezes. Looking down the road toward the village, it occurred to Adela that she might have a visit, and so kindly was her mood that she felt herself competent to a chat with one of her rustic neighbours. As the sun rose higher, she went in and established herself with a piece of embroidery in a deep, bow window in the second story, which, betwixt its muslin curtains and its external frame-work of vines, commanded most insidiously the principal approach to the house. While she drew her threads, she surveyed the road with a deepening conviction that she was destined to have a caller. The air was warm, yet not hot; the dust had been laid during the night by a gentle rain. It had been from the first a source of complaint among Adela's new friends that her courtesies were so thoroughly indiscriminating. Not only had she lent herself to no friendships, but she had committed herself to no preferences. Nevertheless, it was with a by no means impartial fancy that she sat thus expectant at her casement. She had very soon made up her mind that, to answer the exactions of the hour, her visitor should perforce be of

the other sex, and as, thanks to the somewhat uncompromising indifference which, during her residence, she had exhibited to the
jeunesse dorée of the county, her roll-call, in this her hour of need,
was limited to a single name, so her thoughts were now centred
upon the bearer of that name, Mr. Madison Perkins, the Unitarian
minister. If, instead of being Miss Moore's story, this were Mr.
Perkins's, it might easily be condensed into the one pregnant fact
that he was very far gone in love for our heroine. Although of a
different faith from his, she had been so well pleased with one of
his sermons, to which she had allowed herself to lend a tolerant
ear, that, meeting him some time afterward, she had received him
with what she considered a rather knotty doctrinal question; whereupon, gracefully waiving the question, he had asked permission to
call upon her and talk over her 'difficulties'. This short interview
had enshrined her in the young minister's heart; and the half-
dozen occasions on which he had subsequently contrived to see her
had each contributed an additional taper to her shrine. It is but
fair to add, however, that, although a captive, Mr. Perkins was as
yet no captor. He was simply an honourable young man, who happened at this moment to be the most sympathetic companion within reach. Adela, at twenty-five years of age, had both a past and a
future. Mr. Perkins reëchoed the one, and foreshadowed the other.

So, at last, when, as the morning waned toward noon, Adela
descried in the distance a man's figure treading the grassy margin
of the road, and swinging his stick as he came, she smiled to herself with some complacency. But even while she smiled she became
conscious of a most foolish acceleration of the process of her heart.
She rose, and resenting her gratuitous emotion, stood for a moment
half resolved to have herself denied. As she did so, she glanced
along the road again. Her friend had drawn nearer, and, as the
distance lessened, lo! it seemed to her that he was not her friend.
Before many moments her doubts were removed. The gentleman
was a stranger. In front of the house three roads diverged from a
great spreading elm. The stranger came along the opposite side of
the highway, and when he reached the elm stopped and looked
about him as if to verify a direction. Then he deliberately crossed
over. Adela had time to see, unseen, that he was a shapely young
man, with a bearded chin and a straw hat. After the due interval,
Becky, the maid, came up with a card somewhat rudely superscribed in pencil:

THOMAS LUDLOW,
New York.

Turning it over in her fingers, Adela saw that the reverse of a card had been used, abstracted from the basket on her own drawing-room table. The printed name on the other side was dashed out; it ran: *Mr. Madison Perkins.*

'He asked me to give you this, ma'am,' said Becky. 'He helped himself to it out of the tray.'

'Did he ask for me by name?'

'No, ma'am, he asked for Mr. Moore. When I told him Mr. Moore was away, he asked for some of the family. I told him you were all the family, ma'am.'

'Very well,' said Adela, 'I will go down.' But, begging her pardon, we will precede her by a few steps.

Tom Ludlow, as his friends called him, was a young man of twenty-eight, concerning whom you might have heard the most various opinions; for as far as he was known (which, indeed, was not very far), he was at once one of the best liked and one of the best hated of men. Born in one of the lower *strata* of New York society, he was still slightly incrusted, if we may so express it, with his native soil. A certain crudity of manners and of aspect proved him to be one of the great majority of the ungloved. On this basis, however, he was a sufficiently good-looking fellow: a middle-sized, agile figure; a head so well shaped as to be handsome; a pair of inquisitive, responsive eyes, and a large, manly mouth, constituting his heritage of beauty. Turned upon the world at any early age, he had, in the pursuit of a subsistence, tried his head at everything in succession, and had generally found it to be quite as hard as the opposing substance; and his figure may have been thought to reflect this sweet assurance in a look of somewhat aggressive satisfaction with things in general, himself included. He was a man of strong faculties and a strong will, but it is doubtful whether his feelings were stronger than he. He was liked for his directness, his good humour, his general soundness and serviceableness; he was disliked for the same qualities under different names; that is, for his impudence, his offensive optimisms, and his inhuman avidity for facts. When his friends insisted upon his noble disinterestedness, his enemies were wont to reply it was all very well to ignore, to nullify oneself in the pursuit of science, but that to suppress the rest of mankind coincidentally betrayed an excess of zeal. Fortunately for Ludlow, on the whole, he was no great listener; and even if he had been, a certain plebeian thick-skinnedness would have been the guaranty of his equanimity; although it must be added that, if, like a genuine democrat, he was very insensitive, like a genuine democrat, too, he was amazingly proud. His tastes, which

had always been for the natural sciences, had recently led him to
paleontology, that branch of them cultivated by Herbert Moore;
and it was upon business connected with this pursuit that, after a
short correspondence, he had now come to see him.

As Adela went in to him, he came out with a bow from the
window, whence he had been contemplating the lawn. She acknowledged his greeting.

'Miss Moore, I believe,' said Ludlow.

'Miss Moore,' said Adela.

'I beg your pardon for this intrusion, but as I had come from a
distance to see Mr. Moore on business, I thought I might venture
either to ask at headquarters how he may most easily be reached,
or even to charge you with a message.' These words were accompanied with a smile before which it was Adela's destiny to succumb
—if this is not too forcible a term for the movement of feeling with
which she answered them.

'Pray make no apologies,' she said. 'We hardly recognize such a
thing as intrusion in the country. Won't you sit down? My brother
went away only this morning, and I expect him back this afternoon.'

'This afternoon? indeed. In that case I believe I'll wait. It was
very stupid of me not to have dropped a word beforehand. But I
have been in the city all Summer long, and I shall not be sorry to
screw a little vacation out of this business. I'm prodigiously fond
of the country, and I very seldom get a glimpse of it.'

'It's possible,' said Adela, 'that my brother may not come home
until the evening. He was uncertain. You might go to him at
S.'

Ludlow reflected a moment, with his eyes on his hostess. 'If he
does return in the afternoon, at what hour will he arrive?'

'At three.'

'And my own train leaves at four. Allow him a quarter of an hour
to come from town and myself a quarter of an hour to get there (if
he would give me his vehicle, back), I should have half an hour to
see him. We couldn't do much talk, but I could ask him the essential
questions. I wish chiefly to ask him for some letters. It seems a pity
to take two superfluous—that is, possibly superfluous—railway
journeys of an hour apiece, for I should probably come back with
him. Don't you think so?' he asked, very frankly.

'You know best,' said Adela. 'I'm not particularly fond of the
journey to S., even when it's absolutely necessary.'

'Yes; and then this is such a lovely day for a good long ramble in
the fields. That's a thing I haven't done since I don't know when.

I'll stay.' And he placed his hat on the floor beside him.

'I'm afraid, now that I think of it,' said Adela, 'that there is no train until so late an hour that you would have very little time left on your arrival to talk with my brother before the hour at which he himself might have determined to start for home. It's true that you might induce him to remain till the evening.'

'Dear me! I shouldn't like to do that. It might be very inconvenient for him. Besides I shouldn't have time. And then I always like to see a man in his own home—or in my own home; a man, that is, whom I have any regard for—and I have a very great regard for your brother, Miss Moore. When men meet at a half-way house, neither feels at his ease. And then this is such an uncommonly pretty place of yours,' pursued Ludlow, looking about him.

'Yes, it's a very pretty place,' said Adela.

Ludlow got up and walked to the window. 'I want to look at your view,' said he. 'A lovely view it is. You're a happy woman, Miss Moore, to live before such a prospect.'

'Yes, if pretty scenery can make one happy, I ought to be happy.' And Adela was glad to regain her feet and stand on the other side of the table, before the window.

'Don't you think it can?' asked Ludlow, turning around. 'I don't know, though, perhaps it can't. Ugly sights can't make you unhappy, necessarily. I've been working for a year in one of the narrowest, darkest, dirtiest, and busiest streets in New York, with rusty bricks and muddy gutters for scenery. But I think I can hardly set up to be miserable. I wish I could. It might be a claim on your favour.' As he said these words, he stood leaning against the window-shutter, without the curtain, with folded arms. The morning light covered his face, and, mingled with that of his broad laugh, showed Adela that it was a very pleasant face.

'Whatever else he may be,' she said to herself as she stood within the shade of the other curtain, playing with the paper-knife which she had plucked from the table. 'I think he is honest. I am afraid he isn't a gentleman—but he is not a simpleton.' She met his eye frankly for a moment. 'What do you want of my favour?' she asked, with an abruptness of which she was acutely conscious. 'Does he wish to make friends,' she pursued, 'or does he merely wish to pay me a vulgar compliment? There is bad taste, perhaps, in either case, but especially in the latter.' Meanwhile her visitor had already answered her.

'What do I want of your favour? Why, I want to make the most of it.' And Ludlow blushed at his own audacity.

Adela, however, kept her colour. 'I'm afraid it will need all your pulling and stretching,' she said, with a little laugh.

'All right. I'm great at pulling and stretching,' said Ludlow, with a deepening of his great masculine blush, and a broad laugh to match it.

Adela glanced toward the clock on the mantle. She was curious to measure the duration of her acquaintance with this breezy invader of her privacy, with whom she so suddenly found herself bandying florid personalities. She had known him some eight minutes.

Ludlow observed her movement. 'I'm interrupting you and detaining you from your own affairs,' he said; and he moved toward his hat. 'I suppose I must bid you good morning.' And he picked it up.

Adela stood at the table and watched him cross the room. To express a very delicate feeling in terms comparatively broad, she was loth to have him go. She divined, too, that he was loth to go. The knowledge of this feeling on his part, however, affected her composure but slightly. The truth is—we say it with all respect—Adela was an old hand. She was modest, honest and wise; but, as we have said, she had a past—a past of which importunate swains in the guise of morning-callers had been no inconsiderable part; and a great dexterity in what may be called outflanking these gentlemen, was one of her registered accomplishments. Her liveliest emotion at present, therefore, was less one of annoyance at her companion than of surprise at her own gracious impulses, which were yet undeniable. 'Am I dreaming?' she asked herself. She looked out of the window, and then back at Ludlow, who stood grasping his hat and stick, contemplating her face. Should she bid him remain? 'He is honest,' she repeated; 'why should not I be honest for once?' 'I'm sorry you are in a hurry,' she said aloud.

'I am in no hurry,' he answered.

Adela turned her face to the window again, and toward the opposite hills. There was a moment's pause.

'I thought *you* were in a hurry,' said Ludlow.

Adela gave him her eyes. 'My brother would be very glad to have you remain as long as you like. He would expect me to offer you what little hospitality is in my power.'

'Pray, offer it then.'

'That's easily done. This is the parlour, and there, beyond the hall, is my brother's study. Perhaps you would like to look at his books and his collections. I know nothing about them, and I should be a very poor guide. But you are welcome to go in and use your discretion in examining what may interest you.'

'This, I take it, would be but another way of bidding you good-morning.'

'For the present, yes.'

'But I hesitate to take such liberties with your brother's treasures as you prescribe.'

'Prescribe, sir? I prescribe nothing.'

'But if I decline to penetrate into Mr. Moore's *sanctum*, what alternative remains?'

'Really—you must make your own alternative.'

'I think you mentioned the parlour. Suppose I choose that.'

'Just as you please. Here are some books, and, if you like, I will bring you some magazines. Can I serve you in any other way? Are you tired by your walk? Would you like a glass of wine?'

'Tired by my walk?—not exactly. You are very kind, but I feel no immediate desire for a glass of wine. I think you needn't trouble yourself about the magazines, either. I am not exactly in the mood to read.' And Ludlow pulled out his watch and compared it with the clock. 'I'm afraid your clock is fast.'

'Yes;' said Adela, 'very likely.'

'Some ten minutes. Well, I suppose I had better be walking;' and, coming toward Adela, he extended his hand.

She gave him hers. 'It's a day of days for a long, slow ramble,' she said.

Ludlow's only rejoinder was his hand-shake. He moved slowly toward the door, half accompanied by Adela. 'Poor fellow!' she said to herself. The lattice summer-door admitted into the entry a cool, dusky light, in which Adela looked pale. Ludlow divided its wings with his stick, and disclosed a landscape, long, deep and bright, framed by the pillars of the veranda. He stopped on the threshold, swinging his stick. 'I hope I shan't lose my way,' he said.

'I hope not. My brother will not forgive me if you do.'

Ludlow's brows were slightly contracted by a frown, but he contrived to smile with his lips. 'When shall I come back?' he asked abruptly.

Adela found but a low tone—almost a whisper—at her command, to answer. 'Whenever you please,' she said.

The young man turned about, with his back to the bright doorway, and looked into Adela's face, which was now covered with light. 'Miss Moore,' said he, 'it's very much against my will that I leave you at all.'

Adela stood debating within herself. What if her companion should stay? It would, under the circumstances, be an adventure; but was an adventure necessarily unadvisable? It lay wholly with

herself to decide. She was her own mistress, and she had hitherto
been a just mistress. Might she not for once be a generous one? The
reader will observe in Adela's meditation the recurrence of this
saving clause 'for once'. It rests upon the simple fact that she had
begun the day in a romantic mood. She was prepared to be interested; and now that an interesting phenomenon had presented
itself, that it stood before her in vivid human—nay, manly—shape,
instinct with reciprocity, was she to close her hand to the liberality
of fate? To do so would be to court mischance; for it would involve,
moreover, a petty insult to human nature. Was not the man before
her fairly redolent of honesty, and was that not enough? He was
not what Adela had been used to call a gentleman. To this conviction she had made a swallow's flight; but from this assurance she
would start. 'I have seen' (she thus concluded) 'all the gentlemen
can show me; let us try something new.'

'I see no reason why you should run away so fast, Mr. Ludlow,'
she said, aloud.

'I think,' cried Ludlow, 'it would be the greatest piece of folly I
ever committed.'

'I think it would be a pity,' said Adela, with a smile.

'And you invite me into your parlour again? I come as your
visitor, you know. I was your brother's before. It's a simple enough
matter. We are old friends. We have a broad, common ground in
your brother. Isn't that about it?'

'You may adopt whatever theory you please. To my mind, it is,
indeed, a very simple matter.'

'Oh, but I wouldn't have it too simple,' said Ludlow, with a
mighty smile.

'Have it as you please.'

Ludlow leaned back against the doorway. 'Your kindness is too
much for me, Miss Moore,' said he. 'I am passive; I am in your
hands; do with me what you please. I can't help contrasting my fate
with what it might have been but for you. A quarter of an hour ago
I was ignorant of your existence; you weren't in my programme. I
had no idea your brother had a sister. When your servant spoke of
"Miss Moore", upon my word I expected something rather elderly
—something venerable—some rigid old lady, who would say,
"exactly", and "very well, sir", and leave me to spend the rest of the
morning tilting back in a chair on the hotel piazza. It shows what
fools we are to attempt to forecast the future.'

'We must not let our imagination run away with us in any direction,' said Adela.

'Imagination? I don't believe I have any. No, madam,' and Ludlow straightened himself up, 'I live in the present. I write my programme from hour to hour—or, at any rate, I will in the future.'

'I think you are very wise,' said Adela. 'Suppose you write a programme for the present hour. What shall we do? It seems to me a pity to spend so lovely a morning in-doors. I fancy this is the last day of Summer. We ought to celebrate it. How would you like a walk?' Adela had decided that, to reconcile her favours with the proper maintenance of her dignity, her only course was to play the perfect hostess. This decision made, very naturally and gracefully she played her part. It was the one possible part. And yet it did not preclude those delicate sensations with which her novel episode seemed charged: it simply legitimated them. A romantic adventure on so classical a basis would assuredly hurt no one.

'I should like a walk very much,' said Ludlow; 'a walk with a halt at the end of it.'

'Well, if you will consent to a short halt at the beginning of it,' said Adela, 'I will be with you in a very few minutes.' When she returned, in her little hat and shawl, she found her friend seated on the veranda steps. He arose and gave her a card.

'I have been requested, in your absence, to hand you this,' he said.

Adela read with some compunction the name of Mr. Madison Perkins.

'Has he been here?' she asked. 'Why didn't he come in?'

'I told him you were not at home. If it wasn't true then, it was going to be true so soon that the interval was hardly worth taking account of. He addressed himself to me, as I seemed from my position to be quite at home here; but I confess he looked at me as if he doubted my word. He hesitated as to whether he should confide his name to me, or whether he should confide it in that shape to the entry table. I think he wished to show me that he suspected my veracity, for he was making rather grimly for the table when I, fearing that once inside the house he might encounter the living truth, informed him in the most good-humoured tone possible that I would take charge of his little tribute.'

'I think, Mr. Ludlow, that you are a strangely unscrupulous man. How did you know that Mr. Perkins's business was not urgent?'

'I didn't know it. But I knew it could be no more urgent than mine. Depend upon it, Miss Moore, you have no case against me. I only pretend to be a man; to have admitted that charming young gentleman would have been heroic.'

Adela was familiar with a sequestered spot, in the very heart of

the fields, as it seemed to her, to which she now proposed to conduct her friend. The point was to select a goal neither too distant
nor too near, and to adopt a pace neither too rapid nor too slow.
But, although Adela's happy valley was a good two miles away, and
they had measured the interval with the very *minimum* of speed,
yet most sudden seemed their arrival at the stile over which Adela
was used to strike into the meadows. Once on the road, she felt a
precipitate conviction that there could be no evil in an adventure so
essentially wholesome as that to which she had lent herself, and
that there could be no guile in a spirit so deeply sensitive to the
sacred influences of Nature, and to the melancholy aspect of incipient Autumn as that of her companion. A man with an unaffected
relish for small children is a man to inspire young women with a
generous confidence; and so, in a lesser degree, a man with a genuine
feeling for the simple beauties of a common New England landscape may not unreasonably be accepted by the daughters of the
scene as a person worthy of their esteem. Adela was a great observer
of the clouds, the trees and the streams, the sounds and colours, the
echoes and reflections native to her adopted home; and she experienced an honest joy at the sight of Ludlow's keen appreciation of
these modest facts. His enjoyment of them, deep as it was, however,
had to struggle against that sensuous depression natural to a man
who has spent the Summer in a close and fetid laboratory in the
heart of a great city, and against a sensation of a less material order—
the feeling that Adela was a delightful girl. Still, naturally a great
talker, he celebrated his impressions in a generous flow of good-
humoured eloquence. Adela resolved within herself that he was
decidedly a companion for the open air. He was a man to make use,
even to abuse, of the wide horizon and the high ceiling of Nature.
The freedom of his gestures, the sonority of his voice, the keenness
of his vision, the general vivacity of his manners, seemed to neces-
sitate and to justify a universal absence of barriers. They crossed
the stile, and waded through the long grass of several successive
meadows, until the ground began to rise, and stony surfaces to crop
through the turf, when, after a short ascent, they reached a broad
plateau, covered with boulders and shrubs, which lost itself on one
side in a short, steep cliff, whence fields and marshes stretched
down to the opposite river; and on the other, in scattered clumps
of pine and maple, which gradually thickened and multiplied, until
the horizon in that quarter was blue with a long line of woods. Here
was both sun and shade—the unobstructed sky, or the whispering
dome of a circle of pines. Adela led the way to a sunny seat among
the rocks, which commanded the course of the river, and where a

cluster of trees would lend an admonitory undertone to the conversation.

Before long, however, its muffled eloquence became rather importunate, and Adela remarked upon the essential melancholy of the phenomenon.

'It has always seemed to me,' rejoined Ludlow, 'that the wind in the pines expresses tolerably well man's sense of a coming change, simply *as* a change.'

'Perhaps it does,' said Adela. 'The pines are forever rustling, and men are forever changing.'

'Yes, but they can only be said to express it when there is someone there to hear them; and more especially someone in whose life a change is, to his own knowledge, going to take place. Then they are quite prophetic. Don't you know Longfellow says so?'

'Yes, I know Longfellow says so. But you seem to speak from your own feeling.'

'I do.'

'Is there a change pending in your life?'

'Yes, rather an important one.'

'I believe that's what men say when they are going to be married,' said Adela.

'I'm going to be divorced, rather. I'm going to Europe.'

'Indeed! soon?'

'To-morrow,' said Ludlow, after an instant's pause.

'Oh!' said Adela. 'How I envy you!'

Ludlow, who sat looking over the cliff and tossing stones down into the plain, observed a certain inequality in the tone of his companion's two exclamations. The first was nature, the second art. He turned his eyes upon her, but she had turned hers away upon the distance. Then, for a moment, he retreated within himself and thought. He rapidly surveyed his position. Here was he, Tom Ludlow, a hard-headed son of toil, without fortune, without credit, without antecedents, whose lot was cast exclusively with vulgar males, and who had never had a mother, a sister, nor a well-bred sweetheart to pitch his voice for the feminine tympanum; who had seldom come nearer an indubitable young lady than, in a favouring crowd, to receive a mechanical 'thank you' (as if he were a policeman), for some ingeniously provoked service; here he found himself up to his neck in a sudden pastoral with the most ladyish young woman in the land. That it was in him to enjoy the society of such a woman (provided, of course, she were not a fool), he very well knew; but he had not yet suspected that it was possible for him (in the midst of more serious cares) to obtain it. Was he now to infer that this final gift was his—the gift of pleasing women who were worth the pleasing? The inference was at least logical. He had made a good impression. Why else should a modest and discerning girl have so speedily granted him her favour? It was with a little thrill of satisfaction that Ludlow reflected upon the directness of his course. 'It all comes back,' he said to himself, 'to my old theory, that a process can't be too simple. I used no arts. In such an enterprise I shouldn't have known where to begin. It was my ignorance of the regulation method that served me. Women like a gentleman, of course; but they like a man better.' It was the little touch of nature he had discerned in Adela's tone that had set him thinking; but as compared with the frankness of his own attitude it betrayed after all no undue emotion. Ludlow had accepted the fact of his adaptability to the idle mood of a cultivated woman in a thoroughly rational spirit, and he was not now tempted to exaggerate its bearings. He was not the man to be intoxicated by success—this or any other. 'If Miss Moore,' he pursued, 'is so wise—or so foolish—as to like me half an hour for what I am, she is welcome. Assuredly,' he added, as he gazed at her intelligent profile, 'she will not like me for what I am not.' It needs a woman, however, far more intelligent than (thank heaven!) most women are—more intelligent, certainly, than Adela was—to guard her happiness against a strong man's consistent assumption of her intelligence; and doubtless it was from a sense of this general truth, as Ludlow still gazed, he felt an emotion of manly tenderness. 'I wouldn't offend her for the world,' he thought. Just then, Adela, conscious of his gaze, looked about; and before he knew it, Ludlow had repeated aloud, 'Miss Moore, I wouldn't offend you for the world.'

Adela glanced at him for a moment with a little flush that subsided into a smile. 'To what dreadful injury is that the prelude?' she asked.

'It's the prelude to nothing. It refers to the past—to any possible displeasure I may have caused you.'

'Your scruples are unnecessary, Mr. Ludlow. If you had given me offence, I should not have left you to apologize for it. I should not have left the matter to occur to you as you sat dreaming charitably in the sun.'

'What would you have done?'

'Done? nothing. You don't imagine I would have rebuked you—or snubbed you—or answered you back, I take it. I would have left undone—what, I can't tell you. Ask yourself what I have done. I'm sure I hardly know myself,' said Adela, with some intensity. 'At all events, here I am sitting with you in the fields, as if you were a

friend of years. Why do you speak of offence?' And Adela (an uncommon accident with her) lost command of her voice, which
trembled ever so slightly. 'What an odd thought! why should you
offend me? Do I invite it?' Her colour had deepened again, and her
eyes had brightened. She had forgotten herself, and before speaking
had not, as was her wont, sought counsel of that staunch conservative, her taste. She had spoken from a full heart—a heart which had
been filling rapidly since the outset of their walk with a feeling
almost passionate in its quality, and which that little blast of prose
which had brought her Ludlow's announcement of his departure,
had caused to overflow. The reader may give this feeling such a
name as he pleases. We will content ourselves with saying that
Adela had played with fire so effectually that she had been scorched.
The slight vehemence of the speech just quoted had covered her
sensation of pain.

'You pull one up rather short, Miss Moore,' said Ludlow. 'A man
says the best he can.'

Adela made no reply. For a moment she hung her head. Was she
to cry out because she was hurt? Was she to introduce her injured
soul as an impertinent third into the company? No! here our reserved and contemplative heroine is herself again. Her part was still
to be the perfect young lady. For our own part, we can imagine no
figure more bewitching than that of the perfect young lady under
these circumstances; and if Adela had been the most accomplished
coquette in the world she could not have assumed a more becoming
expression than the air of languid equanimity which now covered
her features. But having paid this generous homage to propriety,
she felt free to suffer. Raising her eyes from the ground, she
abruptly addressed her companion with this injunction:

'Mr. Ludlow,' said she, 'tell me something about yourself.'

Ludlow burst into a laugh. 'What shall I tell you?'

'Everything.'

'Everything? Excuse me, I'm not such a fool. But do you know
that's a delicious request you make? I suppose I ought to blush
and hesitate; but I never yet blushed or hesitated in the right place.'

'Very good. There is one fact. Continue. Begin at the beginning.'

'Well, let me see. My name you know. I'm twenty-eight years old.'

'That's the end,' said Adela.

'But you don't want the history of my babyhood, I take it. I
imagine that I was a very big, noisy and ugly baby: what's called
a "splendid infant". My parents were poor, and, of course, honest.
They belonged to a very different set—or "sphere", I suppose you
call it—from any you probably know. They were working people.

My father was a chemist in a small way, and I fancy my mother was
not above using her hands to turn a penny. But although I don't
remember her, I am sure she was a good, sound woman; I feel her
occasionally in my own sinews. I myself have been at work all my
life, and a very good worker I am, let me tell you. I'm not patient,
as I imagine your brother to be—although I have more patience
than you might suppose—but I'm plucky. If you think I'm over-
egotistical, remember 'twas you began it. I don't know whether I'm
clever, and I don't much care; that word is used only by unpractical
people. But I'm clear-headed, and inquisitive, and enthusiastic.
That's as far as I can describe myself. I don't know anything about
my character. I simply suspect I'm a pretty good fellow. I don't
know whether I'm grave or gay, lively or severe. I don't know
whether I'm high-tempered or low-tempered. I don't believe I'm
"high-toned". I fancy I'm good-natured enough, inasmuch as I'm
not nervous. I should not be at all surprised to discover I was prodigiously conceited; but I'm afraid the discovery wouldn't cut me
down, much. I'm desperately hard to snub, I know. Oh, you would
think me a great brute if you knew me. I should hesitate to say
whether I am of a loving turn. I know I'm desperately tired of a
number of persons who are very fond of me; I'm afraid I'm ungrateful. Of course as a man speaking to a woman, there's nothing
for it but to say I'm selfish; but I hate to talk about such windy
abstractions. In the way of positive facts: I'm not educated. I know
no Greek and very little Latin. But I can honestly say that first and
last I have read a great many books—and, thank God, I have a
memory! And I have some tastes, too. I'm very fond of music. I
have a good old voice of my own: *that* I can't help knowing; and
I'm not one to be bullied about pictures. Is that enough? I'm conscious of an utter inability to say anything to the point. To put
myself in a nutshell, I suppose I'm simply a working man; I have
his virtues and I have his defects. I'm a very common fellow.'

'Do you call yourself a very common fellow because you really
believe yourself to be one, or because you are weakly tempted to
disfigure your rather flattering catalogue with a great final blot?'

'I'm sure I don't know. You show more subtlety in that one question than I have shown in my whole string of affirmations. You
women are strong on asking witty questions. Seriously, I believe I
am a common fellow. I wouldn't make the admission to everyone
though. But to you, Miss Moore, who sit there under your parasol
as impartial as the Muse of History, to you I own the truth. I'm no
man of genius. There is something I miss; some final distinction I
lack; you may call it what you please. Perhaps it's humility. Perhaps

you can find it in Ruskin, somewhere. Perhaps it's patience—
perhaps it's imagination. I'm vulgar, Miss Moore. I'm the vulgar
son of vulgar people. I use the word, of course, in its strictest sense.
So much I grant you at the outset, and then I walk ahead.'

'Have you any sisters?'

'Not a sister; and no brothers, nor cousins, nor uncles, nor aunts.'

'And you sail for Europe to-morrow?'

'To-morrow, at ten o'clock.'

'To be away how long?'

'As long as I possibly can. Five years if possible.'

'What do you expect to do in those five years?'

'Study.'

'Nothing but study?'

'It will all come back to that, I fancy. I hope to enjoy myself
reasonably, and to look at the world as I go. But I must not waste
time; I'm growing old.'

'Where are you going?'

'To Berlin. I wanted to get letters from your brother.'

'Have you money? Are you well off?'

'Well off? Not I, no. I'm poor. I travel on a little money that has
just come to me from an unexpected quarter: an old debt owing
my father. It will take me to Germany and keep me for six months.
After that I shall work my way.'

'Are you happy? Are you contented?'

'Just now I'm pretty comfortable, thank you.'

'But will you be so when you get to Berlin?'

'I don't promise to be contented; but I'm pretty sure to be happy.'

'Well!' said Adela, 'I sincerely hope you may be.'

'Amen!' said Ludlow.

Of what more was said at this moment, no record may be given.
The reader has been put into possession of the key of our friends'
conversation; it is only needful to say that substantially upon this
key, it was prolonged for half an hour more. As the minutes elapsed,
Adela found herself drifting further and further away from her
anchorage. When at last she compelled herself to consult her watch,
and remind her companion that there remained but just time
enough for them to reach home, in anticipation of her brother's
arrival, she knew that she was rapidly floating seaward. As she
descended the hill at her companion's side, she felt herself suddenly
thrilled by an acute temptation. Her first instinct was to close her
eyes upon it, in the trust that when she opened them again it would
have vanished; but she found that it was not to be so uncompromis-
ingly dismissed. It importuned her so effectually, that before she had

walked a mile homeward, she had succumbed to it, or had at least
given it the pledge of that quickening of the heart which accompanies a bold resolution. This little sacrifice allowed her no breath
for idle words, and she accordingly advanced with a bent and listening head. Ludlow marched along, with no apparent diminution of
his habitual buoyancy of mien, talking as fast and as loud as at the
outset. He adventured a prophecy that Mr. Moore would not have
returned, and charged Adela with a humorous message of regrets.
Adela had begun by wondering whether the approach of their
separation had wrought within him any sentimental depression at
all commensurate with her own, with that which sealed her lips
and weighed upon her heart; and now she was debating as to
whether his express declaration that he felt 'awfully blue' ought
necessarily to remove her doubts. Ludlow followed up this declaration with a very pretty review of the morning, and a sober
valedictory which, whether intensely felt or not, struck Adela as at
least nobly bare of flimsy compliments. He might be a common
fellow—but he was certainly a very uncommon one. When they
reached the garden gate, it was with a fluttering heart that Adela
scanned the premises for some accidental sign of her brother's
presence. She felt that there would be an especial fitness in his not
having returned. She led the way in. The hall table was bare of his
hat and overcoat. The only object it displayed was Mr. Perkins's
card, which Adela had deposited there on her exit. All that was
represented by that little white ticket seemed a thousand miles
away. Finally, Mr. Moore's absence from his study was conclusive
against his return.

As Adela went back thence into the drawing-room, she simply
shook her head at Ludlow, who was standing before the fire-place;
and as she did so, she caught her reflection in the mantel-glass.
'Verily,' she said to herself, 'I have travelled far.' She had pretty
well unlearned the repose of the Veres of Vere. But she was to break
with it still more completely. It was with a singular hardihood that
she prepared to redeem the little pledge which had been extorted
from her on her way home. She felt that there was no trial to which
her generosity might now be called which she would not hail with
enthusiasm. Unfortunately, her generosity was not likely to be
challenged; although she nevertheless had the satisfaction of assuring herself at this moment that, like the mercy of the Lord, it was
infinite. Should she satisfy herself of her friend's? or should she
leave it delightfully uncertain? These had been the terms of what
has been called her temptation, at the foot of the hill. But inasmuch
as Adela was by no means strictly engaged in the pursuit of pleas-

ure, and as the notion of a grain of suffering was by no means repugnant to her, she had resolved to obtain possession of the one essential fact of her case, even though she should be at heavy costs to maintain it.

'Well, I have very little time,' said Ludlow; 'I must get my dinner and pay my bill and drive to the train.' And he put out his hand.

Adela gave him her own, and looked him full in the eyes. 'You are in a great hurry,' said she.

'It's not I who am in a hurry. It's my confounded destiny. It's the train and the steamer.'

'If you really wished to stay you wouldn't be bullied by the train and the steamer.'

'Very true—very true. But *do* I really wish to stay?'

'That's the question. That's what I want to know.'

'You ask difficult questions, Miss Moore.'

'I mean they shall be difficult.'

'Then, of course, you are prepared to answer difficult ones.'

'I don't know that that's of course, but I am.'

'Well, then, do you wish me to stay? All I have to do is to throw down my hat, sit down and fold my arms for twenty minutes. I lose my train and my ship. I stay in America, instead of going to Europe.'

'I have thought of all that.'

'I don't mean to say it's a great deal. There are pleasures and pleasures.'

'Yes, and especially the former. It is a great deal.'

'And you invite me to accept it?'

'No; I ought not to say that. What I ask of you is whether, if I should so invite you, you would say "yes".'

'That makes the matter very easy for you, Miss Moore. What attractions do you hold out?'

'I hold out nothing whatever, sir.'

'I suppose that means a great deal.'

'It means what it seems to mean.'

'Well, you are certainly a most interesting woman, Miss Moore—a charming woman.'

'Why don't you call me "fascinating" at once, and bid me good morning?'

'I don't know but that I shall have to come to that. But I will give you no answer that leaves you at an advantage. Ask me to stay—command me to stay, if that suits you better—and I will see how it sounds. Come, you must not trifle with a man.' He still held Adela's hand, and they had been looking frankly into each other's eyes. He paused, waiting for an answer.

'Good-bye, Mr. Ludlow,' said Adela. 'God bless you!' And she was about to withdraw her hand; but he held it.

'Are we friends?' said he.

Adela gave a little shrug of her shoulders. 'Friends of three hours.'

Ludlow looked at her with some sternness. 'Our parting could at best hardly have been sweet,' said he; 'but why should you make it bitter, Miss Moore?'

'If it's bitter, why should you try to change it?'

'Because I don't like bitter things.'

Ludlow had caught a glimpse of the truth—that truth of which the reader has had a glimpse—and he stood there at once thrilled and annoyed. He had both a heart and a conscience. 'It's not my fault,' he cried to the latter; but he was unable to add, in all consistency, that it was his misfortune. It would be very heroic, very poetic, very chivalric, to lose his steamer, and he felt that he could do so for sufficient cause—at the suggestion of a fact. But the motive here was less than a fact—an idea; less than an idea—a fancy. 'It's a very pretty little romance as it is,' he said to himself. 'Why spoil it? She is an admirable girl: to have learned that is enough for me.' He raised her hand to his lips, pressed them to it, dropped it, reached the door and bounded out of the garden gate.

The day was ended.

My Friend Bingham

[First appeared in the *Atlantic Monthly*, vol. xix (March 1867), pp. 346-358. Not reprinted during James's lifetime.]

CONSCIOUS AS I AM OF A DEEP AVERSION TO STORIES of a painful nature, I have often asked myself whether, in the events here set forth, the element of pain is stronger than that of joy. An affirmative answer to this question would have stood as a veto upon the publication of my story, for it is my opinion that the literature of horrors needs no extension. Such an answer, however, I am unwilling to pronounce; while, on the other hand, I hesitate to assume the responsibility of a decided negative. I have therefore determined to leave the solution to the reader. I may add, that I am very sensible of the superficial manner in which I have handled my facts. I bore no other part in the accomplishment of these facts than that of a cordial observer; and it was impossible that, even with the best will in the world, I should fathom the emotions of the actors. Yet, as the very faintest reflection of human passions, under the pressure of fate, possesses an immortal interest, I am content to appeal to the reader's sympathy, and to assure him of my own fidelity.

Towards the close of summer, in my twenty-eighth year, I went down to the seaside to rest from a long term of work, and to enjoy, after several years of separation, a *tête-à-tête* with an intimate friend. My friend had just arrived from Europe, and we had agreed to spend my vacation together by the side of the sounding sea, and within easy reach of the city. On taking possession of our lodgings, we found that we should have no fellow-idlers, and we hailed joyously the prospect of the great marine solitudes which each of us declared that he found so abundantly peopled by the other. I hasten to impart to the reader the following facts in regard to the man whom I found so good a companion.

George Bingham had been born and bred among people for whom, as he grew to manhood, he learned to entertain a most generous contempt,—people in whom the hereditary possession of a large property—for he assured me that the facts stood in the relation of cause and effect—had extinguished all intelligent purpose and principle. I trust that I do not speak rhetorically when I describe in these terms the combined ignorance and vanity of my friend's progenitors. It was their fortune to make a splendid figure while they lived, and I feel little compunction in hinting at their poverty in certain human essentials. Bingham was no declaimer, and indeed no great talker; and it was only now and then, in an allusion to the past as the field of a wasted youth, that he expressed his profound resentment. I read this for the most part in the severe humility with which he regarded the future, and under cover of which he seemed to salute it as void at least (whatever other ills it might contain) of those domestic embarrassments which had been the bane of his first manhood. I have no doubt that much may be said, within limits, for the graces of that society against which my friend embodied so violent a reaction, and especially for its good humour,—that home-keeping benevolence which accompanies a sense of material repletion. It is equally probable that to persons of a simple constitution these graces may wear a look of delightful and enduring mystery; but poor Bingham was no simpleton. He was a man of opinions numerous, delicate, and profound. When, with the lapse of his youth, he awoke to a presentiment of these opinions, and cast his first interrogative glance upon the world, he found that in his own little section of it he and his opinions were a piece of melancholy impertinence. Left, at twenty-three years of age, by his father's death, in possession of a handsome property, and absolute master of his actions, he had thrown himself blindly into the world. But, as he afterwards assured me, so superficial was his knowledge of the real world,—the world of labour and inquiry,—that he had found himself quite incapable of intelligent action. In this manner he had wasted a great deal of time. He had travelled much, however; and, being a keen observer of men and women, he had acquired a certain practical knowledge of human nature. Nevertheless, it was not till he was nearly thirty years old that he had begun to live for himself. 'By myself,' he explained, 'I mean something else than this monstrous hereditary faculty for doing nothing and thinking of nothing.' And he led me to believe, or I should rather say he allowed me to believe, that at this moment he had made a serious attempt to study. But upon this point he was not very explicit; for if he blushed for the manner in which he had slighted his opportunities, he blushed equally for the manner in which he had used them. It is my belief that he had but a limited capacity for study, and I am certain that to the end of his days there subsisted in his mind a very friendly relation between fancies and facts.

Bingham was *par excellence* a moralist, a man of sentiment. I know—he knew himself—that, in this busy Western world, this character represents no recognized avocation; but in the absence of such avocation, its exercise was nevertheless very dear to him. I protest that it was very dear to me, and that, at the end of a long morning devoted to my office-desk, I have often felt as if I had

contributed less to the common cause than I have felt after moralizing—or, if you please, sentimentalizing—half an hour with my
friend. He was an idler, assuredly; but his candour, his sagacity, his
good taste, and, above all, a certain diffident enthusiasm which followed its objects with the exquisite trepidation of an unconfessed
and despairing lover,—these things, and a hundred more, redeemed
him from vulgarity. For three years before we came together, as I
have intimated, my impressions of my friend had rested on his
letters; and yet, from the first hour which we spent together, I felt
that they had done him no wrong. We were genuine friends. I don't
know that I can offer better proof of this than by saying that, as our
old personal relations resumed their force, and the time-shrunken
outlines of character filled themselves out, I greeted the reappearance of each familiar foible on Bingham's part quite as warmly as
I did that of the less punctual virtue. Compared, indeed, with the
comrade of earlier years, my actual companion was a well-seasoned
man of the world; but with all his acquired humility and his
disciplined *bonhomie*, he had failed to divest himself of a certain
fastidiousness of mind, a certain formalism of manner, which are
the token and the prerogative of one who has not been obliged to
address himself to practical questions. The charm bestowed by
these facts upon Bingham's conversation—a charm often vainly
invoked in their absence—is explained by his honest indifference to
their action, and his indisposition to turn them to account in the
interest of the picturesque,—an advantage but too easy of conquest
for a young man, rich, accomplished, and endowed with good looks
and a good name. I may say, perhaps, that to a critical mind my
friend's prime distinction would have been his very positive refusal
to drape himself, after the current taste, with those brilliant stuffs
which fortune had strewn at his feet.

Of course, a great deal of our talk bore upon Bingham's recent
travels, adventures, and sensations. One of these last he handled
very frankly, and treated me to a bit of genuine romance. He had
been in love, and had been cruelly jilted, but had now grown able
to view the matter with much of the impartial spirit of those
French critics whose works were his favourite reading. His account
of the young lady's character and motives would indeed have done
credit to many a clever *feuilleton*. I was the less surprised, however,
at his severely dispassionate tone, when, in retracing the process of
his opinions, I discerned the traces—the ravages, I may almost say
—of a solemn act of renunciation. Bingham had forsworn marriage.
I made haste to assure him that I considered him quite too young
for so austere a resolve.

'I can't help it,' said he; 'I feel a foreboding that I shall live and die alone.'

'A foreboding?' said I. 'What's a foreboding worth?'

'Well, then, rationally considered, my marriage is improbable.'

'But it's not to be rationally considered,' I objected. 'It belongs to the province of sentiment.'

'But you deny me sentiment. I fall back upon my foreboding.'

'That's not sentiment,—it's superstition,' I answered. 'Your marrying will depend upon your falling in love; and your falling in love will certainly not depend upon yourself.'

'Upon whom, then?'

'Upon some unknown fair one,—Miss A, B, or C.'

'Well,' said Bingham, submissively, 'I wish she would make haste and reveal herself.'

These remarks had been exchanged in the hollow of a cliff which sloped seaward, and where we had lazily stretched ourselves at length on the grass. The grass had grown very long and brown; and as we lay with our heads quite on a level with it, the view of the immediate beach and the gentle breakers was so completely obstructed by the rank, coarse herbage, that our prospect was reduced to a long, narrow band of deep blue ocean traversing its black fibres, and to the great vault of the sky. We had strolled out a couple of hours before, bearing each a borrowed shot-gun and accompanied by a friendly water-dog, somewhat languidly disposed towards the slaughter of wild ducks. We were neither of us genuine sportsmen, and it is certain that, on the whole, we meant very kindly to the ducks. It was at all events fated that on that day they should suffer but lightly at our hands. For the half-hour previous to the exchange of the remarks just cited, we had quite forgotten our real business; and, with our pieces lost in the grass beside us, and our dog, weary of inaction, wandering far beyond call, we looked like any straw-picking truants. At last Bingham rose to his feet, with the asseveration that it would never do for us to return empty-handed. 'But, behold,' he exclaimed, as he looked down across the breadth of the beach, 'there is our friend of the cottage, with the sick little boy.'

I brought myself into a sitting posture, and glanced over the cliff. Down near the edge of the water sat a young woman, tossing stones into it for the amusement of a child, who stood lustily crowing and clapping his hands. Her title to be called our friend lay in the fact, that on our way to the beach we had observed her issuing from a cottage hard by the hotel, leading by the hand a pale-faced little boy, muffled like an invalid. The hotel, as I have said, was all but deserted, and this young woman had been the first person to engage our idle observation. We had seen that, although plainly dressed, she was young, pretty, and modest; and, in the absence of heavier cares, these facts had sufficed to make her interesting. The question had arisen between us, whether she was a native of the shore, or a visitor like ourselves. Bingham inclined to the former view of the case, and I to the latter. There was, indeed, a certain lowliness in her aspect; but I had contended that it was by no means a rustic lowliness. Her dress was simple, but it was well made and well worn; and I noticed that, as she strolled along, leading her little boy, she cast upon sky and sea the lingering glance of one to whom, in their integrity, these were unfamiliar objects. She was the wife of some small tradesman, I argued, who had brought her child to the seaside by the physician's decree. But Bingham declared that it was utterly illogical to suppose her to be a mother of five years' motherhood; and that, for his part, he saw nothing in her appearance inconsistent with rural influences. The child was her nephew, the son of a married sister, and she a sentimental maiden aunt. Obviously the volume she had in her hand was Tennyson. In the absence on both sides of authentic data, of course the debate was not prolonged; and the subject of it had passed from our memories some time before we again met her on the beach. She soon became aware of our presence, however; and, with a natural sense of intrusion, we immediately resumed our walk. The last that I saw of her, as we rounded a turn in the cliff which concealed the backward prospect, was a sudden grasp of the child's arm, as if to withdraw him from the reach of a hastily advancing wave.

Half an hour's further walk led us to a point which we were not tempted to exceed. We shot between us some half a dozen birds; but as our dog, whose talents had been sadly misrepresented, proved very shy of the deep water, and succeeded in bringing no more than a couple of our victims to shore, we resolved to abstain from further destruction, and to return home quietly along the beach, upon which we had now descended.

'If we meet our young lady,' said Bingham, 'we can gallantly offer her our booty.'

Some five minutes after he had uttered these words, a couple of great sea-gulls came flying landward over our heads, and, after a long gyration in mid-air, boldly settled themselves on the slope of the cliff at some three hundred yards in front of us, a point at which it projected almost into the waves. After a momentary halt, one of them rose again on his long pinions and soared away seaward; the other remained. He sat perched on a jutting boulder some fifteen feet high, sunning his fishy breast.

'I wonder if I could put a shot into him,' said Bingham.

'Try,' I answered; and, as he rapidly charged and levelled his piece, I remember idly repeating, while I looked at the great bird,

> 'God save thee, ancient mariner,
> From the fiends that plague thee thus!
> Why look'st thou so? "With my cross-bow
> I shot the albatross."'

'He's going to rise,' I added.

But Bingham had fired. The creature rose, indeed, half sluggishly, and yet with too hideous celerity. His movement drew from us a cry which was almost simultaneous with the report of Bingham's gun. I cannot express our relation to what followed it better than by saying that it exposed to our sight, beyond the space suddenly left vacant, the happy figure of the child from whom we had parted but an hour before. He stood with his little hands extended, and his face raised toward the retreating bird. Of the sickening sensation which assailed our common vision as we saw him throw back his hands to his head, and reel downwards out of sight, I can give no verbal account, nor of the rapidity with which we crossed the smooth interval of sand, and rounded the bluff.

The child's companion had scrambled up the rocky bank towards the low ledge from which he had fallen, and to which access was of course all too easy. She had sunk down upon the stones, and was wildly clasping the boy's body. I turned from this spectacle to my friend, as to an image of equal woe. Bingham, pale as death, bounded over the stones, and fell on his knees. The woman let him take the child out of her arms, and bent over, with her forehead on a rock, moaning. I have never seen helplessness so vividly embodied as in this momentary group.

'Did it strike his head?' cried Bingham. 'What the devil was he doing up there?'

'I told him he'd get hurt,' said the young woman, with harrowing simplicity. 'To shoot straight at him!—He's killed!'

'Great heavens! Do you mean to say that I saw him?' roared Bingham. 'How did I know he was there? Did you see us?'

The young woman shook her head. 'Of course I didn't see you. I saw you with your guns before. Oh, he's killed!'

'He's not killed. It was mere duck shot. Don't talk such stuff.— My own poor little man!' cried George. 'Charles, where *were* our eyes?'

'He wanted to catch the bird,' moaned our companion. 'Baby, my boy! open your eyes. Speak to your mother. For God's sake, get some help!'

She had put out her hands to take the child from Bingham, who had half angrily lifted him out of her reach. The senseless movement with which, as she disengaged him from Bingham's grasp, he sank into her arms, was clearly the senselessness of death. She burst into sobs. I went and examined the child.

'He *may* not be killed,' I said, turning to Bingham; 'keep your senses. It's not your fault. We *couldn't* see each other.'

Bingham rose stupidly to his feet.

'She must be got home,' I said.

'We must get a carriage. Will you go or stay?'

I saw that he had seen the truth. He looked about him with an expression of miserable impotence. 'Poor little devil!' he said, hoarsely.

'Will you go for a carriage?' I repeated, taking his hand, 'or will you stay?'

Our companion's sobs redoubled their violence.

'I'll stay,' said he. 'Bring some woman.'

I started at a hard run. I left the beach behind me, passed the white cottage at whose garden gate two women were gossiping, and reached the hotel stable, where I had the good fortune to find a vehicle at my disposal. I drove straight back to the white cottage. One of the women had disappeared, and the other was lingering among her flowers,—a middle-aged, keen-eyed person. As I descended and hastily addressed her, I read in her rapid glance an anticipation of evil tidings.

'The young woman who stays with you—' I began.

'Yes,' she said, 'my second-cousin. Well?'

'She's in trouble. She wants you to come to her. Her little boy has hurt himself.' I had time to see that I need fear no hysterics.

'Where did you leave her?' asked my companion.

'On the beach.'

'What's the matter with the child?'

'He fell from a rock. There's no time to be lost.' There was a certain antique rigidity about the woman which was at once irritating and reassuring. I was impelled both to quicken her apprehensions and to confide in her self-control. 'For all I know, ma'am,' said I, 'the child is killed.'

She gave me an angry stare. 'For all you know!' she exclaimed. 'Where were your wits? Were you afraid to look at him?'

'Yes, half afraid.'

She glanced over the paling at my vehicle. 'Am I to get into that?' she asked.

'If you will be so good.'

She turned short about, and re-entered the house, where, I as stood out among the dahlias and the pinks, I heard a rapid opening and shutting of drawers. She shortly reappeared, equipped for driving; and, having locked the house door, and pocketed the key, came and faced me, where I stood ready to help her into the wagon.

'We'll stop for the doctor,' she began.

'The doctor,' said I, 'is of no use.'

A few moments of hard driving brought us to my starting-point. The tide had fallen perceptibly in my absence; and I remember receiving a strange impression of the irretrievable nature of the recent event from the sight of poor Bingham, standing down at the low-water-mark, and looking seaward with his hands in his pockets. The mother of his little victim still sat on the heap of stones where she had fallen, pressing her child to her breast. I helped my companion to descend, which she did with great deliberation. It is my belief that, as we drove along the beach, she derived from the expression of Bingham's figure, and from the patient aversion of his face, a suspicion of his relation to the opposite group. It was not till the elder woman had come within a few steps of her, that the younger became aware of her approach. I merely had time to catch the agonized appeal of her upward glance, and the broad compassion of the other's stooping movement, before I turned my back upon their encounter, and walked down towards my friend. The monotonous murmur of the waves had covered the sound of our wagon-wheels, and Bingham stood all unconscious of the coming of relief,—distilling I know not what divine relief from the simple beauty of sea and sky. I had laid my hand on his shoulder before he turned about. He looked towards the base of the cliff. I knew that a great effusion of feeling would occur in its natural order; but how should I help him across the interval?

'That's her cousin,' I said at random. 'She seems a very capable woman.'

'The child is quite dead,' said Bingham, for all answer. I was struck by the plainness of his statement. In the comparative freedom of my own thoughts I had failed to make allowance for the embarrassed movement of my friend's. It was not, therefore, until afterwards that I acknowledged he had thought to better purpose than I; inasmuch as the very simplicity of his tone implied a positive acceptance (for the moment) of the dreadful fact which he uttered.

'The sooner they get home, the better,' I said. It was evident that the elder of our companions had already embraced this conviction. She had lifted the child and placed him in the carriage, and she was now turning towards his mother and inviting her to ascend. Even at the distance at which I stood, the mingled firmness and tenderness of her gestures were clearly apparent. They seemed, moreover, to express a certain indifference to our movements, an independence of our further interference, which—fanciful as the assertion may look—was not untinged with irony. It was plain that, by whatever rapid process she had obtained it, she was already in possession of our story. 'Thank God for strong-minded women!' I exclaimed;— and yet I could not repress a feeling that it behooved me, on behalf of my friend, to treat as an equal with the vulgar movement of antipathy which he was destined to encounter, and of which, in the irresistible sequence of events, the attitude of this good woman was an index.

We walked towards the carriage together. 'I shall not come home directly,' said Bingham; 'but don't be alarmed about me.'

I looked at my watch. 'I give you two hours,' I said, with all the authority of my affection.

The new-comer had placed herself on the back seat of the vehicle beside the sufferer, who on entering had again possessed herself of her child. As I went about to mount in front, Bingham came and stood by the wheel. I read his purpose in his face,—the desire to obtain from the woman he had wronged some recognition of his *human* character, some confession that she dimly distinguished him from a wild beast or a thunderbolt. One of her hands lay exposed, pressing together on her knee the lifeless little hands of her boy. Bingham removed his hat, and placed his right hand on that of the young woman. I saw that she started at his touch, and that he vehemently tightened his grasp.

'It's too soon to talk of forgiveness,' said he, 'for it's too soon for me to think intelligently of the wrong I have done you. God has brought us together in a very strange fashion.'

The young woman raised her bowed head, and gave my friend, if not just the look he coveted, at least the most liberal glance at her command,—a look which, I fancy, helped him to face the immediate future. But these are matters too delicate to be put into words.

I spent the hours that elapsed before Bingham's return to the inn in gathering information about the occupants of the cottage. Impelled by that lively intuition of calamity which is natural to women, the housekeeper of the hotel, a person of evident kindliness and discretion, lost no time in winning my confidence. I was not unwilling that the tragic incident which had thus arrested our idleness should derive its earliest publicity from my own lips; and I was forcibly struck with the exquisite impartiality with which this homely creature bestowed her pity. Miss Horner, I learned, the mistress of the cottage, was the last representative of a most respectable family, native to the neighbouring town. It had been for some years her practice to let lodgings during the summer. At the close of the present season she had invited her kinswoman, Mrs. Hicks, to spend the autumn with her. That this lady was the widow of a Baptist minister; that her husband had died some three years before; that she was very poor; that her child had been sickly, and that the care of his health had so impeded her exertions for a livelihood, that she had been intending to leave him with Miss Horner for the winter, and obtain a 'situation' in town;—these facts were the salient points of the housekeeper's somewhat prolix recital.

The early autumn dusk had fallen when Bingham returned. He looked very tired. He had been walking for several hours, and, as I fancied, had grown in some degree familiar with his new responsibilities. He was very hungry, and made a vigorous attack upon his supper. I had been indisposed to eat, but the sight of his healthy appetite restored my own. I had grown weary of my thoughts, and I found something salutary in the apparent simplicity and rectitude of Bingham's state of mind.

'I find myself taking it very quietly,' he said, in the course of his repast. 'There is something so absolute in the nature of the calamity, that one is compelled to accept it. I don't see how I could endure to have mutilated the poor little mortal. To kill a human being is, after all, the least injury you can do him.' He spoke these words deliberately, with his eyes on mine, and with an expression of perfect candour. But as he paused, and in spite of my perfect assent to their meaning, I could not help mentally reverting to the really tragic phase of the affair; and I suppose my features revealed to Bingham's scrutiny the process of my thoughts. His pale face flushed a burning crimson, his lips trembled. 'Yes, my boy!' he cried; 'that's where it's damnable.' He buried his head in his hands, and burst into tears.

We had a long talk. At the end of it, we lit our cigars, and came out upon the deserted piazza. There was a lovely starlight, and, after a few turns in silence, Bingham left my side and strolled off towards a bend in the road, in the direction of the sea. I saw him stand motionless for a long time, and then I heard him call me. When I reached his side, I saw that he had been watching a light in the window of the white cottage. We heard the village bell in the distance striking nine.

'Charles,' said Bingham, 'suppose you go down there and make some offer of your services. God knows whom the poor creatures have to look to. She has had a couple of men thrust into her life. She must take the good with the bad.'

I lingered a moment. 'It's a difficult task,' I said. 'What shall I say?'

Bingham silently puffed his cigar. He stood with his arms folded, and his head thrown back, slowly measuring the starry sky. 'I wish she could come out here and look at that sky,' he said at last. 'It's a sight for bereaved mothers. Somehow, my dear boy,' he pursued, 'I never felt less depressed in my life. It's none of my doing.'

'It would hardly do for me to tell her that,' said I.

'I don't know,' said Bingham. 'This isn't an occasion for the exchange of compliments. I'll tell you what you may tell her. I suppose they will have some funeral services within a day or two. Tell her that I should like very much to be present.'

I set off for the cottage. Its mistress in person introduced me into the little parlour.

'Well, sir?' she said, in hard, dry accents.

'I've come,' I answered, 'to ask whether I can be of any assistance to Mrs. Hicks.'

Miss Horner shook her head in a manner which deprived her negation of half its dignity. 'What assistance is possible?' she asked.

'A man,' said I, 'may relieve a woman of certain cares—'

'O, men are a blessed set! You had better leave Mrs. Hicks to me.'

'But will you at least tell me how she is,—if she has in any degree recovered herself?'

At this moment the door of the adjoining room was opened, and Mrs. Hicks stood on the threshold, bearing a lamp,—a graceful and pathetic figure. I now had occasion to observe that she was a woman of decided beauty. Her fair hair was drawn back into a single knot behind her head, and the lamplight deepened the pallor of her face and the darkness of her eyes. She wore a calico dressing-gown and a shawl.

'What do you wish?' she asked, in a voice clarified, if I may so express it, by long weeping.

'He wants to know whether he can be of any assistance,' said the elder lady.

Mrs. Hicks glanced over her shoulder into the room she had left. 'Would you like to look at the child?' she asked, in a whisper.

'Lucy!' cried Miss Horner.

I walked straight over to Mrs. Hicks, who turned and led the way to a little bed. My conductress raised her lamp aloft, and let the light fall gently on the little white-draped figure. Even the bandage about the child's head had not dispelled his short-lived prettiness. Heaven knows that to remain silent was easy enough; but Heaven knows, too, that to break the silence—and to break it as I broke it—was equally easy. 'He must have been a very pretty child,' I said.

'Yes, he was very pretty. He had black eyes. I don't know whether you noticed.'

'No, I didn't notice,' said I. 'When is he to be buried?'

'The day after to-morrow. I am told that I shall be able to avoid an inquest.'

'Mr. Bingham has attended to that,' I said. And then I paused, revolving his petition.

But Mrs. Hicks anticipated it. 'If you would like to be present at the funeral,' she said, 'you are welcome to come.—And so is your friend.'

'Mr. Bingham bade me ask leave. There is a great deal that I should like to say to you for him,' I added, 'but I won't spoil it by trying. It's his own business.'

The young woman looked at me with her deep, dark eyes. 'I pity him from my heart,' she said, pressing her hands to her breast. 'I had rather have my sorrow than his.'

'They are pretty much one sorrow,' I answered. 'I don't see that you can divide it. You are two to bear it. Bingham is a wise, good fellow,' I went on. 'I have shared a great many joys with him. In Heaven's name,' I cried, 'don't bear hard on him!'

'How can I bear hard?' she asked, opening her arms and letting them drop. The movement was so deeply expressive of weakness and loneliness, that, feeling all power to reply stifled in a rush of compassion, I silently made my exit.

On the following day, Bingham and I went up to town, and on the third day returned in time for the funeral. Besides the two ladies, there was no one present but ourselves and the village minister, who of course spoke as briefly as decency allowed. He had accompanied the ladies in a carriage to the graveyard, while Bingham and I had come on foot. As we turned away from the grave, I saw my friend approach Mrs. Hicks. They stood talking beside the freshly-turned earth, while the minister and I attended Miss Horner to the carriage. After she had seated herself, I lingered at the door, exchanging sober commonplaces with the reverend gentleman. At last Mrs. Hicks followed us, leaning on Bingham's arm.

'Margaret,' she said, 'Mr. Bingham and I are going to stay here awhile. Mr. Bingham will walk home with me. I'm *very* much obliged to you, Mr. Bland,' she added, turning to the minister and extending her hand.

I bestowed upon my friend a glance which I felt to be half interrogative and half sympathetic. He gave me his hand, and answered the benediction by its pressure, while he answered the inquiry by his words. 'If you are still disposed to go back to town this afternoon,' he said, 'you had better not wait for me. I may not have time to catch the boat.'

I of course made no scruple of returning immediately to the city. Some ten days elapsed before I again saw Bingham; but I found my attention so deeply engrossed with work, that I scarcely measured the interval. At last, one morning, he came into my office.

'I take for granted,' I said, 'that you have not been all this time at B——.'

'No; I've been on my travels. I came to town the day after you came. I found at my rooms a letter from a lawyer in Baltimore, proposing the sale of some of my property there, and I seized upon it as an excuse for making a journey to that city. I felt the need of movement, of action of some kind. But when I reached Baltimore, I didn't even go to see my correspondent. I pushed on to Washington, walked about for thirty-six hours, and came home.'

He had placed his arm on my desk, and stood supporting his head on his hand, with a look of great physical exhaustion.

'You look very tired,' said I.

'I haven't slept,' said he. 'I had such a talk with that woman!'

'I'm sorry that you should have felt the worse for it.'

'I feel both the worse and the better. She talked about the child.'

'It's well for her,' said I, 'that she was able to do it.'

'She wasn't able, strictly speaking. She began calmly enough, but she very soon broke down.'

'Did you see her again?'

'I called upon her the next day, to tell her that I was going to town, and to ask if I could be useful to her. But she seems to stand in perfect isolation. She assured me that she was in want of nothing.'

'What sort of a woman does she seem to be, taking her in herself?'

'Bless your soul! I can't take her in herself!' cried Bingham, with some vehemence. 'And yet, stay,' he added; 'she's a very pleasing woman.'

'She's very pretty.'

'Yes; she's very pretty. In years, she's little more than a young girl. In her ideas, she's one of "the people".'

'It seems to me,' said I, 'that the frankness of her conduct toward you is very much to her credit.'

'It doesn't offend you, then?'

'Offend me? It gratifies me beyond measure.'

'I think that, if you had seen her as I have seen her, it would interest you deeply. I'm at a loss to determine whether it's the result of great simplicity or great sagacity. Of course, it's absurd to suppose that, ten days ago, it could have been the result of anything but a beautiful impulse. I think that to-morrow I shall again go down to B——.'

I allowed Bingham time to have made his visit and to have brought me an account of his further impressions; but as three days went by without his reappearance, I called at his lodgings. He was still out of town. The fifth day, however, brought him again to my office.

'I've been at B—— constantly,' he said, 'and I've had several interviews with our friend.'

'Well; how fares it?'

'It fares well. I'm forcibly struck with her good sense. In matters of mind—in matters of soul, I may say—she has the touch of an angel, or rather the touch of a woman. That's quite sufficient.'

'Does she keep her composure?'

'Perfectly. You can imagine nothing simpler and less sentimental than her manner. She makes me forget myself most divinely. The child's death colours our talk; but it doesn't confine or obstruct it. You see she has her religion: she can afford to be natural.'

Weary as my friend looked, and shaken by his sudden subjection to care, it yet seemed to me, as he pronounced these words, that his eye had borrowed a purer light and his voice a fresher tone. In short, where I discerned it, how I detected it, I know not; but I felt that he carried a secret. He sat poking with his walking-stick at a nail in the carpet, with his eyes dropped. I saw about his mouth the faint promise of a distant smile,—a smile which six months would bring to maturity.

'George,' said I, 'I have a fancy.'

He looked up. 'What is it?'

'You've lost your heart.'

He stared a moment, with a sudden frown. 'To whom?' he asked.

'To Mrs. Hicks.'

With a frown, I say, but a frown that was as a smile to the effect of my rejoinder. He rose to his feet; all his colour deserted his face and rushed to his eyes.

'I beg your pardon if I'm wrong,' I said.

Bingham had turned again from pale to crimson. 'Don't beg *my* pardon,' he cried. 'You may say what you please. Beg *hers!*' he added, bitterly.

I resented the charge of injustice. 'I've done *her* no wrong!' I answered. 'I haven't said,' I went on with a certain gleeful sense that I was dealing with massive truths,—'I haven't said that she had lost her heart to you!'

'Good God, Charles!' cried Bingham, 'what a horrid imagination you have!'

'I am not responsible for my imagination.'

'Upon my soul, I hope *I'm* not!' cried Bingham, passionately. 'I have enough without that.'

'George,' I said, after a moment's reflection, 'if I thought I had insulted you, I would make amends. But I have said nothing to be ashamed of. I believe that I have hit the truth. Your emotion proves it. I spoke hastily; but you must admit that, having caught a glimpse of the truth, I couldn't stand indifferent to it.'

'The truth! the truth! What truth?'

'Aren't you in love with Mrs. Hicks? Admit it like a man.'

'Like a man! Like a brute. Haven't I done the woman wrong enough?'

'Quite enough, I hope.'

'Haven't I turned her simple joys to bitterness?'

'I grant it.'

'And now you want me to insult her by telling her that I love her?'

'I want you to tell her nothing. What you tell her is your own affair. Remember that, George. It's as little mine as it is the rest of the world's.'

Bingham stood listening, with a contracted brow and his hand grasping his stick. He walked to the dusty office-window and halted a moment, watching the great human throng in the street. Then he turned and came towards me. Suddenly he stopped short. 'God forgive me!' he cried; 'I believe I do love her.'

The fountains of my soul were stirred. 'Combining my own hasty impressions of Mrs. Hicks with yours, George,' I said, 'the consummation seems to me exquisitely natural.'

It was in these simple words that we celebrated the sacred fact. It seemed as if, by tacit agreement, the evolution of this fact was result enough for a single interview.

A few days after this interview, in the evening, I called at Bingham's lodgings. His servant informed me that my friend was out of town, although he was unable to indicate his whereabouts. But as I turned away from the door a hack drew up, and the object of my quest descended, equipped with a travelling-bag. I went down and greeted him under the gas-lamp.

'Shall I go in with you?' I asked; 'or shall I go my way?'

'You had better come in,' said Bingham. 'I have something to say.—I have been down to B——,' he resumed, when the servant had left us alone in his sitting-room. His tone bore the least possible tinge of a confession; but of course it was not as a confessor that I listened.

'Well,' said I, 'how is our friend?'

'Our friend—' answered Bingham. 'Will you have a cigar?'

'No, I thank you.'

'Our friend— Ah, Charles, it's a long story.'

'I sha'n't mind that, if it's an interesting one.'

'To a certain extent it's a painful one. It's painful to come into collision with incurable vulgarity of feeling.'

I was puzzled. 'Has that been your fortune?' I asked.

'It has been my fortune to bring Mrs. Hicks into a great deal of trouble. The case, in three words, is this. Miss Horner has seen fit to resent, in no moderate terms, what she calls the "extraordinary intimacy" existing between Mrs. Hicks and myself. Mrs. Hicks, as was perfectly natural, has resented her cousin's pretension to regulate her conduct. Her expression of this feeling has led to her expulsion from Miss Horner's house.'

'Has she any other friend to turn to?'

'No one, except some relatives of her husband, who are very poor people, and of whom she wishes to ask no favours.'

'Where has she placed herself?'

'She is in town. We came up together this afternoon. I went with her to some lodgings which she had formerly occupied, and which were fortunately vacant.'

'I suppose it's not to be regretted that she has left B——. She breaks with sad associations.'

'Yes; but she renews them too, on coming to town.'

'How so?'

'Why, damn it,' said Bingham, with a tremor in his voice, 'the woman is utterly poor.'

'Has she no resources whatever?'

'A hundred dollars a year, I believe,—worse than nothing.'

'Has she any marketable talents or accomplishments?'

'I believe she is up to some pitiful needle-work or other. Such a woman! O horrible world!'

'Does *she* say so?' I asked.

'She? No indeed. She thinks it's all for the best. I suppose it is. But it seems but a bad best.'

'I wonder,' said I, after a pause, 'whether I might see Mrs. Hicks. Do you think she would receive me?'

Bingham looked at me an instant keenly. 'I suppose so,' said he. 'You can try.'

'I shall go, not out of curiosity,' I resumed, 'but out of—'

'Out of what?'

'Well, in fine, I should like to see her again.'

Bingham gave me Mrs. Hicks's address, and in the course of a few evenings I called upon her. I had abstained from bestowing a fine name upon the impulse which dictated this act; but I am nevertheless free to declare that kindliness and courtesy had a large part in it. Mrs. Hicks had taken up her residence in a plain, small house, in a decent by-street, where, upon presenting myself, I was ushered into a homely sitting-room (apparently her own), and left to await her coming. Her greeting was simple and cordial, and not untinged with a certain implication of gratitude. She had taken for granted, on my part, all possible sympathy and good-will; but as she had regarded me besides as a man of many cares, she had thought it improbable that we should meet again. It was no long time before I became conscious of that generous charm which Bingham had rigorously denominated her good-sense. Good-sense assuredly was there, but good-sense mated and prolific. Never had I seen, it seemed to me, as the moments elapsed, so exquisitely modest a use of such charming faculties,—an intelligence so sensible of its obligations and so indifferent to its privileges. It was obvious that she had been a woman of plain associations: her allusions were to homely facts, and her manner direct and unstudied; and yet, in spite of these limitations, it was equally obvious that she was a person to be neither patronized, dazzled, nor deluded. O the satisfaction which, in the course of that quiet dialogue, I took in this sweet infallibility! How it effaced her loneliness and poverty, and added dignity to her youth and beauty! It made her, potentially at least, a woman of the world. It was an anticipation of the self-possession, the wisdom, and perhaps even in some degree of the wit, which comes through the experience of society,—the result, on Mrs. Hicks's part, of I know not what hours of suffering, despondency, and self-dependence. With whatever intentions, therefore, I might have come before her, I should have found it impossible to address her as any other than an equal, and to regard her affliction as anything less than an absolute mystery. In fact, we hardly touched upon it; and it was only covertly that we alluded to Bingham's melancholy position. I will not deny that in a certain sense I regretted Mrs. Hicks's reserve. It is true that I had a very informal claim upon her confidence; but I had gone to her with a half-defined hope that this claim would be liberally interpreted. It was not even recognized; my vague intentions of counsel and assistance had lain undivined; and I departed with the impression that my social horizon had been considerably enlarged, but that my charity had by no means secured a pensioner.

Mrs. Hicks had given me permission to repeat my visit, and after the lapse of a fortnight I determined to do so. I had seen Bingham several times in the interval. He was of course much interested in my impressions of our friend; and I fancied that my admiration gave him even more pleasure than he allowed himself to express. On entering Mrs. Hicks's parlour a second time, I found him in person standing before the fireplace, and talking apparently with some vehemence to Mrs. Hicks, who sat listening on the sofa. Bingham turned impatiently to the door as I crossed the threshold, and Mrs. Hicks rose to welcome me with all due composure. I was nevertheless sensible that my entrance was ill-timed; yet a retreat was impossible. Bingham kept his place on the hearth-rug, and mechanically gave me his hand,—standing irresolute, as I thought, between annoyance and elation. The fact that I had interrupted a somewhat passionate interview was somehow so obvious, that, at the prompting of a very delicate feeling, Mrs. Hicks hastened to anticipate my apologies.

'Mr. Bingham was giving me a lecture,' she said; and there was perhaps in her accent a faint suspicion of bitterness. 'He will doubtless be glad of another auditor.'

'No,' said Bingham, 'Charles is a better talker than listener. You shall have two lectures instead of one.' He uttered this sally without even an attempt to smile.

'What is your subject?' said I. 'Until I know that, I shall promise neither to talk nor to listen.'

Bingham laid his hand on my arm. 'He represents the world,' he said, addressing our hostess. 'You're afraid of the world. There, make your appeal.'

Mrs. Hicks stood silent for a moment, with a contracted brow and a look of pain on her face. Then she turned to me with a half-smile. 'I don't believe you represent the world,' she said; 'you are too good.'

'She flatters you,' said Bingham. 'You wish to corrupt him, Mrs. Hicks.'

Mrs. Hicks glanced for an instant from my friend to myself. There burned in her eyes a far-searching light, which consecrated the faint irony of the smile which played about her lips. 'O you men!' she said,—'you are so wise, so deep!' It was on Bingham that her eyes rested last; but after a pause, extending her hand, she transferred them to me. 'Mr. Bingham,' she pursued, 'seems to wish you to be admitted to our counsels. There is every reason why his friends should be my friends. You will be interested to know that he has asked me to be his wife.'

'Have you given him an answer?' I asked.

'He was pressing me for an answer when you came in. He conceives me to have a great fear of the judgments of men, and he was saying very hard things about them. But they have very little, after all, to do with the matter. The world may heed it that Mr. Bingham should marry Mrs. Hicks, but it will care very little whether or no Mrs. Hicks marries Mr. Bingham. You are the world, for me,' she cried with beautiful inconsequence, turning to her suitor; 'I know no other.' She put out her hands, and he took them.

I am at a loss to express the condensed force of these rapid words, —the amount of passion, of reflection, of experience, which they seemed to embody. They were the simple utterance of a solemn and intelligent choice; and, as such, the whole phalanx of the Best Society assembled in judgment could not have done less than salute them. What honest George Bingham said, what I said, is of little account. The proper conclusion of my story lies in the highly dramatic fact that out of the depths of her bereavement—out of her loneliness and her pity—this richly gifted woman had emerged, responsive to the passion of him who had wronged her all but as deeply as he loved her. The reader will decide, I think, that this catastrophe offers as little occasion for smiles as for tears. My narrative is a piece of genuine prose.

It was not until six months had elapsed that Bingham's marriage took place. It has been a truly happy one. Mrs. Bingham is now, in the fullness of her bloom, with a single exception, the most charming woman I know. I have often assured her—once too often, possibly—that, thanks to that invaluable good-sense of hers, she is also the happiest. She has made a devoted wife; but—and in occasional moments of insight it has seemed to me that this portion of her fate is a delicate tribute to a fantastic principle of equity—she has never again become a mother. In saying that she has made a devoted wife, it may seem that I have written Bingham's own later history. Yet as the friend of his younger days, the comrade of his *belle jeunesse*, the partaker of his dreams, I would fain give him a sentence apart. What shall it be? He is a truly incorruptible soul; he is a confirmed philosopher; he has grown quite stout.

Poor Richard
A STORY IN THREE PARTS

[First appeared in three instalments in the *Atlantic Monthly*, vol. xix (June 1867), pp. 694-706; vol. xx (July 1867), pp. 32-42; vol. xx (August 1867), pp. 167-78. The tale was heavily revised and reprinted in volume iii of *Stories Revived* (1885).]

PART I

MISS WHITTAKER'S GARDEN COVERED A COUPLE OF acres, behind and beside her house, and at its farther extremity was bounded by a narrow meadow, which in turn was bordered by the old disused towing-path beside the river, at this point a slow and shallow stream. Its low flat banks were unadorned with rocks or trees, and a towing-path is not in itself a romantic promenade. Nevertheless, here sauntered bareheaded, on a certain spring evening, the mistress of the acres just mentioned and many more beside, in sentimental converse with an impassioned and beautiful youth.

She herself had been positively plain, but for the frequent recurrence of a magnificent broad smile,—which imparted loveliness to her somewhat plebeian features,—and (in another degree) for the elegance of her dress, which expressed one of the later stages of mourning, and was of that voluminous abundance proper to women who are massive in person, and rich besides. Her companion's good looks, for very good they were, in spite of several defects, were set off by a shabby suit, as carelessly worn as it was inartistically cut. His manner, as he walked and talked, was that of a nervous, passionate man, wrought almost to desperation; while her own was that of a person self-composed to generous attention. A brief silence, however, had at last fallen upon them. Miss Whittaker strolled along quietly, looking at the slow-mounting moon, and the young man gazed on the ground, swinging his stick. Finally, with a heavy blow, he brought it to earth.

'O Gertrude!' he cried, 'I despise myself.'

'That's very foolish,' said Gertrude.

'And, Gertrude, I adore you.'

'That's more foolish still,' said Gertrude, with her eyes still on the moon. And then, suddenly and somewhat impatiently transferring them to her companion's face, 'Richard,' she asked, 'what do you mean when you say you adore me?'

'Mean?' I mean that I love you.'

'Then, why don't you say what you mean?'

The young man looked at her a moment. 'Will you give me leave,' he asked, 'to say *all* that I mean?'

'Of course.' Then, as he remained silent, 'I listen,' added Gertrude.

Yet he still said nothing, but went striking vehemently at the weeds by the water's edge, like one who may easily burst into tears of rage.

'Gertrude!' he suddenly exclaimed, 'what more do you want than the assurance that I love you!'

'I want nothing more. That assurance is by itself delightful enough. You yourself seemed to wish to add something more.'

'Either you won't understand me,' cried Richard, 'or'—flagrantly vicious for twenty seconds—'you can't!'

Miss Whittaker stopped and looked thoughtfully into his face. 'In our position,' she said, 'if it becomes you to sacrifice reflection to feeling, it becomes me to do the reverse. Listen to me, Richard. I *do* understand you, and better, I fancy, than you understand yourself.'

'O, of course!'

But she continued, heedless of his interruption. 'I thought that, by leaving you to yourself awhile, your feelings might become clearer to you. But they seem to be growing only more confused. I have been so fortunate, or so unfortunate, I hardly know which,'—and she smiled faintly,—'as to please you. That's all very well, but you must not make too much of it. Nothing can make me happier than to please you, or to please anyone. But here it must stop with you, as it stops with others.'

'It does not stop here with others.'

'I beg your pardon. You have no right to say that. It is partly out of justice to others that I speak to you as I am doing. I shall always be one of your best friends, but I shall never be more. It is best I should tell you this at once. I might trifle with you awhile and make you happy (since upon such a thing you are tempted to set your happiness) by allowing you to suppose that I had given you my heart; but the end would soon come, and then where should we be? You may in your disappointment call me heartless now,—I freely give you leave to call me anything that may ease your mind,—but what would you call me then? Friendship, Richard, is a heavenly cure for love. Here is mine,' and she held out her hand.

'No, I thank you,' said Richard, gloomily folding his arms. 'I know my own feelings,' and he raised his voice. 'Haven't I lived with them night and day for weeks and weeks? Great Heavens,

Gertrude, this is no fancy. I'm not of that sort. My whole life has
gone into my love. God has let me idle it away hitherto, only that
I might begin it with you. Dear Gertrude, hear me. I have the heart
of a man. I know I'm not respectable, but I devoutly believe I'm
lovable. It's true that I've neither worked, nor thought, nor studied,
nor turned a penny. But, on the other hand, I've never cared for a
woman before. I've waited for you. And now—now, after all, I'm to
sit down and be *pleased*! The Devil! Please other men, madam!
Me you delight, you intoxicate.'

An honest flush rose to Gertrude's cheek. 'So much the worse for
you!' she cried with a bitter laugh. 'So much the worse for both of
us! But what is your point? Do you wish to marry me?'

Richard flinched a moment under this tacit proposition suddenly
grown vocal; but not from want of heart. 'Of course I do,' he said.
'Well, then, I only pity you the more for your consistency. I can
only entreat you again to rest contented with my friendship. It's
not such a bad substitute, Richard, as I understand it. What my
love might be I don't know,—I couldn't answer for that; but of my
friendship I'm sure. We both have our duties in this matter, and I
have resolved to take a liberal view of mine. I might lose patience
with you, you know, and dismiss you,—leave you alone with your
dreams, and let you break your heart. But it's rather by seeing
more of me than by seeing less, that your feelings will change.'

'Indeed! And yours?'

'I have no doubt they will change, too; not in kind, but in degree.
The better I know you, I am sure, the better I shall like you. The
better too you will like me. Don't turn your back upon me. I speak
the truth. You will get to entertain a serious opinion of me,—which
I'm sure you haven't now, or you wouldn't talk of my intoxicating
you. But you must be patient. It's a singular fact that it takes
longer to like a woman than to love her. A sense of intoxication is
a very poor feeling to marry upon. You wish, of course, to break
with your idleness, and your bad habits,—you see I am so thoroughly
your friend that I'm not afraid of touching upon disagreeable facts,
as I should be if I were your mistress. But you are so indolent, so
irresolute, so undisciplined, so uneducated,'—Gertrude spoke deliberately, and watched the effect of her words,—'that you find a change
of life very difficult. I propose, with your consent, to appoint myself
your counsellor. Henceforth my house will be open to you as to
my dearest friend. Come as often and stay as long as you please.
Not in a few weeks, perhaps, nor even in a few months, but in God's
good time, you will be a noble young man in working order,—
which I don't consider you now, and which I know you don't con-

sider yourself. But I have a great opinion of your talents,' (this was very shrewd of Gertrude,) 'and of your heart. If I turn out to have done you a service, you'll not want to marry me then.'

Richard had silently listened, with a deepening frown. 'That's all very pretty,' he said; 'but'—and the reader will see that, in his earnestness, he was inclined to dispense with courtesy—'it's rotten,—rotten from beginning to end. What's the meaning of all that rigmarole about the inconsistency of friendship and love? Such talk is enough to drive one mad. Refuse me outright, and send me to the Devil, if you must; but don't bemuddle your own brains at the same time. But one little word knocks it all to pieces: I want you for my wife. You make an awful mistake in treating me as a boy,—an awful mistake. I *am* in working order. I have begun life in loving you. I have broken with drinking as effectually as if I hadn't touched a drop of liquor for twenty years. I hate it, I loathe it. I've drunk my last. No, Gertrude, I'm no longer a boy,—you've cured me of that. Hang it, that's why I love you! Don't you see? Ah, Gertrude!'—and his voice fell,—'you're a great enchantress! You have no arts, you have no beauty even, (can't a lover deal with facts now?) but you are an enchantress without them. It's your nature. You are so divinely, damnably honest! That excellent speech just now was meant to smother my passion; but it has only inflamed it. You will say it was nothing but common sense. Very likely; but that is the very point. Your common sense captivates me. It's for that that I love you.'

He spoke with so relentless a calmness that Gertrude was sickened. Here she found herself weaker than he, while the happiness of both of them demanded that she should be stronger.

'Richard Clare,' she said, 'you are unkind!' There was a tremor in her voice as she spoke; and as she ceased speaking, she burst into tears. A selfish sense of victory invaded the young man's breast. He threw his arm about her; but she shook it off. 'You are a coward, sir!' she cried.

'Oho!' said Richard, flushing angrily.

'You go too far; you persist beyond decency.'

'You hate me now, I suppose,' said Richard, brutally, like one at bay.

Gertrude brushed away her tears. 'No indeed,' she answered, sending him a dry, clear glance. 'To hate you, I should have to have loved you. I pity you still.'

Richard looked at her a moment. 'I don't feel tempted to return the feeling, Gertrude,' said he. 'A woman with so much head as you needs no pity.'

'I have not head enough to read your sarcasm, sir; but I have heart enough to excuse it, and I mean to keep a good heart to the end. I mean to keep my temper, I mean to be just, I mean to be conclusive, and not to have to return to this matter. It's not for my pleasure, I would have you know, that I am so explicit. I have nerves as well as you. Listen, then. If I don't love you, Richard, in your way, I don't; and if I can't, I can't. We can't love by will. But with friendship, when it is once established, I believe the will and the reason may have a great deal to do. I will, therefore, put the whole of my mind into my friendship for you, and in that way we shall perhaps be even. Such a feeling—as I shall naturally show it —will, after all, not be very different from that other feeling you ask —as I should naturally show it. Bravely to reconcile himself to such difference as there is, is no more than a man of honour ought to do. Do you understand me?'

'You have an admirable way of putting things. "After all," and "such difference as there is"! The difference is the difference of marriage and no-marriage. I suppose you don't mean that you are willing to live with me without that ceremony?'

'You suppose correctly.'

'Then why do you falsify matters? A woman is either a man's wife, or she isn't.'

'Yes; and a woman is either a man's friend, or she isn't.'

'And you are mine, and I'm an ungrateful brute not to rest satisfied! That's what you mean. Heaven knows you're right,'—and he paused a moment, with his eyes on the ground. 'Don't despise me, Gertrude,' he resumed. 'I'm not so ungrateful as I seem. I'm very much obliged to you for the pains you have taken. Of course I understand your not loving me. You'd be a grand fool if you did; and you're no fool, Gertrude.'

'No, I'm no fool, Richard. It's a great responsibility,—it's dreadfully vulgar; but, on the whole, I'm rather glad.'

'So am I. I could hate you for it; but there is no doubt it's why I love you. If you were a fool, you might love me; but I shouldn't love you, and if I must choose, I prefer that.'

'Heaven has chosen for us. Ah, Richard,' pursued Gertrude, with admirable simplicity, 'let us be good and obey Heaven, and we shall be sure to be happy'—and she held out her hand once more.

Richard took it and raised it to his lips. She felt their pressure and withdrew it.

'Now you must leave me,' she said. 'Did you ride?'

'My horse is at the village.'

'You can go by the river, then. Good night.'

'Good night.'

The young man moved away in the gathering dusk, and Miss Whittaker stood for a moment looking after him.

To appreciate the importance of this conversation, the reader must know that Miss Gertrude Whittaker was a young woman of four-and-twenty, whose father, recently deceased, had left her alone in the world, with a great fortune, accumulated by various enterprises in that part of the State. He had appointed a distant and elderly kinswoman, by name Miss Pendexter, as his daughter's household companion; and an old friend of his own, known to combine shrewdness with integrity, as her financial adviser. Motherless, country-bred, and homely-featured, Gertrude on arriving at maturity had neither the tastes nor the manners of a fine lady. Of a robust and active make, with a warm heart, a cool head, and a very pretty talent for affairs, she was, in virtue, both of her wealth and of her tact, one of the chief figures of the neighbourhood. These facts had forced her into a prominence which she made no attempt to elude, and in which she now felt thoroughly at home. She knew herself to be a power in the land; she knew that, present and absent, she was continually talked about as the rich Miss Whittaker; and although as modest as a woman need be, she was neither so timid nor so nervous as to wish to compromise with her inevitable distinctions. Her feelings were indeed, throughout, strong, rather than delicate; and yet there was in her whole nature, as the world had learned to look at it, a moderation, a temperance, a benevolence, an orderly freedom, which bespoke universal respect. She was impulsive, and yet discreet; economical, and yet generous; humorous, and yet serious; keenly discerning of human distinctions, and yet almost indiscriminately hospitable; with a prodigious fund of common sense beneath all; and yet beyond this,—like the priest behind the king,—and despite her broadly prosaic, and as it were secular tone, a certain latent suggestion of heroic possibilities, which he who had once become insensible of it (supposing him to be young and enthusiastic) would linger about her hoping to detect, as you might stand watchful of a florid and vigorous dahlia, which for an instant, in your passage, should have proved deliciously fragrant. It is upon the actual existence, in more minds than one, of a mystifying sense of this sweet and remote perfume, that our story is based.

Richard Clare and Miss Whittaker were old friends. They had in the first place gone democratically to the town school together as children; and then their divergent growth, as boy and girl, had acknowledged an elastic bond in a continued intimacy between

Gertrude and Fanny Clare, Richard's sister, who, however, in the fullness of time had married, and had followed her husband to California. With her departure the old relations of habit between her brother and her friend had slackened, and gradually ceased. Richard had grown up a rebellious and troublesome boy, with a disposition combining stolid apathy and hot-headed impatience in equal proportions. Losing both of his parents before he was well out of his boyhood, he had found himself at the age of sixteen in possession actual, and as he supposed uncontested, of the paternal farm. It was not long, however, before those turned up who were disposed to question his immediate ability to manage it; the result of which was, that the farm was leased for five years, and that Richard was almost forcibly abducted by a maternal uncle, living on a farm of his own some three hundred miles away. Here our young man spent the remainder of his minority, ostensibly learning agriculture with his cousins, but actually learning nothing. He had very soon established, and had subsequently enjoyed without a day's interval, the reputation of an ill-natured fool. He was dull, disobliging, brooding, lowering. Reading and shooting he liked a little, because they were solitary pastimes; but to common duties and pleasures he proved himself as incompetent as he was averse. It was possible to live with him only because he was at once too selfish and too simple for mischief. As soon as he came of age he resumed possession of the acres on which his boyhood had been passed, and toward which he gravitated under an instinct of mere local affection, rather than from any intelligent purpose. He avoided his neighbours; his father's former associates; he rejected, nay, he violated, their counsel; he informed them that he wanted no help but what he paid for, and that he expected to work his farm for himself and by himself. In short, he proved himself to their satisfaction egregiously ungrateful, conceited, and arrogant. They were not slow to discover that his incapacity was as great as his conceit. In two years he had more than undone the work of the late lessee, which had been an improvement on that of the original owner. In the third year, it seemed to those who observed him that there was something so wanton in his errors as almost to impugn his sanity. He appeared to have accepted them himself, and to have given up all pretence of work. He went about silent and sullen, like a man who feels that he has a quarrel with fate. About this time it became generally known that he was often the worse for liquor; and he hereupon acquired the deplorable reputation of a man worse than unsociable,—a man who drinks alone,—although it was still doubtful whether this practice was the cause or the effect of his poor crops.

About this time, too, he resumed acquaintance with Gertrude Whittaker. For many months after his return he had been held at his distance, together with most of his rural compeers, by the knowledge of her father's bitter hostility to all possible suitors and fortune-hunters; and then, subsequently, by the illness preceding the old man's death; but when at last, on the expiration of her term of mourning, Miss Whittaker had opened to society her long blockaded ports, Richard had, to all the world's amazement, been among the first to profit by this extension of the general privilege, and to cast anchor in the wide and peaceful waters of her friendship. He found himself at this moment, considerably to his surprise, in his twenty-fourth year, that is, a few months Gertrude's junior.

It was impossible that she should not have gathered from mere juxtaposition a vague impression of his evil repute and of his peculiar relation to his neighbours, and to his own affairs. Thanks to this impression, Richard found a very warm welcome,—the welcome of compassion. Gertrude gave him a heavy arrear of news from his sister Fanny, with whom he had dropped correspondence, and, impelled by Fanny's complaints of his long silence, ventured upon a friendly admonition that he should go straight home and write a letter to California. Richard sat before her, gazing at her out of his dark eyes, and not only attempting no defence of his conduct, but rejoicing dumbly in the utter absence of any possible defence, as of an interruption to his companion's virtue. He wished that he might incontinently lay bare all his shortcomings to her delicious reproof. He carried away an extraordinary sense of general alleviation; and forthwith began a series of visits, which in the space of some ten weeks culminated in the interview with which our narrative opens. Painfully diffident in the company of most women, Richard had not from the first known what it was to be shy with Gertrude. As a man of the world finds it useful to refresh his social energies by an occasional *tête-à-tête* of an hour with himself, so Richard, with whom solitude was the rule, derived a certain austere satisfaction from an hour's contact with Miss Whittaker's consoling good sense, her abundance, her decent duties and comforts. Gradually, however, from a salutary process, this became almost an æsthetic one. It was now pleasant to go to Gertrude, because he enjoyed the contagion of her own repose,—because he witnessed her happiness without a sensation of envy,—because he forgot his own entanglements and errors,—because, finally, his soul slept away its troubles beneath her varying glance, very much as his body had often slept away its weariness in the shade of a changing willow. But the soul, like the body, will not sleep long without dreaming; and it will not dream often without wishing at last to tell its dreams. Richard had one day ventured to impart his visions to Gertrude, and the revelation had apparently given her serious pain. The fact that Richard Clare (of all men in the world!) had somehow worked himself into an intimacy with Miss Whittaker very soon became public property among their neighbours; and in the hands of these good people, naturally enough, received an important addition in the inference that he was going to marry her. He was, of course, esteemed a very lucky fellow, and the prevalence of this impression was doubtless not without its effect on the forbearance of certain long-suffering creditors. And even if she was not to marry him, it was further argued, she yet might lend him money; for it was assumed without question that the necessity of raising money was the main-spring of Richard's suit. It is needless to inform the reader that this assumption was—to use a homely metaphor—without a leg to stand upon. Our hero had faults enough, but to be mercenary was not one of them; nor was an excessive concern on the subject of his debts one of his virtues. As for Gertrude, wherever else her perception of her friend's feelings may have been at fault, it was not at fault on this point. That he loved her as desperately as he declared, she indeed doubted; but it never occurred to her to question the purity of his affection. And so, on the other hand, it was strictly out of her heart's indifference that she rejected him, and not for the disparity of their fortunes. In accepting his very simple and natural overtures to friendship, in calling him 'Richard' in remembrance of old days, and in submitting generally to the terms of their old relations, she had foreseen no sentimental catastrophe. She had viewed her friend from the first as an object of lively material concern. She had espoused his interests (like all good women, Gertrude was ever more or less of a partisan) because she loved his sister, and because she pitied himself. She would stand to him *in loco sororis*. The reader has seen that she had given herself a long day's work.

It is not to be supposed that Richard's sober retreat at the close of the walk by the river implied any instinct of resignation to the prospects which Gertrude had opened to him. It is explained rather by an intensity of purpose so deep as to fancy that it can dispense with bravado. This was not the end of his suit, but the beginning. He would not give in until he was positively beaten. It was all very well, he reflected, that Gertrude should reject him. Such a woman as she ought properly to be striven for, and there was something ridiculous in the idea that she should be easily won, whether by himself or by another. Richard was a slow thinker, but he thought more wisely than he talked; and he now took back all his angry boasts of accomplished self-mastery, and humbly surveyed the facts of the case. He was on the way to recovery, but he was by no means cured, and yet his very humility assured him that he was curable. He was no hero, but he was better than his life; he was no scholar, but in his own view at least he was no fool. He was good enough to be better; he was good enough not to sit by the hour soaking his slender brains in whiskey. And at the very least, if he was not worthy to possess Gertrude, he was yet worthy to strive to obtain her, and to live forevermore upon the glory of having been formally refused by the great Miss Whittaker. He would raise himself then to that level from which he could address her as an equal, from which he could borrow that authority of which he was now so shamefully bare. How he would do this, he was at a loss to determine. He was conscious of an immense fund of brute volition, but he cursed his barbarous ignorance, as he searched in vain for those high opposing forces the defeat of which might lend dignity to his struggle. He longed vaguely for some continuous muscular effort, at the end of which he should find himself face to face with his mistress. But as, instead of being a Pagan hero, with an enticing task-list of impossibilities, he was a plain New England farmer, with a bad conscience, and nature with him and not against him,— as, after slaying his dragon, after breaking with liquor, his work was a simple operation in common sense,—in view of these facts he found but little inspiration in his prospect. Nevertheless he fronted it bravely. He was not to obtain Gertrude by making a fortune, but by making himself a man, by learning to think. But as to learn to think is to learn to work, he would find some use for his muscle. He would keep sober and clear-headed; he would retrieve his land and pay his debts. Then let her refuse him if she could,—or if she dared, he was wont occasionally to add.

Meanwhile Gertrude on her side sat quietly at home, revolving in her own fashion a dozen ideal schemes for her friend's redemption and for the diversion of his enthusiasm. Not but that she meant rigorously to fulfil her part of the engagement to which she had invited him in that painful scene by the river. Yet whatever of that firmness, patience, and courtesy of which she possessed so large a stock she might still oppose to his importunities, she could not feel secure against repeated intrusion (for it was by this term that she was disposed to qualify all unsanctioned transgression of those final and immovable limits which she had set to her immense hospitality) without the knowledge of a partial change at least in Richard's own attitude. Such a change could only be effected through some preparatory change in his life; and a change in his life could be brought about only by the introduction of some new influence. This influence, however, was very hard to find. However positively Gertrude had dwelt upon the practical virtue of her own friendship, she was now on further reflection led sadly to distrust the exclusive use of this instrument. He was welcome enough to that, but he needed something more. It suddenly occurred to her, one morning after Richard's image had been crossing and recrossing her mental vision for a couple of hours with wearisome pertinacity, that a world of good might accrue to him through the friendship of a person so unexceptionable as Captain Severn. There was no one, she declared within herself, who would not be better for knowing such a man. She would recommend Richard to his kindness, and him she would recommend to Richard's—what? Here was the rub! Where was there common ground between Richard and such a one as he? To request him to like Richard was easy; to ask Richard to like him was ridiculous. If Richard could only know him, the work were done; he couldn't choose but love him as a brother. But to bespeak Richard's respect for an object was to fill him straightway with aversion for it. Her young friend was so pitiable a creature himself, that it had never occurred to her to appeal to his sentiments of compassion. All the world seemed above him, and he was consequently at odds with all the world. If some worthy being could be found, even less favoured of nature and of fortune than himself, to such a one he might become attached by a useful sympathy. There was indeed nothing particularly enviable in Captain Severn's lot, and herein Richard might properly experience a fellow-feeling for him; but nevertheless he was apparently quite contented with it, and thus he was raised several degrees above Richard, who would be certain to find something aggressive in his equanimity. Still, for all this, Gertrude would bring them together. She had a high estimate of the Captain's generosity, and if Richard should wantonly fail to conform to the situation, the loss would be his own. It may be thought that in this enterprise Captain Severn was somewhat inconsiderately handled. But a generous woman will freely make a missionary of the man she loves. These words suggest the propriety of a short description of the person to whom they refer.

Edmund Severn was a man of eight-and-twenty, who, having for some time combated fortune and his own inclinations as a mathematical tutor in a second-rate country college, had, on the opening of the war, transferred his valour to a more heroic field. His regiment of volunteers, now at work before Richmond, had been raised in Miss Whattaker's district, and beneath her substantial encouragement. His soldiership, like his scholarship, was solid rather than brilliant. He was not destined to be heard of at home, nor to leave his regiment; but on many an important occasion in Virginia he had proved himself in a modest way an excellently useful man. Coming up early in the war with a severe wound, to be nursed by a married sister domiciled in Gertrude's neighbourhood, he was, like all his fellow-sufferers within a wide circuit, very soon honoured with a visit of anxious inquiry from Miss Whittaker, who was as yet known to him only by report, and who transmitted to him the warmest assurances of sympathy and interest, together with the liveliest offers of assistance; and, incidentally as it were to these, a copious selection from the products of her hot-house and store-room. Severn had taken the air for the first time in Gertrude's own great cushioned barouche, which she had sent to his door at an early stage of his convalescence, and which of course he had immediately made use of to pay his respects to his benefactress. He was confounded by the real humility with which, on this occasion, betwixt smiles and tears, she assured him that to be of service to such as him was for her a sacred privilege. Never, thought the Captain as he drove away, had he seen so much rustic breadth combined with so much womanly grace. Half a dozen visits during the ensuing month more than sufficed to convert him into what is called an admirer; but, as the weeks passed by, he felt that there were great obstacles to his ever ripening into a lover. Captain Severn was a serious man; he was conscientious, discreet, deliberate, unused to act without a definite purpose. Whatever might be the intermediate steps, it was necessary that the goal of an enterprise should have become an old story to him before he took the first steps. And, moreover, if the goal seemed a profitable or an honourable station, he was proof against the perils or the discomforts of the journey; while if, on the other hand, it offered no permanent repose, he generally found but little difficulty in resisting the incidental allurements. In pursuance of this habit, or rather in obedience to this principle, of carefully fixing his programme, he had asked himself whether he was prepared to face the logical results of a series of personal attentions to our heroine. Since he had determined a twelvemonth before not to marry until, by some means or another, he should have evoked a sufficient income, no great change had taken place in his fortunes. He was still a poor man and an unsettled one; he was still awaiting his real vocation. Moreover, while subject to the chances of war, he doubted his right to engage a woman's affections: he shrank in horror from the thought of making a widow. Miss Whittaker was one in five thousand. Before the luminous fact of her existence, his dim ideal of the desirable wife had faded into vapour. But should he allow this fact to invalidate all the stern precepts of his reason? He could no more afford to marry a rich woman than a poor one. When he should have earned a subsistense for two, then he would be free to marry whomsoever he might fancy,—a beggar or an heiress. The truth is, that the Captain was a great deal too proud. It was his fault that he could not bring himself to forget the difference between his poverty and Gertrude's wealth. He would of course have resented the insinuation that the superior fortune of the woman he loved should really have force to prevent him from declaring his love; but there is no doubt that in the case before us this fact arrested his passion in its origin. Severn had a most stoical aversion to being in debt. It is certain that, after all, he would have made a very graceful debtor to his mistress or his wife; but while a woman was as yet neither his mistress nor his wife, the idea of being beholden to her was essentially distasteful to him. It would have been a question with one who knew him, whether at this juncture this frigid instinct was destined to resist the warmth of Gertrude's charms, or whether it was destined gradually to melt away. There would have been no question, however, but that it could maintain itself only at the cost of great suffering to its possessor. At this moment, then, Severn had made up his mind that Gertrude was not for him, and that it behooved him to be sternly vigilant both of his impulses and his impressions. That Miss Whittaker, with a hundred rational cares, was anything less than supremely oblivious of him, individually, it never occurred to him to suspect. The truth is, that Gertrude's private and personal emotions were entertained in a chamber of her heart so remote from the portals of speech that no sound of their revelry found its way into the world. She constantly thought of her modest, soldierly, scholarly friend as of one whom a wise woman might find it very natural to love. But what was she to him? A local roadside figure,—at the very most a sort of millionaire Maud Muller,—with whom it was pleasant for a lonely wayfarer to exchange a friendly 'good-morning'. Her duty was to fold her arms resignedly, to sit quietly on the sofa, and watch a great happiness sink below the horizon. With this impression on Gertrude's part it is not surprising that Severn was not wrenched out of himself. The prodigy was apparently to be wrought—if wrought at all—by her common, unbought sweetness. It is true that this was of a potency sufficient almost to work prodigies; but as yet its effect upon Severn had been none other than its effect upon all the world. It kept him

in his kindliest humour. It kept him even in the humour of talking
sentiment; but although, in the broad sunshine of her listening, his
talk bloomed thick with field-flowers, he never invited her to pluck
the least little daisy. It was with perfect honesty, therefore, that she
had rebutted Richard's insinuation that the Captain enjoyed any
especial favour. He was as yet but another of the pensioners of her
good-nature.

The result of Gertrude's meditations was, that she despatched a
note to each of her two friends, requesting them to take tea with
her on the following day. A couple of hours before tea-time she
received a visit from one Major Luttrel, who was recruiting for a
United States regiment at a large town, some ten miles away, and
who had ridden over in the afternoon, in accordance with a general
invitation conveyed to him through an old lady who had bespoken
Miss Whittaker's courtesy for him as a man of delightful manners
and wonderful talents. Gertrude, on her venerable friend's repre-
sentations, had replied, with her wonted alacrity, that she would be
very glad to see Major Luttrel, should he ever come that way, and
then had thought no more about him until his card was brought to
her as she was dressing for the evening. He found so much to say
to her, that the interval passed very rapidly for both of them before
the simultaneous entrance of Miss Pendexter and of Gertrude's
guests. The two officers were already slightly known to each other,
and Richard was accordingly presented to each of them. They eyed
the distracted-looking young farmer with some curiosity. Richard's
was at all times a figure to attract attention; but now he was almost
picturesque (so Severn thought at least) with his careless garments,
his pale face, his dark mistrustful eyes, and his nervous movements.
Major Luttrel, who struck Gertrude as at once very agreeable and
the least bit in the world disagreeable, was, of course, invited
to remain,—which he straightway consented to do; and it soon
became evident to Miss Whittaker that her little scheme was
destined to miscarry. Richard practised a certain defiant silence,
which, as she feared, gave him eventually a decidedly ridiculous
air. His companions displayed toward their hostess that half-avowed
effort to shine and to outshine natural to clever men who find themselves concurring to the entertainment of a young and agreeable
woman. Richard sat by, wondering, in splenetic amazement, whether
he was an ignorant boor, or whether they were only a brace of in-
flated snobs. He decided, correctly enough, in substance, for the
former hypothesis. For it seemed to him that Gertrude's consummate accommodation (for as such he viewed it) of her tone and
her manner to theirs added prodigiously (so his lover's instinct

taught him) to her loveliness and dignity. How magnanimous an impulse on Richard's part was this submission for his sweetheart's sake to a fact damning to his own vanity, could have been determined only by one who knew the proportions of that vanity. He writhed and chafed under the polish of tone and the variety of allusion by which the two officers consigned him to insignificance; but he was soon lost in wonder at the mettlesome grace and vivacity with which Gertrude sustained her share of the conversation. For a moment it seemed to him that her tenderness for his equanimity (for should she not know his mind,—she who had made it?) might reasonably have caused her to forego such an exhibition of her social accomplishments as would but remind him afresh of his own deficiencies; but the next moment he asked himself, with a great revulsion of feeling, whether he, a conscious suitor, should fear to know his mistress in her integrity. As he gulped down the sickening fact of his comparative, nay, his absolute ignorance of the great world represented by his rivals, he felt like anticipating its consequences by a desperate sally into the very field of their conversation. To some such movement Gertrude was continually inviting him by her glances, her smiles, her questions, and her appealing silence. But poor Richard knew that, if he should attempt to talk, he would choke; and this assurance he imparted to his friend in a look piteously eloquent. He was conscious of a sensation of rage under which his heart was fast turning into a fiery furnace, destined to consume all his good resolutions. He could not answer for the future now. Suddenly, as tea was drawing to a close, he became aware that Captain Severn had lapsed into a silence very nearly as profound as his own, and that he was covertly watching the progress of a lively dialogue between Miss Whittaker and Major Luttrel. He had the singular experience of seeing his own feelings reflected in the Captain's face; that is, he discerned there an incipient jealousy. Severn too was in love!

On rising from table, Gertrude proposed an adjournment to the garden, where she was very fond of entertaining her friends at this hour. The sun had sunk behind a long line of hills, far beyond the opposite bank of the river, a portion of which was discernible through a gap in the intervening wood. The high-piled roof and chimney-stacks, the picturesquely crowded surface, of the old patched and renovated farm-house which served Gertrude as a villa, were ruddy with the declining rays. Our friends' long shadows were thrown over the short grass, Gertrude, having graciously anticipated the gentlemen's longing for their cigars, suggested a stroll toward the river. Before she knew it, she had accepted Major

Luttrel's arm; and as Miss Pendexter preferred remaining at home, Severn and Richard found themselves lounging side by side at a short distance behind their hostess. Gertrude, who had marked the reserve which had suddenly fallen upon Captain Severn, and in her simplicity had referred it to some unwitting failure of attention on her own part, had hoped to repair her neglect by having him at her own side. She was in some degree consoled, however, by the sight of his happy juxtaposition with Richard. As for Richard, now that he was on his feet and in the open air, he found it easier to speak.

'Who is that man?' he asked, nodding toward the Major.

'Major Luttrel, of the—the Artillery.'

'I don't like his face much,' said Richard.

'Don't you?' rejoined Severn, amused at his companion's bluntness. 'He's not handsome, but he looks like a soldier.'

'He looks like a rascal, I think,' said Richard.

Severn laughed outright, so that Gertrude glanced back at him. 'Dear me! I think you put it rather strongly. I should call it a very intelligent face.'

Richard was sorely perplexed. He had expected to find acceptance for his bitterest animadversions, and lo! here was the Captain fighting for his enemy. Such a man as that was no rival. So poor a hater could be but a poor lover. Nevertheless, a certain new-born mistrust of his old fashion of measuring human motives prevented him from adopting this conclusion as final. He would try another question.

'Do you know Miss Whittaker well?' he asked.

'Tolerably well. She was very kind to me when I was ill. Since then I've seen her some dozen times.'

'That's a way she has, being kind,' said Richard, with what he deemed considerable shrewdness. But as the Captain merely puffed his cigar responsively, he pursued, 'What do you think of her face?'

'I like it very much,' said the Captain.

'She isn't beautiful,' said Richard, cunningly.

Severn was silent a moment, and then, just as Richard was about to dismiss him from his thoughts, as neither formidable nor satisfactory, he replied, with some emphasis, 'You mean she isn't pretty. She *is* beautiful, I think, in spite of the irregularity of her face. It's a face not to be forgotten. She has no features, no colour, no lilies nor roses, no attitudes; but she has *looks*, expressions. Her face has *character*; and so has her figure. It has no "style", as they call it; but that only belongs properly to a work of art, which Miss Whittaker's figure isn't, thank Heaven! She's as unconscious of it as Nature herself.'

Severn spoke Richard's mind as well as his own. That 'She isn't beautiful' had been an extempore version of the young man's most sacred dogma, namely, She is beautiful. The reader will remember that he had so translated it on a former occasion. Now, all that he felt was a sense of gratitude to the Captain for having put it so much more finely than he, the above being his choicest public expression of it. But the Captain's eyes, somewhat brightened by his short but fervid speech, were following Gertrude's slow steps. Richard saw that he could learn more from them than from any further oral declaration; for something in the mouth beneath them seemed to indicate that it had judged itself to have said enough, and it was obviously not the mouth of a simpleton. As he thus deferred with an unwonted courtesy to the Captain's silence, and transferred his gaze sympathetically to Gertrude's shapely shoulders and to her listening ear, he gave utterance to a tell-tale sigh,—a sigh which there was no mistaking. Severn looked about; it was now his turn to scrutinize. 'Good Heavens!' he exclaimed, 'that boy is in love with her!'

After the first shock of surprise, he accepted this fact with rational calmness. Why shouldn't he be in love with her? '*Je le suis bien*,' said the Captain; 'or, rather, I'm not.' Could it be, Severn pursued, that he was a favourite? He was a mannerless young farmer; but it was plain that he had a soul of his own. He almost wished, indeed, that Richard might prove to be in Gertrude's good graces. 'But if he is,' he reflected, 'why should he sigh? It is true that there is no arguing for lovers. I, who am out in the cold, take my comfort in whistling most impertinently. It may be that my friend here groans for very bliss. I confess, however, that he scarcely looks like a favoured swain.'

And forthwith this faint-hearted gentleman felt a twinge of pity for Richard's obvious infelicity; and as he compared it with the elaborately defensive condition of his own affections, he felt a further pang of self-contempt. But it was easier to restore the equilibrium of his self-respect by an immediate cession of the field, than by contesting it against this woefully wounded knight. 'Whether he wins her or not, he'll fight for her,' the Captain declared; and as he glanced at Major Luttrel, he felt that this was a sweet assurance. He had conceived a singular distrust of the Major.

They had now reached the water's edge, where Gertrude, having arrested her companion, had turned about, expectant of her other guests. As they came up, Severn saw, or thought that he saw (which is a very different thing), that her first look was at Richard. The 'admirer' in his breast rose fratricidal for a moment against the quiet observer; but the next, it was pinioned again. 'Amen,' said the Captain; 'it's none of my business.'

At this moment, Richard was soaring most heroically. The end of his anguish had been a sudden intoxication. He surveyed the scene before him with a kindling fancy. Why should he stand tongue-tied in sullen mistrust of fortune, when all nature beckoned him into the field? There was the river-path where, a fortnight before, he had found an eloquence attested by Gertrude's tears. There was sweet Gertrude herself, whose hand he had kissed and whose waist he had clasped. Surely, he was master here! Before he knew it, he had begun to talk,—rapidly, nervously, and almost defiantly. Major Luttrel having made an observation about the prettiness of the river, Richard entered upon a description of its general course and its superior beauty upon his own place, together with an enumeration of the fish which were to be found in it, and a story about a great overflow ten years before. He spoke in fair, coherent terms, but with singular intensity and vehemence, and with his head thrown back and his eyes on the opposite bank. At last he stopped, feeling that he had given proof of his manhood, and looked towards Gertrude, whose eyes he had been afraid to meet until he had seen his adventure to a close. But she was looking at Captain Severn, under the impression that Richard had secured his auditor. Severn was looking at Luttrel, and Luttrel at Miss Whittaker; and all were apparently so deep in observation that they had marked neither his speech nor his silence. 'Truly,' thought the young man, 'I'm well out of the circle!' But he was resolved to be patient still, which was assuredly, all things considered, a very brave resolve. Yet there was always something spasmodic and unnatural in Richard's magnanimity. A touch in the wrong place would cause it to collapse. It was Gertrude's evil fortune to administer this touch at present. As the party turned about toward the house, Richard stepped to her side and offered her his arm, hoping in his heart—so implicitly did he count upon her sympathy, so almost boyishly, filially, did he depend upon it—for some covert token that his heroism, such as it was, had not been lost upon her.

But Gertrude, intensely preoccupied by the desire to repair her fancied injustice to the Captain, shook her head at him without even meeting his eye. 'Thank you,' she said; 'I want Captain Severn,' who forthwith approached.

Poor Richard felt his feet touch the ground again. He felt that he could have flung the Captain into the stream. Major Luttrel placed himself at Gertrude's other elbow, and Richard stood behind them, almost livid with spite, and half resolved to turn upon his heel and make his way home by the river. But it occurred to him that a more elaborate vengeance would be to follow the trio before him back to the lawn, and there make it a silent and scathing bow. Accordingly, when they reached the house, he stood aloof and bade Gertrude a grim good-night. He trembled with eagerness to see whether she would make an attempt to detain him. But Miss Whittaker, reading in his voice—it had grown too dark to see his face at the distance at which he stood—the story of some fancied affront, and unconsciously contrasting it, perhaps, with Severn's clear and unwarped accents, obeyed what she deemed a prompting of self-respect, and gave him, without her hand, a farewell as cold as his own. It is but fair to add, that, a couple of hours later, as she reviewed the incidents of the evening, she repented most generously of this little act of justice.

PART II

Richard got through the following week he hardly knew how. He found occupation, to a much greater extent than he was actually aware of, in a sordid and yet heroic struggle with himself. For several months now, he had been leading, under Gertrude's inspiration, a strictly decent and sober life. So long as he was at comparative peace with Gertrude and with himself, such a life was more than easy; it was delightful. It produced a moral buoyancy infinitely more delicate and more constant than the gross exhilaration of his old habits. There was a kind of fascination in adding hour to hour, and day to day, in this record of his new-born austerity. Having abjured excesses, he practised temperance after the fashion of a novice: he raised it (or reduced it) to abstinence. He was like an unclean man who, having washed himself clean, remains in the water for the love of it. He wished to be religiously, superstitiously pure. This was easy, as we have said, so long as his goddess smiled, even though it were as a goddess indeed,—as a creature unattainable. But when she frowned, and the heavens grew dark, Richard's sole dependence was in his own will,—as flimsy a trust for an upward scramble, one would have premised, as a tuft of grass on the face of a perpendicular cliff. Flimsy as it looked, however, it served him. It started and crumbled, but it held, if only by a single fibre. When Richard had cantered fifty yards away from Gertrude's gate in a fit of stupid rage, he suddenly pulled up his horse and gulped down his passion, and swore an oath, that, suffer what torments of feeling he might, he would not

at least break the continuity of his gross physical soberness. It was
enough to be drunk in mind; he would not be drunk in body. A
singular, almost ridiculous feeling of antagonism to Gertrude lent
force to this resolution. 'No, madam,' he cried within himself, 'I
shall *not* fall back. Do your best! I shall keep straight.' We often
outweather great offences and afflictions through a certain healthy
instinct of egotism. Richard went to bed that night as grim and
sober as a Trappist monk; and his foremost impulse the next day
was to plunge headlong into some physical labour which should
not allow him a moment's interval of idleness. He found no labour
to his taste; but he spent the day so actively, in the mechanical
annihilation of the successive hours, that Gertrude's image found
no chance squarely to face him. He was engaged in the work of
self-preservation,—the most serious and absorbing work possible to
man. Compared to the results here at stake, his passion for Gertrude
seemed but a fiction. It is perhaps difficult to give a more lively impression of the vigour of this passion, of its maturity and its
strength, than by simply stating that it discreetly held itself in
abeyance until Richard had set at rest his doubts of that which lies
nearer than all else to the heart of man,—his doubts of the strength
of his will. He answered these doubts by subjecting his resolution
to a course of such cruel temptations as were likely either to shiver
it to a myriad of pieces, or to season it perfectly to all the possible
requirements of life. He took long rides over the country, passing
within a stone's throw of as many of the scattered wayside taverns
as could be combined in a single circuit. As he drew near them he
sometimes slackened his pace, as if he were about to dismount,
pulled up his horse, gazed a moment, then, thrusting in his spurs,
galloped away again like one pursued. At other times, in the late
evening, when the window-panes were aglow with the ruddy light
within, he would walk slowly by, looking at the stars, and, after
maintaining this stoical pace for a couple of miles, would hurry
home to his own lonely and black-windowed dwelling. Having successfully performed this feat a certain number of times, he found
his love coming back to him, bereft in the interval of its attendant
jealousy. In obedience to it, he one morning leaped upon his horse
and repaired to Gertrude's abode, with no definite notion of the
terms in which he should introduce himself.

He had made himself comparatively sure of his will; but he was
yet to acquire the mastery of his impulses. As he gave up his horse,
according to his wont, to one of the men at the stable, he saw another steed stalled there which he recognized as Captain Severn's.
'Steady, my boy,' he murmured to himself, as he would have done

to a frightened horse. On his way across the broad court-yard toward the house, he encountered the Captain, who had just taken
his leave. Richard gave him a generous salute (he could not trust
himself to more), and Severn answered with what was at least a
strictly just one. Richard observed, however, that he was very pale,
and that he was pulling a rosebud to pieces as he walked; whereupon our young man quickened his step. Finding the parlour empty,
he instinctively crossed over to a small room adjoining it, which
Gertrude had converted into a modest conservatory; and as he did
so, hardly knowing it, he lightened his heavy-shod tread. The glass
door was open and Richard looked in. There stood Gertrude with
her back to him, bending apart with her hands a couple of tall
flowering plants, and looking through the glazed partition behind
them. Advancing a step, and glancing over the young girl's shoulder,
Richard had just time to see Severn mounting his horse at the stable
door, before Gertrude, startled by his approach, turned hastily
round. Her face was flushed hot, and her eyes brimming with tears.

'You!' she exclaimed, sharply.

Richard's head swam. That single word was so charged with
cordial impatience that it seemed the death-knell of his hope. He
stepped inside the room and closed the door, keeping his hand on
the knob.

'Gertrude,' he said, 'you love that man!'

'Well, sir?'

'Do you confess it?' cried Richard.

'Confess it? Richard Clare, how dare you use such language?
I'm in no humour for a scene. Let me pass.'

Gertrude was angry; but as for Richard, it may almost be said
that he was mad. 'One scene a day is enough, I suppose,' he cried.
'What are these tears about? Wouldn't he have you? Did he refuse
you, as you refused me? Poor Gertrude!'

Gertrude looked at him a moment with concentrated scorn. 'You
fool!' she said, for all answer. She pushed his hand from the latch,
flung open the door, and moved rapidly away.

Left alone, Richard sank down on a sofa and covered his face
with his hands. It burned them, but he sat motionless, repeating to
himself, mechanically, as if to avert thought, 'You fool! you fool!'
At last he got up and made his way out.

It seemed to Gertrude, for several hours after this scene, that she
had at this juncture a strong case against Fortune. It is not our
purpose to repeat the words which she had exchanged with Captain
Severn. They had come within a single step of an *éclaircissement*,
and when but another movement would have flooded their souls

with light, some malignant influence had seized them by the
throats. Had they too much pride? too little imagination? We must
content ourselves with this hypothesis. Severn, then, had walked
mechanically across the yard, saying to himself, 'She belongs to
another'; and adding, as he saw Richard, 'and such another'! Gertrude had stood at her window, repeating, under her breath, 'He
belongs to himself, himself alone.' And as if this was not enough,
when misconceived, slighted, wounded, she had faced about to her
old, passionless, dutiful past, there on the path of retreat to this
asylum Richard Clare had arisen to forewarn her that she should
find no peace even at home. There was something in the violent
impertinence of his appearance at this moment which gave her a
dreadful feeling that fate was against her. More than this. There
entered into her emotions a certain minute particle of awe of the
man whose passion was so uncompromising. She felt that it was out
of place any longer to pity him. He was the slave of his passion; but
his passion was strong. In her reaction against the splendid civility
of Severn's silence, (the real antithesis of which would have been
simply the perfect courtesy of explicit devotion,) she found herself
touching with pleasure on the fact of Richard's brutality. He at
least had ventured to insult her. He had loved her enough to forget
himself. He had dared to make himself odious in her eyes, because
he had cast away his sanity. What cared he for the impression he
made? He cared only for the impression he received. The violence
of this reaction, however, was the measure of its duration. It was
impossible that she should walk backward so fast without stumbling.
Brought to her senses by this accident, she became aware that her
judgment was missing. She smiled to herself as she reflected that it
had been taking holiday for a whole afternoon. 'Richard was right,'
she said to herself. 'I am no fool. I can't be a fool if I try. I'm too
thoroughly my father's daughter for that. I love that man, but I
love myself better. Of course, then, I don't deserve to have him. If
I loved him in a way to merit his love, I would sit down this moment
and write him a note telling him that if he does not come back to
me, I shall die. But I shall neither write the note nor die. I shall live
and grow stout, and look after my chickens and my flowers and my
colts, and thank the Lord in my old age that I have never done
anything unwomanly. Well! I'm as He made me. Whether I can
deceive others, I know not; but I certainly can't deceive myself. I'm
quite as sharp as Gertrude Whittaker; and this it is that has kept
me from making a fool of myself and writing to poor Richard the
note that I wouldn't write to Captain Severn. I needed to fancy
myself wronged. I suffer so little! I needed a sensation! So, shrewd

Yankee that I am, I thought I would get one cheaply by taking up that unhappy boy! Heaven preserve me from the heroics, especially the economical heroics! The one heroic course possible, I decline. What, then, have I to complain of? Must I tear my hair because a man of taste has resisted my unspeakable charms? To be charming, you must be charmed yourself, or at least you must be able to be charmed; and that apparently I'm not. I didn't love him, or he would have known it. Love gets love, and no-love gets none.'

But at this point of her meditations Gertrude almost broke down. She felt that she was assigning herself but a dreary future. Never to be loved but by such a one as Richard Clare was a cheerless prospect; for it was identical with an eternal spinsterhood. 'Am I, then,' she exclaimed, quite as passionately as a woman need do,—'am I, then, cut off from a woman's dearest joys? What blasphemous non-sense! One thing is plain: I am made to be a mother; the wife may take care of herself. I am made to be a wife; the mistress may take care of *her*self. I am in the Lord's hands,' added the poor girl, who, whether or no she could forget herself in an earthly love, had at all events this mark of spontaneous nature, that she could forget her-self in a heavenly one. But in the midst of her pious emotion, she was unable to subdue her conscience. It smote her heavily for her meditated falsity to Richard, for her miserable readiness to succumb to the strong temptation to seek a momentary resting-place in his gaping heart. She recoiled from this thought as from an act cruel and immoral. Was Richard's heart the place for her now, any more than it had been a month before? Was she to apply for comfort where she would not apply for counsel? Was she to drown her decent sorrows and regrets in a base, a dishonest, an extemporized passion? Having done the young man so bitter a wrong in intention, nothing would appease her magnanimous remorse (as time went on) but to repair it in fact. She went so far as keenly to regret the harsh words she had cast upon him in the conservatory. He had been insolent and unmannerly; but he had an excuse. Much should be forgiven him, for he loved much. Even now that Gertrude had imposed upon her feelings a sterner regimen than ever, she could not defend herself from a sweet and sentimental thrill—a thrill in which, as we have intimated, there was something of a tremor—at the recollection of his strident accents and his angry eyes. It was yet far from her heart to desire a renewal, however brief, of this exhibition. She wished simply to efface from the young man's morbid soul the impression of a real contempt; for she knew—or she thought that she knew—that against such an impression he was capable of taking the most fatal and inconsiderate comfort.

Before many mornings had passed, accordingly, she had a horse saddled, and, dispensing with attendance, she rode rapidly over to his farm. The house door and half the windows stood open; but no answer came to her repeated summons. She made her way to the rear of the house, to the barn-yard, thinly tenanted by a few common fowl, and across the yard to a road which skirted its lower extremity and was accessible by an open gate. No human figure was in sight; nothing was visible in the hot stillness but the scattered and ripening crops, over which, in spite of her nervous solicitude, Miss Whittaker cast the glance of a connoisseur. A great uneasiness filled her mind as she measured the rich domain apparently deserted of its young master, and reflected that she perhaps was the cause of its abandonment. Ah, where was Richard? As she looked and listened in vain, her heart rose to her throat, and she felt herself on the point of calling all too wistfully upon his name. But her voice was stayed by the sound of a heavy rumble, as of cart-wheels, beyond a turn in the road. She touched up her horse and cantered along until she reached the turn. A great four-wheeled cart, laden with masses of newly broken stone, and drawn by four oxen, was slowly advancing towards her. Beside it, patiently cracking his whip and shouting monotonously, walked a young man in a slouched hat and a red shirt, with his trousers thrust into his dusty boots. It was Richard. As he saw Gertrude, he halted a moment, amazed, and then advanced, flicking the air with his whip. Gertrude's heart went out towards him in a silent Thank God! Her next reflection was that he had never looked so well. The truth is, that, in this rough adjustment, the native barbarian was duly represented. His face and neck were browned by a week in the fields, his eye was clear, his step seemed to have learned a certain manly dignity from its attendance on the heavy bestial tramp. Gertrude, as he reached her side, pulled up her horse and held out her gloved fingers to his brown dusty hand. He took them, looked for a moment into her face, and for the second time raised them to his lips.

'Excuse my glove,' she said, with a little smile.

'Excuse mine,' he answered, exhibiting his sunburnt, work-stained hand.

'Richard,' said Gertrude, 'you never had less need of excuse in your life. You never looked half so well.'

He fixed his eyes upon her a moment. 'Why, you have forgiven me!' he exclaimed.

'Yes,' said Gertrude, 'I have forgiven you,—both you and myself. We both of us behaved very absurdly, but we both of us had reason. I wish you had come back.'

Richard looked about him, apparently at loss for a rejoinder. 'I have been very busy,' he said, at last, with a simplicity of tone slightly studied. An odd sense of dramatic effect prompted him to say neither more nor less.

An equally delicate instinct forbade Gertrude to express all the joy which this assurance gave her. Excessive joy would have implied undue surprise; and it was a part of her plan frankly to expect the best things of her companion. 'If you have been busy,' she said, 'I congratulate you. What have you been doing?'

'O, a hundred things. I have been quarrying, and draining, and clearing, and I don't know what all. I thought the best thing was just to put my own hands to it. I am going to make a stone fence along the great lot on the hill there. Wallace is forever grumbling about his boundaries. I'll fix them once and for all. What are you laughing at?'

'I am laughing at certain foolish apprehensions that I have been indulging for a week past. You're wiser than I, Richard. I have no imagination.'

'Do you mean that *I* have? I haven't enough to guess what you *do* mean.'

'Why, do you suppose, I have come over this morning?'

'Because you thought I was sulking on account of your having called me a fool.'

'Sulking, or worse. What do I deserve for the wrong I have done you?'

'You have done me no wrong. You reasoned fairly enough. You are not obliged to know me better than I know myself. It's just like you to be ready to take back that bad word, and try to make yourself believe that it was unjust. But was was perfectly just, and therefore I have managed to bear it. I *was* a fool at that moment,— a stupid, impudent fool. I don't know whether that man had been making love to you or not. But you had, I think, been feeling love for him—you looked it; I should have been less than a man, I should be unworthy of your—your affection, if I had failed to see it. I did see it,—I saw it as clearly as I see those oxen now; and yet I bounced in with my own ill-timed claims. To do so was to be a fool. To have been other than a fool would have been to have waited, to have backed out, to have bitten my tongue off before I spoke, to have done anything but what I did. I have no right to claim you, Gertrude, until I can woo you better than that. It was the most fortunate thing in the world that you spoke as you did : it was even kind. It saved me all the misery of groping about for a starting-point. Not to have spoken as you did would have been to fail of justice; and then, probably, I should have sulked, or, as you very considerately say, done worse. I had made a false move in the game, and the only thing to do was to repair it. But you were not obliged to know that I would so readily admit my move to have been false. Whenever I have made a fool of myself before, I have been for sticking it out, and trying to turn all mankind—that is, you—into a fool too, so that I shouldn't be an exception. But this time, I think, I had a kind of inspiration. I felt that my case was desperate. I felt that if I adopted my folly now I adopted it forever. The other day I met a man who had just come home from Europe, and who spent last summer in Switzerland. He was telling me about the mountain-climbing over there,—how they get over the glaciers, and all that. He said that you sometimes came upon great slippery, steep, snow-covered slopes that end short off in a precipice, and that if you stumble or lose your footing as you cross them horizontally, why you go shooting down, and you're gone; that is, but for one little dodge. You have a long walking-pole with a sharp end, you know, and as you feel yourself sliding,—it's as likely as not to be in a sitting posture,—you just take this and ram it into the snow before you, and there you are, stopped. The thing is, of course, to drive it in far enough, so that it won't yield or break; and in any case it hurts infernally to come whizzing down upon this upright pole. But the interruption gives you time to pick yourself up. Well, so it was with me the other day. I stumbled and fell; I slipped, and was whizzing downward; but I just drove in my pole and pulled up short. It nearly tore me in two; but it saved my life.' Richard made this speech with one hand leaning on the neck of Gertrude's horse, and the other on his own side, and with his head slightly thrown back and his eyes on hers. She had sat quietly in her saddle, returning his gaze. He had spoken slowly and deliberately; but without hesitation and without heat. 'This is not romance,' thought Gertrude, 'it's reality.' And this feeling it was that dictated her reply, divesting it of romance so effectually as almost to make it sound trivial.

'It was fortunate you had a walking-pole,' she said.

'I shall never travel without one again.'

'Never, at least,' smiled Gertrude, 'with a companion who has the bad habit of pushing you off the path.'

'O, you may push all you like,' said Richard. 'I give you leave. But isn't this enough about myself?'

'That's as you think.'

'Well, it's all I have to say for the present, except that I am

prodigiously glad to see you, and that of course you will stay
awhile.'

'But you have your work to do.'

'Dear me, never you mind my work. I've earned my dinner this
morning, if you have no objection; and I propose to share it with
you. So we will go back to the house.' He turned her horse's head
about, started up his oxen with his voice, and walked along beside
her on the grassy roadside, with one hand in the horse's mane, and
the other swinging his whip.

Before they reached the yard-gate, Gertrude had revolved his
speech. 'Enough about himself,' she said, silently echoing his words.
'Yes, Heaven be praised, it *is* about himself. I am but a means in
this matter,—he himself, his own character, his own happiness, is
the end.' Under this conviction it seemed to her that her part was
appreciably simplified. Richard was learning wisdom and self-control, and to exercise his reason. Such was the suit that he was
destined to gain. Her duty was as far as possible to remain passive,
and not to interfere with the working of the gods who had selected
her as the instrument of their prodigy. As they reached the gate,
Richard made a trumpet of his hands, and sent a ringing summons
into the fields; whereupon a farm-boy approached, and, with an un-
disguised stare of amazement at Gertrude, took charge of his
master's team. Gertrude rode up to the door-step, where her host
assisted her to dismount, and bade her go in and make herself at
home, while he busied himself with the bestowal of her horse. She
found that, in her absence, the old woman who administered her
friend's household had reappeared, and had laid out the preparations for his mid-day meal. By the time he returned, with his
face and head shining from a fresh ablution, and his shirt-sleeves
decently concealed by a coat, Gertrude had apparently won the
complete confidence of the good wife.

Gertrude doffed her hat, and tucked up her riding-skirt, and sat
down to a *tête-à-tête* over Richard's crumpled table-cloth. The
young man played the host very soberly and naturally; and Gertrude hardly knew whether to augur from his perfect self-possession
that her star was already on the wane, or that it had waxed into a
steadfast and eternal sun. The solution of her doubts was not far
to seek; Richard was absolutely at his ease in her presence. He had
told her indeed that she intoxicated him; and truly, in those
moments when she was compelled to oppose her dewy eloquence
to his fervid importunities, her whole presence seemed to him to
exhale a singularly potent sweetness. He had told her that she was
an enchantress, and this assertion, too, had its measure of truth.

But her spell was a steady one; it sprang not from her beauty, her wit, her figure,—it sprang from her character. When she found herself aroused to appeal or to resistance, Richard's pulses were quickened to what he had called intoxication, not by her smiles, her gestures, her glances, or any accession of that material beauty which she did not possess, but by a generous sense of her virtues in action. In other words, Gertrude exercised the magnificent power of making her lover forget her face. Agreeably to this fact, his habitual feeling in her presence was one of deep repose,—a sensation not unlike that which in the early afternoon, as he lounged in his orchard with a pipe, he derived from the sight of the hot and vaporous hills. He was innocent, then, of that delicious trouble which Gertrude's thoughts had touched upon as a not unnatural result of her visit, and which another woman's fancy would perhaps have dwelt upon as an indispensable proof of its success. 'Porphyro grew faint,' the poet assures us, as he stood in Madeline's chamber on Saint Agnes' eve. But Richard did not in the least grow faint now that his mistress was actually filling his musty old room with her voice, her touch, her looks; that she was sitting in his unfrequented chairs, trailing her skirt over his faded carpet, casting her perverted image upon his mirror, and breaking his daily bread. He was not fluttered when he sat at her well-served table, and trod her muffled floors. Why, then, should he be fluttered now? Gertrude was herself in all places, and once granted that she was at peace) to be at her side was to drink peace as fully in one place as in another.

Richard accordingly ate a great working-day dinner in Gertrude's despite, and she ate a small one for his sake. She asked questions moreover, and offered counsel with most sisterly freedom. She deplored the rents in his table-cloth, and the dismemberments of his furniture; and although by no means absurdly fastidious in the matter of household elegance, she could not but think that Richard would be a happier and a better man if he were a little more comfortable. She forbore, however, to criticise the poverty of his *entourage*, for she felt that the obvious answer was, that such a state of things was the penalty of his living alone; and it was desirable, under the circumstances, that this idea should remain implied.

When at last Gertrude began to bethink herself of going, Richard broke a long silence by the following question: 'Gertrude, *do* you love that man?'

'Richard,' she answered, 'I refused to tell you before, because you asked the question as a right. Of course you do so no longer. No. I do not love him. I have been near it,—but I have missed it. And now good-bye.'

For a week after her visit, Richard worked as bravely and steadily as he had done before it. But one morning he woke up lifeless, morally speaking. His strength had suddenly left him. He had been straining his faith in himself to a prodigious tension, and the chord had suddenly snapped. In the hope that Gertrude's tender fingers might repair it, he rode over to her towards evening. On his way through the village, he found people gathered in knots, reading fresh copies of the Boston newspapers over each other's shoulders, and learned that tidings had just come of a great battle in Virginia, which was also a great defeat. He procured a copy of the paper from a man who had read it out, and made haste to Gertrude's dwelling.

Gertrude received his story with those passionate imprecations and regrets which were then in fashion. Before long, Major Luttrel presented himself, and for half an hour there was no talk but about the battle. The talk, however, was chiefly between Gertrude and the Major, who found considerable ground for difference, she being a great radical and he a decided conservative. Richard sat by, listening apparently, but with the appearance of one to whom the matter of the discourse was of much less interest than the manner of those engaged in it. At last, when tea was announced, Gertrude told her friends, very frankly, that she would not invite them to remain,— that her heart was too heavy with her country's woes, and with the thought of so great a butchery, to allow her to play the hostess,— and that, in short, she was in the humour to be alone. Of course there was nothing for the gentlemen but to obey; but Richard went out cursing the law, under which, in the hour of his mistress's sorrow, his company was a burden and not a relief. He watched in vain, as he bade her farewell, for some little sign that she would fain have him stay, but that as she wished to get rid of his companion civility demanded that she should dismiss them both. No such sign was forthcoming, for the simple reason that Gertrude was sensible of no conflict between her desires. The men mounted their horses in silence, and rode slowly along the lane which led from Miss Whittaker's stables to the high-road. As they approached the top of the lane, they perceived in the twilight a mounted figure coming towards them. Richard's heart began to beat with an angry foreboding, which was confirmed as the rider drew near and disclosed Captain Severn's features. Major Luttrel and he, being bound in courtesy to a brief greeting, pulled up their horses; and as an attempt to pass them in narrow quarters would have been a greater incivility than even Richard was prepared to commit, he likewise halted.

'This is ugly news, isn't it?' said Severn. 'It has determined me to go back to-morrow.'

'Go back where?' asked Richard.

'To my regiment.'

'Are you well enough?' asked Major Luttrel. 'How is that wound?'

'It's so much better that I believe it can finish getting well down there as easily as here. Good-bye, Major. I hope we shall meet again.' And he shook hands with Major Luttrel. 'Good-bye, Mr. Clare.' And, somewhat to Richard's surprise, he stretched over and held out his hand to him.

Richard felt that it was tremulous, and, looking hard into his face, he thought it wore a certain unwonted look of excitement. And then his fancy coursed back to Gertrude, sitting where he had left her, in the sentimental twilight, alone with her heavy heart. With a word, he reflected, a single little word, a look, a motion, this happy man whose hand I hold can heal her sorrows. 'Oh!' cried Richard, 'that by this hand I might hold him fast forever!'

It seemed to the Captain that Richard's grasp was needlessly protracted and severe. 'What a grip the poor fellow has!' he thought. 'Good-bye,' he repeated aloud, disengaging himself.

'Good-bye,' said Richard. And then he added, he hardly knew why, 'Are you going to bid good-bye to Miss Whittaker?'

'Yes. Isn't she at home?'

Whether Richard really paused or not before he answered, he never knew. There suddenly arose such a tumult in his bosom that it seemed to him several moments before he became conscious of his reply. But it is probable that to Severn it came only too soon. 'No,' said Richard; 'she's not at home. We have just been calling.' As he spoke, he shot a glance at his companion, armed with defiance of his impending denial. But the Major just met his glance and then dropped his eyes. This slight motion was a horrible revelation. He had served the Major too.

'Ah? I'm sorry,' said Severn, slacking his rein,—'I'm sorry.' And from his saddle he looked down toward the house more longingly and regretfully than he knew.

Richard felt himself turning from pale to consuming crimson. There was a simple sincerity in Severn's words which was almost irresistible. For a moment he felt like shouting out a loud denial of his falsehood: 'She is there! she's alone and in tears, awaiting you. Go to her—and be damned!' But before he could gather his words into his throat, they were arrested by Major Luttrel's cool, clear voice, which in its calmness seemed to cast scorn upon his weakness.

'Captain,' said the Major, 'I shall be very happy to take charge of your farewell.'

'Thank you, Major. Pray do. Say how extremely sorry I was. Good-bye again.' And Captain Severn hastily turned his horse about, gave him his spurs, and galloped away, leaving his friends standing alone in the middle of the road. As the sound of his retreat expired, Richard, in spite of himself, drew a long breath. He sat motionless in the saddle, hanging his head.

'Mr. Clare,' said the Major, at last, 'that was very cleverly done.'

Richard looked up. 'I never told a lie before,' said he.

'Upon my soul, then, you did it uncommonly well. You did it so well I almost believed you. No wonder that Severn did.'

Richard was silent. Then suddenly he broke out, 'In God's name, sir, why don't you call me a blackguard? I've done a beastly act!'

'O, come,' said the Major, 'you needn't mind that, with me. We'll consider that said. I feel bound to let you know that I'm very, very much obliged to you. If you hadn't spoken, how do you know but that I might?'

'If you had, I would have given you the lie, square in your teeth.'

'Would you, indeed? It's very fortunate, then, I held my tongue. If you will have it so, I won't deny that your little improvisation sounded very ugly. I'm devilish glad I didn't make it, if you come to that.'

Richard felt his wit sharpened by a most unholy scorn,—a scorn far greater for his companion than for himself. 'I am glad to hear that it did sound ugly,' he said. 'To me, it seemed beautiful, holy, and just. For the space of a moment, it seemed absolutely right that I should say what I did. But you saw the lie in its horrid nakedness, and yet you let it pass. You have no excuse.'

'I beg your pardon. You are immensely ingenious, but you are immensely wrong. Are you going to make out that I am the guilty party? Upon my word, you're a cool hand. I *have* an excuse. I have the excuse of being interested in Miss Whittaker's remaining unengaged.'

'So I suppose. But you don't love her. Otherwise—'

Major Luttrel laid his hand on Richard's bridle. 'Mr. Clare,' said he, 'I have no wish to talk metaphysics over this matter. You had better say no more. I know that your feelings are not of an enviable kind, and I am therefore prepared to be good-natured with you. But you must be civil yourself. You have done a shabby deed; you are ashamed of it, and you wish to shift the responsibility upon me, which is more shabby still. My advice is, that you behave like a man of spirit, and swallow your apprehensions. I trust that you are not going to make a fool of yourself by an apology or retraction in any quarter. As for its having seemed holy and just to do what you did, that is mere bosh. A lie is a lie, and as such is often excusable. As anything else,—as a thing beautiful, holy, or just,—it's quite inexcusable. Yours was a lie to you, and a lie to me. It serves me, and I accept it. I suppose you understand me. I adopt it. You don't suppose it was because I was frightened by those big black eyes of yours that I held my tongue. As for my loving or not loving Miss Whittaker, I have no report to make to you about it. I will simply say that I intend, if possible, to marry her.'

'She'll not have you. She'll never marry a cold-blooded rascal.'

'I think she'll prefer him to a hot-blooded one. Do you want to pick a quarrel with me? Do you want to make me lose my temper? I shall refuse you that satisfaction. You have been a coward, and you want to frighten someone before you go to bed to make up for it. Strike me, and I'll strike you in self-defence, but I'm not going to mind your talk. Have you anything to say? No? Well, then, good evening.' And Major Luttrel started away.

It was with rage that Richard was dumb. Had he been but a cat's-paw after all? Heaven forbid! He sat irresolute for an instant, and then turned suddenly and cantered back to Gertrude's gate. Here he stopped again; but after a short pause he went in over the gravel with a fast-beating heart. O, if Luttrel were but there to see him! For a moment he fancied he heard the sound of the Major's returning steps. If he would only come and find him at confession! It would be so easy to confess before him! He went along beside the house to the front, and stopped beneath the open drawing-room window.

'Gertrude!' he cried softly, from his saddle.

Gertrude immediately appeared. 'You, Richard!' she exclaimed.

Her voice was neither harsh nor sweet; but her words and her intonation recalled vividly to Richard's mind the scene in the conservatory. He fancied them keenly expressive of disappointment. He was invaded by a mischievous conviction that she had been expecting Captain Severn, or that at the least she had mistaken his voice for the Captain's. The truth is that she had half fancied it might be,—Richard's call having been little more than a loud whisper. The young man sat looking up at her, silent.

'What do you want?' she asked. 'Can I do anything for you?'

Richard was not destined to do his duty that evening. A certain infinitesimal dryness of tone on Gertrude's part was the inevitable result of her finding that that whispered summons came only from Richard. She was preoccupied. Captain Severn had told her a fort-

night before, that, in case of news of a defeat, he should not await
the expiration of his leave of absence to return. Such news had now
come, and her inference was that her friend would immediately
take his departure. She could not but suppose that he would come
and bid her farewell, and what might not be the incidents, the
results, of such a visit? To tell the whole truth, it was under the
pressure of these reflections that, twenty minutes before, Gertrude
had dismissed our two gentlemen. That this long story should be
told in the dozen words with which she greeted Richard, will seem
unnatural to the disinterested reader. But in those words, poor
Richard, with a lover's clairvoyance, read it at a single glance. The
same resentful impulse, the same sickening of the heart, that he had
felt in the conservatory, took possession of him once more. To be
witness of Severn's passion for Gertrude,—that he could endure. To
be witness of Gertrude's passion for Severn,—against that obligation
his reason rebelled.

'What is it you wish, Richard?' Gertrude repeated. 'Have you
forgotten anything?'

'Nothing! nothing!' cried the young man. 'It's no matter!'

He gave a great pull at his bridle, and almost brought his horse
back on his haunches, and then, wheeling him about on himself, he
thrust in his spurs and galloped out of the gate.

On the highway he came upon Major Luttrel, who stood looking
down the lane.

'I'm going to the Devil, sir!' cried Richard. 'Give me your hand
on it.'

Luttrel held out his hand. 'My poor young man,' said he, 'you're
out of your head. I'm sorry for you. You haven't been making a
fool of yourself?'

'Yes, a damnable fool of myself!'

Luttrel breathed freely. 'You'd better go home and go to bed,' he
said. 'You'll make yourself ill by going on at this rate.'

'I—I'm afraid to go home,' said Richard, in a broken voice. 'For
God's sake, come with me!'—and the wretched fellow burst into
tears. 'I'm too bad for any company but yours,' he cried, in his sobs.

The Major winced, but he took pity. 'Come, come,' said he, 'we'll
pull through. I'll go home with you.'

They rode off together. That night Richard went to bed miserably drunk; although Major Luttrel had left him at ten o'clock,
adjuring him to drink no more. He awoke the next morning in a
violent fever; and before evening the doctor, whom one of his hired
men had brought to his bedside, had come and looked grave and
pronounced him very ill.

PART III

In country districts, where life is quiet, incidents do duty as
events; and accordingly Captain Severn's sudden departure for his
regiment became very rapidly known among Gertrude's neighbours.
She herself heard it from her coachman, who had heard it in the
village, where the Captain had been seen to take the early train.
She received the news calmly enough to outward appearance, but a
great tumult rose and died in her breast. He had gone without a
word of farewell! Perhaps he had not had time to call upon her.
But bare civility would have dictated his dropping her a line of
writing,—he who must have read in her eyes the feeling which her
lips refused to utter, and who had been the object of her tenderest
courtesy. It was not often that Gertrude threw back into her friends'
teeth their acceptance of the hospitality which it had been placed
in her power to offer them; but if she now mutely reproached
Captain Severn with ingratitude, it was because he had done more
than slight her material gifts: he had slighted that constant moral
force with which these gifts were accompanied, and of which they
were but the rude and vulgar token. It is but natural to expect that
our dearest friends will accredit us with our deepest feelings; and
Gertrude had constituted Edmund Severn her dearest friend. She
had not, indeed, asked his assent to this arrangement, but she had
borne it out by a subtile devotion which she felt that she had a
right to exact of him that he should repay,—repay by letting her
know that, whether it was lost on his heart or not, it was at least
not lost to his senses,—that, if he could not return it, he could at
least remember it. She had given him the flower of her womanly
tenderness, and, when his moment came, he had turned from her
without a look. Gertrude shed no tears. It seemed to her that she
had given her friend tears enough, and that to expend her soul in
weeping would be to wrong herself. She would think no more of
Edmund Severn. He should be as little to her for the future as she
was to him.

It was very easy to make this resolution: to keep it, Gertrude
found another matter. She could not think of the war, she could not
talk with her neighbours of current events, she could not take up a
newspaper, without reverting to her absent friend. She found herself constantly harassed with the apprehension that he had not
allowed himself time really to recover, and that a fortnight's exposure would send him back to the hospital. At last it occurred to

her that civility required that she should make a call upon Mrs. Martin, the Captain's sister; and a vague impression that this lady might be the depositary of some farewell message—perhaps of a letter—which she was awaiting her convenience to present, led her at once to undertake this social duty. The carriage which had been ordered for her projected visit was at the door, when, within a week after Severn's departure, Major Luttrel was announced. Gertrude received him in her bonnet. His first care was to present Captain Severn's adieus, together with his regrets that he had not had time to discharge them in person. As Luttrel made his speech, he watched his companion narrowly, and was considerably reassured by the un-flinching composure with which she listened to it. The turn he had given to Severn's message had been the fruit of much mischievous cogitation. It had seemed to him that, for his purposes, the assumption of a hasty, and as it were mechanical, allusion to Miss Whit-taker, was more serviceable than the assumption of no allusion at all, which would have left a boundless void for the exercise of Gert-rude's fancy. And he had reasoned well; for although he was tempted to infer from her calmness that his shot had fallen short of the mark, yet, in spite of her silent and almost smiling assent to his words, it had made but one bound to her heart. Before many minutes, she felt that those words had done her a world of good. 'He had not had time!' Indeed, as she took to herself their full expression of perfect indifference, she felt that her hard, forced smile was broadening into the sign of a lively gratitude to the Major.

Major Luttrel had still another task to perform. He had spent half an hour on the preceding day at Richard's bedside, having ridden over to the farm, in ignorance of his illness, to see how matters stood with him. The reader will already have surmised that the Major was not pre-eminently a man of conscience: he will, therefore, be the less surprised and shocked to hear that the sight of the poor young man, prostrate, fevered, and delirious, and to all appearance rapidly growing worse, filled him with an emotion the reverse of creditable. In plain terms, he was very glad to find Richard a prisoner in bed. He had been racking his brains for a scheme to keep his young friend out of the way, and now, to his exceeding satisfaction, Nature had relieved him of this trouble-some care. If Richard was condemned to typhoid fever, which his symptoms seemed to indicate, he would not, granting his recovery, be able to leave his room within a month. In a month, much might be done; nay, with energy, all might be done. The reader has been all but directly informed that the Major's present purpose was to secure Miss Whittaker's hand. He was poor, and he was ambitious, and he was, moreover, so well advanced in life—being thirty-six years of age—that he had no heart to think of building up his fortune by slow degrees. A man of good breeding, too, he had become sensible, as he approached middle age, of the many advantages of a luxurious home. He had accordingly decided that a wealthy marriage would most easily unlock the gate to prosperity. A girl of a somewhat lighter calibre than Gertrude would have been the woman—we cannot say of his heart; but, as he very generously argued, beggars can't be choosers. Gertrude was a woman with a mind of her own; but, on the whole, he was not afraid of her. He was abundantly prepared to do his duty. He had, of course, as became a man of sense, duly weighed his obstacles against his advantages; but an impartial scrutiny had found the latter heavier in the balance. The only serious difficulty in his path was the possibility that, on hearing of Richard's illness, Gertrude, with her confounded benevolence, would take a fancy to nurse him in person, and that, in the course of her ministrations, his delirious ramblings would force upon her mind the damning story of the deception practised upon Captain Severn. There was nothing for it but bravely to face this risk. As for that other fact, which many men of a feebler spirit would have deemed an invincible obstacle, Luttrel's masterly understanding had immediately converted it into the prime agent of success,—the fact, namely, that Gertrude's heart was preoccupied. Such knowledge as he possessed of the relations between Miss Whittaker and his brother officer he had gained by his unaided observations and his silent deductions. These had been logical; for, on the whole, his knowledge was accurate. It was at least what he might have termed a good working knowledge. He had calculated on a passionate reactionary impulse on Gertrude's part, consequent on Severn's simulated offence. He knew that, in a generous woman, such an impulse, if left to itself, would not go very far. But on this point it was that his policy bore. He would not leave it to itself: he would take it gently into his hands, attenuate it, prolong it, economize it, and mould it into the clew to his own good-fortune. He thus counted much upon his skill and his tact; but the likewise placed a becoming degree of reliance upon his solid personal qualities,—qualities too sober and too solid, perhaps, to be called *charms*, but thoroughly adapted to inspire confidence. The Major was not handsome in feature; he left that to younger men and to lighter women; but his ugliness was of a masculine, aristocratic, intelligent stamp. His figure, moreover, was good enough to compensate for the absence of a straight nose and

a fine mouth; and his general bearing offered a most pleasing com-
bination of the gravity of the man of affairs and the versatility of
the man of society.

In her sudden anxiety on Richard's behalf, Gertrude soon forgot
her own immaterial woes. The carriage which was to have conveyed her to Mrs. Martin's was used for a more disinterested
purpose. The Major, prompted by a strong faith in the salutary
force of his own presence, having obtained her permission to accompany her, they set out for the farm, and soon found themselves in
Richard's chamber. The young man was wrapped in a heavy sleep,
from which it was judged imprudent to arouse him. Gertrude, sighing as she compared his thinly furnished room with her own
elaborate apartments, drew up a mental list of essential luxuries
which she would immediately send him. Not but that he had
received, however, a sufficiency of homely care. The doctor was
assiduous, and the old woman who nursed him was full of rough
good-sense.

'He asks very often after you, Miss,' she said, addressing Gertrude,
but with a sly glance at the Major. 'But I think you'd better not
come too often. I'm afraid you'd excite him more than you'd quiet
him.'

'I'm afraid you would, Miss Whittaker,' said the Major, who
could have hugged the goodwife.

'Why should I excite him?' asked Gertrude, 'I'm used to sick-
rooms. I nursed my father for a year and a half.'

'O, it's very well for an old woman like me, but it's no place for a
fine young lady like you,' said the nurse, looking at Gertrude's
muslins and laces.

'I'm not so fine as to desert a friend in distress,' said Gertrude. 'I
shall come again, and if it makes the poor fellow worse to see me,
I shall stay away. I am ready to do anything that will help him to
get well.'

It had already occurred to her that, in his unnatural state, Richard
might find her presence a source of irritation, and she was prepared
to remain in the background. As she returned to her carriage, she
caught herself reflecting with so much pleasure upon Major Luttrel's
kindness in expending a couple of hours of his valuable time on so
unprofitable an object as poor Richard, that, by way of intimating
her satisfaction, she invited him to come home and dine with her.

After a short interval she paid Richard a second visit, in company
with Miss Pendexter. He was a great deal worse; he lay emaciated,
exhausted, and stupid. The issue was doubtful. Gertrude immediately pushed forward to M——, a larger town than her own, sought

out a professional nurse, and arranged with him to relieve the old woman from the farm, who was worn out with her vigilance. For a fortnight, moreover, she received constant tidings from the young man's physician. During this fortnight, Major Luttrel was assiduous, and proportionately successful.

It may be said, to his credit, that he had by no means conducted his suit upon that narrow programme which he had drawn up at the outset. He very soon discovered that Gertrude's resentment— if resentment there was—was a substance utterly impalpable even to his most delicate tact, and he had accordingly set to work to woo her like an honest man, from day to day, from hour to hour, trusting so devoutly for success to momentary inspiration, that he felt his suit dignified by a certain flattering *faux air* of genuine passion. He occasionally reminded himself, however, that he might really be owing more to the subtle force of accidental contrast than Gertrude's life-long reserve—for it was certain she would not depart from it—would ever allow him to measure.

It was as an honest man, then, a man of impulse and of action, that Gertrude had begun to like him. She was not slow to perceive whither his operations tended; and she was almost tempted at times to tell him frankly that she would spare him the intermediate steps, and meet him at the goal without further delay. It was not that she was prepared to love him, but she would make him an obedient wife. An immense weariness had somehow come upon her, and a sudden sense of loneliness. A vague suspicion that her money had done her an incurable wrong inspired her with a profound distaste for the care of it. She felt cruelly hedged out from human sympathy by his bristling possessions. 'If I had had five hundred dollars a year,' she said in a frequent parenthesis, 'I might have pleased him.' Hating her wealth, accordingly, and chilled by her isolation, the temptation was strong upon her to give herself up to that wise, brave gentleman who seemed to have adopted such a happy medium betwixt loving her for her money and fearing her for it. Would she not always stand between men who would represent the two extremes? She would anticipate security by an alliance with Major Luttrel.

One evening, on presenting himself, Luttrel read these thoughts so clearly in her eyes, that he made up his mind to speak. But his mind was burdened with a couple of facts, of which it was necessary that he should discharge it before it could enjoy the freedom of action which the occasion required. In the first place, then, he had been to see Richard Clare, and had found him suddenly and decidedly better. It was unbecoming, however,—it was impossible,

—that he should allow Gertrude to linger over this pleasant announcement.

'I tell the good news first,' he said, gravely. 'I have some very bad news, too, Miss Whittaker.'

Gertrude sent him a rapid glance. 'Someone has been killed,' she said.

'Captain Severn has been shot,' said the Major,—'shot by a guerilla.'

Gertrude was silent. No answer seemed possible to that uncompromising fact. She sat with her head on her hand, and her elbow on the table beside her, looking at the figures on the carpet. She uttered no words of commonplace regret; but she felt as little like giving way to serious grief. She had lost nothing, and, to the best of her knowledge, *he* had lost nothing. She had an old loss to mourn, —a loss a month old, which she had mourned as she might. To give way to passion would have been but to impugn the solemnity of her past regrets. When she looked up at her companion, she was pale, but she was calm, yet with a calmness upon which a single glance of her eye directed him not inconsiderately to presume. She was aware that this glance betrayed her secret; but in view both of Severn's death and of the Major's attitude, such betrayal mattered less. Luttrel had prepared to act upon her hint, and to avert himself gently from the topic, when Gertrude, who had dropped her eyes again, raised them with a slight shudder. 'I'm cold,' she said. 'Will you shut that window beside you, Major? Or stay, suppose you give me my shawl from the sofa.'

Luttrel brought the shawl, placed it on her shoulders, and sat down beside her. 'These are cruel times,' he said, with studied simplicity. 'I'm sure I hardly know what's to come of it all.'

'Yes, they are cruel times,' said Gertrude. 'They make one feel cruel. They make one doubt of all he has learnt from his pastors and masters.'

'Yes, but they teach us something new also.'

'I'm sure I don't know,' said Gertrude, whose heart was so full of bitterness that she felt almost malignant. 'They teach us how mean we are. War is an infamy, Major, though it *is* your trade. It's very well for you, who look at it professionally, and for those who go and fight; but it's a miserable business for those who stay at home, and do the thinking and the sentimentalizing. It's a miserable business for women; it makes us more spiteful than ever.'

'Well, a little spite isn't a bad thing, in practice,' said the Major. 'War is certainly an abomination, both at home and in the field. But as wars go, Miss Whittaker, our own is a very satisfactory one.

It involves something. It won't leave us as it found us. We're in the midst of a revolution, and what's a revolution but a turning upside down? It makes sad work with our habits and theories and our traditions and convictions. But, on the other hand,' Luttrel pursued, warming to his task, 'it leaves something untouched, which is better than these,—I mean our feelings, Miss Whittaker.' And the Major paused until he had caught Gertrude's eyes, when, having engaged them with his own, he proceeded. 'I think they are the stronger for the downfall of so much else, and, upon my soul, I think it's in them we ought to take refuge. Don't you think so?'

'Yes, if I understand you.'

'I mean our serious feelings, you know,—not our tastes nor our passions. I don't advocate fiddling while Rome is burning. In fact it's only poor, unsatisfied devils that are tempted to fiddle. There is one feeling which is respectable and honourable, and even sacred, at all times and in all places, whatever they may be. It doesn't depend upon circumstances, but they upon it; and with its help, I think, we are a match for any circumstances. I don't mean religion, Miss Whittaker,' added the Major, with a sober smile.

'If you don't mean religion,' said Gertrude, 'I suppose you mean love. That's a very different thing.'

'Yes, a very different thing; so I've always thought, and so I'm glad to hear you say. Some people, you know, mix them up in the most extraordinary fashion. I don't fancy myself an especially religious man; in fact, I believe I'm rather otherwise. It's my nature. Half mankind are born so, or I suppose the affairs of this world wouldn't move. But I believe I'm a good lover, Miss Whittaker.'

'I hope for your own sake you are, Major Luttrel.'

'Thank you. Do you think now you could entertain the idea for the sake of anyone else?'

Gertrude neither dropped her eyes, nor shrugged her shoulders, nor blushed. If anything, indeed, she turned somewhat paler than before, as she sustained her companion's gaze, and prepared to answer him as directly as she might.

'If I loved you, Major Luttrel,' she said, 'I should value the idea for my own sake.'

The Major, too, blanched a little. 'I put my question condition-ally,' he answered, 'and I have got, as I deserved, a conditional reply. I will speak plainly, Miss Whittaker. *Do* you value the fact for your own sake? It would be plainer still to say, Do you love me? but I confess I'm not brave enough for that. I will say, Can you? or I will even content myself with putting it in the conditional again, and asking you if you could; although, after all, I hardly know what the *if* understood can reasonably refer to. I'm not such a fool as to ask of any woman—least of all of you—to love me contingently. You can only answer for the present, and say yes or no. I shouldn't trouble you to say either, if I didn't conceive that I had given you time to make up your mind. It doesn't take forever to know James Luttrel. I'm not one of the great unfathomable ones. We've seen each other more or less intimately for a good many weeks; and as I'm conscious, Miss Whittaker, of having shown you my best, I take for granted that if you don't fancy me now, you won't a month hence, when you shall have seen my faults. Yes, Miss Whittaker, I can solemnly say,' continued the Major, with genuine feeling, 'I have shown you my best, as every man is in honour bound to do who approaches a woman with those predispositions with which I have approached you. I have striven hard to please you,'—and he paused. 'I can only say, I hope I have succeeded.'

'I should be very insensible,' said Gertrude, 'if all your kindness and your courtesy had been lost upon me.'

'In Heaven's name, don't talk about courtesy,' cried the Major.

'I am deeply conscious of your devotion, and I am very much obliged to you for urging your claims so respectfully and considerately. I speak seriously, Major Luttrel,' pursued Gertrude. 'There is a happy medium of expression, and you have taken it. Now it seems to me that there is a happy medium of affection, with which you might be content. Strictly, I don't love you. I question my heart, and it gives me that answer. The feeling that I have is not a feeling to work prodigies.'

'May it at least work the prodigy of allowing you to be my wife?'

'I don't think I shall over-estimate its strength, if I say that it may. If you can respect a woman who gives you her hand in cold blood, you are welcome to mine.'

Luttrel moved his chair and took her hand. 'Beggars can't be choosers,' said he, raising it to his moustache.

'O Major Luttrel, don't say that,' she answered. 'I give you a great deal; but I keep a little,—a little,' said Gertrude, hesitating, 'which I suppose I shall give to God.'

'Well, I shall not be jealous,' said Luttrel.

'The rest I give to you, and in return I ask a great deal.'

'I shall give you all. You know I told you I'm not religious.'

'No, I don't want more than I give,' said Gertrude.

'But, pray,' asked Luttrel, with a delicate smile, 'what am I to do with the difference?'

'You had better keep it for yourself. What I want is your protection, sir, and your advice, and your care. I want you to take me
away from this place, even if you have to take me down to the army.
I want to see the world under the shelter of your name. I shall give
you a great deal of trouble. I'm a mere mass of possessions: what I
am, is nothing to what I have. But ever since I began to grow up,
what I am has been the slave of what I have. I am weary of my
chains, and you must help me to carry them,'—and Gertrude rose
to her feet as if to inform the Major that his audience was at an
end.

He still held her right hand; she gave him the other. He stood
looking down at her, an image of manly humility, while from his
silent breast went out a brief thanksgiving to favouring fortune.

At the pressure of his hands, Gertrude felt her bosom heave. She
burst into tears. 'O, you must be very kind to me!' she cried, as he
put his arm about her, and she dropped her head upon his shoulder.

When once Richard's health had taken a turn for the better, it
began very rapidly to improve. 'Until he is quite well,' Gertrude
said, one day, to her accepted suitor, 'I had rather he heard nothing
of our engagement. He was once in love with me himself,' she
added, very frankly. 'Did you ever suspect it? But I hope he will
have got better of that sad malady, too. Nevertheless, I shall expect
nothing of his good judgment until he is quite strong; and as he
may hear of my new intentions from other people, I propose that,
for the present, we confide them to no one.'

'But if he asks me point-blank,' said the Major, 'what shall I
answer?'

'It's not likely he'll ask you. How should he suspect anything?'

'O,' said Luttrel, 'Clare is one that suspects everything.'

'Tell him we're not engaged, then. A woman in my position may
say what she pleases.'

It was agreed, however, that certain preparations for the marriage
should meanwhile go forward in secret; and that the marriage itself
should take place in August, as Luttrel expected to be ordered back
into service in the autumn. At about this moment Gertrude was
surprised to receive a short note from Richard, so feebly scrawled
in pencil as to be barely legible. 'Dear Gertrude,' it ran, 'don't come
to see me just yet. I'm not fit. You would hurt me, and *vice versa*.
God bless you! R. CLARE.' Miss Whittaker explained his request, by
the supposition that a report had come to him of Major Luttrel's
late assiduities (which it was impossible should go unobserved);
that, leaping at the worst, he had taken her engagement for granted;

and that, under this impression, he could not trust himself to see her. She despatched him an answer, telling him that she would await his pleasure, and that, if the doctor would consent to his having letters, she would meanwhile occasionally write to him. 'She will give me good advice,' thought Richard impatiently; and on this point, accordingly, she received no account of his wishes. Expecting to leave her house and close it on her marriage, she spent many hours in wandering sadly over the meadow-paths and through the woodlands which she had known from her childhood. She had thrown aside the last ensigns of filial regret, and now walked sad and splendid in the uncompromising colours of an affianced bride. It would have seemed to a stranger that, for a woman who had freely chosen a companion for life, she was amazingly spiritless and sombre. As she looked at her pale cheeks and heavy eyes in the mirror, she felt ashamed that she had no fairer countenance to offer to her destined lord. She had lost her single beauty, her smile; and she would make but a ghastly figure at the altar. 'I ought to wear a calico dress and an apron,' she said to herself, 'and not this glaring finery.' But she continued to wear her finery, and to lay out her money, and to perform all her old duties to the letter. After the lapse of what she deemed a sufficient interval, she went to see Mrs. Martin, and to listen dumbly to her narration of her brother's death, and to her simple eulogies.

Major Luttrel performed his part quite as bravely, and much more successfully. He observed neither too many things nor too few; he neither presumed upon his success, nor mistrusted it. Having on his side received no prohibition from Richard, he resumed his visits at the farm, trusting that, with the return of reason, his young friend might feel disposed to renew that anomalous alliance in which, on the hapless evening of Captain Severn's farewell, he had taken refuge against his despair. In the long, languid hours of his early convalescence, Richard had found time to survey his position, to summon back piece by piece the immediate past, and to frame a general scheme for the future. But more vividly than anything else, there had finally disengaged itself from his meditations a profound aversion to James Luttrel.

It was in this humour that the Major found him; and as he looked at the young man's gaunt shoulders, supported by pillows, at his face, so livid and aquiline, at his great dark eyes, luminous with triumphant life, it seemed to him that an invincible spirit had been sent from a better world to breathe confusion upon his hopes. If Richard hated the Major, the reader may guess whether the Major loved Richard. Luttrel was amazed at his first remark.

'I suppose you're engaged by this time,' Richard said, calmly enough.

'Not quite,' answered the Major. 'There's a chance for you yet.'

To this Richard made no rejoinder. Then, suddenly, 'Have you had any news of Captain Severn?' he asked.

For a moment the Major was perplexed at his question. He had assumed that the news of Severn's death had come to Richard's ears, and he had been half curious, half apprehensive as to its effect. But an instant's reflection now assured him that the young man's estrangement from his neighbours had kept him hitherto and might still keep him in ignorance of the truth. Hastily, therefore, and inconsiderately, the Major determined to confirm this ignorance. 'No,' said he; 'I've had no news. Severn and I are not on such terms as to correspond.'

The next time Luttrel came to the farm, he found the master sitting up in a great, cushioned, chintz-covered armchair which Gertrude had sent him the day before out of her own dressing-room.

'Are you engaged yet?' asked Richard.

There was a strain as if of defiance in his tone. The Major was irritated. 'Yes,' said he, 'we *are* engaged now.'

The young man's face betrayed no emotion.

'Are you reconciled to it?' asked Luttrel.

'Yes, practically I am.'

'What do you mean by practically? Explain yourself.'

'A man in my state can't explain himself. I mean that, however I feel about it, I shall accept Gertrude's marriage.'

'You're a wise man, my boy,' said the Major, kindly.

'I'm growing wise. I feel like Solomon on his throne in this chair. But I confess, sir, I don't see how she could have you.'

'Well, there's no accounting for tastes,' said the Major, good-humouredly.'

'Ah, if it's been a matter of taste with her,' said Richard, 'I have nothing to say.'

They came to no more express understanding than this with regard to the future. Richard continued to grow stronger daily, and to defer the renewal of his intercourse with Gertrude. A month before, he would have resented as a bitter insult the intimation that he would ever be so resigned to lose her as he now found himself. He would not see her for two reasons: first, because he felt that it would be—or that at least in reason it ought to be—a painful experience to look upon his old mistress with a coldly critical eye; and secondly, because, justify to himself as he would his new-born in-

difference, he could not entirely cast away the suspicion that it was
a last remnant of disease, and that, when he stood on his legs again
in the presence of those exuberant landscapes with which he had
long since established a sort of sensuous communion, he would feel,
as with a great tumultuous rush, the return of his impetuous manhood and of his old capacity. When he had smoked a pipe in the
outer sunshine, when he had settled himself once more to the long
elastic bound of his mare, then he would see Gertrude. The reason
of the change which had come upon him was that she had disappointed him,—she whose magnanimity it had once seemed that
his fancy was impotent to measure. She had accepted Major Luttrel,
a man whom he despised; she had so mutilated her magnificent
heart as to match it with his. The validity of his dislike to the
Major, Richard did not trouble himself to examine. He accepted it
as an unerring instinct; and, indeed, he might have asked himself,
had he not sufficient proof? Moreover he laboured under the sense
of a gratuitous wrong. He had suffered an immense torment of
remorse to drive him into brutishness, and thence to the very gate
of death, for an offence which he had deemed mortal, and which
was after all but a phantasm of his impassioned conscience. What
a fool he had been! a fool for his nervous fears, and a fool for his
penitence. Marriage with Major Luttrel,—such was the end of Gertrude's fancied anguish. Such, too, we hardly need add, was the end
of that idea of reparation which had been so formidable to Luttrel.
Richard had been generous; he would now be just.

Far from impeding his recovery, these reflections hastened it.
One morning in the beginning of August, Gertrude received notice
of Richard's presence. It was a still, sultry day, and Miss Whittaker,
her habitual pallor deepened by the oppressive heat, was sitting
alone in a white morning-dress, languidly fanning aside at once the
droning flies and her equally importunate thoughts. She found
Richard standing in the middle of the drawing-room, booted and
spurred.

'Well, Richard,' she exclaimed, with some feeling, 'you're at last
willing to see me!'

As his eyes fell upon her, he started and stood almost paralysed,
heeding neither her words nor her extended hand. It was not Gertrude he saw, but her ghost.

'In Heaven's name what has happened to you?' he cried. 'Have
you been ill?'

Gertrude tried to smile in feigned surprise at his surprise; but
her muscles relaxed. Richard's words and looks reflected more
vividly than any mirror the dejection of her person; and this, the

misery of her soul. She felt herself growing faint. She staggered back to a sofa and sank down.

Then Richard felt as if the room were revolving about him, and as if his throat were choked with imprecations,—as if his old erratic passion had again taken possession of him, like a mingled legion of devils and angels. It was through pity that his love returned. He went forward and dropped on his knees at Gertrude's feet. 'Speak to me!' he cried, seizing her hands. 'Are you unhappy? Is your heart broken? O Gertrude! what have you come to?'

Gertrude drew her hands from his grasp and rose to her feet. 'Get up, Richard,' she said. 'Don't talk to wildly. I'm not well. I'm very glad to see you. *You* look well.'

'I've got my strength again,—and meanwhile you've been failing. You're unhappy, you're wretched! Don't say you're not, Gertrude: it's as plain as day. You're breaking your heart.'

'The same old Richard!' said Gertrude, trying to smile again.

'Would that you were the same old Gertrude! Don't try to smile; you can't!'

'I *shall*!' said Gertrude, desperately. 'I'm going to be married, you know.'

'Yes, I know. I don't congratulate you.'

'I have not counted upon that honour, Richard. I shall have to do without it.'

'You'll have to do without a great many things!' cried Richard, horrified by what seemed to him her blind self-immolation.

'I have all I ask,' said Gertrude.

'You haven't all *I* ask then! You haven't all your friends ask.'

'My friends are very kind, but I marry to suit myself.'

'You've not suited yourself!' retorted the young man. 'You've suited—God knows what!—your pride, your despair, your resent-ment.' As he looked at her, the secret history of her weakness seemed to become plain to him, and he felt a mighty rage against the man who had taken a base advantage of it. 'Gertrude!' he cried, 'I entreat you to go back. It's not for my sake,—*I*'ll give you up,—I'll go a thousand miles away, and never look at you again. It's for your own. In the name of your happiness, break with that man! Don't fling yourself away. Buy him off, if you consider yourself bound. Give him your money. That's all he wants.'

As Gertrude listened, the blood came back to her face, and two flames into her eyes. She looked at Richard from head to foot. 'You are not weak,' she said, 'you are in your senses, you are well and strong; you shall tell me what you mean. You insult the best friend I have. Explain yourself! you insinuate foul things,—speak them out!' Her eyes glanced toward the door, and Richard's followed them. Major Luttrel stood on the threshold.

'Come in, sir!' cried Richard. 'Gertrude swears she'll believe no harm of you. Come and tell her that she's wrong! How can you keep on harassing a woman whom you've brought to this state? Think of what she was three months ago, and look at her now!'

Luttrel received this broadside without flinching. He had over-heard Richard's voice from the entry, and he had steeled his heart for the encounter. He assumed the air of having been so amazed by the young man's first words as only to have heard his last; and he glanced at Gertrude mechanically as if to comply with them. 'What's the matter?' he asked, going over to her, and taking her hand; 'are you ill?' Gertrude let him have her hand, but she forbore to meet his eyes.

'Ill! of course she's ill!' cried Richard, passionately. 'She's dying,—she's consuming herself! I know I seem to be playing an odious part here, Gertrude, but, upon my soul, I can't help it. I look like a betrayer, an informer, a sneak, but I don't feel like one! Still, I'll leave you, if you say so.'

'Shall he go, Gertrude?' asked Luttrel, without looking at Richard.

'No. Let him stay and explain himself. He has accused you,—let him prove his case.'

'I know what he is going to say,' said Luttrel. 'It will place me in a bad light. Do you still wish to hear it?'

Gertrude drew her hand hastily out of Luttrel's. 'Speak, Richard!' she cried, with a passionate gesture.

'I will speak,' said Richard. 'I've done you a dreadful wrong, Gertrude. How great a wrong, I never knew until I saw you to-day so miserably altered. When I heard that you were to be married, I fancied that it was no wrong, and that my remorse had been wasted. But I understand it now; and *he* understands it, too. You once told me that you had ceased to love Captain Severn. It wasn't true. You never ceased to love him. You love him at this moment. If he were to get another wound in the next battle, how would you feel? How would you bear it?' And Richard paused for an instant with the force of his interrogation.

'For God's sake,' cried Gertrude, 'respect the dead!'

'The dead! Is he dead?'

Gertrude covered her face with her hands.

'You beast!' cried Luttrel.

Richard turned upon him savagely. 'Shut your infernal mouth!' he roared. 'You told me he was alive and well!'

Gertrude made a movement of speechless distress.

'You would have it, my dear,' said Luttrel, with a little bow.

Richard had turned pale, and began to tremble. 'Excuse me, Gertrude,' he said, hoarsely, 'I've been deceived. Poor, unhappy woman! Gertrude,' he continued, going nearer to her, and speaking in a whisper, '*I* killed him.'

Gertrude fell back from him, as he approached her, with a look of unutterable horror. 'I and *he*,' said Richard, pointing at Luttrel.

Gertrude's eyes followed the direction of his gesture, and transferred their scorching disgust to her suitor. This was too much for Luttrel's courage. 'You idiot!' she shouted at Richard, 'speak out!'

'He loved you, though you believed he didn't,' said Richard. 'I saw it the first time I looked at him. To everyone but you it was as plain as day. Luttrel saw it too. But he was too modest, and he never fancied you cared for him. The night before he went back to the army, he came to bid you good-bye. If he had seen you, it would have been better for everyone. You remember that evening, of course. We met him, Luttrel and I. He was all on fire,—he meant to speak. I knew it, you knew it, Luttrel: it was in his fingers' ends. I intercepted him. I turned him off,—I lied to him and told you you were away. I was a coward, and I did neither more nor less than that. I knew you were waiting for him. It was stronger than my will,—I believe I should do it again. Fate was against him, and he went off. I came back to tell you, but my damnable jealousy strangled me. I went home and drank myself into a fever. I've done you a wrong that I can never repair. I'd go hang myself if I thought it would help you.' Richard spoke slowly, softly, and explicitly, as if irresistible Justice in person had her hand upon his neck, and were forcing him down upon his knees. In the presence of Gertrude's dismay nothing seemed possible but perfect self-conviction. In Luttrel's attitude, as he stood with his head erect, his arms folded, and his cold grey eye fixed upon the distance, it struck him that there was something atrociously insolent; not insolent to him,—for that he cared little enough,—but insolent to Gertrude and to the dreadful solemnity of the hour. Richard sent the Major a look of the most aggressive contempt. 'As for Major Luttrel,' he said, '*he* was but a passive spectator. No, Gertrude, by Heaven!' he burst out; 'he was worse than I! I loved you, and he didn't!'

'Our friend is correct in his facts, Gertrude,' said Luttrel, quietly. 'He is incorrect in his opinions. I *was* a passive spectator of his deception. He appeared to enjoy a certain authority with regard to your wishes,—the source of which I respected both of you sufficiently never to question,—and I accepted the act which he has described as an exercise of it. You will remember that you had sent us away on the ground that you were in no humour for company. To deny you, therefore, to another visitor, seemed to me rather officious, but still pardonable. You will consider that I was wholly ignorant of your relations to that visitor; that whatever you may have done for others, Gertrude, to me you never vouchsafed a word of information on the subject, and that Mr. Clare's words are a revelation to me. But I am bound to believe nothing that he says. I am bound to believe that I have injured you only when I hear it from your own lips.'

Richard made a movement as if to break out upon the Major; but Gertrude, who had been standing motionless with her eyes upon the ground, quickly raised them, and gave him a look of imperious prohibition. She had listened, and she had chosen. She turned to Luttrel. 'Major Luttrel,' she said, 'you *have* been an accessory in what has been for me a serious grief. It is my duty to tell you so. I mean, of course, a profoundly unwilling accessory. I pity you more than I can tell you. I think your position more pitiable than mine. It is true that I never made a confidant of you. I never made one of Richard. I had a secret, and he surprised it. You were less fortunate.' It might have seemed to a thoroughly dispassionate observer that in these last four words there was an infinitesimal touch of tragic irony. Gertrude paused a moment while Luttrel eyed her intently, and Richard, from a somewhat tardy instinct of delicacy, walked over to the bow-window. 'This is the most painful moment of my life,' she resumed. 'I hardly know where my duty lies. The only thing that is plain to me is, that I must ask you to release me from my engagement. I ask it most humbly, Major Luttrel,' Gertrude continued, with warmth in her words, and a chilling coldness in her voice,—a coldness which it sickened her to feel there, but which she was unable to dispel. 'I can't expect that you should give me up easily; I know that it's a great deal to ask, and'—she forced the chosen words out of her mouth—'I should thank you more than I can say if you would put some condition upon my release. You have done honourably by me, and I repay you with ingratitude. But I can't marry you.' Her voice began to melt. 'I have been false from the beginning. I have no heart to give you. I should make you a despicable wife.'

The Major, too, had listened and chosen, and in this trying conjuncture he set the seal to his character as an accomplished man.

He saw that Gertrude's movement was final, and he determined to respect the inscrutable mystery of her heart. He read in the glance of her eye and the tone of her voice that the perfect dignity had fallen from his character,—that his integrity had lost its bloom; but he also read her firm resolve never to admit this fact to her own mind, nor to declare it to the world, and he honoured her forbearance. His hopes, his ambitions, his visions, lay before him like a colossal heap of broken glass; but he would be as graceful as she was. She had divined him; but she had spared him. The Major was inspired.

'You have at least spoken to the point,' he said. 'You leave no room for doubt or for hope. With the little light I have, I can't say I understand your feelings, but I yield to them religiously. I believe so thoroughly that you suffer from the thought of what you ask of me, that I will not increase your suffering by assuring you of my own. I care for nothing but your happiness. You have lost it, and I give you mine to replace it. And although it's a simple thing to say,' he added, 'I must say simply that I thank you for your implicit faith in my integrity,'—and he held out his hand. As she gave him hers, Gertrude felt utterly in the wrong; and she looked into his eyes with an expression so humble, so appealing, so grateful, that, after all, his exit may be called triumphant.

When he had gone, Richard turned from the window with an enormous sense of relief. He had heard Gertrude's speech, and he knew that perfect justice had not been done; but still there was enough to be thankful for. Yet now that his duty was accomplished, he was conscious of a sudden lassitude. Mechanically he looked at Gertrude, and almost mechanically he came towards her. She, on her side, looking at him as he walked slowly down the long room, his face indistinct against the deadened light of the white-draped windows behind him, marked the expression of his figure with another pang. 'He has rescued me,' she said to herself; 'but his passion has perished in the tumult. Richard,' she said aloud, uttering the first words of vague kindness that came into her mind, 'I forgive you.'

Richard stopped. The idea had lost its charm. 'You're very kind,' he said, wearily. 'You're far too kind. How do you know you forgive me? Wait and see.'

Gertrude looked at him as she had never looked before; but he saw nothing of it. He saw a sad, plain girl in a white dress, nervously handling her fan. He was thinking of himself. If he had been thinking of her, he would have read in her lingering, up-ward gaze, that he had won her; and if, so reading, he had opened his arms, Gertrude would have come to them. We trust the reader is not shocked. She neither hated him nor despised him, as she ought doubtless in consistency to have done. She felt that he was abundantly a man, and she loved him. Richard on his side felt humbly the same truth, and he began to respect himself. The past had closed abruptly behind him, and tardy Gertrude had been shut in. The future was dimly shaping itself without her image. So he did not open his arms.

'Good-bye,' he said, holding out his hand. 'I may not see you again for a long time.'

Gertrude felt as if the world were deserting her. 'Are you going away?' she asked, tremulously.

'I mean to sell out and pay my debts, and go to the war.'

She gave him her hand, and he silently shook it. There was no contending with the war, and she gave him up.

With their separation our story properly ends, and to say more would be to begin a new story. It is perhaps our duty, however, expressly to add, that Major Luttrel, in obedience to a logic of his own, abstained from revenge; and that, if time has not avenged him, it has at least rewarded him. General Luttrel, who lost an arm before the war was over, recently married Miss Van Winkel of Philadelphia, and seventy thousand a year. Richard engaged in the defence of his country, on a captain's commission, obtained with some difficulty. He saw a great deal of fighting, but he has no scars to show. The return of peace found him in his native place, without a home, and without resources. One of his first acts was to call dutifully and respectfully upon Miss Whittaker, whose circle of acquaintance had apparently become very much enlarged, and now included a vast number of gentlemen. Gertrude's manner was kindness itself, but a more studied kindness than before. She had lost much of her youth and her simplicity. Richard wondered whether she had pledged herself to spinsterhood, but of course he didn't ask her. She inquired very particularly into his material prospects and intentions, and offered most urgently to lend him money, which he declined to borrow. When he left her, he took a long walk through her place and beside the river, and, wandering back to the days when he had yearned for her love, assured himself that no woman would ever again be to him what she had been. During his stay in this neighbourhood he found himself impelled to a species of submission to one of the old agricultural magnates whom he had insulted in his unregenerate days, and through whom he was glad to obtain some momentary employment. But his present position is very distasteful to him, and he is eager to try his fortunes in the West. As yet, however, he has lacked even the means to get as far as St. Louis. He drinks no more than is good for him. To speak of Gertrude's impressions of Richard would lead us quite too far. Shortly after his return she broke up her household, and came to the bold resolution (bold, that is, for a woman young, unmarried, and ignorant of manners in her own country) to spend some time in Europe. At our last accounts she was living in the ancient city of Florence. Her great wealth, of which she was wont to complain that it excluded her from human sympathy, now affords her a most efficient protection. She passes among her fellow-countrymen abroad for a very independent, but a very happy woman; although, as she is by this time twenty-seven years of age, a little romance is occasionally invoked to account for her continued celibacy.

The Story of a Masterpiece

IN TWO PARTS

[First appeared in two instalments in the *Galaxy*, vol. v (January 1868), pp. 5-21; vol. v (February 1868), pp. 133-43. The serial text carried one illustration by Gaston Fay. Not reprinted during James's lifetime.]

PART I

NO LONGER AGO THAN LAST SUMMER, DURING A SIX weeks' stay at Newport, John Lennox became engaged to Miss Marian Everett of New York. Mr. Lennox was a widower, of large estate, and without children. He was thirty-five years old, of a sufficiently distinguished appearance, of excellent manners, of an unusual share of sound information, of irreproachable habits and of a temper which was understood to have suffered a trying and salutary probation during the short term of his wedded life. Miss Everett was, therefore, all things considered, believed to be making a very good match and to be having by no means the worst of the bargain.

And yet Miss Everett, too, was a very marriageable young lady —the pretty Miss Everett, as she was called, to distinguish her from certain plain cousins, with whom, owing to her having no mother and no sisters, she was constrained, for decency's sake, to spend a great deal of her time—rather to her own satisfaction, it may be conjectured, than to that of these excellent young women.

Marian Everett was penniless, indeed; but she was richly endowed with all the gifts which make a woman charming. She was, without dispute, the most charming girl in the circle in which she lived and moved. Even certain of her elders, women of a larger experience, of a heavier calibre, as it were, and, thanks to their being married ladies, of greater freedom of action, were practically not so charming as she. And yet, in her emulation of the social graces of these, her more fully licensed sisters, Miss Everett was quite guiltless of any aberration from the strict line of maidenly dignity. She professed an almost religious devotion to good taste, and she looked with horror upon the boisterous graces of many of her companions. Beside being the most entertaining girl in New York, she was, therefore, also the most irreproachable. Her beauty was, perhaps,

contestable, but it was certainly uncontested. She was the least bit below the middle height, and her person was marked by a great fullness and roundness of outline; and yet, in spite of this comely ponderosity, her movements were perfectly light and elastic. In complexion, she was a genuine blonde—a warm blonde; with a midsummer bloom upon her cheek, and the light of a midsummer sun wrought into her auburn hair. Her features were not cast upon a classical model, but their expression was in the highest degree pleasing. Her forehead was low and broad, her nose small, and her mouth—well, by the envious her mouth was called *enormous*. It is certain that it had an immense capacity for smiles, and that when she opened it to sing (which she did with infinite sweetness) it emitted a copious flood of sound. Her face was, perhaps, a trifle too circular, and her shoulders a trifle too high; but, as I say, the general effect left nothing to be desired. I might point out a dozen discords in the character of her face and figure, and yet utterly fail to invalidate the impression they produced. There is something essentially uncivil, and, indeed, unphilosophical, in the attempt to verify or to disprove a woman's beauty in detail, and a man gets no more than he deserves when he finds that, in strictness, the aggregation of the different features fails to make up the total. Stand off, gentlemen, and let *her* make the addition. Beside her beauty, Miss Everett shone by her good nature and her lively perceptions. She neither made harsh speeches nor resented them; and, on the other hand, she keenly enjoyed intellectual cleverness, and even cultivated it. Her great merit was that she made no claims or pretensions. Just as there was nothing artificial in her beauty, so there was nothing pedantic in her acuteness and nothing sentimental in her amiability. The one was all freshness and the others all *bonhommie*.

John Lennox saw her, then loved her and offered her his hand. In accepting it Miss Everett acquired, in the world's eye, the one advantage which she lacked—a complete stability and regularity of position. Her friends took no small satisfaction in contrasting her brilliant and comfortable future with her somewhat precarious past. Lennox, nevertheless, was congratulated on the right hand and on the left; but none too often for his faith. That of Miss Everett was not put to so severe a test, although she was frequently reminded by acquaintances of a moralizing turn that she had reason to be very thankful for Mr. Lennox's choice. To these assurances Marian listened with a look of patient humility, which was extremely becoming. It was as if for *his* sake she could consent even to be bored.

Within a fortnight after their engagement had been made known, both parties returned to New York. Lennox lived in a house of his own, which he now busied himself with repairing and refurnishing; for the wedding had been fixed for the end of October. Miss Everett lived in lodgings with her father, a decayed old gentleman, who rubbed his idle hands from morning till night over the prospect of his daughter's marriage.

John Lennox, habitually a man of numerous resources, fond of reading, fond of music, fond of society and not averse to politics, passed the first weeks of the Autumn in a restless, fidgetty manner. When a man approaches middle age he finds it difficult to wear gracefully the distinction of being engaged. He finds it difficult to discharge with becoming alacrity the various *petits soins* incidental to the position. There was a certain pathetic gravity, to those who knew him well, in Lennox's attentions. One-third of his time he spent in foraging in Broadway, whence he returned half-a-dozen times a week, laden with trinkets and gimcracks, which he always finished by thinking it puerile and brutal to offer his mistress. Another third he passed in Mr. Everett's drawing-room, during which period Marian was denied to visitors. The rest of the time he spent, as he told a friend, God knows how. This was stronger language than his friend expected to hear, for Lennox was neither a man of precipitate utterance, nor, in his friend's belief, of a strongly passionate nature. But it was evident that he was very much in love; or at least very much off his balance.

'When I'm with her it's all very well,' he pursued, 'but when I'm away from her I feel as if I were thrust out of the ranks of the living.'

'Well, you must be patient,' said his friend; 'you're destined to live hard, yet.'

Lennox was silent, and his face remained rather more sombre than the other liked to see it.

'I hope there's no particular difficulty,' the latter resumed; hoping to induce him to relieve himself of whatever weighed upon his consciousness.

'I'm afraid sometimes I—afraid sometimes she doesn't really love me.'

'Well, a little doubt does no harm. It's better than to be too sure of it, and to sink into fatuity. Only be sure you love her.'

'Yes,' said Lennox, solemnly, 'that's the great point.'

One morning, unable to fix his attention on books and papers, he bethought himself of an expedient for passing an hour.

He had made, at Newport, the acquaintance of a young artist named Gilbert, for whose talent and conversation he had conceived a strong relish. The painter, on leaving Newport, was to go to the

Adirondacks, and to be back in New York on the first of October, after which time he begged his friend to come and see him.

It occurred to Lennox on the morning I speak of that Gilbert must already have returned to town, and would be looking for his visit. So he forthwith repaired to his studio.

Gilbert's card was on the door, but, on entering the room, Lennox found it occupied by a stranger—a young man in painter's garb, at work before a large panel. He learned from this gentleman that he was a temporary sharer of Mr. Gilbert's studio, and that the latter had stepped out for a few moments. Lennox accordingly prepared to await his return. He entered into conversation with the young man, and, finding him very intelligent, as well as, apparently, a great friend of Gilbert, he looked at him with some interest. He was of something less than thirty, tall and robust, with a strong, joyous, sensitive face, and a thick auburn beard. Lennox was struck with his face, which seemed both to express a great deal of human sagacity and to indicate the essential temperament of a painter.

'A man with that face,' he said to himself, 'does work at least worth looking at.'

He accordingly asked his companion if he might come and look at his picture. The latter readily assented, and Lennox placed himself before the canvas.

It bore a representation of a half-length female figure, in a costume and with an expression so ambiguous that Lennox remained uncertain whether it was a portrait or a work of fancy: a fair-haired young woman, clad in a rich mediæval dress, and looking like a countess of the Renaissance. Her figure was relieved against a sombre tapestry, her arms loosely folded, her head erect and her eyes on the spectator, toward whom she seemed to move—'*Dans un flôt de velours traînant ses petits pieds.*'

As Lennox inspected her face it seemed to reveal a hidden likeness to a face he well knew—the face of Marian Everett. He was of course anxious to know whether the likeness was accidental or designed.

'I take this to be a portrait,' he said to the artist, 'a portrait "in character".'

'No,' said the latter, 'it's a mere composition: a little from here and a little from there. The picture has been hanging about me for the last two or three years, as a sort of receptacle of waste ideas. It has been the victim of innumerable theories and experiments. But it seems to have survived them all. I suppose it possesses a certain amount of vitality.'

'Do you call it anything?'

'I called it originally after something I'd read—Browning's poem, "My Last Duchess." Do you know it?'

'Perfectly.'

'I am ignorant of whether it's an attempt to embody the poet's impression of a portrait actually existing. But why should I care? This is simply an attempt to embody my own private impression of the poem, which has always had a strong hold on my fancy. I don't know whether it agrees with your own impression and that of most readers. But I don't insist upon the name. The possessor of the picture is free to baptize it afresh.'

The longer Lennox looked at the picture the more he liked it, and the deeper seemed to be the correspondence between the lady's expression and that with which he had invested the heroine of Browning's lines. The less accidental, too, seemed that element which Marian's face and the face on the canvas possessed in common. He thought of the great poet's noble lyric and of its exquisite significance, and of the physiognomy of the woman he loved having been chosen at the fittest exponent of that significance.

He turned away his head; his eyes filled with tears. 'If I were possessor of the picture,' he said, finally, answering the artist's last words, 'I should feel tempted to call it by the name of a person of whom it very much reminds me.'

'Ah?' said Baxter; and then, after a pause—'a person in New York?'

It had happened, a week before, that, at her lover's request, Miss Everett had gone in his company to a photographer's and had been photographed in a dozen different attitudes. The proofs of these photographs had been sent home for Marian to choose from. She had made a choice of half a dozen—or rather Lennox had made it —and the latter had put them in his pocket, with the intention of stopping at the establishment and giving his orders. He now took out his pocket-book and showed the painter one of the cards.

'I find a great resemblance,' said he, 'between your Duchess and that young lady.'

The artist looked at the photograph. 'If I am not mistaken,' he said, after a pause, 'the young lady is Miss Everett.'

Lennox nodded assent.

His companion remained silent for a few moments, examining the photograph with considerable interest; but, as Lennox observed, without comparing it with his picture.

'My Duchess very probably bears a certain resemblance to Miss Everett, but a not exactly intentional one,' he said, at last. 'The picture was begun before I ever saw Miss Everett. Miss Everett, as you see—or as you know—has a very charming face, and, during the few weeks in which I saw her, I continued to work upon it. You know how a painter works—how artists of all kinds work: they claim their property wherever they find it. What I found to my purpose in Miss Everett's appearance I didn't hesitate to adopt; especially as I had been feeling about in the dark for a type of countenance which her face effectually realized. The Duchess was an Italian, I take it; and I had made up my mind that she was to be a blonde. Now, there is a decidedly southern depth and warmth of tone in Miss Everett's complexion, as well as that breadth and thickness of feature which is common in Italian women. You see the resemblance is much more a matter of type than of expression. Nevertheless, I'm sorry if the copy betrays the original.'

'I doubt,' said Lennox, 'whether it would betray it to any other perception than mine. I have the honour,' he added, after a pause, 'to be engaged to Miss Everett. You will, therefore, excuse me if I ask whether you mean to sell her picture?'

'It's already sold—to a lady,' rejoined the artist, with a smile; 'a maiden lady, who is a great admirer of Browning.'

At this moment Gilbert returned. The two friends exchanged greetings, and their companion withdrew to a neighbouring studio. After they had talked a while of what had happened to each since they parted, Lennox spoke of the painter of the Duchess and of his remarkable talent, expressing surprise that he shouldn't have heard of him before, and that Gilbert should never have spoken of him.

'His name is Baxter—Stephen Baxter,' said Gilbert, 'and until his return from Europe, a fortnight ago, I knew little more about him than you. He's a case of improvement. I met him in Paris in '62; at that time he was doing absolutely nothing. He has learned what you see in the interval. On arriving in New York he found it impossible to get a studio big enough to hold him. As, with my little sketches, I need only occupy one corner of mine, I offered him the use of the other three, until he should be able to bestow himself to his satisfaction. When he began to unpack his canvases I found I had been entertaining an angel unawares.'

Gilbert then proceeded to uncover, for Lennox's inspection, several of Baxter's portraits, both of men and women. Each of these works confirmed Lennox's impression of the painter's power. He returned to the picture on the easel. Marian Everett reappeared at his silent call, and looked out of the eyes with a most penetrating tenderness and melancholy.

'He may say what he pleases,' thought Lennox, 'the resemblance *is*, in some degree, also a matter of expression. Gilbert,' he added, wishing to measure the force of the likeness, 'whom does it remind you of?'

'I know,' said Gilbert, 'of whom it reminds *you*.'

'And do you see it yourself?'

'They are both handsome, and both have auburn hair. That's all I can see.'

Lennox was somewhat relieved. It was not without a feeling of discomfort—a feeling by no means inconsistent with his first moment of pride and satisfaction—that he thought of Marian's peculiar and individual charms having been subjected to the keen appreciation of another than himself. He was glad to be able to conclude that the painter had merely been struck with what was most superficial in her appearance, and that his own imagination supplied the rest. It occurred to him, as he walked home, that it would be a not unbecoming tribute to the young girl's loveliness on his own part, to cause her portrait to be painted by this clever young man. Their engagement had as yet been an affair of pure sentiment, and he had taken an almost fastidious care not to give himself the vulgar appearance of a mere purveyor of luxuries and pleasures. Practically, he had been as yet for his future wife a poor man—or rather a man, pure and simple, and not a millionaire. He had ridden with her, he had sent her flowers, and he had gone with her to the opera. But he had neither sent her sugar-plums, nor made bets with her, nor made her presents of jewellery. Miss Everett's female friends had remarked that he hadn't as yet given her the least little betrothal ring, either of pearls or of diamonds. Marian, however, was quite content. She was, by nature, a great artist in the *mise en scène* of emotions, and she felt instinctively that this classical moderation was but the converse presentment of an immense matrimonial abundance. In his attempt to make it impossible that his relations with Miss Everett should be tinged in any degree with the accidental condition of the fortunes of either party, Lennox had thoroughly understood his own instinct. He knew that he should some day feel a strong and irresistible impulse to offer his mistress some visible and artistic token of his affection, and that his gift would convey a greater satisfaction from being sole of its kind. It seemed to him now that his chance had come. What gift could be more delicate than the gift of an opportunity to contribute by her patience and good-will to her husband's possession of a perfect likeness of her face?'

On that same evening Lennox dined with his future father-in-law, as it was his habit to do once a week.

'Marian,' he said, in the course of the dinner, 'I saw, this morning, an old friend of yours.'

'Ah,' said Marian, 'who was that?'

'Mr. Baxter, the painter.'

Marian changed colour—ever so little; no more, indeed, than was natural to an honest surprise.

Her surprise, however, could not have been great, inasmuch as she now said that she had seen his return to America mentioned in a newspaper, and as she knew that Lennox frequented the society of artists. 'He was well, I hope,' she added, 'and prosperous.'

'Where did you know this gentleman, my dear?' asked Mr. Everett.

'I knew him in Europe two years ago—first in the Summer in Switzerland, and afterward in Paris. He is a sort of cousin of Mrs. Denbigh.' Mrs. Denbigh was a lady in whose company Marian had recently spent a year in Europe—a widow, rich, childless, an invalid, and an old friend of her mother. 'Is he always painting?'

'Apparently, and extremely well. He has two or three as good portraits there as one may reasonably expect to see. And he has, moreover, a certain picture which reminded me of you.'

'His "Last Duchess?"' asked Marian, with some curiosity. 'I should like to see it. If you think it's like me, John, you ought to buy it up.'

'I wanted to buy it, but it's sold. You know it then?'

'Yes, through Mr. Baxter himself. I saw it in its rudimentary state, when it looked like nothing that I should care to look like. I shocked Mrs. Denbigh very much by telling him I was glad it was his "last". The picture, indeed, led to our acquaintance.'

'And not *vice versa*,' said Mr. Everett, facetiously.

'How *vice versa*?' asked Marian, innocently. 'I met Mr. Baxter for the first time at a party in Rome.'

'I thought you said you met him in Switzerland,' said Lennox.

'No, in Rome. It was only two days before we left. He was introduced to me without knowing I was with Mrs. Denbigh, and indeed without knowing that she had been in the city. He was very shy of Americans. The first thing he said to me was that I looked very much like a picture he had been painting.'

'That you realized his ideal, etc.'

'Exactly, but not at all in that sentimental tone. I took him to Mrs. Denbigh; they found they were sixth cousins by marriage; he came to see us the next day, and insisted upon our going to his studio. It was a miserable place. I believe he was very poor. At least Mrs. Denbigh offered him some money, and he frankly accepted it.

She attempted to spare his sensibilities by telling him that, if he liked, he could paint her a picture in return. He said he would if he had time. Later, he came up into Switzerland, and the following Winter we met him in Paris.'

If Lennox had had any mistrust of Miss Everett's relations with the painter, the manner in which she told her little story would have effectually blighted it. He forthwith proposed that, in consideration not only of the young man's great talent, but of his actual knowledge of her face, he should be invited to paint her portrait.

Marian assented without reluctance and without alacrity, and Lennox laid his proposition before the artist. The latter requested a day or two to consider, and then replied (by note) that he would be happy to undertake the task.

Miss Everett expected that, in view of the projected renewal of their old acquaintance, Stephen Baxter would call upon her, under the auspices of her lover. He called in effect, alone, but Marian was not at home, and he failed to repeat the visit. The day for the first sitting was therefore appointed through Lennox. The artist had not as yet obtained a studio of his own, and the latter cordially offered him the momentary use of a spacious and well-lighted apartment in his house, which had been intended as a billiard room, but was not yet fitted up. Lennox expressed no wishes with regard to the portrait, being content to leave the choice of position and costume to the parties immediately interested. He found the painter perfectly well acquainted with Marian's 'points', and he had an implicit confidence in her own good taste.

Miss Everett arrived on the morning appointed, under her father's escort, Mr. Everett, who prided himself largely upon doing things in proper form, having caused himself to be introduced beforehand to the painter. Between the latter and Marian there was a brief exchange of civilities, after which they addressed themselves to business. Miss Everett professed the most cheerful deference to Baxter's wishes and fancies, at the same time that she made no secret of possessing a number of strong convictions as to what should be attempted and what should be avoided.

It was no surprise to the young man to find her convictions sound and her wishes thoroughly sympathetic. He found himself called upon to make no compromise with stubborn and unnatural prejudices, nor to sacrifice his best intentions to a short-sighted vanity.

Whether Miss Everett was vain or not need not here be declared. She had at least the wit to perceive that the interests of an enlightened sagacity would best be served by a painting which should be good from the painter's point of view, inasmuch as these are the painting's chief end. I may add, moreover, to her very great credit, that she thoroughly understood how great an artistic merit should properly attach to a picture executed at the behest of a passion, in order that it should be anything more than a mockery—a parody—of the duration of that passion; and that she knew instinctively that there is nothing so chilling to an artist's heat as the inteference of illogical self-interest, either on his own behalf or that of another.

Baxter worked firmly and rapidly, and at the end of a couple of hours he felt that he had begun his picture. Mr. Everett, as he sat by, threatened to be a bore; labouring apparently under the impression that it was his duty to beguile the session with cheap aesthetic small talk. But Marian good-humouredly took the painter's share of the dialogue, and he was not diverted from his work.

The next sitting was fixed for the morrow. Marian wore the dress which she had agreed upon with the painter, and in which, as in her position, the 'picturesque' element had been religiously suppressed. She read in Baxter's eyes that she looked supremely beautiful, and she saw that his fingers tingled to attack his subject. But she caused Lennox to be sent for, under the pretense of obtaining his adhesion to her dress. It was black, and he might object to black. He came, and she read in his kindly eyes an augmented edition of the assurance conveyed in Baxter's. He was enthusiastic for the black dress, which, in truth, seemed only to confirm and enrich, like a grave maternal protest, the young girl's look of undiminished youth.

'I expect you,' he said to Baxter, 'to make a masterpiece.'

'Never fear,' said the painter, tapping his forehead. 'It's made.'

On this second occasion, Mr. Everett, exhausted by the intellectual strain of the preceding day, and encouraged by his luxurious chair, sank into a tranquil sleep. His companions remained for some time, listening to his regular breathing; Marian with her eyes patiently fixed on the opposite wall, and the young man with his glance mechanically travelling between his figure and the canvas. At last he fell back several paces to survey his work. Marian moved her eyes, and they met his own.

'Well, Miss Everett,' said the painter, in accents which might have been tremulous if he had not exerted a strong effort to make them firm.

'Well, Mr. Baxter,' said the young girl.

And the two exchanged a long, firm glance, which at last ended in a smile—a smile which belonged decidedly to the family of the famous laugh of the two angels behind the altar in the temple.

'Well, Miss Everett,' said Baxter, going back to his work; 'such is life!'

'So it appears,' rejoined Marian. And then, after a pause of some moments: 'Why didn't you come and see me?' she added.

'I came and you weren't at home.'

'Why didn't you come again?'

'What was the use, Miss Everett?'

'It would simply have been more decent. We might have become reconciled.'

'We seem to have done that as it is.'

'I mean "in form".'

'That would have been absurd. Don't you see how true an instinct I had? What could have been easier than our meeting? I assure you that I should have found any talk about the past, and mutual assurances or apologies extremely disagreeable.'

Miss Everett raised her eyes from the floor and fixed them on her companion with a deep, half-reproachful glance, 'Is the past, then,' she asked, 'so utterly disagreeable?'

Baxter stared, half amazed. 'Good heavens!' he cried, 'of course it is.'

Miss Everett dropped her eyes and remained silent.

I may as well take advantage of the moment, rapidly to make plain to the reader the events to which the above conversation refers.

Miss Everett had found it expedient, all things considered, not to tell her intended husband the whole story of her acquaintance with Stephen Baxter; and when I have repaired her omissions, the reader will probably justify her discretion.

She had, as she said, met this young man for the first time at Rome, and there in the course of two interviews had made a deep impression upon his heart. He had felt that he would give a great deal to meet Miss Everett again. Their reunion in Switzerland was therefore not entirely fortuitous; and it had been the more easy for Baxter to make it possible, for the reason that he was able to claim a kind of roundabout relationship with Mrs. Denbigh, Marian's companion. With this lady's permission he had attached himself to their party. He had made their route of travel his own, he had stopped when they stopped and been prodigal of attentions and civilities. Before a week was over, Mrs. Denbigh, who was the soul of confiding good nature, exulted in the discovery of an invaluable kinsman. Thanks not only to her naturally unexacting disposition, but to the apathetic and inactive habits induced by constant physical suffering, she proved a very insignificant third in her companions' spending of the hours. How delightfully these hours were spent, it requires no great effort to imagine. A suit conducted in the midst of the most romantic scenery in Europe is already half won. Marian's social graces were largely enhanced by the satisfaction which her innate intelligence of natural beauty enabled her to take in the magnificent scenery of the Alps. She had never appeared to such advantage; she had never known such perfect freedom and frankness and gaiety. For the first time in her life she had made a captive without suspecting it. She had surrendered her heart to the mountains and the lakes, the eternal snows and the pastoral valleys, and Baxter, standing by, had intercepted it. He felt his long-projected Swiss tour vastly magnified and beautiful by Miss Everett's part in it—by the constant feminine sympathy which gushed within earshot, with the coolness and clearness of a mountain spring. Oh! if only it too had not been fed by the eternal snows! And then her beauty—her indefatigable beauty—was a continual enchantment. Miss Everett looked so thoroughly in her place in a drawing-room that it was almost logical to suppose that she looked well nowhere else. But in fact, as Baxter learned, she looked quite well enough in the character of what ladies call a 'fright'—that is, sunburnt, travel-stained, overheated, exilarated and hungry—to elude all invidious comparisons.

At the end of three weeks, one morning as they stood together on the edge of a falling torrent, high above the green concavities of the hills, Baxter felt himself irresistibly urged to make a declaration. The thunderous noise of the cataract covered all vocal utterance; so, taking out his sketch-book, he wrote three short words on a blank leaf. He handed her the book. She read his message with a beautiful change of colour and a single rapid glance at his face. She then tore out the leaf.

'Don't tear it up!' cried the young man.

She understood him by the movement of his lips and shook her head with a smile. But she stooped, picked up a little stone, and wrapped it in the bit of paper, prepared to toss it into the torrent.

Baxter, uncertain, put out his hand to take it from her. She passed it into the other hand and gave him the one he attempted to take.

She threw away the paper, but she let him keep her hand.

Baxter had still a week at his disposal, and Marian made it a very happy one. Mrs. Denbigh was tired; they had come to a halt, and there was no interruption to their being together. They talked a great deal of the long future, which, on getting beyond the sound of the cataract, they had expeditiously agreed to pursue in common. It was their misfortune both to be poor. They determined, in view of this circumstance, to say nothing of their engagement until Baxter, by dint of hard work, should have at least quadrupled his income. This was cruel, but it was imperative, and Marian made no complaint. Her residence in Europe had enlarged her conception of the material needs of a pretty woman, and it was quite natural that she should not, close upon the heels of this experience, desire to rush into marriage with a poor artist. At the end of some days Baxter started for Germany and Holland, portions of which he wished to visit for purposes of study. Mrs. Denbigh and her young friend repaired to Paris for the Winter. Here, in the middle of February, they were rejoined by Baxter, who had achieved his German tour. He had received, while absent, five little letters from Marian, full of affection. The number was small, but the young man detected in the very temperance of his mistress a certain delicious flavour of implicit constancy. She received him with all the frankness and sweetness that he had a right to expect, and listened with great interest to his account of the improvement in his prospects. He had sold three of his Italian pictures and had made an invaluable collection of sketches. He was on the high road to wealth and fame, and there was no reason their engagement should not be announced. But to this latter proposition Marian demurred —demurred so strongly, and yet on grounds so arbitrary, that a somewhat painful scene ensued. Stephen left her, irritated and per- plexed. The next day, when he called, she was unwell and unable to see him; and the next—and the next. On the evening of the day that he had made his third fruitless call at Mrs. Denbigh's, he over- heard Marian's name mentioned at a large party. The interlocutors were two elderly women. On giving his attention to their talk, which they were taking no pains to keep private, he found that his mistress was under accusal of having trifled with the affections of an un- happy young man, the only son of one of the ladies. There was apparently no lack of evidence or of facts which might be construed as evidence. Baxter went home, *la mort dans l'âme*, and on the following day called again on Mrs. Denbigh. Marian was still in her room, but the former lady received him. Stephen was in great trouble, but his mind was lucid, and he addressed himself to the task of interrogating his hostess. Mrs. Denbigh, with her habitual indolence, had remained unsuspicious of the terms on which the young people stood.

'I'm sorry to say,' Baxter began, 'that I heard Miss Everett accused last evening of very sad conduct.'

'Ah, for heaven's sake, Stephen,' returned his kinswoman, 'don't go back to that. I've done nothing all Winter but defend and palliate her conduct. It's hard work. Don't make me do it for you. You know her as well as I do. She was indiscreet, but I know she is penitent, and for that matter she's well out of it. He was by no means a desirable young man.'

'The lady whom I heard talking about the matter,' said Stephen, 'spoke of him in the highest terms. To be sure, as it turned out, she was his mother.'

'His mother? You're mistaken. His mother died ten years ago.'

Baxter folded his arms with a feeling that he needed to sit firm. '*Allons*,' said he, 'of whom do you speak?'

'Of young Mr. King.'

'Good heavens,' cried Stephen. 'So there are two of them?'

'Pray, of whom do *you* speak?'

'Of a certain Mr. Young. The mother is a handsome old woman with white curls.'

'You don't mean to say there has been anything between Marian and Frederic Young?'

'*Voilà!* I only repeat what I hear. It seems to me, my dear Mrs. Denbigh, that you ought to know.'

Mrs. Denbigh shook her head with a melancholy movement. 'I'm sure I don't,' she said. 'I give it up. I don't pretend to judge. The manners of young people to each other are very different from what they were in my day. One doesn't know whether they mean nothing or everything.'

'You know, at least, whether Mr. Young has been in your drawing-room?'

'Oh, yes, frequently. I'm very sorry that Marian is talked about. It's very unpleasant for me. But what can a sick woman do?'

'Well,' said Stephen, 'so much for Mr. Young. And now for Mr. King.'

'Mr. King is gone home. It's a pity he ever came away.'

'In what sense?'

'Oh, he's a silly fellow. He doesn't understand young girls.'

'Upon my word,' said Stephen, 'with expression,' as the music sheets say, 'he might be very wise and not do that.'

'Not but that Marian was injudicious. She meant only to be amiable, but she went too far. She became adorable. The first thing she knew he was holding her to an account.'

'Is he good-looking?'

'Well enough.'

'And rich?'

'Very rich, I believe.'

'And the other?'

'What other—Marian?'

'No, no; your friend Young?'

'Yes, he's quite handsome.'

'And rich, too?'

'Yes, I believe he's also rich.'

Baxter was silent a moment. 'And there's no doubt,' he resumed, 'that they were both far gone?'

'I can only answer for Mr. King.'

'Well, I'll answer for Mr. Young. His mother wouldn't have talked as she did unless she'd seen her son suffer. After all, then, it's perhaps not so much to Marian's discredit. Here are two handsome young millionaires, madly smitten. She refuses them both. She doesn't care for good looks and money.'

'I don't say that,' said Mrs. Denbigh, sagaciously. 'She doesn't care for those things alone. She wants talent, and all the rest of it. Now, if you were only rich, Stephen—' added the good lady, innocently.

Baxter took up his hat. 'When you wish to marry Miss Everett,' he said, 'you must take good care not to say too much about Mr. King and Mr. Young.'

Two days after this interview, he had a conversation with the young girl in person. The reader may like him the less for his easily-shaken confidence, but it is a fact that he had been unable to make light of these lightly-made revelations. For him his love had been a passion; for *her*, he was compelled to believe, it had been a vulgar pastime. He was a man of violent temper; he went straight to the point.

'Marian,' he said, 'you've been deceiving me.'

Marian knew very well what he meant; she knew very well that she had grown weary of her engagement and that, however little of a fault her conduct had been to Messrs. Young and King, it had been an act of grave disloyalty to Baxter. She felt that the blow was struck and that their engagement was clean broken. She knew that Stephen would be satisfied with no half-excuses or half-denials; and she had none others to give. A hundred such would not make a perfect confession. Making no attempt, therefore, to save her 'prospects', for which she had ceased to care, she merely attempted to save her dignity. Her dignity for the moment was well enough secured by her natural half-cynical coolness of temper. But this same vulgar placidity left in Stephen's memory an impression of heartlessness and shallowness, which in that particular quarter, at least, was destined to be forever fatal to her claims to real weight and worth. She denied the young man's right to call her to account and to interfere with her conduct; and she almost anticipated his proposal that they should consider their engagement at an end. She even declined the use of the simple logic of tears. Under these circumstances, of course, the interview was not of long duration.

'I regard you,' said Baxter, as he stood on the threshold, 'as the most superficial, most heartless of women.'

He immediately left Paris and went down into Spain, where he remained till the opening of the Summer. In the month of May Mrs. Denbigh and her *protégé* went to England, where the former, through her husband, possessed a number of connections, and where Marian's thoroughly un-English beauty was vastly admired. In September they sailed for America. About a year and a half, therefore, had elapsed between Baxter's separation from Miss Everett and their meeting in New York.

During this interval the young man's wounds had had time to heal. His sorrow, although violent, had been short-lived, and when he finally recovered his habitual equanimity, he was very glad to have purchased exemption at the price of a simple heart-ache. Reviewing his impressions of Miss Everett in a calmer mood, he made up his mind that she was very far from being the woman of his desire, and that she had not really been the woman of his choice. 'Thank God,' he said to himself, 'it's over. She's irreclaimably light. She's hollow, trivial, vulgar.' There had been in his addresses something hasty and feverish, something factitious and unreal in his fancied passion. Half of it had been the work of the scenery, of the weather, of mere juxtaposition, and, above all, of the young girl's picturesque beauty; to say nothing of the almost suggestive tolerance and indolence of poor Mrs. Denbigh. And finding himself very much interested in Velasquez, at Madrid, he dismissed Miss Everett from his thoughts. I do not mean to offer his judgment of Miss Everett as final; but it was at least conscientious. The ample justice, moreover, which, under the illusion of sentiment, he had rendered to her charms and graces, gave him a right, when free from that illusion, to register the estimate of the arid spaces of her nature. Miss Everett might easily have accused him of injustice and brutality; but this fact would still stand to plead in his favour, that he cared with all his strength for truth. Marian, on the contrary, was quite indifferent to it. Stephen's angry sentence on her conduct had awakened no echo in her contracted soul.

The reader has now an adequate conception of the feelings with which these two old friends found themselves face to face. It is needful to add, however, that the lapse of time had very much diminished the force of those feelings. A woman, it seems to me,

ought to desire no easier company, none less embarrassed or embarrassing, than a disenchanted lover; premising, of course, that
the process of disenchantment is thoroughly complete, and that
some time has elapsed since its completion.

Marian herself was perfectly at her ease. She had not retained
her equanimity—her philosophy, one might almost call it—during
that painful last interview, to go and lose it now. She had no ill
feeling toward her old lover. His last words had been—like all words
in Marian's estimation—a mere *façon de parler*. Miss Everett was
in so perfect a good humour during these last days of her maiden-
hood that there was nothing in the past that she could not have
forgiven.

She blushed a little at the emphasis of her companion's remark;
but she was not discountenanced. She summoned up her good
humour. 'The truth is, Mr. Baxter,' she said, 'I feel at the present
moment on perfect good terms with the world; I see everything *en
rose*; the past as well as the future.'

'I, too, am on very good terms with the world,' said Baxter, 'and
my heart is quite reconciled to what you call the past. But, nevertheless, it's very disagreeable to me to think about it.'

'Ah then,' said Miss Everett, with great sweetness, 'I'm afraid
you're not reconciled.'

Baxter laughed—so loud that Miss Everett looked about at her
father. But Mr. Everett still slept the sleep of gentility. 'I've no
doubt,' said the painter, 'that I'm far from being so good a Christian
as you. But I assure you I'm very glad to see you again.'

'You've but to say the word and we're friends,' said Marian.

'We were very foolish to have attempted to be anything else.'

' "Foolish," yes. But it was a pretty folly.'

'Ah no, Miss Everett. I'm an artist, and I claim a right of property
in the word "pretty". You mustn't stick it in there. Nothing could
be pretty which had such an ugly termination. It was all false.'

'Well—as you will. What have you been doing since we parted?'

'Travelling and working. I've made great progress in my trade.
Shortly before I came home I became engaged.'

'Engaged?—*à la bonne heure*. Is she good?—is she pretty?'

'She's not nearly so pretty as you.'

'In other words, she's infinitely more good. I'm sure I hope she is.
But why did you leave her behind you?'

'She's with a sister, a sad invalid, who is drinking mineral waters
on the Rhine. They wished to remain there to the cold weather.
They're to be home in a couple of weeks, and we are straightway
to be married.'

'I congratulate you, with all my heart,' said Marian.

'Allow me to do as much, sir,' said Mr. Everett, waking up; which he did by instinct whenever the conversation took a ceremonious turn.

Miss Everett gave her companion but three more sittings, a large part of his work being executed with the assistance of photographs. At these interviews also, Mr. Everett was present, and still delicately sensitive to the soporific influences of his position. But both parties had the good taste to abstain from further references to their old relations, and to confine their talk to less personal themes.

PART II

One afternoon, when the picture was nearly finished, John Lennox went into the empty painting-room to ascertain the degree of its progress. Both Baxter and Marian had expressed a wish that he should not see it in its early stages, and this, accordingly, was his first view. Half an hour after he had entered the room, Baxter came in, unannounced, and found him sitting before the canvas, deep in thought. Baxter had been furnished with a house-key, so that he might have immediate and easy access to his work whenever the humour came upon him.

'I was passing,' he said, 'and I couldn't resist the impulse to come in and correct an error which I made this morning, now that a sense of its enormity is fresh in my mind.' He sat down to work, and the other stood watching him.

'Well,' said the painter, finally, 'how does it satisfy you?'

'Not altogether.'

'Pray develop your objections. It's in your power materially to assist me.'

'I hardly know how to formulate my objections. Let me, at all events, in the first place, say that I admire your work immensely. I'm sure it's the best picture you've painted.'

'I honestly believe it is. Some parts of it,' said Baxter, frankly, 'are excellent.'

'It's obvious. But either those very parts or others are singularly disagreeable. That word isn't criticism, I know; but I pay you for the right to be arbitrary. They are too hard, too strong, of too frank a reality. In a word, your picture frightens me, and if I were Marian I should feel as if you'd done me a certain violence.'

'I'm sorry for what's disagreeable; but I meant it all to be real. I go in for reality; you must have seen that.'

'I approve you; I can't too much admire the broad and firm

methods you've taken for reaching this same reality. But you can be real without being brutal—without attempting, as one may say, to be *actual*.'

'I deny that I'm brutal. I'm afraid, Mr. Lennox, I haven't taken quite the right road to please you. I've taken the picture too much *au sérieux*. I've striven too much for completeness. But if it doesn't please you it will please others.'

'I've no doubt of it. But that isn't the question. The picture is good enough to be a thousand times better.'

'That the picture leaves room for infinite improvement, I, of course, don't deny; and, in several particulars, I see my way to make it better. But, substantially, the portrait is there. I'll tell you what you miss. My work isn't "classical"; in fine, I'm not a man of genius.'

'No; I rather suspect you are. But, as you say, your work isn't classical. I adhere to my term *brutal*. Shall I tell you? It's too much of a study. You've given poor Miss Everett the look of a professional model.'

'If that's the case I've done very wrong. There never was an easier, a less conscious sitter. It's delightful to look at her.'

'Confound it, you've given all her ease, too. Well, I don't know what's the matter. I give up.'

'I think,' said Baxter, 'you had better hold your verdict in abeyance until the picture is finished. The classical element is there, I'm sure; but I've not brought it out. Wait a few days, and it will rise to the surface.'

Lennox left the artist alone; and the latter took up his brushes and painted hard till nightfall. He laid them down only when it was too dark to see. As he was going out, Lennox met him in the hall.

'*Exegi monumentum*,' said Baxter; 'it's finished. Go and look at your ease. I'll come to-morrow and hear your impressions.'

The master of the house, when the other had gone, lit half a dozen lights and returned to the study of the picture. It had grown prodigiously under the painter's recent handling, and whether it was that, as Baxter had said, the classical element had disengaged itself, or that Lennox was in a more sympathetic mood, it now impressed him as an original and powerful work, a genuine portrait, the deliberate image of a human face and figure. It was Marian, in very truth, and Marian most patiently measured and observed. Her beauty was there, her sweetness, and her young loveliness and her aerial grace, imprisoned forever, made inviolable and perpetual. Nothing could be more simple than the conception and composition of the picture. The figure sat peacefully, looking slightly to the right, with the head erect and the hands—the virginal hands, without rings or bracelets—lying idle on its knees. The blonde hair was gathered into a little knot of braids on the top of the head (in the fashion of the moment), and left free the almost childish contour of the ears and cheeks. The eyes were full of colour, contentment and light; the lips were faintly parted. Of colour in the picture, there was, in strictness, very little; but the dark draperies told of reflected sunshine, and the flesh-spaces of human blushes and pallors, of throbbing life and health. The work was strong and simple, the figure was thoroughly void of affectation and stiffness, and yet supremely elegant.

'That's what it is to be an artist,' thought Lennox. 'All this has been done in the past two hours.'

It was his Marian, assuredly, with all that had charmed him—with all that still charmed him when he saw her: her appealing confidence, her exquisite lightness, her feminine enchantments. And yet, as he looked, an expression of pain came into his eyes, and lingered there, and grew into a mortal heaviness.

Lennox had been as truly a lover as a man may be; but he loved with the discretion of fifteen years' experience of human affairs. He had a penetrating glance, and he liked to use it. Many a time when Marian, with eloquent lips and eyes, had poured out the treasures of her nature into his bosom, and he had taken them in his hands and covered them with kisses and passionate vows; he had dropped them all with a sudden shudder and cried out in silence, 'But ah! where is the heart?' One day he had said to her (irrelevantly enough, doubtless), 'Marian, where *is* your heart?'

'*Where*—what do you mean?' Miss Everett had said.

'I think of you from morning till night. I put you together and take you apart, as people do in that game where they make words out of a parcel of given letters. But there's always one letter wanting. I can't put my hand on your heart.'

'My heart, John,' said Marian, ingeniously, 'is the whole word. My heart's everywhere.'

This may have been true enough. Miss Everett had distributed her heart impartially throughout her whole organism, so that, as a natural consequence, its native seat was somewhat scantily occupied. As Lennox sat and looked at Baxter's consummate handiwork, the same question rose again to his lips; and if Marian's portrait suggested it, Marian's portrait failed to answer it. It took Marian to do that. It seemed to Lennox that some strangely potent agency had won from his mistress the confession of her inmost soul, and had written it there upon the canvas in firm yet passionate lines.

Marian's person was lightness—her charm was lightness; could it be that her soul was levity too? Was she a creature without faith and without conscience? What else was the meaning of that horrible blankness and deadness that quenched the light in her eyes and stole away the smile from her lips? These things were the less to be eluded because in so many respects the painter had been profoundly just. He had been as loyal and sympathetic as he had been intelligent. Not a point in the young girl's appearance had been slighted; not a feature but had been forcibly and delicately rendered. Had Baxter been a man of marvellous insight—an unparalleled observer; or had he been a mere patient and unflinching painter, building infinitely better than he knew? Would not a mere painter have been content to paint Miss Everett in the strong, rich, objective manner of which the work was so good an example, and to do nothing more? For it was evident that Baxter had done more. He had painted with something more than knowledge—with imagination, with feeling. He had almost *composed*; and his composition had embraced the truth. Lennox was unable to satisfy his doubts. He would have been glad to believe that there was no imagination in the picture but what his own mind supplied; and that the unsubstantial sweetness on the eyes and lips of the image was but the smile of youth and innocence. He was in a muddle—he was absurdly suspicious and capricious; he put out the lights and left the portrait in kindly darkness. Then, half as a reparation to his mistress, and half as a satisfaction to himself, he went up to spent an hour with Marian. She, at least, as he found, had no scruples. She thought the portrait altogether a success, and she was very willing to be handed down in that form to posterity. Nevertheless, when Lennox came in, he went back into the painting-room to take another glance. This time he lit but a single light. Faugh! it was worse than with a dozen. He hastily turned out the gas.

Baxter came the next day, as he had promised. Meanwhile poor Lennox had had twelve hours of uninterrupted reflection, and the expression of distress in his eyes had acquired an intensity which, the painter saw, proved it to be of far other import than a mere tribute to his power.

'Can the man be jealous?' thought Baxter. Stephen had been so innocent of any other design than that of painting a good portrait, that his conscience failed to reveal to him the source of his companion's trouble. Nevertheless he began to pity him. He had felt tempted, indeed, to pity him from the first. He had liked him and esteemed him; he had taken him for a man of sense and of feeling, and he had thought it a matter of regret that such a man—a creature of strong spiritual needs—should link his destiny with that of Marian Everett. But he had very soon made up his mind that Lennox knew very well what he was about, and that he needed no enlightenment. He was marrying with his eyes open, and had weighed the risks against the profits. Everyone had his particulai taste, and at thirty-five years of age John Lennox had no need to be told that Miss Everett was not quite all that she might be. Baxter had thus taken for granted that his friend had designedly selected as his second wife a mere pretty woman—a woman with a genius for receiving company, and who would make a picturesque use of his money. He knew nothing of the serious character of the poor man's passion, nor of the extent to which his happiness was bound up in what the painter would have called his delusion. His only concern had been to do his work well; and he had done it the better because of his old interest in Marian's bewitching face. It is very certain that he had actually infused into his picture that force of characterization and that depth of reality which had arrested his friend's attention; but he had done so wholly without effort and without malice. The artistic half of Baxter's nature exerted a lusty dominion over the human half—fed upon its disappointments and grew fat upon its joys and tribulations. This, indeed, is simply saying that the young man was a true artist. Deep, then, in the unfathomed recesses of his strong and sensitive nature, his genius had held communion with his heart and had transferred to canvas the burden of its disenchantment and its resignation. Since his little affair with Marian, Baxter had made the acquaintance of a young girl whom he felt that he could love and trust forever; and, sobered and strengthened by this new emotion, he had been able to resume with more distinctness the shortcomings of his earlier love. He had, therefore, painted with feeling. Miss Everett could not have expected him to do otherwise. He had done his honest best, and conviction had come in unbidden and made it better.

Lennox had begun to feel very curious about the history of his companion's acquaintance with his destined bride; but he was far from feeling jealous. Somehow he felt that he could never again be jealous. But in ascertaining the terms of their former intercourse, it was of importance that he should not allow the young man to suspect that he discovered in the portrait any radical defect.

'Your old acquaintance with Miss Everett,' he said, frankly, 'has evidently been of great use to you.'

'I suppose it has,' said Baxter. 'Indeed, as soon as I began to paint, I found her face coming back to me like a half-remembered tune. She was wonderfully pretty at that time.'

'She was two years younger.'

'Yes, and I was two years younger. Decidedly, you are right. I *have* made use of my old impressions.'

Baxter was willing to confess to so much; but he was resolved not to betray anything that Marian had herself kept secret. He was not surprised that she had not told her lover of her former engagement; he expected as much. But he would have held it inexcusable to attempt to repair her omission.

Lennox's faculties were acutely sharpened by pain and suspicion, and he could not help detecting in his companion's eyes an intention of reticence. He resolved to baffle it.

'I am curious to know,' he said, 'whether you were ever in love with Miss Everett?'

'I have no hesitation in saying Yes,' rejoined Baxter; fancying that a general confession would help him more than a particular denial. 'I'm one of a thousand, I fancy. Or one, perhaps, of only a hundred. For you see I've got over it. I'm engaged to be married.'

Lennox's countenance brightened. 'That's it,' said he. 'Now I know what I didn't like in your picture—the point of view. I'm not jealous,' he added. 'I should like the picture better if I were. You evidently care nothing for the poor girl. You have got over your love rather too well. You loved her, she was indifferent to you, and now you take your revenge.' Distracted with grief, Lennox was taking refuge in irrational anger.

Baxter was puzzled. 'You'll admit,' said he, with a smile, 'that it's a very handsome revenge.' And all his professional self-esteem rose to his assistance. 'I've painted for Miss Everett the best portrait that has yet been painted in America. She herself is quite satisfied.'

'Ah!' said Lennox, with magnificent dissimulation; 'Marian is generous.'

'Come, then,' said Baxter; 'what do you complain of? You accuse me of scandalous conduct, and I'm bound to hold you to an account.' Baxter's own temper was rising, and with it his sense of his picture's merits. 'How have I perverted Miss Everett's expression? How have I misrepresented her? What does the portrait lack? Is it ill-drawn? Is it vulgar? Is it ambiguous? Is it immodest?' Baxter's patience gave out as he recited these various charges. 'Fiddle-sticks!' he cried; 'you know as well as I do that the picture is excellent.'

'I don't pretend to deny it. Only I wonder that Marian was willing to come to you.'

It is very much to Baxter's credit that he still adhered to his resolution not to betray the young girl, and that rather than do so he was willing to let Lennox suppose that he had been a rejected adorer.

'Ah, as you say,' he exclaimed, 'Miss Everett is so generous!'

Lennox was foolish enough to take this as an admission. 'When I say, Mr. Baxter,' he said, 'that you have taken your revenge, I don't mean that you've done so wantonly or consciously. My dear fellow, how could you help it? The disappointment was proportionate to the loss and the reaction to the disappointment.'

'Yes, that's all very well; but, meanwhile, I wait in vain to learn wherein I've done wrong.'

Lennox looked from Baxter to the picture, and from the picture back to Baxter.

'I defy you to tell me,' said Baxter. 'I've simply kept Miss Everett as charming as she is in life.'

'Oh, damn her charms!' cried Lennox.

'If you were not the gentleman, Mr. Lennox,' continued the young man, 'which, in spite of your high temper, I believe you to be, I should believe you—'

'Well, you should believe me?'

'I should believe you simply bent on cheapening the portrait.'

Lennox made a gesture of vehement impatience. The other burst out laughing and the discussion closed. Baxter instinctively took up his brushes and approached his canvas with a vague desire to detect latent errors, while Lennox prepared to take his departure.

'Stay!' said the painter, as he was leaving the room; 'if the picture really offends you, I'll rub it out. Say the word,' and he took up a heavy brush, covered with black paint.

But Lennox shook his head with decision and went out. The next moment, however, he reappeared. 'You *may* rub it out,' he said. 'The picture is, of course, already mine.'

But now Baxter shook his head. 'Ah! now it's too late,' he answered. 'Your chance is gone.'

Lennox repaired directly to Mr. Everett's apartments. Marian was in the drawing-room with some morning callers, and her lover sat by until she had got rid of them. When they were alone together, Marian began to laugh at her visitors and to parody certain of their affectations, which she did with infinite grace and spirit. But Lennox cut her short and returned to the portrait. He had thought better of his objections of the preceding evening; he liked it.

'But I wonder, Marian,' he said, 'that you were willing to go to Mr. Baxter.'

'Why so?' asked Marian, on her guard. She saw that her lover

knew something, and she intended not to commit herself until she
knew how much he knew.

'An old lover is always dangerous.'

'An old lover?' and Marian blushed a good honest blush. But she
rapidly recovered herself. 'Pray where did you get that charming
news?'

'Oh, it slipped out,' said Lennox.

Marian hesitated a moment. Then with a smile: 'Well, I was
brave,' she said. 'I went.'

'How came it,' pursued Lennox, 'that you didn't tell me?'

'Tell you what, my dear John?'

'Why, about Baxter's little passion. Come, don't be modest.'

Modest! Marian breathed freely. 'What do you mean, my dear,
by telling your wife not to be modest? Pray don't ask me about Mr.
Baxter's passions. What do I know about them?'

'Did you know nothing of this one?'

'Ah, my dear, I know a great deal too much for my comfort. But
he's got bravely over it. He's engaged.'

'Engaged, but not quite disengaged. He's an honest fellow, but
he remembers his *penchant*. It was as much as he could do to keep
his picture from turning to the sentimental. He saw you as he
fancied you—as he wished you; and he has given you a little look
of what he imagines moral loveliness, which comes within an ace
of spoiling the picture. Baxter's imagination isn't very strong, and
this same look expresses, in point of fact, nothing but inanity.
Fortunately he's a man of extraordinary talent, and a real painter,
and he has made a good portrait in spite of himself.'

To such arguments as these was John Lennox reduced, to stifle
the evidence of his senses. But when once a lover begins to doubt,
he cannot cease at will. In spite of his earnest efforts to believe in
Marian as before, to accept her without scruple and without second
thought, he was quite unable to repress an impulse of constant mistrust and aversion. The charm was broken, and there is no mending
a charm. Lennox stood half-aloof, watching the poor girl's countenance, weighing her words, analyzing her thoughts, guessing at her
motives.

Marian's conduct under this trying ordeal was truly heroic. She
felt that some subtle change had taken place in her future husband's
feelings, a change which, although she was powerless to discover its
cause, yet obviously imperilled her prospects. Something had
snapped between them; she had lost half of her power. She was
horribly distressed, and the more so because that superior depth of
character which she had all along gladly conceded to Lennox,

might now, as she conjectured, cover some bold and portentous design. Could he meditate a direct rupture? Could it be his intention to dash from her lips the sweet, the spiced and odorous cup of being the wife of a good-natured millionaire? Marian turned a tremulous glance upon her past, and wondered if he had discovered any dark spot. Indeed, for that matter, might she not defy him to do so? She had done nothing really amiss. There was no visible blot in her history. It was faintly discoloured, indeed, by a certain vague moral dinginess; but it compared well enough with that of other girls. She had cared for nothing but pleasure; but to what else were girls brought up? On the whole, might she not feel at ease? She assured herself that she might; but she nevertheless felt that if John wished to break off his engagement, he would do it on high abstract grounds, and not because she had committed a naughtiness the more or the less. It would be simply because he had ceased to love her. It would avail her but little to assure him that she would kindly overlook this circumstance and remit the obligations of the heart. But, in spite of her hideous apprehensions, she continued to smile and smile.

The days passed by, and John consented to be still engaged. Their marriage was only a week off—six days, five days, four. Miss Everett's smile became less mechanical. John had apparently been passing through a crisis—a moral and intellectual crisis, inevitable in a man of his constitution, and with which she had nothing to do. On the eve of marriage he had questioned his heart; he had found that it was no longer young and capable of the vagaries of passion, and he had made up his mind to call things by their proper names, and to admit to himself that he was marrying not for love, but for friendship, and a little, perhaps, for prudence. It was only out of regard for what he supposed Marian's own more exalted theory of the matter, that he abstained from revealing to her this common-sense view of it. Such was Marian's hypothesis.

Lennox had fixed his wedding-day for the last Thursday in October. On the preceding Friday, as he was passing up Broadway, he stopped at Goupil's to see if his order for the framing of the portrait had been fulfilled. The picture had been transferred to the shop, and, when duly framed, had been, at Baxter's request and with Lennox's consent, placed for a few days in the exhibition room. Lennox went up to look at it.

The portrait stood on an easel at the end of the hall, with three spectators before it—a gentleman and two ladies. The room was otherwise empty. As Lennox went toward the picture, the gentleman turned out to be Baxter. He proceeded to introduce his friend

to his two companions, the younger of whom Lennox recognized as
the artist's betrothed. The other, her sister, was a plain, pale woman,
with the look of ill health, who had been provided with a seat and
made no attempt to talk. Baxter explained that these ladies had
arrived from Europe but the day before, and that his first care had
been to show them his masterpiece.

'Sarah,' said he, 'has been praising the model very much to the
prejudice of the copy.'

Sarah was a tall, black-haired girl of twenty, with irregular
features, a pair of luminous dark eyes, and a smile radiant of white
teeth—evidently an excellent person. She turned to Lennox with
a look of frank sympathy, and said in a deep, rich voice:

'She must be very beautiful.'

'Yes, she's very beautiful,' said Lennox, with his eyes lingering on
her own pleasant face. 'You must know her—she must know you.'

'I'm sure I should like very much to see her,' said Sarah.

'This is very nearly as good,' said Lennox. 'Mr. Baxter is a great
genius.'

'I know Mr. Baxter is a genius. But what is a picture, at the best?
I've seen nothing but pictures for the last two years, and I haven't
seen a single pretty girl.'

The young girl stood looking at the portrait in very evident
admiration, and, while Baxter talked to the elder lady, Lennox
bestowed a long, covert glance upon his *fiancée*. She had brought
her head into almost immediate juxtaposition with that of Marian's
image, and, for a moment, the freshness and the strong animation
which bloomed upon her features seemed to obliterate the lines and
colours on the canvas. But the next moment, as Lennox looked, the
roseate circle of Marian's face blazed into remorseless distinctness,
and her careless blue eyes looked with cynical familiarity into his
own.

He bade an abrupt good morning to his companions, and went
toward the door. But beside it he stopped. Suspended on the wall
was Baxter's picture, *My Last Duchess*. He stood amazed. Was *this*
the face and figure that, a month ago, had reminded him of his
mistress? Where was the likeness now? It was utterly absent as if it
had never existed. The picture, moreover, was a very inferior work
to the new portrait. He looked back at Baxter, half tempted to
demand an explanation, or at least to express his perplexity. But
Baxter and his sweetheart had stooped down to examine a minute
sketch near the floor, with their heads in delicious contiguity.

How the week elapsed, it were hard to say. There were moments
when Lennox felt as if death were preferable to the heartless union

which now stared him in the face, and as if the only opposite course was to transfer his property to Marian and to put an end to his existence. There were others, again, when he was fairly reconciled to his fate. He had but to gather his old dreams and fancies into a faggot and break them across his knee, and the thing were done. Could he not collect in their stead a comely cluster of moderate and rational expectations, and bind them about with a wedding favour? His love was dead, his youth was dead; that was all. There was no need of making a tragedy of it. His love's vitality had been but small, and since it was to be short-lived it was better that it should expire before marriage than after. As for marriage, that should stand, for that was not of necessity a matter of love. He lacked the brutal consistency necessary for taking away Marian's future. If he had mistaken her and overrated her, the fault was his own, and it was a hard thing that she should pay the penalty. Whatever were her failings, they were profoundly involuntary, and it was plain that with regard to himself her intentions were good. She would be no companion, but she would be at least a faithful wife.

With the help of this grim logic, Lennox reached the eve of his wedding day. His manner toward Miss Everett during the preceding week had been inveterately tender and kind. He felt that in losing his love she had lost a heavy treasure, and he offered her instead the most unfailing devotion. Marian had questioned him about his lassitude and his preoccupied air, and he had replied that he was not very well. On the Wednesday afternoon, he mounted his horse and took a long ride. He came home toward sunset, and was met in the hall by his old housekeeper.

'Miss Everett's portrait, sir,' she said, 'has just been sent home, in the most beautiful frame. You gave no directions, and I took the liberty of having it carried into the library. I thought,' and the old woman smiled deferentially, 'you'd like best to have it in your own room.'

Lennox went into the library. The picture was standing on the floor, back to back with a high arm-chair, and catching, through the window, the last horizontal rays of the sun. He stood before it a moment, gazing at it with a haggard face.

'Come!' said he, at last, 'Marian may be what God has made her; but *this* detestable creature I can neither love nor respect!'

He looked about him with an angry despair, and his eye fell on a long, keen poinard, given him by a friend who had bought it in the East, and which lay as an ornament on his mantel-shelf. He seized it and thrust it, with barbarous glee, straight into the lovely face of the image. He dragged it downward, and made a long fissure in the living canvas. Then, with half-a-dozen strokes, he wantonly hacked it across. The act afforded him an immense relief.

I need hardly add that on the following day Lennox was married.* He had locked the library door on coming out the evening before, and he had the key in his waistcoat pocket as he stood at the altar. As he left town, therefore, immediately after the ceremony, it was not until his return, a fortnight later, that the fate of the picture became known. It is not necessary to relate how he explained his exploit to Marian and how he disclosed it to Baxter. He at least put on a brave face. There is a rumour current of his having paid the painter an enormous sum of money. The amount is probably exaggerated, but there can be no doubt that the sum was very large. How he has fared—how he is destined to fare—in matrimony, it is rather too early to determine. He has been married scarcely three months.

* In a letter to one of the editors of the *Galaxy*, dated October 23, 1867, James wrote: '... As for adding a paragraph I should strongly object to it. It doesn't seem to me necessary. Silence on the subject will prove to the reader, I think, that the marriage *did* come off. I have little fear that the reader will miss a positive statement to that effect and the story closes in a more dramatic manner, to my apprehension, just as I have left it.' MS. Letter in the W.C. Church Collection in the New York Public Library.

The Romance of Certain Old Clothes

[First appeared in the *Atlantic Monthly*, vol. xxi (February 1868), pp. 209-20. The tale was revised and reprinted in *A Passionate Pilgrim* (1875). The 1875 text was later revised and reprinted in volume iii of *Stories Revived* (1885).]

TOWARD THE MIDDLE OF THE EIGHTEENTH CENTURY there lived in the Province of Massachusetts a widowed gentlewoman, the mother of three children. Her name is of little account: I shall take the liberty of calling her Mrs. Willoughby,—a name, like her own, of a highly respectable sound. She had been left a widow after some six years of marriage, and had devoted herself to the care of her children. These latter grew up in a manner to reward her tender care and to gratify her fondest hopes. The first-born was a son, whom she had called Bernard, after his father. The others were daughters,—born at an interval of three years apart. Good looks were traditional in the family, and these young persons were not likely to allow the tradition to perish. The boy was of that fair and ruddy complexion and of that athletic mould which in those days (as in these) were the sign of genuine English blood,—a frank, affectionate young fellow, a capital son and brother, and a steadfast friend. Clever, however, he was not; the wit of the family had been apportioned chiefly to his sisters. Mr. Willoughby had been a great reader of Shakespeare, at a time when this pursuit implied more penetration of mind than at the present day, and in a community where it required much courage to patronize the drama even in the closet; and he had wished to record his admiration of the great poet by calling his daughters out of his favourite plays. Upon the elder he had bestowed the charming name of Viola; and upon the younger, the more serious one of Perdita, in memory of a little girl born between them, who had lived but a few weeks.

When Bernard Willoughby came to his sixteenth year, his mother put a brave face upon it, and prepared to execute her husband's last request. This had been an earnest entreaty that, at the proper age, his son should be sent out to England, there to complete his education at the University of Oxford, which had been the seat of his own studies. Mrs. Willoughby valued her son three times as much as she did her two daughters together; but she valued her husband's wishes more. So she swallowed her sobs, and made up her boy's trunk and his simple provincial outfit, and sent him on his way across the seas. Bernard was entered at his father's college, and spent five years in England, without great honour, indeed, but with a vast deal of pleasure and no discredit. On leaving the University he made the journey to France. In his twenty-third year he took ship for home, prepared to find poor little New England (New England was very small in those days) an utterly intolerable place of abode. But there had been changes at home, as well as in Mr. Bernard's opinions. He found his mother's house quite habitable, and his sisters grown into two very charming young ladies, with all the accomplishments and graces of the young women of Britain, and a certain native-grown gentle *brusquerie* and wildness, which, if it was not an accomplishment, was certainly a grace the more. Bernard privately assured his mother that his sisters were fully a match for the most genteel young women in England; whereupon poor Mrs. Willoughby quite came into conceit of her daughters. Such was Bernard's opinion, and such, in a tenfold higher degree, was the opinion of Mr. Arthur Lloyd. This gentleman, I hasten to add, was a college-mate of Mr. Bernard, a young man of reputable family, of a good person and a handsome inheritance; which latter appurtenance he prepared to invest in trade in this country. He and Bernard were warm friends; they had crossed the ocean together, and the young American had lost no time in presenting him at his mother's house, where he had made quite as good an impression as that which he had received, and of which I have just given a hint.

The two sisters were at this time in all the freshness of their youthful bloom; each wearing, of course, this natural brilliancy in the manner that became her best. They were equally dissimilar in appearance and character. Viola, the elder—now in her twenty-second year,—was tall and fair, with calm grey eyes and auburn tresses; a very faint likeness to the Viola of Shakespeare's comedy, whom I imagine as a brunette (if you will), but a slender, airy creature, full of the softest and finest emotions. Miss Willoughby, with her rich, fair skin, her fine arms, her majestic height, and her slow utterance, was not cut out for adventures. She would never have put on a man's jacket and hose; and, indeed, being a very plump beauty, it is perhaps as well that she wouldn't. Perdita, too, might very well have exchanged the sweet melancholy of her name against something more in consonance with her aspect and disposition. She was a positive brunette, short of stature, light of foot, with dark brown eyes full of fire and animation. She had been from her childhood a creature of smiles and gaiety; and so far from making you wait for an answer to your speech, as her hand-

some sister was wont to do (while she gazed at you with her somewhat cold grey eyes), she had given you the choice of half a dozen,
suggested by the successive clauses of your proposition, before you
had got to the end of it.

The young girls were very glad to see their brother once more;
but they found themselves quite able to maintain a reserve of good-
will for their brother's friend. Among the young men, their friends
and neighbours, the *belle jeunesse* of the Colony, there were many
excellent fellows, several devoted swains, and some two or three
who enjoyed the reputation of universal charmers and conquerors.
But the home-bred arts and the somewhat boisterous gallantry of
these honest young colonists were completely eclipsed by the good
looks, the fine clothes, the respectful *empressement*, the perfect
elegance, the immense information, of Mr. Arthur Lloyd. He was
in reality no paragon; he was an honest, resolute, intelligent young
man, rich in pounds sterling, in his health and comfortable hopes,
and his little capital of uninvested affections. But he was a gentleman; he had a handsome face; he had studied and travelled; he
spoke French, he played on the flute, and he read verses aloud
with very great taste. There were a dozen reasons why Miss
Willoughby and her sister should forthwith have been rendered
fastidious in the choice of their male acquaintance. The imagination of women is especially adapted to the various little conven-
tions and mysteries of polite society. Mr. Lloyd's talk told our little
New England maidens a vast deal more of the ways and means of
people of fashion in European capitals than he had any idea of
doing. It was delightful to sit by and hear him and Bernard discourse upon the fine people and fine things they had seen. They
would all gather round the fire after tea, in the little wainscoted
parlour,—quite innocent then of any intention of being picturesque
or of being anything else, indeed, than economical, and saving the
expense of stamped papers and tapestries,—and the two young
men would remind each other, across the rug, of this, that, and the
other adventure. Viola and Perdita would often have given their
ears to know exactly what adventure it was, and where it happened,
and who was there, and what the ladies had on; but in those days
a well-bred young woman was not expected to break into conversation of her own movement or to ask too many questions; and
the poor girls used therefore to sit fluttering behind the more
languid—or more discreet—curiosity of their mother.

That they were both very nice girls Arthur Lloyd was not slow
to discover; but it took him some time to satisfy himself as to the
balance of their charms. He had a strong presentiment—an emotion

of a nature entirely too cheerful to be called a foreboding—that he was destined to marry one of them; yet he was unable to arrive at a preference, and for such a consummation a preference was certainly indispensable, inasmuch as Lloyd was quite too much of a young man to reconcile himself to the idea of making a choice by lot and being cheated of the heavenly delight of falling in love. He resolved to take things easily, and to let his heart speak. Meanwhile, he was on a very pleasant footing. Mrs. Willoughby showed a dignified indifference to his 'intentions', equally remote from a carelessness of her daughters' honour and from that hideous alacrity to make him commit himself, which, in his quality of a young man of property, he had but too often encountered in the venerable dames of his native islands. As for Bernard, all that he asked was that his friend should take his sisters as his own; and as for the fair creatures themselves, however each may have secretly longed for the monopoly of Mr. Lloyd's attentions, they observed a very decent and modest and contented demeanour.

Towards each other, however, they were somewhat more on the offensive. They were good sisterly friends, betwixt whom it would take more than a day for the seeds of jealousy to sprout and bear fruit; but the young girls felt that the seeds had been sown on the day that Mr. Lloyd came into the house. Each made up her mind that, if she should be slighted, she would bear her grief in silence, and that no one should be any the wiser; for if they had a great deal of love, they had also a great deal of pride. But each prayed in secret, nevertheless, that upon *her* the glory might fall. They had need of a vast deal of patience, of self-control, and of dissimulation. In those days a young girl of decent breeding could make no advances whatever, and barely respond, indeed, to those that were made. She was expected to sit still in her chair with her eyes on the carpet, watching the spot where the mystic handkerchief should fall. Poor Arthur Lloyd was obliged to undertake his wooing in the little wainscoted parlour, before the eyes of Mrs. Willoughby, her son, and his prospective sister-in-law. But youth and love are so cunning that a hundred little signs and tokens might travel to and fro, and not one of these three pair of eyes detect them in their passage. The young girls had but one chamber and one bed between them, and for long hours together they were under each other's direct inspection. That each knew that she was being watched, however, made not a grain of difference in those little offices which they mutually rendered, or in the various household tasks which they performed in common. Neither flinched nor fluttered beneath the silent batteries of her sister's eyes. The only apparent change in their habits was that they had less to say to each other. It was impossible to talk about Mr. Lloyd, and it was ridiculous to talk about anything else. By tacit agreement they began to wear all their choice finery, and to devise such little implements of coquetry, in the way of ribbons and top-knots and furbelows as were sanctioned by indubitable modesty. They executed in the same inarticulate fashion a little agreement of sincerity on these delicate matters. 'It is better so?' Viola would ask, tying a bunch of ribbons on her bosom, and turning about from her glass to her sister. Perdita would look up gravely from her work, and examine the decoration. 'I think you had better give it another loop,' she would say, with great solemnity, looking hard at her sister with eyes that added, 'upon my honour'. So they were forever stitching and trimming their petticoats, and pressing out their muslins, and contriving washes and ointments and cosmetics, like the ladies in the household of the vicar of Wakefield. Some three or four months went by; it grew to be midwinter, and as yet Viola knew that if Perdita had nothing more to boast of than she, there was not much to be feared from her rivalry. But Perdita by this time, the charming Perdita, felt that her secret had grown to be tenfold more precious than her sister's.

One afternoon Miss Willoughby sat alone before her toilet-glass, combing out her long hair. It was getting too dark to see; she lit the two candles in their sockets on the frame of her mirror, and then went to the window to draw her curtains. It was a grey December evening; the landscape was bare and bleak, and the sky heavy with snow-clouds. At the end of the long garden into which her window looked was a wall with a little postern door, opening into a lane. The door stood ajar, as she could vaguely see in the gathering darkness, and moved slowly to and fro, as if someone were swaying it from the lane without. It was doubtless a servant-maid. But as she was about to drop her curtain, Viola saw her sister step within the garden, and hurry along the path toward the house. She dropped the curtain, all save a little crevice for her eyes. As Perdita came up the path, she seemed to be examining something in her hand, holding it close to her eyes. When she reached the house she stopped a moment, looked intently at the object, and pressed it to her lips.

Poor Viola slowly came back to her chair, and sat down before her glass, where, if she had looked at it less abstractedly, she would have seen her handsome features sadly disfigured by jealousy. A moment afterwards, the door opened behind her, and her sister came into the room, out of breath, and her cheeks aglow with the chilly air.

Perdita started. 'Ah,' said she, 'I thought you were with mamma.' The ladies were to go to a tea-party, and on such occasions it was the habit of one of the young girls to help their mother to dress. Instead of coming in, Perdita lingered at the door.

'Come in, come in,' said Viola. 'We've more than an hour yet. I should like you very much to give a few strokes to my hair.' She knew that her sister wished to retreat, and that she could see in the glass all her movements in the room. 'Nay, just help me with my hair,' she said, 'and I'll go to mamma.'

Perdita came reluctantly, and took the brush. She saw her sister's eyes, in the glass, fastened hard upon her hands. She had not made three passes, when Viola clapped her own right hand upon her sister's left, and started out of her chair. 'Whose ring is that?' she cried, passionately, drawing her towards the light.

On the young girl's third finger glistened a little gold ring, adorned with a couple of small rubies. Perdita felt that she need no longer keep her secret, yet that she must put a bold face on her avowal. 'It's mine,' she said proudly.

'Who gave it to you?' cried the other.

Perdita hesitated a moment. 'Mr. Lloyd.'

'Mr. Lloyd is generous, all of a sudden.'

'Ah no,' cried Perdita, with spirit, 'not all of a sudden. He offered it to me a month ago.'

'And you need a month's begging to take it?' said Viola, looking at the little trinket; which indeed was not especially elegant, although it was the best that the jeweller of the Province could furnish. 'I shouldn't have taken it in less than two.'

'It isn't the ring,' said Perdita, 'it's what it means!'

'It means that you're not a modest girl,' cried Viola. 'Pray does mamma know of your conduct? does Bernard?'

'Mamma has approved my "conduct", as you call it. Mr. Lloyd has asked my hand, and mamma has given it. Would you have had him apply to you, sister?'

Viola gave her sister a long look, full of passionate envy and sorrow. Then she dropped her lashes on her pale cheeks, and turned away. Perdita felt that it had not been a pretty scene; but it was her sister's fault. But the elder girl rapidly called back her pride, and turned herself about again. 'You have my very best wishes,' she said with a low courtesy. 'I wish you every happiness, and a very long life.'

Perdita gave a bitter laugh. 'Don't speak in that tone,' she cried.

'I'd rather you cursed me outright. Come, sister,' she added, 'he couldn't marry both of us.'

'I wish you very great joy,' Viola repeated mechanically, sitting down to her glass again, 'and a very long life, and plenty of children.'

There was something in the sound of these words not at all to Perdita's taste. 'Will you give me a year, at least?' she said. 'In a year I can have one little boy,—or one little girl at least. If you'll give me your brush again, I'll do your hair.'

'Thank you,' said Viola. 'You had better go to mamma. It isn't proper that a young lady with a promised husband should wait on a girl with none.'

'Nay,' said Perdita, good-humouredly, 'I have Arthur to wait upon me. You need my service more than I need yours.'

But her sister motioned her away, and she left the room. When she had gone, poor Viola fell on her knees before her dressing-table, buried her head in her arms, and poured out a flood of tears and sobs. She felt very much the better for this effusion of sorrow. When her sister came back, she insisted upon helping her to dress, and upon her wearing her prettiest things. She forced upon her acceptance a bit of lace of her own, and declared that now that she was to be married she should do her best to appear worthy of her lover's choice. She discharged these offices in stern silence; but, such as they were, they had to do duty as an apology and an atonement; she never made any other.

Now that Lloyd was received by the family as an accepted suitor, nothing remained but to fix the wedding-day. It was appointed for the following April, and in the interval preparations were diligently made for the marriage. Lloyd, on his side, was busy with his commercial arrangements, and with establishing a correspondence with the great mercantile house to which he had attached himself in England. He was therefore not so frequent a visitor at Mrs. Willoughby's as during the months of his diffidence and irresolution, and poor Viola had less to suffer than she had feared from the sight of the mutual endearments of the young lovers. Touching his future sister-in-law Lloyd had a perfectly clear conscience. There had not been a particle of sentiment uttered between them, and he had not the slightest suspicion that she coveted anything more than his fraternal regard. He was quite at his ease; life promised so well, both domestically and financially. The lurid clouds of revolution were as yet twenty years beneath the horizon, and that his connubial felicity should take a tragic turn it was absurd, it was blasphemous, to apprehend. Meanwhile at Mrs. Willoughby's there was a greater rustling of silks, a more rapid clicking of scissors, and flying of needles than ever. Mrs. Willoughby had determined that her daughter should carry from home the most elegant outfit that her money could buy, or that the country could furnish. All the sage women in the county were convened, and their united taste was brought to bear on Perdita's wardrobe. Viola's situation, at this moment, was assuredly not to be envied. The poor girl had an inordinate love of dress, and the very best taste in the world, as her sister perfectly well knew. Viola was tall, she was full and stately, she was made to carry stiff brocade and masses of heavy lace, such as belong to the toilet of a rich man's wife. But Viola sat aloof, with her beautiful arms folded and her head averted, while her mother and sister and the venerable women aforesaid worried and wondered over their materials, oppressed by the multitude of their resources. One day there came in a beautiful piece of white silk, brocaded with heavenly blue and silver, sent by the bridegroom himself,—it not being thought amiss in those days that the husband elect should contribute to the bride's *trousseau*. Perdita was quite at a loss to imagine a pattern and trimmings which should do sufficient honour to the splendour of the material.

'Blue's your colour, sister, more than mine,' she said with appealing eyes. 'It's a pity it's not for you. You'd know what to do with it.'

Viola got up from her place, and looked at the great shining fabric as it lay spread over the back of a chair. Then she took it up in her hands and felt it,—lovingly, as Perdita could see,—and turned about toward the mirror with it. She let it roll down to her feet, and flung the other end over her shoulder, gathering it in about her waist with her white arm bare to the elbow. She threw back her head, and looked at her image, and a hanging tress of her auburn hair fell upon the gorgeous surface of the silk. It made a dazzling picture. The women standing about uttered a little 'Ah!' of admiration. 'Yes, indeed,' said Viola, quietly, 'blue is my colour.' But Perdita could see that her fancy had been stirred, and that she would now fall to work and solve all their silken riddles. And indeed she behaved very well, as Perdita, knowing her insatiable love of millinery, was quite ready to declare. Yards and yards of lovely silks and satins, of muslins, velvets, and laces, passed through her cunning hands, without a word of envy coming from her lips. Thanks to her efforts, when the wedding-day came Perdita was prepared to espouse more of the vanities of life than any fluttering young bride who had yet challenged the sacramental blessing of a New England divine.

It had been arranged that the young couple should go out and spend the first days of their wedded life at the country house of an English gentleman,—a man of rank, and a very kind friend to Lloyd. He was an unmarried man; he professed himself delighted to withdraw and leave them for a week to their billing and cooing. After the ceremony at church,—it had been performed by an English priest,—young Mrs. Lloyd hastened back to her mother's house to change her wedding gear for a riding-dress. Viola helped her to effect the change, in the little old room in which they had been fond sisters together. Perdita then hurried off to bid farewell to her mother, leaving Viola to follow. The parting was short; the horses were at the door, and Arthur impatient to start. But Viola had not followed, and Perdita hastened back to her room, opening the door abruptly. Viola, as usual, was before the glass, but in a position which caused the other to stand still, amazed. She had dressed herself in Perdita's cast-off wedding veil and wreath, and on her neck she had hung the heavy string of pearls which the young girl had received from her husband as a wedding-gift. These things had been hastily laid aside, to wait their possessor's disposal on her return from the country. Bedizened in this unnatural garb, Viola stood at the mirror, plunging a long look into its depths, and reading Heaven knows what audacious visions. Perdita was shocked and pained. It was a hideous image of their old rivalry come to life again. She made a step toward her sister, as if to pull off the veil and the flowers. But catching her eyes in the glass, she stopped.

'Farewell, Viola,' she said. 'You might at least have waited till I had got out of the house.' And she hurried away from the room.

Mr. Lloyd had purchased in Boston a house which, in the taste of those days, was considered a marvel of elegance and comfort; and here he very soon established himself with his young wife. He was thus separated by a distance of twenty miles from the residence of his mother-in-law. Twenty miles in that primitive era of roads and conveyances were as good as a hundred at the present day, and Mrs. Willoughby saw but little of her daughter during the first twelvemonth of her marriage. She suffered in no small degree from her absence; and her affliction was not diminished by the fact that Viola had fallen into a spiritless and languid state, which made change of scene and of air essential to her restoration. The real cause of the young girl's dejection the reader will not be slow to suspect. Mrs. Willoughby and her gossips, however, deemed her complaint a purely physical one, and doubted not that she would obtain relief from the remedy just mentioned. Her mother accordingly proposed on her behalf a visit to certain relatives on the paternal side, established in New York, who had long complained that they were able to see so little of their New England cousins. Viola was despatched to these good people, under a suitable escort, and remained with them for several months. In the interval her brother Bernard, who had begun the practice of the law, made up his mind to take a wife. Viola came home to the wedding, apparently cured of her heartache, with honest roses and lilies in her face, and a proud smile on her lips. Arthur Lloyd came over from Boston to see his brother-in-law married, but without his wife, who was expecting shortly to be confined. It was nearly a year since Viola had seen him. She was glad—she hardly knew why—that Perdita had stayed at home. Arthur looked happy, but he was more grave and solemn than before his marriage. She thought he looked 'interesting'—for although the word in its modern sense was not then invented, we may be sure that the idea was. The truth is, he was simply preoccupied with his wife's condition. Nevertheless he by no means failed to observe Viola's beauty and splendour, and how she quite effaced the poor little bride. The allowance that Perdita had enjoyed for her dress had now been transferred to her sister, who certainly made the most of it. On the morning after the wedding, he had a lady's saddle put on the horse of the servant who had come with him from town, and went out with the young girl for a ride. It was a keen, clear morning in January; the ground was bare and hard, and the horses in good condition,—to say nothing of Viola, who was charming in her hat and plume, and her dark blue riding-coat, trimmed with fur. They rode all the morning, they lost their way, and were obliged to stop for dinner at a farmhouse. The early winter dusk had fallen when they got home. Mrs. Willoughby met them with a long face. A messenger had arrived at noon from Mrs. Lloyd; she was beginning to be ill, and desired her husband's immediate return. The young man swore at the thought that he had lost several hours, and that by hard riding he might already have been with his wife. He barely consented to stop for a mouthful of supper, but mounted the messenger's horse and started off at a gallop.

He reached home at midnight. His wife had been delivered of a little girl. 'Ah, why weren't you with me?' she said, as he came to her bedside.

'I was out of the house when the man came. I was with Viola,' said Lloyd, innocently.

Mrs. Lloyd made a little moan, and turned about. But she continued to do very well, and for a week her improvement was uninterrupted. Finally, however, through some excess of diet or of exposure, it was checked, and the poor lady grew rapidly worse.

Lloyd was in despair. It very soon became evident that the relapse was fatal. Mrs. Lloyd came to a sense of her approaching end, and declared that she was reconciled with death. On the third evening after the change took place she told her husband that she felt she would not outlast the night. She dismissed her servants, and also requested her mother to withdraw,—Mrs. Willoughby having arrived on the preceding day. She had had her infant placed on the bed beside her, and she lay on her side, with the child against her breast, holding her husband's hands. The night-lamp was hidden behind the heavy curtains of the bed, but the room was illumined with a red glow from the immense fire of logs on the hearth.

'It seems strange to die by such a fire as that,' the young woman said, feebly trying to smile. 'If I had but a little of such fire in my veins! But I've given it all to this little spark of mortality.' And she dropped her eyes on her child. Then raising them she looked at her husband with a long penetrating gaze. The last feeling which lingered in her heart was one of mistrust. She had not recovered from the shock which Arthur had given her by telling her that in the hour of her agony he had been with Viola. She trusted her husband very nearly as well as she loved him; but now that she was called away forever, she felt a cold horror of her sister. She felt in her soul that Viola had never ceased to envy her good fortune; and a year of happy security had not effaced the young girl's image, dressed in her wedding garments, and smiling with fancied triumph. Now that Arthur was to be alone, what might not Viola do? She was beautiful, she was engaging; what arts might she not use, what impression might she not make upon the young man's melancholy heart? Mrs. Lloyd looked at her husband in silence. It seemed hard, after all, to doubt of his constancy. His fine eyes were filled with tears; his face was convulsed with weeping; the clasp of his hands was warm and passionate. How noble he looked, how tender, how faithful and devoted! 'Nay,' thought Perdita, 'he's not for such as Viola. He'll never forget me. Nor does Viola truly care for him; she cares only for vanities and finery and jewels.' And she dropped her eyes on her white hands, which her husband's liberality had covered with rings, and on the lace ruffles which trimmed the edge of her nightdress. 'She covets my rings and my laces more than she covets my husband.'

At this moment the thought of her sister's rapacity seemed to cast a dark shadow between her and the helpless figure of her little girl. 'Arthur,' she said, 'you must take off my rings. I shall not be buried in them. One of these days my daughter shall wear them,— my rings and my laces and silks. I had them all brought out and shown me to-day. It's a great wardrobe,—there's no such another in the Province; I can say it without vanity now that I've done with it. It will be a great inheritance for my daughter, when she grows into a young woman. There are things there that a man never buys twice, and if they're lost you'll never again see the like. So you'll watch them well. Some dozen things I've left to Viola; I've named them to my mother. I've given her that blue and silver; it was meant for her; I wore it only once, I looked ill in it. But the rest are to be sacredly kept for this little innocent. It's such a providence that she should be my colour; she can wear my gowns; she has her mother's eyes. You know the same fashions come back every twenty years. She can wear my gowns as they are. They'll lie there quietly waiting till she grows into them,—wrapped in camphor and rose-leaves, and keeping their colours in the sweet-scented darkness. She shall have black hair, she shall wear my carnation satin. Do you promise me, Arthur?'

'Promise you what, dearest?'

'Promise me to keep your poor little wife's old gowns.'

'Are you afraid I'll sell them?'

'No, but that they may get scattered. My mother will have them properly wrapped up, and you shall lay them away under a double-lock. Do you know the great chest in the attic, with the iron bands? There's no end to what it will hold. You can lay them all there. My mother and the housekeeper will do it, and give you the key. And you'll keep the key in your secretary, and never give it to anyone but your child. Do you promise me?'

'Ah, yes, I promise you,' said Lloyd, puzzled at the intensity with which his wife appeared to cling to this idea.

'Will you swear?' repeated Perdita.

'Yes, I swear.'

'Well—I trust you—I trust you,' said the poor lady, looking into his eyes with eyes in which, if he had suspected her vague apprehensions, he might have read an appeal quite as much as an assurance.

Lloyd bore his bereavement soberly and manfully. A month after his wife's death, in the course of commerce, circumstances arose which offered him an opportunity of going to England. He embraced it as an alleviation to his sadness. He was absent nearly a year, during which his little girl was tenderly nursed and cherished by her grandmother. On his return he had his house again thrown open, and announced his intention of keeping the same state as during his wife's lifetime. It very soon came to be predicted that he would marry again, and there were at least a dozen young women of whom one may say that it was by no fault of theirs that, for six months after his return, the prediction did not come true. During this interval he still left his little daughter in Mrs. Willoughby's hands, the latter assuring him that a change of residence at so tender an age was perilous to her health. Finally, however, he declared that his heart longed for the little creature's presence, and that she must be brought up to town. He sent his coach and his housekeeper to fetch her home. Mrs. Willoughby was in terror lest something should befall her on the road; and, in accordance with this feeling, Viola offered to ride along with her. She could return the next day. So she went up to town with her little niece, and Mr. Lloyd met her on the threshold of his house, overcome with her kindness and with gratitude. Instead of returning the next day, Viola stayed out the week; and when at last she reappeared, she had only come for her clothes. Arthur would not hear of her coming home, nor would the baby. She cried and moaned if Viola left her; and at the sight of her grief Arthur lost his wits, and swore that she was going to die. In fine, nothing would suit them but that Viola should remain until the little thing had grown used to strange faces.

It took two months for this consummation to be brought about; for it was not until this period had elapsed that Viola took leave of her brother-in-law. Mrs. Willoughby had fretted and fumed over her daughter's absence; she had declared that it was not becoming, and that it was the talk of the town. She had reconciled herself to it only because, during the young girl's visit, the household enjoyed an unwonted term of peace. Bernard Willoughby had brought his wife home to live, between whom and her sister-in-law there existed a bitter hostility. Viola was perhaps no angel; but in the daily practice of life she was a sufficiently good-natured girl, and if she quarrelled with Mrs. Bernard it was not without provocation. Quarrel, however, she did, to the great annoyance not only of her antagonist, but the two spectators of these constant altercations. Her stay in the household of her brother-in-law, therefore, would have been delightful, if only because it removed her from contact with the object of her antipathy at home. It was doubly—it was ten times—delightful, inasmuch as it kept her near the object of her old passion. Mrs. Lloyd's conjectures had fallen very far short of the truth, touching Viola's feeling for her husband. It had been a passion at first and a passion it remained,—a passion of whose radiant heat, tempered to the delicate state of his feelings, Mr. Lloyd very soon felt the influence. Lloyd, as I have said, was no paragon; it was not in his nature to practise an ideal constancy. He had not

been many days in the house with his sister-in-law before he began
to assure himself that she was, in the language of that day, a
devilish fine woman. Whether Viola really practised those insidious
arts that her sister had been tempted to impute to her it is needless
to inquire. It is enough to say that she found means to appear to the
very best advantage. She used to seat herself every morning before
the great fireplace in the dining-room, at work upon a piece of
tapestry, with her little niece disporting herself on the carpet at her
feet, or on the train of her dress, and playing with her woollen balls.
Lloyd would have been a very stupid fellow if he had remained
insensible to the rich suggestions of this charming picture. He was
prodigiously fond of his little girl, and was never weary of taking
her in his arms and tossing her up and down, and making her crow
with delight. Very often, however, he would venture upon greater
liberties than the little creature was yet prepared to allow, and she
would suddenly vociferate her displeasure. Viola would then drop
her tapestry, and put out her handsome hands with the serious smile
of the young girl whose virgin fancy has revealed to her all a
mother's healing arts. Lloyd would give up the child, their eyes
would meet, their hands would touch, and Viola would extinguish
the little girl's sobs upon the snowy folds of the kerchief that crossed
her bosom. Her dignity was perfect, and nothing could be less
obtrusive than the manner in which she accepted her brother-in-
law's hospitality. It may be almost said, perhaps, that there was
something harsh in her reserve. Lloyd had a provoking feeling that
she was in the house, and yet that she was unapproachable. Half an
hour after supper, at the very outset of the long winter evenings,
she would light her candle, and make the young man a most respectful courtesy, and march off to bed. If these were arts, Viola
was a great artist. But their effect was so gentle, so gradual, they
were calculated to work upon the young widower's fancy with such
a finely shaded *crescendo*, that, as the reader has seen, several weeks
elapsed before Viola began to feel sure that her return would cover
her outlay. When this became morally certain, she packed up her
trunk, and returned to her mother's house. For three days she
waited; on the fourth Mr. Lloyd made his appearance, a respectful
but ardent suitor. Viola heard him out with great humility, and
accepted him with infinite modesty. It is hard to imagine that Mrs.
Lloyd should have forgiven her husband; but if anything might
have disarmed her resentment, it would have been the ceremonious
continence of this interview. Viola imposed upon her lover but a
short probation. They were married, as was becoming, with great
privacy,—almost with secrecy,—in the hope, perhaps, as was wag-

gishly remarked at the time, that the late Mrs. Lloyd wouldn't hear of it.

The marriage was to all appearance a happy one, and each party obtained what each had desired,—Lloyd 'a devilish fine woman', and Viola—but Viola's desires, as the reader will have observed, have remained a good deal of a mystery. There were, indeed, two blots upon their felicity; but time would, perhaps, efface them. During the three first years of her marriage Mrs. Lloyd failed to become a mother, and her husband on his side suffered heavy losses of money. This latter circumstance compelled a material retrenchment in his expenditure, and Viola was perforce less of a great lady than her sister had been. She contrived, however, to sustain with unbroken consistency the part of an elegant woman, although it must be confessed that it required the exercise of more ingenuity than belongs to your real aristocratic repose. She had long since ascertained that her sister's immense wardrobe had been sequestrated for the benefit of her daughter, and that it lay languishing in thankless gloom in the dusty attic. It was a revolting thought that these glorious fabrics should wait on the bidding of a little girl who sat in a high chair, and ate bread-and-milk with a wooden spoon. Viola had the good taste, however, to say nothing about the matter until several months had expired. Then, at last, she timidly broached it to her husband. Was it not a pity that so much finery should be lost?—for lost it would be, what with colours fading, and moths eating it up, and the change of fashions. But Lloyd gave so abrupt and peremptory a negative to her inquiry, that she saw that for the present her attempt was vain. Six months went by, however, and brought with them new needs and new fancies. Viola's thoughts hovered lovingly about her sister's relics. She went up and looked at the chest in which they lay imprisoned. There was a sullen defiance in its three great padlocks and its iron bands, which only quickened her desires. There was something exasperating in its incorruptible immobility. It was like a grim and grizzled old household servant, who locks his jaws over a family secret. And then there was a look of capacity in its vast extent, and a sound as of dense fullness, when Viola knocked its side with the toe of her little slipper, which caused her to flush with baffled longing. 'It's absurd,' she cried; 'it's improper, it's wicked,' and she forthwith resolved upon another attack upon her husband. On the following day, after dinner, when he had had his wine, she bravely began it. But he cut her short with great sternness.

'Once for all, Viola,' said he, 'it's out of the question. I shall be gravely displeased if you return to the matter.'

'Very good,' said Viola. 'I'm glad to learn the value at which I'm held. Great Heaven!' she cried, 'I'm a happy woman. It's a delightful thing to feel one's self sacrificed to a caprice!' And her eyes filled with tears of anger and disappointment.

Lloyd had a good-natured man's horror of a woman's sobs, and he attempted—I may say he condescended—to explain. 'It's not a caprice, dear, it's a promise,' he said,—'an oath.'

'An oath? It's a pretty matter for oaths! and to whom, pray?'

'To Perdita,' said the young man, raising his eyes for an instant, but immediately dropping them.

'Perdita,—ah, Perdita!' And Viola's tears broke forth. Her bosom heaved with stormy sobs,—sobs which were the long-deferred counterpart of the violent fit of weeping in which she had indulged herself on the night when she discovered her sister's betrothal. She had hoped, in her better moments, that she had done with her jealousy; but here it raged again as fierce as ever. 'And pray what right,' she cried, 'had Perdita to dispose of my future? What right had she to bind you to meanness and cruelty? Ah, I occupy a dignified place, and I make a very fine figure! I'm welcome to what Perdita has left! And what has she left? I never knew till now how little! Nothing, nothing, nothing!'

This was very poor logic, but it was very good passion. Lloyd put his arm around his wife's waist and tried to kiss her, but she shook him off with magnificent scorn. Poor fellow! he had coveted a 'devilish fine woman', and he had got one. Her scorn was intolerable. He walked away with his ears tingling,—irresolute, distracted. Before him was his secretary, and in it the sacred key which with his own hand he had turned in the triple lock. He marched up and opened it, and took the key from a secret drawer, wrapped in a little packet which he had sealed with his own honest bit of blazonry. *Teneo*, said the motto,—'I hold.' But he was ashamed to put it back. He flung it upon the table beside his wife.

'Keep it!' she cried. 'I want it not. I hate it!'

'I wash my hands of it,' cried her husband. 'God forgive me!'

Mrs. Lloyd gave an indignant shrug of her shoulders, and swept out of the room, while the young man retreated by another door. Ten minutes later Mrs. Lloyd returned, and found the room occupied by her little step-daughter and the nursery-maid. The key was not on the table. She glanced at the child. The child was perched on a chair with the packet in her hands. She had broken the seal with her own little fingers. Mrs. Lloyd hastily took possession of the key.

At the habitual supper-hour Arthur Lloyd came back from his

counting-room. It was the month of June, and supper was served by daylight. The meal was placed on the table, but Mrs. Lloyd failed to make her appearance. The servant whom his master sent to call her came back with the assurance that her room was empty, and that the women informed him that she had not been seen since dinner. They had in truth observed her to have been in tears, and, supposing her to be shut up in her chamber, had not disturbed her. Her husband called her name in various parts of the house, but without response. At last it occurred to him that he might find her by taking the way to the attic. The thought gave him a strange feeling of discomfort, and he bade his servants remain behind, wishing no witness in his quest. He reached the foot of the staircase leading to the topmost flat, and stood with his hand on the banisters, pronouncing his wife's name. His voice trembled. He called again, louder and more firmly. The only sound which disturbed the absolute silence was a faint echo of his own voice, repeating his question under the great eaves. He nevertheless felt irresistibly moved to ascend the staircase. It opened upon a wide hall, lined with wooden closets, and terminating in a window which looked westward, and admitted the last rays of the sun. Before the window stood the great chest. Before the chest, on her knees, the young man saw with amazement and horror the figure of his wife. In an instant he crossed the interval between them, bereft of utterance. The lid of the chest stood open, exposing, amid their perfumed napkins, its treasure of stuffs and jewels. Viola had fallen backward from a kneeling posture, with one hand suporting her on the floor and the other pressed to her heart. On her limbs was the stiffness of death, and on her face, in the fading light of the sun, the terror of something more than death. Her lips were parted in entreaty, in dismay, in agony; and on her bloodless brow and cheeks there glowed the marks of ten hideous wounds from two vengeful ghostly hands.

A Most Extraordinary Case

[First appeared in the *Atlantic Monthly*, vol. xxi (April 1868), pp. 461-485. The tale was revised and reprinted in volume iii of *Stories Revived* (1885).]

LATE IN THE SPRING OF THE YEAR 1865, JUST AS THE war had come to a close, a young invalid officer lay in bed in one of the uppermost chambers of one of the great New York hotels. His meditations were interrupted by the entrance of a waiter, who handed him a card superscribed *Mrs. Samuel Mason*, and bearing on its reverse the following words in pencil: 'Dear Colonel Mason, I have only just heard of your being here, ill and alone. It's too dreadful. Do you remember me? Will you see me? If you do, I think you *will* remember me. I insist on coming up. M. M.'

Mason was undressed, unshaven, weak, and feverish. His ugly little hotel chamber was in a state of confusion which had not even the merit of being picturesque. Mrs. Mason's card was at once a puzzle and a heavenly intimation of comfort. But all that it represented was so dim to the young man's enfeebled perception that it took him some moments to collect his thoughts.

'It's a lady, sir,' said the waiter, by way of assisting him.

'Is she young or old?' asked Mason.

'Well, sir, she's a little of both.'

'I can't ask a lady to come up here,' groaned the invalid.

'Upon my word, sir, you look beautiful,' said the waiter. 'They like a sick man. And I see she's of your own name,' continued Michael, in whom constant service had bred great frankness of speech; 'the more shame to her for not coming before.'

Colonel Mason concluded that, as the visit had been of Mrs. Mason's own seeking, he would receive her without more ado. 'If she doesn't mind it, I'm sure I needn't,' said the poor fellow, who hadn't the strength to be over-punctilious. So in a very few moments his visitor was ushered up to his bedside. He saw before him a handsome, middle-aged blonde woman, stout of figure, and dressed in the height of the fashion, who displayed no other embarrassment than such as was easily explained by the loss of breath consequent on the ascent of six flights of stairs.

'Do you remember me?' she asked, taking the young man's hand.

He lay back on his pillow, and looked at her. 'You used to be my aunt,—my aunt Maria,' he said.

'I'm your aunt Maria, still,' she answered. 'It's very good of you not to have forgotten me.'

'It's very good of you not to have forgotten *me*,' said Mason, in a tone which betrayed a deeper feeling than the wish to return a civil speech.

'Dear me, you've had the war and a hundred dreadful things. I've been living in Europe, you know. Since my return I've been living in the country, in your uncle's old house on the river, of which the lease had just expired when I came home. I came to town yesterday on business, and accidentally heard of your condition and your whereabouts. I knew you'd gone into the army, and I had been wondering a dozen times what had become of you, and whether you wouldn't turn up now that the war's at last over. Of course I didn't lose a moment in coming to you. I'm *so* sorry for you.' Mrs. Mason looked about her for a seat. The chairs were encumbered with odds and ends belonging to her nephew's wardrobe and to his equipment, and with the remnants of his last repast. The good lady surveyed the scene with the beautiful mute irony of compassion.

The young man lay watching her comely face in delicious submission to whatever form of utterance this feeling might take. 'You're the first woman—to call a woman—I've seen in I don't know how many months,' he said, contrasting her appearance with that of his room, and reading her thoughts.

'I should suppose so. I mean to be as good as a dozen.' She disembarrassed one of the chairs, and brought it to the bed. Then, seating herself, she ungloved one of her hands, and laid it softly on the young man's wrist. 'What a great full-grown young fellow you've become!' she pursued. 'Now, tell me, are you very ill?'

'You must ask the doctor,' said Mason. 'I actually don't know. I'm extremely uncomfortable, but I suppose it's partly my circumstances.'

'I've no doubt it's more than half your circumstances. I've seen the doctor. Mrs. Van Zandt is an old friend of mine; and when I come to town, I always go to see her. It was from her I learned this morning that you were here in this state. We had begun by rejoicing over the new prospects of peace; and from that, of course, we had got to lamenting the numbers of young men who are to enter upon it with lost limbs and shattered health. It happened that Mrs. Van Zandt mentioned several of her husband's patients as examples, and yourself among the number. You were an excellent young man, miserably sick, without family or friends, and with no asylum but a suffocating little closet in a noisy hotel. You may imagine that I pricked up my ears, and asked your baptismal name.

Dr. Van Zandt came in, and told me. Your name is luckily an uncommon one: it's absurd to suppose that there could be two
Ferdinand Masons. In short, I felt that you were my husband's
brother's child, and that at last I too might have my little turn at
hero-nursing. The little that the Doctor knew of your history agreed
with the little that I knew, though I confess I was sorry to hear that
you had never spoken of our relationship. But why should you? At
all events you've got to acknowledge it now. I regret your not having
said something about it before, only because the Doctor might have
brought us together a month ago, and you would now have been
well.'

'It will take me more than a month to get well,' said Mason, feeling that, if Mrs. Mason was meaning to exert herself on his behalf,
she should know the real state of the case. 'I never spoke of you,
because I had quite lost sight of you. I fancied you were still in
Europe; and indeed,' he added, after a moment's hesitation, 'I
heard that you had married again.'

'Of course you did,' said Mrs. Mason, placidly. 'I used to hear it
once a month myself. But I had a much better right to fancy you
married. Thank Heaven, however, there's nothing of that sort
between us. We can each do as we please. I promise to cure you in
a month, in spite of yourself.'

'What's your remedy?' asked the young man, with a smile very
courteous, considering how sceptical it was.

'My first remedy is to take you out of this horrible hole. I talked
it all over with Dr. Van Zandt. He says you must get into the country. Why, my dear boy, this is enough to kill you outright,—one
Broadway outside of your window and another outside of your
door! Listen to me. My house is directly on the river, and only two
hours' journey by rail. You know I've no children. My only companion is my niece, Caroline Hofmann. You shall come and stay
with us until you are as strong as you need be,—if it takes a dozen
years. You shall have sweet, cool air, and proper food, and decent
attendance, and the devotion of a sensible woman. I shall not listen
to a word of objection. You shall do as you please, get up when you
please, dine when you please, go to bed when you please, and say
what you please. I shall ask nothing of you but to let yourself be
very dearly cared for. Do you remember how, when you were a boy
at school, after your father's death, you were taken with measles,
and your uncle had you brought to our own house? I helped to
nurse you myself, and I remember what nice manners you had in
the very midst of your measles. Your uncle was very fond of you;
and if he had had any considerable property of his own, I know he

would have remembered you in his will. But of course he couldn't leave away his wife's money. What I wish to do for you is a very small part of what he would have done, if he had only lived, and heard of your gallantry and your sufferings. So it's settled. I shall go home this afternoon. Tomorrow morning I shall despatch my man-servant to you with instructions. He's an Englishman. He thoroughly knows his business, and he will put up your things, and save you every particle of trouble. You've only to let yourself be dressed, and driven to the train. I shall, of course, meet you at your journey's end. Now don't tell me you're not strong enough.'

'I feel stronger at this moment than I've felt in a dozen weeks,' said Mason. 'It's useless for me to attempt to thank you.'

'Quite useless. I shouldn't listen to you. And I suppose,' added Mrs. Mason, looking over the bare walls and scanty furniture of the room, 'you pay a fabulous price for this bower of bliss. Do you need money?'

The young man shook his head.

'Very well, then,' resumed Mrs. Mason, conclusively, 'from this moment you're in my hands.'

The young man lay speechless from the very fulness of his heart; but he strove by the pressure of his fingers to give her some assur-ance of his gratitude. His companion rose, and lingered beside him, drawing on her glove, and smiling quietly with the look of a long-baffled philanthropist who has at last discovered a subject of infinite capacity. Poor Ferdinand's weary visage reflected her smile. Finally, after the lapse of years, he too was being cared for. He let his head sink into the pillow, and silently inhaled the perfume of her sober elegance and her cordial good-nature. He felt like taking her dress in his hand, and asking her not to leave him,—now that solitude would be bitter. His eyes, I suppose, betrayed this touching appre-hension,—doubly touching in a war-wasted young officer. As she prepared to bid him farewell, Mrs. Mason stooped, and kissed his forehead. He listened to the rustle of her dress across the carpet, to the gentle closing of the door, and to her retreating footsteps. And then, giving way to his weakness, he put his hands to his face, and cried like a homesick school-boy. He had been reminded of the exquisite side of life.

Matters went forward as Mrs. Mason had arranged them. At six o'clock on the following evening Ferdinand found himself deposited at one of the way stations of the Hudson River Railroad, exhausted by his journey, and yet excited at the prospect of its drawing to a close. Mrs. Mason was in waiting in a low basket-phaeton, with a magazine of cushions and wrappings. Ferdinand transferred himself to her side, and they drove rapidly homeward. Mrs. Mason's house was a cottage of liberal make, with a circular lawn, a sinuous avenue, and a well-grown plantation of shrubbery. As the phaeton drew up before the porch, a young lady appeared in the doorway. Mason will be forgiven if he considered himself presented *ex officio*, as I may say, to this young lady. Before he really knew it, and in the absence of the servant, who, under Mrs. Mason's directions, was busy in the background with his trunk, he had availed himself of her proffered arm, and had allowed her to assist him through the porch, across the hall, and into the parlour, where she graciously consigned him to a sofa which, for his especial use, she had caused to be wheeled up before a fire kindled for his especial comfort. He was unable, however, to take advantage of her good offices. Prudence dictated that without further delay he should betake himself to his room.

On the morning after his arrival he got up early, and made an attempt to be present at breakfast; but his strength failed him, and he was obliged to dress at his leisure, and content himself with a simple transition from his bed to his arm-chair. The chamber assigned him was designedly on the ground-floor, so that he was spared the trouble of measuring his strength with the staircase,—a charming room, brightly carpeted and upholstered, and marked by a certain fastidious freshness which betrayed the uncontested dominion of women. It had a broad high window, draped in chintz and crisp muslin and opening upon the greensward of the lawn. At this window, wrapped in his dressing-gown, and lost in the embrace of the most unresisting of arm-chairs, he slowly discussed his simple repast. Before long his hostess made her appearance on the lawn outside the window. As this quarter of the house was covered with warm sunshine, Mason ventured to open the window and talk to her, while she stood out on the grass beneath her parasol.

'It's time to think of your physician,' she said. 'You shall choose for yourself. The great physician here is Dr. Gregory, a gentleman of the old school. We have had him but once, for my niece and I have the health of a couple of dairy-maids. On that one occasion he —well, he made a fool of himself. His practice is among the "old families", and he only knows how to treat certain old-fashioned, obsolete complaints. Anything brought about by the war would be quite out of his range. And then he vacillates, and talks about his own maladies *à lui*. And, to tell the truth, we had a little repartee which makes our relations somewhat embiguous.'

'I see he would never do,' said Mason, laughing. 'But he's not your only physician?'

'No: there is a young man, a newcomer, a Dr. Knight, whom I

don't know, but of whom I've heard very good things. I confess that
I have a prejudice in favour of the young men. Dr. Knight has a
position to establish, and I suppose he's likely to be especially
attentive and careful. I believe, moreover, that he's been an army
surgeon.'

'I knew a man of his name,' said Mason. 'I wonder if this is he.
His name was Horace Knight,—a light-haired, near-sighted
man.'

'I don't know,' said Mrs. Mason; 'perhaps Caroline knows.' She
retreated a few steps, and called to an upper window: 'Caroline,
what's Dr. Knight's first name?'

Mason listened to Miss Hofmann's answer,—'I haven't the least
idea.'

'Is it Horace?'

'I don't know.'

'Is he light or dark?'

'I've never seen him.'

'Is he near-sighted?'

'How in the world should I know?'

'I fancy he's as good as anyone,' said Ferdinand. 'With you, my
dear aunt, what does the doctor matter?'

Mrs. Mason accordingly sent for Dr. Knight, who, on arrival,
turned out to be her nephew's old acquaintance. Although the
young men had been united by no greater intimacy than the superficial comradeship resulting from a winter in neighbouring quarters,
they were very well pleased to come together again. Horace Knight
was a young man of good birth, good looks, good faculties, and good
intentions, who, after a three years' practice of surgery in the army,
had undertaken to push his fortune in Mrs. Mason's neighbourhood.
His mother, a widow with a small income, had recently removed to
the country for economy, and her son had been unwilling to leave
her to live alone. The adjacent country, moreover, offered a
promising field for a man of energy,—a field well stocked with large
families of easy income and of those conservative habits which lead
people to make much of the cares of a physician. The local prac-
titioner had survived the glory of his prime, and was not, perhaps,
entirely guiltless of Mrs. Mason's charge, that he had not kept up
with the progress of the 'new diseases'. The world, in fact, was
getting too new for him, as well as for his old patients. He had had
money invested in the South,—precious sources of revenue, which
the war had swallowed up at a gulp; he had grown frightened and
nervous and querulous; he had lost his presence of mind and his
spectacles in several important conjunctures; he had been repeat-

edly and distinctly fallible; a vague dissatisfaction pervaded the breasts of his patrons; he was without competitors: in short, fortune was propitious to Dr. Knight. Mason remembered the young physician only as a good-humoured, intelligent companion; but he soon had reason to believe that his medical skill would leave nothing to be desired. He arrived rapidly at a clear understanding of Ferdinand's case; he asked intelligent questions, and gave simple and definite instructions. The disorder was deeply seated and virulent, but there was no apparent reason why unflinching care and prudence should not subdue it.

'Your strength is very much reduced,' he said, as he took his hat and gloves to go; 'but I should say you had an excellent constitution. It seems to me, however,—if you will pardon me for saying so, —to be partly your own fault that you have fallen so low. You have opposed no resistance; you haven't cared to get well.'

'I confess that I haven't,—particularly. But I don't see how you should know it.'

'Why, it's obvious.'

'Well, it was natural enough. Until Mrs. Mason discovered me, I hadn't a friend in the world. I had become demoralized by solitude. I had almost forgotten the difference between sickness and health. I had nothing before my eyes to remind me in tangible form of that great mass of common human interests for the sake of which —under whatever name he may disguise the impulse—a man continues in health and recovers from disease. I had forgotten that I ever cared for books or ideas, or anything but the preservation of my miserable carcass. My carcass had become quite too miserable to be an object worth living for. I was losing time and money at an appalling rate; I was getting worse rather than better; and I therefore gave up resistance. It seemed better to die easy than to die hard. I put it all in the past tense, because within these three days I've become quite another man.'

'I wish to Heaven I could have heard of you,' said Knight. 'I would have made you come home with me, if I could have done nothing else. It was certainly not a rose-coloured prospect; but what do you say now?' he continued, looking around the room. 'I should say that at the present moment rose-colour was the prevailing hue.'

Mason assented with an eloquent smile.

'I congratulate you from my heart. Mrs. Mason—if you don't mind my speaking of her—is so thoroughly (and, I should suppose, incorrigbly) good-natured, that it's quite a surprise to find her extremely sensible.'

'Yes; and so resolute and sensible in her better moments,' said

Ferdinand, 'that it's quite a surprise to find her good-natured. She's a fine woman.'

'But I should say that your especial blessing was your servant. He looks as if he had come out of an English novel.'

'My especial blessing! You haven't seen Miss Hofmann, then?'

'Yes: I met her in the hall. She looks as if she had come out of an American novel. I don't know that that's great praise; but, at all events, I make her come out of it.'

'You're bound in honour, then,' said Mason, laughing, 'to put her into another.'

Mason's conviction of his newly made happiness needed no enforcement at the Doctor's hands. He felt that it would be his own fault if these were not among the most delightful days of his life. He resolved to give himself up without stint to his impressions,— utterly to vegetate. His illness alone would have been a sufficient excuse for a long term of intellectual laxity; but Mason had other good reasons besides. For the past three years he had been stretched without intermission on the rack of duty. Although constantly exposed to hard service, it had been his fortune never to receive a serious wound; and, until his health broke down, he had taken fewer holidays than any officer I ever heard of. With an abundance of a certain kind of equanimity and self control,—a faculty of ready self-adaptation to the accomplished fact, in any direction,—he was yet in his innermost soul a singularly nervous, over-scrupulous person. On the few occasions when he had been absent from the scene of his military duties, although duly authorized and warranted in the act, he had suffered so acutely from the apprehension that something was happening, or was about to happen, which not to have witnessed or to have had a hand in would be matter of eternal mortification, that he can be barely said to have enjoyed his recreation. The sense of lost time was, moreover, his perpetual bugbear,—the feeling that precious hours were now fleeting uncounted, which in more congenial labours would suffice almost for the building of a monument more lasting than brass. This feeling he strove to propitiate as much as possible by assiduous reading and study in the intervals of his actual occupations. I cite the fact merely as an evidence of the uninterrupted austerity of his life for a long time before he fell sick. I might triple this period, indeed, by a glance at his college years, and at certain busy months which intervened between this close of his youth and the opening of the war. Mason had always worked. He was fond of work to begin with; and, in addition, the complete absence of family ties had allowed him to follow his tastes without obstruction or diversion. This circumstance

had been at once a great gain to him and a serious loss. He reached
his twenty-seventh year a very accomplished scholar, as scholars go,
but a great dunce in certain social matters. He was quite ignorant
of all those lighter and more evanescent forms of conviviality
attached to being somebody's son, brother, or cousin. At last, however, as he reminded himself, he was to discover what it was to
be the nephew of somebody's husband. Mrs. Mason was to teach
him the meaning of the adjective *domestic*. It would have been
hard to learn it in a pleasanter way. Mason felt that he was to learn
something from his very idleness, and that he would leave the house
a wiser as well as a better man. It became probable, thanks to that
quickening of the faculties which accompanies the dawning of a
sincere and rational attachment, that in this last respect he would
not be disappointed. Very few days sufficed to reveal to him the
many excellent qualities of his hostess,—her warm capacious heart,
her fairness of mind, her good temper, her good taste, her vast fund
of experience and of reminiscence, and, indeed, more than all, a
certain passionate devotedness, to which fortune, in leaving her
a childless widow, had done but scant justice. The two accordingly
established a friendship,—a friendship that promised as well for
the happiness of each as any that ever undertook to meddle with
happiness. If I were telling my story from Mrs. Mason's point of
view, I take it that I might make a very good thing of the statement that this lady had deliberately and solemnly conferred her
affection upon my hero; but I am compelled to let it stand in this
simple shape. Excellent, charming person that she was, she had
every right to the rich satisfaction which belonged to a liberal—
yet not too liberal—estimate of her guest. She had divined him,—
so much the better for her. That it was very much the better for
him is obviously one of the elementary facts of my narrative; a fact
of which Mason became to rapidly and profoundly sensible, that he
was soon able to dismiss it from his thoughts to his life,—its proper
sphere.

In the space of ten days, then, most of the nebulous impressions
evoked by change of scene had gathered into substantial form.
Others, however, were still in the nebulous state,—diffusing a gentle
light upon Ferdinand's path. Chief among these was the mild radiance of which Miss Hofmann was the centre. For three days after his
arrival Mason had been confined to his room by the aggravation
of his condition consequent upon his journey. It was not till the
fourth day, therefore, that he was able to renew the acquaintance so
auspiciously commenced. When at last, at dinner-time, he reappeared in the drawing-room, Miss Hofmann greeted him almost

as an old friend. Mason had already discovered that she was young and gracious; he now rapidly advanced to the conclusion that she was uncommonly pretty. Before dinner was over, he had made up his mind that she was neither more nor less than beautiful. Mrs. Mason had found time to give him a full account of her life. She had lost her mother in infancy, and had been adopted by her aunt in the early years of this lady's widowhood. Her father was a man of evil habits,—a drunkard, a gambler, and a rake, outlawed from decent society. His only dealings with his daughter were to write her every month or two a begging letter, she being in possession of her mother's property. Mrs. Mason had taken her niece to Europe, and given her every advantage. She had had an expensive education; she had travelled; she had gone into the world; she had been presented, like a good republican, to no less than three European sovereigns; she had been admired; she had had half a dozen offers of marriage to her aunt's knowledge, and others, perhaps, of which she was ignorant, and had refused them all. She was now twenty-six years of age, beautiful, accomplished, and *au mieux* with her bankers. She was an excellent girl, with a will of her own. 'I'm very fond of her,' Mrs. Mason declared, with her habitual frankness; 'and I suppose she's equally fond of me; but we long ago gave up all idea of playing at mother and daughter. We have never had a disagreement since she was fifteen years old; but we have never had an agreement either. Caroline is no sentimentalist. She's honest, good-tempered, and perfectly discerning. She foresaw that we were still to spend a number of years together, and she wisely declined at the outset to affect a range of feelings that wouldn't stand the wear and tear of time. She knew that she would make a poor daughter, and she contented herself with being a good niece. A capital niece she is. In fact we're almost sisters. There are moments when I feel as if she were ten years older than I, and as if it were absurd in me to attempt to interfere with her life. I never do. She has it quite in her own hands. My attitude is little more than a state of affectionate curiosity as to what she will do with it. Of course she'll marry, sooner or later; but I'm curious to see the man of her choice. In Europe, you know, girls have no acquaintances but such as they share with their parents and guardians; and in that way I know most of the gentlemen who have tried to make themselves acceptable to my niece. There were some excellent young men in the number; but there was not one—or, rather, there was but one—for whom Caroline cared a straw. That one she loved, I believe; but they had a quarrel, and she lost him. She's very discreet and conciliating. I'm sure no girl ever before got rid of half a dozen suitors with so little offence. Ah, she's a dear, good girl!' Mrs. Mason pursued. 'She's saved me a world of trouble in my day. And when I think what she might have been, with her beauty, and what not! She has kept all her suitors as friends. There are two of them who write to her still. She doesn't answer their letters; but once in a while she meets them, and thanks them for writing, and that contents them. The others are married, and Caroline remains single. I take for granted it won't last forever. Still, although she's *not* a sentimentalist, she'll not marry a man she doesn't care for, merely because she's growing old. Indeed, it's only the sentimental girls, to my belief, that do that. They covet a man for his money or his looks, and then give the feeling some fine name. But there's one thing, Mr. Ferdinand,' added Mrs. Mason, at the close of these remarks, 'you will be so good as not to fall in love with my niece. I can assure you that she'll not fall in love with you, and a hopeless passion will not hasten your recovery. Caroline is a charming girl. You can live with her very well without that. She's good for common daylight, and you'll have no need of wax-candles and ecstasies.'

'Be reassured,' said Ferdinand, laughing. 'I'm quite too attentive to myself at present to think of anyone else. Miss Hofmann might be dying for a glance of my eye, and I shouldn't hesitate to sacrifice her. It takes more than half a man to fall in love.'

At the end of ten days summer had fairly set in; and Mason found it possible, and indeed profitable, to spend a large portion of his time in the open air. He was unable either to ride or to walk; and the only form of exercise which he found practicable was an occasional drive in Mrs. Mason's phaeton. On these occasions Mrs. Mason was his habitual companion. The neighbourhood offered an interminable succession of beautiful drives; and poor Ferdinand took a truly exquisite pleasure in reclining idly upon a pile of cushions, warmly clad, empty-handed, silent, with only his eyes in motion, and rolling rapidly between fragrant hedges and springing crops, and beside the outskirts of woods, and along the heights which overlooked the river. Detested war was over, and all nature had ratified the peace. Mason used to gaze up into the cloudless sky until his eyes began to water, and you would have actually supposed he was shedding sentimental tears. Besides these comfortable drives with his hostess, Mason had adopted another method of inhaling the sunshine. He used frequently to spend several hours at a time on a veranda beside the house, sheltered from the observation of visitors. Here, with an arm-chair and a footstool, a cigar and half a dozen volumes of novels, to say nothing of the society of either of the ladies, and sometimes of both, he suffered the mornings to pass unmeasured and uncounted. The chief incident of these mornings was the Doctor's visit, in which, of course, there was a strong element of prose,—and very good prose, as I may add, for the Doctor was turning out an excellent fellow. But, for the rest, time unrolled itself like a gentle strain of music. Mason knew so little, from direct observation, of the *vie intime* of elegant, intelligent women, that their habits, their manners, their household motions, their principles, possessed in his view all the charm of a spectacle,— a spectacle which he contemplated with the indolence of an invalid, the sympathy of a man of taste, and a little of the awkwardness which women gladly allow, and indeed provoke, in a soldier, for the pleasure of forgiving it. It was a very simple matter to Miss Hofmann that she should be dressed in fresh crisp muslin, that her hands should be white and her attitudes felicitous; she had long since made her peace with these things. But to Mason, who was familiar only with books and men, they were objects of constant, half-dreamy contemplation. He would sit for half an hour at once, with a book on his knees and the pages unturned, scrutinizing with ingenious indirectness the simple mass of colours and contours which made up the physical personality of Miss Hofmann. There was no question as to her beauty, or as to its being a warm, sympathetic beauty, and not the cold perfection of poetry. She was the least bit taller than most women, and neither stout nor the reverse. Her hair was of a dark and lustrous brown, turning almost to black, and lending itself readily to those multitudinous ringlets which were then in fashion. Her forehead was broad, open, and serene; and her eyes of that deep and clear sea-green that you may observe of a summer's afternoon, when the declining sun shines through the rising of a wave. Her complexion was the colour of perfect health. These, with her full, mild lips, her generous and flexible figure, her magnificent hands, were charms enough to occupy Mason's attention, and it was but seldom that he allowed it to be diverted. Mrs. Mason was frequently called away by her household cares, but Miss Hofmann's time was apparently quite her own. Nevertheless, it came into Ferdinand's head one day, that she gave him her company only from a sense of duty, and when, according to his wont, he had allowed this impression to ripen in his mind, he ventured to assure her that, much as he valued her society, he should be sorry to believe that her gracious bestowal of it interfered with more profitable occupations. 'I'm no companion,' he said. 'I don't pretend to be one. I sit here deaf and dumb, and blind and halt, patiently waiting to be healed,—waiting till this vagabond Nature of ours strolls my way, and brushes me with the hem of her garment.'

'I find you very good company,' Miss Hofmann replied on this occasion. 'What do you take me for? The hero of a hundred fights, a young man who has been reduced to a shadow in the service of his country,—I should be very fastidious if I asked for anything better.'

'O, if it's on theory!' said Mason. And, in spite of Miss Hofmann's protest, he continued to assume that it *was* on theory that he was not intolerable. But she remained true to her post, and with a sort of placid inveteracy which seemed to the young man to betray either a great deal of indifference or a great deal of self-command. 'She thinks I'm stupid,' he said to himself. 'Of course she thinks I'm stupid. How should she think otherwise? She and her aunt have talked me over. Mrs. Mason has enumerated my virtues, and Miss Hofmann has added them up: total, a well-meaning bore. She has armed herself with patience. I must say it becomes her very well.' Nothing was more natural, however, than that Mason should exaggerate the effect of his social incapacity. His remarks were desultory, but not infrequent; often trivial, but always good-humoured and informal. The intervals of silence, indeed, which enlivened his conversation with Miss Hofmann, might easily have been taken for the confident pauses in the talk of old friends.

Once in a while Miss Hofmann would sit down at the piano and play to him. The veranda communicated with the little sitting-room by means of a long window, one side of which stood open. Mason would move his chair to this aperture, so that he might see the music as well as hear it. Seated at the instrument, at the farther end of the half-darkened room, with her figure in half-profile, and her features, her movements, the colour of her dress, but half defined in the cool obscurity, Miss Hofmann would discourse infinite melody. Mason's eyes rested awhile on the vague white folds of her dress, on the heavy convolutions of her hair, and the gentle movement of her head in sympathy with the music. Then a single glance in the other direction revealed another picture,—the dazzling midday sky, the close-cropped lawn, lying almost black in its light, and the patient, round-backed gardener, in white shirt-sleeves, clipping the hedge or rolling the gravel. One morning, what with the music, the light, the heat, and the fragrance of the flowers,—from the perfect equilibrium of his senses, as it were,—Mason manfully went to sleep. On waking he found that he had slept an hour, and that the sun had invaded the veranda. The music had ceased; but on looking into the parlour he saw Miss Hofmann still at the piano. A gentleman was leaning on the instrument with his back toward the window, intercepting her face. Mason sat for some moments, hardly sensible, at first, of his transition to consciousness, languidly guessing at her companion's identity. In a short time his observation was quickened by the fact that the picture before him was animated by no sound of voices. The silence was unnatural, or, at the least, disagreeable. Mason moved his chair, and the gentleman looked round. The gentleman was Horace Knight. The Doctor called out, 'Good morning!' from his place, and finished his conversation with Miss Hofmann before coming out to his patient. When he moved away from the piano, Mason saw the reason for his friends' silence. Miss Hofmann had been trying to decipher a difficult piece of music, the Doctor had been trying to assist her, and they had both been brought to a stop.

'What a clever fellow he is!' thought Mason. 'There he stands, rattling off musical terms as if he had never thought of anything else. And yet, when he talks medicine, it's impossible to talk more to the point.' Mason continued to be very well satisfied with Knight's intelligence of his case, and with his treatment of it. He had been in the country now for three weeks, and he would hesitate indeed to affirm that he felt materially better; but he felt more comfortable. There were moments when he feared to push the inquiry as to his real improvement, because he had a sickening apprehension that he would discover that in one or two important particulars he was worse. In the course of time he imparted these fears to his physician. 'But I may be mistaken,' he added, 'and for this reason. During the last fortnight I have become much more sensible of my condition than while I was in town. I then accepted each additional symptom as a matter of course. The more the better, I thought. But now I expect them to give an account of themselves. Now I have a positive wish to recover.'

Dr. Knight looked at his patient for a moment curiously. 'You are right,' he said; 'a little impatience is a very good thing.'

'O, I'm not impatient. I'm patient to a most ridiculous extent. I allow myself a good six months, at the very least.'

'That is certainly not unreasonable,' said Knight. 'And will you allow me a question? Do you intend to spend those six months in this place?'

'I'm unable to answer you. I suppose I shall finish the summer here, unless the summer finishes me. Mrs. Mason will hear of nothing else. In September I hope to be well enough to go back to town, even if I'm not well enough to think of work. What do you advise?'

'I advise you to put away all thoughts of work. That is imperative. Haven't you been at work all your life long? Can't you spare a pitiful little twelve-month to health and idleness and pleasure?'

'Ah, pleasure, pleasure!' said Mason, ironically.

'Yes, pleasure,' said the Doctor. 'What has she done to you that you should speak of her in that manner?'

'O, she bothers me,' said Mason.

'You are very fastidious. It's better to be bothered by pleasure than by pain.'

'I don't deny it. But there is a way of being indifferent to pain. I don't mean to say that I have found it out, but in the course of my illness I have caught a glimpse of it. But it's beyond my strength to be indifferent to pleasure. In two words, I'm afraid of dying of kindness.'

'O, nonsense!'

'Yes, it's nonsense; and yet it's not. There would be nothing miraculous in my not getting well.'

'It will be your fault if you don't. It will prove that you're fonder of sickness than health, and that you're not fit company for sensible mortals. Shall I tell you?' continued the Doctor, after a moment's hesitation. 'When I knew you in the army, I always found you a step beyond my comprehension. You took things too hard. You had scruples and doubts about everything. And on top of it all you were devoured with the mania of appearing to take things easily and to be perfectly indifferent. You played your part very well, but you must do me the justice to confess that it *was* a part.'

'I hardly know whether that's a compliment or an impertinence. I hope, at least, that you don't mean to accuse me of playing a part at the present moment.'

'On the contrary. I'm your physician; you're frank.'

'It's not because you're my physician that I'm frank,' said Mason. 'I shouldn't think of burdening you in that capacity with my miserable caprices and fancies;' and Ferdinand paused a moment. 'You're a man!' he pursued, laying his hand on his companion's arm. 'There's nothing here but women, Heaven reward them! I'm saturated with whispers and perfumes and smiles, and the rustling of dresses. It takes a man to understand a man.'

'It takes more than a man to understand you, my dear Mason,' said Knight, with a kindly smile. 'But I listen.'

Mason remained silent, leaning back in his chair, with his eyes wandering slowly over the wide patch of sky disclosed by the window, and his hands languidly folded on his knees. The Doctor examined him with a look half amused, half perplexed. But at last his face grew quite sober, and he contracted his brow. He placed his hand on Mason's arm and shook it gently, while Ferdinand met his gaze. The Doctor frowned, and, as he did so, his companion's mouth expanded into a placid smile. 'If you don't get well,' said Knight,—'if you don't get well—' and he paused.

'What will be the consequences?' asked Ferdinand, still smiling.

'I shall hate you,' said Knight, half smiling too.

Mason broke into a laugh. 'What shall I care for that?'

'I shall tell people that you were a poor, spiritless fellow,—that you are no loss.'

'I give you leave,' said Ferdinand.

The Doctor got up. 'I don't like obstinate patients,' he said.

Ferdinand burst into a long loud laugh, which ended in a fit of coughing.

'I'm getting too amusing,' said Knight; 'I must go.'

'Nay, laugh and grow fat,' cried Ferdinand. 'I promise to get well.' But that evening, at least, he was no better, as it turned out, for his momentary exhilaration. Before turning in for the night, he went into the drawing-room to spend half an hour with the ladies. The room was empty, but the lamp was lighted, and he sat down by the table and read a chapter in a novel. He felt excited, light-headed, light-hearted, half-intoxicated, as if he had been drinking strong coffee. He put down his book, and went over to the mantelpiece, above which hung a mirror, and looked at the reflection of his face. For almost the first time in his life he examined his features, and wondered if he were good-looking. He was able to conclude only that he looked very thin and pale, and utterly unfit for the business of life. At last he heard an opening of doors overhead, and a rustling of voluminous skirts on the stairs. Mrs. Mason came in, fresh from the hands of her maid, and dressed for a party.

'And is Miss Hofmann going?' asked Mason. He felt that his heart was beating, and that he hoped Mrs. Mason would say no. His momentary sense of strength, the mellow lamplight, the open piano, and the absence of the excellent woman before him, struck him as so many reasons for her remaining at home. But the sound of the young lady's descent upon the stairs was an affirmative to his question. She forthwith appeared upon the threshold, dressed in crape of a kind of violent blue, with desultory clusters of white roses. For some ten minutes Mason had the pleasure of being witness of that series of pretty movements and preparations with which women in full dress beguile the interval before their carriage is announced; their glances at the mirror, their slow assumption of their gloves, their mutual revisions and felicitations.

'Isn't she lovely?' said Miss Hofmann to the young man, nodding at her aunt, who looked every inch the handsome woman that she was.

'Lovely, lovely, lovely!' said Ferdinand, so emphatically, that Miss Hofmann transferred her glance to him; while Mrs. Mason good-humouredly turned her back, and Caroline saw that Mason was engaged in a survey of her own person.

Miss Hofmann smiled discreetly. 'I wish very much you might come,' she said.

'I shall go to bed,' answered Ferdinand, simply.

'Well, that's much better. We shall go to bed at two o'clock. Meanwhile I shall caper about the rooms to the sound of a piano and fiddle, and Aunt Maria will sit against the wall with her toes tucked under a chair. Such is life!'

'You'll dance then,' said Mason.

'I shall dance. Dr. Knight has invited me.'

'Does he dance well, Caroline?' asked Mrs. Mason.

'That remains to be seen. I have a strong impression that he does not.'

'Why?' asked Ferdinand.

'He does so many other things well.'

'That's no reason,' said Mrs. Mason. 'Do you dance, Ferdinand?' Ferdinand shook his head.

'I like a man to dance,' said Caroline, 'and yet I like him not to dance.'

'That's a very womanish speech, my dear,' said Mrs. Mason.

'I suppose it is. It's inspired by my white gloves and my low dress, and my roses. When once a woman gets on such things, Colonel Mason, expect nothing but nonsense.—Aunt Maria,' the young lady continued, 'will you button my glove?'

'Let me do it,' said Ferdinand. 'Your aunt has her gloves on.'

'Thank you.' And Miss Hofmann extended a long white arm, and drew back with her other hand the bracelet from her wrist. Her glove had three buttons, and Mason performed the operation with great deliberation and neatness.

'And now,' said he, gravely, 'I hear the carriage. You want me to put on your shawl?'

'If you please,'— Miss Hofmann passed her full white drapery into his hands, and then turned about her fair shoulders. Mason solemnly covered them, while the waiting-maid, who had come in, performed the same service for the elder lady.

'Good-bye,' said the latter, giving him her hand. 'You're not to come out into the air.' And Mrs. Mason, attended by her maid, transferred herself to the carriage. Miss Hofmann gathered up her loveliness, and prepared to follow. Ferdinand stood leaning against the parlour door, watching her; and as she rustled past him she nodded farewell with a silent smile. A characteristic smile, Mason thought it,—a smile in which there was no expectation of triumph and no affectation of reluctance, but just the faintest suggestion of perfectly good-humoured resignation. Mason went to the window and saw the carriage roll away with its lighted lamps, and then stood looking out into the darkness. The sky was cloudy. As he turned away the maid-servant came in, and took from the table a pair of rejected gloves. 'I hope you're feeling better, sir,' she said, politely.

'Thank you, I think I am.'

'It's a pity you couldn't have gone with the ladies.'

'I'm not well enough yet to think of such things,' said Mason, trying to smile. But as he walked across the floor he felt himself attacked by a sudden sensation, which cannot be better described than as a general collapse. He felt dizzy, faint, and sick. His head swam and his knees trembled. 'I'm ill,' he said, sitting down on the sofa; 'you must call William.'

William speedily arrived, and conducted the young man to his room. 'What on earth had you been doing, sir?' asked this most irreproachable of serving-men, as he helped him to undress.

Ferdinand was silent a moment. 'I had been putting on Miss Hofmann's shawl,' he said.

'Is that all, sir?'

'And I had been buttoning her glove.'

'Well, sir, you must be very prudent.'

'So it appears,' said Ferdinand.

He slept soundly, however, and the next morning was the better for it. 'I'm certainly better,' he said to himself, as he slowly proceeded to his toilet. 'A month ago such an attack as that of last evening would have effectually banished sleep. Courage, then. The Devil isn't dead, but he's dying.'

In the afternoon he received a visit from Horace Knight. 'So you danced last evening at Mrs. Bradshaw's,' he said to his friend.

'Yes, I danced. It's a great piece of frivolity for a man in my position; but I thought there would be no harm in doing it just once, to show them I know how. My abstinence in future will tell the better. Your ladies were there. I danced with Miss Hofmann. She was dressed in blue, and she was the most beautiful woman in the room. Everyone was talking about it.'

'I saw her,' said Mason, 'before she went off.'

'You should have seen her there,' said Knight. 'The music, the excitement, the spectators, and all that, bring out a woman's beauty.'

'So I suppose,' said Ferdinand.

'What strikes me,' pursued the Doctor, 'is her—what shall I call it?—her vitality, her quiet buoyancy. Of course, you didn't see her when she came home? If you had, you would have noticed, unless I'm very much mistaken, that she was as fresh and elastic at two o'clock as she had been at ten. While all the other women looked tired and jaded and used up, she alone showed no signs of exhaustion. She was neither pale nor flushed, but still light-footed, rosy, and erect. She's solid. You see I can't help looking at such things as a physician. She has a magnificent organization. Among all those other poor girls she seemed to have something of the inviolable strength of a goddess;' and Knight smiled frankly as he entered the region of eloquence. 'She wears her artificial roses and dew-drops as if she had gathered them on the mountain tops, instead of buying them in Broadway. She moves with long steps, her dress rustles, and to a man of fancy it's the sound of Diana on the forest-leaves.'

Ferdinand nodded assent. 'So you're a man of fancy,' he said.

'Of course I am,' said the Doctor.

Ferdinand was not inclined to question his friend's estimate of Miss Hofmann, nor to weigh his words. They only served to confirm an impression which was already strong in his own mind. Day by day he had felt the growth of this impression. 'He must be a strong man who would approach her,' he said to himself. 'He must be as vigorous and elastic as she herself, or in the progress of courtship she will leave him far behind. He must be able to forget his lungs and his liver and his digestion. To have broken down in his country's defence, even, will avail him nothing. What is that to her? She needs a man who has defended his country without breaking down, —a being complete, intact, well seasoned, invulnerable. Then,— then,' thought Ferdinand, 'perhaps she will consider him. Perhaps it will be to refuse him. Perhaps, like Diana, to whom Knight compares her, she is meant to live alone. It's certain, at least, that she is able to wait. She will be young at forty-five. Women who are young at forty-five are perhaps not the most interesting women. They are likely to have felt for nobody and for nothing. But it's often less their own fault than that of the men and women about them. This one at least *can* feel; the thing is to move her. Her soul is an instrument of a hundred strings, only it takes a strong hand to draw sound. Once really touched, they will reverberate for ever and ever.'

In fine, Mason was in love. It will be seen that his passion was not arrogant nor uncompromising; but, on the contrary, patient, discreet, and modest,—almost timid. For ten long days, the most memorable days of his life,—days which, if he had kept a journal, would have been left blank,—he held his tongue. He would have suffered anything rather than reveal his emotions, or allow them to come accidentally to Miss Hofmann's knowledge. He would cherish them in silence until he should feel in all his sinews that he was himself again, and then he would open his heart. Meanwhile he would be patient; he would be the most irreproachable, the most austere, the most insignificant of convalescents. He was as yet unfit to touch her, to look at her, to speak to her. A man was not to go a-wooing in his dressing-gown and slippers.

There came a day, however, when, in spite of his high resolves, Ferdinand came near losing his balance. Mrs. Mason had arranged with him to drive in the phaeton after dinner. But it befell that, an hour before the appointed time, she was sent for by a neighbour who had been taken ill.

'But it's out of the question that you should lose your drive,' said Miss Hofmann, who brought him her aunt's apologies. 'If you are still disposed to go, I shall be happy to take the reins. I shall not be as good company as Aunt Maria, but perhaps I shall be as good company as Thomas.' It was settled, accordingly, that Miss Hofmann should act as her aunt's substitute, and at five o'clock the phaeton left the door. The first half of their drive was passed in silence; and almost the first words they exchanged were as they finally drew near to a space of enclosed ground, beyond which, through the trees at its farther extremity, they caught a glimpse of a turn in the river. Miss Hofmann involuntarily pulled up. The sun had sunk low, and the cloudless western sky glowed with rosy yellow. The trees which concealed the view flung over the grass a great screen of shadow, which reached out into the road. Between their scattered stems gleamed the broad white current of the Hudson. Our friends both knew the spot. Mason had seen it from a boat, when one morning a gentleman in the neighbourhood, thinking to do him a kindness, had invited him to take a short sail; and with Miss Hofmann it had long been a frequent resort.

'How beautiful!' she said, as the phaeton stopped.

'Yes, if it wasn't for those trees,' said Ferdinand. 'They conceal the best part of the view.'

'I should rather say they indicate it,' answered his companion. 'From here they conceal it; but they suggest to you to make your way in, and lose yourself behind them, and enjoy the prospect in privacy.'

'But you can't take a vehicle in.'

'No: there is only a footpath, although I have ridden in. One of these days, when you're stronger, you must drive to this point, and get out, and walk over to the bank.'

Mason was silent a moment,—a moment during which he felt in his limbs the tremor of a bold resolution. 'I noticed the place the day I went out on the water with Mr. McCarthy. I immediately marked it as my own. The bank is quite high, and the trees make a little amphitheatre on its summit. I think there's a bench.'

'Yes, there are two benches,' said Caroline.

'Suppose, then, we try it now,' said Mason, with an effort.

'But you can never walk over that meadow. You see it's broken ground. And, at all events, I can't consent to your going alone.'

'That, madam,' said Ferdinand, rising to his feet in the phaeton, 'is a piece of folly I should never think of proposing. Yonder is a house, and in it there are people. Can't we drive thither, and place the horse in their custody?'

'Nothing is more easy, if you insist upon it. The house is occupied by a German family with a couple of children, who are old friends of mine. When I come here on horseback they always clamour for "coppers". From their little garden the walk is shorter.'

So Miss Hofmann turned the horse toward the cottage, which stood at the head of a lane, a few yards from the road. A little boy and girl, with bare heads and bare feet,—the former members very white and the latter very black,—came out to meet her. Caroline greeted them good-humouredly in German. The girl, who was the elder, consented to watch the horse, while the boy volunteered to show the visitors the shortest way to the river. Mason reached the point in question without great fatigue, and found a prospect which would have repaid even greater trouble. To the right and to the left, a hundred feet below them, stretched the broad channel of the seaward-shifting waters. In the distance rose the gentle masses of the Catskills with all the intervening region vague and neutral in the gathering twilight. A faint odour of coolness came up to their faces from the stream below.

'You can sit down,' said the little boy, doing the honours.

'Yes, Colonel, sit down,' said Caroline. 'You've already been on your feet too much.'

Ferdinand obediently seated himself, unable to deny that he was glad to do so. Miss Hofmann released from her grasp the skirts which she had gathered up in her passage from the phaeton, and strolled to the edge of the cliff, where she stood for some moments talking with her little guide. Mason could only hear that she was speaking German. After the lapse of a few moments Miss Hofman turned back, still talking—or rather listening—to the child.

'He's very pretty,' she said in French, as she stopped before Ferdinand.

Mason broke into a laugh. 'To think,' said he, 'that that little youngster should forbid us the use of two languages! Do you speak French, my child?'

'No,' said the boy, sturdily, 'I speak German.'

'Ah, there I can't follow you!'

The child stared a moment, and then replied, with pardonable irrelevancy, 'I'll show you the way down to the water.'

'There I can't follow you either. I hope *you*'ll not go, Miss Hofmann,' added the young man, observing a movement on Caroline's part.

'Is it hard?' she asked of the child.

'No, it's easy.'

'Will I tear my dress?'

The child shook his head; and Caroline descended the bank under his guidance.

As some moments elapsed before she reappeared, Ferdinand ventured to the edge of the cliff, and looked down. She was sitting on a rock on the narrow margin of sand, with her hat in her lap, twisting the feather in her fingers. In a few moments it seemed to Ferdinand that he caught the tones of her voice, wafted upward as if she were gently singing. He listened intently, and at last succeeded in distinguishing several words; they were German. 'Confound her German!' thought the young man. Suddenly Miss Hofmann rose from her seat, and, after a short interval, reappeared on the platform. 'What did you find down there?' asked Ferdinand, almost savagely.

'Nothing,—a little strip of a beach and a pile of stones.'

'You *have* torn your dress,' said Mason.

Miss Hofmann surveyed her drapery. 'Where, if you please?'

'There, in front.' And Mason extended his walking-stick, and inserted it into the injured fold of muslin. There was a certain graceless *brusquerie* in the movement which attracted Miss Hofmann's attention. She looked at her companion, and, seeing that his face was discomposed, fancied that he was annoyed at having been compelled to wait.

'Thank you,' she said; 'it's easily mended. And now suppose we go back.'

'No, not yet,' said Ferdinand. 'We have plenty of time.'

'Plenty of time to catch cold,' said Miss Hofmann, kindly.

Mason had planted his stick where he had let it fall on withdrawing it from contact with his companion's skirts, and stood leaning against it, with his eyes on the young girl's face. 'What if I do catch cold?' he asked abruptly.

'Come, don't talk nonsense,' said Miss Hofmann.

'I never was more serious in my life.' And, pausing a moment, he drew a couple of steps nearer. She had gathered her shawl closely about her, and stood with her arms lost in it, holding her elbows. 'I don't mean that quite literally,' Mason continued. 'I wish to get well, on the whole. But there are moments when this perpetual self-coddling seems beneath the dignity of man, and I'm tempted to purchase one short hour of enjoyment, of happiness, at the cost— well, at the cost of my life if necessary!'

This was a franker speech than Ferdinand had yet made; the reader may estimate his habitual reserve. Miss Hofmann must have been somewhat surprised, and even slightly puzzled. But it was plain that he expected a rejoinder.

'I don't know what temptation you may have had,' she answered, smiling; 'but I confess that I can think of none in your present circumstances likely to involve the great sacrifice you speak of. What you say, Colonel Mason, is half—'

'Half what?'

'Half ungrateful. Aunt Maria flatters herself that she has made existence as easy and as peaceful for you—as stupid, if you like— as it can possibly be for a—a clever man. And now, after all, to accuse her of introducing temptations.'

'Your aunt Maria is the best of women, Miss Hofmann,' said Mason. 'But I'm not a clever man. I'm deplorably weak-minded. Very little things excite me. Very small pleasures are gigantic temptations. I would give a great deal, for instance, to stay here with you for half an hour.'

It is a delicate question whether Miss Hofmann now ceased to be perplexed; whether she discerned in the young man's accents —it was his tone, his attitude, his eyes that were fully significant, rather than his words—an intimation of that sublime and simple truth in the presence of which a wise woman puts off coquetry and prudery, and stands invested with perfect charity. But charity is nothing if not discreet; and Miss Hofmann may very well have effected the little transaction I speak of, and yet have remained, as she did remain, gracefully wrapped in her shawl, with the same serious smile on her face. Ferdinand's heart was thumping under his waistcoat; the words in which he might tell her that he loved her were fluttering there like frightened birds in a storm-shaken cage. Whether his lips would form them or not depended on the next words she uttered. On the faintest sign of defiance or of impatience he would really give her something to coquet withal. I repeat that I do not undertake to follow Miss Hofmann's feelings; I only know that her words were those of a woman of great instincts. 'My dear Colonel Mason,' she said, 'I wish we might remain here the whole evening. The moments are quite too pleasant to be wantonly sacrificed. I simply put you on your conscience. If you believe that you can safely do so,—that you'll not have some dreadful chill in consequence,—let us by all means stay awhile. If you do not so believe, let us go back to the carriage. There is no good reason, that I see, for our behaving like children.'

If Miss Hofmann apprehended a scene,—I do not assert that she did,—she was saved. Mason extracted from her words a delicate assurance that he could afford to wait. 'You're an angel, Miss Hofmann,' he said, as a sign that this kindly assurance had been taken. 'I think we had better go back.'

Miss Hofmann accordingly led the way along the path, and Ferdinand slowly followed. A man who has submitted to a woman's wisdom generally feels bound to persuade himself that he has surrendered at discretion. I suppose it was in this spirit that Mason said to himself as he walked along, 'Well, I got what I wanted.'

The next morning he was again an invalid. He woke up with symptoms which as yet he had scarcely felt at all; and he was obliged to acknowledge the bitter truth that, small as it was, his adventure had exceeded his strength. The walk, the evening air, the dampness of the spot, had combined to produce a violent attack of fever. As soon as it became plain that, in vulgar terms, he was 'in for it', he took his heart in his hands and succumbed. As his condition grew worse, he was fortunately relieved from the custody of this valuable organ, with all it contained of hopes delayed and broken projects, by several intervals of prolonged unconsciousness.

For three weeks he was a very sick man. For a couple of days his recovery was doubted of. Mrs. Mason attended him with inexhaustible patience and with the solicitude of real affection. She was resolved that greedy Death should not possess himself, through any fault of hers, of a career so full of bright possibilities and of that active gratitude which a good-natured elderly woman would relish, as she felt that of her *protégé* to be. Her vigils were finally rewarded. One fine morning poor long-silent Ferdinand found words to tell her that he was better. His recovery was very slow, however, and it ceased several degrees below the level from which he had originally fallen. He was thus twice a convalescent,—a sufficiently miserable fellow. He professed to be very much surprised to find himself still among the living. He remained silent and grave, with a newly contracted fold in his forehead, like a man honestly perplexed at the vagaries of destiny. 'It must be,' he said to Mrs. Mason,—'it must be that I am reserved for great things.'

In order to insure absolute quiet in the house, Ferdinand learned Miss Hofmann had removed herself to the house of a friend, at a distance of some five miles. On the first day that the young man was well enough to sit in his arm-chair Mrs. Mason spoke of her niece's return, which was fixed for the morrow. 'She will want very much to see you,' she said. 'When she comes, may I bring her into your room?'

'Good heavens, no!' said Ferdinand, to whom the idea was very disagreeable. He met her accordingly at dinner, three days later. He left his room at the dinner hour, in company with Dr. Knight, who was taking his departure. In the hall they encountered Mrs. Mason, who invited the Doctor to remain, in honour of his patient's reappearance in society. The Doctor hesitated a moment, and, as he did so, Ferdinand heard Miss Hofmann's step descending the stair. He turned towards her just in time to catch on her face the vanishing of a glance of intelligence. As Mrs. Mason's back was against the staircase, her glance was evidently meant for Knight. He excused himself on the plea of an engagement, to Mason's regret, while the latter greeted the younger lady. Mrs. Mason proposed another day,—the following Sunday; the Doctor assented, and it was not till some time later that Ferdinand found himself wondering why Miss Hofmann should have forbidden him to remain. He rapidly perceived that during the period of their separation this young lady had lost none of her charms; on the contrary, they were more irresistible than ever. It seemed to Mason, moreover, that they were bound together by a certain pensive gentleness, a tender, submissive look, which he had hitherto failed to observe. Mrs. Mason's own remarks assured him that he was not the victim of an illusion.

'I wonder what is the matter with Caroline,' she said. 'If it were not that she tells me that she never was better, I should believe she is feeling unwell. I've never seen her so simple and gentle. She looks like a person who has a great fright,—a fright not altogether unpleasant.'

'She has been staying in a house full of people,' said Mason. 'She has been excited, and amused, and preoccupied; she returns to you and me (excuse the juxtaposition,—it exists)—a kind of reaction asserts itself.' Ferdinand's explanation was ingenious rather than plausible.

Mrs. Mason had a better one. 'I have an impression,' she said, 'George Stapleton, the second of the sons, is an old admirer of Caroline's. It's hard to believe that he could have been in the house with her for a fortnight without renewing his suit, in some form or other.'

Ferdinand was not made uneasy, for he had seen and talked with Mr. George Stapleton,—a young man, very good-looking, very good-natured, very clever, very rich, and very unworthy, as he conceived, of Miss Hofmann. 'You don't mean to say that your niece has listened to him,' he answered, calmly enough.

'Listened, yes. He has made himself agreeable, and he has succeeded in making an impression,—a temporary impression,' added Mrs. Mason with a business-like air.

'I can't believe it,' said Ferdinand.

'Why not? He's a very nice fellow.'

'Yes,—yes,' said Mason, 'very nice indeed. He's very rich too.' And here the talk was interrupted by Caroline's entrance.

On Sunday the two ladies went to church. It was not till after they had gone that Ferdinand left his room. He came into the little parlour, took up a book, and felt something of the stir of his old intellectual life. Would he ever again know what it was to work? In the course of an hour the ladies came in, radiant with devotional millinery. Mrs. Mason soon went out again, leaving the others together. Miss Hofmann asked Ferdinand what he had been reading; and he was thus led to declare that he really believed he should, after all, get the use of his head again. She listened with all the respect which an intelligent woman who leads an idle life necessarily feels for a clever man when he consents to make her in some degree the confidant of his intellectual purposes. Quickened by her delicious sympathy, her grave attention, and her intelligent questions, he was led to unbosom himself of several of his dearest convictions and projects. It was easy that from this point the conversation should advance to matters of belief and hope in general. Before he knew it, it had done so; and he had thus the great satisfaction of discussing with the woman on whom of all others his selfish and personal happiness was most dependent those great themes in whose expansive magnitude persons and pleasures and passions are absorbed and extinguished, and in whose austere effulgence the brightest divinities of earth remit their shining. Serious passions are a good preparation for the highest kinds of speculation. Although Ferdinand was urging no suit whatever upon his companion, and consciously, at least, making use in no degree of the emotion which accompanied her presence, it is certain that, as they formed themselves, his conceptions were the clearer for being the conceptions of a man in love. And, as for Miss Hofmann, her attention could not, to all appearances, have been more lively, nor her perception more delicate, if the atmosphere of her own intellect had been purified by the sacred fires of a responsive passion.

Knight duly made his appearance at dinner, and proved himself once more the entertaining gentleman whom our friends had long since learned to appreciate. But Mason, fresh from his contest with morals and metaphysics, was forcibly struck with the fact that he was one of those men from whom these sturdy beggars receive more kicks than halfpence. He was nevertheless obliged to admit, that, if he was not a man of principles, he was thoroughly a man of honour. After dinner the company adjourned to the piazza, where, in the course of half an hour, the Doctor proposed to Miss Hofmann to take a turn in the grounds. All around the lawn there wound a narrow footpath, concealed from view in spots by clusters of shrubbery. Ferdinand and his hostess sat watching their retreating figures as they slowly measured the sinuous strip of gravel; Miss Hofmann's light dress and the Doctor's white waistcoat gleaming at intervals through the dark verdure. At the end of twenty minutes they returned to the house. The Doctor came back only to make his bow and to take his departure; and, when he had gone, Miss Hofmann retired to her own room. The next morning she mounted her horse, and rode over to see the friend with whom she had stayed during Mason's fever. Ferdinand saw her pass his window, erect in the saddle, with her horse scattering the gravel with his nervous steps. Shortly afterwards Mrs. Mason came into the room, sat down by the young man, made her habitual inquiries as to his condition, and then paused in such a way as that he instantly felt that she had something to tell him. 'You've something to tell me,' he said; 'what is it?'

Mrs. Mason blushed a little, and laughed. 'I was first made to promise to keep it a secret,' she said. 'If I'm so transparent now that I have leave to tell it, what should I be if I hadn't? Guess.'

Ferdinand shook his head peremptorily. 'I give it up.'

'Caroline is engaged.'

'To whom?'

'Not to Mr. Stapleton,—to Dr. Knight.'

Ferdinand was silent a moment; but he neither changed colour nor dropped his eyes. Then, at last, 'Did she wish you not to tell me?' he asked.

'She wished me to tell no one. But I prevailed upon her to let me tell you.'

'Thank you,' said Ferdinand with a little bow—and an immense irony.

'It's a great surprise,' continued Mrs. Mason. 'I never suspected it. And there I was talking about Mr. Stapleton! I don't see how they have managed it. Well, I suppose it's for the best. But it seems odd that Caroline should have refused so many superior offers, to put up at last with Dr. Knight.'

Ferdinand had felt for an instant as if the power of speech was deserting him; but volition nailed it down with a great muffled hammer-blow.

'She might do worse,' he said mechanically.

Mrs. Mason glanced at him as if struck by the sound of his voice. 'You're not surprised, then?'

'I hardly know. I never fancied there was anything between them, and yet, now that I look back, there has been nothing against it. They have talked to each other neither too much nor too little. Upon my soul, they're an accomplished couple!' Glancing back at his friend's constant reserve and self-possession, Ferdinand—strange as it may seem—could not repress a certain impulse of sympathetic admiration. He had had no vulgar rival. 'Yes,' he repeated gravely, 'she might do worse.'

'I suppose she might. He's poor, but he's clever; and I'm sure I hope to Heaven he loves her!'

Ferdinand said nothing.

'May I ask,' he resumed at length, 'whether they became engaged yesterday, on that walk around the lawn?'

'No; it would be fine if they had, under our very noses! It was all done while Caroline was at the Stapletons'. It was agreed between them yesterday that she should tell me at once.'

'And when are they to be married?'

'In September, if possible. Caroline told me to tell you that she counts upon your staying for the wedding.'

'Staying where?' asked Mason, with a little nervous laugh.

'Staying here, of course,—in the house.'

Ferdinand looked his hostess full in the eyes, taking her hand as he did so. ' "The funeral baked meats did coldly furnish forth the marriage tables." '

'Ah, hold your tongue!' cried Mrs. Mason, pressing his hand. 'How can you be so horrible? When Caroline leaves me, Ferdinand, I shall be quite alone. The tie which binds us together will be very much slackened by her marriage. I can't help thinking that it was never very close, when I consider that I've had no part in the most important step of her life. I don't complain. I suppose it's natural enough. Perhaps it's the fashion,—come in with striped petticoats and pea-jackets. Only it makes me feel like an old woman. It removes me twenty years at a bound from my own engagement, and the day I burst out crying on my mother's neck because your uncle had told a young girl I knew, that he thought I had beautiful eyes. Now-a-days I suppose they tell the young ladies themselves, and have them cry on their own necks. It's a great saving of time. But I shall miss Caroline all the same; and then, Ferdinand, I shall make a great deal of you.'

'The more the better,' said Ferdinand, with the same laugh; and at this moment Mrs. Mason was called away.

Ferdinand had not been a soldier for nothing. He had received a heavy blow, and he resolved to bear it like a man. He refused to allow himself a single moment of self-compassion. On the contrary, he spared himself none of the hard names offered by his passionate vocabulary. For not guessing Caroline's secret, he was perhaps excusable. Women were all inscrutable, and this one especially so. But Knight was a man like himself,—a man whom he esteemed, but whom he was loath to credit with a deeper and more noiseless current of feeling than his own, for his own was no babbling brook, betraying its course through green leaves. Knight had loved modestly and decently, but frankly and heartily, like a man who was not ashamed of what he was doing, and if he had not found it out it was his own fault. What else had he to do? He had been a besotted daydreamer, while his friend had simply been a genuine lover. He deserved his injury, and he would bear it in silence. He had been unable to get well on an illusion; he would now try getting well on a truth. This was stern treatment, the reader will admit, likely to kill if it didn't cure.

Miss Hofmann was absent for several hours. At dinner-time she had not returned, and Mrs. Mason and the young man accordingly sat down without her. After dinner Ferdinand went into the little parlour, quite indifferent as to how soon he met her. Seeing or not seeing her, time hung equally heavy. Shortly after her companions had risen from table, she rode up to the door, dismounted, tired and hungry, passed directly into the dining-room, and sat down to eat in her habit. In half an hour she came out, and, crossing the hall on her way upstairs, saw Mason in the parlour. She turned round, and, gathering up her long skirts with one hand, while she held a little sweet-cake to her lips with the other, stopped at the door to bid him good day. He left his chair, and went towards her. Her face wore a somewhat weary smile.

'So you're going to be married,' he began abruptly.

Miss Hofmann assented with a slight movement of her head.

'I congratulate you. Excuse me if I don't do it with the last grace. I feel all I dare to feel.'

'Don't be afraid,' said Caroline, smiling, and taking a bite from her cake.

'I'm not sure that it's not more unexpected than even such things have a right to be. There's no doubt about it?'

'None whatever.'

'Well, Knight's a very good fellow. I haven't seen him yet,' he pursued, as Caroline was silent. 'I don't know that I'm in any hurry to see him. But I mean to talk to him. I mean to tell him that if he doesn't do his duty by you, I shall—'

'Well?'

'I shall remind him of it.'

'O, I shall do that,' said Miss Hofmann.

Ferdinand looked at her gravely. 'By Heaven! you know,' he cried with intensity, 'it must be either one thing or the other.'

'I don't understand you.'

'O, I understand myself. You're not a woman to be thrown away, Miss Hofmann.'

Caroline made a gesture of impatience. 'I don't understand you,' she repeated. 'You must excuse me. I'm very tired.' And she went rapidly upstairs.

On the following day Ferdinand had an opportunity to make his compliments to the Doctor. 'I don't congratulate you on doing it,' he said, 'so much as on the way you've done it.'

'What do you know about the way?' asked Knight.

'Nothing whatever. That's just it. You took good care of that. And you're to be married in the autumn?'

'I hope so. Very quietly, I suppose. The parson to do it, and Mrs. Mason and my mother and you to see it's done properly.' And the Doctor put his hand on Ferdinand's shoulder.

'O, I'm the last person to choose,' said Mason. 'If he were to omit anything, I should take good care not to cry out.' It is often said, that, next to great joy, no state of mind is so frolicsome as great distress. It was in virtue of this truth, I suppose, that Ferdinand was able to be facetious. He kept his spirits. He talked and smiled and lounged about with the same deferential languor as before. During the interval before the time appointed for the wedding it was agreed between the parties interested that Miss Hofmann should go over and spend a few days with her future mother-in-law, where she might partake more freely and privately than at home of the pleasure of her lover's company. She was absent a week; a week during which Ferdinand was thrown entirely upon his hostess for entertainment and diversion,—things he had a very keen sense of needing. There were moments when it seemed to him that he was living by mere force of will, and that, if he loosened the screws for a single instant, he would sink back upon his bed again, and never leave it. He had forbidden himself to think of Caroline, and had prescribed a course of meditation upon that other mistress, his first love, with whom he had long since exchanged pledges,— she of a hundred names,—work, letters, philosophy, fame. But, after Caroline had gone, it was supremely difficult not to think of her. Even in absence she was supremely conspicuous. The most that Ferdinand could do was to take refuge in books,—an immense number of which he now read, fiercely, passionately, voraciously,— in conversation with Mrs. Mason, and in such society as he found in his path. Mrs. Mason was a great gossip,—a gossip on a scale so magnificent as to transform the foible into a virtue. A gossip, moreover, of imagination, dealing with the future as well as the present and the past,—with a host of delightful half-possibilities, as well as with stale hyper-verities. With her, then, Ferdinand talked of his own future, into which she entered with the most outspoken and intelligent sympathy. 'A man,' he declared, 'couldn't do better; and a man certainly would do worse.' Mrs. Mason arranged a European tour and residence for her nephew, in the manner of one who knew her ground. Caroline once married, she herself would go abroad, and fix herself in one of the several capitals in which an American widow with an easy income may contrive to support existence. She would make her dwelling a base of supplies—a *pied à terre*—for Ferdinand, who should take his time to it, and visit every accessible spot in Europe and the East. She would leave him free to go and come as he pleased, and to live as he listed; and I may say that, thanks to Mrs. Mason's observation of Continental manners, this broad allowance covered in her view quite as much as it did in poor Ferdinand's, who had never been out of his own country. All that she would ask of him would be to show himself say twice a year in her drawing-room, and to tell her stories of what he had seen; that drawing-room which she already saw in her mind's eye,—a compact little *entresol* with tapestry hangings in the doorways and a coach-house in the court attached. Mrs. Mason was not a severe moralist; but she was quite too sensible a woman to wish to demoralize her nephew, and to persuade him to trifle with his future,—that future of which the war had already made light, in its own grim fashion. Nay, she loved him; she thought him the cleverest, the most promising, of young men. She looked to the day when his name would be on men's lips, and it would be a great piece of good fortune to have very innocently married his uncle. Herself a great observer of men and manners, she wished to give him advantages which had been sterile in her own case.

In the way of society, Ferdinand made calls with his hostess, went out twice to dine, and caused Mrs. Mason herself to entertain company at dinner. He presided on these occasions with distinguished good grace. It happened, moreover, that invitations had been out some days for a party at the Stapletons',—Miss Hofmann's friends,—and that, as there was to be no dancing, Ferdinand boldly announced his intention of going thither. 'Who knows?' he said; 'it may do me more good than harm. We can go late, and come away early.' Mrs. Mason doubted of the wisdom of the act; but she finally assented, and prepared herself. It was late when they left home, and when they arrived the rooms—rooms of exceptional vastness—were at their fullest. Mason received on this his first appearance in society a most flattering welcome, and in a very few moments found himself in exclusive possession of Miss Edith Stapleton, Caroline's particular friend. This young lady has had no part in our story, because our story is perforce short, and condemned to pick and choose its constituent elements. With the least bit wider compass we might long since have whispered to the reader, that Miss Stapleton—who was a charming girl—had conceived a decided preference for our Ferdinand over all other men whomsoever. That Ferdinand was utterly ignorant of the circumstances is our excuse for passing it by; and we linger upon it, therefore, only long enough to suggest that the young girl must have been very happy at this particular moment.

'Is Miss Hofmann here?' Mason asked as he accompanied her into an adjoining room.

'Do you call that being here?' said Miss Stapleton, looking across the apartment. Mason, too, looked across.

There he beheld Miss Hofmann, full-robed in white, standing fronted by a semicircle of no less than five gentlemen,—all good-looking and splendid. Her head and shoulders rose serene from the *bouillonnement* of her beautiful dress, and she looked and listened with that half-abstracted air which is pardonable in a woman beset by half-a-dozen admirers. When Caroline's eyes fell upon her friend, she stared a moment, surprised, and then made him the most gracious bow in the world,—a bow so gracious that her little circle half divided itself to let it pass, and looked around to see where the deuce it was going. Taking advantage of this circumstance, Miss Hofmann advanced several steps. Ferdinand went towards her, and there, in sight of a hundred men and as many women, she gave him her hand, and smiled upon him with extraordinary sweetness. They went back together to Miss Stapleton, and Caroline made him sit down, she and her friend placing themselves on either side. For half an hour Ferdinand had the honour of engrossing the attention of the two most charming girls present,—and, thanks to this distinction, indeed the attention of the whole company. After which the two young ladies had him introduced successively to every maiden and matron in the assembly in the least remarkable for loveliness or wit. Ferdinand rose to the level of the occasion, and conducted himself with unprecedented gallantry. Upon others he made, of course, the best impression, but to himself he was an object almost of awe. I am compelled to add, however, that he was obliged to fortify himself with repeated draughts of wine; and that even with the aid of this artificial stimulant he was unable to conceal from Mrs. Mason and his physician that he was looking far too much like an invalid to be properly where he was.

'Was there ever anything like the avidity of these dreadful girls?' said Mrs. Mason to the Doctor. 'They'll let a man swoon at their feet sooner than abridge a *tête-à-tête* that amuses them. Then they'll have up another. Look at little Miss McCarthy, yonder, with Ferdinand and George Stapleton before her. She's got them contradicting each other, and she looks like a Roman fast lady at the circus. What does she care so long as she makes her evening? They like a man to look as if he were going to die,—it's interesting.'

Knight went over to his friend, and told him sternly that it was high time he should be at home and in bed. 'You're looking horribly,' he added shrewdly, as Ferdinand resisted.

'You're *not* looking horribly, Colonel Mason,' said Miss McCarthy, a very audacious little person, overhearing this speech.

'It isn't a matter of taste, madam,' said the Doctor, angrily; 'it's a fact.' And he led away his patient.

Ferdinand insisted that he had not hurt himself, that, on the contrary, he was feeling uncommonly well; but his face contradicted him. He continued for two or three days more to play at 'feeling well', with a courage worthy of a better cause. Then at last he let disease have its way. He settled himself on his pillows, and fingered his watch, and began to wonder how many revolutions he would still witness of those exquisite little needles. The Doctor came, and gave him a sound rating for what he called his imprudence. Ferdinand heard him out patiently; and then assured him that prudence or imprudence had nothing to do with it; that death had taken fast hold of him, and that now his only concern was to make easy terms with his captor. In the course of the same day he sent for a lawyer and altered his will. He had no known relatives, and his modest patrimony stood bequeathed to a gentleman of his acquaintance who had no real need of it. He now divided it into two unequal portions, the smaller of which he devised to William Bowles, Mrs. Mason's man-servant and his personal attendant; and the larger—which represented a considerable sum—to Horace Knight. He informed Mrs. Mason of these arrangements, and was pleased to have her approval.

From this moment his strength began rapidly to ebb, and the shattered fragments of his long-resisting will floated down its shallow current into dissolution. It was useless to attempt to talk, to beguile the interval, to watch the signs, or to count the hours. A constant attendant was established at his side, and Mrs. Mason appeared only at infrequent moments. The poor woman felt that her heart was broken, and spent a great deal of time in weeping. Miss Hofmann remained, naturally, at Mrs. Knight's. 'As far as I can judge,' Horace had said, 'it will be a matter of a week. But it's the most extraordinary case I ever heard of. The man was steadily getting well.' On the fifth day he had driven Miss Hofmann home, at her suggestion that it was no more than decent that she should give the young man some little sign of sympathy. Horace went up to Ferdinand's bedside, and found the poor fellow in the languid middle condition between sleeping and waking in which he had passed the last forty-eight hours. 'Colonel,' he asked gently, 'do you think you could see Caroline?'

For all answer, Ferdinand opened his eyes. Horace went out, and led his companion back into the darkened room. She came softly up to the bedside, stood looking down for a moment at the sick man, and then stooped over him.

'I thought I'd come and make you a little visit,' she said. 'Does it disturb you?'

'Not in the least,' said Mason, looking her steadily in the eyes. 'Not half as much as it would have done a week ago. Sit down.'

'Thank you. Horace won't let me. I'll come again.'

'You'll not have another chance,' said Ferdinand. 'I'm not good for more than two days yet. Tell them to go out. I wish to see you alone. I wouldn't have sent for you, but, now that you're here, I might as well take advantage of it.'

'Have you anything particular to say?' asked Knight, kindly.

'O, come,' said Mason, with a smile which he meant to be good-natured, but which was only ghastly; 'you're not going to be jealous of me at this time of day.'

Knight looked at Miss Hofmann for permission, and then left the room with the nurse. But a minute had hardly elapsed before Miss Hofmann hurried into the adjoining apartment, with her face pale and discomposed.

'Go to him!' she exclaimed. 'He's dying!'

When they reached him he was dead.

In the course of a few days his will was opened, and Knight came to the knowledge of his legacy. 'He was a good, generous fellow, he said to Mrs. Mason and Miss Hofmann, 'and I shall never be satisfied that he mightn't have recovered. It was a most extraordinary case.' He was considerate enough of his audience to abstain from adding that he would give a great deal to have been able to make an autopsy. Miss Hofmann's wedding was, of course, not deferred. She was married in September, 'very quietly'. It seemed to her lover, in the interval, that she was very silent and thoughtful. But this was certainly natural under the circumstances.

A Problem

[First appeared in the *Galaxy*, vol. v (June 1868), pp. 697-707. The serial text carried one illustration by W. J. Hennessy. Not reprinted during James's' lifetime.]

SEPTEMBER WAS DRAWING TO AN END, AND WITH IT THE honeymoon of two young persons in whom I shall be glad to interest the reader. They had stretched it out in sovereign contempt of the balance of the calendar. That September hath thirty days is a truth known to the simplest child; but our young lovers had given it at least forty. Nevertheless, they were on the whole not sorry to have the overture play itself out, and to see the curtain rise on the drama in which they had undertaken the leading parts. Emma thought very often of the charming little house which was awaiting her in town, and of the servants whom her dear mother had promised to engage; and, indeed, for that matter, the young wife let her imagination hover about the choice groceries with which she expected to find her cupboards stocked through the same kind agency. Moreover, she had left her wedding-gown at home—thinking it silly to carry her finery into the country—and she felt a great longing to refresh her memory as to the particular shade of a certain lavender silk, and the exact length of a certain train. The reader will see that Emma was a simple, unsophisticated person, and that her married life was likely to be made up of small joys and vexations. She was simple and gentle and pretty and young; she adored her husband. He, too, had begun to feel that it was time they were married in earnest. His thoughts wandered back to his counting-room and his vacant desk, and to the possible contents of the letters which he had requested his fellow-clerk to open in his absence. For David, too, was a simple, natural fellow, and although he thought his wife the sweetest of human creatures—or, indeed, for that very reason—he was unable to forget that life is full of bitter inhuman necessities and perils which muster in force about you when you stand idle. He was happy, in short, and he felt it unfair that he should any longer have his happiness for nothing.

The two, therefore, had made up their trunks again, and ordered the vehicle in time for the morrow's train. Twilight had come on, and Emma sat at the window empty-handed, taking a silent farewell of the landscape, which she felt that they had let into the secret of their young love. They had sat in the shade of every tree, and watched the sunset from the top of every rock.

David had gone to settle his account with the landlord, and to bid good-bye to the doctor, who had been of such service when Emma had caught cold by sitting for three hours on the grass after a day's rain.

Sitting alone was dull work. Emma crossed the threshold of the long window, and went to the garden gate to look for her husband. The doctor's house was a mile away, close to the village. Seeing nothing of David, she strolled along the road, bareheaded, in her shawl. It was a lovely evening. As there was no one to say so to, Emma, said so, with some fervour, to herself; and to this she added a dozen more remarks, equally original and eloquent—and equally sincere. That David was, ah! so good, and that she ought to be so happy. That she would have a great many cares, but that she would be orderly, and saving, and vigilant, and that her house should be a sanctuary of modest elegance and good taste; and, then, that she might be a mother.

When Emma reached this point, she ceased to meditate and to whisper virtuous nothings to her conscience. She rejoiced; she walked more slowly, and looked about at the dark hills, rising in soft undulations against the luminous west, and listened to the long pulsations of sound mounting from woods and hedges and the margins of pools. Her ears rang, and her eyes filled with tears.

Meanwhile she had walked a half-mile, and as yet David was not in sight. Her attention, however, was at this moment diverted from her quest. To her right, on a level with the road, stretched a broad, circular space, half meadow, half common, enclosed in the rear by a wood. At some distance, close to the wood, stood a couple of tents, such as are used by the vagrant Indians who sell baskets and articles of bark. In front, close to the road, on a fallen log, sat a young Indian woman, weaving a basket, with two children beside her. Emma looked at her curiously as she drew near.

'Good evening,' said the woman, returning her glance with hard, bright black eyes. 'Don't you want to buy something?'

'What have you got to sell?' asked Emma, stopping.

'All sorts of things. Baskets, and pincushions, and fans.'

'I should like a basket well enough—a little one—if they're pretty.'

'Oh, yes, they're pretty, you'll see.' And she said something to one of the children, in her own dialect. He went off, in compliance, to the tents.

While he was gone, Emma looked at the other child, and pronounced it very handsome; but without touching it, for the little savage was in the last degree unclean. The woman doggedly continued her work, examining Emma's person from head to foot, and staring at her dress, her hands, and her rings.

In a few moments the child came back with a number of baskets strung together, followed by an old woman, apparently the mother of the first. Emma looked over the baskets, selected a pretty one, and took out her purse to pay for it. The price was a dollar, but Emma had nothing smaller than a two-dollar note, and the woman professed herself unable to give change.

'Give her the money,' said the old woman, 'and, for the difference, I'll tell your fortune.'

Emma looked at her, hesitating. She was a repulsive old squaw, with sullen, black eyes, and her swarthy face hatched across with a myriad wrinkles.

The younger woman saw that Emma looked a little frightened, and said something in her barbarous native gutturals to her companion. The latter retorted, and the other burst out into a laugh.

'Give me your hand,' said the old woman, 'and I'll tell your fortune.' And, before Emma found time to resist, she came and took hold of her left hand. She held it awhile, with the back upwards, looking at its fair surface, and at the diamonds on her third finger. Then, turning up the palm, she began to mutter and grumble. Just as she was about to speak, Emma saw her look half-defiantly at someone apparently behind her. Turning about, she saw that her husband had come up unperceived. She felt relieved. The woman had a horribly vicious look, and she exhaled, moreover, a strong odour of whiskey. Of this David immediately became sensible.

'What is she doing?' he asked of his wife.

'Don't you see. She's telling my fortune.'

'What has she told you?'

'Nothing yet. She seems to be waiting for it to come to her.'

The squaw looked at David cunningly, and David returned her gaze with ill-concealed disgust. 'She'll have to wait a long time,' he said to his wife. 'She has been drinking.'

He had lowered his voice, but the woman heard him. The other began to laugh, and said something in her own tongue to her mother. The latter still kept Emma's hand and remained silent.

'This your husband?' she said, at last, nodding at David.

Emma nodded assent. The woman again examined her hand. 'Within the year,' she said, 'you'll be a mother.'

'That's wonderful news,' said David. 'Is it to be a boy or a girl?'

The woman looked hard at David. 'A girl,' she said. And then she transferred her eyes to Emma's palm.

'Well, is that all?' said Emma.

'She'll be sick.'

'Very likely,' said David. 'And we'll send for the doctor.'

'The doctor'll do no good.'

'Then we shall send for another,' said Emma, laughing—but not without an effort.

'He'll do no good. She'll die.'

The young squaw began to laugh again. Emma drew her hand away, and looked at her husband. He was a little pale, and Emma put her hand into his arm.

'We're very much obliged to you for the information,' said David. 'At what age is our little girl to die?'

'Oh, very young.'

'How young?'

'Oh, very young.' The old woman seemed indisposed to commit herself further, and David led his wife away.

'Well,' said Emma, 'she gave us a good dollar's worth.'

'I think,' said David, 'she had been giving herself a good dollar's worth. She was full of liquor.'

From this assurance Emma drew for twenty-four hours to come a good deal of comfort. As for David, in the course of an hour he had quite forgotten the prophecy.

The next day they went back to town. Emma found her house all that she had desired, and her lavender silk not a shade too pale, nor her train an inch too short. The winter came and went, and she was still a very happy woman. The spring arrived, the summer drew near, and her happiness increased. She became the mother of a little girl.

For some time after the child was born Emma was confined to her room. She used to sit with the infant on her lap, nursing her, counting her breathings, wondering whether she would be pretty. David was at his place of business, with his head full of figures. A dozen times Emma recurred to the old woman's prophecy, sometimes with a tremor, sometimes with indifference, sometimes almost with defiance. Then, she declared that it was silly to remember it. A tipsy old squaw—a likely providence for her precious child. She was, perhaps, dead herself by this time. Nevertheless, her prophecy was odd; she seemed so positive. And the other woman laughed so disagreeably. Emma had not forgotten that laugh. She might well laugh, with her own lusty little savages beside her.

The first day that Emma left her room, one evening, at dinner, she couldn't help asking her husband whether he remembered the Indian woman's prediction. David was taking a glass of wine. He nodded.

'You see it's half come true,' said Emma. 'A little girl.'

'My dear,' said David, 'one would think you believed it.'

'Of course she'll be sick,' said Emma. 'We must expect that.'

'Do you think, my dear,' pursued David, 'that it's a little girl because that venerable person said so?'

'Why no, of course not. It's only a coincidence.'

'Well, then, if it's merely a coincidence, we may let it rest. If the old woman's *dictum* was a real prediction, we may also let it rest. That it has half come true lessens the chances for the other half.'

The reader may detect a flaw in David's logic; but it was quite good enough for Emma. She lived upon it for a year, at the end of which it was in a manner put to the test.

It were certainly incorrect to say that Emma guarded and cherished her little girl any the more carefully by reason of the old woman's assurance; her natural affection was by itself a guaranty of perfect vigilance. But perfect vigilance is not infallible. When the child was a twelvemonth old it fell grievously sick, and for a week its little life hung by a thread. During this time I am inclined to think that Emma quite forgot the sad prediction suspended over the infant's head; it is certain, at least, that she never spoke of it to her husband, and that he made no attempt to remind her of it. Finally, after a hard struggle, the little girl came out of the cruel embrace of disease, panting and exhausted, but uninjured. Emma felt as if her child was immortal, and as if, henceforth, life would have no trials for her. It was not till then that she thought once more of the prophecy of the swarthy sybil.

She was sitting on the sofa in her chamber, with the child lying asleep in her lap, watching the faint glow of returning life in its poor wasted cheeks. David came in from his day's labour and sat down beside her.

'I wonder,' said Emma, 'what our friend Magawisca—or whatever her name is—would say to that.'

'She would feel desperately snubbed,' said David. 'Wouldn't she, little transcendent convalescent?' And he gently tickled the tip of his little girl's nose with the end of his moustache. The baby softly opened her eyes, and, vaguely conscious of her father, lifted her hand and languidly clutched his nose. 'Upon my soul,' said David, 'she's positively boisterous. There's life in the old dog yet.'

'Oh, David, how can you?' said Emma. But she sat watching her husband and child with a placid, gleeful smile. Gradually, her smile grew the least bit serious, and then vanished, though she still looked like the happy woman that she was. The nurse came up from supper, and took possession of the baby. Emma let it go, and remained sitting on the sofa. When the nurse had gone into the adjoining room, she laid her hand in one of her husband's.

'David,' she said, 'I have a little secret.'

'I've no doubt,' said David, 'that you have a dozen. You're the most secretive, clandestine, shady sort of woman I ever came across.'

It is needless to say that this was merely David's exuberant humour; for Emma was the most communicative, sympathetic soul in the world. She practised, in a quiet way, a passionate devotion to her husband, and it was a part of her religion to make him her confidant. She had, of course, in strictness, very little to confide to him. But she confided to him her little, in the hope that he would one day confide to her what she was pleased to believe his abundance.

'It's not exactly a secret,' Emma pursued; 'only I've kept it so long that it almost seems like one. You'll think me very silly, David. I couldn't bear to mention it so long as there was any chance of truth in the talk of that horrible old squaw. But now, that it's disproved, it seems absurd to keep it on my mind; not that I really ever felt it there, but if I said nothing about it, it was for your sake. I'm sure you'll not mind it; and if you don't, David, I'm sure I needn't.'

'My dear girl, what on earth is coming?' said David. '"If you don't, I'm sure I needn't!"—you make a man's flesh crawl.'

'Why, it's another prophecy,' said Emma.

'Another prophecy? Let's have it, then, by all means.'

'But you don't mean, David, that you're going to believe it?'

'That depends. If it's to my advantage, of course I shall.'

'To your advantage! Oh, David!'

'My dear Emma, prophecies are not to be sneered at. Look at this one about the baby.'

'Look at the baby, I should say.'

'Exactly. Isn't she a girl? hasn't she been at death's door?'

'Yes; but the old woman made her go through.'

'Nay; you've no imagination. Of course, they pull off short of the catastrophe; but they give you a good deal, by the way.'

'Well, my dear, since you're so determined to believe in them, I should be sorry to prevent you. I make you a present of this one.'

'Was it a squaw, this time?'

'No, it was an old Italian—a woman who used to come on Saturday mornings at school and sell us sugar-plums and trinkets. You see it was ten years ago. Our teachers used to dislike her; but we let her into the garden by a back-gate. She used to carry a little tray, like a pedler. She had candy and cakes, and kid-gloves. One day, she offered to tell our fortunes with cards. She spread out her cards on the top of her tray, and half a dozen of us went through the ceremony. The rest were afraid. I believe I was second. She told me a long rigmarole that I have forgotten, but said nothing about lovers or husbands. That, of course, was all we wanted to hear; and, though I was disappointed, I was ashamed to ask any questions. To the girls who came after me, she promised successively the most splendid marriages. I wondered whether I was to be an old maid. The thought was horrible, and I determined to try and conjure such a fate. "But I?" I said, as she was going to put up her cards; "am I never to be married?" She looked at me, and then looked over her cards again. I suppose she wished to make up for her neglect. "Ah, you, Miss," she said—"you are better off than any of them. You are to marry twice!" Now, my dear,' Emma added, 'make the most of that.' And she leaned her head on her husband's shoulder and looked in his face, smiling.

But David smiled not at all. On the contrary, he looked grave. Hereupon, Emma put by her smile, and looked grave, too. In fact, she looked pained. She thought it positively unkind of David to take her little story in such stiff fashion.

'It's very strange,' said David.

'It's very silly,' said Emma. 'I'm sorry I told you, David.'

'I'm very glad. It's extremely curious. Listen, and you'll see—I, too, have a secret, Emma.'

'Nay, I don't want to hear it,' said Emma.

'You shall hear it,' said the young man. 'I never mentioned it before, simply because I had forgotten it—utterly forgotten it. But your story calls it back to my memory. I, too, once had my fortune told. It was neither a squaw nor a gypsy. It was a young lady, in company. I forget her name. I was less than twenty. It was at a party, and she was telling people's fortunes. She had cards; she pretended to have a gift. I don't know what I had been saying. I suppose that, as boys of that age are fond of doing, I had been showing off my wit at the expense of married life. I remember a young lady introducing me to this person, and saying that here was a young man who declared he never would marry. Was it true? She looked at her cards, and said it was completely false, and that I should marry twice. The company began to laugh. I was mortified. "Why don't you say three times?" I said. "Because," answered the young lady, "my cards say only twice."' David had got up from the sofa, and stood before his wife. 'Don't you think it's curious?' he said.

'Curious enough. One would say you thought it something more.'

'You know,' continued David, 'we can't both marry twice.'

' "You know," ' cried Emma. 'Bravo, my dear. "You know" is delightful. Perhaps you would like me to withdraw and give you a chance.'

David looked at his wife, half surprised at the bitterness of her words. He was apparently on the point of making some conciliatory speech; but he seemed forcibly struck, afresh, with the singular agreement of the two predictions. 'Upon my soul!' he said, 'it's preternaturally odd!' He burst into a fit of laughter.

Emma put her hands to her face and sat silent. Then, after a few moments: 'For my part,' she said, 'I think it's extremely disagreeable!' Overcome by the effort to speak, she burst into tears.

Her husband again placed himself at her side. He still took the humorous view of the case—on the whole, perhaps, indiscreetly. 'Come, Emma,' he said, 'dry your tears, and consult your memory. Are you sure you've never been married before?'

Emma shook off his caresses and got up. Then, suddenly turning around, she said, with vehemence, 'And you, sir?'

For an answer David laughed afresh; and then, looking at his wife a moment, he rose and followed her. 'Où diable la jalousie va-t-elle se nicher?' he cried. He put his arm about her, she yielded, and he kissed her. At this moment a little wail went up from the baby in the neighbouring room. Emma hastened away.

Where, indeed, as David had asked, will jealousy stow herself away? In what odd, unlikely corners will she turn up? She made herself a nest in poor Emma's innocent heart, and, at her leisure, she lined and feathered it. The little scene I have just described left neither party, indeed, as it found them. David had kissed his wife and shown the folly of her tears, but he had not taken back his story. For ten years he hadn't thought of it; but, now that he had been reminded of it, he was quite unable to dismiss it from his thoughts. It besieged him, and harassed and distracted him; it thrust itself into his mind at the most inopportune moments; it buzzed in his ears and danced among the columns of figures in his great folio account books. Sometimes the young lady's prediction conjoined itself with a prodigious array of numerals, and roamed away from its modest place among the units into the hundreds of thousands. David read himself a million times a husband. But, after all, as he reflected, the oddity was not in his having been predestined, according to the young lady, to marry twice; but in poor Emma having drawn exactly the same lot. It was a conflict of oracles. It would be an interesting inquiry, although now, of course, quite impracticable, to ascertain which of the two was more to be trusted. For how under the sun could both have

revealed the truth? The utmost ingenuity was powerless to reconcile their mutual incompatibility. Could either of the soothsayers
have made her statement in a figurative sense? It seemed to David
that this was to fancy them a grain too wise. The simplest solution
—except not to think of the matter at all, which he couldn't bring
himself to accomplish—was to fancy that each of the prophecies
nullified the other, and that when he became Emma's husband,
their counterfeit destinies had been put to confusion.

Emma found it quite impossible to take the matter so easily.
She pondered it night and day for a month. She admitted that the
prospect of a second marriage was, of necessity, unreal for one of
them; but her heart ached to discover for which of them it was
real. She had laughed at the folly of the Indian's threat; but she
found it impossible to laugh at the extraordinary coincidence of
David's promised fate with her own. That it was absurd and illogical
made it only the more painful. It filled her life with a horrible
uncertainty. It seemed to indicate that whether or no the silly
gossip of a couple of jugglers was, on either side, strictly fulfilled;
yet there was some dark cloud hanging over their marriage. Why
should an honest young couple have such strange things said of
them? Why should they be called upon to read such an illegible
riddle? Emma repented bitterly of having told her secret. And yet,
too, she rejoiced; for it was a dreadful thought that David, un-
prompted to reveal his own adventure should have kept such a
dreadful occurrence locked up in his breast, shedding, Heaven
knows what baleful influence, on her life and fortunes. Now she
could live it down; she could combat it, laugh at it. And David,
too, could do as much for the mysterious prognostic of his own
extinction. Never had Emma's fancy been so active. She placed
the two faces of her destiny in every conceivable light. At one
moment, she imagined that David might succumb to the pressure
of his fancied destiny, and leave her a widow, free to marry again;
and at another that he would grow enamoured of the thought of
obeying his own oracle, and crush her to death by the masculine
vigour of his will. Then, again, she felt as if her own will were
strong, and as if she bore on her head the protecting hand of fate.
Love was much, assuredly, but fate was more. And here, indeed,
what was fate but love? As she had loved David, so she would
love another. She racked her poor little brain to conjure up this
future master of her life. But, to do her justice, it was quite in vain.
She could not forget David. Nevertheless, she felt guilty. And then
she thought of David, and wondered whether he was guilty, too—
whether he was dreaming of another woman.

In this way it was that Emma became jealous. That she was a very silly girl I don't pretend to deny. I have expressly said that she was a person of a very simple make; and in proportion to the force of her old straightforward confidence in her husband, was that of her present suspicion and vagaries.

From the moment that Emma became jealous, the household angel of peace shook its stainless wings and took a melancholy flight. Emma immediately betrayed herself. She accused her husband of indifference, and of preferring the society of other women. Once she told him that he might, if he pleased. It was *à propos* of an evening party, to which they had both been asked. During the afternoon, while David was still at his business, the baby had been taken sick, and Emma had written a note to say that they should not be able to come. When David returned, she told him of her note, and he laughed and said that he wondered whether their intended hostess would fancy that it was his practice to hold the baby. For his part, he declared that he meant to go; and at nine o'clock he appeared, dressed. Emma looked at him, pale and indignant.

'After all,' she said, 'you're right. Make the most of your time.'

These were horrible words, and, as was natural, they made a vast breach between the husband and wife.

Once in a while Emma felt an impulse to take her revenge, and look for happiness in society, and in the sympathy and attention of agreeable men. But she never went very far. Such happiness seemed but a troubled repose, and the world at large had no reason to suspect that she was not on the best of terms with her husband.

David, on his side, went much further. He was gradually transformed from a quiet, home-keeping, affectionate fellow, into a nervous, restless, querulous man of pleasure, a diner-out and a haunter of clubs and theatres. From the moment that he detected their influence on his life, he had been unable to make light of the two prophecies. Then one, now the other, dominated his imagination, and, in either event, it was impossible to live as he would have lived in ignorance. Sometimes, at the thought of an early death, he was seized with a passionate attachment to the world, and an irresistible desire to plunge into worldly joys. At other moments, thinking of his wife's possible death, and her place being taken by another woman, he felt a fierce and unnatural impatience of all further delay in the evolution of events. He wished to annihilate the present. To live in expectation so acute and so feverish was not to live. Poor David was occasionally tempted by desperate expedients to kill time. Gradually the perpetual oscillation from one phase of his destiny to the other, and the constant change from passionate exaltation to equally morbid depression, induced a state of chronic excitement, not far removed from insanity.

At about this moment he made the acquaintance of a young unmarried woman whom I may call Julia—a very charming, superior person, of a character to exert a healing, soothing influence upon his troubled spirit. In the course of time, he told her the story of his domestic revolution. At first, she was very much amused; she laughed at him, and called him superstitious, fantastic, and puerile. But he took her levity so ill, that she changed her tactics, and humoured his delusion.

It seemed to her, however, that his case was serious, and that, if some attempt were not made to arrest his growing alienation from his wife, the happiness of both parties might depart forever. She believed that the flimsy ghost of their mysterious future could be effectually laid only by means of a reconciliation. She doubted that their love was dead and gone. It was only dormant. If she might once awaken it, she would retire with a light heart, and leave it lord of the house.

So, without informing David of her intention, Julia ventured to call upon Emma, with whom she had no personal acquaintance. She hardly knew what she should say; she would trust to the inspiration of the moment; she merely wished to kindle a ray of light in the young wife's darkened household. Emma, she fancied, was a simple, sensitive person; she would be quickly moved by proffered kindness.

But, although she was unacquainted with Emma, the young wife had considerable knowledge of Julia. She had had her pointed out to her in public: Julia was handsome. Emma hated her. She thought of her as her husband's temptress and evil genius. She assured herself that they were longing for her death, so that they might marry. Perhaps he was already her lover. Doubtless they would be glad to kill her. In this way it was that, instead of finding a gentle, saddened, sensitive person, Julia found a bitter, scornful woman, infuriated by a sense of insult and injury. Julia's visit seemed to Emma the climax of insolence. She refused to listen to her. Her courtesy, her gentleness, her attempt at conciliation, struck her as a mockery and a snare. Finally, losing all self-control, she called her a very hard name.

Then Julia, who had a high temper of her own, plucked up a spirit, and struck a blow for her dignity—a blow, however, which unfortunately rebounded on David. 'I had steadily refused, Madam,' she said, 'to believe that you are a fool. But you quite persuade me.'

With these words she withdrew. But it mattered little to Emma whether she remained or departed. She was conscious only of one thing, that David had called her a fool to another woman. 'A fool?' she cried. 'Truly I have been. But I shall be no longer.'

She immediately made her preparations for leaving her husband's house, and when David came home he found her with her child and a servant on the point of departure. She told him in a few words that she was going to her mother's, that in his absence he had employed persons to insult her in her own house, it was necessary that she should seek protection in her family. David offered no resistance. He made no attempt to resent her accusation. He was prepared for anything. It was fate.

Emma accordingly went to her mother's. She was supported in this extraordinary step, and in the long months of seclusion which followed it, by an exalted sense of her own comparative integrity and virtue. She, at least, had been a faithful wife. She had endured, she had been patient. Whatever her destiny might be, she had made no indecent attempt to anticipate it. More than ever she devoted herself to her little girl. The comparative repose and freedom of her life gave her almost a feeling of happiness. She felt that deep satisfaction which comes upon the spirit when it has purchased contentment at the expense of reputation. There was now, at least, no falsehood in her life. She neither valued her marriage nor pretended to value it.

As for David, he saw little of any one but Julia. Julia, I have said, was a woman of great merit and of perfect generosity. She very soon ceased to resent the check she had received from Emma, and not despairing, still, of seeing peace once more established in the young man's household, she made it a matter of conscience to keep David by her influence in as sane and unperverted a state of mind as circumstances would allow. 'She may hate me,' thought Julia, 'but I'll keep him for her.' Julia's, you see, in all this business was the only wise head.

David took his own view of their relations. 'I shall certainly see you as often as I wish,' he declared. 'I shall take consolation where I find it. She has her child—her mother. Does she begrudge me a friend? She may thank her stars I don't take to drink or to play.'

For six months David saw nothing of his wife. Finally, one evening, when he was at Julia's house, he received this note:

'Your daughter died this morning, after several hours' suffering. She will be buried to-morrow morning.   E.'

David handed the note to Julia. 'After all,' he said, 'she was right.'

'Who was right, my poor friend?' asked Julia.

'The old squaw. We cried out too soon.'

The next morning he went to the house of his mother-in-law. The servant, recognizing him, ushered him into the room in which the remains of his poor little girl lay, ready for burial. Near the darkened window stood his mother-in-law, in conversation with a gentleman—a certain Mr. Clark—whom David recognized as a favourite clergyman of his wife, and whom he had never liked. The lady, on his entrance, made him a very grand curtsy—if, indeed, that curtsy may be said to come within the regulations which govern salutations of this sort, in which the head is tossed up in proportion as the body is depressed—and swept out of the room. David bowed to the clergyman, and went and looked at the little remnant of mortality which had once been his daughter. After a decent interval, Mr. Clark ventured to approach him.

'You have met with a great trial, sir,' said the clergyman.

David assented in silence.

'I suppose,' continued Mr. Clark, 'it is sent, like all trials, to remind us of our feeble and dependent condition—to purge us of pride and stubbornness—to make us search our hearts and see whether we have not by chance allowed the noisome weeds of folly to overwhelm and suffocate the modest flower of wisdom.'

That Mr. Clark had deliberately prepared this speech, with a view to the occasion, I should hesitate to affirm. Gentlemen of his profession have these little parcels of sentiment ready to their hands. But he was, of course, acquainted with Emma's estrangement from her husband (although not with its original motives), and, like a man of genuine feeling, he imagined that under the softening action of a common sorrow, their two hardened hearts might be made to melt and again to flow into one. 'The more we lose, my friend,' he pursued, 'the more we should cherish and value what is left.'

At this moment the door opened, and Emma came in—pale, and clad in black. She stopped, apparently unprepared to see her husband. But, on David's turning toward her, she came forward.

David felt as if Heaven had sent an angel to give the lie to his last words. His face flushed—firstwith shame, and then with joy. He put out his arms. Emma halted an instant, struggling with her pride, and looked at the clergyman. He raised his hand, with a pious sacramental gesture, and she fell on her husband's neck.

The clergyman took hold of David's hand and pressed it; and, although, as I have said, the young man had never been particularly

'AND SHE FELL ON HER HUSBAND'S NECK.'

fond of Mr. Clark, he devoutly returned the pressure.

'Well,' said Julia, a fortnight later—for in the interval Emma had been brought to consent to her husband's maintaining his acquaintance with this lady, and even herself to think of her a very good sort of person—'well, I don't see but that the terrible problem is at last solved, and that you have each been married twice.'

De Grey: A Romance

[First appeared in the *Atlantic Monthly*, vol. xxii (July 1868), pp. 57-78. Not reprinted during James's lifetime.]

IT WAS THE YEAR 1820, AND MRS. DE GREY, BY THE SAME token, as they say in Ireland (and, for that matter, out of it), had reached her sixty-seventh spring. She was, nevertheless, still a handsome woman, and, what is better yet, still an amiable woman. The untroubled, unruffled course of her life had left as few wrinkles on her temper as on her face. She was tall and full of person, with dark eyes and abundant white hair, which she rolled back from her forehead over a cushion, or some such artifice. The freshness of youth and health had by no means faded out of her cheeks, nor had the smile of her imperturbable courtesy expired on her lips. She dressed, as became a woman of her age and a widow, in black garments, but relieved with a great deal of white, with a number of handsome rings on her fair hands. Frequently, in the spring, she wore a little flower or a sprig of green leaves in the bosom of her gown. She had been accused of receiving these little floral ornaments from the hands of Mr. Herbert (of whom I shall have more to say); but the charge is unfounded, inasmuch as they were very carefully selected from a handful cut in the garden by her maid.

That Mrs. De Grey should have been just the placid and elegant old lady that she was, remained, in the eyes of the world at large, in spite of an abundance of a certain sort of evidence in favour of such a result, more or less of a puzzle and a problem. It is true, that every one who knew anything about her knew that she had enjoyed great material prosperity, and had suffered no misfortunes. She was mistress in her own right of a handsome property and a handsome house; she had lost her husband, indeed, within a year after marriage; but, as the late George De Grey had been of a sullen and brooding humour,—to that degree, indeed, as to incur the suspicion of insanity,—her loss, leaving her well provided for, might in strictness have been accounted a gain. Her son, moreover, had never given her a moment's trouble; he had grown up a charming young man, handsome, witty, and wise; he was a model of filial devotion. The lady's health was good; she had half a dozen perfect servants; she had the perpetual company of the incomparable Mr. Herbert; she was as fine a figure of an elderly woman as any in town; she might, therefore, very well have been happy and have looked so. On the other hand, a dozen sensible women had been known to declare with emphasis, that not for all her treasures and her felicity would they have consented to be Mrs. De Grey. These ladies were, of course, unable to give a logical reason for so strong an aversion. But it is certain that there hung over Mrs. De Grey's history and circumstances a film, as it were, a shadow of mystery, which struck a chill upon imaginations which might easily have been kindled into envy of her good fortune. 'She lives in the dark,' some one had said of her. Close observers did her the honour to believe that there was a secret in her life, but of a wholly undefined character. Was she the victim of some lurking sorrow, or the mistress of some clandestine joy? These imputations, we may easily believe, are partially explained by the circumstance that she was a Catholic, and kept a priest in her house. The unexplained portion might very well, moreover, have been discredited by Mrs. De Grey's perfectly candid and complacent demeanour. It was certainly hard to conceive, in talking with her, to what part of her person one might pin a mystery,—whether on her clear, round eyes or her handsome, benevolent lips. Let us say, then, in defiance of the voice of society, that she was no tragedy queen. She was a fine woman, a perfect gentlewoman. She had taken life, as she liked a cup of tea,—weak, with an exquisite aroma and plenty of cream and sugar. She had never lost her temper, for the excellent reason that she had none to lose. She was troubled with no fears, no doubts, no scruples, and blessed with no sacred certainties. She was fond of her son, of the church, of her garden, and of her toilet. She had the very best taste; but, morally, one may say that she had had no history.

Mrs. De Grey had always lived in seclusion; for a couple of years previous to the time of which I speak she had lived in solitude. Her son, on reaching his twenty-third year, had gone to Europe for a long visit, in pursuance of a plan discussed at intervals between his mother and Mr. Herbert during the whole course of his boyhood. They had made no attempt to forecast his future career, or to prepare him for a profession. Strictly, indeed, he was at liberty, like his late father, to dispense with a profession. Not that it was to be wished that he should take his father's life as an example. It was understood by the world at large, and, of course, by Mrs. De Grey and her companion in particular, that this gentleman's existence had been blighted, at an early period, by an unhappy love-affair; and it was notorious that, in consequence, he had spent the few years of his maturity in gloomy idleness and dissipation. Mrs. De Grey, whose own father was an Englishman, reduced to poverty, but with claims to high gentility, professed herself unable to understand why Paul should not live decently on his means. Mr. Herbert declared that in America, in any walk of life, idleness was indecent; and that he hoped the young man would—nominally at least—select a career. It was agreed on both sides, however, that there was no need for haste; and that it was proper, in the first place, he should see the world. The world, to Mrs. De Grey, was little more than a name; but to Mr. Herbert, priest as he was, it was a vivid reality. Yet he felt that the generous and intelligent youth upon whose education he had lavished all the treasures of his tenderness and sagacity, was not unfitted, either by nature or culture, to measure his sinews against its trials and temptations; and that he should love him the better for coming home at twenty-five an accomplished gentleman and a good Catholic, sobered and seasoned by experience, sceptical in small matters, confident in great, and richly replete with good stories. When he came of age, Paul received his walking-ticket, as they say, in the shape of a letter of credit for a handsome sum on certain London bankers. But the young man pocketed the letter, and remained at home, poring over books, lounging in the garden, and scribbling heroic verses. At the end of a year, he plucked up a little ambition, and took a turn through the country, travelling much of the way on horseback. He came back an ardent American, and felt that he might go abroad without danger. During his absence in Europe he had written home innumerable long letters,—compositions to elaborate (in the taste of that day, recent as it is) and so delightful, that, between their pride in his epistolary talent, and their longing to see his face, his mother and his ex-tutor would have been at a loss to determine whether he gave them more satisfaction at home or abroad.

With his departure the household was plunged in unbroken repose. Mrs. De Grey neither went out nor entertained company. An occasional morning call was the only claim made upon her hospitality. Mr. Herbert, who was a great scholar, spent all his hours in study; and his patroness sat for the most part alone, arrayed with a perfection of neatness which there was no one to admire (unless it be her waiting-maid, to whom it remained a constant matter of awe), reading a pious book or knitting under-garments for the orthodox needy. At times, indeed, she wrote long letters to her son, —the contents of which Mr. Herbert found it hard to divine. This was accounted a dull life forty years ago; now, doubtless, it would be considered no life at all. It is no matter of wonder, therefore, that finally, one April morning, in her sixty-seventh year, as I have said, Mrs. De Grey suddenly began to suspect that she was lonely.

Another long year, at least, was to come and go before Paul's return. After meditating for a while in silence, Mrs. De Grey resolved to take counsel with Father Herbert.

This gentleman, an Englishman by birth, had been an intimate friend of George De Grey, who had made his acquaintance during a visit to Europe, before his marriage. Mr. Herbert was a younger son of an excellent Catholic family, and was at the time beginning, on small resources, the practice of the law. De Grey met him in London, and the two conceived a strong mutual sympathy. Herbert had neither taste for his profession nor apparent ambition of any sort. He was, moreover, in weak health; and his friend found no difficulty in persuading him to accept the place of travelling companion through France and Italy. De Grey carried a very long purse, and was a most liberal friend and patron; and the two young men accomplished their progress as far as Venice in the best spirits and on the best terms. But in Venice, for reasons best known to themselves, they bitterly and irretrievably quarrelled. Some persons said it was over a card-table, and some said it was about a woman. At all events, in consequence, De Grey returned to America, and Herbert repaired to Rome. He obtained admission into a monastery, studied theology, and finally was invested with priestly orders. In America, in his thirty-third year, De Grey married the lady whom I have described. A few weeks after his marriage he wrote to Herbert, expressing a vehement desire to be reconciled. Herbert felt that the letter was that of a most unhappy man; he had already forgiven him; he pitied him, and after a short delay succeeded in obtaining an ecclesiastical mission to the United States. He reached New York and presented himself at his friend's house, which from this moment became his home. Mrs. De Grey had recently given birth to a son; her husband was confined to his room by illness, reduced to a shadow of his former self by repeated sensual excesses. He survived Herbert's arrival but a couple of months; and after his death the rumour went abroad that he had by his last will settled a handsome income upon the priest, on condition that he would continue to reside with his widow, and take the entire charge of his boy's education.

This rumour was confirmed by the event. For twenty-five years, at the time of which I write, Herbert had lived under Mrs. De Grey's roof as her friend and companion and counsellor, and as her son's tutor. Once reconciled to his friend, he had gradually dropped his priestly character. He was of an essentially devout temperament, but he craved neither parish nor pulpit. On the other hand, he had become an indefatigable student. His late friend had bequeathed

to him a valuable library, which he gradually enlarged. His passion
for study, however, appeared singularly disinterested, inasmuch as,
for many years, his little friend Paul was the sole witness and
receptacle of his learning. It is true that he composed a large portion
of a History of the Catholic Church in America, which, although
the manuscript exists, has never seen, and, I suppose, is never
destined to see, the light. It is in the very best keeping, for it
contains an immense array of facts. The work is written, not from
a sympathetic, but from a strictly respectful point of view; but it
has a fatal defect,—it lacks unction.

The same complaint might have been made of Father Herbert's
personal character. He was the soul of politeness, but it was a cold
and formal courtesy. When he smiled, it was, as the French say,
with the end of his lips, and when he took your hand, with the end
of his fingers. He had had a charming face in his younger days, and,
when gentlemen dressed their hair with powder, his fine black eyes
must have produced the very best effect. But he had lost his hair,
and he wore on his naked crown a little black silk cap. Round his
neck he had a black cravat of many folds, without any collar. He
was short and slight, with a stoop in his shoulders, and a handsome
pair of hands.

'If it were not for a sad sign to the contrary,' said Mrs. De Grey,
in pursuance of her resolve to take counsel of her friend, 'I should
believe I am growing younger.'

'What is the sign to the contrary?' asked Herbert.

'I'm losing my eyes. I can't see to read. Suppose I should become
blind.'

'And what makes you suspect that you are growing young again?'

'I feel lonely. I lack company. I miss Paul.'

'You will have Paul back in a year.'

'Yes; but in the meanwhile I shall be miserable. I wish I knew
some nice person whom I might ask to stay with me.'

'Why don't you take a companion,—some poor gentlewoman in
search of a home? She would read to you, and talk to you.'

'No; that would be dreadful. She would be sure to be old and
ugly. I should like someone to take Paul's place,—someone young
and fresh like him. We're all so terribly old, in the house. You're at
least seventy; I'm sixty-five' (Mrs. De Grey was pleased to say);
'Deborah is sixty, the cook and coachman are fifty-five apiece.'

'You want a young girl then?'

'Yes, some nice, fresh young girl, who would laugh once in a
while, and make a little music,—a little sound in the house.

'Well,' said Herbert, after reflecting a moment, 'you had better suit yourself before Paul comes home. You have only a year.'

'Dear me,' said Mrs. De Grey; 'I shouldn't feel myself obliged to turn her out on Paul's account.'

Father Herbert looked at his companion with a penetrating glance. 'Nevertheless, my dear lady,' he said, 'you know what I mean.'

'O yes, I know what you mean,—and you, Father Herbert, know know what I think.'

'Yes, madam, and, allow me to add, that I don't greatly care. Why should I? I hope with all my heart that you'll never find yourself compelled to think otherwise.'

'It is certain,' said Mrs. De Grey, 'that Paul has had time to play out his little tragedy a dozen times over.'

'His father,' rejoined Herbert, gravely, 'was twenty-six years old.'

At these words Mrs. De Grey looked at the priest with a slight frown and a flushed cheek. But he took no pains to meet her eyes, and in a few moments she had recovered, in silence, her habitual calmness.

Within a week after this conversation Mrs. De Grey observed at church two persons who appeared to be strangers in the congregation: an elderly woman, meanly clad, and evidently in ill health, but with a great refinement of person and manner; and a young girl whom Mrs. De Grey took for her daughter. On the following Sunday she again found them at their devotions, and was forcibly struck by a look of sadness and trouble in their faces and attitude. On the third Sunday they were absent; but it happened that during the walk, going to confession, she met the young girl, pale, alone, and dressed in mourning, apparently just leaving the confessional. Something in her gait and aspect assured Mrs. De Grey that she was alone in the world, friendless and helpless; and the good lady, who at times was acutely sensible of her own isolation in society, felt a strong and sympathetic prompting to speak to the stranger, and ask the secret of her sorrow. She stopped her before she left the church, and, addressing her with the utmost kindness, succeeded so speedily in winning her confidence that in half an hour she was in possession of the young girl's entire history. She had just lost her mother, and she found herself in the great city penniless, and all but houseless. They were from the South; her father had been an officer in the navy, and had perished at sea, two years before. Her mother's health had failed, and they had come to New York, ill-advisedly enough, to consult an eminent physician. He had been very kind, he had taken no fees, but his skill had been applied in vain. Their money had melted away in other directions,—for food and lodging and clothing. There had been enough left to give the poor lady a decent burial; but no means of support save her own exertions remained for the young girl. She had no relatives to look to, but she professed herself abundantly willing to work. 'I look weak,' she said, 'and pale, but I'm really strong. It's only that I'm tired,—and sad. I'm ready to do anything. But I don't know where to look.' She had lost her colour and the roundness and elasticity of youth; she was thin and ill-dressed; but Mrs. De Grey saw that at her best she must be properly a very pretty creature, and that she was evidently, by rights, a charming girl. She looked at the elder lady with lustrous, appealing blue eyes from under the hideous black bonnet in which her masses of soft light hair were tucked away. She assured her that she had received a very good education, and that she played on the piano-forte. Mrs. De Grey fancied her divested of her rusty weeds, and dressed in a white frock and a blue ribbon, reading aloud at an open window, or touching the keys of her old not unmelodious spinnet; for if she took her (as she mentally phrased it) Mrs. De Grey was resolved that she would not be harassed with the sight of her black garments. It was plain that, frightened and faint and nervous as she was, the poor child would take any service unconditionally. She kissed her then tenderly within the sacred precinct, and led her away to her carriage, quite forgetting her business with her confessor. On the following day Margaret Aldis (such was the young girl's name) was transferred in the same vehicle to Mrs. De Grey's own residence.

This edifice was demolished some years ago, and the place where it stood forms at the present moment the very centre of a turbulent thoroughfare. But at the period of which I speak it stood on the outskirts of the town, with as vast a prospect of open country in one direction as in the other of close-built streets. It was an excellent old mansion, moreover, in the best taste of the time, with large square rooms and broad halls and deep windows, and, above all, a delightful great garden, hedged off from the road by walls of dense verdure. Here, steeped in repose and physical comfort, rescued from the turbid stream of common life, and placed apart in the glow of tempered sunshine, valued, esteemed, caressed, and yet feeling that she was not a mere passive object of charity, but that she was doing her simple utmost to requite her protectress, poor Miss Aldis bloomed and flowered afresh. With rest and luxury and leisure, her natural gaiety and beauty came back to her. Her beauty was not dazzling, indeed, nor her gaiety obtrusive; but, united, they were the flower of girlish grace. She still retained a certain tenuity and fragility of aspect, a lightness of tread, a softness of voice, a faint-

ness of colouring, which suggested an intimate acquaintance with
suffering. But there seemed to burn, nevertheless, in her deep blue
eyes the light of an almost passionate vitality; and there sat on her
firm, pale lips the utterance of a determined, devoted will. It seemed
at times as if she gave herself up with a sensuous, reckless, half-
thankless freedom to the mere consciousness of security. It was
evident that she had an innate love of luxury. She would sometimes
sit, motionless, for hours, with her head thrown back, and her eyes
slowly wandering, in a silent ecstasy of content. At these times
Father Herbert, who had observed her attentively from the moment
of her arrival (for, scholar and recluse as he was, he had not lost
the faculty of appreciating feminine grace),—at these times the old
priest would watch her covertly and marvel at the fantastic, soul-
less creature whom Mrs. De Grey had taken to her side. One evening, after a prolonged stupor of this sort, in which the young girl
had neither moved nor spoken, sitting like one whose soul had
detached itself and was wandering through space, she rose, on Mrs.
De Grey's at last giving her an order, and moved forward as if in
compliance; and then, suddenly rushing toward the old woman, she
fell on her knees, and buried her head in her lap and burst into a
paroxysm of sobs. Herbert, who had been standing by, went and
laid one hand on her head, and with the other made over it the
sign of the cross, in the manner of a benediction,—a consecration
of the passionate gratitude which had finally broken out into utterance. From this moment he loved her.

Margaret read aloud to Mrs. De Grey, and on Sunday evenings
sang in a clear, sweet voice the chants of their Church, and occupied herself constantly with fine needle-work, in which she possessed great skill. They spent the long summer mornings together, in
reading and work and talk. Margaret told her companion the
simple, sad details of the history of which she had already given
her the outline; and Mrs. De Grey, who found it natural to look
upon them as a kind of practical romance organized for her entertainment, made her repeat them over a dozen times. Mrs. De Grey,
too, honoured the young girl with a recital of her own biography,
which, in its vast vacuity, produced upon Margaret's mind a vague
impression of grandeur. The vacuity, indeed, was relieved by the
figure of Paul, whom Mrs. De Grey never grew weary of describing,
and of whom, finally, Margaret grew very fond of thinking. She
listened most attentively to Mrs. De Grey's eulogies of her son, and
thought it a great pity he was not at home. And then she began to
long for his return, and then, suddenly, she began to fear it. Perhaps
he would dislike her being in the house, and turn her out of doors.

It was evident that his mother was not prepared to contradict him. Perhaps—worse still—he would marry some foreign woman, and bring her home, and she would turn wickedly jealous of Margaret (in the manner of foreign women). De Grey, roaming through Europe, took her for granted, piously enough, that he was never absent from his good mother's thoughts; but he remained superbly unconscious of the dignity which he had usurped in the meditations of her humble companion. Truly, we know where our lives begin, but who shall say where they end? Here was a careless young gentleman whose existence enjoyed a perpetual echo in the soul of a poor girl utterly unknown to him. Mrs. De Grey had two portraits of her son, which, of course, she lost no time in exhibiting to Margaret,—one taken in his boyhood with brilliant red hair and cheeks, the lad's body encased in a bright blue jacket, and his neck encircled in a frill, open very low; the other, executed just before his departure, a handsome young man in a buff waistcoat, clean shaven, with an animated countenance, dark, close-curling auburn hair, and very fine eyes. The former of these designs Margaret thought a very pretty child; but to the other the poor girl straightway lost her heart,—the more easily that Mrs. De Grey assured her, that, although the picture was handsome enough, it conveyed but the faintest idea of her boy's adorable flesh and blood. In a couple of months arrived a long-expected letter from Paul, and with it another portrait,—a miniature, painted in Paris by a famous artist. Here Paul appeared a far more elegant figure than in the work of the American painter. In what the change consisted it was hard to tell; but his mother declared that it was easy to see that he had spent two years in the best company in Europe.

'O, the best company!' said Father Herbert, who knew the force of his term. And, smiling a moment with inoffensive scorn, he relapsed into his wonted gravity.

'I think he looks very sad,' said Margaret, timidly.

'Fiddlesticks!' cried Herbert, impatiently. 'He looks like a coxcomb. Of course, it's the Frenchman's fault,' he added, more gently. 'Why on earth does he send us his picture at all? It's a great piece of impertinence. Does he think we've forgotten him? When I want to remember my boy, I have something better to look to than that flaunting bit of ivory.'

At these words the two ladies went off, carrying the portrait with them, to read Paul's letter in private. It was in eight pages, and Margaret read it aloud. Then, when she had finished, she read it again; and in the evening she read it once more. The next day, Mrs. De Grey, taking the young girl into her confidence, brought out a large packet containing his earlier letters, and Margaret spent the whole morning in reading them over aloud. That evening she took a stroll in the garden alone,—the garden in which *he* had played as a boy, and lounged and dreamed as a young man. She found his name—his beautiful name—rudely cut on a wooden bench. Introduced, as it seemed to her that she had been by his letters, into the precincts of his personality, the mystery of his being, the magic circle of his feelings and opinions and fancies; wandering by his side, unseen, over Europe, and treading, unheard, the sounding pavements of famous churches and palaces, she felt that she tasted for the first time of the substance and sweetness of life. Margaret walked about for an hour in the starlight, among the dusky, perfumed alleys. Mrs. De Grey, feeling unwell, had gone to her room. The young girl heard the far-off hum of the city slowly decrease and expire, and then, when the stillness of the night was unbroken, she came back into the parlour across the long window, and lit one of the great silver candlesticks that decorated the ends of the mantel. She carried it to the wall where Mrs. De Grey had suspended her son's miniature, having first inserted it in an immense gold frame, from which she had expelled a less valued picture. Margaret felt that she must see the portrait before she went to bed. There was a certain charm and ravishment in beholding it privately by candle-light. The wind had risen,—a warm west wind,—and the long white curtains of the open windows swayed and bulged in the gloom in a spectral fashion. Margaret guarded the flame of the candle with her hand, and gazed at the polished surface of the portrait, warm in the light, beneath its glittering plate of glass. What an immensity of life and passion was concentrated into those few square inches of artificial colour. The young man's eyes seemed to gaze at her with a look of profound recognition. They held her fascinated; she lingered on the spot, unable to move. Suddenly the clock on the chimney-piece rang out a single clear stroke. Margaret started and turned about, at the thought that it was already half past ten. She raised her candle aloft to look at the dial-plate; and perceived three things: that it was one o'clock in the morning, that her candle was half burnt out, and that someone was watching her from the other side of the room. Setting down her light, she recognized Father Herbert.

'Well, Miss Aldis,' he said, coming into the light, 'what do you think of it?'

Margaret was startled and confused, but not abashed. 'How long have I been here?' she asked, simply.

'I have no idea. I myself have been here half an hour.'

'It was very kind of you not to disturb me,' said Margaret, less simply.

'It was a very pretty picture,' said Herbert.

'O, it's beautiful!' cried the young girl, casting another glance at the portrait over her shoulder.

The old man smiled sadly, and turned away, and then, coming back, 'How do you like our young man, Miss Aldis?' he asked, apparently with a painful effort.

'I think he's very handsome,' said Margaret, frankly.

'He's not so handsome as that,' said Herbert.

'His mother says he's handsomer.'

'A mother's testimony in such cases is worth very little. Paul is well enough, but he's no miracle.'

'I think he looks sad,' said Margaret. 'His mother says he's very gay.'

'He may have changed vastly within two years. Do you think,' the old man added, after a pause, 'that he looks like a man in love?'

'I don't know,' said Margaret, in a low voice. 'I never saw one.'

'Never?' said the priest, with an earnestness which surprised the young girl.

She blushed a little. 'Never, Father Herbert.'

The priest's dark eyes were fixed on her with a strange intensity of expression. 'I hope, my child, you never may,' he said, solemnly.

The tone of his voice was not unkind, but it seemed to Margaret as if there were something cruel and chilling in the wish. 'Why not I as well as another?' she asked.

The old man shrugged his shoulders. 'O, it's a long story,' he said.

The summer passed away and flushed into autumn, and the autumn slowly faded, and finally expired in the cold embrace of December. Mrs. De Grey had written to her son of her having taken Margaret into her service. At this time came a letter in which the young man was pleased to express his satisfaction at this measure. 'Present my compliments to Miss Aldis,' he wrote, 'and assure her of my gratitude for the comfort she has given my dear mother,—of which, indeed, I hope before very long to inform her in person.' In writing these good-natured words Paul De Grey little suspected the infinite reverberation they were to have in poor Margaret's heart. A month later arrived a letter, which was handed to Mrs. De Grey at breakfast. 'You will have received my letter of December 3rd,' it began (a letter which had miscarried and failed to arrive), 'and will have formed your respective opinions of its contents.' As Mrs. De Grey read these words, Father Herbert looked at Margaret; she had turned pale. 'Favourable or not,' the letter continued, 'I am sorry to be obliged to bid you undo them again. But my engagement to Miss L. is broken off. It had become impossible. As I made no attempt to give you a history of it, or to set forth my motives, so I shall not now attempt to go into the logic of rupture. But it's broken clean off, I assure you. Amen.' And the letter passed to other matters, leaving our friends sadly perplexed. They awaited the arrival of the missing letter; but all in vain; it never came. Mrs. De Grey immediately wrote to her son, urgently requesting an explanation of the events to which he had referred. His next letter, however, contained none of the desired information. Mrs. De Grey repeated her request. Whereupon Paul wrote that he would tell her the story when he had reached home. He hated to talk about it. 'Don't be uneasy, dear mother,' he added; 'Heaven has insured me against a relapse. Miss L. died three weeks ago at Naples.' As Mrs. De Grey read these words, she laid down the letter and looked at Father Herbert, who had been called to hear it. His pale face turned ghastly white, and he returned the old woman's gaze with compressed lips and a stony immobility in his eyes. Then, suddenly, a fierce, inarticulate cry broke from his throat, and, doubling up his fist, he brought it down with a terrible blow on the table. Margaret sat watching him, amazed. He rose to his feet, seized her in his arms, and pressed her on his neck.

'My child! my child!' he cried, in a broken voice, 'I have always loved you! I have been harsh and cold and crabbed. I was fearful. The thunder has fallen! Forgive me, child. I'm myself again.' Margaret, frightened, disengaged herself, but he kept her hand. 'Poor boy!' he cried, with a tremulous sigh.

Mrs. De Grey sat smelling her vinaigrette, but not visibly discomposed. 'Poor boy!' she repeated, but without a sigh,—which gave the words an ironical sound.—'He had ceased to care for her,' she said.

'Ah, madam!' cried the priest, 'don't blaspheme. Go down on your knees, and thank God that *we* have been spared that hideous sight!'

Mystified and horrified, Margaret drew her hand from his grasp, and looked with wondering eyes at Mrs. De Grey. She smiled faintly, touched her forefinger to her forehead, tapped it, raised her eyebrows, and shook her head.

From counting the months that were to elapse before Paul's return, our friends came to counting the weeks, and then the days. The month of May arrived; Paul had sailed from England. At this time Mrs. De Grey opened her son's room, and caused it to be prepared for occupation. The contents were just as he had left them;

she bade Margaret come in and see it. Margaret looked at her face
in his mirror, and sat down a moment on his sofa, and examined
the books on his shelves. They seemed a prodigious array; they
were in several languages, and gave a deep impression of their
owner's attainments. Over the chimney hung a small sketch in
pencil, which Margaret made haste to inspect,—a likeness of a
young girl, skilfully enough drawn. The original had apparently
been very handsome, in the dark style; and in the corner of the
sketch was written the artist's name,—*De Grey*. Margaret looked at
the portrait in silence, with quickened heartbeats.

'Is this Mr. Paul's?' she asked at last of her companion.

'It belongs to Paul,' said Mrs. De Grey. 'He used to be very fond
of it, and insisted upon hanging it there. His father sketched it
before our marriage.'

Margaret drew a breath of relief. 'And who is the lady?' she
asked.

'I hardly know. Some foreign person, I think, that Mr. De Grey
had been struck with. There's something about her in the other
corner.'

In effect, Margaret detected on the opposite side of the sketch,
written in minute characters, the word '*obiit*, 1786.'

'You don't know Latin, I take it, my dear,' said Mrs. De Grey, as
Margaret read the inscription. 'It means that she died thirty-four
good years ago.'

'Poor girl!' said Margaret, softly. As they were leaving the room,
she lingered on the threshold and looked about her, wishing that
she might leave some little memento of her visit. 'If we knew just
when he would arrive,' she said, 'I would put some flowers on his
table. But they might fade.'

As Mrs. De Grey assured her that the moment of his arrival was
quite uncertain, she left her fancied nosegay uncut, and spent the
rest of the day in a delightful tremor of anticipation, ready to see
the dazzling figure of a young man, equipped with strange foreign
splendour, start up before her and look at her in cold surprise, and
hurry past her in search of his mother. At every sound of footsteps
or of an opening door she laid down her work, and listened
curiously. In the evenings, as if by a common instinct of expectancy, Father Herbert met Mrs. De Grey in the front drawing-room,
—an apartment devoted exclusively to those festivities which never
occurred in the annals of this tranquil household.

'A year ago to-day, madam,' said Margaret, as they all sat silent
among the gathering shadows, 'I came into your house. To-day
ends a very happy year.'

'Let us hope,' said Father Herbert, sententiously, 'that to-morrow will begin another.'

'Ah, my dear lady,' cried Margaret, with emotion; 'my good father,—my only friends,—what harm can come to me with you? It was you who rescued me from harm.' Her heart was swollen with gratitude, and her eyes with rising tears. She gave a long shudder at the thought of the life that might have been her fate. But, feeling a natural indisposition to obtrude her peculiar sensations upon the attention of persons so devoutly absorbed in the thought of a coming joy, she left her place, and wandered away into the garden. Before many minutes, a little gate opened in the paling, not six yards from where she stood. A man came in, whom, in the dim light, she knew to be Paul De Grey. Approaching her rapidly, he made a movement as if to greet her, but stopped suddenly, and removed his hat.

'Ah, you're Miss—the young lady,' he said.

He had forgotten her name. This was something other, something less felicitous, than the cold surprise of the figure in Margaret's vision. Nevertheless, she answered him, audibly enough: 'They are in the drawing-room; they expect you.'

He bounded along the path, and entered the house. She followed him slowly to the window, and stood without, listening. The silence of the young man's welcome told of its warmth.

Paul De Grey had made good use of his sojourn in Europe; he had lost none of his old merits, and had gained a number of new ones. He was by nature and culture an intelligent, amiable, accomplished fellow. It was his fortune to possess a peculiar, indefinable charm of person and manner. He was tall and slight of structure, but compact, firm, and active, with a clear, fair complexion, an open, prominent brow, crisp auburn hair, and eyes—a glance, a smile—radiant with youth and intellect. His address was frank, manly, and direct; and yet it seemed to Margaret that his bearing was marked by a certain dignity and elegance—at times even verging upon formalism—which distinguished it from that of other men. It was not, however, that she detected in his character any signs of that strange principle of melancholy which had exerted so powerful an action upon the other members of the household (and, from what she was able to gather, on his father). She fancied, on the contrary, that she had never known less levity associated with a more exquisite mirth. If Margaret had been of a more analytical turn of mind, she would have told herself that Paul De Grey's nature was eminently aristocratic. But the young girl contented herself with understanding it less, and secretly loving it more; and

when she was in want of an epithet, she chose a simpler term. Paul
was like a ray of splendid sunshine in the dull, colourless lives of
the two women; he filled the house with light and heat and joy. He
moved, to Margaret's fancy, in a circle of almost supernatural glory.
His words, as they fell from his lips, seemed diamonds and pearls;
and, in truth, his conversation, for a month after his return, was in
the last degree delightful. Mrs. De Grey's house was *par excellence*
the abode of leisure,—a castle of indolence; and Paul in talking,
and his companions in listening, were conscious of no jealous stress
of sordid duties. The summer days were long, and Paul's daily fund
of loquacity were inexhaustible. A week after his arrival, after breakfast, Father Herbert contracted the habit of carrying him off to his
study; and Margaret, passing the half-open door, would hear the
changeful music of his voice. She begrudged the old man, at these
times, the exclusive enjoyment of so much eloquence. She felt that
with his tutor, Paul's talk was far wiser and richer than it was possible it should be with two simple-minded women; and the young
girl had a pious longing to hear him, to see him, at his best. A
brilliant best it was to Father Herbert's mind; for Paul had surpassed
his fondest hopes. He had amassed such a store of knowledge; he
had learned all the good that the old man had enjoined upon him;
and, although he had not wholly ignored the evil against which the
priest had warned him, he judged it so wisely and wittily! Women
and priests, as a general thing, like a man none the less for not
being utterly innocent. Father Herbert took an unutterable satisfaction in the happy development of Paul's character. He was more
than the son of his loins: he was the child of his intellect, his
patience, and devotion.

The afternoons and evenings Paul was free to devote to his
mother, who, out of her own room, never dispensed for an hour
with Margaret's attendance. This, thanks to the young girl's delicate
tact and sympathy, had now become an absolute necessity. Margaret
sat by with her work, while Paul talked, and marvelled at his inexhaustible stock of gossip and anecdote and forcible, vivid description. He made cities and churches and galleries and playhouses
swarm and shine before her enchanted senses, and reproduced the
people he had met and the scenery through which he had travelled,
until the young girl's head turned at the rapid succession of images
and pictures. And then, at time, he would seem to grow weary, and
would sink into silence; and Margaret, looking up askance from
her work, would see his eyes absently fixed, and a faint smile on his
face, or else a cold gravity, and she would wonder what far-off
memory had called back his thoughts to that unknown European

world. Sometimes, less frequently, when she raised her eyes, she found him watching her own figure, her bent head, and the busy movement of her hands. But (as yet, at least) he never turned away his glance in confusion; he let his eyes rest, and justified his scrutiny by some simple and natural remark.

But as the weeks passed by, and the summer grew to its fullness, Mrs. De Grey contracted the habit of going after dinner to her own room, where, we may respectfully conjecture, she passed the afternoon in dishabille and slumber. But De Grey and Miss Aldis tacitly agreed together that, in the prime and springtime of life, it was stupid folly to waste in any such fashion the longest and brightest hours of the year; and so they, on their side, contracted the habit of sitting in the darkened drawing-room, and gossiping away the time until within an hour of tea. Sometimes, for a change, they went across the garden into a sort of summer-house, which occupied a central point in the enclosure, and stood with its face averted from the mansion, and looking to the north, and with its sides covered with dense, clustering vines. Within, against the wall, was a deep garden bench, and in the middle a table, upon which Margaret placed her work-basket, and the young man the book, which, under the pretence of meaning to read, he usually carried in his hand. Within was coolness and deep shade and silence, and without the broad glare of the immense summer sky. When I say there was silence, I mean that there was nothing to interrupt the conversation of these happy idlers. Their talk speedily assumed that desultory, volatile character, which is the sign of great intimacy. Margaret found occasion to ask Paul a great many questions which she had not felt at liberty to ask in the presence of his mother, and to demand additional light upon a variety of little points which Mrs. De Grey had been content to leave in obscurity. Paul was perfectly communicative. If Miss Aldis cared to hear, he was assuredly glad to talk. But suddenly it struck him that her attitude of mind was a singular provocation to egotism, and that for six weeks, in fact, he had done nothing but talk about himself,—his own adventures, sensations, and opinions.

'I declare, Miss Aldis,' he cried, 'you're making me a monstrous egotist. That's all you women are good for. I shall not say another word about Mr. Paul De Grey. Now it's your turn.'

'To talk about Mr. Paul De Grey?' asked Margaret, with a smile.

'No, about Miss Margaret Aldis,—which, by the way, is a very pretty name.'

'By the way, indeed!' said Margaret. 'By the way for you, perhaps. But for me, my pretty name is all I have.'

'If you mean, Miss Aldis,' cried Paul, 'that your beauty is all in your name—'

'I'm sadly mistaken. Well, then, I don't. The rest is in my imagination.'

'Very likely. It's certainly not in mine.'

Margaret was, in fact, at this time, extremely pretty; a little pale with the heat, but rounded and developed by rest and prosperity, and animated—half inspired, I may call it—with tender gratitude. Looking at her as he said these words, De Grey was forcibly struck with the interesting character of her face. Yes, most assuredly, her beauty was a potent reality. The charm of her face was forever refreshed and quickened by the deep loveliness of her soul.

'I mean literally, Miss Aldis,' said the young man, 'that I wish you to talk about yourself. I want to hear *your* adventures. I demand it, —I need it.'

'My adventures?' said Margaret. 'I have never had any.'

'Good!' cried Paul; 'that in itself is an adventure.'

In this way it was that Margaret came to relate to her companion the short story of her young life. The story was not all told, however, short as it was, in a single afternoon; that is, a whole week after she began, the young girl found herself setting Paul right with regard to a matter of which he had received a false impression.

'Nay, he is married,' said Margaret; 'I told you so.'

'O, he is married?' said Paul.

'Yes; his wife's an immense fat woman.'

'O, his wife's an immense fat woman?'

'Yes; and he thinks all the world of her.'

'O, he thinks all the world of her!'

It was natural that, in this manner, with a running commentary supplied by Paul, the narrative should proceed slowly. But, in addition to the observations here quoted, the young man maintained another commentary, less audible and more profound. As he listened to this frank and fair-haired maiden, and reflected that in the wide world she might turn in confidence and sympathy to other minds than his,—as he found her resting her candid thoughts and memories on his judgment, as she might lay her white hand on his arm, —it seemed to him that the pure intentions with which she believed his soul to be peopled took in her glance a graver and higher cast. All the gorgeous colour faded out of his recent European reminiscences and regrets, and he was sensible only of Margaret's presence, and of the tender rosy radiance in which she sat and moved, as in a sort of earthly halo. Could it be, he asked himself, that while he was roaming about Europe, in a vague, restless search for his future, his end, his aim, these things were quietly awaiting him at his own deserted hearth-stone, gathered together in the immaculate person of the sweetest and fairest of women? Finally, one day, this view of the case struck him so forcibly, that he cried out in an ecstasy of belief and joy.

'Margaret,' he said, 'my mother found you in church, and there, before the altar, she kissed you and took you into her arms. I have often thought of that scene. It makes it no common adoption.'

'I'm sure I have often thought of it,' said Margaret.

'It makes it sacred and everlasting,' said Paul. 'On that blessed day you came to us for ever and ever.'

Margaret looked at him with a face tremulous between smiles and tears. 'For as long as you will keep me,' she said. 'Ah, Paul!' For an instant the young man had expressed all his longing and his passion.

With the greatest affection and esteem for his mother, Paul had always found it natural to give precedence to Father Herbert in matters of appeal and confidence. The old man possessed a delicacy of intellectual tact which made his sympathy and his counsel alike delightful. Some days after the conversation upon a few of the salient points of which I have lightly touched, Paul and Margaret renewed their mutual vows in the summer-house. They now possessed that deep faith in the sincerity of their own feelings, and that undoubting delight in each other's reiterated protests, which left them nothing to do but to take their elders into their confidence. They came through the garden together, and on reaching the threshold Margaret found that she had left her scissors in the garden hut; whereupon Paul went back in search of them. The young girl came into the house, reached the foot of the staircase, and waited for her lover. At this moment Father Herbert appeared in the open doorway of his study, and looked at Margaret with a melancholy smile. He stood, passing one hand slowly over another, and gazing at her with kindly, darksome looks.

'It seems to me, Mistress Margaret,' he said, 'that you keep all this a marvellous secret from your poor old Doctor Herbert.'

In the presence of this gentle and venerable scholar, Margaret felt that she had no need of vulgar blushing and simpering and negation. 'Dear Father Herbert,' she said, with heavenly simpleness, 'I have just been begging Paul to tell you.'

'Ah, my daughter,'—and the old man but half stifled a sigh,— 'it's all a strange and terrible mistery.'

Paul came in and crossed the hall with the light step of a lover. 'Paul,' said Margaret, 'Father Herbert knows.'

'Father Herbert knows!' repeated the priest,—'Father Herbert knows everything. You're very innocent for lovers.'

'You're very wise, sir, for a priest,' said Paul, blushing.

'I knew it a week ago,' said the old man, gravely.

'Well, sir,' said Paul, 'we love you none the less for loving each other so much more. I hope you'll not love us the less.'

'Father Herbert thinks it's "terrible",' said Margaret, smiling.

'O Lord!' cried Herbert, raising his hand to his head as if in pain. He turned about, and went into his room.

Paul drew Margaret's hand through his arm and followed the priest. 'You suffer, sir,' he said, 'at the thought of losing us,—of our leaving you. That certainly needn't trouble you. Where should we go? As long as you live, as long as my mother lives, we shall all make but a single household.'

The old man appeared to have recovered his composure. 'Ah!' he said; 'be happy, no matter where, and I shall be happy. You're very young.'

'Not so young,' said Paul, laughing, but with a natural disinclination to be placed in too boyish a light. 'I'm six-and-twenty. *F'ai vécu*,—I've lived.'

'He's been through everything,' said Margaret, leaning on his arm.

'Not quite everything.' And Paul, bending his eyes, with a sober smile, met her upward glance.

'O, he's modest,' murmured Father Herbert.

'Paul's been all but married already,' said Margaret.

The young man made a gesture of impatience. Herbert stood with his eyes fixed on his face.

'Why do you speak of that poor girl?' said Paul. Whatever satisfaction he may have given Margaret on the subject of his projected marriage in Europe, he had since his return declined, on the plea that it was extremely painful, to discuss the matter either with his mother or with his old tutor.

'Miss Aldis is perhaps jealous,' said Herbert, cunningly.

'O Father Herbert!' cried Margaret.

'There is little enough to be jealous of,' said Paul.

'There's a fine young man!' cried Herbert. 'One would think he had never cared for her.'

'It's perfectly true.'

'Oh!' said Herbert, in a tone of deep reproach, laying his hand on the young man's arm. 'Don't say that.'

'Nay, sir, I shall say it. I never said anything less to her. She enchanted me, she entangled me, but, before Heaven, I never loved her!'

'O, God help you!' cried the priest. He sat down, and buried his face in his hands.

Margaret turned deadly pale, and recalled the scene which had occurred on the receipt of Paul's letter, announcing the rupture of his engagement. 'Father Herbert,' she cried, 'what horrible, hideous mystery do you keep locked up in your bosom? If it concerns me,—if it concerns Paul,—I demand of you to tell us.

Moved apparently by the young girl's tone of agony to a sense of the needfulness of self-control, Herbert uncovered his face, and directed to Margaret a rapid glance of entreaty. She perceived that it meant that, at any cost, she should be silent. Then, with a sublime attempt at dissimulation, he put out his hands, and laid one on each of his companions' shoulders. 'Excuse me, Paul,' he said, 'I'm a foolish old man. Old scholars are a sentimental, a superstitious race. We believe still that all women are angels, and that all men—'

'That all men are fools,' said Paul, smiling.

'Exactly. Whereas, you see,' whispered Father Herbert, 'there are no fools but ourselves.'

Margaret listened to this fantastic bit of dialogue with a beating heart, fully determined not to content herself with any such flimsy explanation of the old man's tragical allusions. Meanwhile, Herbert urgently besought Paul to defer for a few days making known his engagement to his mother.

The next day but one was Sunday, the last in August. The heat for a week had been oppressive, and the air was now sullen and brooding, as if with an approaching storm. As she left the breakfast-table, Margaret felt her arm touched by Father Herbert.

'Don't go to church,' he said, in a low voice. 'Make a pretext, and stay at home.

'A pretext?—'

'Say you've letters to write.'

'Letters?' and Margaret smiled half bitterly. 'To whom should I write letters?'

'Dear me, then say you're ill. I give you absolution. When they're gone, come to me.'

At church-time, accordingly, Margaret feigned a slight indisposition; and Mrs. De Grey, taking her son's arm, mounted into her ancient deep-seated coach, and rolled away from the door. Margaret immediately betook herself to Father Herbert's apartment. She saw in the old man's face the portent of some dreadful avowal. His whole figure betrayed the weight of an inexorable necessity.

'My daughter,' said the priest, 'you are a brave, pious girl—'

'Ah!' cried Margaret, 'it's something horrible, or you wouldn't say that. Tell me at once!'

'You need all your courage.'

'Doesn't he love me?—Ah, in Heaven's name, speak!'

'If he didn't love you with a damning passion, I should have nothing to say.'

'O, then, say what you please!' said Margaret.

'Well, then,—you must leave this house.'

'Why?—when?—where must I go?'

'This moment, if possible. You must go anywhere,—the further the better,—the further from *him*. Listen, my child,' said the old man, his bosom wrung by the stunned, bewildered look of Margaret's face; 'it's useless to protest, to weep, to resist. It's the voice of fate!'

'And pray, sir,' said Margaret, 'of what do you accuse me?'

'I accuse no one. I don't even accuse Heaven.'

'But there's a reason,—there's a motive—'

Herbert laid his hand on his lips, pointed to a seat, and, turning to an ancient chest on the table, unlocked it, and drew from it a small volume, bound in vellum, apparently an old illuminated missal. 'There's nothing for it,' he said, 'but to tell you the whole story.'

He sat down before the young girl, who held herself rigid and expectant. The room grew dark with the gathering storm-clouds, and the distant thunder muttered.

'Let me read you ten words,' said the priest, opening at a fly-leaf of the volume, on which a memorandum or register had been inscribed in a great variety of hands, all minute and some barely legible. 'God be with you!' and the old man crossed himself. Involuntarily, Margaret did the same. ' "George De Grey," ' he read, ' "met and loved, September, 1786, Antonietta Gambini, of Milan. She died October 9th, same year. John De Grey married, April 4th, 1749, Henrietta Spencer. She died May 7th. George De Grey engaged himself October, 1710, to Mary Fortescue. She died October 31st. Paul de Grey, aged nineteen, betrothed June, 1672, at Bristol, England, to Lucretia Lefevre, aged thirty-one, of that place. She died July 27th. John De Grey, affianced January 10th, 1649, to Blanche Ferrars, of Castle Ferrars, Cumberland. She died, by her lover's hand, January 12th. Stephen De Grey offered his hand to Isabel Stirling, October, 1619. She died within the month. Paul De Grey exchanged pledges with Magdalen Scrope, August, 1586. She died in childbirth, September, 1587." ' Father Herbert paused. 'Is it enough?' he asked, looking up with glowing eyes. 'There are two pages more. The De Greys are an ancient line; they keep their records.'

Margaret had listened with a look of deepening, fierce, passionate horror,—a look more of anger and of wounded pride than of terror. She sprang towards the priest with the lightness of a young cat, and dashed the hideous record from his hand.

'What abominable nonsense is this!' she cried. 'What does it mean? I barely heard it; I despise it; I laugh at it!'

The old man seized her arm with a firm grasp. 'Paul De Grey,' he said, in an awful voice, 'exchanged pledges with Margaret Aldis, August, 1821. She died—with the falling leaves.'

Poor Margaret looked about her for help, inspiration, comfort of some kind. The room contained nothing but serried lines of old parchment-covered books, each seeming a grim repetition of the volume at her feet. A vast peal of thunder resounded through the noonday stillness. Suddenly her strength deserted her; she felt her weakness and loneliness, the grasp of the hand of fate. Father Herbert put out his arms, she flung herself on his neck, and burst into tears.

'Do you still refuse to leave him?' asked the priest. 'If you leave him, you're saved.'

'Saved?' cried Margaret, raising her head; 'and Paul?'

'Ah, there it is.—He'll forget you.'

The young girl pondered a moment. 'To have him do that,' she said, 'I should apparently have to die.' Then wringing her hands with a fresh burst of grief, 'Is it certain,' she cried, 'that there are no exceptions?'

'None, my child'; and he picked up the volume. 'You see it's the first love, the first passion. After that, they're innocent. Look at Mrs. De Grey. The race is accursed. It's an awful, inscrutable mystery. I fancied that you were safe, my daughter, and that that poor Miss L. had borne the brunt. But Paul was at pains to undeceive me. I've searched his life, I've probed his conscience: it's a virgin heart. Ah, my child, I dreaded it from the first. I trembled when you came into the house. I wanted Mrs. De Grey to turn you off. But she laughs at it,—she calls it an old-wife's tale. *She* was safe enough; her husband didn't care two straws for her. But there's a little dark-eyed maiden buried in Italian soil who could tell her another story. She withered, my child. She was life itself,—an incarnate ray of her own Southern sun. She died of De Grey's kisses. Don't ask me how it began, it's always been so. It goes back to the night of time. One of the race, they say, came home from the East, from the crusades, infected with the germs of the plague. He had pledged his love-

faith to a young girl before his departure, and it had been arranged
that the wedding should immediately succeed his return. Feeling
unwell, he consulted an elder brother of the bride, a man versed in
fantastic medical lore, and supposed to be gifted with magical skill.
By him he was assured that he was plague-stricken, and that he was
in duty bound to defer the marriage. The young knight refused to
comply, and the physician, infuriated, pronounced a curse upon his
race. The marriage took place; within a week the bride expired, in
horrible agony; the young man, after a slight illness, recovered; the
curse took effect.'

Margaret took the quaint old missal into her hand, and turned
to the grisly register of death. Her heart grew cold as she thought
of her own sad sisterhood with all those miserable women of the
past. Miserable women, but ah! tenfold more miserable men,—
helpless victims of their own baleful hearts. She remained silent,
with her eyes fixed on the book, abstractedly; mechanically, as it
were, she turned to another page, and read a familiar orison to the
blessed Virgin. Then raising her head, with her deep-blue eyes
shining with the cold light of an immense resolve,—a prodigious act
of volition,—'Father Herbert,' she said, in low, solemn accents, 'I
revoke the curse. I undo it. *I curse it!*'

From this moment, nothing would induce her to bestow a
moment's thought on salvation by flight. It was too late, she declared. If she was destined to die, she had already imbibed the fatal
contagion. But they should see. She cast no discredit on the existence or the potency of the dreadful charm; she simply assumed,
with deep self-confidence which filled the old priest with mingled
wonder and anguish, that it would vainly expend its mystic force
once and forever upon her own devoted, impassioned life. Father
Herbert folded his trembling hands resignedly. He had done his
duty; the rest was with God. At times, living as he had done for
years in dread of the moment which had now arrived, with his
whole life darkened by its shadow, it seemed to him among the
strange possibilities of nature that this frail and pure young girl
might indeed have sprung, at the command of outraged love, to the
rescue of the unhappy line to which he had dedicated his manhood.
And then at other moments it seemed as if she were joyously casting herself into the dark gulf. At all events, the sense of peril had
filled Margaret herself with fresh energy and charm. Paul, if he had
not been too enchanted with her feverish gaiety and grace to
trouble himself about their motive and origin, would have been at
loss to explain their sudden morbid intensity. Forthwith, at her
request, he announced his engagement to his mother, who put on

a very gracious face, and honoured Margaret with a sort of official kiss.

'Ah me!' muttered Father Herbert, 'and now she thinks she has bound them fast.' And later, the next day, when Mrs. De Grey, talking of the matter, avowed that it really did cost her a little to accept as a daughter a girl to whom she had paid a salary,—'A salary, madam!' cried the priest with a bitter laugh; 'upon my word, I think it was the least you could do.'

'*Nous verrons*,' said Mrs. De Grey, composedly.

A week passed by, without ill omens. Paul was in a manly ecstasy of bliss. At moments he was almost bewildered by the fullness with which his love and faith had been requited. Margaret was transfigured, glorified, by the passion which burned in her heart. 'Give a plain girl, a common girl, a lover,' thought Paul, 'and she grows pretty, charming. Give a charming girl a lover—' and if Margaret was present, his eloquent eyes uttered the conclusion; if she was absent, his restless steps wandered in search of her. Her beauty within the past ten days seemed to have acquired an unprecedented warmth and richness. Paul went so far as to fancy that her voice had grown more deep and mellow. She looked older; she seemed in an instant to have overleaped a year of her development, and to have arrived at the perfect maturity of her youth. One might have imagined that, instead of the further, she stood just on the hither verge of marriage. Meanwhile Paul grew conscious of he hardly knew what delicate change in his own emotions. The exquisite feeling of pity, the sense of her appealing weakness, her heavenly dependence, which had lent its tender strain to swell the concert of his affections, had died away, and given place to a vague profound instinct of respect. Margaret was, after all, no such simple body; her nature, too, had its mysteries. In truth, thought Paul, tenderness, gentleness, is its own reward. He had bent to pluck this pallid flower of sunless household growth; he had dipped its slender stem in the living waters of his love, and lo! it had lifted its head, and spread its petals, and brightened into splendid purple and green. This glowing potency of loveliness filled him with a tremor which was almost a foreboding. He longed to possess her; he watched her with covetous eyes; he wished to call her utterly his own.

'Margaret,' he said to her, 'you fill me with a dreadful delight. You grow more beautiful every day. We must be married immediately, or, at this rate, by our wedding-day, I shall have grown mortally afraid of you. By the soul of my father, I didn't bargain for this! Look at yourself in that glass.' And he turned her about

to a long mirror; it was in his mother's dressing-room; Mrs. De Grey
had gone into the adjoining chamber.

Margaret saw herself reflected from head to foot in the glassy
depths, and perceived the change in her appearance. Her head rose
with a sort of proud serenity from the full curve of her shoulders;
her eyes were brilliant, her lips trembled, her bosom rose and fell
with all the insolence of her deep devotion. 'Blanche Ferrars, of
Castle Ferrars,' she silently repeated, 'Isabel Stirling, Magdalen
Scrope,—poor foolish women! You were not women, you were
children. It's your fault, Paul,' she cried, aloud, 'if I look other than
I should! Why is there such a love between us?' And then, seeing
the young man's face beside her own, she fancied he looked pale.
'My Paul,' she said, taking his hands, 'you're pale. What a face for
a happy lover! You're impatient. Well-a-day, sir! it shall be when
you please.'

The marriage was fixed for the last of September; and the two
women immediately began to occupy themselves with the purchase
of the bridal garments. Margaret, out of her salary, had saved a
sufficient sum to buy a handsome wedding gown; but, for the other
articles of her wardrobe, she was obliged to be indebted to the
liberality of Mrs. De Grey. She made no scruple, indeed, of expending large sums of money, and, when they were expended, of asking
for more. She took an active, violent delight in procuring quantities
of the richest stuffs. It seemed to her that, for the first time, she had
parted with all flimsy dignity and conventional reticence and coy-
ness, as if she had flung away her conscience to be picked up by
vulgar, happy, unimperilled women. She gathered her marriage
finery together in a sort of fierce defiance of impending calamity.
She felt excited to outstrip it, to confound it, to stare it out of
countenance.

One day she was crossing the hall, with a piece of stuff just sent
from the shop. It was a long morsel of vivid pink satin, and, as she
held it, a portion of it fell over her arm to her feet. Father Herbert's
door stood ajar; she stopped, and went in.

'Excuse me, reverend sir,' said Margaret; 'but I thought it a pity
not to show you this beautiful bit of satin. Isn't it a lovely pink?—
it's almost red,—it's carnation. It's the colour of our love,—of my
death. Father Herbert,' she cried, with a shrill, resounding laugh,
'*it's my shroud*! Don't you think it would be a pretty shroud?—
pink satin, and blonde-lace, and pearls?'

The old man looked at her with a haggard face. 'My daughter,'
he said, 'Paul will have an incomparable wife.'

'Most assuredly, if you compare me with those ladies in your

prayer-book. Ah! Paul shall have a wife, at least. That's very
certain.'

'Well,' said the old man, 'you're braver than I. You frighten me.'

'Dear Father Herbert, didn't you once frighten me?'

The old man looked at Margaret with mingled tenderness and
horror. 'Tell me, child,' he said, 'in the midst of all this, do you ever
pray?'

'God forbid!' cried the poor creature. 'I have no heart for prayer.'

She had long talks with Paul about their future pleasures, and
the happy life they should lead. He declared that he would set
their habits to quite another tune, and that the family should no
longer be buried in silence and gloom. It was an absurd state of
things, and he marvelled that it should ever have come about. They
should begin to live like other people, and occupy their proper place
in society. They should entertain company, and travel, and go to
the play of an evening. Margaret had never seen a play; after their
marriage, if she wished, she should see one every week for a year.
'Have no fears, my dear,' cried Paul, 'I don't mean to bury you
alive; I'm not digging your grave. If I expected you to be content
to live as my poor mother lives, we might as well be married by the
funeral service.'

When Paul talked with this buoyant energy, looking with a firm,
undoubting gaze on the long, blissful future, Margaret drew from
his words fortitude and joy, and scorn of all danger. Father
Herbert's secret seemed a vision, a fantasy, a dream, until, after a
while, she found herself again face to face with the old man, and
read in his haggard features that to him, at least, it was a deep
reality. Nevertheless, among all her feverish transitions from hope
to fear, from exaltation to despair, she never, for a moment, ceased
to keep a cunning watch upon her physical sensations, and to lie in
wait for morbid symptoms. She wondered that, with this ghastly
burden on her consciousness, she had not long since been goaded
to insanity, or crushed into utter idiocy. She fancied that, sad as it
would have been to rest in ignorance of the mystery in which her
life had been involved, it was yet more terrible to know it. During
the week after her interview with Father Herbert, she had not slept
half an hour of the daily twenty-four; and yet, far from missing her
sleep, she felt, as I have attempted to show, intoxicated, electrified,
by the unbroken vigilance and tension of her will. But she well knew
that this could not last forever. One afternoon, a couple of days
after Paul had uttered those brilliant promises, he mounted his
horse for a ride. Margaret stood at the gate, watching him regretfully, and, as he galloped away, he kissed her his hand. An hour

before tea she came out of her room, and entered the parlour, where Mrs. De Grey had established herself for the evening. A moment later, Father Herbert, who was in the act of lighting his study-lamp, heard a piercing shriek resound through the house.

His heart stood still. 'The hour is come,' he said. 'It would be a pity to miss it.' He hurried to the drawing-room, together with the servants, also startled by the cry. Margaret lay stretched on the sofa, pale, motionless, panting, with her eyes closed and her hand pressed to her side. Herbert exchanged a rapid glance with Mrs. De Grey, who was bending over the young girl, holding her other hand.

'Let us at least have no scandal,' she said, with dignity, and straightway dismissed the servants. Margaret gradually revived, declared that it was nothing,—a mere sudden pain,—that she felt better, and begged her companions to make no commotion. Mrs. De Grey went to her room, in search of a phial of smelling-salts, leaving Herbert alone with Margaret. He was on his knees on the floor, holding her other hand. She raised herself to a sitting posture.

'I know what you are going to say,' she cried, 'but it's false. Where's Paul?'

'Do you mean to tell him?' asked Herbert.

'Tell him?' and Margaret started to her feet. 'If I were to die, I should wring his heart; if I were to tell him, I should break it.'

She started up, I say; she had heard and recognized her lover's rapid step in the passage. Paul opened the door and came in precipitately, out of breath and deadly pale. Margaret came towards him with her hand still pressed to her side, while Father Herbert mechanically rose from his kneeling posture. 'What has happened?' cried the young man. 'You've been ill!'

'Who told you that anything has happened?' said Margaret.

'What is Herbert doing on his knees?'

'I was praying, sir,' said Herbert.

'Margaret,' repeated Paul, 'in Heaven's name, what *is* the matter?'

'What's the matter with you, Paul? It seems to me that I should ask the question.'

De Grey fixed a dark, searching look on the young girl, and then closed his eyes, and grasped at the back of a chair, as if his head were turning. 'Ten minutes ago,' he said, speaking slowly, 'I was riding along by the river-side; suddenly I heard in the air the sound of a distant cry, which I knew to be yours. I turned and galloped. I made three miles in eight minutes.'

'A cry, dear Paul? what should I cry about? and to be heard three miles! A pretty compliment to my lungs.'

'Well,' said the young man, 'I suppose, then, it was my fancy. But my horse heard it too; he lifted his ears, and plunged and started.'

'It must have been his fancy too! It proves you an excellent rider, —you and your horse feeling as one man!'

'Ah, Margaret, don't trifle!'

'As one horse, then!'

'Well, whatever it may have been, I'm not ashamed to confess that I'm thoroughly shaken. I don't know what has become of my nerves.'

'For pity's sake, then, don't stand there shivering and staggering like a man in an ague-fit. Come, sit down on the sofa.' She took hold of his arm, and led him to the couch. He, in turn, clasped her arm in his own hand, and drew her down beside him. Father Herbert silently made his exit, unheeded. Outside of the door he met Mrs. De Grey, with her smelling-salts.

'I don't think she needs them now,' he said. 'She has Paul.' And the two adjourned together to the tea-table. When the meal was half finished, Margaret came in with Paul.

'How do you feel, dear?' said Mrs. De Grey.

'He feels much better,' said Margaret, hastily.

Mrs. De Grey smiled complacently. 'Assuredly,' she thought, 'my future daughter-in-law has a very pretty way of saying things.'

The next day, going into Mrs. De Grey's room, Margaret found Paul and his mother together. The latter's eyes were red, as if she had been weeping; and Paul's face wore an excited look, as if he had been making some painful confession. When Margaret came in, he walked to the window and looked out, without speaking to her. She feigned to have come in search of a piece of needle-work, obtained it, and retired. Nevertheless, she felt deeply wounded. What had Paul been doing, saying? Why had he not spoken to her? Why had he turned his back upon her? It was only the evening before, when they were alone in the drawing-room, that he had been so unutterably tender. It was a cruel mystery; she would have no rest until she learned it,—although, in truth, she had little enough as it was. In the afternoon, Paul again ordered his horse, and dressed himself for a ride. She waylaid him as he came downstairs, booted and spurred; and, as his horse was not yet at the door, she made him go with her into the garden.

'Paul,' she said, suddenly, 'what were you telling your mother this morning? Yes,' she continued, trying to smile, but without success, 'I confess it,—I'm jealous.'

'O my soul!' cried the young man, wearily, putting both his hands to his face.

'Dear Paul,' said Margaret, taking his arm, 'that's very beautiful, but it's not an answer.'

Paul stopped in the path, took the young girl's hands and looked steadfastly into her face, with an expression that was in truth a look of weariness,—of worse than weariness, of despair. 'Jealous, you say?'

'Ah, not now!' she cried, pressing his hands.

'It's the first foolish thing I have heard you say.'

'Well, it was foolish to be jealous of your mother; but I'm still jealous of your solitude,—of these pleasures in which I have no share,—of your horse,—your long rides.'

'You wish me to give up my ride?'

'Dear Paul, where are your wits? To wish it is—to wish it. To say I wish it is to make a fool of myself.'

'My wits are with—with something that's forever gone!' And he closed his eyes and contracted his forehead as if in pain. 'My youth, my hope,—what shall I call it?—my happiness.'

'Ah!' said Margaret, reproachfully, 'you have to shut your eyes to say that.'

'Nay, what is happiness without youth?'

'Upon my word, one would think I was forty,' cried Margaret.

'Well, so long as I'm sixty!'

The young girl perceived that behind these light words there was something very grave. 'Paul,' she said, 'the trouble simply is that you're unwell.'

He nodded assent, and with his assent it seemed to her that an unseen hand had smitten the life out of her heart.

'That is what you told your mother?'

He nodded again.

'And what you were unwilling to tell me?'

He blushed deeply. 'Naturally,' he said.

She dropped his hands and sat down, for very faintness, on a garden bench. Then rising suddenly, 'Go, and take your ride,' she rejoined. 'But, before you go, kiss me once.'

And Paul kissed her, and mounted his horse. As she went into the house, she met Father Herbert, who had been watching the young man ride away, from beneath the porch, and who was returning to his study.

'My dear child,' said the priest, 'Paul is very ill. God grant that, if you manage not to die, it may not be at his expense!'

For all answer, Margaret turned on him, in her passage, a face so cold, ghastly, and agonized, that it seemed a vivid response to his heart-shaking fears. When she reached her room, she sat down

on her little bed, and strove to think clearly and deliberately. The
old man's words had aroused a deep-sounding echo in the vast
spiritual solitudes of her being. She was to find, then, after her long
passion, that the curse was absolute, inevitable, eternal. It could
be shifted, but not eluded; in spite of the utmost strivings of human
agony, it insatiably claimed its victim. Her own strength was exhausted; what was she to do? All her borrowed splendour of brilliancy and bravery suddenly deserted her, and she sat alone,
shivering in her weakness. Deluded fool that she was, for a day,
for an hour, to have concealed her sorrow from her lover! The
greater her burden, the greater should have been her confidence.
What neither might endure alone, they might have surely endured together. But she blindly, senselessly, remorselessly drained
the life from his being. As she bloomed and prospered, he drooped
and languished. While she was living for him, he was dying of her.
Execrable, infernal comedy! What would help her now? She thought
of suicide, and she thought of flight;—they were about equivalent.
If it were certain that by the sudden extinction of her own life
she might liberate, exonerate Paul, it would cost her but an instant's
delay to plunge a knife into her heart. But who should say that,
enfeebled, undermined as he was, the shock of her death might
not give him his quietus? Worse than all was the suspicion that
he had begun to dislike her, and that a dim perception of her
noxious influence had already taken possession of his senses. He
was cold and distant. Why else, when he had begun really to feel
ill, had he not spoken first to her? She was distasteful, loathsome.
Nevertheless, Margaret still grasped, with all the avidity of despair,
at the idea that it was still not too late to take him into her counsels,
and to reveal to him all the horrors of her secret. Then at least,
whatever came, death or freedom, they should meet it together.

Now that the enchantment of her fancied triumph had been
taken from her, she felt utterly exhausted and overwhelmed. Her
whole organism ached with the desire for sleep and forgetfulness.
She closed her eyes, and sank into the very stupor of repose. When
she came to her senses, her room was dark. She rose, and went to
her window, and saw the stars. Lighting a candle, she found that
her little clock indicated nine. She had slept five hours. She hastily
dressed herself, and went down stairs.

In the drawing-room, by an open window, wrapped in a shawl,
with a lighted candle, sat Mrs. De Grey.

'You're happy, my dear,' she cried, 'to be able to sleep so soundly,
when we are all in such a state.'

'What state, dear lady?'

'Paul has not come in.'

Margaret made no reply; she was listening intently to the distant sound of a horse's steps. She hurried out of the room, to the front door, and across the court-yard to the gate. There, in the dark starlight, she saw a figure advancing, and the rapid ring of hoofs. The poor girl suffered but a moment's suspense. Paul's horse came dashing along the road—riderless. Margaret, with a cry, plunged forward, grasping at his bridle; but he swerved, with a loud neigh, and, scarcely slackening his pace, swept into the enclosure at a lower entrance, where Margaret heard him clattering over the stones on the road to the stable, greeted by shouts and ejaculations from the hostler.

Madly, precipitately, Margaret rushed out into the darkness, along the road, calling upon Paul's name. She had not gone a quarter of a mile, when she heard an answering voice. Repeating her cry, she recognized her lover's accents.

He was upright, leaning against a tree, and apparently uninjured, but with his face gleaming through the darkness like a mask of reproach, white with the phosphorescent dews of death. He had suddenly felt weak and dizzy, and in the effort to keep himself in the saddle had frightened his horse, who had fiercely plunged, and unseated him. He leaned on Margaret's shoulder for support, and spoke with a faltering voice.

'I have been riding,' he said, 'like a madman. I felt ill when I went out, but without the shadow of a cause. I was determined to work it off by motion and the open air.' And he stopped, gasping.

'And you feel better, dearest?' murmured Margaret.

'No, I feel worse. I'm a dead man.'

Margaret clasped her lover in her arms with a long, piercing moan, which resounded through the night.

'I'm yours no longer, dear unhappy soul,—I belong, by I don't know what fatal, inexorable ties, to darkness and death and nothingness. They stifle me. Do you hear my voice?'

'Ah, senseless clod that I am, I have killed you!'

'I believe it's true. But it's strange. What is it, Margaret?—you're enchanted, baleful, fatal!' He spoke barely above a whisper, as if his voice were leaving him; his breath was cold on her cheek, and his arm heavy on her neck.

'Nay,' she cried, 'in Heaven's name, go on! Say something that will kill me.'

'Farewell, farewell!' said Paul, collapsing.

Margaret's cry had been, for the startled household she had left behind her, an index to her halting-place. Father Herbert drew near hastily, with servants and lights. They found Margaret sitting by the roadside, with her feet in a ditch, clasping her lover's inanimate head in her arms, and covering it with kisses, wildly moaning. The sense had left her mind as completely as his body, and it was likely to come back to one as little as to the other.

A great many months naturally elapsed before Mrs. De Grey found herself in the humour to allude directly to the immense calamity which had overwhelmed her house; and when she did so, Father Herbert was surprised to find that she still refused to accept the idea of a supernatural pressure upon her son's life, and that she quietly cherished the belief that he had died of the fall from his horse.

'And suppose Margaret had died? Would to Heaven she had!' said the priest.

'Ah, suppose!' said Mrs. De Grey. 'Do you make that wish for the sake of your theory?'

'Suppose that Margaret had had a lover,—a passionate lover,— who had offered her his heart before Paul had ever seen her; and then that Paul had come, bearing love and death.'

'Well, what then?'

'Which of the three, think you, would have had most cause for sadness?'

'It's always the survivors of a calamity who are to be pitied,' said Mrs. De Grey.

'Yes, madam, it's the survivors,—even after fifty years.'

Osborne's Revenge

[First appeared in the *Galaxy*, vol. vi (July 1868), pp. 5-31. The serial text carried one illustration by W. J. Hennessy. Not reprinted during James's lifetime.]

I

PHILIP OSBORNE AND ROBERT GRAHAM WERE INTIMATE friends. The latter had been spending the summer at certain medicinal springs in New York, the use of which had been recommended by his physician. Osborne, on the other hand—a lawyer by profession, and with a rapidly increasing practice—had been confined to the city, and had suffered June and July to pass, not unheeded, heaven knows, but utterly unhonoured. Toward the middle of July he began to feel uneasy at not hearing from his friend, habitually the best of correspondents. Graham had a charming literary talent, and plenty of leisure, being without a family, and without business. Osborne wrote to him, asking the reason of his silence, and demanding an immediate reply. He received in the course of a few days the following letter:

> DEAR PHILIP: I am, as you conjectured, not well. These infernal waters have done me no good. On the contrary—they have poisoned me. They have poisoned my life, and I wish to God I had never come to them. Do you remember the *White Lady* in *The Monastery*, who used to appear to the hero at the spring? There is such a one here, at this spring—which you know tastes of sulphur. Judge of the quality of the young woman. She has charmed me, and I can't get away. But I mean to try again. Don't think I'm cracked, but expect me next week. Yours always,
>
> R.G.

The day after he received this letter, Osborne met, at the house of a female friend detained in town by the illness of one of her children, a lady who had just come from the region in which Graham had fixed himself. This lady, Mrs. Dodd by name, and a widow, had seen a great deal of the young man, and she drew a very long face and threw great expression into her eyes as she spoke of him. Seeing that she was inclined to be confidential, Osborne made it possible that she should converse with him privately. She assured him, behind her fan, that his friend was dying of a broken heart. Something should be done. The story was briefly this. Graham had made the acquaintance, in the early part of the summer, of a young lady, a certain Miss Congreve, who was living in the neighbourhood with a married sister. She was not pretty, but she was clever, graceful, and pleasing, and Graham had immediately fallen in love with her. She had encouraged his addresses, to the knowledge of all their friends, and at the end of a month—heart-histories are very rapid at the smaller watering places—their engagement, although not announced, was hourly expected. But at this moment a stranger had effected an entrance into the little society of which Miss Congreve was one of the most brilliant ornaments—a Mr. Holland, out of the West—a man of Graham's age, but better favoured in person. Heedless of the circumstance that her affections were notoriously preoccupied, he had immediately begun to be attentive to the young girl. Equally reckless of the same circumstance, Henrietta Congreve had been all smiles—all seduction. In the course of a week, in fact, she had deliberately transferred her favours from the old love to the new. Graham had been turned out into the cold; she had ceased to look at him, to speak to him, to think of him. He nevertheless remained at the springs, as if he found a sort of fascination in the sense of his injury, and in seeing Miss Congreve and Holland together. Besides, he doubtless wished people to fancy that, for good reasons, he had withdrawn his suit, and it was therefore not for him to hide himself. He was proud, reserved, and silent, but his friends had no difficulty in seeing that his pain was intense, and that his wound was almost mortal. Mrs. Dodd declared that unless he was diverted from his sorrow, and removed from contact with the various scenes and objects which reminded him of his unhappy passion—and above all, deprived of the daily chance of meeting Miss Congreve— she would not answer for his sanity.

Osborne made all possible allowance for exaggeration. A woman, he reflected, likes so to round off her story—especially if it is a dismal one. Nevertheless he felt very anxious, and he forthwith wrote his friend a long letter, asking him to what extent Mrs. Dodd's little romance was true, and urging him to come immediately to town, where, if it was substantially true, he might look for diversion. Graham answered by arriving in person. At first, Osborne was decidedly relieved. His friend looked better and stronger than he had looked for months. But on coming to talk with him, he found him morally, at least, a sad invalid. He was listless, abstracted, and utterly inactive in mind. Osborne observed with regret that he

made no response to his attempts at interrogation and to his proffered sympathy. Osborne had by nature no great respect for sentimental woes. He was not a man to lighten his tread because his
neighbour below stairs was laid up with a broken heart. But he saw
that it would never do to poke fun at poor Graham, and that he
was quite proof against the contagion of gaiety. Graham begged
him not to think him morbid or indifferent to his kindness, and
to allow him not to speak of his trouble until it was over. He had
resolved to forget it. When he had forgotten it—as one forgets
such things—when he had contrived to push the further end of it
at least into the past—then he would tell him all about it. For the
present he must occupy his thoughts with something else. It was
hard to decide what to do. It was hard to travel without an aim.
Yet the intolerable heat made it impossible that he should stay
in New York. He might go to Newport.

'A moment,' said Osborne. 'Has Miss Congreve gone to Newport?'

'Not that I know of.'

'Does she intend to go?'

Graham was silent. 'Good heavens!' he cried, at last, 'forbid it
then! All I want is to have it forbidden. *I* can't forbid it. Did you
ever see a human creature so degraded?' he added, with a ghastly
smile. 'Where *shall* I go?'

Philip went to his table and began to overhaul a mass of papers
fastened with red tape. He selected several of these documents and
placed them apart. Then turning to his friend, 'You're to go out to
Minnesota,' he said, looking him in the eyes. The proposal was a
grave one, and gravely as it was meant, Osborne would have been
glad to have Graham offer some resistance. But he sat looking
at him with a solemn stare which (in the light of subsequent events)
cast a lugubrious shade over the whole transaction. 'The deuce!'
thought Osborne. 'Has it made him stupid?—What you need,' he
said aloud, 'is to have something else to think about. An idle man
can't expect to get over such troubles. I have some business to
be done at St. Paul, and I know that if you'll give your attention
to it, you're as well able to do it as any man. It's a simple matter,
but it needs a trustworthy person. So I shall depend upon
you.'

Graham came and took up the papers and looked over them
mechanically.

'Never mind them now,' said Osborne; 'it's past midnight; you
must go to bed. To-morrow morning I'll put you *au fait*, and the
day after, if you like, you can start.'

The next morning Graham seemed to have recovered a considerable portion of his old cheerfulness. He talked about indifferent matters, laughed, and seemed for a couple of hours to have forgotten Miss Congreve. Osborne began to doubt that the journey was necessary, and he was glad to be able to think, afterwards, that he had expressed his doubts, and that his friend had strongly combatted them and insisted upon having the affair explained to him. He mastered it, to Osborne's satisfaction, and started across the continent.

During the ensuing week Philip was so pressed with business that he had very little time to think of the success of Graham's mission. Within the fortnight he received the following letter:

DEAR PHILIP: Here I am, safe, but anything but sound. I don't know what to think of it, but I have completely forgotten the terms of my embassy. I can't for my life remember what I'm to do or say, and neither the papers nor your notes assist me a whit. 12th.—I wrote so much yesterday and then went out to take a walk and collect my thoughts. I *have* collected them, once for all. Do you understand, dearest Philip? Don't call me insane, or impious, or anything that merely expresses your own impatience and intolerance, without throwing a ray of light on the state of my own mind. He only can understand it who has felt it, and he who has felt it can do but as I do. Life has lost, I don't say it's charm—that I could willingly dispense with—but its meaning. I shall live in your memory and your love, which is a vast deal better than living in my own self-contempt. Farewell.   R.G.

Osborne learned the circumstances of his friend's death three days later, through his correspondent at St. Paul—the person to whom Graham had been addressed. The unhappy young man had shot himself through the head in his room at the hotel. He had left money, and written directions for the disposal of his remains—directions which were, of course, observed. As Graham possessed no near relative, the effect of his death was confined to a narrow circle; to the circle, I may say, of Philip Osborne's capacious personality. The two young men had been united by an almost passionate friendship. Now that Graham had ceased to be, Osborne became sensible of the strength of this bond; he felt that he cared more for it than for any human tie. They had known each other ten years, and their intimacy had grown with their growth during the most active period of their lives. It had been strengthened within and without by the common enjoyment of so many pleasures, the experience of so many hazards, the exchange of so much advice, so much confidence, and so many pledges of mutual interest, that each had grown to regard it as the single absolute certainty in life, the one fixed fact in a shifting world. As constantly happens with intimate friends, the two were perfectly diverse in character, tastes and appearance. Graham was three years the elder, slight, under-sized, feeble in health, sensitive, indolent, whimsical, generous, and in reality of a far finer clay than his friend, as the latter, moreover, perfectly well knew. Their intimacy was often a puzzle to observers. Disinterested parties were at loss to discover how Osborne had come to set his heart upon an insignificant, lounging invalid, who, in general company, talked in monosyllables, in a weak voice, and gave himself the airs of one whom nature had endowed with the right to be fastidious, without ever having done a stroke of work. Graham's partisans, on the other hand, who were chiefly women (which, by the way, effectually relieves him from the accusation occasionally brought against him of being 'effeminate') were quite unable to penetrate the motives of his interest in a commonplace, hard-work-ing lawyer, who addressed a charming woman as if he were exhort-ing a jury of grocers and undertakers, and viewed the universe as one vast 'case'. This account of Osborne's mind and manners would have been too satirical to be wholly just, and yet it would have been excusable as an attempt to depict a figure in striking contrast with poor Graham. Osborne was in all respects a large fellow. He was six feet two in height, with a chest like a boxing-master, and a clear, brown complexion, which successfully resisted the deleterious action of a sedentary life. He was, in fact, without a particle of vanity, a particularly handsome man. His character corresponded to his person, or, as one may say, continued and completed it, and his mind kept the promise of his character. He was all of one piece—all health and breadth, capacity and energy. Graham had once told his friend somewhat brutally—for in his little, weak voice Graham said things far more brutal than Osborne, just as he said things far more fine—he had told him that he worked like a horse and loved like a dog.

Theoretically, Osborne's remedy for mental trouble was work. He redoubled his attention to his professional affairs, and strove to reconcile himself, once for all, to his loss. But he found his grief far stronger than his will, and felt that it obstinately refused to be pacified without some act of sacrifice or devotion. Osborne had an essentially kind heart and plenty of pity and charity for deserv-ing objects; but at the bottom of his soul there lay a well of bitter-ness and resentment which, when his nature was strongly shaken by a sense of wrong, was sure to ferment and raise its level, and at last to swamp his conscience. These bitter waters had been stirred, and he felt that they were rising fast. His thoughts travelled back with stubborn iteration from Graham's death to the young girl who figured in the prologue to the tragedy. He felt in his breast a savage need of hating her. Osborne's friends observed in these days that he looked by no means pleasant; and if he had not been such an excellent fellow he might easily have passed for an intolerable brute. He was not softened and mellowed by suffering; he was exasperated. It seemed to him that justice cried aloud that Henrietta Congreve should be confronted with the results of her folly, and made to carry forever in her thoughts, in all the hideousness of suicide, the image of her miserable victim. Osborne was, perhaps, in error, but he was assuredly sincere; and it is strong evidence of the energy of genuine affection that this lusty intellect should have been brought, in the interest of another, to favour a scheme which it would have deemed wholly, ludicrously impotent to assuage the injured dignity of its own possessor. Osborne must have been very fond of his friend not to have pronounced him a drivelling fool. It is true that he had always pitied him as much as he loved him, although Graham's incontestable gifts and virtues had kept this feeling in the background. Now that he was gone, pity came uppermost, and bade fair to drive him to a merciless disallowance of all claims to extenuation on the part of the accused. It was unlikely that, for a long time at least, he would listen to anything but that Graham had been foully wronged, and that the light of his life had been wantonly quenched. He found it impossible to sit down in resignation. The best that he could do, indeed, would not call Graham back to life; but he might at least discharge his gall, and have the comfort of feeling that Miss Congreve was the worse for it. He was quite unable to work. He roamed about for three days in a disconsolate, angry fashion. On the third, he called upon Mrs. Dodd, from whom he learned that Miss Congreve had gone to Newport, to stay with a second married sister. He went home and packed up a valise, and—without knowing why, feeling only that to do so was to do something, and to put himself in the way of doing more—drove down to the Newport boat.

II

His first inquiry on his arrival, after he had looked up several of his friends and encountered a number of acquaintances, was about Miss Congreve's whereabouts and habits. He found that she was very little known. She lived with her sister, Mrs. Wilkes, and as yet had made but a single appearance in company. Mrs. Wilkes, moreover, he learned, was an invalid and led a very quiet life. He ascertained the situation of her house and gave himself the satisfaction of walking past it. It was a pretty place, on a secluded by-road, marked by various tokens of wealth and comfort. He heard, as he passed, through the closed shutters of the drawing-room window, the sound of a high melodious voice, warbling and trilling to the accompaniment of a piano. Osborne had no soul for music, but he stopped and listened, and as he did so, he remembered Graham's passion for the charming art and fancied that these were the very accents that had lured him to his sorrow. Poor Graham! here too, as in all things, he had showed his taste. The singer discharged a magnificent volley of roulades and flourishes and became silent. Osborne, fancying he heard a movement of the lattice of the shutters, slowly walked away. A couple of days later he found himself strolling, alone and disconsolate, upon the long avenue which runs parallel to the Newport cliffs, which, as all the world knows, may be reached by five minutes' walk from any part of it. He had been on the field, now, for nearly a week, and he was no nearer his revenge. His unsatisfied desire haunted his steps and hovered in a ghostly fashion about thoughts which perpetual contact with old friends and new, and the entertaining spectacle of a heterogeneous throng of pleasure seekers and pleasure venders, might have made free and happy. Osborne was very fond of the world, and while he still clung to his resentment, he yet tacitly felt that it lurked as a skeleton at his banquet. He was fond of nature, too, and betwixt these two predilections, he grew at moments ashamed of his rancour. At all events, he felt a grateful sense of relief when as he pursued his course along this sacred way of fashion, he caught a glimpse of the deep blue expanse of the ocean, shining at the end of a cross-road. He forthwith took his way down to the cliffs. At the point where the road ceased, he found an open barouche, whose occupants appeared to have wandered out of sight. Passing this carriage, he reached a spot where the surface of the cliff communicates with the beach, by means of an abrupt footpath. This path he descended and found himself on a level with the broad expanse of sand and the rapidly rising tide. The wind was blowing fresh from the sea and the little breakers tumbling in with their multitudinous liquid clamour. In a very few moments Osborne felt a sensible exhilaration of spirits. He had not advanced many steps under the influence of this joyous feeling, when, on turning a slight projection in the cliff, he described a sight which caused him to hasten forward. On a broad flat rock, at about a dozen yards from the shore, stood a child of some five years—a handsome boy, fair-haired and well dressed—stamping his feet and wringing his hands in an apparent agony of terror. It was easy to understand the situation. The child had ventured out on the rock while the water was still low, and had become so much absorbed in paddling with his little wooden spade among the rich marine deposits on its surface, that he had failed to observe the advance of the waves, which had now completely covered the intermediate fragments of rock and were foaming and weltering betwixt him and the shore. The poor little fellow stood screaming to the winds and waters, and quite unable to answer Osborne's shouts of interrogation and comfort. Meanwhile, the latter prepared to fetch him ashore. He saw with some disgust that the channel was too wide to warrant a leap, and yet, as the child's companions might at any moment appear, in the shape of distracted importunate women, he judged it imprudent to divest himself of any part of his apparel. He accordingly plunged in without further ado, waded forward, seized the child and finally restored him to *terra firma*. He felt him trembling in his arms like a frightened bird. He set him on his feet, soothed him, and asked him what had become of his guardians.

The boy pointed toward a rock, lying at a certain distance, close under the cliff, and Osborne, following his gesture, distinguished what seemed to be the hat and feather of a lady sitting on the further side of it.

'That's Aunt Henrietta,' said the child.

'Aunt Henrietta deserves a scolding,' said Osborne. 'Come, we'll go and give it to her.' And he took the boy's hand and led him toward his culpable relative. They walked along the beach until they came abreast of the rock, and approached the lady in front. At the sound of their feet on the stones, she raised her head. She was a young woman, seated on a boulder, with an album in her lap, apparently absorbed in the act of sketching. Seeing at a glance that something was amiss, she rose to her feet and thrust the album into her pocket. Osborne's wet trousers and the bespattered garments and discomposed physiognomy of the child revealed the nature of the calamity. She held out her arms to her little nephew. He dropped Philip's hand, and ran and threw himself on his aunt's neck. She raised him up and kissed him, and looked interrogatively at Osborne.

'I couldn't help seeing him safely in your hands,' said the latter, removing his hat. 'He has had a terrific adventure.'

'What is it, darling?' cried the young lady, again kissing the little fellow's bloodless face.

'He came into the water after me,' cried the boy. 'Why did you leave me there?'

'What has happened, sir?' asked the young girl, in a somewhat peremptory tone.

'You had apparently left him on that rock, madam, with a channel betwixt him and the shore deep enough to drown him. I took the liberty of displacing him. But he's more frightened than hurt.'

The young girl had a pale face and dark eyes. There was no beauty in her features; but Osborne had already perceived that they were extremely expressive and intelligent. Her face flushed a little, and her eyes flashed; the former, it seemed to Philip, with mortification at her own neglect, and the latter with irritation at the reproach conveyed in his accents. But he may have been wrong. She sat down on the rock, with the child on her knees, kissing him repeatedly and holding him with a sort of convulsive pressure. When she looked up, the flashes in her eyes had melted into a couple of tears. Seeing that Philip was a gentleman, she offered a few words of self-justification. She had kept the boy constantly within sight, and only within a few minutes had allowed her attention to be drawn away. Her apology was interrupted by the arrival of a second young woman—apparently a nursery-maid—who emerged from the concealment of the neighbouring rocks, leading a little girl by the hand. Instinctively, her eyes fell upon the child's wet clothes.

'Ah! Miss Congreve,' she cried, in true nursery-maid style, 'what'll Mrs. Wilkes say to that?'

'She will say that she is very thankful to this gentleman,' said Miss Congreve, with decision.

Philip had been looking at the young girl as she spoke, forcibly struck by her face and manner. He detected in her appearance a peculiar union of modesty and frankness, of youthful freshness and elegant mannerism, which suggested vague possibilities of further acquaintance. He had already found it pleasant to observe her. He had been for ten days in search of a wicked girl, and it was a momentary relief to find himself suddenly face to face with a charming one. The nursery-maid's apostrophe was like an electric shock.

It is, nevertheless, to be supposed that he concealed his surprise, inasmuch as Miss Congreve gave no sign of having perceived that he was startled. She had come to a tardy sense of his personal discomfort. She besought him to make use of her carriage, which he would find on the cliff, and quickly return home. He thanked her and declined her offer, declaring that it was better policy to walk. He put out his hand to his little friend and bade him good-bye. Miss Congreve liberated the child and he came and put his hand in Philip's.

'One of these days,' said Osborne, 'you'll have long legs, too, and then you'll not mind the water.' He spoke to the boy, but he looked hard at Miss Congreve, who, perhaps, thought he was asking for some formal expression of gratitude.

'His mother,' she said, 'will give herself the pleasure of thanking you.'

'The trouble,' said Osborne, 'the very unnecessary trouble. Your best plan,' he added, with a smile (for, wonderful to tell, he actually smiled) 'is to say nothing about it.'

'If I consulted my own interests alone,' said the young girl, with a gracious light in her dark eyes, 'I should certainly hold my tongue. But I hope my little victim is not so ungrateful as to promise silence.'

Osborne stiffened himself up; for this was more or less of a compliment. He made his bow in silence and started for home at a rapid pace. On the following day he received this note by post:

> Mrs. Wilkes begs to thank Mr. Osborne most warmly for the prompt and generous relief afforded to her little boy. She regrets that Mr. Osborne's walk should have been interrupted, and hopes that his exertions have been attended with no bad effects.

Enclosed in the note was a pocket-handkerchief, bearing Philip's name, which he remembered to have made the child take, to wipe his tears. His answer was, of course, brief.

> Mr. Osborne begs to assure Mrs. Wilkes that she exaggerates the importance of the service rendered to her son, and that he has no cause to regret his very trifling efforts. He takes the liberty of presenting his compliments to Master Wilkes, and of hoping that he has recovered from his painful sensations.

The correspondence naturally went no further, and for some days no additional light was thrown upon Miss Congreve. Now that Philip had met her, face to face, and found her a commonplace young girl—a clever girl, doubtless, for she looked it, and an agree-able one—but still a mere young lady, mindful of the proprieties, with a face innocent enough, and even a trifle sad, and a couple of pretty children who called her 'aunt', and whom, indeed, in a moment of enthusiastic devotion to nature and art, she left to the mercy of the waves, but whom she finally kissed and comforted and handled with all due tenderness—now that he had met Miss Congreve under these circumstances, he felt his mission sitting more lightly on his conscience. Ideally she had been repulsive; actually, she was a person whom, if he had not been committed to detest her, he would find it very pleasant to like. She had been humanized, to his view, by the mere accidents of her flesh and blood. Philip was by no means prepared to give up his resentment. Poor Graham's ghost sat grim and upright in his memory, and fed the flickering flame. But it was something of a problem to reconcile the heroine of his vengeful longings, with the heroine of the little scene on the beach, and to accommodate this inoffensive figure, in turn, to the colour of his retribution. A dozen matters conspired to keep him from coming to the point, and to put him in a comparatively good humour. He was invited to the right and the left; he lounged and bathed, and talked, and smoked, and rode, and dined out, and saw an endless succession of new faces, and in short, reduced the vestments of his outward mood to a suit of very cheerful half-mourning. And all this, moreover, without any sense of being faithless to his friend. Oddly enough, Graham had never seemed so living as now that he was dead. In the flesh, he had possessed but a half-vitality. His spirit had been exquisitely willing, but his flesh had been fatally weak. He was at best a baffled, disappointed man. It was his spirit, his affections, his sympathies and perceptions, that were warm and active, and Osborne knew that he had fallen sole heir to these. He felt his bosom swell with a wholesome sense of the magnitude of the heritage, and he was conscious with each successive day, of less desire to invoke poor Graham in dark corners, and mourn him in lonely places. By a single solemn, irrevocable aspiration, he had placed his own tough organism and his energetic will at the service of his friend's virtues. So as he found his excursion turning into a holiday, he stretched his long limbs and with the least bit of a yawn whispered *Amen*.

Within a week after his encounter with Miss Congreve, he went with a friend to witness some private theatricals, given in the house of a lady of great social repute. The entertainment consisted of two plays, the first of which was so flat and poor that when the curtain fell Philip prepared to make his escape, thinking he might easily bring the day to some less impotent conclusion. As he passed along the narrow alley between the seats and the wall of the drawing-room, he brushed a printed programme out of a lady's hand. Stooping to pick it up, his eye fell upon the name of Miss Congreve among the performers in the second piece. He immediately retraced his steps. The overture began, the curtain rose again, and several persons appeared on the stage, arrayed in the

powder and patches of the last century. Finally, amid loud acclama-
tions, walked on Miss Congreve, as the heroine, powdered and
patched in perfection. She represented a young countess—a widow
in the most interesting predicament—and for all good histrionic
purposes, she was irresistibly beautiful. She was dressed, painted,
and equipped with great skill and in the very best taste. She looked
as if she had stepped out of the frame of one of those charming
full-length pastel portraits of fine ladies in Louis XV.'s time,
which they show you in French palaces. But she was not alone all
grace and elegance and *finesse*; she had dignity; she was serious
at moments, and severe; she frowned and commanded; and, at the
proper time, she wept the most natural tears. It was plain that Miss
Congreve was a true artist. Osborne had never seen better acting—
never, indeed, any so good; for here was an actress who was at once
a perfect young lady and a consummate mistress of dramatic effect.
The audience was roused to the highest pitch of enthusiasm, and
Miss Congreve's fellow-players were left quite in the lurch. The
beautiful Miss Latimer, celebrated in polite society for her face
and figure, who had undertaken the second female part, was compelled for the nonce to have neither figure nor face. The play had
been marked in the bills as adapted from the French 'especially
for this occasion'; and when the curtain fell for the last time, the
audience, in great good humour clamoured for the adapter. Some
time elapsed before any notice was taken of their call, which they
took as a provocation of their curiosity. Finally, a gentleman made
his way before the curtain, and proclaimed that the version of the
piece which his associates had had the honour of performing was
from the accomplished pen of the young lady who had won their
applause in the character of the heroine. At this announcement,
a dozen enthusiasts lifted their voices and demanded that Miss
Congreve should be caused to reappear; but the gentleman cut
short their appeal by saying that she had already left the house.
This was not true, as Osborne subsequently learned. Henrietta was
sitting on a sofa behind the scenes, waiting for her carriage, fingering an immense bouquet, and listening with a tired smile to compliments—hard by Miss Latimer, who sat eating an ice beside her
mother, the latter lady looking in a very grim fashion at that very
plain, dreadfully thin Miss Congreve.

Osborne walked home thrilled and excited, but decidedly bewildered. He felt that he had reckoned without his host, and that
Graham's fickle mistress was not a person to be snubbed and done
for. He was utterly at a loss as to what to think of her. She broke
men's hearts and turned their heads; whatever she put her hand

to she marked with her genius. She was a coquette, a musician, an artist, an actress, an author—a prodigy. Of what stuff was she made? What had she done with her heart and her conscience? She painted her face, and frolicked among lamps and flowers to the clapping of a thousand hands, while poor Graham lay imprisoned in eternal silence. Osborne was put on his mettle. To draw a penitent tear from those deep and charming eyes was assuredly a task for a clever man.

The plays had been acted on a Wednesday. On the following Saturday Philip was invited to take part in a picnic, organized by Mrs. Carpenter, the lady who had conducted the plays, and who had a mania for making up parties. The persons whom she had now enlisted were to proceed by water to a certain pastoral spot consecrated by nature to picnics, and there to have lunch upon the grass, to dance and play nursery-games. They were carried over in two large sailing boats, and during the transit Philip talked awhile with Mrs. Carpenter, whom he found a very amiable, loquacious person. At the further end of the boat in which, with his hostess, he had taken his place, he observed a young girl in a white dress, with a thick, blue veil drawn over her face. Through the veil, directed toward his own person, he perceived the steady glance of two fine dark eyes. For a moment he was at a loss to recognize their possessor; but his uncertainty was rapidly dispelled.

'I see you have Miss Congreve,' he said to Mrs. Carpenter—'the actress of the other evening.'

'Yes,' said Mrs. Carpenter, 'I persuaded her to come. She's all the fashion since Wednesday.'

'Was she unwilling to come?' asked Philip.

'Yes, at first. You see she's a good, quiet girl; she hates to have a noise made about her.'

'She had enough noise the other night. She has wonderful talent.'

'Wonderful, wonderful. And heaven knows where she gets it. Do you know her family? The most matter-of-fact, least dramatic, least imaginative people in the world—people who are shy of the theatre on moral grounds.'

'I see. They won't go to the theatre; the theatre comes to them.'

'Exactly. It serves them right. Mrs. Wilkes, Henrietta's sister, was in a dreadful state about her attempting to act. But now, since Henrietta's success, she's talking about it to all the world.'

When the boat came to shore, a plank was stretched from the prow to an adjacent rock for the accommodation of the ladies. Philip stood at the head of the plank, offering his hand for their assistance. Mrs. Carpenter came last, with Miss Congreve, who

declined Osborne's aid but gave him a little bow, through her veil.
Half an hour later Philip again found himself at the side of his
hostess, and again spoke of Miss Congreve. Mrs. Carpenter warned
him that she was standing close at hand, in a group of young girls.

'Have you heard,' he asked, lowering his voice, 'of her being engaged to be married—or of her having been?'

'No,' said Mrs. Carpenter, 'I've heard nothing. To whom?—stay.
I've heard vaguely of something this summer at Sharon. She had
a sort of flirtation with some man, whose name I forget.'

'Was it Holland?'

'I think not. He left her for that very silly little Mrs. Dodd—
who hasn't been a widow six months. I think the name was
Graham.'

Osborne broke into a peal of laughter so loud and harsh that his
companion turned upon him in surprise. 'Excuse me,' said he.
'It's false.'

'You ask questions, Mr. Osborne,' said Mrs. Carpenter, 'but you
seem to know more about Miss Congreve than I do.'

'Very likely. You see I knew Robert Graham.' Philip's words were
uttered with such emphasis and resonance that two or three of the
young girls in the adjoining group turned about and looked at him.

'She heard you,' said Mrs. Carpenter.

'She didn't turn round,' said Philip.

'That proves what I say. I meant to introduce you, and now I
can't.'

'Thank you,' said Philip. 'I shall introduce myself.' Osborne felt
in his bosom all the heat of his old resentment. This perverse and
heartless girl, then, his soul cried out, not content with driving poor
Graham to impious self-destruction, had caused it to be believed
that he had killed himself from remorse at his own misconduct.
He resolved to strike while the iron was hot. But although he was
an avenger, he was still a gentleman, and he approached the young
girl with a very civil face.

'If I am not mistaken,' he said, removing his hat, 'you have
already done me the honour of recognizing me.'

Miss Congreve's bow, as she left the boat, had been so obviously
a sign of recognition, that Philip was amazed at the vacant smile
with which she received his greeting. Something had happened
in the interval to make her change her mind. Philip could think
of no other motive than her having overheard his mention of
Graham's name.

'I have an impression,' she said, 'of having met you before; but
I confess that I'm unable to place you.'

Osborne looked at her a moment. 'I can't deny myself,' he said, 'the pleasure of asking about little Mr. Wilkes.'

'I remember you now,' said Miss Congreve, simply. 'You carried my nephew out of the water.'

'I hope he has got over his fright.'

'He denies, I believe, that he was frightened. Of course, for my credit, I don't contradict him.'

Miss Congreve's words were followed by a long pause, by which she seemed in no degree embarrassed. Philip was confounded by her apparent self-possession—to call it by no worse name. Considering that she had Graham's death on her conscience, and that, hearing his name on Osborne's lips, she must have perceived the latter to be identical with that dear friend of whom Graham must often have spoken, she was certainly showing a very brave face. But had she indeed heard of Graham's death? For a moment Osborne gave her the benefit of the doubt. He felt that he would take a grim satisfaction in being bearer of the tidings. In order to confer due honour on the disclosure, he saw that it was needful to detach the young girl from her companions. As, therefore, the latter at this moment began to disperse in clusters and couples along the shore, he proposed that they should stroll further a-field. Miss Congreve looked about at the other young girls as if to call one of them to her side, but none of them seemed available. So she slowly moved forward under Philip's guidance, with a half-suppressed look of reluctance. Philip began by paying her a very substantial compliment upon her acting. It was a most inconsequential speech, in the actual state of his feelings, but he couldn't help it. She was perhaps as wicked a girl as you shall easily meet, but her acting was perfect. Having paid this little tribute to equity, he broke ground for Graham.

'I don't feel, Miss Congreve,' he said, 'as if you were a new acquaintance. I have heard you a great deal talked about.' This was not literally true, the reader will remember. All Philip's information had been acquired in his half hour with Mrs. Dodd.

'By whom, pray?' asked Henrietta.

'By Robert Graham.'

'Ah, yes. I was half prepared to hear you speak of him. I remember hearing him speak of a person of your name.'

Philip was puzzled. Did she know, or not? 'I believe you knew him quite well yourself,' he said, somewhat peremptorily.

'As well as he would let me—I doubt if any one knew him well.'

'So you've heard of his death,' said Philip.

'Yes, from himself.'

'He wrote me a letter, in his last hours, leaving his approaching end to be inferred, rather than positively announcing it. I wrote an answer, with the request that if my letter was not immediately called for, it should be returned by the post-office. It was returned within a week.—And now, Mr. Osborne,' the young girl added, 'let me make a request.'

Philip bowed.

'I shall feel particularly obliged if you will say no more about Mr. Graham.'

This was a stroke for which Osborne was not prepared. It had at least the merit of directness. Osborne looked at his companion. There was a faint flush in her cheeks, and a serious light in her eyes. There was plainly no want of energy in her wish. He felt that he must suspend operations and make his approach from another quarter. But it was some moments before he could bring himself to accede to her request. She looked at him, expecting an answer, and he felt her dark eyes on his face.

'Just as you please,' he said, at last, mechanically.

They walked along for some moments in silence. Then, suddenly coming upon a young married woman, whom Mrs. Carpenter had pressed into her service as a lieutenant, Miss Congreve took leave of Philip, on a slight pretext, and entered into talk with this lady. Philip strolled away and walked about for an hour alone. He had met with a check, but he was resolved that, though he had fallen back, it would be only to leap the further. During the half-hour that Philip sauntered along by the water, the dark cloud suspended above poor Miss Congreve's head doubled its portentous volume. And, indeed, from Philip's point of view, could anything well be more shameless and more heartless than the young girl's request?

At last Osborne remembered that he was neglecting the duties laid upon him by Mrs. Carpenter. He retraced his steps and made his way back to the spot devoted to the banquet. Mrs. Carpenter called him to her, said that she had been looking for him for an hour, and, when she learned how he had been spending his time, slapped him with her parasol, called him a horrid creature, and declared she would never again invite him to anything of hers. She then introduced him to her niece, a somewhat undeveloped young lady, with whom he went and sat down over the water. They found very little to talk about. Osborne was thinking of Miss Congreve, and Mrs. Carpenter's niece, who was very timid and fluttering, having but one foot yet, as one may say, in society, was abashed and unnerved at finding herself alone with so very tall and mature and handsome a gentleman as Philip. He gave her a

little confidence in the course of time, however, by making little
stones skip over the surface of the water for her amusement. But
he still kept thinking of Henrietta Congreve, and he at last bethought himself of asking his companion whether she knew her.
Yes, she knew her slightly; but she threw no light on the subject.
She was evidently not of an analytical turn of mind, and she was
too innocent to gossip. She contented herself with saying that she
believed Henrietta was wonderfully clever, and that she read Latin
and Greek.

'Clever, clever,' said Philip, 'I hear nothing else. I shall begin to
think she's a demon.'

'No, Henrietta Congreve is very good,' said his companion. 'She's
very religious. She visits the poor and reads sermons. You know
the other night she acted for the poor. She's anything but a demon.
I think she's so nice.'

Before long the party was summoned to lunch. Straggling couples
came wandering into sight, gentlemen assisting young girls out of
rocky retreats into which no one would have supposed them capable
of penetrating, and to which—more wonderful still—no one had
observed them to direct their steps.

The table was laid in the shade, on the grass, and the feasters sat
about on rugs and shawls. As Osborne took his place along with
Mrs. Carpenter's niece, he noticed that Miss Congreve had not yet
reappeared. He called his companion's attention to the circumstance, and she mentioned it to her aunt, who said that the young
girl had last been seen in company with Mr. Stone—a person
unknown to Osborne—and that she would, doubtless, soon turn
up.

'I suppose she's quite safe,' said Philip's neighbour—innocently
or wittily, he hardly knew which; 'she's with a clergyman.'

In a few moments the missing couple appeared on the crest of an
adjacent hill. Osborne watched them as they came down. Mr.
Stone was a comely-faced young man, in a clerical necktie and
garments of an exaggerated sacerdotal cut—a divine, evidently of
strong 'ritualistic' tendencies. Miss Congreve drew near, pale, graceful, and grave, and Philip, with his eyes fixed on her in the interval,
lost not a movement of her person, nor a glance of her eyes. She
wore a white muslin dress, short, in the prevailing fashion, with
trimmings of yellow ribbon inserted in the skirt; and round her
shoulders a shawl of heavy black lace, crossed over her bosom and
tied in a big knot behind. In her hand she carried a great bunch of
wild flowers, with which, as Philip's neighbour whispered to him,
she had 'ruined' her gloves. Osborne wondered whether there was

any meaning in her having taken up with a clergyman. Had she
suddenly felt the tardy pangs of remorse, and been moved to seek
spiritual advice? Neither on the countenance of her ecclesiastical
gallant, nor on her own, were there any visible traces of pious discourse. On the contrary, poor Mr. Stone looked sadly demoralized;
their conversation had been wholly of profane things. His white
cravat had lost its conservative rigidity, and his hat its unimpas-
sioned equipoise. Worse than all, a little blue forget-me-not had
found its way into his button-hole. As for Henrietta, her face wore
that look of half-severe serenity which was its wonted expression,
but there was no sign of her having seen her lover's ghost.

Osborne went mechanically through the movements of being
attentive to the insipid little person at his side. But his thoughts
were occupied with Miss Congreve and his eyes constantly turning
to her face. From time to time, they met her own. A fierce disgust
muttered in his bosom. What Henrietta Congreve needed, he said
to himself, was to be used as she used others, as she was evidently
now using this poor little parson. He was already over his ears
in love—vainly feeling for bottom in midstream, while she sat dry-
shod on the brink. She needed a lesson; but who should give it?
She knew more than all her teachers. Men approached her only to
be dazzled and charmed. If she could only find her equal or her
master! One with as clear a head, as lively a fancy, as relentless
a will as her own; one who would turn the tables, anticipate her,
fascinate her, and then suddenly look at his watch and bid her
good morning. Then, perhaps, Graham might settle to sleep in his
grave. Then she would feel what it was to play with hearts, for then
her own would have been as glass against bronze. Osborne looked
about the table, but none of Mrs. Carpenter's male guests bore the
least resemblance to the hero of his vision—a man with a heart of
bronze and a head of crystal. They were, indeed very proper swains
for the young ladies at their sides, but Henrietta Congreve was not
one of these. She was not a mere twaddling ball-room flirt. There
was in her coquetry something serious and exalted. It was an intellectual joy. She drained honest men's hearts to the last drop, and
bloomed white upon the monstrous diet. As Philip glanced around
the circle, his eye fell upon a young girl who seemed for a moment
to have forgotten her neighbours, her sandwiches and her cham-
pagne, and was very innocently contemplating his own person. As
soon as she perceived that he had observed her, she of course
dropped her eyes on her plate. But Philip had read the meaning
of her glance. It seemed to say—this lingering virginal eyebeam—
in language easily translated, Thou art the man! It said, in other

words, in less transcendental fashion, My dear Mr. Osborne, you are a very good looking fellow. Philip felt his pulse quicken; he had received his baptism. Not that good looks were a sufficient outfit for breaking Miss Congreve's heart; but they were the outward sign of his mission.

The feasting at last came to an end. A fiddler, who had been brought along, began to tune his instrument, and Mrs. Carpenter proceeded to organize a dance. The *débris* of the collation was cleared away, and the level space thus uncovered converted into a dancing floor. Osborne, not being a dancing man, sat at a distance, with two or three other spectators, among whom was the Rev. Mr. Stone. Each of these gentlemen watched with close attention the movements of Henrietta Congreve. Osborne, however, occasionally glanced at his companion, who, on his side, was quite too absorbed in looking at Miss Congreve to think of anyone else.

'They look very charming, those young ladies,' said Philip, addressing the young clergyman, to whom he had just been introduced. 'Some of them dance particularly well.'

'Oh, yes!' said Mr. Stone, with fervour. And then, as if he feared that he had committed himself to an invidious distinction unbecoming his cloth: 'I think they all dance well.'

But Philip, as a lawyer, naturally took a different view of the matter from Mr. Stone, as a clergyman. 'Some of them very much better than others, it seems to me. I had no idea that there could be such a difference. Look at Miss Congreve, for instance.'

Mr. Stone, whose eyes were fixed on Miss Congreve, obeyed this injunction by moving them away for a moment, and directing them to a very substantial and somewhat heavy-footed young lady, who was figuring beside her. 'Oh, yes, she's very graceful,' he said, with unction. 'So light, so free, so quiet!'

Philip smiled. 'You, too, most excellent simpleton,' he said, to himself—'you, too, shall be avenged.' And then—'Miss Congreve is a very remarkable person,' he added, aloud.

'Oh, very!'

'She has extraordinary versatility.'

'Most extraordinary.'

'Have you seen her act?'

'Yes—yes; I infringed upon my usage in regard to entertainments of that nature, and went the other evening. It was a most brilliant performance.'

'And you know she wrote the play.'

'Ah, not exactly,' said Mr. Stone, with a little protesting gesture; 'she translated it.'

'Yes; but she had to write it quite over. Do you know it in French?'—and Philip mentioned the original title.

Mr. Stone signified that he was unacquainted with the work.

'It would never have done, you know,' said Philip, 'to play it as it stands. I saw it in Paris. Miss Congreve eliminated the little difficulties with uncommon skill.'

Mr. Stone was silent. The violin uttered a long-drawn note, and the ladies curtsied low to their gentlemen. Miss Congreve's partner stood with his back to our two friends, and her own obeisance was, therefore, executed directly in front of them. As she bent toward the ground, she raised her eyes and looked at them. If Mr. Stone's enthusiasm had been damped by Philip's irreverent freedom, it was rekindled by this glance. 'I suppose you've heard her sing,' he said, after a pause.

'Yes, indeed,' said Philip, without hesitation.

'She sings sacred music with the most beautiful fervour.'

'Yes, so I'm told. And I'm told, moreover, that she's very learned —that she has a passion for books.'

'I think it very likely. In fact, she's quite an accomplished theologian. We had this morning a very lively discussion.'

'You differed, then?' said Philip.

'Oh,' said Mr. Stone, with charming *naïveté*, '*I* didn't differ. It was she!'

'Isn't she a little—the least bit—' and Philip paused, to select his word.

'The least bit?' asked Mr. Stone, in a benevolent tone. And then, as Philip still hesitated—'The least bit heterodox?'

'The least bit of a coquette?'

'Oh, Mr. Osborne!' cried the young divine—'that's the last thing I should call Miss Congreve.'

At this moment, Mrs. Carpenter drew nigh. 'What is the last thing you should call Miss Congreve?' she asked, overhearing the clergyman's words.

'A coquette.'

'It seems to me,' said the lady, 'that it's the first thing I should call her. You have to come to it, I fancy. You always do, you know. I should get it off my mind at once, and then I should sing her charms.'

'Oh, Mrs. Carpenter!' said Mr. Stone.

'Yes, my dear young man. She's quiet but she's deep—I see Mr. Osborne knows,' and Mrs. Carpenter passed on.

'She's deep—that's what I say,' said Mr. Stone, with mild firmness. —'What do you know, Mr. Osborne?'

Philip fancied that the poor fellow had turned pale; he certainly looked grave.

'Oh, I know nothing,' said Philip. 'I affirmed nothing. I merely inquired.'

'Well then, my dear sir'—and the young man's candid visage flushed a little with the intensity of his feelings—'I give you my word for it, that I believe Miss Congreve to be not only the most accomplished, but the most noble-minded, the most truthful, the most truly christian young lady—in this whole assembly.'

'I'm sure, I'm much obliged to you for the assurance,' said Philip. 'I shall value it and remember it.'

It would not have been hard for Philip to set down Mr. Stone as a mere soft-hearted, philandering parson—a type ready made to his hand. Mrs. Carpenter, on the other hand, was a shrewd sagacious woman. But somehow he was impressed by the minister's words, and quite untouched by those of the lady. At last those of the dancers who were tired of the sport, left the circle and wandered back to the shore. The afternoon was drawing to a close, the western sky was beginning to blush crimson and the shadows to grow long on the grass. Only half an hour remained before the moment fixed for the return to Newport. Philip resolved to turn it to account. He followed Miss Congreve to a certain rocky platform, overlooking the water, whither, with a couple of elderly ladies, she had gone to watch the sunset. He found no difficulty in persuading her to wander aside from her companions. There was no mistrust in her keen and delicate face. It was incredible that she should have meant defiance; but her very repose and placidity had a strangely irritating action upon Philip. They affected him as the climax of insolence. He drew from his breast-pocket a small portfolio, containing a dozen letters, among which was the last one he had received from Graham.

'I shall take the liberty, for once, Miss Congreve,' he said, 'of violating the injunction which you laid upon me this morning with regard to Robert Graham. I have here a letter which I should like you to see.'

'From Mr. Graham himself?'

'From Graham himself—written just before his death.' He held it out, but Henrietta made no movement to take it.

'I have no desire to see it,' she said. 'I had rather not. You know he wrote also to me at that moment.'

'I'm sure,' said Philip, 'I should not refuse to see your letter.'

'I can't offer to show it to you. I immediately destroyed it.'

'Well, you see I've kept mine.—It's not long,' Osborne pursued.

Miss Congreve, as if with a strong effort, put out her hand and took the document. She looked at the direction for some moments, in silence, and then raised here eyes toward Osborne. 'Do you value it?' she asked. 'Does it contain anything you wish to keep?'

'No; I give it to you, for that matter.'

'Well then!' said Henrietta. And she tore the letter twice across, and threw the scraps into the sea.

'Ah!' cried Osborne, 'what the devil have you done?'

'Don't be violent, Mr. Osborne,' said the young girl. 'I hadn't the slightest intention of reading it. You are properly punished for having disobeyed me.'

Philip swallowed his rage at a gulp, and followed her as she turned away.

III

In the middle of September Mrs. Dodd came to Newport, to stay with a friend—somewhat out of humour at having been invited at the fag-end of the season, but on the whole very much the same Mrs. Dodd as before; or rather not quite the same, for, in her way, she had taken Graham's death very much to heart. A couple of days after her arrival, she met Philip in the street, and stopped him. 'I'm glad to find *someone* still here,' she said; for she was with her friend, and having introduced Philip to this lady, she begged him to come and see her. On the next day but one, accordingly, Philip presented himself, and saw Mrs. Dodd alone. She began to talk about Graham; she became very much affected, and with a little more encouragement from Osborne, she would certainly have shed tears. But, somehow, Philip was loth to countenance her grief; he made short responses. Mrs. Dodd struck him as weak and silly and morbidly sentimental. He wondered whether there could have been any truth in the rumour that Graham had cared for her. Not certainly if there was any truth in the story of his passion for Henrietta Congreve. It was impossible that he should have cared for both. Philip made this reflection, but he stopped short of adding that Mrs. Dodd failed signally to please him, because during the past three weeks he had constantly enjoyed Henrietta's society.

For Mrs. Dodd, of course, the transition was easy from Graham to Miss Congreve. 'I'm told Miss Congreve is still here,' she said. 'Have you made her acquaintance?'

'Perfectly,' said Philip.

'You seem to take it very easily. I hope you have brought her to

'AND SHE TORE THE LETTER TWICE ACROSS, AND THREW THE SCRAPS INTO
THE SEA.'

a sense of her iniquities. There's a task, Mr. Osborne. You ought to convert her.'

'I've not attempted to convert her. I've taken her as she is.'

'Does she wear mourning for Mr. Graham? It's the least she can do.'

'Wear mourning?' said Philip. 'Why, she has been going to a party every other night.'

'Of course I don't suppose she has put on a black dress. But does she mourn *here*?' And Mrs. Dodd laid her hand on her heart.

'You mean in her heart? Well, you know, it's problematical that she has one.'

'I suppose she disapproves of suicide,' said Mrs. Dodd, with a little acrid smile. 'Bless my soul, so do I.'

'So do I, Mrs. Dodd,' said Philip. And he remained for a moment thoughtful. 'I wish to heaven,' he cried, 'that Graham were here! It seems to me at moments that he and Miss Congreve might have come to an understanding again.'

Mrs. Dodd threw out her hands in horror. 'Why, has she given up her last lover?'

'Her last lover? Whom do you mean?'

'Why, the man I told you of—Mr. Holland.'

Philip appeared quite to have forgotten this point in Mrs. Dodd's recital. He broke into a loud, nervous laugh. 'I'll be hanged,' he cried, 'if I know! One thing is certain,' he pursued, with emphasis, recovering himself; 'Mr. Holland—whoever he is—has for the past three weeks seen nothing of Miss Congreve.'

Mrs. Dodd sat silent, with her eyes lowered. At last, looking up, 'You, on the other hand, I infer,' she said, 'have seen a great deal of her.'

'Yes, I've seen her constantly.'

Mrs. Dodd raised her eyebrows and distended her lips in a smile which was emphatically not a smile. 'Well, you'll think it an odd question, Mr. Osborne,' she said, 'but how do you reconcile your intimacy with Miss Congreve with your devotion to Mr. Graham?'

Philip frowned—quite too severely for good manners. Decidedly, Mrs. Dodd was extremely silly. 'Oh,' he rejoined, 'I reconcile the two things perfectly. Moreover, my dear Mrs. Dodd, allow me to say that it's my own business. At all events,' he added, more gently, 'perhaps, one of these days, you'll read the enigma.'

'Oh, if it's an enigma,' cried the lady, 'perhaps I can guess it.'

Philip had risen to his feet to take his leave, and Mrs. Dodd threw herself back on the sofa, clasped her hands in her lap, and looked up at him with a penetrating smile. She shook her finger at him reproachfully. Philip saw that she had an idea; perhaps it was the right one. At all events, he blushed. Upon this Mrs. Dodd cried out.

'I've guessed it,' she said. 'Oh, Mr. Osborne!'

'What have you guessed?' asked Philip, not knowing why in the world he should blush.

'If I've guessed right,' said Mrs. Dodd, 'it's a charming idea. It does you credit. It's quite romantic. It would do in a novel.'

'I doubt,' said Philip, 'whether I know what you are talking about.'

'Oh, yes, you do. I wish you good luck. To another man I should say it was a dangerous game. But to you!'—and with an insinuating movement of her head, Mrs. Dodd measured with a glance the length and breadth of Philip's fine person.

Osborne was inexpressibly disgusted, and without further delay he took his leave.

The reader will be at a loss to understand why Philip should have been disgusted with the mere foreshadowing on the part of another, of a scheme which, three weeks before, he had thought a very happy invention. For we may as well say outright, that although Mrs. Dodd was silly, she was not so silly but that she had divined his original intentions with regard to Henrietta. The fact is that in three weeks Philip's humour had undergone a great change. The reader has gathered for himself that Henrietta Congreve was no ordinary girl, that she was, on the contrary, a person of distinguished gifts and remarkable character. Until within a very few months she had seen very little of the world, and her mind and talents had been gradually formed in seclusion, study, and, it is not too much to say, meditation. Thanks to her circumscribed life and her long contemplative leisures, she had reached a pitch of rare intellectual perfection. She was educated, one may say, in a sense in which the term may be used of very few young girls, however richly endowed by nature. When at a later period than most girls, owing to domestic circumstances which it is needless to unfold, she made her entrance into society and learned what it was to be in the world and of the world, to talk and listen, to please and be pleased, to be admired, flattered and interested, her admirable faculties and beautiful intellect, ripened in studious solitude, burst into luxuriant bloom and bore the fairest fruit. Miss Congreve was accordingly a person for whom a man of taste and of feeling could not help entertaining a serious regard. Philip Osborne was emphatically such a man; the manner in which he was affected by his friend's death proves, I think, that he had feeling; and it is ample evidence of his taste that he had chosen such a friend. He had no sooner begun to act in obedience to the impulse mystically be-

stowed, as it were, at the close of Mrs. Carpenter's feast—he had
no sooner obtained an introduction at Mrs. Wilkes's, and, with
excellent tact and discretion, made good his footing there, than
he began to feel in his inmost heart that in staking his life upon
Miss Congreve's favour, poor Graham had indeed revealed the
depths of his exquisite sensibility. For a week at least—a week during which, with unprecedented good fortune and a degree of
assurance worthy of a better cause, Philip contrived in one way
and another to talk with his fair victim no less than a dozen times
—he was under the empire of a feverish excitement which kept
him from seeing the young girl in all her beautiful integrity. He
was preoccupied with his own intentions and the effect of his own
manoeuvres. But gradually he quite forgot himself while he was in
her presence, and only remembered that he had a sacred part to
play, after he had left the house. Then it was that he conceived
the intensity of Graham's despair, and then it was that he began
to be sadly, woefully puzzled by the idea that a woman could unite
so much loveliness with so much treachery, so much light with so
much darkness. He was as certain of the bright surface of her
nature as of its cold and dark reverse, and he was utterly unable
to discover a link of connection between the two. At moments he
wondered how in the world he had become saddled with this meta-
physical burden: *que diable venait-il faire dans cette galère?* But
nevertheless he was afloat; he must row his boat over the current to where the restless spirit of his friend paced the opposite
shore.

Henrietta Congreve, after a first movement of apparent aversion,
was very well pleased to accept Osborne as a friend and as an
habitué of her sister's house. Osborne fancied that he might believe
without fatuity—for whatever the reader may think, it is needless
to say that Philip was very far from supposing his whole course to
be a piece of infatuated coxcombry—that she preferred him to most
of the young men of her circle. Philip had a just estimate of his
own endowments, and he knew that for the finer social purposes,
if not for strictly sentimental ones, he contained the stuff of an
important personage. He had no taste for trivialities, but trivialities
played but a small part in Mrs. Wilkes's drawing-room. Mrs. Wilkes
was a simple woman, but she was neither silly nor frivolous; and
Miss Congreve was exempt from these foibles for even better reasons. 'Women really care only for men who can tell them something,' Osborne remembered once to have heard Graham say, not
without bitterness. 'They are always famished for news.' Philip now
reflected with satisfaction that he could give Miss Congreve more

news than most of her constituted gossips. He had an admirable memory and a very lively observation. In these respects Henrietta was herself equally well endowed; but Philip's experience of the world had of course been tenfold more extensive, and he was able continually to complete her partial inductions and to rectify her false conjectures. Sometimes they seemed to him wonderfully shrewd, and sometimes delightfully innocent. He nevertheless frequently found himself in a position to make her acquainted with facts possessing the charm of absolute novelty. He had travelled and seen a great variety of men and women, and of course he had read a number of books which a woman is not expected to read. Philip was keenly sensible of these advantages; but it nevertheless seemed to him that if the exhibition of his mental treasures furnished Miss Congreve with a great deal of entertainment, her attention, on the other hand, had a most refreshing effect upon his mind.

At the end of three weeks Philip might, perhaps not unreasonably, have supposed himself in a position to strike his blow. It is true that, for a woman of sense, there is a long step between thinking a man an excellent friend and a charming talker, and surrendering her heart to him. Philip had every reason to believe that Henrietta thought these good things of himself; but if he had hereupon turned about to make his exit, with the conviction that when he had closed the parlour door behind him he should, by lending an attentive ear, hear her fall in a swoon on the carpet, he might have been sadly snubbed and disappointed. He longed for an opportunity to test the quality of his empire. If he could only pretend for a week to be charmed by another woman, Miss Congreve might perhaps commit herself. Philip flattered himself that he could read very small signs. But what other woman could decently serve as the object of a passion thus extemporized? The only woman Philip could think of was Mrs. Dodd; and to think of Mrs. Dodd was to give it up. For a man who was intimate with Miss Congreve to pretend to care for any other woman (except a very old friend) was to act in flagrant contempt of all verisimilitude. Philip had, therefore, to content himself with playing off his own assumed want of heart against Henrietta's cordial regard. But at this rate the game moved very slowly. Work was accumulating at a prodigious rate at his office, and he couldn't dangle about Miss Congreve forever. He bethought himself of a harmless artifice for drawing her out. It seemed to him that his move was not altogether unsuccessful, and that, at a pinch, Henrietta might become jealous of a rival in his affections. Nevertheless, he was strongly tempted to take up his hand and leave the game. It was too confoundedly exciting.

The incident of which I speak happened within a few days after Osborne's visit to Mrs. Dodd. Finding it impossible to establish an imaginary passion for an actual, visible young lady, Philip resolved to invent not only the passion, but the young lady, too. One morning, as he was passing the show-case of one of the several photographers who came to Newport for the season, he was struck by the portrait of a very pretty young girl. She was fair in colour, graceful, well dressed, well placed, her face was charming, she was plainly a lady. Philip went in and asked who she was. The photographer had destroyed the negative and had kept no register of her name. He remembered her, however, distinctly. The portrait had not been taken during the summer; it had been taken during the preceding winter, in Boston, the photographer's headquarters. 'I kept it,' he said, 'because I thought it so very perfect a picture. And such a charming sitter! We haven't many like that.' He added, however, that it was too good to please the masses, and that Philip was the first gentleman who had had the taste to observe it.

'So much the better,' thought Philip, and forthwith proposed to the man to part with it. The latter, of course, had conscientious scruples; it was against his principles to dispose of the portraits of ladies who came to him in confidence. To do him justice, he adhered to his principles, and Philip was unable to persuade him to sell it. He consented, however, to give it to Mr. Osborne, *gratis*. Mr. Osborne deserved it, and he had another for himself. By this time Philip had grown absolutely fond of the picture; at this latter intelligence he looked grave, and suggested that if the artist would not sell one, perhaps he would sell two. The photographer declined, reiterated his offer, and Philip finally accepted. By way of compensation, however, he proceeded to sit for his own portrait. In the course of half an hour the photographer gave him a dozen reflections of his head and shoulders, distinguished by as many different attitudes and expressions.

'You sit first-rate, sir,' said the artist. 'You take beautifully. You're quite a match for my young lady.'

Philip went off with his dozen prints, promising to examine them at his leisure, select and give a liberal order.

In the evening he went to Mrs. Wilkes's. He found this lady on her verandah, drinking tea in the open air with a guest, whom in the darkness he failed to recognize. As Mrs. Wilkes proceeded to introduce him, her companion graciously revealed herself as Mrs. Dodd. 'How on earth,' thought Philip, 'did she get here?' To find

Mrs. Dodd instead of Miss Congreve was, of course, a gross dis-comfiture. Philip sat down, however, with a good grace, to all appearance, hoping that Henrietta would turn up. Finally, moving his chair to a line with the drawing room window, he saw the young girl within, reading by the lamp. She was alone and intent upon her book. She wore a dress of white grenadine, covered with ornaments and arabesques of crimson silk, which gave her a some-what fantastical air. For the rest, her expression was grave enough, and her brows contracted, as if she were completely absorbed in her book. Her right elbow rested on the table, and with her hand she mechanically twisted the long curl depending from her *chignon*. Watching his opportunity, Osborne escaped from the ladies on the verandah and made his way into the drawing-room. Miss Congreve received him as an old friend, without rising from her chair.

Philip began by pretending to scold her for shirking the society of Mrs. Dodd.

'Shirking!' said Henrietta. 'You are very polite to Mrs. Dodd.'

'It seems to me,' rejoined Osborne, 'that I'm quite as polite as you.'

'Well, perhaps you are. To tell the truth, I'm not very polite. At all events, she doesn't care to see me. She must have come to see my sister.'

'I didn't know she knew Mrs. Wilkes.'

'It's an acquaintance of a couple of hours' standing. I met her, you know, at Sharon in July. She was once very impertinent to me, and I fancied she had quite given me up. But this afternoon, during our drive, as my sister and I got out of the carriage, on the rocks, who should I see but Mrs. Dodd, wandering about alone, with a bunch of sea-weed as big as her head. She rushed up to me; I introduced her to Anna, and finding that she had walked quite a distance, Anna made her get into the carriage. It appears that she's staying with a friend, who has no carriage, and she's very miserable. We drove her about for an hour. Mrs. Dodd was fascinating, she threw away her sea-weed, and Anna asked her to come home to tea. After tea, having endured her for two mortal hours, I took refuge here.'

'If she was fascinating,' said Philip, 'why do you call it enduring her?'

'It's all the more reason, I assure you.'

'I see, you have not forgiven her impertinence.'

'No, I confess I have not. The woman was positively revolting.'

'She appears nevertheless, to have forgiven you.'

'She has nothing to forgive.'

In a few moments, Philip took his photographs out of his pocket, handed them to Henrietta, and asked her advice as to which he should choose. Miss Congreve inspected them attentively, and selected but one. 'This one is excellent,' she said. 'All the others are worthless in comparison.'

'You advise me then to order that alone?'

'Why, you'll do as you please. I advise you to order that, at any rate. If you do, I shall ask you for one; but I shall care nothing for the rest.'

Philip protested that he saw very little difference between this favoured picture and the others, and Miss Congreve declared that there was all the difference in the world. As Philip replaced the specimens in his pocket-book, he dropped on the carpet the portrait of the young lady of Boston.

'Ah,' said Henrietta, 'a young lady. I suppose I may see it.'

'On one condition,' said Philip, picking it up. 'You'll please not to look at the back of the card.'

I am very much ashamed to have to tell such things of poor Philip; for in point of fact, the back of the card was a most innocent blank. If Miss Congreve had ventured to disobey him, he would have made a very foolish figure. But there was so little that was boisterous in Henrietta's demeanour, that Osborne felt that he ran no risk.

'Who is she?' asked Henrietta, looking at the portrait. 'She's charming.'

'She's a Miss Thompson, of Philadelphia.'

'Dear me, not Dora Thompson, assuredly.'

'No indeed,' said Philip, a little nervously. 'Her name's not Dora —nor anything like it.'

'You needn't resent the insinuation, sir. Dora's a very pretty name.'

'Yes, but her own is prettier.'

'I'm very curious to hear it.'

Philip suddenly found himself in deep waters. He struck out blindly and answered at random, 'Angelica.'

Miss Congreve smiled—somewhat ironically, it seemed to Philip. 'Well,' she said, 'I like her face better than her name.'

'Dear me, if you come to that, so do I!' cried Philip, with a laugh.

'Tell me about her, Mr. Osborne,' pursued Henrietta. 'She must be, with that face and figure, just the nicest girl in the world.'

'Well, well, well,' said Philip, leaning back in his chair, and looking at the ceiling—'perhaps she is—or at least, you'll excuse me if I say I think she is.'

'I should think it inexcusable if you didn't say so,' said Henrietta, giving him the card. 'I'm sure I've seen her somewhere.'

'Very likely. She comes to New York,' said Philip. And he thought it prudent, on the whole, to divert the conversation to another topic. Miss Congreve remained silent and he fancied pensive. Was she jealous of Angelica Thompson? It seemed to Philip that, without fatuity, he might infer that she was, and that she was too proud to ask questions.

Mrs. Wilkes had enabled Mrs. Dodd to send tidings to her hostess of her whereabouts, and had promised to furnish her with an escort on her return. When Mrs. Dodd prepared to take her leave, Philip, finding himself also ready to depart, offered to walk home with her.

'Well, sir,' said the lady, when they had left the house, 'your little game seems to be getting on.'

Philip said nothing.

'Ah, Mr. Osborne,' said Mrs. Dodd, with ill-concealed impatience, 'I'm afraid you're too good for it.'

'Well, I'm afraid I am.'

'If you hadn't been in such a hurry to agree with me,' said Mrs. Dodd, 'I should have said that I meant, in other words, that you're too stupid.'

'Oh, I agree to that, too,' said Philip.

The next day he received a letter from his partner in business, telling him of a great pressure of work, and urging him to return at his earliest convenience. 'We are told,' added this gentleman, 'of a certain Miss ——, I forget the name. If she's essential to your comfort, bring her along; but, at any rate, come yourself. In your absence the office is at a stand-still—a fearful case of repletion without digestion.'

This appeal came home to Philip's mind, to use a very old metaphor, like the sound of the brazen trumpet to an old cavalry charger. He felt himself overwhelmed with a sudden shame at the thought of the precious hours he had wasted and the long mornings he had consigned to perdition. He had been burning incense to a shadow, and the fumes had effaced it. In the afternoon he walked down toward the cliffs, feeling woefully perplexed, and exasperated in mind, and longing only to take a farewell look at the sea. He was not prepared to admit that he had played with fire and burned his fingers; but it was certain that he had gained nothing at the game. How the deuce had Henrietta Congreve come to thrust herself into his life—to steal away his time and his energies and to put him into a savage humour with himself? He would have given a great deal to be able to banish her from his thoughts; but she remained, and, while she remained, he hated her. After all, he had not been wholly cheated of his revenge. He had begun by hating her and he hated her still. On his way to the cliffs he met Mrs. Wilkes, driving alone. Henrietta's place, vacant beside her, seemed to admonish him that she was at home, and almost, indeed, that she expected him. At all events, instead of going to bid farewell to the sea, he went to bid farewell to Miss Congreve. He felt that his farewell might easily be cold and formal, and indeed bitter.

He was admitted, he passed through the drawing-room to the veranda, and found Henrietta sitting on the grass, in the garden, holding her little nephew on her knee and reading him a fairy tale. She made room for him on the garden bench beside her, but kept the child. Philip felt himself seriously discomposed by this spectacle. In a few moments he took the boy upon his own knees. He then told Miss Congreve briefly that he intended that evening to leave Newport. 'And you,' he said, 'when are you coming?'

'My sister,' said Henrietta, 'means to stay till Christmas. I hope to be able to remain as long.'

Poor Philip bowed his head and heard his illusions tumbling most unmusically about his ears. His blow had smitten but the senseless air. He waited to see her colour fade, or to hear her voice tremble. But he waited in vain. When he looked up and his eyes met Henrietta's, she was startled by the expression of his face.

'Tom,' she said to the child, 'go and ask Jane for my fan.'

The child walked off, and Philip rose to his feet. Henrietta, hesitating a moment, also rose. 'Must you go?' she asked.

Philip made no answer, but stood looking at her with blood-shot eyes, and with an intensity which puzzled and frightened the young girl.

'Miss Congreve,' he said, abruptly, 'I'm a miserable man!'

'Oh, no!' said Henrietta, gently.

'I love a woman who doesn't care a straw for me!'

'Are you sure?' said Henrietta, innocently.

'Sure! I adore her!'

'Are you sure she doesn't care for you?'

'Ah, Miss Congreve!' cried Philip. 'If I could imagine, if I could hope—' and he put out his hand, as if to take her own.

Henrietta drew back, pale and frowning, carrying her hand to her heart. 'Hope for nothing!' she said.

At this moment, little Tom Wilkes reappeared, issuing from the drawing-room window. 'Aunt Henrietta,' he cried, 'here's a new gentleman!'

Miss Congreve and Philip turned about, and saw a young man step out upon the verandah from the drawing-room. Henrietta, with a little cry, hastened to meet him. Philip stood in his place.

Miss Congreve exchanged a cordial greeting with the stranger, and led him down to the lawn. As she came toward him, Philip saw that Henrietta's pallor had made way for a rosy flush. She was beautiful.

'Mr. Osborne,' she said, 'Mr. Holland.'

Mr. Holland bowed graciously; but Philip bowed not at all. 'Good-bye, then,' he said, to the young girl.

She bowed, without speaking.

'Who's your friend, Henrietta?' asked her companion, when they were alone.

'He's a Mr. Osborne, of New York,' said Miss Congreve; 'a friend of poor Mr. Graham.'

'By the way, I suppose you've heard of poor Graham's death.'

'Oh, yes; Mr. Osborne told me. And, indeed—what do you think? Mr. Graham wrote to me that he expected to die.'

'Expected? Is that what he said?'

'I don't remember his words. I destroyed the letter.'

'I must say, I think it would have been in better taste not to write.'

'Taste! He had long since parted company with taste.'

'I don't know. There was a method in his madness; and, as a rule, when a man kills himself, he shouldn't send out circulars.'

'Kills himself? Good heavens, George! what do you mean?' Miss Congreve had turned pale, and stood looking at her companion with eyes dilated with horror.

'Why, my dear Henrietta,' said the young man, 'excuse my abruptness. Didn't you know it?'

'How strange—how fearful!' said Henrietta, slowly. 'I wish I had kept his letter.'

'I'm glad you didn't,' said Holland. 'It's a horrible business. Forget it.'

'Horrible—horrible,' murmured the young girl, in a tremulous tone. Her voice was shaken with irrepressible tears. Poor girl! in the space of five minutes, she had been three times surprised. She gave way to her emotion and burst into sobs. George Holland drew her against him, and pressed his arm about her, and kissed her, and whispered comfort in her ear.

In the evening, Philip started for New York. On the steamer, he found Mrs. Dodd, who had come to an end of her visit. She was accompanied by a certain Major Dodd, of the Army, a brother of her deceased husband, and in addition, as it happened, her cousin. He was an unmarried man, a good-natured man, and a very kind friend to his sister-in-law, who had no family of her own, and who was in a position to be grateful for the services of a gentleman. In spite of a general impression to the contrary, I may affirm that the Major had no desire to make his little services a matter of course. 'I'm related to Maria twice over already,' he had been known to say, in a moment of expansion. 'If I ever marry, I shall prefer to do it not quite so much in the family.' He had come to Newport to conduct his sister home, who forthwith introduced him to Philip.

It was a clear, mild night, and, when the steamer had got under way, Mrs. Dodd and the two gentlemen betook themselves to the upper deck, and sat down in the starlight. Philip, it may be readily imagined, was in no humour for conversation; but he felt that he could not wholly neglect Mrs. Dodd. Under the influence of the beautiful evening, the darkly-shining sea, the glittering constellations, this lady became rabidly sentimental. She talked of friendship, and love, and death, and immortality. Philip saw what was coming. Before many moments, she had the bad taste (considering the Major's presence, as it seemed to Philip) to take poor Graham as a text for a rhapsody. Osborne lost patience, and interrupted her by asking if she would mind his lighting a cigar. She was scandalized, and immediately announced that she would go below. Philip had no wish to be uncivil. He attempted to restore himself to her favour by offering to see her down to the cabin. She accepted his escort, and he went with her to the door of her state-room, where she gave him her hand for good-night.

'Well,' she said—'and Miss Congreve?'

Philip positively scowled. 'Miss Congreve,' he said, 'is engaged to be married.'

'To Mr.——?'

'To Mr. Holland.'

'Ah!' cried Mrs. Dodd, dropping his hand, 'why didn't you break the engagement!'

'My dear Mrs. Dodd,' said Philip, 'you don't know what you're talking about.'

Mrs. Dodd smiled a pitiful smile, shrugged her shoulders, and turned away. 'Poor Graham!' she said.

Her words came to Philip like a blow in the face. 'Graham!' he cried. 'Graham was a fool!' He had struck back; he couldn't help it.

He made his way upstairs again, and came out on the deck, still trembling with the violence of his retort. He walked to the edge of the boat and leaned over the railing, looking down into the black gulfs of water which foamed and swirled in the wake of the vessel. He knocked off the end of his cigar, and watched the red particles fly downward and go out in the darkness. He was a disappointed, saddened man. There in the surging, furious darkness, yawned instant death. Did it tempt him, too? He drew back with a shudder, and returned to his place by Major Dodd.

The Major preserved for some moments a meditative silence. Then, at last, with a half apologetic laugh, 'Mrs. Dodd,' he said, 'labours under a singular illusion.'

'Ah?' said Philip.

'But you knew Mr. Graham yourself?' pursued the Major.

'Oh, yes; I knew him.'

'It was a very melancholy case,' said Major Dodd.

'A very melancholy case;' and Philip repeated his words.

'I don't know how it is that Mrs. Dodd was beguiled into such fanaticism on the subject. I believe she went so far as once to blow out at the young lady.'

'The young lady?' said Philip.

'Miss Congreve, you know, the object of his persecutions.'

'Oh, yes,' said Philip, painfully mystified.

'The fact is,' said the Major, leaning over, and lowering his voice confidentially, 'Mrs. Dodd was in love with him—as far, that is, as a woman can be in love with a man in that state.'

'Is it possible?' said Philip, disgusted and revolted at he knew not what, for his companion's allusions were an enigma.

'Oh, I was at Sharon for three weeks,' the Major continued; 'I went up for my sister-in-law; I saw it all. I wanted to bring poor Graham away, but he wouldn't listen to me—not that he wasn't very quiet. He made no talk, and opened himself only to Mrs. Dodd and me—we lived in the same house, you know. Of course, I very soon saw through it, and I felt very sorry for poor Miss Congreve. She bore it very well, but it must have been very annoying.'

Philip started up from his chair. 'For heaven's sake, Major Dodd,' he cried, 'what are you talking about?'

The Major stared a moment, and then burst into a peal of laughter. 'You agree, then, with Mrs. Dodd?' he said, recovering himself.

'I understand Mrs. Dodd no better than I do you.'

'Why, my dear sir,' said the Major, rising to his feet and extending his hand, 'I beg a hundred pardons. But you must excuse me if I adhere to my opinion.'

'First, please, be so good as to inform me of your opinion.'

'Why, sir, the whole story is simply bosh.'

'Good heavens,' cried Philip, 'that's no opinion!'

'Well, then, sir, if you will have it: the man was as mad as a March hare.'

'Oh!' cried Philip. His exclamation said a great many things, but the Major took it as a protest.

'He was a monomaniac.'

Philip said nothing.

'The idea is not new to you?'

'Well,' said Philip, 'to tell the truth, it is.'

'Well,' said the Major, with a courteous flourish, 'there you have it—for nothing.'

Philip drew a long breath. 'Ah, no!' he said, gravely, 'not for nothing.' He stood silent for some time, with his eyes fixed on the deck. Major Dodd puffed his cigar and eyed him askance. At last Philip looked up. 'And Henrietta Congreve?'

'Henrietta Congreve,' said the major, with military freedom and gallantry, 'is the sweetest girl in the world. Don't talk to me! I know her.'

'She never became engaged to Graham?'

'Engaged? She never looked at him.'

'But he was in love with her.'

'Ah, that was his own business. He worried her to death. She tried gentleness and kindness—it made him worse. Then, when she declined to see him, the poor fellow swore that she had jilted him. It was a fixed idea. He got Mrs. Dodd to believe it.'

Philip's silent reflections—the hushed eloquence of his amazed unburdened heart—we have no space to interpret. But as the major lightened the load with one hand, he added to it with the other. Philip had never pitied his friend till now. 'I knew him well,' he said, aloud. 'He was the best of men. She might very well have cared for him.'

'Good heavens! my dear sir, how could the woman love a madman'

'You use strong language. When I parted with him in June, he was as sane as you or I.'

'Well, then, apparently, he lost his mind in the interval. He was in wretched health.'

'But a man doesn't lose his mind without a cause.'

'Let us admit, then,' said the major, 'that Miss Congreve was the cause. I insist that she was the innocent cause. How should she have trifled with him? She was engaged to another man. The ways of the Lord are inscrutable. Fortunately,' continued the Major, 'she doesn't know the worst.'

'How, the worst'

'Why, you know he shot himself.'

'Bless your soul, Miss Congreve knows it.'

'I think you're mistaken. She didn't know it this morning.'

Philip was sickened and bewildered by the tissue of horrors in which he found himself entangled. 'Oh,' he said, bitterly, 'she has forgotten it then. She knew it a month ago.'

'No, no, no,' rejoined the major, with decision. 'I took the liberty, this morning, of calling upon her, and as we had had some conversation upon Mr. Graham at Sharon, I touched upon his death. I saw she had heard of it, and I said nothing more—'

'Well then?' said Philip.

'Well, then, my dear sir, she thinks he died in his bed. May she never think otherwise!'

In the course of that night—he sat out on deck till two o'clock, alone—Philip, revolving many things, fervently echoed this last wish of Major Dodd.

Aux grands maux les grands remèdes. Philip is now a married man; and curious to narrate, his wife bears a striking likeness to the young lady whose photograph he purchased for the price of six dozen of his own. And yet her name is not Angelica Thompson— nor even Dora.

A Light Man

[First appeared in the *Galaxy*, vol. viii (July 1869), pp. 49-68. The tale was heavily revised and reprinted in volume v of *Stories by American Authors* (1884). The 1884 text was later revised and reprinted in volume i of *Stories Revived* (1885).]

> And I—what I seem to my friend, you see—
>   What I soon shall seem to his love, you guess.
> What I seem to myself, do you ask of me?
>   No hero, I confess.
>   A LIGHT WOMAN. BROWNING'S MEN AND WOMEN.

APRIL 4, 1857.—I HAVE CHANGED MY SKY WITHOUT changing my mind. I resume these old notes in a new world. I hardly know of what use they are; but it's easier to preserve the habit than to break it. I have been at home now a week—at home, forsooth! And yet after all, it is home. I'm dejected, I'm bored, I'm blue. How can a man be more at home than that? Nevertheless, I'm the citizen of a great country, and for that matter, a great city. I walked to-day some ten miles or so along Broadway, and on the whole I don't blush for my native land. We're a capable race and a good-looking withal; and I don't see why we shouldn't prosper as well as another. This, by the way, ought to be a very encouraging reflection. A capable fellow and a good looking withal; I don't see why he shouldn't die a millionaire. At all events he must set bravely to work. When a man has, at thirty-two, a net income of considerably less than nothing, he can scarcely hope to overtake a fortune before he himself is overtaken by age and philosophy—two deplorable obstructions. I'm afraid that one of them has already planted itself in my path. What am I? What do I wish? Whither do I tend? What do I believe? I am constantly beset by these impertinent whisperings. Formerly it was enough that I was Maximus Austin; that I was endowed with a cheerful mind and a good digestion; that one day or another, when I had come to the end, I should return to America and begin at the beginning; that, meanwhile, existence was sweet in—in the Rue Tranchet. But now! Has the sweetness really passed out of life? Have I eaten the plums and left nothing but the bread and milk and corn-starch, or whatever the horrible concoction is?—we had it to-day for dinner. Pleasure, at least, I imagine—pleasure pure and simple, pleasure crude, brutal and vulgar—this poor flimsy delusion has lost all its prettiness. I shall never again care for certain things—and indeed for certain persons. Of such things, of such persons, I firmly maintain, however, that I was never an enthusiastic votary. It would be more to my credit, I suppose, if I had been. More would be forgiven me if I had loved a little more, if into all my folly and egotism I had put a little more *naïveté* and sincerity. Well, I did the best I could, I was at once too bad and too good for it all. At present, it's far enough off; I've put the sea between us. I'm stranded. I sit high and dry, scanning the horizon for a friendly sail, or waiting for a high tide to set me afloat. The wave of pleasure has planted me here in the sand. Shall I owe my rescue to the wave of pain? At moments my heart throbs with a sort of ecstatic longing to expiate my stupid peccadilloes. I see, as through a glass, darkly, the beauty of labour and love. Decidedly, I'm willing to work. It's written.

7th.—My sail is in sight; it's at hand; I've all but boarded the vessel. I received this morning a letter from the best man in the world. Here it is:

DEAR MAX: I see this very moment, in the old newspaper which had already passed through my hands without yielding up its most precious item, the announcement of your arrival in New York. To think of your having perhaps missed the grasp of my hand. Here it is, dear Max—to rap on the knuckles, if you like. When I say I have just read of your arrival, I mean that twenty minutes have elapsed by the clock. These have been spent in conversation with my excellent friend Mr. Frederick Sloane—your excellent self being the subject. I haven't time to say more about Mr. Sloane than that he is very anxious to make your acquaintance, and that, if your time is not otherwise predestined, he would esteem it a particular favour to have you pass a month under his roof—the ample roof which covers my own devoted head. It appears that he knew your mother very intimately, and he has a taste for visiting the amenities of the parents upon the children; the original ground of my own connection with him was that he had been a particular friend of my father. You may have heard your mother speak of him—a perfect eccentric, but a charming one. He will make you most welcome. But whether or no you come for his sake, come for mine. I have a hundred questions on the end of my pen, but I can't drop them, lest I should lose the mail. You'll not refuse me without an excellent reason, and I shan't excuse you, even then. So the sooner the better. Yours more than ever,

THEODORE LISLE.

Theodore's letter is of course very kind, but it's perfectly obscure. My mother may have had the highest regards for Mr. Sloane, but she never mentioned his name in my hearing. Who is he, what is he, and what is the nature of his relations with Theodore? I shall learn betimes. I have written to Theodore that I gladly accept (I believe I suppressed the 'gladly' though) his friend's invitation, and that I shall immediately present myself. What better can I do? I shall, at the narrowest calculation, obtain food and lodging while I invoke the fates. I shall have a basis of operations. D., it appears, is a long day's journey, but delicious when you reach it. I'm curious to see a delicious American town. And a month's stay! Mr. Frederick Sloane, whoever you are, *vous faites bien les choses*, and the little that I know of you is very much to your credit. You enjoyed the friendship of my dear mother, you possess the esteem of my incomparable Theodore, you commend yourself to my own affection. At this rate, I shan't grudge it.

D——, 14th.—I have been here since Thursday evening—three days. As we rattled up to the tavern in the village, I perceived from the top of the coach, in the twilight, Theodore beneath the porch, scanning the vehicle, with all his affectionate soul in his eyes. I made hardly more than two downward strides into his arms—or, at all events, into his hands. He has grown older, of course, in these five years, but less so than I had expected. His is one of those smooth unwrinkled souls that infuse a perennial fairness and freshness into the body. As tall as ever, moreover, and as lean and clean. How short and fat and dark and debauched he makes one feel! By nothing he says or means, of course, but merely by his old unconscious purity and simplicity—that slender aspiring rectitude which makes him remind you of the tower of an English abbey. He greeted me with smiles, and stares, and formidable blushes. He assures me that he never would have known me, and that five years have quite transformed my physiognomy. I asked him if it was for the better? He looked at me hard for a moment, with his eyes of blue, and then, for all answer, he blushed again.

On my arrival we agreed to walk over from the village. He dismissed his wagon with my trunk, and we went arm-in-arm through the dusk. The town is seated at the foot of certain mountains, whose names I have yet to learn, and at the head of a vast sheet of water which, as yet, too, I know only as 'The Lake'. The road hitherward soon leaves the village and wanders in rural loveliness by the lake side. Sometimes the water is hidden by clumps of trees, behind which we heard it lapping and gurgling in the darkness; sometimes it stretches out from your feet in unspotted beauty, offering its broad white bosom to the embrace of the dark fraternal hills. The walk from the tavern takes some half an hour, in which space Theodore had explained his position to my comparative satisfaction. Mr. Sloane is old, widowed and rich; his age is seventy-two, and as his health is thoroughly broken, is practically even greater; and his fortune—Theodore, characteristically, doesn't know its numerical formula. It's probably a round million. He has lived much abroad, and in the thick of things; he has had adventures and passions and all that sort of thing; and now, in the evening of his days, like an old French diplomat, he takes it into his head to write his memoirs. To this end he has taken poor Theodore to his generous side, to serve as his guide, philosopher and friend. He has been a great scribbler, says Theodore, all his days, and he proposes to incorporate a large amount of promiscuous literary matter into this singular record of his existence. Theodore's principal function seems to be to get him to leave things out. In fact, the poor boy seems troubled in conscience. His patron's lucubrations have taken the turn of all memoirs; and become *tout bonnement* immoral. On the whole, he declares they are a very odd mixture—a jumble of pretentious trash and of excellent good sense. I can readily understand it. The old man bores me, puzzles me, and amuses me.

He was in waiting to receive me. We found him in his library—which, by the way, is simply the most delightful apartment that I ever smoked a cigar in—a room for a lifetime. At one end stands a great fireplace, with a florid, fantastic mantel-piece in carved white marble—an importation, of course, and as one may say, an interpolation; the groundwork of the house, the 'fixtures', being throughout plain, solid and domestic. Over the mantel-shelf is a large landscape painting, a *soi-distant* Gainsborough, full of the mellow glory of an English summer. Beneath it stands a fantastic litter of French bronzes and outlandish *chinoiseries*. Facing the door, as you enter, is a vast window set in a recess, with cushioned seats and large clear panes, stationed as it were at the very apex of the lake (which forms an almost perfect oval) and commanding a view of its whole extent. At the other end, opposite the fire-place, the wall is studded, from floor to ceiling, with choice foreign paintings, placed in relief against the orthodox crimson screen. Elsewhere the walls are covered with books, arranged neither in formal regularity nor quite helter-skelter, but in a sort of genial mutual incongruity, which tells that sooner or later each volume feels sure of leaving the ranks and returning into different company. Mr. Sloane uses his books. His two passions, according to Theodore, are reading and talking; but to talk he must have a book in his hand. The charm of the room lies in the absence of the portentous soberness—the browns, and blacks, and greys—which distinguish most rooms of its class. It's a sort of female study. There are half a dozen light colours scattered about—pink in the carpet, tender blue in the curtains, yellow in the chairs. The result is a general look of brightness, and lightness, and unpedantic elegance. You perceive the place to be the home, not of a man of learning, but of a man of fancy.

He rose from his chair—the man of fancy, to greet me—the man of fact. As I looked upon him, in the lamp-light, it seemed to me, for the first five minutes, that I had seldom seen a worse-favoured human creature. It took me then five minutes to get the point of view; then I began to admire. He is undersized, or at best of my own moderate stature, bent and contracted with years; thin, however, where I am stout, and light where I am heavy. In colour we're about equally dark. Mr. Sloane, however, is curiously pale, with a dead opaque yellow pallor. Literally, it's a magnificent yellow. His skin is of just the hue and apparent texture of some old crumpled Oriental scroll. I know a dozen painters who would give more than they have to arrive at the exact 'tone' of his thick-veined saffron-coloured hands—his polished ivory knuckles. His eyes are circled with red, but within their unhealthy orbits they scintillate like black diamonds. His nose, owing to the falling away of other portions of his face, has assumed a grotesque, unnatural prominence; it describes an immense arch, gleaming like parchment stretched on ivory. He has kept his teeth, but replaced his hair by a dead black wig; of course he's clean shaven. In his dress he has a muffled, waddled look, and an apparent aversion to linen, inasmuch as none is visible on his person. He seems neat enough, but not fastidious. At first, as I say, I fancied him monstrously ugly; but on further acquaintance I perceived that what I had taken for ugliness is nothing but the incomplete remains of remarkable good looks. The lines of his features are delicate; his nose, *ceteris paribus*, would be extremely handsome; his eyes are the eyes of a mind, not of a body. There is intelligence on his brow and sweetness on his lips.

He offered his two hands, as Theodore introduced me; I gave him my own, and he stood smiling upon me like some quaint old image in ivory and ebony, scanning my face with the sombre sparkle of his gaze. 'Good heaven!' he said, at last, 'how much you look like your father.' I sat down, and for half an hour we talked of many things; of my journey, of my impressions of home, of my reminiscences of Europe, and, by implication, of my prospects. His voice is aged and cracked, but he uses it with immense energy. Mr. Sloane is not yet in his dotage, by a long shot. He nevertheless makes himself out a woefully old man. In reply to an inquiry I made about his health, he favoured me with a long list of his infirmities (some of which are very trying, certainly) and assured me that he had but a mere pinch of vitality left.

'I live,' he said, 'out of mere curiosity.'

'I have heard of people dying,' I answered, 'from the same motive.'

He looked at me a moment, as if to ascertain whether I was making light of his statement. And then, after a pause, 'Perhaps you don't know,' said he, with a certain vague pomposity, 'that I disbelieve in a future life.'

Poor Theodore! at these words he got up and walked to the fire.

'Well, we shan't quarrel about that,' said I. Theodore turned round, staring.

'Do you mean that you agree with me?' the old man asked.

'I certainly haven't come here to talk theology. Dear me, Mr. Sloane,' I said, 'don't ask me to disbelieve, and I'll never ask you to believe.'

'Come,' cried Mr. Sloane, rubbing his hands, 'you'll not persuade me you're a Christian—like your friend Theodore there.'

'Like Theodore—assuredly not.' And then, somehow, I don't know why, at the thought of Theodore's Christianism, I burst into a laugh. 'Excuse me, my dear fellow,' I said, 'you know, for the last ten years I have lived in Catholic countries.'

'Good, good, good!' cried Mr. Sloane, rubbing his hands and clapping them together, and laughing with high relish.

'Dear me,' said Theodore, smiling, but vaguely apprehensive, too —and a little touched, perhaps by my involuntary reflection upon the quality of his faith, 'I hope you're not a Roman Catholic.'

I saw the old man, with his hands locked, eyeing me shrewdly, and waiting for my answer. I pondered a moment in mock gravity. 'I shall make my confession,' I said. 'I've been in the East, you know. I'm a Mohammedan!'

Hereupon Mr. Sloane broke out into a wheezy ecstasy of glee. Verily, I thought, if he lives for curiosity, he's easily satisfied.

We went into dinner, in the constitution of which I should have been at loss to suggest the shadow of an improvement. I observed, by the way, that for a victim of paralysis, neuralgia, dyspepsia, and a thousand other ills, Mr. Sloane plies a most inconsequential knife and fork. Sweets, and spices, and condiments seem to be the chief of his diet. After dinner he dismissed us, in consideration of my natural desire to see my friend in private. Theodore has capital quarters—a chamber and sitting-room as luxurious as a man (or as a woman, for that matter) could possibly wish. We talked till

near midnight—of ourselves and of our lemon-coloured host below.
That is, I spoke of myself, and Theodore listened; and then Theodore told of Mr. Sloane and I listened. His commerce with the old
man has sharpened his wits. Sloane has taught him to observe and
judge, and Theodore turns around, observes, judges—him! He has
become quite the critic and analyst. There is something very
pleasant in the sagacity of virtue, in discernment without bitterness,
penetration without spite. Theodore has all these unalloyed graces,
to say nothing of an angelic charity. At midnight we repaired to
the library to take leave of our host till the morrow—an attention
which, under all circumstances, he formally exacts. As I gave him
my hand he held it again and looked at me as he had done on my
arrival. 'Good heavens,' he said, at last, 'how much you look like
your mother!'

To-night, at the end of my third day, I begin to feel decidedly at
home. The fact is, I'm supremely comfortable. The house is
pervaded by an indefinable, irresistible air of luxury and privacy.
Mr. Frederick Sloane must be a horribly corrupt old mortal. Already
in his hateful, delightful presence I have become heartily reconciled
to doing nothing. But with Theodore on one side, I honestly believe
I can defy Mr. Sloane on the other. The former asked me this morning, with real solicitude, in allusion to the bit of dialogue I have
quoted above on matters of faith, if I had actually ceased to care
for divine things. I assured him that I would rather utterly lose my
sense of the picturesque, than do anything to detract from the
splendour of religious worship. Some of the happiest hours of my
life, I told him, have been spent in cathedrals. He looked at me
awhile, in friendly sadness. 'I hardly know,' he said, 'whether you
are worse than Mr. Sloane, or better.'

But Theodore is, after all, in duty bound to give a man a long
rope in these matters. His own rope is one of the longest. He reads
Voltaire with Mr. Sloane, and Emerson in his own room. He's the
stronger man of the two; he has the bigger stomach. Mr. Sloane
delights, of course, in Voltaire, but he can't read a line of Emerson.
Theodore delights in Emerson, and has excellent taste in the matter
of Voltaire. It appears that since we parted in Paris, five years ago,
his conscience has dwelt in many lands. *C'est toute une histoire*—
which he tells very nicely. He left college determined to enter the
ministry, and came abroad to lay the basis of his theological great-
ness in some German repository of science. He appears to have
studied, not wisely but too well. Instead of faith full-armed and
serene, there sprang from the labour of his brain a myriad abortive
doubts, piping for sustenance. He went for a winter to Italy, where,

I take it, he was not quite so much afflicted as he ought to have been, at the sight of the beautiful spiritual repose which he had missed. It was after this that we spent those three months together in Brittany—the best-spent three months of my whole ten years abroad. Theodore inoculated me, I think, with a little of his sacred fermentation, and I infused into his conscience something of my vulgar indifference; and we agreed together that there were a few good things left—health, friendship, a summer sky, and the lovely by-ways of an old French province. He came home, returned to theology, accepted a 'call', and made an attempt to respond to it. But the inner voice failed him. His outlook was cheerless enough. During his absence his married sister, the elder one, had taken the other to live with her, relieving Theodore of the charge of contribution to her support. But suddenly, behold the husband, the brother-in-law, dies, leaving a mere fragment of property; and the two ladies, with their two little girls, are afloat in the wide world. Theodore finds himself at twenty-six without an income, without a profession, and with a family of four females to support. Well, in his quiet way, he draws on his courage. The history of the two years which preceded his initiation here is a simple record of practical manly devotion. He rescued his sisters and nieces from the deep waters, placed them high and dry, established them somewhere in decent gentility—and then found at last that his strength had left him—had dropped dead like an over-ridden horse. In short, he had worked himself ill. It was now his sisters' turn. They nursed him with all the added tenderness of gratitude for the past and terror of the future, and brought him safely through a grievous malady. Meanwhile Mr. Sloane, having decided to treat himself to a private secretary and suffered dreadful mischance in three successive experiments, had heard of Theodore's situation and his merits; had furthermore recognized in him the son of an early and intimate friend, and had finally offered him the very comfortable position which he now occupies. There is a decided incongruity between Theodore as a man—as Theodore, in fine—and the dear fellow as the intellectual agent, confidant, complaisant, purveyor, pander—what you will—of a battered old cynic and worldly dilettante. There seems at first sight a perfect want of agreement between his character and his function. One is gold and the other brass, or something very like it. But on reflection I perfectly conceive that he should, under the circumstances, have accepted Mr. Sloane's offer and been content to do his duties. Just heaven! Theodore's contentment in such a case is a theme for the moralist—a better moralist than I. The best and purest mortals are an odd mixture, and in none of us does honesty exist, *totus, teres, atque rotundus.* Ideally, Theodore hasn't the smallest business *dans cette galère.* It offends my sense of propriety to find him here. I feel like admonishing him as a friend that he has knocked at the wrong door, and that he had better retreat before he is brought to the blush. Really, as I say, I suppose he might as well be here, as reading Emerson 'evenings', in the back parlour; to those two very plain sisters—judging from their photographs. Practically it hurts no one to compromise with his tendencies. Poor Theodore was weak, depressed, out of work. Mr. Sloane offers him a lodging and a salary in return for—after all, merely a little forbearance. All he has to do is to read to the old man, lay down the book awhile, with his finger in the place, and let him talk; take it up again, read another dozen pages and submit to another commentary. Then to write a dozen pages under his dictation—to suggest a word, polish off a period, or help him out with a reluctant idea or a half-remembered fact. This is all, I say; and yet this is much. Theodore's apparent success proves it to be much, as well as the old man's satisfaction. It's a part; he plays it. He uses tact; he has taken a reef in his pride; he has clipped the sting of his conscience, he listens, he talks, conciliates, accommodates, flatters— does it as well as many a worse man—does it far better than I. I might dominate Mr. Sloane, but I doubt that I could serve him. But after all, it's not a matter of better and worse. In every son of woman there are two men—the practical man and the dreamer. We live for our dreams—but, meanwhile, we live by our wits. When the dreamer is a poet, his brother is an artist. Theodore is essentially a man of taste. If he were not destined to become a high priest among moralists, he might be a prince among connoisseurs. He plays his part then, artistically, with taste, with relish—with all the *finesse* of his delicate fancy. How can Mr. Sloane fail to believe that he possesses a paragon? He is no such fool as to misconceive a *belle âme* when a *belle âme* comes in his way. He confidentially assured me this morning that Theodore has the most beautiful mind in the world, but that it's a pity he's so simple as not to suspect it. If he only doesn't ruin him with his flattery!

19th.—I'm certainly fortunate among men. This morning when, tentatively, I spoke of understaying my month, Mr. Sloane rose from his seat in horror, and declared that for the present I must regard his house as my home. 'Come, come,' he said, 'when you leave this place where do you intend to go?' Where, indeed? I graciously allowed Mr. Sloane to have the best of the argument. Theodore assures me that he appreciates these and other affabilities, and that I have made what he calls a 'conquest' of his venerable heart. Poor, battered, bamboozled old organ! he would have one believe that it has a most tragical record of capture and recapture. At all events, it appears that I'm master of the citadel. For the present I have no wish to evacuate. I feel, nevertheless, in some far-off corner of my soul, that I ought to shoulder my victorious banner and advance to more fruitful triumphs.

I blush for my slothful inaction. It isn't that I'm willing to stay here a month, but that I'm willing to stay here six. Such is the charming, disgusting truth. Have I actually outlived the age of energy? Have I survived my ambition, my integrity, my self-respect? Verily I ought to have survived the habit of asking myself silly questions. I made up my mind long ago that I care deeply for nothing save my own personal comfort, and I don't care for that sufficiently to secure it at the cost of acute temporary suffering. I have a passion for nothing—not even for life. I know very well the appearance I make in the world. I pass for intelligent, well-informed, accomplished, amiable, strong. I'm supposed to have a keen relish for letters, for music, for science, for art. There was a time when I fancied I cared for scientific research; but I know now that I care for it as little as I really do for Shakespeare, for Rubens, for Rossini. When I was younger, I used to find a certain entertainment in the contemplation of men and women. I liked to see them hurrying on each other's heals across the stage. But I'm sick and tired of them now; not that I'm a misanthrope, God forbid. They're not worth hating. I never knew but one creature who was, and her I went and loved. To be consistent, I ought to have hated my mother—and now I ought to hate Theodore. But I don't—truly, on the whole, I don't —any more than I love him. I firmly believe that a large portion of his happiness rests upon his devout conviction that I really care for him. He believes in that, as he believes in all the rest of it—in my knowledge, my music, my underlying 'earnestness', my sense of beauty and love of truth. Oh, for a *man* among them all—a fellow with eyes in his head—eyes that would look me through and through, and flash out in scorn of my nothingness. Then, perhaps, I might answer him with rage; *then*, perhaps, I might feel a simple, healthy emotion.

In the name of bare nutrition—in the fear of starvation—what am I to do? (I was obliged this morning to borrow ten dollars from Theodore, who remembered gleefully that he has been owing me no less than twenty-five dollars for the past four years, and in fact has preserved a note to this effect). Within the last week I have hatched a desperate scheme. I have deliberately conceived the idea of marrying money. Why not accept and utilize the goods of the gods? It is not my fault, after all, if I pass for a superior fellow. Why not admit that practically, mechanically—as I may say— maritally, I *may* be a superior fellow? I warrant myself, at least, thoroughly gentle. I should never beat my wife; I doubt that I should ever snub her. Assume that her fortune has the proper num- ber of zeros and that she herself is one of them, and I can actually imagine her adoring me. It's not impossible that I've hit the nail and solved my riddle. Curiously, as I look back upon my brief career, it all seems to tend in a certain way to this consummation. It has its graceful curves and crooks, indeed, and here and there a passionate tangent; but on the whole, if I were to unfold it here *à la* Hogarth, what better legend could I scrawl beneath the series of pictures than So-and-So's Progress to a Mercenary Marriage?

Coming events do what we all know with their shadows. My glorious destiny is, perhaps, not far off. I already feel throughout my person a magnificent languor—as from the possession of past opulence. Or is it simply my sense of perfect well-being in this perfectly appointed home? Is it simply the absolutely comfortable life I lead in this delicious old house? At all events, the house *is* delicious, and my only complaint of Mr. Sloane is, that instead of an old widower, he's not an old widow (or I a young maid), so that I might marry him, survive him, and dwell forever in this rich and mellow home. As I write here, at my bedroom table, I have only to stretch out an arm and raise the window-curtain, to see the thick- planted garden budding and breathing, and growing in the moon- shine. Far above, in the liquid darkness, sails the glory-freighted orb of the moon; beneath, in its light, lies the lake, in murmuring, troubled sleep; around stand the gentle mountains, wearing the cold reflection on their shoulders, or hiding it away in their glens. So much for midnight. To-morrow the sun will be lovely with the beauty of day. Under one aspect or another I have it always before me. At the end of the garden is moored a boat, in which Theodore and I have repeatedly explored the surface of the lake, and visited the mild wilderness of its shores. What lovely landward coves and bays—what alder-smothered creeks—what lily-sheeted pools—what sheer steep hill-sides, darkening the water with the downward image of their earthy greenness. I confess that in these excursions Theo- dore does the rowing and I the contemplation. Mr. Sloane avoids the water—on account of the dampness, he says; but because he's afraid of drowning, I suspect.

22nd.—Theodore is right. The *bonhomme* has taken me into his favour. I protest I don't see how he was to escape it. I doubt that there has ever been a better flattered man. I don't blush for it. In

one coin or another I must repay his hospitality—which is certainly
very liberal. Theodore advises him, helps him, comforts him; I
amuse him, surprise him, deprave him. This is speaking vastly well
for my power. He pretends to be surprised at nothing, and to
possess in perfection—poor, pitiable old fop—the art *nil admirari*;
but repeatedly, I know, I have clear outskipped his fancy. As for his
depravity, it's a very pretty piece of wickedness, but it strikes me as
a purely intellectual matter. I imagine him never to have had any
downright senses. He may have been unclean; morally, he's not
over savoury now; but he never can have been what the French call
a *viveur*. He's too delicate, he's of a feminine turn; and what woman
was ever a *viveur*? He likes to sit in his chair, and read scandal, talk
scandal, make scandal, so far as he may without catching a cold or
incurring a headache. I already feel as if I had known him a lifetime. I read him as clearly, I think, as if I had. I know the type to
which he belongs; I have encountered, first and last, a round dozen
of specimens. He's neither more nor less than a gossip—a gossip
flanked by a coxcomb and an egotist. He's shallow, vain, cold, superstitious, timid, pretentious, capricious; a pretty jumble of virtues!
And yet, for all this, he has his good points. His caprices are sometimes generous, I imagine; and his aversion to the harsh, cruel, and
hideous, frequently takes the form of positive kindness and charity.
His memory (for trifles) is remarkable, and (where his own perform-
ances are not involved) his taste is excellent. He has no will for evil
more than for good. He is the victim, however, of more illusions
with regard to himself than I ever knew a human heart to find
lodging for. At the age of twenty, poor, ignorant and remarkably
handsome, he married a woman of immense wealth, many years his
senior. At the end of three years she very considerately went out of
the world, and left him to the enjoyment of his freedom and riches.
If he had remained poor, he might from time to time have rubbed
at random against the truth, and would still be wearing a few of its
sacred smutches on his sleeve. But he wraps himself in his money
as in a wadded dressing gown, and goes trundling through life on
his little gold wheels, as warm and close as an unweaned baby. The
greater part of his career, from his marriage to within fifteen years
ago, was spent in Europe, which, superficially, he knows very well.
He has lived in fifty places, known hundreds of people, and spent
thousands of dollars. At one time, I believe, he spent a few thousands
too many, trembled for an instant on the verge of a pecuniary
crash; but recovered himself, and found himself more frightened
than hurt, but loudly admonished to lower his pitch. He passed five
years in a species of penitent seclusion on the lake of—I forget what

(his genius seems to be partial to lakes), and formed the rudiments of his present magnificent taste for literature; I can't call it anything but magnificent, so long as it must needs have Theodore Lisle as a ministrant. At the close of this period, by economy, he had become a rich man again. The control and discipline exercised during these years upon his desires and his natural love of luxury, must have been the sole act of real resolution in the history of Mr. Sloane's life. It was rendered possible by his morbid, his actually pusillanimous dread of poverty; he doesn't feel safe without half a million between him and starvation. Meanwhile he had turned from a young man into an old man; his health was broken, his spirit was jaded, and I imagine, to do him justice, that he began to feel certain natural, filial longings for this dear American mother of us all. They say the most hopeless truants and triflers have come to it. He came to it, at all events; he packed up his books and pictures and gimcracks, and bade farewell to Europe. This house which he now occupies belonged to his wife's estate. She had, for sentimental reasons of her own, commended it to his particular regard. On his return he came to see it, fancied it, turned a parcel of carpenters and upholsterers into it, and by inhabiting it for twelve years, transformed it into the perfect dwelling which I find it. Here he has spent all his time, with the exception of a regular winter's visit to New York—a practice recently discontinued, owing to the aggravation of his physical condition and the projection of these famous memoirs. His life has finally come to be passed in comparative solitude. He tells of various distant relatives, as well as intimate friends of both sexes, who used formerly to be largely entertained at his cost, but with each of them, in the course of time, he seems to have clipped the thread of intercourse. Throughout life, evidently, he has shown great delicacy of tact in keeping himself clean of parasites. Rich, lonely and vain, he must have been fair game for the race of social sycophants and cormorants; and it's richly to the credit of his shrewdness and good sense, that he has suffered so little havoc in substance and happiness. Apparently they've been a sad lot of bunglers. I maintain that he's to be—how shall I say it? —possessed. But you must work in obedience to certain definite laws. Doctor Jones, his physician, tells me that in point of fact he has had for the past ten years an unbroken series of favourites, *protégés*, and heirs presumptive; but that each, in turn, by some fatally false movement, has fairly unjointed his nose. The doctor declares, moreover, that they were, at best, a woefully common set of people. Gradually the old man seems to have developed a preference for two or three strictly exquisite intimates, over a throng of your vulgar charmers. His tardy literary schemes, too—fruit of his all but sapless senility—have absorbed more and more of his time and attention. The end of it all is, therefore, that Theodore and I have him quite to ourselves, and that it behooves us to keep our noses on our faces, and our heads on our shoulders

Poor, pretentious old simpleton! It's not his fault, after all, that he fancies himself a great little man. How are you to judge of the stature of mankind when men have forever addressed you on their knees? Peace and joy to his innocent fatuity! He believes himself the most rational of men; in fact, he's the most vapidly sentimental. He fancies himself a philosopher, a thinker, a student. His philosophy and his erudition are quite of a piece; they would lie at ease in the palm of Theodore's hand. He prides himself on his good manners, his urbanity, his unvarying observance of the becoming. My private impression is, that his cramped old bosom contains unsuspected treasures of cunning impertinence. He takes his stand on his speculative audacity—his direct, undaunted gaze at the universe; in truth, his mind is haunted by a hundred dingy old-world spectres and theological phantasms. He fancies himself one of the weightiest of men; he is essentially one of the lightest. He deems himself ardent, impulsive, passionate, magnanimous—capable of boundless enthusiasm for an idea or a sentiment. It is clear to me that, on no occasion of pure, disinterested action can he ever have taken a timely, positive second step. He fancies, finally, that he has drained the cup of life to the dregs; that he has known in its bitterest intensity, every emotion of which the human spirit is capable; that he has loved, struggled, and suffered. Stuff and nonsense, all of it. He has never loved anyone but himself; he has never suffered from anything but an undigested supper or an exploded pretension; he has never touched with the end of his lips the vulgar bowl from which the mass of mankind quaffs its great floods of joy and sorrow. Well, the long and short of it all is, that I honestly pity him. He may have given sly knocks in his life, but he can't hurt *me*. I pity his ignorance, his weakness, his timidity. He has tasted the real sweetness of life no more than its bitterness; he has never dreamed, or wandered, or dared; he has never known any but mercenary affection; neither men nor women have risked aught for *him*—for his good spirits, his good looks, and his poverty. How I should like to give him, for once, a real sensation!

26th.—I took a row this morning with Theodore a couple of miles along the lake, to a point where we went ashore and lounged away an hour in the sunshine, which is still very comfortable. Poor Theodore seems troubled about many things. For one, he is troubled about me; he is actually more anxious about my future than I myself; he thinks better of me than I do of myself; he is so deucedly conscientious, so scrupulous, so averse to giving offence or to *brusquer* any situation before it has played itself out, that he shrinks from betraying his apprehensions or asking any direct questions. But I know that he is dying to extort from me some positive profession of practical interest and faith. I catch myself in the act of taking—heaven forgive me!—a half-malicious joy in confounding his expectations—leading his generous sympathies off the scent by various extravagant protestations of mock cynicism and malignity. But in Theodore I have so firm a friend that I shall have a long row to hoe if I ever find it needful to make him forswear his devotion— abjure his admiration. He admires me—that's absolute; he takes my moral infirmities for the eccentricities of genius, and they only impart an extra flavour—a *haut goût*—to the richness of my charms. Nevertheless, I can see that he is disappointed. I have even less to show, after this lapse of years, than he had hoped. Heaven help us! little enough it must strike him as being. What an essential absurdity there is in our being friends at all. I honestly believe we shall end with hating each other. They are all very well now—our diversity, our oppugnancy, our cross purposes; now that we are at play together they serve as a theme for jollity. But when we settle down to work—ah me! for the tug of war. I wonder, as it is, that Theodore keeps his patience with me. His education since we parted should tend logically to make him despise me. He has studied, thought, suffered, loved—loved those very plain sisters and nieces. Poor me! how should I be virtuous? I have no sisters, plain or pretty!—nothing to love, work for, live for. Friend Theodore, if you are going one of these days to despise me and drop me—in the sacred name of comfort, come to the point at once, and make an end of our common agony!

He is troubled, too, about Mr. Sloane. His attitude toward the *bonhomme* quite passes my comprehension. It's the queerest jumble of contraries. He penetrates him, contemns him—yet respects and admires him. It all comes of the poor boy's shrinking New England conscience. He's afraid to give his perceptions a fair chance, lest, forsooth, they should look over his neighbour's wall. He'll not understand that he may as well sacrifice the old man for a lamb as for a sheep. His view of the gentleman, therefore, is a perfect tissue of cobwebs—a jumble of half-way sorrows, and wide-drawn charities, and hair-breadth 'scapes from utter damnation, and sudden platitudes of generosity; fit, all of it, to make an angel curse!

'The man's a perfect egotist and fool,' say I, 'but I like him.' Now

Theodore likes him—or rather wants to like him; but he can't reconcile it to his self-respect—fastidious deity!—to like a fool. Why the deuce can't he leave it alone altogether? It's a purely practical matter. He ought to do the duties of his place all the better for having his head clear of officious sentiment. I don't believe in disinterested service; and Theodore is too desperately bent on preserving his disinterestedness. With me, it's different. I'm perfectly free to love the *bonhomme*—for a fool. I'm neither a scribe nor a Pharisee; I'm—ah me, *what* am I?

And then, Theodore is troubled about his sisters. He's afraid he's not doing his duty by them. He thinks he ought to be with them—to be getting a larger salary—to be teaching his nieces. I'm not versed in such questions. Perhaps he ought.

MAY 3d.—This morning Theodore sent me word that he was ill and unable to get up; upon which I immediately repaired to his bedside. He had caught cold, was sick and a little feverish. I urged him to make no attempt to leave his room, and assured him that I would do what I could to reconcile Mr. Sloane to his non-attendance. This I found an easy matter. I read to him for a couple of hours, wrote four letters—one in French—and then talked a good two hours more. I have done more talking, by the way, in the last fortnight, than in any previous twelve months—much of it, too, none of the wisest, nor, I may add, of the most fastidiously veracious. In a little discussion, two or three days ago, with Theodore, I came to the point and roundly proclaimed that in gossiping with Mr. Sloane I made no scruple, for our common satisfaction, of discreetly using the embellishments of fiction. My confession gave him 'that turn', as Mrs. Gamp would say, that his present illness may be the result of it. Nevertheless, poor, dear fellow, I trust he'll be on his legs to-morrow. This afternoon, somehow, I found myself really in the humour of talking. There was something propitious in the circumstances; a hard, cold rain without, a wood-fire in the library, the *bonhomme* puffing cigarettes in his arm-chair, beside him a portfolio of newly imported prints and photographs, and—Theodore tucked safely away in bed. Finally, when I brought our *tête-à-tête* to a close (taking good care to understay my welcome) Mr. Sloane seized me by both hands and honoured me with one of his venerable grins. 'Max,' he said—'you must let me call you Max—you're the most delightful man I ever knew.'

Verily, there's some virtue left in me yet. I believe I fairly blushed. 'Why didn't I know you ten years ago?' the old man went on. 'Here are ten years lost.'

'Ten years ago, my dear Mr. Sloane,' quoth Max, 'I was hardly worth your knowing.'

'But I did know you!' cried the *bonhomme*. 'I knew you in knowing your mother.'

Ah! my mother again. When the old man begins that chapter I feel like telling him to blow out his candle and go to bed.

'At all events,' he continued, 'we must make the most of the years that remain. I'm a poor sick old fellow, but I've no notion of dying. You'll not get tired of me and want to go away?'

'I'm devoted to you, sir,' I said. 'But I must be looking up some work, you know.'

'Work! Bah! I'll give you work. I'll give you wages.'

'I'm afraid,' I said, with a smile, 'that you'll want to give me the wages without the work.' And then I declared that I must go up and look at poor Theodore.

The *bonhomme* still kept my hands. 'I wish very much,' he said, 'that I could get you to love me as well as you do poor Theodore.'

'Ah, don't talk about love, Mr. Sloane. I'm no lover.'

'Don't you love your friend?'

'Not as he deserves.'

'Nor as he loves you, perhaps?'

'He loves me, I'm afraid, far more than I deserve.'

'Well, Max,' my host pursued, 'we can be good friends, all the same. We don't need a hocus-pocus of false sentiment. We are *men*, aren't we?—men of sublime good sense.' And just here, as the old man looked at me the pressure of his hands deepened to a convulsive grasp, and the bloodless mask of his countenance was suddenly distorted with a nameless fear. 'Ah, my dear young man!' he cried, 'come and be a son to me—the son of my age and desolation! For God's sake don't leave me to pine and die alone!'

I was amazed—and I may say I was moved. Is it true, then, that this poor old heart contains such measureless depths of horror and longing? I take it that he's mortally afraid of death. I assured him on my honour that he may henceforth call upon me for any service.

8th.—Theodore's indisposition turned out more serious than I expected. He has been confined to his room till to-day. This evening he came down to the library in his dressing gown. Decidedly, Mr. Sloane is an eccentric, but hardly, as Theodore thinks, a 'charming' one. There is something extremely curious in the exhibition of his caprices—the incongruous fits and starts, as it were, of his taste. For some reason, best known to himself, he took it into his head to deem it a want of delicacy, of respect, of *savoir-vivre*—of heaven knows what—that poor Theodore, who is still weak and languid, should enter the sacred precinct of his study in the vulgar drapery of a dressing-gown. The sovereign trouble with the *bonhomme* is an absolute lack of the instinct of justice. He's of the real feminine turn—I believe I have written it before—without a ray of woman's virtues. I honestly believe that I might come into his study in my night-shirt and he would smile upon it as a picturesque *déshabillé*. But for poor Theodore to-night there was nothing but scowls and frowns, and barely a civil inquiry about his health. But poor Theodore is not such a fool, either; he'll not die of a snubbing; I never said he was a weakling. Once he fairly saw from what quarter the wind blew, he bore the master's brutality with the utmost coolness and gallantry. Can it be that Mr. Sloane really wishes to drop him? The delicious old brute! He understands favour and friendship only as a selfish rapture—a reaction, an infatuation, an act of aggressive, exclusive patronage. It's not a bestowal with him, but a transfer, and half his pleasure in causing his sun to shine is that —being woefully near its setting—it will produce a number of delectable shadows. He wants to cast my shadow, I suppose, on Theodore; fortunately I'm not altogether an opaque body. Since Theodore was taken ill he has been into his room but once, and has sent him none but the scantiest messages. I, too, have been much less attentive than I should have wished to be; but my time has not been my own. It has been, every moment of it, at Mr. Sloane's disposal. He actually runs after me; he devours me; he makes a fool of himself, and is trying hard to make one of me. I find that he will stand—that, in fact, he actually enjoys—a certain kind of humorous snubbing. He likes anything that will tickle his fancy, impart a flavour to our relations, remind him of his old odds and ends of novels and memoirs. I have fairly stepped into Theodore's shoes, and done—with what I feel in my bones to be vastly inferior skill and taste—all the reading, writing, condensing, expounding, transcribing and advising that he has been accustomed to do. I have driven with the *bonhomme*; played chess and cribbage with him; and beaten him, bullied him, contradicted him; and forced him into going out on the water under my charge. Who shall say, after this, that I haven't done my best to discourage his advances, confound his benevolence? As yet, my efforts are vain; in fact they quite turn to my own confusion. Mr. Sloane is so vastly thankful at having escaped from the lake with his life that he seems actually to look upon me as a kind of romantic preserver and protector. Faugh! what tiresome nonsense it all is! But one thing is certain, it can't last forever. Admit that he *has* cast Theodore out and

taken me in. He will speedily discover that he has made a pretty
mess of it, and that he had much better have left well enough
alone. He likes my reading and writing now, but in a month he'll
begin to hate them. He'll miss Theodore's healthy, unerring, impersonal judgment. What an advantage that pure and luminous
nature has over mine, after all. I'm for days, he's for years; he for
the long run, I for the short. I, perhaps, am intended for success,
but he alone for happiness. He holds in his heart a tiny sacred particle, which leavens his whole being and keeps it pure and sound
—a faculty of admiration and respect. For him human nature is
still a wonder and a mystery; it bears a divine stamp—Mr. Sloane's
tawdry organism as well as the best.

13th.—I have refused, of course, to supplant Theodore further,
in the exercise of his functions, and he has resumed his morning
labours with Mr. Sloane. I, on my side, have spent these morning
hours in scouring the country on that capital black mare, the use
of which is one of the perquisites of Theodore's place. The days
have been magnificent—the heat of the sun tempered by a murmuring, wandering wind, the whole north a mighty ecstasy of sound
and verdure, the sky a far-away vault of bended blue. Not far from
the mill at M., the other end of the lake, I met, for the third time,
that very pretty young girl, who reminds me so forcibly of A. L.
She makes so very frank and fearless a use of her eyes that I ventured to stop and bid her good-morning. She seems nothing loth
to an acquaintance. She's an out-and-out barbarian in speech, but
her eyes look as if they had drained the noon-day heavens of their
lustre. These rides do me good; I had got into a sadly worrying,
brooding habit of thought.

What has got into Theodore I know not; his illness seems to
have left him strangely affected. He has fits of sombre reserve,
alternating with spasms of extravagant gaiety. He avoids me at
times for hours together, and then he comes and looks at me with
an inscrutable smile, as if he were on the verge of a burst of confidence—which again is swallowed up in the darkness of his silence.
Is he hatching some astounding benefit to his species? Is he working
to bring about my removal to a higher sphere of action? *Nous
verrons bien.*

18th.—Theodore threatens departure. He received this morning
a letter from one of his sisters—the young widow—announcing her
engagement to a minister whose acquaintance she has recently
made, and intimating her expectation of an immediate union with
the gentleman—a ceremony which would require Theodore's attendance. Theodore, in high good humour, read the letter aloud at

breakfast—and to tell the truth a charming letter it was. He then spoke of his having to go on to the wedding; a proposition to which Mr. Sloane graciously assented—but with truly startling amplitude. 'I shall be sorry to lose you after so happy a connection,' said the old man. Theodore turned pale, stared a moment, and then, recovering his colour and his composure, declared that he should have no objection in life to coming back.

'Bless my soul!' cried the *bonhomme*, 'you don't mean to say you'll leave your little sister all alone?'

To which Theodore replied that he would arrange for her to live with his brother-in-law. 'It's the only proper thing,' he declared, in a tone which was not to be gainsaid. It has come to this, that Mr. Sloane actually wants to turn him out of the house. Oh, the precious old fool! He keeps smiling an uncanny smile, which means, as I read it, that if the poor boy once departs he shall never return on the old footing—for all his impudence!

20th.—This morning, at breakfast, we had a terrific scene. A letter arrives for Theodore; he opens it, turns white and red, frowns, falters, and then informs us that the clever widow has broken off her engagement. No wedding, therefore, and no departure for Theodore. The *bonhomme* was furious. In his fury he took the liberty of calling poor Mrs. Parker (the sister) a very impolite name. Theodore rebuked him, with perfect good taste, and kept his temper.

'If my opinions don't suit you, Mr. Lisle,' the old man broke out, 'and my mode of expressing them displeases you, you know you can easily remove yourself from within my jurisdiction.'

'My dear Mr. Sloane,' said Theodore, 'your opinions, as a general rule, interest me deeply, and have never ceased to act most beneficially upon the formation of my own. Your mode of expressing them is charming, and I wouldn't for the world, after all our pleasant intercourse, separate from you in bitterness. Only, I repeat, your qualification of my sister's conduct was perfectly uncalled for. If you knew her, you would be the first to admit it.'

There was something in Theodore's aspect and manner, as he said these words, which puzzled me all the morning. After dinner, finding myself alone with him, I told him I was glad he was not obliged to go away. He looked at me with the mysterious smile I have mentioned—a smile which actually makes him handsome—thanked me and fell into meditation. As this bescribbled chronicle is the record of my follies, as well as of my *haut faits*, I needn't hesitate to say that, for a moment, I was keenly exasperated. What business has poor, transparent Theodore to put on the stony mask of the sphinx and play the inscrutable? What right has he to do so with me especially, in whom he has always professed an absolute confidence? Just as I was about to cry out, 'Come, my dear boy, this affectation of mystery has lasted quite long enough—favour me at last with the result of your cogitation!'—as I was on the point of thus expressing my impatience of his continued solemnity of demeanour, the oracle at last addressed itself to utterance.

'You see, my dear Max,' he said, 'I can't, in justice to myself, go away in obedience to any such intimation as that vouchsafed to me this morning. What do you think of my actual footing here?'

Theodore's actual footing here seemed to me essentially uncomfortable; of course I said so.

'Nay, I assure you it's not,' he answered. 'I should feel, on the contrary, very uncomfortable to think that I'd come away, except by my own choice. You see a man can't afford to cheapen himself. What are you laughing at?'

'I'm laughing, in the first place, my dear fellow, to hear on your lips the language of cold calculation; and in the second place, at your odd notion of the process by which a man keeps himself up in the market.'

'I assure you that it's the correct notion. I came here as a favour to Mr. Sloane; it was expressly understood so. The occupation was distasteful to me. I had from top to bottom to accommodate myself to my duties. I had to compromise with a dozen convictions, preferences, prejudices. I don't take such things easily; I take them hard; and when once the labour is achieved I can't consent to have it thrown away. If Mr. Sloane needed me then, he needs me still. I am ignorant of any change having taken place in his intentions, or in his means of satisfying them. I came not to amuse him, but to do a certain work; I hope to remain until the work is completed. To go away sooner is to make a confession of incapacity which, I protest, costs too great a sacrifice to my vanity.'

Theodore spoke these words with a face which I have never seen him wear; a fixed, mechanical smile; a hard, dry glitter in his eyes; a harsh, strident tone in his voice—in his whole physiognomy a gleam, as it were, a note of defiance. Now I confess that for defiance I have never been conscious of an especial relish. When I'm defied, I'm ugly. 'My dear man,' I replied, 'your sentiments do you prodigious credit. Your very ingenious theory of your present situation, as well as your extremely pronounced sense of your personal value, are calculated to insure you a degree of practical success which can very well dispense with the furtherance of my poor good wishes.' Oh, the grimness of his listening smile—and I suppose I may add of my own physiognomy! But I have ceased to be puzzled. Theodore's

conduct for the past ten days is suddenly illumined with a backward, lurid ray. Here are a few plain truths, which it behooves
me to take to heart—commit to memory. Theodore is jealous of
me. Theodore hates me. Theodore has been seeking for the past
three months to see his name written, last but not least, in a certain
testamentary document: 'Finally, I bequeath to my dear young
friend, Theodore Lisle, in return for invaluable services and unfailing devotion, the bulk of my property, real and personal, consisting
of—' (hereupon follows an exhaustive enumeration of houses, lands,
public securities, books, pictures, horses, and dogs). It is for this
that he has toiled, and watched, and prayed; submitted to intellectual weariness and spiritual torture; made his terms with levity,
blasphemy, and insult. For this he sets his teeth and tightens his
grasp; for this he'll fight. Merciful powers! it's an immense weight
off one's mind. There are nothing, then, but vulgar, common laws;
no sublime exceptions, no transcendent anomalies. Theodore's a
knave, a hypo—nay, nay; stay, irreverent hand!—Theodore's a
man! Well, that's all I want. *He* wants fight—he shall have it. Have
I got, at last, my simple, natural emotion?

  21st.—I have lost no time. This evening, late, after I had heard
Theodore go to his room (I had left the library early, on the pretext of having letters to write), I repaired to Mr. Sloane, who had not
yet gone to bed, and informed him that it is necessary I shall at
once leave him, and seek some occupation in New York. He felt
the blow; it brought him straight down on his marrow-bones. He
went through the whole gamut of his arts and graces; he blustered,
whimpered, entreated, flattered. He tried to drag in Theodore's
name; but this I, of course, prevented. But, finally, why, *why*, WHY,
after all my promises of fidelity, must I thus cruelly desert him?
Then came my supreme avowal: I have spent my last penny; while
I stay, I'm a beggar. The remainder of this extraordinary scene I
have no power to describe: how the *bonhomme*, touched, inflamed,
inspired, by the thought of my destitution, and at the same time
annoyed, perplexed, bewildered at having to commit himself to
any practical alleviation of it, worked himself into a nervous frenzy
which deprived him of a clear sense of the value of his words and
his actions; how I, prompted by the irresistible spirit of my desire
to leap astride of his weakness, and ride it hard into the goal of my
dreams, cunningly contrived to keep his spirit at the fever point,
so that strength, and reason, and resistance should burn themselves
out. I shall probably never again have such a sensation as I enjoyed
to-night—actually feel a heated human heart throbbing, and turning, and struggling in my grasp; know its pants, its spasms, its

convulsions, and its final senseless quiescence. At half-past one o'clock, Mr. Sloane got out of his chair, went to his secretary, opened a private drawer, and took out a folded paper. 'This is my will,' he said, 'made some seven weeks ago. If you'll stay with me, I'll destroy it.'

'Really, Mr. Sloane,' I said, 'if you think my purpose is to exert any pressure upon your testamentary inclinations—'

'I'll tear it in pieces,' he cried; 'I'll burn it up. I shall be as sick as a dog to-morrow; but I'll do it. A-a-h!'

He clapped his hand to his side, as if in sudden, overwhelming pain, and sank back fainting into his chair. A single glance assured me that he was unconscious. I possessed myself of the paper, opened it, and perceived that the will is almost exclusively in Theodore's favour. For an instant, a savage, puerile feeling of hate sprang erect in my bosom, and I came within an ace of obeying my foremost impulse—that of casting the document into the fire. Fortunately, my reason overtook my passion, though for a moment 'twas an even race. I replaced the paper in the secretary, closed it, and rang the bell for Robert (the old man's servant). Before he came I stood watching the poor, pale remnant of mortality before me, and wondering whether those feeble life-gasps were numbered. He was as white as a sheet, grimacing with pain—horribly ugly. Suddenly, he opened his eyes; they met my own; I fell on my knees and took his hands. They closed on mine with a grasp strangely akin to the rigidity of death. Nevertheless, since then he has revived, and has relapsed again into a comparatively healthy sleep. Robert seems to know how to deal with him.

22nd.—Mr. Sloane is seriously ill—out of his mind and unconscious of people's identity. The doctor has been here, off and on, all day, but this evening reports improvement. I have kept out of the old man's room, and confined myself to my own, reflecting largely upon the odd contingency of his immediate death. Does Theodore know of the will? Would it occur to him to divide the property? Would it occur to me, in his place? We met at dinner, and talked in a grave, desultory, friendly fashion. After all, he's an excellent fellow. I don't hate him. I don't even dislike him. He jars on me, *il m'agace*; but that's no reason why I should do him an evil turn. Nor shall I. The property is a fixed idea, that's all. I shall get it if I can. We're fairly matched. Before heaven, no, we're not fairly matched! Theodore has a conscience.

23rd.—I'm restless and nervous—and for good reasons. Scribbling here keeps me quiet. This morning Mr. Sloane is better; feeble and uncertain in mind, but unmistakably on the mend. I may confess now that I feel relieved of a weighty burden. Last night I hardly slept a wink. I lay awake listening to the pendulum of my clock. It seemed to say 'He lives—he dies.' I fully expected to hear it stop suddenly at *dies*. But it kept going all the morning, and to a decidedly more lively tune. In the afternoon the old man sent for me. I found him in his great muffled bed, with his face the colour of damp chalk, and his eyes glowing faintly, like torches half-stamped out. I was forcibly struck with the utter loneliness of his lot. For all human attendance, my villainous self grinning at his bedside, and old Robert without, listening, doubtless, at the keyhole. The *bonhomme* stared at me stupidly; then seemed to know me, and greeted me with a sickly smile. It was moments before he was able to speak. At last he faintly bade me to descend into the library, open the secret drawer of the secretary (which he contrived to direct me how to do), possess myself of his will, and burn it up. He appears to have forgotten his having removed it, night before last. I told him that I had an insurmountable aversion to any personal dealings with the document. He smiled, patted the back of my hand, and requested me, in that case, to get it, at least, and bring it to him. I couldn't deny him that favour? No, I couldn't, indeed. I went down to the library, therefore, and on entering the room found Theodore standing by the fireplace with a bundle of papers. The secretary was open. I stood still, looking from the ruptured cabinet to the documents in his hand. Among them I recognized, by its shape and size, the paper of which I had intended to possess myself. Without delay I walked straight up to him. He looked surprised, but not confused. 'I'm afraid I shall have to trouble you,' I said, 'to surrender one of those papers.'

'Surrender, Max? To anything of your own you are perfectly welcome. I didn't know, however, that you made use of Mr. Sloane's secretary. I was looking up some notes of my own making, in which I conceive I have a property.'

'This is what I want, Theodore,' I said; and I drew the will, unfolded, from between his hands. As I did so his eyes fell upon the superscription, 'Last Will and Testament. March. F. S.' He flushed a splendid furious crimson. Our eyes met. Somehow—I don't know how or why, or for that matter why not—I burst into a violent peal of laughter. Theodore stood staring, with two hot, bitter tears in his eyes.

'Of course you think,' he said, 'that I came to ferret out that thing.'

I shrugged my shoulders—those of my body only. I confess, morally, I was on my knees with contrition, but there was a fascination in it—a fatality. I remembered that in the hurry of my movements, the other evening, I had replaced the will simply in one of the outer drawers of the cabinet, among Theodore's own papers; doubtless where he had taken it up. 'Mr. Sloane sent me for it,' I said.

'Very good, I'm glad to hear he's well enough to think of such things.'

'He means to destroy it.'

'I hope, then, he has another made.'

'Mentally, I suppose he has.'

'Unfortunately, his weakness isn't mental—or exclusively so.'

'Oh, he'll live to make a dozen more,' I said. 'Do you know the purport of this one?'

Theodore's colour, by this time, had died away into a sombre paleness. He shook his head. The doggedness of the movement provoked me. I wished to arouse his curiosity. 'I have his commission,' I rejoined, 'to destroy it.'

Theodore smiled superbly. 'It's not a task I envy you,' he said.

'I should think not—especially if you knew the import of the will.' He stood with folded arms, regarding me with the remote contempt of his rich blue eyes. I couldn't stand it. 'Come, it's your property,' I cried. 'You're sole legatee. I give it up to you.' And I thrust the paper into his hand.

He received it mechanically; but after a pause, bethinking himself, he unfolded it and cast his eyes over the contents. Then he slowly refolded it and held it a moment with a tremulous hand. 'You say that Mr. Sloane directed you to destroy it?' he finally asked.

'I say so.'

'And that you know the contents?'

'Exactly.'

'And that you were about to comply?'

'On the contrary, I declined.'

Theodore fixed his eyes, for a moment, on the superscription, and then raised them again to my face. 'Thank you, Max,' he said. 'You've left me a real satisfaction.' He tore the sheet across and threw the bits into the fire. We stood watching them burn. 'Now he can make another,' said Theodore.

'Twenty others,' I replied.

'No,' said Theodore, 'you'll take care of that.'

'Upon my soul,' I cried, 'you're bitter!'

'No, not now. I worked off all my bitterness in these few words.'

'Well, in consideration of that, I excuse them.'

'Just as you please.'

'Ah,' said I, 'there's a little bitterness left!'

'No, nothing but indifference. Farewell.' And he put out his hand.

'Are you going away?'

'Of course I am. Farewell.'

'Farewell, then. But isn't your departure rather sudden?'

'I ought to have gone three weeks ago—three weeks ago.' I had taken his hand, he pulled it away, covered his face, and suddenly burst into tears.

'Is *that* indifference?' I asked.

'It's something you'll never know,' he cried. 'It's shame! I'm not sorry you should see it. It will suggest to you, perhaps, that my heart has never been in this filthy contest. Let me assure you, at any rate, that it hasn't; that it has had nothing but scorn for the base perversion of my pride and my ambition. These tears are tears of joy at their return—the return of the prodigals! Tears of sorrow—sorrow—'

He was unable to go on. He sank into a chair, burying his face in his handkerchief.

'For God's sake, Theodore,' I said, 'stick to the joy.'

He rose to his feet again. 'Well,' he said, 'it was for your sake that I parted with my self-respect; with your assistance I recover it.'

'How for my sake?'

'For whom but you would I have gone as far as I did? For what other purpose than that of keeping our friendship whole would I have borne you company into this narrow pass? A man whom I loved less I would long since have parted with. You were indeed— you and your incomparable gifts—to bring me to this. You ennobled, exalted, enchanted the struggle. I *did* value my prospects of coming into Mr. Sloane's property. I valued them for my poor sister's sake, as well as for my own, so long as they were the natural reward of conscientious service, and not the prize of hypocrisy and cunning. With another man than you I never would have contested such a prize. But I loved you, even as my rival. You played with me, deceived me, betrayed me. I held my ground, hoping and longing to purge you of your error by the touch of your old pledges of affection. I carried them in my heart. For Mr. Sloane, from the moment that, under your magical influence, he revealed his extraordinary foibles, I had nothing but contempt.'

'And for me now?'

'Don't ask me. I don't trust myself.'

'Hate, I suppose.'

'Is that the best you can imagine? Farewell.'

'Is it a serious farewell—farewell forever?'

'How can there be any other?'

'I'm sorry that such should be your point of view. It's characteristic. All the more reason then that I should say a word in self-defence. You accuse me of having "played with you, deceived you, betrayed you". It seems to me that you're quite off the track. You say you loved me. If so, you ought to love me still. It wasn't for my virtue; for I never had any, or pretended to any. In anything I have done recently, therefore, there has been no inconsistency. I never pretended to love you. I don't understand the word, in the sense you attach to it. I don't understand the feeling, between men. To me, love means quite another thing. You give it a meaning of your own; you enjoy the profit of your invention; it's no more than just that you should pay the penalty. Only, it seems to me rather hard that *I* should pay it.' Theodore remained silent; but his brow slowly contracted into an inexorable frown. 'Is it still a "serious farewell?"' I went on. 'It seems a pity. After this clearing up, it actually seems to me that I shall be on better terms with you. No man can have a deeper appreciation of your excellent faculties, a keener enjoyment of your society, your talk. I should very much regret the loss of them.'

'Have we, then, all this while,' said Theodore, 'understood each other so little?'

'Don't say "we" and "each other". I think I have understood you.'

'Very likely. It's not for want of my having confessed myself.'

'Well, Theodore, I do you justice. To me you've always been over generous. Try now, and be just.'

Still he stood silent, with his cold, hard frown. It was plain that, if he was to come back to me, it would be from a vast distance. What he was going to answer I know not. The door opened, and Robert appeared, pale, trembling, his eyes starting in his head.

'I verily believe, gentlemen,' he cried, 'that poor Mr. Sloane is dead in bed.'

There was a moment's perfect silence. 'Amen,' said I. 'Yes, Theodore, try and be just.' Mr. Sloane had quietly died in my absence.

24th.—Theodore went up to town this morning, having shaken hands with me in silence before he started. Doctor Jones, and Brookes the attorney, have been very officious; and, by their advice, I have telegraphed to a certain Miss Meredith, a maiden lady, by their account the nearest of kin; or, in other words, simply a discarded half-niece of the defunct. She telegraphs back that she will arrive in person for the funeral. I shall remain till she comes. I have lost a fortune; but have I irretrievably lost a friend? I'm sure I can't say.

Gabrielle De Bergerac

[First appeared in three instalments in the *Atlantic Monthly*, vol. xxiv (July 1869), pp. 55-71; vol. xxiv (August 1869), pp. 231-41; vol. xxiv (September 1869), pp. 352-61. Not reprinted during James's lifetime.]

PART I

MY GOOD OLD FRIEND, IN HIS WHITE FLANNEL DRESSING-gown, with his wig 'removed', as they say of the dinner-service, by a crimson nightcap, sat for some moments gazing into the fire. At last he looked up. I knew what was coming. 'Apropos, that little debt of mine—'

Not that the debt was really very little. But M. de Bergerac was a man of honour, and I knew I should receive my dues. He told me frankly that he saw no way, either in the present or the future, to reimburse me in cash. His only treasures were his paintings; would I choose one of them? Now I had not spent an hour in M. de Bergerac's little parlour twice a week for three winters, without learning that the Baron's paintings were, with a single exception, of very indifferent merit. On the other hand, I had taken a great fancy to the picture thus excepted. Yet, as I knew it was a family portrait, I hesitated to claim it. I refused to make a choice. M. de Bergerac, however, insisted, and I finally laid my finger on the charming image of my friend's aunt. I of course insisted, on my side, that M. de Bergerac should retain it during the remainder of his life, and so it was only after his decease that I came into possession of it. It hangs above my table as I write, and I have only to glance up at the face of my heroine to feel how vain it is to attempt to describe it. The portrait represents, in dimensions several degrees below those of nature, the head and shoulders of a young girl of two-and-twenty. The execution of the work is not especially strong, but it is thoroughly respectable, and one may easily see that the painter deeply appreciated the character of the face. The countenance is interesting rather than beautiful,—the forehead broad and open, the eyes slightly prominent, all the features full and firm and yet replete with gentleness. The head is slightly thrown back, as if in movement, and the lips are parted in a half-smile. And yet, in spite of this tender smile, I always fancy that the eyes are sad. The hair, dressed without powder, is rolled back over a high cushion (as I suppose), and adorned just above the left ear

with a single white rose; while, on the other side, a heavy tress from
behind hangs upon the neck with a sort of pastoral freedom. The
neck is long and full, and the shoulders rather broad. The whole
face has a look of mingled softness and decision, and seems to
reveal a nature inclined to revery, affection, and repose, but capable
of action and even of heroism. Mlle de Bergerac died under the
axe of the Terrorists. Now that I had acquired a certain property
in this sole memento of her life, I felt a natural curiosity as to her
character and history. Had M. de Bergerac known his aunt? Did
he remember her? Would it be a tax on his good-nature to suggest
that he should favour me with a few reminiscences? The old man
fixed his eyes on the fire, and laid his hand on mine, as if his
memory were fain to draw from both sources—from the ruddy
glow and from my fresh young blood—a certain vital, quickening
warmth. A mild, rich smile ran to his lips, and he pressed my
hand. Somehow,—I hardly know why,—I felt touched almost to
tears. Mlle. de Bergerac had been a familiar figure in her nephew's
boyhood, and an important event in her life had formed a sort of
episode in his younger days. It was a simple enough story; but
such as it was, then and there, settling back into his chair, with the
fingers of the clock wandering on to the small hours of the night,
he told it with a tender, lingering garrulity. Such as it is, I repeat
it. I shall give, as far as possible, my friend's words, or the English
of them; but the reader will have to do without his inimitable
accents. For them there is no English.

My father's household at Bergerac (said the Baron) consisted,
exclusive of the servants, of five persons,—himself, my mother, my
aunt (Mlle. de Bergerac), M. Coquelin (my preceptor), and
M. Coquelin's pupil, the heir of the house. Perhaps, indeed,
I should have numbered M. Coquelin among the servants.
It is certain that my mother did. Poor little woman! she
was a great stickler for the rights of birth. Her own birth was all she
had, for she was without health, beauty, or fortune. My father,
on his side, had very little of the last; his property of Bergerac
yielded only enough to keep us without discredit. We gave no
entertainments, and passed the whole year in the country; and as
my mother was resolved that her weak health should do her a kindness as well as an injury, it was put forward as an apology for
everything. We led at best a simple, somnolent sort of life. There
was a terrible amount of leisure for rural gentlefolks in those good
old days. We slept a great deal; we slept, you will say, on a volcano.
It was a very different world from this patent new world of yours,

and I may say that I was born on a different planet. Yes, in 1789, there came a great convulsion; the earth cracked and opened and broke, and this poor old *pays de France* went whirling through space. When I look back at my childhood, I look over a gulf. Three years ago, I spent a week at a country house in the neighbourhood of Bergerac, and my hostess drove me over to the site of the château. The house has disappeared, and there's a homœopathic —hydropathic—what do you call it?—establishment erected in its place. But the little town is there, and the bridge on the river, and the church where I was christened, and the double row of lime-trees on the market-place, and the fountain in the middle. There's only one striking difference: the sky is changed. I was born under the old sky. It was black enough, of course, if we had only had eyes to see it; but to me, I confess, it looked divinely blue. And in fact it was very bright,—the little patch under which I cast my juvenile shadow. An odd enough little shadow, you would have thought it. I was promiscuously cuddled and fondled. I was M. le Chevalier, and prospective master of Bergerac; and when I walked to church on Sunday, I had a dozen yards of lace on my coat and a little sword at my side. My poor mother did her best to make me good for nothing. She had her maid to curl my hair with the tongs, and she used, with her own fingers, to stick little black patches on my face. And yet I was a good deal neglected too, and I would go for days with black patches of another sort. I'm afraid I should have got very little education if a kind Providence hadn't given me poor M. Coquelin. A kind Providence, that is, and my father; for with my mother my tutor was no favourite. She thought him—and, indeed, she called him—a bumpkin, a clown. There was a very pretty abbé among her friends, M. Tiblaud by name, whom she wished to install at the château as my intellectual, and her spiritual, adviser; but my father, who, without being anything of an *esprit fort*, had an incurable aversion to a priest out of church, very soon routed this pious scheme. My poor father was an odd figure of a man. He belonged to a type as completely obsolete as the biggest of those big-boned, pre-historic monsters discovered by M. Cuvier. He was not overburdened with opinions or principles. The only truth that was absolute to his perception was that the house of Bergerac was *de bonne noblesse.* His tastes were not delicate. He was fond of the open air, of long rides, of the smell of the game-stocked woods in autumn, of playing at bowls, of a drinking-cup, of a dirty pack of cards, and a free-spoken tavern Hebe. I have nothing of him but his name. I strike you as an old fossil, a relic, a mummy. Good heavens! you should have seen him,—his good, his bad manners, his arrogance, his *bonhomie*, his stupidity and pluck.

My early years had promised ill for my health; I was listless and languid, and my father had been content to leave me to the women, who, on the whole, as I have said, left me a good deal to myself. But one morning he seemed suddenly to remember that he had a little son and heir running wild. It was I remember, in my ninth year, a morning early in June, after breakfast, at eleven o'clock. He took me by the hand and led me out on the terrace, and sat down and made me stand between his knees. I was engaged upon a great piece of bread and butter, which I had brought away from the table. He put his hand into my hair, and, for the first time that I could remember, looked me straight in the face. I had seen him take the forelock of a young colt in the same way, when he wished to look at its teeth. What did he want? Was he going to send me for sale? His eyes seemed prodigiously black and his eyebrows terribly thick. They were very much the eyebrows of that portrait. My father passed his other hand over the muscles of my arms and the sinews of my poor little legs.

'Chevalier,' said he, 'you're dreadfully puny. What's one to do with you?'

I dropped my eyes and said nothing. Heaven knows I felt puny.

'It's time you knew how to read and write. What are you blushing at?'

'I *do* know how to read,' said I.

My father stared. 'Pray, who taught you?'

'I learned in a book.'

'What book?'

I looked up at my father before I answered. His eyes were bright, and there was a little flush in his face,—I hardly knew whether of pleasure or anger. I disengaged myself and went into the drawing-room, where I took from a cupboard in the wall an odd volume of Scarron's *Roman comique*. As I had to go through the house, I was absent some minutes. When I came back I found a stranger on the terrace. A young man in poor clothes, with a walking-stick, had come up from the avenue, and stood before my father, with his hat in his hand. At the farther end of the terrace was my aunt. She was sitting on the parapet, playing with a great black crow, which we kept in a cage in the dining-room window. I betook myself to my father's side with my book, and stood staring at our visitor. He was a dark-eyed, sunburnt, young man, of about twenty-eight, of middle height, broad in the shoulders and short in the neck, with a slight lameness in one of his legs. He looked travel-stained and weary and pale. I remember there was something prepossessing in his being pale. I didn't know that the paleness came simply from his being horribly hungry.

'In view of these facts,' he said, as I came up, 'I have ventured to presume upon the good-will of M. le Baron.'

My father sat back in his chair, with his legs apart and a hand on each knee and his waistcoat unbuttoned, as was usual after a meal. 'Upon my word,' he said, 'I don't know what I can do for you. There's no place for you in my own household.'

The young man was silent a moment. 'Has M. le Baron any children?' he asked, after a pause.

'I have my son whom you see here.'

'May I inquire if M. le Chevalier is supplied with a preceptor?'

My father glanced down at me. 'Indeed, he seems to be,' he cried. 'What have you got there?' And he took my book. 'The little rascal has M. Scarron for a teacher. This is his preceptor!'

I blushed very hard, and the young man smiled. 'Is that your only teacher?' he asked.

'My aunt taught me to read,' I said, looking round at her.

'And did your aunt recommend this book?' asked my father.

'My aunt gave me M. Plutarque,' I said.

My father burst out laughing, and the young man put his hat up to his mouth. But I could see that above it his eyes had a very good-natured look. My aunt, seeing that her name had been mentioned, walked slowly over to where we stood, still holding her crow on her hand. You have her there before you; judge how she looked. I remember that she frequently dressed in blue, my poor aunt, and I know that she must have dressed simply. Fancy her in a light stuff gown, covered with big blue flowers, with a blue ribbon in her dark hair, and the points of her high-heeled blue slippers peeping out under her stiff white petticoat. Imagine her strolling along the terrace of the château with a villanous black crow perched on her wrist. You'll admit it's a picture.

'Is all this true, sister?' said my father. 'Is the Chevalier such a scholar?'

'He's a clever boy,' said my aunt, putting her hand on my head.

'It seems to me that at a pinch he could do without a preceptor,' said my father. 'He has such a learned aunt.'

'I've taught him all I know. He had begun to ask me questions that I was quite unable to answer.'

'I should think he might,' cried my father, with a broad laugh, 'when once he had got into M. Scarron!'

'Questions out of Plutarch,' said Mlle. de Bergerac, 'which you must know Latin to answer.'

'Would you like to know Latin, M. le Chevalier?' said the young man, looking at me with a smile.

'Do you know Latin,—you?' I asked.

'Perfectly,' said the young man, with the same smile.

'Do you want to learn Latin, Chevalier?' said my aunt.

'Every gentleman learns Latin,' said the young man.

I looked at the poor fellow, his dusty shoes and his rusty clothes. 'But you're not a gentleman,' said I.

He blushed up to his eyes. 'Ah, I only teach it,' he said.

In this way it was that Pierre Coquelin came to be my governor. My father, who had a mortal dislike to all kinds of cogitation and inquiry, engaged him on the simple testimony of his face and of his own account of his talents. His history, as he told it, was in three words as follows: He was of our province, and neither more nor less than the son of a village tailor. He is my hero: *tirez-vous de là*. Showing a lively taste for books, instead of being promoted to the paternal bench, he had been put to study with the Jesuits. After a residence of some three years with these gentlemen, he had incurred their displeasure by a foolish breach of discipline, and had been turned out into the world. Here he had endeavoured to make capital out of his excellent education, and had gone up to Paris with the hope of earning his bread as a scribbler. But in Paris he scribbled himself hungry and nothing more, and was in fact in a fair way to die of starvation. At last he encountered an agent of the Marquis de Rochambeau, who was collecting young men for the little army which the latter was prepared to conduct to the aid of the American insurgents. He had engaged himself among Rochambeau's troops, taken part in several battles, and finally received a wound in his leg of which the effect was still perceptible. At the end of three years he had returned to France, and repaired on foot, with what speed he might, to his native town; but only to find that in his absence his father had died, after a tedious illness, in which he had vainly lavished his small earnings upon the physicians, and that his mother had married again, very little to his taste. Poor Coquelin was friendless, penniless, and homeless. But once back on his native soil, he found himself possessed again by his old passion for letters, and, like all starving members of his craft, he had turned his face to Paris. He longed to make up for his three years in the wilderness. He trudged along, lonely, hungry, and weary, till he came to the gates of Bergerac. Here, sitting down to rest on a stone, he saw us come out on the terrace to digest our breakfast in the sun. Poor Coquelin! he had the stomach of a gentleman. He was filled with an irresistible longing to rest awhile from his struggle with destiny, and it seemed to him that for a mess of smoking pottage he would gladly exchange his vague and dubious future. In obedience to this simple impulse, —an impulse touching in its humility, when you knew the man,— he made his way up the avenue. We looked affable enough,—an honest country gentleman, a young girl playing with a crow, and a little boy eating bread and butter; and it turned out, we were as kindly as we looked.

For me, I soon grew extremely fond of him, and I was glad to think in later days that he had found me a thoroughly docile child. In those days, you know, thanks to Jean Jacques Rousseau, there was a vast stir in men's notions of education, and a hundred theories afloat about the perfect teacher and the perfect pupil. Coquelin was a firm devotee of Jean Jacques, and very possibly applied some of his precepts to my own little person. But of his own nature Coquelin was incapable of anything that was not wise and gentle, and he had no need to learn humanity in books. He was, never-theless, a great reader, and when he had not a volume in his hand he was sure to have two in his pockets. He had half a dozen little copies of the Greek and Latin poets, bound in yellow parchment, which, as he said, with a second shirt and a pair of white stockings, constituted his whole library. He had carried these books to America, and read them in the wilderness, and by the light of camp-fires, and in crowded, steaming barracks in winter-quarters. He had a passion for Virgil. M. Scarron was very soon dismissed to the cupboard, among the dice-boxes and the old packs of cards, and I was confined for the time to Virgil and Ovid and Plutarch, all of which, with the stimulus of Coquelin's own delight, I found very good reading. But better than any of the stories I read were those stories of his wanderings, and his odd companions and en-counters, and charming tales of pure fantasy, which, with the best grace in the world, he would recite by the hour. We took long walks, and he told me the names of the flowers and the various styles of the stars, and I remember that I often had no small trouble to keep them distinct. He wrote a very bad hand, but he made very pretty drawings of the subjects then in vogue,—nymphs and heroes and shepherds and pastoral scenes. I used to fancy that his knowledge and skill were inexhaustible, and I pestered him so for entertainment that I certainly proved that there were no limits to his patience.

When he first came to us he looked haggard and thin and weary;

but before the month was out, he had acquired a comfortable rotundity of person, and something of the sleek and polished look which befits the governor of a gentleman's son. And yet he never lost a certain gravity and reserve of demeanour which was nearly akin to a mild melancholy. With me, half the time, he was of course intolerably bored, and he must have had hard work to keep from yawning in my face,—which, as he knew I knew, would have been an unwarrantable liberty. At table, with my parents, he seemed to be constantly observing himself and inwardly regulating his words and gestures. The simple truth, I take it, was that he had never sat at a gentleman's table, and although he must have known himself incapable of a real breach of civility,—essentially delicate as he was in his feelings,—he was too proud to run the risk of violating etiquette. My poor mother was a great stickler for cere-mony, and she would have had her majordomo to lift the covers, even if she had had nothing to put into the dishes. I remember a cruel rebuke she bestowed upon Coquelin, shortly after his arrival. She could never be brought to forget that he had been picked up, as she said, on the roads. At dinner one day, in the absence of Mlle. de Bergerac, who was indisposed, he inadvertently occupied her seat, taking me as a *vis-à-vis* instead of a neighbour. Shortly after-wards, coming to offer wine to my mother, he received for all response a stare so blank, cold, and insolent, as to leave no doubt of her estimate of his presumption. In my mother's simple philo-sophy, Mlle. de Bergerac's seat could be decently occupied only by herself, and in default of her presence should remain conspicuously and sacredly vacant. Dinner at Bergerac was at best, indeed, a cold and dismal ceremony. I see it now,—the great dining-room, with its high windows and their faded curtains, and the tiles upon the floor, and the immense wainscots, and the great white marble chimney-piece, reaching to the ceiling,—a triumph of delicate carving,—and the panels above the doors, with their *galant* mythological paint-ings. All this had been the work of my grandfather, during the Regency, who had undertaken to renovate and beautify the château; but his funds had suddenly given out, and we could boast but a desultory elegance. Such talk as passed at table was between my mother and the Baron, and consisted for the most part of a series of insidious attempts on my mother's part to extort information which the latter had no desire, or at least no faculty, to impart. My father was constitutionally taciturn and apathetic, and he in-variably made an end of my mother's interrogation by proclaiming that he hated gossip. He liked to take his pleasure and have done with it, or at best, to ruminate his substantial joys within the conservative recesses of his capacious breast. The Baronne's inquisitive tongue was like a lambent flame, flickering over the sides of a rock. She had a passion for the world, and seclusion had only sharpened the edge of her curiosity. She lived on old memories—shabby, tarnished bits of intellectual finery—and vagrant rumours, anecdotes, and scandals.

Once in a while, however, her curiosity held high revel; for once a week we had the Vicomte de Treuil to dine with us. This gentleman was, although several years my father's junior, his most intimate friend and the only constant visitor at Bergerac. He brought with him a sort of intoxicating perfume of the great world, which I myself was not too young to feel. He had a marvellous fluency of talk; he was polite and elegant; and he was constantly getting letters from Paris, books, newspapers, and prints, and copies of the new songs. When he dined at Bergerac, my mother used to rustle away from table, kissing her hand to him, and actually light-headed from her deep potations of gossip. His conversation was a constant popping of corks. My father and the Vicomte, as I have said, were firm friends,—the firmer for the great diversity of their characters. M. de Bergerac was dark, grave, and taciturn, with a deep, sonorous voice. He had in his nature a touch of melancholy, and, in default of piety, a broad vein of superstition. The foundations of his soul, moreover, I am satisfied, in spite of the somewhat ponderous superstructure, were laid in a soil of rich tenderness and pity. Gaston de Treuil was of a wholly different temper. He was short and slight, without any colour, and with eyes as blue and lustrous as sapphires. He was so careless and gracious and mirthful, that to an unenlightened fancy he seemed the model of a joyous, reckless, gallant, impenitent *veneur*. But it sometimes struck me that, as he revolved an idea in his mind, it produced a certain flinty ring, which suggested that his nature was built, as it were, on rock, and that the bottom of his heart was hard. Young as he was, besides, he had a tired, jaded, exhausted look, which told of his having played high at the game of life, and, very possibly, lost. In fact, it was notorious that M. de Treuil had run through his property, and that his actual business in our neighbourhood was to repair the breach in his fortunes by constant attendance on a wealthy kinsman, who occupied an adjacent chateau, and who was dying of age and his infirmities. But while I thus hint at the existence in his composition of these few base particles, I should be sorry to represent him as substantially less fair and clear and lustrous than he appeared to be. He possessed an irresistible charm, and that of itself is a virtue. I feel sure, moreover, that my father would never have

reconciled himself to a real scantiness of masculine worth. The
Vicomte enjoyed, I fancy, the generous energy of my father's
good-fellowship, and the Baron's healthy senses were flattered by
the exquisite perfume of the other's infallible *savoir-vivre*. I offer
a hundred apologies, at any rate, to the Vicomte's luminous shade,
that I should have ventured to cast a dingy slur upon his name.
History has commemorated it. He perished on the scaffold, and
showed that he knew how to die as well as to live. He was the last
relic of the lily-handed youth of the *bon temps*; and as he looks
at me out of the poignant sadness of the past, with a reproachful
glitter in his cold blue eyes, and a scornful smile on his fine lips,
I feel that, elegant and silent as he is, he has the last word in our
dispute. I shall think of him henceforth as he appeared one night,
or rather one morning, when he came home from a ball with my
father, who had brought him to Bergerac to sleep. I had my bed
in a closet out of my mother's room, where I lay in a most un-
wholesome fashion among her old gowns and hoops and cosmetics.
My mother slept little; she passed the night in her dressing-gown,
bolstered up in her bed, reading novels. The two gentlemen came
in at four o'clock in the morning and made their way up to the
Baronne's little sitting-room, next to her chamber. I suppose they
were highly exhilarated, for they made a great noise of talking and
laughing, and my father began to knock at the chamber door.
He called out that he had M. de Treuil, and that they were cold
and hungry. The Baronne said that she had a fire and they might
come in. She was glad enough, poor lady, to get news of the ball,
and to catch their impressions before they had been dulled by
sleep. So they came in and sat by the fire, and M. de Treuil looked
for some wine and some little cakes where my mother told him. I
was wide awake and heard it all. I heard my mother protesting
and crying out, and the Vicomte laughing, when he looked into the
wrong place; and I am afraid that in my mother's room there were
a great many wrong places. Before long, in my little stuffy, dark
closet, I began to feel hungry too; whereupon I got out of bed and
ventured forth into the room. I remember the whole picture, as
one remembers isolated scenes of childhood: my mother's bed,
with its great curtains half drawn back at the side, and her little
eager face and dark eyes peeping out of the recess; then the two
men at the fire,—my father with his hat on, sitting and looking
drowsily into the flames, and the Vicomte standing before the
hearth, talking, laughing, and gesticulating, with the candlestick
in one hand and a glass of wine in the other,—dropping the wax
on one side and the wine on the other. He was dressed from head

to foot in white velvet and white silk, with embroideries of silver, and an immense *jabot*. He was very pale, and he looked lighter and slighter and wittier and more elegant than ever. He had a weak voice, and when he laughed, after one feeble little spasm, it went off into nothing, and you only knew he was laughing by his nodding his head and lifting his eyebrows and showing his handsome teeth. My father was in crimson velvet, with tarnished gold facings. My mother bade me get back into bed, but my father took me on his knees and held out my bare feet to the fire. In a little while, from the influence of the heat, he fell asleep in his chair, and I sat in my place and watched M. de Treuil as he stood in the firelight drinking his wine and telling stories to my mother, until at last I too relapsed into the innocence of slumber. They were very good friends, the Vicomte and my mother. He admired the turn of her mind. I remember his telling me several years later, at the time of her death, when I was old enough to understand him, that she was a very brave, keen little woman, and that in her musty solitude of Bergerac she said a great many more good things than the world ever heard of.

During the winter which preceded Coquelin's arrival, M. de Treuil used to show himself at Bergerac in a friendly manner; but about a month before this event, his visits became more frequent and assumed a special import and motive. In a word, my father and his friend between them had conceived it to be a fine thing that the latter should marry Mlle. de Bergerac. Neither from his own nor from his friend's point of view was Gaston de Treuil a marrying man or a desirable *parti*. He was too fond of pleasure to conciliate a rich wife, and too poor to support a penniless one. But I fancy that my father was of the opinion that if the Vicomte came into his kinsman's property, the best way to insure the preservation of it, and to attach him to his duties and responsibilities, would be to unite him to an amiable girl, who might remind him of the beauty of a domestic life and lend him courage to mend his ways. As far as the Vicomte was concerned, this was assuredly a benevolent scheme, but it seems to me that it made small account of the young girl's own happiness. M. de Treuil was supposed, in the matter of women, to have known everything that can be known, and to be as *blasé* with regard to their charms as he was proof against their influence. And, in fact, his manner of dealing with women, and of discussing them, indicated a profound disenchant-ment,— no bravado of contempt, no affectation of cynicism, but a cold, civil, absolute lassitude. A simply charming woman, therefore, would never have served the purpose of my father's theory. A very sound and liberal instinct led him to direct his thoughts to his sister. There were, of course, various auxiliary reasons for such disposal of Mlle. de Bergerac's hand. She was now a woman grown, and she had as yet received no decent proposals. She had no marriage portion of her own, and my father had no means to endow her. Her beauty, moreover, could hardly be called a dowry. It was without those vulgar allurements which, for many a poor girl, replace the glitter of cash. If within a very few years more she had not succeeded in establishing herself creditably in the world, nothing would be left for her but to withdraw from it, and to pledge her virgin faith to the chilly sanctity of a cloister. I was destined in the course of time to assume the lordship and the slender revenues of Bergerac, and it was not to be expected that I should be burdened on the very threshold of life with the maintenance of a dowerless maiden aunt. A marriage with M. de Treuil would be in all senses a creditable match, and, in the event of his becoming his kinsman's legatee, a thoroughly comfortable one.

It was some time before the colour of my father's intentions, and the milder hue of the Vicomte's acquiescence, began to show in our common daylight. It is not the custom, as you know, in our excellent France, to admit a lover on probation. He is expected to make up his mind on a view of the young lady's endowments, and to content himself before marriage with the bare cognition of her face. It is not thought decent (and there is certainly reason in it) that he should dally with his draught, and hold it to the light, and let the sun play through it, before carrying it to his lips. It was only on the ground of my father's warm good-will to Gaston de Treuil, and the latter's affectionate respect for the Baron, that the Vicomte was allowed to appear as a lover, before making his proposals in form. M. de Treuil, in fact, proceeded gradually, and made his approaches from a great distance. It was not for several weeks, therefore, that Mlle. de Bergerac became aware of them. And now, as this dear young girl steps into my story, where, I ask you, shall I find words to describe the broad loveliness of her person, to hint at the perfect beauty of her mind, to suggest the sweet mystery of her first suspicion of being sought, from afar, in marriage? Not in my fancy, surely; for there I should disinter the flimsy elements and tarnished properties of a superannuated comic opera. My taste, my son, was formed once for all fifty years ago. But if I wish to call up Mlle. de Bergerac, I must turn to my earliest memories, and delve in the sweet-smelling virgin soil of my heart.

For Mlle. de Bergerac is no misty sylphid nor romantic moonlit nymph. She rises before me now, glowing with life, with the sound of her voice just dying in the air,—the more living for the mark of her crimson death-satin.

There was every good reason why her dawning consciousness of M. de Treuil's attentions—although these were little more than projected as yet—should have produced a serious tremor in her heart. It was not that she was aught of a coquette; I honestly believe that there was no latent coquetry in her nature. At all events, whatever she might have become after knowing M. de Treuil, she was no coquette to speak of in her ignorance. Her ignorance of men, in truth, was great. For the Vicomte himself, she had as yet known him only distantly, formally, as a gentleman of rank and fashion; and for others of his quality, she had seen but a small number, and not seen them intimately. These few words suffice to indicate that my aunt led a life of unbroken monotony. Once a year she spent six weeks with certain ladies of the Visitation, in whose convent she had received her education, and of whom she continued to be very fond. Half a dozen times in the twelve-month she went to a ball, under convoy of some haply ungrudging *châtelaine*. Two or three times a month, she received a visit at Bergerac. The rest of the time she paced, with the grace of an angel and the patience of a woman, the dreary corridors and un-clipt garden walks of Bergerac. The discovery, then, that the brilliant Vicomte de Treuil was likely to make a proposal for her hand was an event of no small importance. With precisely what feelings she awaited its coming, I am unable to tell; but I have no hesitation in saying that even at this moment (that is, in less than a month after my tutor's arrival) her feelings were strongly modified by her acquaintance with Pierre Coquelin.

The word 'acquaintance' perhaps exaggerates Mlle. de Bergerac's relation to this excellent young man. Twice a day she sat facing him at table, and half a dozen times a week she met him on the staircase, in the saloon, or in the park. Coquelin had been accommodated with an apartment in a small untenanted pavilion, within the enclosure of our domain, and except at meals, and when his presence was especially requested at the château, he confined himself to his own precinct. It was there, morning and evening, that I took my lesson. It was impossible, therefore, that an intimacy should have arisen between these two young persons, equally separated as they were by material and conventional barriers. Nevertheless, as the sequel proved, Coquelin must, by his mere presence, have begun very soon to exert a subtle action on Mlle. de Bergerac's thoughts.

As for the young girl's influence on Coquelin, it is my belief that
he fell in love with her the very first moment he beheld her,—that
morning when he trudged wearily up our avenue. I need certainly
make no apology for the poor fellow's audacity. You tell me that
you fell in love at first sight with my aunt's portrait; you will
readily excuse the poor youth for having been smitten with the
original. It is less logical perhaps, but it is certainly no less natural,
that Mlle. de Bergerac should have ventured to think of my governor
as a decidedly interesting fellow. She saw so few men that one the
more or the less made a very great difference. Coquelin's importance, moreover, was increased rather than diminished by the fact
that, as I may say, he was a son of the soil. Marked as he was, in
aspect and utterance, with the genuine plebeian stamp, he opened
a way for the girl's fancy into a vague, unknown world. He stirred
her imagination, I conceive, in very much the same way as such
a man as Gaston de Treuil would have stirred—actually had stirred,
of course—the grosser sensibilities of many a little *bourgeoise*.
Mlle. de Bergerac was so thoroughly at peace with the consequences
of her social position, so little inclined to derogate in act or in
thought from the perfect dignity of her birth, that with the best
conscience in the world, she entertained, as they came, the feelings
provoked by Coquelin's manly virtues and graces. She had been
educated in the faith that *noblesse oblige*, and she had seen none
but gentlefolks and peasants. I think that she felt a vague, unavowed curiosity to see what sort of a figure you might make when
you were under no obligations to nobleness. I think, finally, that
unconsciously and in the interest simply of her unsubstantial dreams,
(for in those long summer days at Bergerac, without finery, without
visits, music, or books, or anything that a well-to-do grocer's daughter enjoys at the present day, she must, unless she was a far greater
simpleton than I wish you to suppose, have spun a thousand airy,
idle visions,) she contrasted Pierre Coquelin with the Vicomte de
Treuil. I protest that I don't see how Coquelin bore the contrast.
I frankly admit that, in her place, I would have given all my
admiration to the Vicomte. At all events, the chief result of any
such comparison must have been to show how, in spite of real
trials and troubles, Coquelin had retained a certain masculine freshness and elasticity, and how, without any sorrows but those of his
own wanton making, the Vicomte had utterly rubbed off this
primal bloom of manhood. There was that about Gaston de Treuil
that reminded you of an actor by daylight. His little row of foot-
lights had burned itself out. But this is assuredly a more pedantic

view of the cast than any that Mlle. de Bergerac was capable of taking. The Vicomte had but to learn his part and declaim it, and the illusion was complete.

Mlle. de Bergerac may really have been a great simpleton, and my theory of her feelings—vague and imperfect as it is—may be put together quite after the fact. But I see you protest; you glance at the picture; you frown. *C'est bon*; give me your hand. She received the Vicomte's gallantries, then, with a modest, conscious dignity, and courtesied to exactly the proper depth when he made her one of his inimitable bows.

One evening—it was, I think, about ten days after Coquelin's arrival—she was sitting reading to my mother, who was ill in bed. The Vicomte had been dining with us, and after dinner we had gone into the drawing-room. At the drawing-room door Coquelin had made his bow to my father, and carried me off to his own apartment. Mlle. de Bergerac and the two gentlemen had gone into the drawing-room together. At dusk I had come back to the château, and, going up to my mother, had found her in company with her sister-in-law. In a few moments my father came in, looking stern and black.

'Sister,' he cried, 'why did you leave us alone in the drawing-room? Didn't you see I wanted you to stay?'

Mlle. de Bergerac laid down her book and looked at her brother before answering. 'I had to come to my sister,' she said: 'I couldn't leave her alone.'

My mother, I'm sorry to say, was not always just to my aunt. She used to lose patience with her sister's want of coquetry, of ambition, of desire to make much of herself. She divined wherein my aunt had offended. 'You're very devoted to your sister, suddenly,' she said. 'There are duties and duties, mademoiselle. I'm very much obliged to you for reading to me. You can put down the book.'

'The Vicomte swore very hard when you went out,' my father went on.

Mlle. de Bergerac laid aside her book. 'Dear me!' she said, 'if he was going to swear, it's very well I went.'

'Are you afraid of the Vicomte?' said my mother. 'You're twenty-two years old. You're not a little girl.'

'Is she twenty-two?' cried my father. 'I told him she was twenty-one.'

'Frankly, brother,' said Mlle. de Bergerac, 'what does he want? Does he want to marry me?'

My father stared a moment. *'Pardieu!'* he cried.

'She looks as if she didn't believe it,' said my mother. 'Pray, did you ever ask him?'

'No, madam; did you? You are very kind.' Mlle. de Bergerac was excited; her cheek flushed.

'In the course of time,' said my father, gravely, 'the Vicomte proposes to demand your hand.'

'What is he waiting for?' asked Mlle. de Bergerac, simply.

'*Fi donc, mademoiselle!*' cried my mother.

'He is waiting for M. de Sorbières to die,' said I, who had got this bit of news from my mother's waiting-woman.

My father stared at me, half angrily; and then,—'He expects to inherit,' he said, boldly. 'It's a very fine property.'

'He would have done better, it seems to me,' rejoined Mlle. de Bergerac, after a pause, 'to wait till he had actually come into possession of it.'

'M. de Sorbières,' cried my father, 'has given him his word a dozen times over. Besides, the Vicomte loves you.'

Mlle. de Bergerac blushed, with a little smile, and as she did so her eyes fell on mine. I was standing gazing at her as a child gazes at a familiar friend who is presented to him in a new light. She put out her hand and drew me towards her. 'The truth comes out of the mouths of children,' she said. 'Chevalier, does he love me?'

'Stuff!' cried the Baronne; 'one doesn't speak to children of such things. A young girl should believe what she's told. I believed my mother when she told me that your brother loved me. He didn't, but I believed it, and as far as I know I'm none the worse for it.'

For ten days after this I heard nothing more of Mlle. de Bergerac's marriage, and I suppose that, childlike, I ceased to think of what I had already heard. One evening, about midsummer, M. de Treuil came over to supper, and announced that he was about to set out in company with poor M. de Sorbières for some mineral springs in the South, by the use of which the latter hoped to prolong his life.

I remember that, while we sat at table, Coquelin was appealed to as an authority upon some topic broached by the Vicomte, on which he found himself at variance with my father. It was the first time, I fancy, that he had been so honoured and that his opinions had been deemed worth hearing. The point under discussion must have related to the history of the American War, for Coquelin spoke with the firmness and fulness warranted by personal knowledge. I fancy that he was a little frightened by the sound of his own voice, but he acquitted himself with perfect good grace and success. We all sat attentive; my mother even staring a little surprised to find in a beggarly pedagogue a perfect *beau diseur*. My father, as became so great a gentleman, knew by a certain rough instinct when a man had something amusing to say. He leaned back, with his hands in his pockets, listening and paying the poor fellow the tribute of a half-puzzled frown. The Vicomte, like a man of taste, was charmed. He told stories himself, he was a good judge.

After supper we went out on the terrace. It was a perfect summer night, neither too warm nor too cool. There was no moon, but the stars flung down their languid light, and the earth, with its great dark masses of vegetation and the gently swaying tree-tops, seemed to answer back in a thousand vague perfumes. Somewhere, close at hand, out of an enchanted tree, a nightingale raved and carolled in delirious music. We had the good taste to listen in silence. My mother sat down on a bench against the house, and put out her hand and made my father sit beside her. Mlle. de Bergerac strolled to the edge of the terrace, and leaned against the balustrade, whither M. de Treuil soon followed her. She stood motionless, with her head raised, intent upon the music. The Vicomte seated himself upon the parapet, with his face towards her and his arms folded. He may perhaps have been talking, under cover of the nightingale. Coquelin seated himself near the other end of the terrace, and drew me between his knees. At last the nightingale ceased. Coquelin got up, and bade good night to the company, and made his way across the park to his lodge. I went over to my aunt and the Vicomte.

'M. Coquelin is a clever man,' said the Vicomte, as he disappeared down the avenue. 'He spoke very well this evening.'

'He never spoke so much before,' said I. 'He's very shy.'

'I think,' said my aunt, 'he's a little proud.'

'I don't understand,' said the Vicomte, 'how a man with any pride can put up with the place of a tutor. I had rather dig in the fields.'

'The Chevalier is much obliged to you,' said my aunt, laughing. 'In fact, M. Coquelin has to dig a little, hasn't he, Chevalier?'

'Not at all,' said I. 'But he keeps some plants in pots.'

At this my aunt and the Vicomte began to laugh. 'He keeps one precious plant,' cried my aunt, tapping my face with her fan.

At this moment my mother called me away. 'He makes them laugh,' I heard her say to my father, as I went to her.

'She had better laugh about it than cry,' said my father.

Before long, Mlle. de Bergerac and her companion came back toward the house.

'M. le Vicomte, brother,' said my aunt, 'invites me to go down and walk in the park. May I accept?'

'By all means,' said my father. 'You may go with the Vicomte as you would go with me.'

'Ah!' said the Vicomte.

'Come then, Chevalier,' said my aunt. 'In my turn, I invite you.'

'My son,' said the Baronne, 'I forbid you.'

'But my brother says,' rejoined Mlle. de Bergarac, 'that I may go with himself. He would not object to my taking my nephew.' And she put out her hand.

'One would think,' said my mother, 'that you were setting out for Siberia.'

'For Siberia!' cried the Vicomte, laughing; 'O no!'

I paused, undecided. But my father gave me a push. 'After all,' he said, 'it's better.'

When I overtook my aunt and her lover, the latter, losing no time, appeared to have come quite to the point.

'Your brother tells me, mademoiselle,' he had begun, 'that he has spoken to you.'

The young girl was silent.

'You may be indifferent,' pursued the Vicomte, 'but I can't believe you're ignorant.'

'My brother has spoken to me,' said Mlle. de Bergerac at last, with an apparent effort,—'my brother has spoken to me of his project.'

'I'm very glad he seemed to you to have espoused my cause so warmly that you call it his own. I did my best to convince him that I possess what a person of your merit is entitled to exact of the man who asks her hand. In doing so, I almost convinced myself. The point is now to convince you.'

'I listen.'

'You admit, then, that your mind is not made up in advance against me.'

'Mon Dieu!' cried my aunt, with some emphasis, 'a poor girl like me doesn't make up her mind. You frighten me, Vicomte. This is a serious question. I have the misfortune to have no mother. I can only pray God. But prayer helps me not to choose, but only to be resigned.'

'Pray often, then, mademoiselle. I'm not an arrogant lover, and since I have known you a little better, I have lost all my vanity. I'm not a good man nor a wise one. I have no doubt you think me very light and foolish, but you can't begin to know how light and foolish

I am. Marry me and you'll never know. If you don't marry me, I'm afraid you'll never marry.'

'You're very frank, Vicomte. If you think I'm afraid of never marrying, you're mistaken. One can be very happy as an old maid. I spend six weeks every year with the ladies of the Visitation. Several of them are excellent women, charming women. They read, they educate young girls, they visit the poor—'

The Vicomte broke into a laugh. 'They get up at five o'clock in the morning; they breakfast on boiled cabbage; they make flannel waistcoats, and very good sweetmeats! Why do you talk so, mademoiselle? Why do you say that you would like to lead such a life? One might almost believe it is coquetry. *Tenez*, I believe it's ignorance,—ignorance of your own feelings, your own nature, and your own needs.' M. de Treuil paused a moment, and, although I had a very imperfect notion of the meaning of his words, I remember being struck with the vehement look of his pale face, which seemed fairly to glow in the darkness. Plainly, he was in love. 'You are not made for solitude,' he went on; 'you are not made to be buried in a dingy old château, in the depths of a ridiculous province. You are made for the world, for the court, for pleasure, to be loved, admired, and envied. No, you don't know yourself, nor does Bergerac know you, nor his wife! I, at least, appreciate you. I know that you are supremely beautiful—'

'Vicomte,' said Mlle. de Bergerac, 'you forget—the child.'

'Hang the child! Why did you bring him along? *You* are no child. You can understand me. You are a woman, full of intelligence and goodness and beauty. They don't know you here, they think you a little demoiselle in pinafores. Before Heaven, mademoiselle, there is that about you,—I see it, I feel it here at your side, in this rustling darkness,—there is that about you that a man would gladly die for.'

Mlle. de Bergerac interrupted him with energy. 'You talk extravagantly. I don't understand you; you frighten me.'

'I talk as I feel. I frighten you? So much the better. I wish to stir your heart and get some answer to the passion of my own.'

Mlle. de Bergerac was silent a moment, as if collecting her thoughts. 'If I talk with you on this subject, I must do it with my wits about me,' she said at last. 'I must know exactly what we each mean.'

'It's plain then that I can't hope to inspire you with any degree of affection.'

'One doesn't promise to love. Vicomte; I can only answer for the present. My heart is so full of good wishes toward you that it costs me comparatively little to say I don't love you.'

'And anything I may say of my own feelings will make no difference to you?'

'You have said you love me. Let it rest there.'

'But you look as if you doubted my word.'

'You can't see how I look; Vicomte, I believe you.'

'Well, then, there is one point gained. Let us pass to the others. I'm thirty years old. I have a very good name and a very bad reputation. I honestly believe that, though I've fallen below my birth, I've kept above my fame. I believe that I have no vices of temper; I'm neither brutal, nor jealous, nor miserly. As for my fortune, I'm obliged to admit that it consists chiefly in my expectations. My actual property is about equal to your brother's, and you know how your sister-in-law is obliged to live. My expectations are thought particularly good. My great-uncle, M. de Sorbières, posses- ses, chiefly in landed estates, a fortune of some three millions of livres. I have no important competitors, either in blood or devotion. He is eighty-seven years old and paralytic, and within the past year I have been laying siege to his favour with such constancy that his surrender, like his extinction, is only a question of time. I received yesterday a summons to go with him to the Pyrenees, to drink certain medicinal waters. The least he can do, on my return, is to make me a handsome allowance, which with my own revenues will make—*en attendant* better things—a sufficient income for a reason- able couple.'

There was a pause of some moments, during which we slowly walked along in the obstructed starlight, the silence broken only by the train of my aunt's dress brushing against the twigs and pebbles.

'What a pity,' she said, at last, 'that you are not able to speak of all this good fortune as in the present rather than in the future.'

'There it is! Until I came to know you, I had no thoughts of marriage. What did I want of wealth? If five years ago I had fore- seen this moment, I should stand here with something better than promises.'

'Well, Vicomte,' pursued the young girl, with singular composure, 'you do me the honour to think very well of me: I hope you will not be vexed to find that prudence is one of my virtues. If I marry, I wish to marry well. It's not only the husband, but the marriage that counts. In accepting you as you stand, I should make neither a sentimental match nor a brilliant one.'

'Excellent. I love you, prudence and all. Say, then, that I present myself here three months hence with the titles and tokens of property amounting to a million and a half of livres, will you consider that I am a *parti* sufficiently brilliant to make you forget that you don't love me?'

'I should never forget that.'

'Well, nor I either. It makes a sort of sorrowful harmony! If three months hence, I repeat, I offer you a fortune instead of this poor empty hand, will you accept the one for the sake of the other?'

My aunt stopped short in the path. 'I hope, Vicomte,' she said, with much apparent simplicity, 'that you are going to do nothing indelicate.'

'God forbid, mademoiselle! It shall be a clean hand and a clean fortune.'

'If you ask then a promise, a pledge—'

'You'll not give it. I ask then only for a little hope. Give it in what form you will.'

We walked a few steps farther and came out from among the shadows, beneath the open sky. The voice of M. de Treuil, as he uttered these words, was low and deep and tender and full of entreaty. Mlle. de Bergerac cannot but have been deeply moved. I think she was somewhat awe-struck at having called up such a force of devotion in a nature deemed cold and inconstant. She put out her hand. 'I wish success to any honourable efforts. In any case you will be happier for your wealth. In one case it will get you a wife, and in the other it will console you.'

'Console me! I shall hate it, despise it, and throw it into the sea!'

Mlle. de Bergerac had no intention, of course, of leaving her companion under an illusion. 'Ah, but understand, Vicomte,' she said, 'I make no promise. My brother claims the right to bestow my hand. If he wishes our marriage now, of course he will wish it three months hence. I have never gainsaid him.'

'From now to three months a great deal may happen.'

'To you perhaps, but not to me.'

'Are you going to your friends of the Visitation?'

'No, indeed. I have no wish to spend the summer in a cloister. I prefer the green fields.'

'Well, then, *va* for the green fields! They're the next best thing. I recommend you to the Chevalier's protection.'

We had made half the circuit of the park, and turned into an alley which stretched away towards the house, and about midway in its course separated into two paths, one leading to the main avenue, and the other to the little pavilion inhabited by Coquelin. At the point where the alley was divided stood an enormous oak of great circumference, with a circular bench surrounding its trunk. It occupied, I believe, the central point of the whole domain. As we reached the oak, I looked down along the footpath towards the pavilion, and saw Coquelin's light shining in one of the windows. I immediately proposed that we should pay him a visit. My aunt objected, on the ground that he was doubtless busy and would not thank us for interrupting him. And then, when I insisted, she said it was not proper.

'How not proper?'

'It's not proper for me. A lady doesn't visit young men in their own apartments.'

At this the Vicomte cried out. He was partly amused, I think, at my aunt's attaching any compromising power to poor little Coquelin, and partly annoyed at her not considering his own company, in view of his pretensions, a sufficient guaranty.

'I should think,' he said, 'that with the Chevalier and me you might venture—'

'As you please, then,' said my aunt. And I accordingly led the way to my governor's abode.

It was a small edifice of a single floor, standing prettily enough among the trees, and still habitable, although very much in disrepair. It had been built by that same ancestor to whom Bergerac was indebted, in the absence of several of the necessities of life, for many of its elegant superfluities, and had been designed, I suppose, as a scene of pleasure,—such pleasure as he preferred to celebrate elsewhere than beneath the roof of his domicile. Whether it had ever been used I know not; but it certainly had very little of the look of a pleasure-house. Such furniture as it had once possessed had long since been transferred to the needy saloons of the chateau, and it now looked dark and bare and cold. In front, the shrubbery had been left to grow thick and wild and almost totally to exclude the light from the windows; but behind, outside of the two rooms which he occupied, and which had been provided from the chateau with the articles necessary for comfort, Coquelin had obtained my father's permission to effect a great clearance in the foliage, and he now enjoyed plenty of sunlight and a charming view of the neighbouring country. It was in the larger of these two rooms, arranged as a sort of study, that we found him.

He seemed surprised and somewhat confused by our visit, but he very soon recovered himself sufficiently to do the honours of his little establishment.

'It was an idea of my nephew,' said Mlle. de Bergerac. 'We were walking in the park, and he saw your light. Now that we are here, Chevalier, what would you have us do?'

'M. Coquelin has some very pretty things to show you,' said I.

Coquelin turned very red. 'Pretty things, Chevalier? Pray, what do you mean? I have some of your nephew's copy-books,' he said, turning to my aunt.

'Nay, you have some of your own,' I cried. 'He has books full of drawings, made by himself.'

'Ah, you draw?' said the Vicomte.

'M. le Chevalier does me the honour to think so. My drawings are meant for no critics but children.'

'In the way of criticism,' said my aunt, gently, 'we too are children. Her beautiful eyes, as she uttered these words, must have been quite as gentle as her voice. Coquelin looked at her, thinking very modestly of his little pictures, but loth to refuse the first request she had ever made him.

'Show them, at any rate,' said the Vicomte, in a somewhat peremptory tone. In those days, you see, a man occupying Coquelin's place was expected to hold all his faculties and talents at the disposal of his patron, and it was thought an unwarrantable piece of assumption that he should cultivate any of the arts for his own peculiar delectation. In withholding his drawings, therefore, it may have seemed to the Vicomte that Coquelin was unfaithful to the service to which he was held,—that, namely, of instructing, diverting, and edifying the household of Bergerac. Coquelin went to a little cupboard in the wall, and took out three small albums and a couple of portfolios. Mlle. de Bergerac sat down at the table, and Coquelin drew up the lamp and placed his drawings before her. He turned them over, and gave such explanations as seemed necessary. I have only my childish impressions of the character of these sketches, which, in my eyes, of course, seemed prodigiously clever. What the judgment of my companions was worth I know not, but they appeared very well pleased. The Vicomte probably knew a good sketch from a poor one, and he very good-naturedly pronounced my tutor an extremely knowing fellow. Coquelin had drawn anything and everything,—peasants and dumb brutes, landscapes and Parisian types and figures, taken indifferently from high and low life. But the best pieces in the collection were a series of illustrations and reminiscences of his adventures with the American army, and of the figures and episodes he had observed in the Colonies. They were for the most part rudely enough executed, owing to his want of time and materials, but they were full of *finesse* and character. M. de Treuil was very much amused at the rude equipments of your ancestors. There were sketches of the enemy too, whom Coquelin had apparently not been afraid to look in the face. While he was turning over these designs for Mlle. de

Bergerac, the Vicomte took up one of his portfolios, and, after a short inspection, drew from it, with a cry of surprise, a large portrait in pen and ink.

'*Tiens!*' said I; it's my aunt!'

Coquelin turned pale. Mlle. de Bergerac looked at him, and turned the least bit red. As for the Vicomte, he never changed colour. There was no eluding the fact that it was a likeness, and Coquelin had to pay the penalty of his skill.

'I didn't know,' he said, at random, 'that it was in that portfolio. Do you recognize it, mademoiselle?'

'Ah,' said the Vicomte, dryly, 'M. Coquelin meant to hide it.'

'It's too pretty to hide,' said my aunt; 'and yet it's too pretty to show. It's flattered.'

'Why should I have flattered you, mademoiselle?' asked Coquelin. 'You were never to see it.'

'That's what it is, mademoiselle,' said the Vicomte, 'to have such dazzling beauty. It penetrates the world. Who knows where you'll find it reflected next?'

However pretty a compliment this may have been to Mlle. de Bergerac, it was decidedly a back-handed blow to Coquelin. The young girl perceived that he felt it.

She rose to her feet. 'My beauty,' she said, with a slight tremor in her voice, 'would be a small thing without M. Coquelin's talent. We are much obliged to you I hope that you'll bring your pictures to the château, so that we may look at the rest.'

'Are you going to leave him this?' asked M. de Treuil, holding up the portrait.

'If M. Coquelin will give it to me, I shall be very glad to have it.'

'One doesn't keep one's own portrait,' said the Vicomte. 'It ought to belong to me.' In those days, before the invention of our sublime machinery for the reproduction of the human face, a young fellow was very glad to have his mistress's likeness in pen and ink.

But Coquelin had no idea of contributing to the Vicomte's gallery. 'Excuse me,' he said, gently, but looking the nobleman in the face. 'The picture isn't good enough for Mlle de Bergerac, but it's too good for anyone else'; and he drew it out of the other's hands, tore it across, and applied it to the flame of the lamp.

We went back to the château in silence. The drawing-room was empty; but as we went in, the Vicomte took a lighted candle from a table and raised it to the young girl's face. '*Parbleu!*' he exclaimed, 'the vagabond had looked at you to good purpose!'

Mlle. de Bergerac gave a half-confused laugh. 'At any rate,' she said, 'he didn't hold a candle to me as if I were my old smoke-

stained grandame, yonder!' and she blew out the light. 'I'll call my
brother,' she said, preparing to retire.

'A moment,' said her lover; 'I shall not see you for some weeks. I
shall start to-morrow with my uncle. I shall think of you by day,
and dream of you by night. And meanwhile I shall very much
doubt whether you think of me.'

Mlle. de Bergerac smiled. 'Doubt, doubt. It will help you to pass
the time. With faith alone it would hang very heavy.'

'It seems hard,' pursued M. de Treuil, 'that I should give you so
many pledges, and that you should give me none.'

'I give all I ask.'

'Then, for Heaven's sake, ask for something!'

'Your kind words are all I want.'

'Then give me some kind word yourself.'

'What shall I say, Vicomte?'

'Say,—say that you'll wait for me.'

They were standing in the centre of the great saloon, their figures
reflected by the light of a couple of candles in the shining inlaid
floor. Mlle. de Bergerac walked away a few steps with a look of
agitation. Then turning about, 'Vicomte,' she asked, in a deep, full
voice, 'do you truly love me?'

'Ah, Gabrielle!' cried the young man.

I take it that no woman can hear her baptismal name uttered
for the first time as that of Mlle. de Bergerac then came from her
suitor's lips without being thrilled with joy and pride.

'Well, M. de Treuil,' she said, 'I will wait for you.'

PART II

I remember distinctly the incidents of that summer at Bergerac;
or at least its general character, its tone. It was a hot, dry season;
we lived with doors and windows open. M. Coquelin suffered very
much from the heat, and sometimes, for days together, my lessons
were suspended. We put our books away and rambled out for a long
day in the fields. My tutor was perfectly faithful; he never allowed
me to wander beyond call. I was very fond of fishing, and I used
to sit for hours, like a little old man, with my legs dangling over
the bank of our slender river, patiently awaiting the bite that so
seldom came. Near at hand, in the shade, stretched at his length on
the grass, Coquelin read and re-read one of his half dozen Greek
and Latin poets. If we had walked far from home, we used to go
and ask for some dinner at the hut of a neighbouring peasant. For

a very small coin we got enough bread and cheese and small fruit
to keep us over till supper. The peasants, stupid and squalid as they
were, always received us civilly enough, though on Coquelin's
account quite as much as on my own. He addressed them with an
easy familiarity, which made them feel, I suppose, that he was, if
not quite one of themselves, at least by birth and sympathies much
nearer to them than to the future Baron de Bergerac. He gave me
in the course of these walks a great deal of good advice; and without perverting my signorial morals or instilling any notions that
were treason to my rank and position, he kindled in my childish
breast a little democratic flame which has never quite become
extinct. He taught me the beauty of humanity, justice, and tolerance; and whenever he detected me in a precocious attempt to
assert my baronial rights over the wetched little *manants* who
crossed my path, he gave me morally a very hard drubbing. He had
none of the base complaisance and cynical nonchalence of the traditional tutor of our old novels and comedies. Later in life I might
have found him too rigorous a moralist; but in those days I liked
him all the better for letting me sometimes feel the curb. It gave
me a highly agreeable sense of importance and maturity. It was a
tribute to half-divined possibilities of naughtiness. In the afternoon,
when I was tired of fishing, he would lie with his thumb in his book
and his eyes half closed and tell me fairy-tales till the eyes of both
of us closed together. Do the instructors of youth nowadays con-
descend to the fairy-tale pure and simple? Coquelin's stories belonged to the old, old world: no political economy, no physics, no
application to anything in life. Do you remember in Doré's illustrations to Perrault's tales, the picture of the enchanted castle of
the Sleeping Beauty? Back in the distance, in the bosom of an
ancient park and surrounded by thick baronial woods which
blacken all the gloomy horizon, on the farther side of a great
abysmal hollow of tangled forest verdure, rise the long façade, the
moss-grown terraces, the towers, the purple roofs, of a château of
the time of Henry IV. Its massive foundations plunge far down into
the wild chasm of the woodland, and its cold pinnacles of slate
tower upwards, close to the rolling autumn clouds. The afternoon
is closing in and a chill October wind is beginning to set the forest
a-howling. In the foreground, on an elevation beneath a mighty
oak, stand a couple of old woodcutters pointing across into the enchanted distance and answering the questions of the young prince.
They are the bent and blackened woodcutters of old France, of La
Fontaine's Fables and the *Médecin malgré lui*. What does the castle
contain? What secret is locked in its stately walls? What revel is

enacted in its long saloons? What strange figures stand aloof from
its vacant windows? You ask the question, and the answer is a long
revery. I never look at the picture without thinking of those summer afternoons in the woods and of Coquelin's long stories. His
fairies were the fairies of the *Grand Siècle*, and his princes and
shepherds the godsons of Perrault and Madame d'Aulnay. They
lived in such palaces and they hunted in such woods.

Mlle. de Bergerac, to all appearance, was not likely to break her
promise to M. de Treuil,—for lack of the opportunity, quite as
much as of the will. Those bright summer days must have seemed
very long to her, and I can't for my life imagine what she did with
her time. But she, too, as she had told the Vicomte, was very fond
of the green fields; and although she never wandered very far from
the house, she spent many an hour in the open air. Neither here
nor within doors was she likely to encounter the happy man of
whom the Vicomte might be jealous. Mlle. de Bergerac had a
friend, a single intimate friend, who came sometimes to pass the
day with her, and whose visits she occasionally returned. Marie de
Chalais, the granddaughter of the Marquis de Chalais, who lived
some ten miles away, was in all respects the exact counterpart and
foil of my aunt. She was extremely plain, but with that sprightly,
highly seasoned ugliness which is often so agreeable to men. Short,
spare, swarthy, light, with an immense mouth, a most impertinent
little nose, an imperceptible foot, a charming hand, and a delightful voice, she was, in spite of her great name and her fine clothes,
the very idea of the old stage *soubrette*. Frequently, indeed, in her
dress and manner, she used to provoke a comparison with this incomparable type. A cap, an apron, and a short petticoat were all
sufficient; with these and her bold, dark eyes she could impersonate
the very genius of impertinence and intrigue. She was a thoroughly
light creature, and later in life, after her marriage, she became
famous for her ugliness, her witticisms, and her adventures; but
that she had a good heart is shown by her real attachment to my
aunt. They were forever at cross-purposes, and yet they were excellent friends. When why aunt wished to walk, Mlle. de Chalais
wished to sit still; when Mlle. de Chalais wished to laugh, my aunt
wished to meditate; when my aunt wished to talk piety, Mlle. de
Chalais wished to talk scandal. Mlle de Bergerac, however, usually
carried the day and set the tune. There was nothing on earth that
Marie de Chalais so despised as the green fields; and yet you might
have seen her a dozen times that summer wandering over the
domain of Bergerac, in a short muslin dress and a straw hat, with
her arm entwined about the waist of her more stately friend. We

used often to meet them, and as we drew near Mlle. de Chalais would always stop and offer to kiss the Chevalier. By this pretty trick Coquelin was subjected for a few moments to the influence of her innocent *agaceries*; for rather than have no man at all to prick with the little darts of her coquetry, the poor girl would have gone off and made eyes at the scarecrow in the wheat-field. Coquelin was not at all abashed by her harmless advances; for although, in addressing my aunt, he was apt to lose his voice or his countenance, he often showed a very pretty wit in answering Mlle. de Chalais.

On one occasion she spent several days at Bergerac, and during her stay she proffered an urgent entreaty that my aunt should go back with her to her grandfather's house, where, having no parents, she lived with her governess. Mlle. de Bergerac declined, on the ground of having no gowns fit to visit in; whereupon Mlle de Chalais went to my mother, begged the gift of an old blue silk dress, and with her own cunning little hands made it over for my aunt's figure. That evening Mlle. de Bergerac appeared at supper in this renovated garment,—the first silk gown she had ever worn. Mlle. de Chalais had also dressed her hair, and decked her out with a number of trinkets and furbelows; and when the two came into the room together, they reminded me of the beautiful Duchess in Don Quixote, followed by a little dark-visaged Spanish waiting-maid. The next morning Coquelin and I rambled off as usual in search of adventures, and the day after that they were to leave the château. Whether we met with any adventures or not I forget; but we found ourselves at dinner-time at some distance from home, very hungry after a long tramp. We directed our steps to a little road-side hovel, where we had already purchased hospitality, and made our way in unannounced. We were somewhat surprised at the scene that met our eyes.

On a wretched bed at the farther end of the hut lay the master of the household, a young peasant whom we had seen a fortnight before in full health and vigour. At the head of the bed stood his wife, moaning, crying, and wringing her hands. Hanging about her, clinging to her skirts, and adding their piping cries to her own lamentations, were four little children, unwashed, unfed, and half clad. At the foot, facing the dying man, knelt his old mother—a horrible hag, so bent and brown and wrinkled with labour and age that there was nothing womanly left of her but her coarse, rude dress and cap, nothing of maternity but her sobs. Beside the pillow stood the priest, who had apparently just discharged the last offices of the Church. On the other side, on her knees, with the poor fellow's hand in her own, knelt Mlle. de Bergerac, like a consoling angel. On a stool near the door, looking on from a distance, sat Mlle. de Chalais, holding a little bleating kid in her arms. When she saw us, she started up. 'Ah, M. Coquelin!' she cried, 'do persuade Mlle. de Bergerac to leave this horrible place.'

I saw Mlle. de Bergerac look at the curé and shake her head, as if to say that it was all over. She rose from her knees and went round to the wife, telling her the same tale with her face. The poor, squalid *paysanne* gave a sort of savage, stupid cry, and threw herself and her rags on the young girl's neck. Mlle. de Bergerac caressed her, and whispered heaven knows what divinely simple words of comfort. Then, for the first time, she saw Coquelin and me, and beckoned us to approach.

'Chevalier,' she said, still holding the woman on her breast, 'have you got any money?'

At these words the woman raised her head. I signified that I was penniless.

My aunt frowned impatiently. 'M. Coquelin, have you?'

Coquelin drew forth a single small piece, all that he possessed; for it was the end of his month. Mlle. de Bergerac took it, and pursued her inquiry.

'Curé, have you any money?'

'Not a sou,' said the curé, smiling sweetly.

'Bah!' said Mlle. de Bergerac, with a sort of tragic petulance. 'What can I do with twelve sous?'

'Give it all the same,' said the woman, doggedly, putting out her hand.

'They want money,' said Mlle. de Bergerac, lowering her voice to Coquelin. 'They have had this great sorrow, but a *louis d'or* would dull the wound. But we're all penniless. O for the sight of a little gold!'

'I have a *louis* at home,' said I; and I felt Coquelin lay his hand on my head.

'What was the matter with the husband?' he asked.

'*Mon Dieu!*' said my aunt, glancing round at the bed. 'I don't know.'

Coquelin looked at her, half-amazed, half worshipping.

'Who are they, these people? What are they?' she asked.

'Mademoiselle,' said Coquelin, fervently, 'you're an angel!'

'I wish I were,' said Mlle. de Bergerac, simply; and she turned to the old mother.

We walked home together,—the curé with Mlle. de Chalais and me, and Mlle. de Bergerac in front with Coquelin. Asking how the two young girls had found their way to the death-bed we had just left, I learned from Mlle. de Chalais that they had set out for a stroll together, and, striking into a footpath across the fields, had gone farther than they supposed, and lost their way. While they were trying to recover it, they came upon the wretched hut where we had found them, and were struck by the sight of two children, standing crying at the door. Mlle. de Bergerac had stopped and questioned them to ascertain the cause of their sorrow, which with some difficulty she found to be that their father was dying of a fever. Whereupon, in spite of her companion's lively opposition, she had entered the miserable abode, and taken her place at the wretched couch, in the position in which we had discovered her. All this, doubtless, implied no extraordinary merit on Mlle. de Bergerac's part; but it placed her in a gracious, pleasing light.

The next morning the young girls went off in the great coach of M. de Chalais, which had been sent for them overnight, my father riding along as an escort. My aunt was absent a week, and I think I may say we keenly missed her. When I say we, I mean Coquelin and I, and when I say Coquelin and I, I mean Coquelin in particular; for it had come to this, that my tutor was roundly in love with my aunt. I didn't know it then, of course; but looking back, I see that he must already have been stirred to his soul's depths. Young as I was, moreover, I believe that I even then suspected his passion, and, loving him as I did, watched it with a vague, childish awe and sympathy. My aunt was to me, of course, a very old story, and I am sure she neither charmed nor dazzled my boyish fancy. I was quite too young to apprehend the meaning or the consequences of Coquelin's feelings; but I knew that he had a secret, and I wished him joy of it. He kept so jealous a guard on it that I would have defied my elders to discover the least reason for accusing him; but with a simple child of ten, thinking himself alone and uninterrupted, he showed himself plainly a lover. He was absent, restless, pre-occupied; now steeped in languid revery, now pacing up and down with the exaltation of something akin to hope. Hope itself he could never have felt; for it must have seemed to him that his passion was so audacious as almost to be criminal. Mlle. de Bergerac's absence showed him, I imagine, that to know her had been the event of his life; to see her across the table, to hear her voice, her tread, to pass her, to meet her eye, a deep, consoling, healing joy. It revealed to him the force with which she had grasped his heart, and I think he was half frightened at the energy of is passion.

One evening, while Mlle. de Bergerac was still away, I sat in his window, committing my lesson for the morrow by the waning light. He was walking up and down among the shadows. 'Chevalier,' said he, suddenly, 'what should you do if I were to leave you?'

My poor little heart stood still. 'Leave me?' I cried, aghast; 'why should you leave me?'

'Why, you know I didn't come to stay forever.'

'But you came to stay till I'm a man grown. Don't you like your place?'

'Perfectly.'

'Don't you like my father?'

'Your father is excellent.'

'And my mother?'

'Your mother is perfect.'

'And me, Coquelin?'

'You, Chevalier, are a little goose.'

And then, from a sort of unreasoned instinct that Mlle. de Bergerac was somehow connected with his idea of going away, 'And my aunt?' I added.

'How, your aunt?'

'Don't you like her?'

Coquelin had stopped in his walk, and stood near me and above me. He looked at me some moments without answering, and then sat down beside me in the window-seat, and laid his hand on my head.

'Chevalier,' he said, 'I will tell you something.'

'Well?' said I, after I had waited some time.

'One of these days you will be a man grown, and I shall have left you long before that. You'll learn a great many things that you don't know now. You'll learn what a strange, vast world it is, and what strange creatures men are—and women; how strong, how weak, how happy, how unhappy. You'll learn how many feelings and passions they have, and what a power of joy and of suffering. You'll be Baron de Bergerac and master of the château and of this little house. You'll sometimes be very proud of your title, and you'll sometimes feel very sad that it's so little more than a bare title. But neither your pride nor your grief will come to anything beside this, that one day, in the prime of your youth and strength and good looks, you'll see a woman whom you will love more than all these things,—more than your name, your lands, your youth, and strength, and beauty. It happens to all men, especially the good ones, and you'll be a good one. But the woman you love will be far out of your reach. She'll be a princess, perhaps she'll be the Queen. How can a poor little Baron de Bergerac expect her to look at him? You will give up your life for a touch of her hand; but what will she care for your life or your death? You'll curse your love, and yet you'll bless it, and perhaps—not having your living to get—you'll come up here and shut yourself up with your dreams and regrets. You'll come perhaps into this pavilion, and sit here alone in the twilight. And then, my child, you'll remember this evening; that I foretold it all and gave you my blessing in advance and—kissed you.' He bent over, and I felt his burning lips on my forehead.

I understood hardly a word of what he said; but whether it was that I was terrified by his picture of the possible insignificance of a Baron de Bergerac, or that I was vaguely overawed by his deep, solemn tones, I know not; but my eyes very quietly began to emit a flood of tears. The effect of my grief was to induce him to assure me that he had no present intention of leaving me. It was not, of course, till later in life, that, thinking over the situation, I understood his impulse to arrest his hopeless passion for Mlle. de Bergerac by immediate departure. He was not brave in time.

At the end of a week she returned one evening as we were at supper. She came in with M. de Chalais, an amiable old man, who had been so kind as to accompany her. She greeted us severally, and nodded to Coquelin. She talked, I remember, with great volubility, relating what she had seen and done in her absence, and laughing with extraordinary freedom. As we left the table, she took my hand, and I put out the other and took Coquelin's.

'Has the Chevalier been a good boy?' she asked.

'Perfect,' said Coquelin; 'but he has wanted his aunt sadly.'

'Not at all,' said I, resenting the imputation as derogatory to my independence.

'You have had a pleasant week, mademoiselle?' said Coquelin.

'A charming week. And you?'

M. Coquelin has been very unhappy,' said I. 'He thought of going away.'

'Ah?' said my aunt.

Coquelin was silent.

'You think of going away?'

'I merely spoke of it, mademoiselle. I must go away some time, you know. The Chevalier looks upon me as something eternal.'

'What's eternal?' asked the Chevalier.

'There is nothing eternal, my child,' said Mlle. de Bergerac. 'Nothing lasts more than a moment.'

'O,' said Coquelin. 'I don't agree with you!'

'You don't believe that in this world everything is vain and fleeting and transitory?'

'By no means; I believe in the permanence of many things.'

'Of what, for instance?'

'Well, of sentiments and passions.'

'Very likely. But not of the hearts that hold them. "Lovers die, but love survives." I heard a gentleman say that at Chalais.'

'It's better, at least, than if he had put it the other way. But lovers last too. They survive; they outlive the things that would fain destroy them,—indifference, denial, and despair.'

'But meanwhile the loved object disappears. When it isn't one, it's the other.'

'O, I admit that it's a shifting world. But I have a philosophy for that.'

'I'm curious to know your philosophy.'

'It's a very old one. It's simply to make the most of life while it lasts. I'm very fond of life,' said Coquelin, laughing.

'I should say that as yet, from what I know of your history, you have had no great reason to be.'

'Nay, it's like a cruel mistress,' said Coquelin. 'When once you love her, she's absolute. Her hard usage doesn't affect you. And certainly I have nothing to complain of now.'

'You're happy here then?'

'Profoundly, mademoiselle, in spite of the Chevalier.'

'I should suppose that with your tastes you would prefer something more active, more ardent.'

'*Mon Dieu*, my tastes are very simple. And then—happiness, *cela ne se raisonne pas*. You don't find it when you go in quest of it. It's like fortune; it comes to you in your sleep.'

'I imagine,' said Mlle. de Bergerac, 'that I was never happy.'

'That's a sad story,' said Coquelin.

The young girl began to laugh. 'And never unhappy.'

'Dear me, that's still worse. Never fear, it will come.'

'What will come?'

'That which is both bliss and misery at once.'

Mlle. de Bergerac hesitated a moment. 'And what is this strange thing?' she asked.

On his side Coquelin was silent. 'When it comes to you,' he said, at last, 'you'll tell me what you call it.'

About a week after this, at breakfast, in pursuance of an urgent request of mine, Coquelin proposed to my father to allow him to take me to visit the ruins of an ancient feudal castle some four leagues distant, which he had observed and explored while he trudged across the country on his way to Bergerac, and which, indeed, although the taste for ruins was at that time by no means so general as since the Revolution (when one may say it was in a measure created), enjoyed a certain notoriety throughout the province. My father good-naturedly consented; and as the distance was too great to be achieved on foot, he placed his two old coach-horses at our service. You know that although I affected, in boyish sort, to have been indifferent to my aunt's absence, I was really very fond of her, and it occurred to me that our excursion would be more solemn and splendid for her taking part in it. So I appealed to my father and asked if Mlle. de Bergerac might be allowed to go with us. What the Baron would have decided had he been left to himself I know not; but happily for our cause my mother cried out that, to her mind, it was highly improper that her sister-in-law should travel twenty miles alone with two young men.

'One of your young men is a child,' said my father, 'and her nephew into the bargain; and the other,'—and he laughed, coarsely but not ill-humouredly,—'the other is—Coquelin!'

'Coquelin is not a child nor is mademoiselle either,' said my mother.

'All the more reason for their going. Gabrielle, will you go?' My father I fear, was not remarkable in general for his tenderness or his *prévenance* for the poor girl whom fortune had given him to protect; but from time to time he would wake up to a downright sense of kinship and duty, kindled by the pardonable aggressions of my mother, between whom and her sister-in-law there existed a singular antagonism of temper.

Mlle. de Bergerac looked at my father intently and with a little blush. 'Yes, brother, I'll go. The Chevalier can take me *en croupe.*'

So we started, Coquelin on one horse, and I on the other, with my aunt mounted behind me. Our sport for the first part of the journey consisted chiefly in my urging my beast into a somewhat ponderous gallop, so as to terrify my aunt, who was not very sure of her seat, and who, at moments between pleading and laughing, had hard work to preserve her balance. At these times Coquelin would ride close alongside us, at the same cumbersome pace, declaring himself ready to catch the young girl if she fell. In this way we jolted along, in a cloud of dust, with shouts and laughter.

'Madame the Baronne was wrong,' said Coquelin, 'in denying that we are children.'

'O, this is nothing yet,' cried my aunt.

The castle of Fossy lifted its dark and crumbling towers with a decided air of feudal arrogance from the summit of a gentle eminence in the recess of a shallow gorge among the hills. Exactly when it had flourished and when it had decayed I knew not, but in the year of grace of our pilgrimage it was a truly venerable, almost a formidable, ruin. Two great towers were standing,—one of them

diminished by half its upper elevation, and the other sadly scathed
and shattered, but still exposing its hoary head to the weather, and
offering the sullen hospitality of its empty skull to a colony of
swallows. I shall never forget that day at Fossy; it was one of those
long raptures of childhood which seem to imprint upon the mind
an ineffaceable stain of light. The novelty and mystery of the
dilapidated fortress,—its antiquity, its intricacy, its sounding vaults
and corridors, its inaccessible heights and impenetrable depths, the
broad sunny glare of its grass-grown courts and yards, the twilight
of its passages and midnight of its dungeons, and along with all
this my freedom to rove and scramble, my perpetual curiosity, my
lusty absorption of the sun-warmed air, and the contagion of my
companions' careless and sensuous mirth,—all these things combined to make our excursion one of the memorable events of my
youth. My two companions accepted the situation and drank in
the beauty of the day and the richness of the spot with all my own
reckless freedom. Coquelin was half mad with the joy of spending
a whole unbroken summer's day with the woman whom he secretly
loved. He was all motion and humour and resonant laughter; and
yet intermingled with his random gaiety there lurked a solemn
sweetness and reticence, a feverish concentration of thought, which
to a woman with a woman's senses must have fairly betrayed his
passion. Mlle. de Bergerac, without quite putting aside her natural
dignity and gravity of mien, lent herself with a charming girlish
energy to the undisciplined spirit of the hour.

Our first thoughts, after Coquelin had turned the horses to
pasture in one of the grassy courts of the castle, were naturally
bestowed upon our little basket of provisions; and our first act was
to sit down on a heap of fallen masonry and divide its contents.
After that we wandered. We climbed the still practicable stair-
cases, and wedged ourselves into turrets and strolled through the
chambers and halls; we started from their long repose every echo
and bat and owl within the innumerable walls.

Finally, after we had rambled a couple of hours, Mlle. de Bergerac betrayed signs of fatigue. Coquelin went with her in search of
a place of rest, and I was left to my own devices. For an hour I
found plenty of diversion, at the end of which I returned to my
friends. I had some difficulty in finding them. They had mounted
by an imperfect and somewhat perilous ascent to one of the upper
platforms of the castle. Mlle. de Bergerac was sitting in a listless
posture on a block of stone, against the wall, in the shadow of the
still surviving tower; opposite, in the light, half leaning, half sitting
on the parapet of the terrace, was her companion.

'For the last half-hour, mademoiselle,' said Coquelin, as I came up, 'you've not spoken a word.'

'All the morning,' said Mlle. de Bergerac, 'I've been scrambling and chattering and laughing. Now, by reaction, I'm *triste.*'

'I protest, so am I,' said Coquelin. 'The truth is, this old feudal fortress is a decidedly melancholy spot. It's haunted with the ghost of the past. It smells of tragedies, sorrows, and cruelties.' He uttered these words with singular emphasis. 'It's a horrible place,' he pursued, with a shudder.

Mlle. de Bergerac began to laugh. 'It's odd that we should only just now have discovered it!'

'No, it's like the history of that abominable past of which it's a relic. At the first glance we see nothing but the great proportions, the show, and the splendour, but when we come to explore, we detect a vast underground world of iniquity and suffering. Only half this castle is above the soil; the rest is dungeons and vaults and *oubliettes.*'

'Nevertheless,' said the young girl, 'I should have liked to live in those old days. Shouldn't you?'

'Verily, no, mademoiselle!' And then after a pause, with a certain irrepressible bitterness: 'Life is hard enough now.'

Mlle. de Bergerac stared but said nothing.

'In those good old days,' Coquelin resumed, 'I should have been a brutal, senseless peasant, yoked down like an ox, with my forehead in the soil. Or else I should have been a trembling, groaning, fasting monk, moaning my soul away in the ecstasies of faith.'

Mlle. de Bergerac rose and came to the edge of the platform. 'Was no other career open in those days?'

'To such a one as me,—no. As I say, mademoiselle, life is hard now, but it was a mere dead weight then. I know it was. I feel in my bones and pulses that awful burden of despair under which my wretched ancestors struggled. *Tenez,* I'm the great man of the race. My father came next; he was one of four brothers, who all thought it a prodigious rise in the world when he became the village tailor. If we had lived five hundred years ago, in the shadow of these great towers, we should never have risen at all. We should have stuck with our feet in the clay. As I'm not a fighting man, I suppose I should have gone into the Church. If I hadn't died from an overdose of inanition, very likely I might have lived to be a cardinal.'

Mlle. de Bergerac leaned against the parapet, and with a meditative droop of the head looked down the little glen toward the plain and the highway. 'For myself,' she said, 'I can imagine very charming things of life in this castle of Fossy.'

'For yourself, very likely.'

'Fancy the great moat below filled with water and sheeted with lilies, and the drawbridge lowered, and a company of knights riding into the gates. Within, in one of those vaulted, quaintly timbered rooms, the châtelaine stands ready to receive them, with her women, her chaplain, her physician, and her little page. They come clanking up the staircase, with ringing swords, sweeping the ground with their plumes. They are all brave and splendid and fierce, but one of them far more than the rest. They each bend a knee to the lady—'

'But he bends two,' cried Coquelin. 'They wander apart into one of those deep embrasures and spin the threads of perfect love. Ah, I could fancy a sweet life, in those days, mademoiselle, if I could only fancy myself a knight!'

'And you can't,' said the young girl, gravely, looking at him.

'It's an idle game; it's not worth trying.'

'Apparently then, you're a cynic; you have an equally small opinion of the past and the present.'

'No; you do me injustice.'

'But you say that life is hard.'

'I speak not for myself, but for others; for my brothers and sisters and kinsmen in all degrees; for the great mass of *petits gens* of my own class.'

'Dear me, M. Coquelin, while you're about it, you can speak for others still; for poor portionless girls, for instance.'

'Are they very much to be pitied?'

Mlle. de Bergerac was silent. 'After all,' she resumed, 'they oughtn't to complain.'

'Not when they have a great name and beauty,' said Coquelin.

'O heaven!' said the young girl, impatiently, and turned away. Coquelin stood watching her, his brow contracted, his lips parted. Presently, she came back. 'Perhaps you think,' she said, 'that I care for my name,—my great name, as you call it.'

'Assuredly, I do.'

She stood looking at him, blushing a little and frowning. As he said these words, she gave an impatient toss of the head and turned away again. In her hand she carried an ornamented fan, an antiquated and sadly dilapidated instrument. She suddenly raised it above her head, swung it a moment, and threw it far across the parapet. 'There goes the name of Bergerac!' she said; and sweeping round, made the young man a very low courtesy.

There was in the whole action a certain passionate freedom which set poor Coquelin's heart a-throbbing. 'To have a good name, mademoiselle,' he said, 'and to be indifferent to it, is the sign of a noble mind.' (In parenthesis, I may say that I think he was quite wrong.)

'It's quite as noble, monsieur,' returned my aunt, 'to have a small name and not to blush for it.'

With these words I fancy they felt as if they had said enough; the conversation was growing rather too pointed.

'I think,' said my aunt, 'that we had better prepare to go.' And she cast a farewell glance at the broad expanse of country which lay stretched out beneath us, striped with the long afternoon shadows.

Coquelin followed the direction of her eyes. 'I wish very much,' he said, 'that before we go we might be able to make our way up into the summit of the great tower. It would be worth the attempt. The view from here, charming as it is, must be only a fragment of what you see from that topmost platform.'

'It's not likely,' said my aunt, 'that the staircase is still in a state to be used.'

'Possibly not; but we can see.'

'Nay,' insisted my aunt, 'I'm afraid to trust the Chevalier. There are great breaches in the sides of the ascent, which are so many open doors to destruction.'

I strongly opposed this view of the case; but Coquelin, after scanning the elevation of the tower and such of the fissures as were visible from our standpoint, declared that my aunt was right and that it was my duty to comply. 'And you, too, mademoiselle,' he said, 'had better not try it, unless you pride yourself on your strong head.'

'No, indeed, I have a particularly weak one. And you?'

'I confess I'm very curious to see the view. I always want to read to the end of a book, to walk to the turn of a road, and to climb to the top of a building.'

'Good,' said Mlle. de Bergerac. 'We'll wait for you.'

Although in a straight line from the spot which we occupied, the distance through the air to the rugged sides of the great cylinder of masonry which frowned above us was not more than thirty yards, Coquelin was obliged, in order to strike at the nearest accessible point the winding staircase which clung to its massive ribs, to retrace his steps through the interior of the castle and make a *détour* of some five minutes' duration. In ten minutes more he showed himself at an aperture in the wall, facing our terrace.

'How do you prosper?' cried my aunt, raising her voice.

'I've mounted eighty steps,' he shouted; 'I've a hundred more.'

Presently he appeared again at another opening. 'The steps have stopped,' he cried.

'You've only to stop too,' rejoined Mlle. de Bergerac. Again he was lost to sight and we supposed he was returning. A quarter of an hour elapsed, and we began to wonder at his not having over-taken us, when we heard a loud call high above our heads. There he stood, on the summit of the edifice, waving his hat. At this point he was so far above us that it was difficult to communicate by sounds, in spite of our curiosity to know how, in the absence of a staircase, he had effected the rest of the ascent. He began to represent, by gestures of pretended rapture, the immensity and beauty of the prospect. Finally Mlle. de Bergerac beckoned to him to descend, and pointed to the declining sun, informing him at the same time that we would go down and meet him in the lower part of the castle. We left the terrace accordingly, and, making the best of our way through the intricate passages of the edifice, at last, not without a feeling of relief, found ourselves on the level earth. We waited quite half an hour without seeing anything of our com-panion. My aunt, I could see, had become anxious, although she endeavoured to appear at her ease. As the time elapsed, however, it became so evident that Coquelin had encountered some serious obstacle to his descent, that Mlle. de Bergerac proposed we should, in so far as was possible, betake ourselves to his assistance. The point was to approach him within speaking distance.

We entered the body of the castle again, climbed to one of the upper levels, and reached a spot where an extensive destruction of the external wall partially exposed the great tower. As we approached this crumbling breach, Mlle. de Bergerac drew back from its brink with a loud cry of horror. It was not long before I discerned the cause of her movement. The side of the tower visible from where we stood presented a vast yawning fissure, which ex-plained the interruption of the staircase, the latter having fallen for want of support. The central column, to which the steps had been fastened, seemed, nevertheless, still to be erect, and to have formed, with the agglomeration of fallen fragments and various occasional projections of masonry, the means by which Coquelin, with extraordinary courage and skill, had reached the topmost plat-form. The ascent, then, had been possible; the descent, curiously enough, he seemed to have found another matter; and after striving in vain to retrace his footsteps, had been obliged to commit himself to the dangerous experiment of passing from the tower to the external surface of the main fortress. He had accomplished half his journey and now stood directly over against us in a posture which caused my young limbs to stiffen with dismay. The point to which he had directed himself was apparently the breach at which we stood; meanwhile he had paused, clinging in mid-air to heaven knows what narrow ledge or flimsy iron clump in the stone-work, and straining his nerves to an agonized tension in the effort not to fall, while his eyes vaguely wandered in quest of another footing. The wall of the castle was so immensely thick, that wherever he could embrace its entire section, progress was comparatively easy; the more especially as, above our heads, this same wall had been demolished in such a way as to maintain a rapid upward inclina-tion to the point where it communicated with the tower.

I stood staring at Coquelin with my heart in my throat, forgetting (or rather too young to reflect) that the sudden shock of seeing me where I was might prove fatal to his equipoise. He perceived me, however, and tried to smile. 'Don't be afraid,' he cried, 'I'll be with you in a moment.' My aunt, who had fallen back, returned to the aperture, and gazed at him with pale cheeks and clasped hands. He made a long step forward, successfully, and, as he recovered himself, caught sight of her face and looked at her with fearful intentness. Then seeing, I suppose, that she was sickened by his insecurity, he disengaged one hand and motioned her back. She retreated, paced in a single moment the length of the enclosure in which we stood, returned and stopped just short of the point at which she would have seen him again. She buried her face in her hands, like one muttering a rapid prayer, and then advanced once more within range of her friend's vision. As she looked at him, clinging in mid-air and planting step after step on the jagged and treacherous edge of the immense perpendicular chasm, she repressed another loud cry only by thrusting her handkerchief into her mouth. He caught her eyes again, gazed into them with piercing keenness, as if to drink in coolness and confidence, and then, as she closed them again in horror, motioned me with his head to lead her away. She returned to the farther end of the apartment and leaned her head against the wall. I remained staring at poor Coquelin, fascinated by the spectacle of his mingled danger and courage. Inch by inch, yard by yard, I saw him lessen the interval which threatened his life. It was a horrible, beautiful sight. Some five minutes elapsed; they seemed life fifty. The last few yards he accomplished with a rush; he reached the window which was the goal of his efforts, swung himself in and let himself down by a prodigious leap to the level on which we stood. Here he stopped, pale, lacerated, and drenched with perspiration. He put out his hand to Mlle. de Bergerac, who, at the sound of his steps, had turned herself about. On seeing him she made a few steps forward and burst into tears. I took his extended hand. He bent over me and kissed me, and then giving me a push, 'Go and kiss your poor aunt,' he said. Mlle. de Bergerac clasped me to her breast with a most convulsive pressure. From that moment till we reached home, there was very little said. Both my companions had matter for silent reflection,—Mlle. de Bergerac in the deep significance of that offered hand, and Coquelin in the rich avowal of her tears.

PART III

A week after this memorable visit to Fossy, in emulation of my good preceptor, I treated my friends, or myself at least, to a five minutes' fright. Wandering beside the river one day when Coquelin had been detained within doors to overlook some accounts for my father, I amused myself, where the bank projected slightly over the stream, with kicking the earth away in fragments, and watching it borne down the current. The result may be anticipated: I came very near going the way of those same fragments. I lost my foothold and fell into the stream, which, however, was so shallow as to offer no great obstacle to self-preservation. I scrambled ashore, wet to the bone, and, feeling rather ashamed of my misadventure, skulked about in the fields for a couple of hours, in my dripping clothes. Finally, there being no sun and my garments remaining inexorably damp, my teeth began to chatter and my limbs to ache. I went home and surrendered myself. Here again the result may be foreseen: the next day I was laid up with a high fever.

Mlle. de Bergerac, as I afterwards learned, immediately appointed herself my nurse, removed me from my little sleeping-closet to her own room, and watched me with the most tender care. My illness lasted some ten days, my convalescence a week. When I began to mend, my bed was transferred to an unoccupied room adjoining my aunt's. Here, late one afternoon, I lay languidly singing to myself and watching the western sunbeams shimmering on the opposite wall. If you were ever ill as a child, you will remember such moments. You look by the hour at your thin, white hands; you listen to the sounds in the house, the opening of doors and the tread of feet; you murmur strange odds and ends of talk; and you watch the fading of the day and the dark flowering of the night. Presently my aunt came in, introducing Coquelin, whom she left by my bedside. He sat with me a long time, talking in the old, kind way, and gradually lulled me to sleep with the gentle murmur of his voice. When I awoke again it was night. The sun was quenched on the opposite wall, but through a window on the same side came a broad ray of moonlight. In the window sat Coquelin, who had apparently not left the room. Near him was Mlle. de Bergerac.

Some time elapsed between my becoming conscious of their presence and my distinguishing the sense of the words that were passing between them. When I did so, if I had reached the age when one ponders and interprets what one hears, I should readily have perceived that since those last thrilling moments at Fossy their friendship had taken a very long step, and that the secret of each heart had changed place with its mate. But even now there was little that was careless and joyous in their young love; the first words of Mlle. de Bergerac that I distinguished betrayed the sombre tinge of their passion.

'I don't care what happens now,' she said. 'It will always be something to have lived through these days.'

'You're stronger than I, then,' said Coquelin. 'I haven't the courage to defy the future. I'm afraid to think of it. Ah, why can't we make a future of our own?'

'It would be a greater happiness than we have a right to. Who are you, Pierre Coquelin, that you should claim the right to marry the girl you love, when she's a demoiselle de Bergerac to begin with? And who am I, that I should expect to have deserved a greater blessing than that one look of your eyes, which I shall never, never forget? It is more than enough to watch you and pray for you and worship you in silence.'

'What am I? what are you? We are two honest mortals, who have a perfect right to repudiate the blessings of God. If ever a passion deserved its reward, mademoiselle, it's the absolute love I bear you. It's not a spasm, a miracle, or a delusion; it's the most natural emotion of my nature.'

'We don't live in a natural world, Coquelin. If we did, there would be no need of concealing this divine affection. Great heaven! who's natural? Is it my sister-in-law? Is it M. de Treuil? Is it my brother? My brother is sometimes so natural that he's brutal. Is it I myself? There are moments when I'm afraid of my nature.'

It was too dark for me to distinguish my companions' faces in the course of this singular dialogue; but it's not hard to imagine how, as my aunt uttered these words, with a burst of sombre *naïveté*, her lover must have turned upon her face the puzzled brightness of his eyes.

'What do you mean?' he asked.

'*Mon Dieu!* think how I have lived! What a senseless, thoughtless life! What solitude, ignorance, and languor! What trivial duties and petty joys! I have fancied myself happy at times, for it was God's mercy that I didn't know what I lacked. But now that my soul begins to stir and throb and live, it shakes me with its mighty pulsations. I feel as if in the mere wantonness of strength and joy it might drive me to some extravagance. I seem to feel myself making a great rush, with my eyes closed and my heart in my throat. And then the earth sinks away from under my feet, and in my ears is the sound of a dreadful tumult.'

'Evidently we have very different ways of feeling. For you our love is action, passion; for me it's rest. For you it's romance; for me it's reality. For me it's a necessity; for you (how shall I say it?) it's a luxury. In point of fact, mademoiselle, how should it be otherwise? When a demoiselle de Bergerac bestows her heart upon an obscure adventurer, a man born in poverty and servitude, it's a matter of charity, of noble generosity.'

Mlle. de Bergerac received this speech in silence, and for some moments nothing was said. At last she resumed: 'After all that has passed between us, Coquelin, it seems to me a matter neither of generosity nor of charity to allude again to that miserable fact of my birth.'

'I was only trying to carry out your own idea, and to get at the truth with regard to our situation. If our love is worth a straw, we needn't be afraid of that. Isn't it true—blessedly true, perhaps, for all I know—that you shrink a little from taking me as I am? Except for my character, I'm so little! It's impossible to be less of a *personage*. You can't quite reconcile it to your dignity to love a nobody, so you fling over your weakness a veil of mystery and romance and exaltation. You regard your passion, perhaps, as more of an escapade, an adventure, than it needs to be.'

'My "nobody",' said Mlle. de Bergerac, gently, 'is a very wise man, and a great philosopher. I don't understand a word you say.'

'Ah, so much the better!' said Coquelin with a little laugh.

'Will you promise me,' pursued the young girl, 'never again by word or deed to allude to the difference of our birth? If you refuse, I shall consider you an excellent pedagogue, but no lover.'

'Will you in return promise me—'

'Promise you what?'

Coquelin was standing before her, looking at her, with folded arms. 'Promise me likewise to forget it!'

Mlle. de Bergerac stared a moment, and also rose to her feet. 'Forget it! Is this generous?' she cried. 'Is it delicate? I had pretty well forgot it, I think, on that dreadful day at Fossy!' Her voice trembled and swelled; she burst into tears. Coquelin attempted to remonstrate, but she motioned him aside, and swept out of the room.

It must have been a very genuine passion between these two, you'll observe, to allow this handling without gloves. Only a plant of hardy growth could have endured this chilling blast of discord and disputation. Ultimately, indeed, its effect seemed to have been to fortify and consecrate their love. This was apparent several days later; but I know not what manner of communication they had had in the interval. I was much better, but I was still weak and languid. Mlle. de Bergerac brought me my breakfast in bed, and then, having helped me to rise and dress, led me out into the garden, where she had caused a chair to be placed in the shade. While I sat watching the bees and butterflies, and pulling the flowers to pieces, she strolled up and down the alley close at hand, taking slow stitches in a piece of embroidery. We had been so occupied about ten minutes, when Coquelin came towards us from his lodge, —by appointment, evidently, for this was a roundabout way to the house. Mlle. de Bergerac met him at the end of the path, where I could not hear what they said, but only see their gestures. As they came along together, she raised both hands to her ears, and shook her head with vehemence, as if to refuse to listen to what he was urging. When they drew near my resting-place, she had interrupted him.

'No, no, no!' she cried, 'I will never forget it to my dying day. How should I? How can I look at you without remembering it? It's in your face, your figure, your movements, the tones of your voice. It's you,—it's what I love in you! It was that which went through my heart that day at Fossy. It was the look, the tone, with which you called the place horrible; it was your bitter plebeian hate. When you spoke of the misery and baseness of your race, I could have cried out in an anguish of love! When I contradicted you, and pretended that I prized and honoured all these tokens of your servitude,—just heaven! you know now what my words were worth!'

Coquelin walked beside her with his hands clasped behind him, and his eyes fixed on the ground with a look of repressed sensibility. He passed his poor little convalescent pupil without heeding him. When they came down the path again, the young girl was still talking with the same feverish volubility.

'But most of all, the first day, the first hour, when you came up the avenue to my brother! I had never seen any one like you. I had seen others, but you had something that went to my soul. I devoured you with my eyes,—your dusty clothes, your uncombed hair, your pale face, the way you held yourself not to seem tired. I went down on my knees, then; I haven't been up since.'

The poor girl, you see, was completely possessed by her passion, and yet she was in a very strait place. For her life she wouldn't recede; and yet how was she to advance? There must have been an odd sort of simplicity in her way of bestowing her love; or perhaps you'll think it an odd sort of subtlety. It seems plain to me now, as I tell the story, that Coquelin, with his perfect good sense, was right, and that there was, at this moment, a large element of romance in the composition of her feelings. She seemed to feel no desire to realize her passion. Her hand was already bestowed; fate was inexorable. She wished simply to compress a world of bliss into her few remaining hours of freedom.

The day after this interview in the garden I came down to dinner; on the next I sat up to supper, and for some time afterwards, thanks to my aunt's preoccupation of mind. On rising from the table, my father left the château; my mother, who was ailing, returned to her room. Coquelin disappeared, under pretence of going to his own apartments; but, Mlle. de Bergerac having taken me into the drawing-room and detained me there some minutes, he shortly rejoined us.

'Great heaven, mademoiselle, this must end!' he cried, as he came into the room. 'I can stand it no longer.'

'Nor can I,' said my aunt. 'But I have given my word.'

'Take back your word, then! Write him a letter—go to him— send me to him—anything! I can't stay here on the footing of a thief and an impostor. I'll do anything,' he continued, as she was silent. 'I'll go to him in person; I'll go to your brother; I'll go to your sister even. I'll proclaim it to the world. Or, if you don't like that, I'll keep it a mortal secret. I'll leave the château with you without an hour's delay. I'll defy pursuit and discovery. We'll go to America,—anywhere you wish, if it's only action. Only spare me the agony of seeing you drift along into that man's arms.'

Mlle. de Bergerac made no reply for some moments. At last, 'I will never marry M. de Treuil,' she said.

To this declaration Coquelin made no response; but after a pause, 'Well, well, well?' he cried.

'Ah, you're pitiless!' said the young girl.

'No, mademoiselle, from the bottom of my heart I pity you.'

'Well, then, think of all you ask! Think of the inexpiable criminality of my love. Think of me standing here,—here before my mother's portrait,—murmuring out my shame, scorched by my sister's scorn, buffeted by my brother's curses! Gracious heaven,

Coquelin, suppose after all I were a bad, hard girl!'

'I'll suppose nothing; this is no time for hair-splitting.' And then, after a pause, as if with a violent effort, in a voice hoarse and yet soft: 'Gabrielle, passion is blind. Reason alone is worth a straw. I'll not counsel you in passion, let us wait till reason comes to us.' He put out his hand; she gave him her own; he pressed it to his lips and departed.

On the following day, as I still professed myself too weak to resume my books, Coquelin left the château alone, after breakfast, for a long walk. He was going, I suppose, into the woods and meadows in quest of Reason. She was hard to find, apparently, for he failed to return to dinner. He reappeared, however, at supper, but now my father was absent. My mother, as she left the table, expressed the wish that Mlle. de Bergerac should attend her to her own room. Coquelin, meanwhile, went with me into the great saloon, and for half an hour talked to me gravely and kindly about my studies, and questioned me on what we had learned before my illness. At the end of this time Mlle. de Bergerac returned.

'I got this letter to-day from M. de Treuil,' she said, and offered him a missive which had apparently been handed to her since dinner.

'I don't care to read it,' he said.

She tore it across and held the pieces to the flame of the candle. 'He is to be here to-morrow,' she added finally.

'Well?' asked Coquelin gravely.

'You know my answer.'

'Your answer to him, perfectly. But what is your answer to me?'

She looked at him in silence. They stood for a minute, their eyes locked together. And then, in the same posture,—her arms loose at her sides, her head slightly thrown back,—'To you,' she said, 'my answer is—farewell.'

The word was little more than whispered; but, though he heard it, he neither started nor spoke. He stood unmoved, all his soul trembling under his brows and filling the space between his mistress and himself with a sort of sacred stillness. Then, gradually, his head sank on his breast, and his eyes dropped on the ground.

'It's reason,' the young girl began. 'Reason has come to me. She tells me that if I marry in my brother's despite, and in opposition to all the traditions that have been kept sacred in my family, I shall neither find happiness nor give it. I must choose the simplest course. The other is a gulf; I can't leap it. It's harder than you think. Something in the air forbids it,—something in the very look of these old walls, within which I was born and I've lived. I shall never marry; I shall go into religion. I tried to fling away my name; it was sowing dragons' teeth. I don't ask you to forgive me. It's small enough comfort that you should have the right to think of me as a poor, weak heart. Keep repeating that: it will console you. I shall not have the compensation of doubting the perfection of what I love.'

Coquelin turned away in silence. Mlle. de Bergerac sprang after him. 'In Heaven's name,' she cried, 'say something! Rave, storm, swear, but don't let me think I've broken your heart.'

'My heart's sound,' said Coquelin, almost with a smile. 'I regret nothing that has happened. O, how I love you!'

The young girl buried her face in her hands.

'This end,' he went on, 'is doubtless the only possible one. It's thinking very lightly of life to expect any other. After all, what call had I to interrupt your life,—to burden you with a trouble, a choice, a decision? As much as anything that I have ever known in you I admire your beautiful delicacy of conscience.'

'Ah,' said the young girl, with a moan, 'don't kill me with fine names!'

And then came the farewell. 'I feel,' said poor Coquelin, 'that I can't see you again. We must not meet. I will leave Bergerac immediately,—to-night,—under pretext of having been summoned home by my mother's illness. In a few days I will write to your brother that circumstances forbid me to return.'

My own part in this painful interview I shall not describe at length. When it began to dawn upon my mind that my friend was actually going to disappear, I was seized with a convulsion of rage and grief. 'Ah,' cried Mlle. de Bergerac bitterly, 'that was all that was wanting!' What means were taken to restore me to composure, what promises were made me, what pious deception was practised, I forget; but, when at last I came to my senses, Coquelin had made his exit.

My aunt took me by the hand and prepared to lead me up to bed, fearing naturally that my ruffled aspect and swollen visage would arouse suspicion. At this moment I heard the clatter of hoofs in the court, mingled with the sound of voices. From the window, I saw M. de Treuil and my father alighting from horseback. Mlle. de Bergerac, apparently, made the same observation; she dropped my hand and sank down in a chair. She was not left long in suspense. Perceiving a light in the saloon, the two gentlemen immediately made their way to this apartment. They came in together, arm in arm, the Vicomte dressed in mourning. Just within the threshold they stopped; my father disengaged his arm, took his companion by the hand and led him to Mlle. de Bergerac. She rose to her feet as you may imagine a sitting statue to rise. The Vicomte bent his knee.

'At last, mademoiselle,' said he,—'sooner than I had hoped,—my long probation is finished.'

The young girl spoke, but no one would have recognized her voice. 'I fear, M. le Vicomte,' she said, 'that it has only begun.'

The Vicomte broke into a harsh, nervous laugh.

'Fol de rol, mademoiselle,' cried my father, 'your pleasantry is in very bad taste.'

But the Vicomte had recovered himself. 'Mademoiselle is quite right,' he declared; 'she means that I must now begin to deserve my happiness.' This little speech showed a very brave fancy. It was in flagrant discord with the expression of the poor girl's figure, as she stood twisting her hands together and rolling her eyes,— an image of sombre desperation.

My father felt there was a storm in the air. 'M. le Vicomte is in mourning for M. de Sorbrières,' he said. 'M. le Vicomte is his sole legatee. He comes to exact the fulfilment of your promise.'

'I made no promise,' said Mlle. de Bergerac.

'Excuse me, mademoiselle; you gave your word that you'd wait for me.'

'Gracious heaven!' cried the young girl; 'haven't I waited for you!'

'*Ma toute belle*,' said the Baron, trying to keep his angry voice within the compass of an undertone, and reducing it in the effort to a very ugly whisper, 'if I had supposed you were going to make us a scene, *nom de Dieu!* I would have taken my precautions before-hand! You know what you're to expect. Vicomte, keep her to her word. I'll give you half an hour. Come, Chevalier.' And he took me by the hand.

We had crossed the threshold and reached the hall, when I heard the Vicomte give a long moan, half plaintive, half indignant. My father turned, and answered with a fierce, inarticulate cry, which I can best describe as a roar. He straightway retraced his steps, I, of course, following. Exactly what, in the brief interval, had passed between our companions I am unable to say; but it was plain that Mlle. de Bergerac, by some cruelly unerring word or act, had dis-charged the bolt of her refusal. Her gallant lover had sunk into a chair, burying his face in his hands, and stamping his feet on the floor in a frenzy of disappointment. She stood regarding him in a sort of helpless, distant pity. My father had been going to break out into a storm of imprecations; but he suppressed them, and folded his arms.

'And now, mademoiselle,' he said, 'will you be so good as to inform me of your intentions.'

Beneath my father's gaze the softness passed out of my aunt's face and gave place to an angry defiance, which he must have recognized as cousin-german, at least, to the passion in his own breast. 'My intentions had been,' she said, 'to let M. le Vicomte know that I couldn't marry him, with as little offence as possible. But you seem determined, my brother, to thrust in a world of offence somewhere.'

You must not blame Mlle. de Bergerac for the sting of her retort. She foresaw a hard fight; she had only sprung to her arms.

My father looked at the wretched Vicomte, as he sat sobbing and stamping like a child. His bosom was wrung with pity for his friend. 'Look at that dear Gaston, that charming man, and blush for your audacity.'

'I know a great deal more about my audacity than you, brother. I might tell you things that would surprise you.'

'Gabrielle, you are mad!' the Baron broke out.

'Perhaps I am,' said the young girl. And then, turning to M. de Treuil, in a tone of exquisite reproach, 'M. le Vicomte, you suffer less well than I had hoped.'

My father could endure no more. He seized his sister by her two wrists, so that beneath the pressure her eyes filled with tears. 'Heartless fool!' he cried, 'do you know what I can do to you?'

'I can imagine, from this specimen,' said the poor creature.

The Baron was beside himself with passion. 'Down, down on your knees,' he went on, 'and beg our pardon all round for your senseless, shameless perversity!' As he spoke, he increased the pressure of his grasp to that degree that, after a vain struggle to free herself, she uttered a scream of pain. The Vicomte sprang to his feet. 'In heaven's name, Gabrielle,' he cried,—and it was the only real *naïveté* that he had ever uttered,—'isn't it all a horrible jest?'

Mlle. de Bergerac shook her head. 'It seems hard, Vicomte,' she said, 'that I should be answerable for your happiness.'

'You hold it there in your hand. Think of what I suffer. To have lived for weeks in the hope of this hour, and to find it what you would fain make it! To have dreamed of rapturous bliss, and to wake to find it hideous misery! Think of it once again!'

'She shall have a chance to think of it,' the Baron declared; 'she shall think of it quite at her ease. Go to your room, mademoiselle, and remain there till further notice.'

Gabrielle prepared to go, but, as she moved away, 'I used to fear you, brother,' she said with homely scorn, 'but I don't fear you now. Judge whether it's because I love you more!'

'Gabrielle,' the Vicomte cried out, 'I haven't given you up.'

'Your feelings are your own, M. le Vicomte. I would have given more than I can say rather than have caused you to suffer. Your asking my hand has been the great honour of my life; my withholding it has been the great trial.' And she walked out of the room with the step of unacted tragedy. My father, with an oath, despatched me to bed in her train. Heavy-headed with the recent spectacle of so much half-apprehended emotion, I speedily fell asleep.

I was aroused by the sound of voices, and the grasp of a heavy hand on my shoulder. My father stood before me, holding a candle, with M. de Treuil beside him. 'Chevalier,' he said, 'open your eyes like a man, and come to your senses.'

Thus exhorted, I sat up and stared. The Baron sat down on the edge of the bed. 'This evening,' he began, 'before the Vicomte and I came in, were you alone with your aunt?'—My dear friend, you see the scene from here. I answered with the cruel directness of my years. Even if I had had the wit to dissemble, I should have lacked the courage. Of course I had no story to tell. I had drawn no inferences; I didn't say that my tutor was my aunt's lover. I simply said that he had been with us after supper, and that he wanted my aunt to go away with him. Such was my part in the play. I see the whole picture again,—my father brandishing the candlestick, and devouring my words with his great flaming eyes; and the Vicomte behind, portentously silent, with his black clothes and his pale face.

They had not been three minutes out of the room when the door leading to my aunt's chamber opened and Mlle. de Bergerac appeared. She had heard sounds in my apartment, and suspected the visit of the gentlemen and its motive. She immediately won from me the recital of what I had been forced to avow. 'Poor Chevalier,' she cried, for all commentary. And then, after a pause, 'What made them suspect that M. Coquelin had been with us?'

'They saw him, or some one, leave the château as they came in.'

'And where have they gone now?'

'To supper. My father said to M. de Treuil that first of all they must sup.'

Mlle. de Bergerac stood a moment in meditation. Then suddenly, 'Get up, Chevalier,' she said, 'I want you to go with me.'

'Where are you going?'

'To M. Coquelin's.'

I needed no second admonition. I hustled on my clothes; Mlle. de Bergerac left the room and immediately returned, clad in a light mantle. We made our way undiscovered to one of the private entrances of the château, hurried across the park and found a light in the window of Coquelin's lodge. It was about half past nine. Mlle. de Bergerac gave a loud knock at the door, and we entered her lover's apartment.

Coquelin was seated at his table writing. He sprang to his feet with a cry of amazement. Mlle. de Bergerac stood panting, with one hand pressed to her heart, while rapidly moving the other as if to enjoin calmness.

'They are come back,' she began,—'M. de Treuil and my brother!'

'I thought he was to come to-morrow. Was it a deception?'

'Ah, no! not from him,—an accident. Pierre Coquelin, I've had such a scene! But it's not your fault.'

'What made the scene?'

'My refusal, of course.'

'You turned off the Vicomte?'

'Holy Virgin! You ask me?'

'Unhappy girl!' cried Coquelin.

'No, I was a happy girl to have had a chance to act as my heart bade me. I had faltered enough. But it was hard!'

'It's all hard.'

'The hardest is to come,' said my aunt. She put out her hand; he sprang to her and seized it, and she pressed his own with vehemence. 'They have discovered our secret,—don't ask how. It was Heaven's will. From this moment, of course—'

'From this moment, of course,' cried Coquelin, 'I stay where I am!'

With an impetuous movement she raised his hand to her lips and kissed it. 'You stay where you are. We have nothing to conceal, but we have nothing to avow. We have no confessions to make. Before God we have done our duty. You may expect them, I fancy to-night; perhaps, too, they will honour me with a visit. They are supping between two battles. They will attack us with fury, I know; but let them dash themselves against our silence as against a wall of stone. I have taken my stand. My love, my errors, my longings, are my own affair. My reputation is a sealed book. Woe to him who would force it open!'

The poor girl had said once, you know, that she was afraid of her nature. Assuredly it had now sprung erect in its strength; it came hurrying into action on the wings of her indignation.

'Remember, Coquelin,' she went on, 'you are still and always my friend. You are the guardian of my weakness, the support of my strength.'

'Say it all, Gabrielle!' he cried. 'I'm for ever and ever your lover!'

Suddenly, above the music of his voice, there came a great rattling knock at the door. Coquelin sprang forward; it opened in his face and disclosed my father and M. de Treuil. I have no words in my dictionary, no images in my rhetoric, to represent the sudden horror that leaped into my father's face as his eye fell upon his sister. He staggered back a step and then stood glaring, until his feelings found utterance in a single word: *'Coureuse!'* I have never been able to look upon the word as trivial since that moment.

The Vicomte came striding past him into the room, like a bolt of lightning from a rumbling cloud, quivering with baffled desire, and looking taller by the head for his passion. 'And it was for this, mademoiselle,' he cried, 'and for *that!*' and he flung out a scornful hand toward Coquelin. 'For a beggarly, boorish, ignorant pedagogue!'

Coquelin folded his arms. 'Address me directly, M. le Vicomte,' he said; 'don't fling mud at me over mademoiselle's head.'

'You? Who are you?' hissed the nobleman. 'A man doesn't address you; he sends his lackeys to flog you!'

'Well, M. le Vicomte, you're complete,' said Coquelin, eying him from head to foot.

'Complete?' and M. de Treuil broke into an almost hysterical laugh. 'I only lack having married your mistress!'

'Ah!' cried Mlle. de Bergerac.

'O, you poor, insensate fool!' said Coquelin.

'Heaven help me,' the young man went on, 'I'm ready to marry her still.'

While these words were rapidly exchanged, my father stood choking with the confusion of amazement and rage. He was stupefied at his sister's audacity,—at the dauntless spirit which ventured to flaunt its shameful passion in the very face of honour and authority. Yet that simple interjection which I have quoted from my aunt's lips stirred a secret tremor in his heart; it was like the striking of some magic silver bell, portending monstrous things. His passion faltered, and, as his eyes glanced upon my innocent head (which, it must be confessed, was sadly out of place in that pernicious scene), alighted on this smaller wrong. 'The next time you go on your adventures, mademoiselle,' he cried, 'I'd thank you not to pollute my son by dragging him at your skirts.'

'I'm not sorry to have my family present,' said the young girl, who had had time to collect her thoughts. 'I should be glad even if my sister were here. I wish simply to bid you farewell.'

Coquelin, at these words, made a step towards her. She passed her hand through his arm. 'Things have taken place—and chiefly within the last moment—which change the face of the future. You've done the business, brother,' and she fixed her glittering eyes on the Baron; 'you've driven me back on myself. I spared you, but you never spared me. I cared for my name; you loaded it with dishonour. I chose between happiness and duty,—duty as you would have laid it down: I preferred duty. But now that happiness has become one with simple safety from violence and insult, I go back to happiness. I give you back your name; though I have kept it more jealously than you. I have another ready for me. O Messieurs!' she cried, with a burst of rapturous exaltation, 'for what you have done to me I thank you.'

My father began to groan and tremble. He had grasped my hand in his own, which was clammy with perspiration. 'For the love of God, Gabrielle,' he implored, 'or the fear of the Devil, speak so that a sickened, maddened Christian can understand you! For what purpose did you come here to-night?'

'*Mon Dieu*, it's a long story. You made short work with it. I might in justice do as much. I came here, brother, to guard my reputation, and not to lose it.'

All this while my father had neither looked at Coquelin nor spoken to him, either because he thought him not worth his words, or because he had kept some transcendent insult in reserve. Here my governor broke in. 'It seems to me time, M. le Baron, that I should inquire the purpose of your own visit.'

My father stared a moment. 'I came, M. Coquelin, to take you by the shoulders and eject you through that door, with the further impulsion, if necessary, of a vigorous kick.'

'Good! And M. le Vicomte?'

'M. le Vicomte came to see it done.'

'Perfect! A little more and you had come too late. I was on the point of leaving Bergerac. I can put the story into three words. I have been so happy as to secure the affections of Mlle. de Bergerac. She asked herself, devoutly, what course of action was possible under the circumstances. She decided that the only course was that we should immediately separate. I had no hesitation in bringing my residence with M. le Chevalier to a sudden close. I was to have quitted the château early to-morrow morning, leaving mademoiselle at absolute liberty. With her refusal of M. de Treuil I have nothing to do. Her action in this matter seems to have been strangely precipitated, and my own departure anticipated in consequence. It was at her adjuration that I was preparing to depart. She came here this evening to command me to stay. In our relations there was nothing that the world had a right to lay a finger upon. From the moment that they were suspected it was of the first importance to the security and sanctity of Mlle. de Bergerac's position that there should be no appearance on my part of elusion or flight. The relations I speak of had ceased to exist; there was, therefore, every reason why for the present I should retain my place. Mlle. de Bergerac had been here some three minutes, and had just made known her wishes, when you arrived with the honourable intentions which you avow, and under that illusion the perfect stupidity of which is its least reproach. In my own turn, Messieurs, I thank you!'

'Gabrielle,' said my father, as Coquelin ceased speaking, 'the long and short of it appears to be that after all you needn't marry this man. Am I to understand that you intend to?'

'Brother, I mean to marry M. Coquelin.'

My father stood looking from the young girl to her lover. The Vicomte walked to the window, as if he were in want of air. The night was cool and the window closed. He tried the sash, but for some reason it resisted. Whereupon he raised his sword-hilt and with a violent blow shivered a pane into fragments. The Baron went on: 'On what do you propose to live?'

'It's for me to propose,' said Coquelin. 'My wife shall not suffer.'

'Whither do you mean to go?'

'Since you're so good as to ask,—to Paris.'

My father had got back his fire. 'Well, then,' he cried, 'my bitterest unforgiveness go with you, and turn your unholy pride to abject woe! My sister may marry a base-born vagrant if she wants, but I shall not give her away. I hope you'll enjoy the mud in which you've planted yourself. I hope your marriage will be blessed in the good old fashion, and that you'll regard philosophically the sight of a half-dozen starving children. I hope you'll enjoy the company of chandlers and cobblers and scribblers!' The Baron could go no further. 'Ah, my sister!' he half exclaimed. His voice broke; he gave a great convulsive sob, and fell into a chair.

'Coquelin,' said my aunt, 'take me back to the château.'

As she walked to the door, her hand in the young man's arm, the Vicomte turned short about from the window, and stood with his drawn sword, grimacing horribly.

'Not if I can help it!' he cried through his teeth, and with a sweep of his weapon he made a savage thrust at the young girl's breast, Coquelin, with equal speed, sprang before her, threw out his arm, and took the blow just below the elbow.

'Thank you, M. le Vicomte,' he said, 'for the chance of calling you a coward! There was something I wanted.'

Mlle. de Bergerac spent the night at the château, but by early dawn she had disappeared. Whither Coquelin betook himself with his gratitude and his wound, I know not. He lay, I suppose, at some neighbouring farmer's. My father and the Vicomte kept for an hour a silent, sullen vigil in my preceptor's vacant apartment,—for an hour and perhaps longer, for at the end of this time I fell asleep, and when I came to my senses, the next morning, I was in my own bed.

M. de Bergerac had finished his tale.

'But the marriage,' I asked, after a pause,—'was it happy?'

'Reasonably so, I fancy. There is no doubt that Coquelin was an excellent fellow. They had three children, and lost them all. They managed to live. He painted portraits and did literary work.'

'And his wife?'

'Her history, I take it, is that of all good wives: she loved her husband. When the Revolution came, they went into politics; but here, in spite of his base birth, Coquelin acted with that superior temperance which I always associate with his memory. He was no *sans-culotte*. They both went to the scaffold among the Girondists.'

TEXTUAL VARIANTS

INTRODUCTION

IN PREPARING THIS RECORD OF ALL SUBSTANTIVE variants in the six revised tales of the period some decisions of an editorial nature had to be taken: this introduction explains those decisions.

The variants listed below are keyed to the periodical versions of the tales—the original creations of which all later changes are, so to speak, offshoots—as reprinted in the present edition. I have taken all book editions of a tale published during James's lifetime and subjected them to textual comparison with the periodical text. The substantive variants that the collation revealed have been compiled in this record.

The overall authority of the revisions examined cannot be questioned: the two principal collections—*A Passionate Pilgrim* and *Stories Revived*—where most of the revised versions of the tales first appeared—as well as the first revised form of 'A Light Man', which appeared in a separate collection, were all prepared by James himself. And 'the process of retouching' to which the tales had been subjected was to be an important feature of the 'reintroduced' works.[1] The authority of individual instances of alteration, however, is impossible to establish as only one of the six manuscript revisions has survived.[2] In the absence of such evidence for comparison, the problem becomes a critical one. Needless to say, all substantive variants listed have been critically examined from the viewpoint of style and structure, and were found to conform to the context of meanings established in the originals. Remarkably few misprints have been noticed in the revised editions.

The decision to ignore all accidentals—variants of punctuation, contractions (I have/I've), expanded forms (I've/I have), paragraph division, spelling variants, etc.,—is of course arbitrary. It is influenced by two factors. First, it is extremely difficult, if not altogether impossible, to record the variants of punctuation in a complex and large body of multiple texts such as the 112 tales of Henry James. Secondly, as readers of James know, in the matter of punctuation he was not very consistent. The difference between the early system of punctuation and that of the New York Edition is so great that the latter cannot be treated as anything but a new, highly idiosyncratic style. It was decided, therefore, to treat this aspect of the revisions separately in an essay to appear in the final volume of

---

[1] See Appendix I.
[2] See headnote to 'A Light Man' below.

the edition. For the present it should suffice to say that the revised texts are lightly punctuated, and that most contractions have been expanded in them. Although I have generally ignored the accidentals, the punctuation variants in all substantively revised passages have been recorded.

Each of the six lists opens with a brief headnote which singles out the texts that have been collated. The note does not mention that sample collations of all available reprints of the revised editions have been taken privately. For works with more than one revised form, the initial letters of the titles in which the revised forms appeared have been used as identifying symbols for the two stages of revision. These symbols are explained in the first note and later appear against each entry. In most cases, the first note is followed by another set of notes which record the revised division of chapters, revised names of the characters, and other similar peculiarities of the revision.

For each entry, the page and line references are to the text in the present edition. The usual square bracket divides the original from the revised form. Wherever possible, I have tried to divide the revisions into very small units of text, the original form of which is indicated preceding the square bracket. In the case of longer passages, however, three dots (...) have been used to cover the matter, of all lengths, left out. The ellipses cover not only substantive matter but also punctuation, including full stops and quotation marks.

James often makes changes towards the end of his sentences and these usually add new matter. In recording such additions, the full stop at the end of the original sentence has *not* been indicated—unless the revised form closes with a different punctuation mark. The same treatment has been given to all punctuation marks coming *at the end* of a passage which has been revised without any change in the original punctuation mark.

A frequent, and significant, feature of the revisions is the readjustment of editorial directions in the dialogues—the changes made in the placing of such fictional props as 'he said', 'she said', etc. Since many of these alterations affect only the directions, and not the speeches, a method had to be evolved to avoid long passages of unrevised matter. The following should explain the procedure adopted to deal with the problem. If, for example,

'No, I do not agree with you.'

is changed to

'No,' he said, 'I do not agree with you.'

the list would record the variant thus:

No, I do not] No,' he said, 'I do not

In other words, in the case of revisions involving dialogue, *only the relevant part* of the quotation marks has been indicated. And the same principle is employed in recording revisions where James has added something before or after a speech, or has omitted the stage direction. Finally, in order to save space, the usual practice of transcribing dialogue in separate units has not been kept.

A LANDSCAPE PAINTER

Notes:

1, The variants recorded below are based on a collation of the original serial text of the tale (*Atlantic Monthly*, 1866) and its revised version in *Stories Revived* (1885).

2. The following are the revised forms of proper names. Only the first occurrence of these forms is recorded.

Mrs. M] Mrs. Monkhouse
Richard Blunt] Richard Quarterman
Esther Blunt] Miriam Quarterman
Mr. Johnson] Mr. Prendergast
John Banister] Alfred Banister
Dorothy] Cynthia

A Landscape Painter] A Landscape-Painter

57:16	assigned] attributed
22	rupture] break
34–35	I took ... eldest born] it was not impossible for me to believe that her first-born had also shown the cloven foot
58:7–8	towards] toward
9	on the sea-shore] at the seaside
16–17	detail, a ... my hands] go into, a good many of his personal belongings have become mine
18	elegant] cultivated
18–19	seriously ... letters] fond of reading, wrote a little, and painted a good deal
19	very bad poetry] rather amateurish verse
21	all] many
21	adapted] calculated
22	portion] few
22	that which] that portion which
27	great painter] charming artist
31	decease] passing away
34	Cragthorpe] Chowderville
35	pondering] wondering
36	these ... idleness] this occasional history of nothing at all
38–9	my life ... dullest] I have had least to say
39–40	launched ... life] I have had a sufficient dose of dulness
59:3	while] om.
4	strong and clear] immensely refreshed
7	without] outside
11	Mrs. M—,] Mrs. Monkhouse
12–14	before, it seems ... and cloud] before have I seen such a

	pretty little coast—never before have I been so taken with wave and rock and cloud
59:14	a sensuous] om.
15	unparalleled] om.
15–17	stricken ... and as yet] enamoured of all the moods and tenses of the ocean; and as yet
20	for the victories] if you please, for the prodigies
30	did I see] have I seen
37	three or four miles,] four or five miles
40	a little cove! So] a dear little cove—so
41	the town] Chowderville
41	off] om.
60:2	about] round
10	over] on
12	my steps] the miles
12–13	cloudy ... horizon] flitting, gleaming sails
13–14	killing ... suckers] passing the time anyhow
32	feeling ... compassion, I] disposition might not be hostile —he didn't look like a wild islander—I
41	insidious] violent
61:3	bargain] exchange
3	Richard Blunt] Richard Quarterman
4	Captain, for short] Cap'n, for respect
8	that I have broken] I have simply broken
12–13	hundred thousand a year] large income
17	own] om.
18	millions] dollars
19–20	To be ... be poor,—] To be young, strong and poor—
22	pure] om.
23	the Captain] Captain Quarterman
27–8	cultivating ... health] studying and sketching coast-scenery; toning myself up with the sea air
30	a good deal of an economist] of a very frugal mind
32	ill success of the] want of success in the
33	an odd union] a queer mixture
34	old fashioned,] om.
34:5	I suppose ... convertible.] om.
41	house] tenement
62:1	dearest] sweetest
3	graveyard] churchyard
22	smiles propitious] makes no objection
24	housed] domiciled, almost domesticated
25	skirting the harbour] which skirts the harbour
29	slippers. He] slippers—he
32	well-bred woman] superior being
33	Miss Blunt's] the young lady's
34	violet ribbon at] blue ribbon on

62:35	thereto] to the button-hole
37	deference] gaiety
39	very frank] pleasing
39	her hospitality] their taking me in
63:2	refuse outright] simply tell you so
2	Bravo] Brava
4	rather plump] with roundness in her lines
7	a florid brunette] a brunette with colour
11–20	Her mouth ... red red rose!] She has perfect teeth, and her smile is almost unnaturally brilliant. Her chin is surpassingly round. She has a capital movement, too, and looked uncommonly well as she strolled in the garden-path with a big spray of geranium lifted to her nose.
22	with a ... smile] she doesn't hesitate to laugh very musically
24	matters] mysteries
26	quite ... very proud] fond of keeping herself *to* herself, as the phrase is, and is even, possibly, very proud
27–8	at full ... a lady] at as full length as I can paint you
31–2	the *effect* ... touch] her stately way of sitting at the instrument, than by the quality of her playing, though that is evidently high
34	vast] large
35	southern light] north-light
37–8	in as ... fashion] so as to make it look as much like a studio
39	looked] snuffed
41	deferential silence] prudent reserve
64:8	got] obtained
11	Blunt] the Captain
15	Miss Blunt's] The young lady's
20–1	practical ... her own] second-hand acquaintance with life
22	'Zanoni'] *The Missing Bride*
24	New-York heiresses] daughters of gold, in New York
29	out] om.
29–30	left to] left quite to
32	sturdy] pure
34	and] om.
65:3	kind of] om.
4–5	seems ... sobriety] only deepens the impression of vanished uses
5	implies ... obstructed] seems to say that the protecting
6	are in ... decline] look down on their decline and can't help them
13	terrors] bitterness
15	harbour] bay

65:16   fields] uplands
16   established ... *rendezvous*] taken a kind of tryst
22   labour] industry
29   how they can frown!] they have also lachrymal moods.
31   Miss Blunt sallies] Miss Miriam—her name is Miriam, and it exactly fits her—sallies
36   red] rich
37-8   profoundly ... spectacle] very honourable figure
39   an ... This] a familiar, but not a vulgar, nod. The
41   of loveliness and dignity] om.
66:1   simplicity] fine effect
12   bends ... depth] hangs
12   horizon] horizon a canopy of denser tissue
16   quite a] a really
18   deep] om.
20   beach] sand
21   it as upon] it—poorly—as they might upon
22-3   I seek it] I have to look for it
23-8   great mossy ... several days] large stones which hold up to the sun a shoulder coated with delicate gray, figured over with fine, pale, sea-green moss, or else in one of the long, shallow dells where a tangle of blackberry-bushes hedges about a pool that reflects the sky. I am giving my best attention to a plain brown hillside, and trying to make it look like something in nature; and as we have now had the same clear sky for several days
30   furnishes ... napkin full] supplies me with a little parcel
31   hours] hour
35   day after day] always
40   calico] light
42   footsteps] footstep
67:7   darkling] darkening
12   thinks] believes
13   Esther] Miriam
13-14   a newly inducted daughter-in-law] some new arrival—say a daughter-in-law lately brought home
14   indeed] *à propos* of daughters-in-law
20-1   It is ... courtesy] It is natural enough that they should like me, because I have tried to please them
27-9   I have prided ... is, however,] I have done my best to be nice to the stately Miriam without making love to her. That I haven't done *that*, however, is
32:3   lady, without ... I record] lady. Those animated eyes have a power to keep people in their place. I mention
43   an excellent memory] a retentive faculty
68:5   old cosmopolitanism] worldly lore
8   sympathetic] submissive

68:9–10	amiable garrulities] traveller's tales
10	relation] understanding
15–16	prepared for ... the transition] in condition to be practised upon. Sometimes his artless fables don't 'take' at all
18–19	shallow ... apprehension] dry climate of my land-bred mind
29	I fancy ... whole,] I take for granted that
30	my part] my little part
30	come] comes
31	experience] find
31–2	hundred ... luxuries,] old luxuries and pleasures
41	meeting] a place of worship
69:12	festival,' said I.] festival.'
20	Mr. Johnson] Mr. Prendergast
34	roundly] frankly
35	*tête-à-tête*] conversation
40	said she] she remarked
70:3	Your claim ... pray] You have had all the attention I am capable of. Have I been so very rude
4	uncivil ... inconsiderate] so very rude, perhaps, but rather inconsiderate
5–6	which you ... relish] whom you can't expect me to care much about
12	improper] weak
12	That's an] That's a very
19–20	charges ... obliquity] accusations and rebukes
21	sex] sexes
22	morally ... each other] to scan each other's faults
25	little] wee
32	read] peruse
33	Meanwhile,' I asked, 'what] Meanwhile what
35	'I haven't.'] 'My Bible,' I said, 'is the female mind.'
38–40	What a ... feminine piety] In what a terrible tradition she has been reared, and what an edifying spectacle is the piety of women
71:2	assumes it] puts it on
5–6	Dear ... holiday faith!] 'Dear me, what a comfort it is to have a nice, fresh, holiday-creed!'
6	Miss Blunt] Miriam
8	her soberly] her, without chaffing,
9	reading ... me] reading, and she answered me in the same tone
15	you, then, so poor] you so very poor
15–16	asked ... abruptly.] om.
17	under thirty] om.
18	poor?' I answered. 'Upon] poor? Upon

71:23   a couple] half-a-one
25   **yet] also**
26   repulsive] difficult to live with
30   compliment] lump of sugar
31   paid you a compliment] given you one
33–4   angle with ... bait] put out your paws and bark
34   inartistic] slap-dash
35   repulsive] very difficult to live with
37   compliment] lump of sugar
38–40   charming ... sociable.] very indulgent. You let us off easily, but you wouldn't like us a bit if you didn't pity us. Don't I go deep? Sociable? ah, well, no—decidedly not!

43   eloquent] striking
72:1–8   You call ... I think not] You call poor Mr. Prendergast conceited; but, really, I believe he has more humility than you. He envies my father and me—thinks us so cultivated. You don't envy any one, and yet I don't think you're a saint. You treat us kindly because you think virtue in a lowly station ought to be encouraged. Would you take the same amount of pains for a person you thought your equal, a person equally averse with yourself to being under an obligation? There are differences
72:8   it's delightful to charm] it's very delightful to fascinate
9–10   charmer does not sit] fascinator doesn't set
11   charmed] dazzled
12   convinced and refuted] listened to, counted with
15–16   the principal of the school] Miss Blackenberg
16–17   women without ... thought] people without any *arrière-pensée*. Of course the people I see are mainly women
18   natural] agreeable
22–4   You are incapable ... I have] You are incapable of exposing yourself to be bored, whereas I take it as my waterproof takes the rain. You have no idea what heroism I show
25   precious] om.
29   narrowness] smallness
30–1   don't. I like to go] don't, I like to bleed; to go
32   of the house] om.
32   well-dressed and] very much dressed, very
37   pluck] patience
39   agreeable] selfish
41   their applause] their good opinion
73:3   I beg your pardon] be so good as to excuse me
5   swims ... I don't] swims. Sugar, did you say? I don't
6   attacking me or praising me] giving me sugar or vitriol
16   gamut] scales

73:19   poor ... stupid] poor and has a hump
    39   an] if
    43   severely] richly
74:2   greatest] finest
    13   harbour] port
    18   woman] female
    21   it's] it be
    25   a gentleman] one of the old sort
    36   dry expression of mouth] dry, edifying expression
    38   dreary] dismal
75:4   she was engaged] she had passed her word
    7   "When John grows rich enough,"] "When Alfred"—his name was Alfred—"grows rich enough,"
    11   came no nearer to his fortune] hadn't accumulated very much
    15   Has John ... fortune] Has Alfred made his little pile
    27   John Banister] Alfred Banister
    30-1   accumulating ... fast] amassing considerable wealth
    37   gentleman] mariner
    38   maid-servant] black domestic
    39   Dorothy] Cynthia
    41-2   wrapt ... slumber] sleeping like a log
76:1   open] best
    5   midsummer! What] midsummer—what
    8   kingdom of light] luminosity
    10   loveliest] handsomest
    13   her. She] her, and besides she
    13   Confound it] Damn her drudgery
    15   Mrs. Dorothy] the dusky Cynthia
    16   said I] I said
    20   Miss Blunt] Miss Quarterman, colouring
    23   things,' ... 'a sentimental] things, a sentimental
    24   despicable.'] despicable!' she exclaimed.
    26   things,' ... 'a woman] things a woman
    27   unlovely] wanting in sweetness
    28   loveliness] sweetness
    42   wagon] vehicle
77:2   time] spin
    3   hard] breezy
    5   yesterday, which had] last night which has
    6   had] have
    10   lofty] om.
    13   loved so well] sometimes painted
    15-16   whose prows ... waves] which had rounded the curve of the globe
    17   plunge down ... beach,] begin
    18-20   moments ... into powder] time looking at their long,

diminishing, crooked perspective, blue and dun as it re-
ceded, with the white surge playing at their feet

77:23	the old man] my host
24	picturesque embrace] osculation
24–5	that ... that smile] that confiding hand-shake
25	failed] fail
27	upstairs] om.
78:1	broken] disappointed
5	my story] my little story
10	said Miss Esther] Miriam said
14	nice] neat
15	Fort Pudding] Fort Plunkett
19	warmly ... project] entered into the project with passion
20–1	when ... pushed] when—about ten o'clock—we pushed
22	it. We] it; and we
31	mossy] delicate
33–5	gleaming ... raised aloft] which looked like masses of black lace. The steep, straggling sides of the cliffs lifted
37	heavy shadow] cool darkness
39	figure] picture
40	this Cragthorpe air] the air of this place
41	approached] surpassed
79:4	lovely it was] it animated the whole scene
5	short white skirt] white petticoat
6–7	the crimson ... her arm,] om.
10	out of which] where
10–12	happy mouth ... the picture] parted lips said things I lost—these are some of the points I hastily noted
17	accessories] aerial perspective
20	devilish pretty] infernally handsome
26-7	reappeared] returned
27	handkerchief] pocket-handkerchief
30	who was] for
35	a dollar] so much
35	in Cragthorpe] at Chowderville
36	would] should
80:2	nonsense] cheap fun
2	like] om.
5–6	soon ... cool spring] immediately discovered flowing water
8	Blunt and I] he and I
12	poetry and ... long] sweetness and artless revelry of this interminable
13	ate, drank,] ate and drank
15	wild] perfect
16	Blunt] The Captain
19	register] notice

80:20–1   fool on ... about it] one to criticise us we were brilliant
           enough
    24   lingered] dawdled
    24–5   the livelong ... prospect with] in the same place, and
           drowned the prospect with
    29   remind] recall to
    32   big] rich
    35   That's ... programme.] om.
    41   pannier] hamper
81:4   Miss Blunt said,] My companion remarked
    5   believed she would] supposed she ought to
    6–7   her crimson ... silk sack] it being an old shawl of faded
           red (Canton crape, I believe they call it), which I have
           seen very often
    10   I placed her ... own head] I spun her hat round on my
           stick
    19–29 I think I ... listener she is!] I think I may trust it to the
           keeping of my memory; it was the sort of thing that
           comes back to one—after. If something ever happens
           which I think *may*, that apparently idle hour will seem,
           as one looks back, very symptomatic, and what we didn't
           say be perceived to have been more significant than what
           we did. There was something between us—there *is* some-
           thing between us—and we listened to its impalpable
           presence—I liken it to the hum (very faint) of an un-
           seen insect—in the golden stillness of the afternoon. I
           must add that if she expects, foresees, if she waits, she
           does so with a supreme serenity. If she is my fate (and
           she has the air of it), she is conscious that it's *her* fate
           to be so.
    37–8   chilly ... fallen] autumnal weather; dusk has gathered
    41   room] place
82:2   an armful of wood] half-a-dozen logs
    7–8   have pretended ... all that] at least have made a show of
           calling the negress. I should have had my own day, but
           we have changed all that
    9–11   word. I sat ... she] word, but sat considering my fate and
           watching it come nearer and nearer. For the first time
           since I have known her (my fate) she
    12   her she] her (I remember such things) she
    13   purple] blue
    21   this] the
    41   my coming] that I should come here
83:3   told father] told my father
    4   play. Leaning] play, and leaning
    7   Yes.] Well, sir?
    9   but I] but, you know, I

83:28-9   without knowing it] the merest accident
35   but I mean it] but you exasperate me
36   thoughts] attention
38-40   silently ... might not] put my arm round her waist and kiss her; but I decided that I might do nothing of the sort
84:3   I stopped a moment.] om.
5   vice,' ... 'and] vice, and
8   a rather shrill] rather a shrill
13   Honestly ... express it.] Do you think me capable of deceiving you?
21   God's] pity's
24   I am open to conviction.] How can I help believing what you tell me?
25   Thank God!] Dearest, bravest of women,
30-3   'I certainly sha'n't whisper ... fact.] I don't know whether *she* whispered or not, but before I left her she consented.
34   within] in about
39   not rich] so very poor
40   said I] I remarked
85:1   rich or not] poor or not
2   am] am rich
8   *giving* which I experienced] *buying* which I suffered from
8-10   I was ... at all events] That intercourse was conducted by means of little parcels, and I have resolved that this engagement, at all events
11   balked] cheated
11-13   I don't ... hands] Fortunately there is not much danger of this, for my mistress is positively lyrical
13   a very pretty] an enthusiastic
17   grey] pink
19-20   garment ... generally] garment, upon which all the art and taste and eyesight, and all the velvet and lace, of Chowderville have been lavished
23   it,' ... 'and] it and
24   fortune. All] fortune,' said I. 'All
26-7   said Esther] Miriam replied
30   the schoolmistress] Miss Blackenberg (the schoolmistress)
32-33   take care of itself] leak out as occasion helps it
34   be *à refaire*] have to be done over again
35   Clifton] Cragthorpe
36   free of city-people] purged of cockneys
86:1   inland] to New York
4   and] om.
8   the little ... her heart] the infant a kiss, bless her tender heart
23   a hundred thousand a year] ever so much money

86:25	born] fitted by nature
26	I believe] I verily believe
29	here about my sensations] now about what passed through me when you asked me to—to do *this*
39	You deceived ... you] You cheated me and I mystified you
39–41	your deception ... across me.] you tell me your secret I can tell you mine. *Now* we are free, with the fortune that you know. Excuse me, but it sometimes comes over me!
87:6	shouldn't] wouldn't
9–10	No,—simply ... be a man!'] No, it was the act of any woman—placed as I was placed. You don't believe it?' And she began to smile. 'Come, you may abuse me in your diary if you like—I shall never peep into it again!'

A DAY OF DAYS

Notes:

1. The variants recorded below are based on a collation of the original serial text of the tale (*Galaxy*, 1866) and its revised version in *Stories Revived* (1885).

2. The following are the revised forms of proper names. Only the first occurrence of these forms is recorded.

Laura B] Laura Benton
Madison Perkins] Weatherby Pynsent
S.] Slowfield

88:1	some] the highest
9	very] om.
13–14	a Summer] a summer or two
16	in Havana] in the Havana
16	means beautiful] means perfectly beautiful
20	'society'] the best company
89:3	couple of years] period
4	not be unprofitable] yield a fine refreshment
9	and of] and
13–14	prove ... growth] check the morbid development of her brain-power
14–15	live in ... books from] merely vegetate; walk and ride, and read the old-fashioned books in
17	very prettily housed at] established in a very pretty house, at
19	small college] small but ancient college
21-2	it was very soon made] there were no barriers to break down
23	delicate] conscientious
24	had a vague] had had a vague
27–8	discovered ... temperence] became aware that his sister led almost an ascetic life
29	bought back] recovered
35	was about] was now about
36	lapsed] declined
37–8	suffered a ... distinguished] rubbed off the social facility, the 'knowledge of the world' for which she was formerly distinguished
39	*tête-à-tête*] intimate conversation
40	but also that she had] but had also
43	Laura B.,] Laura Benton,
90:6	S.,] Slowfield,
7	home, and] home, or

90:8	until the evening] till the night
9	during Adela's] during the term of Adela's
11–12	nevertheless] om.
12–13	a sort ... days] a return of that condition
15	half laughing] with the smile that she reserved for her maidenly monologues
15	fair] good
17	pay a ... morning calls] call on a lot of tiresome local people
19	delicious] delectable
28	kindly] human
28–9	she felt ... neighbours] if any of the local people were to come to her she felt it was in her to humour them
33	vines] high-creeping plants
38–9	her courtesies ... indiscriminating] she was equally gracious to all men, and, what was more remarkable, to all women
39	lent] dedicated
41–2	a by no means ... casement] an imagination by no means severely impartial that she sat communing with her open casement
43	exactions] requirements
43	should perforce] must
91:1–3	the other sex ... of the county] a sex as different as possible from her own; and as, thanks to the few differences in favour of any individual she had been able to discover among the young males of the country-side
5	Mr. Madison Perkins] Mr. Weatherby Pynsent
7–8	one pregnant ... heroine] simple statement that he was very far gone indeed
8–9	of a ... from his] affiliated to a richer ceremonial than his own
5–6	half-dozen] half a dozen
7	an additional taper to her shrine] another candle to her altar
19	young man] young parson
22	reëchoed ... the other] reminded her of the one and gave her a foretaste of the other
27	of a most ... of her heart] that her heart was beating quite idiotically
29	have herself denied] see no one at all
31	lessened, lo! it seemed to her] lessened she began to perceive
33–4	diverged ... elm] went their different ways, and a spreading elm, tall and slim, like the feathery sheaf of a gleaner, with an ancient bench beneath it, made an informal *rond-point*

91:36	a direction] some direction that had been given him
37	shapely] robust
38	straw] soft white
92:1–2	that the ... been used,] the gentleman had made use of the reverse of a paste-board
9	were all] was all
17	*strata*] walks
18–19	society ... native soil] life, he still seemed always to move in his native element
19	manners and of] manner and
20	be one of ... ungloved] belong to the great vulgar, muscular, popular majority
24	his heritage of beauty] the most expressive part of his equipment
27	figure] person
28–9	sweet assurance ... included] experience in an air of taking success too much for granted
31	He was liked] People liked him
32–3	he was disliked] and disliked him
34	and] om.
37–8	to nullify oneself ... coincidentally] to suppress, one's own sensibilities in the pursuit of knowledge, but to trample on the rest of mankind at the same time
40–1	have been ... equanimity] always have saved his tender parts
43	amazingly] unexpectedly
93:2	paleontology ... them] the study of fossil remains, the branch
5	in] om.
5	with a bow] om.
6	whence] where
6	contemplating] looking at
7	his greeting] the friendly nod which he apparently intended for a greeting
13	charge you with a message] give you a message for him
14–16	before which ... them] under the influence of which it had been written on the scroll of Adela's fate that she was to descend from her pedestal
18	the country] this simple little place
24	screw] squeeze
24	prodigiously] tremendously
25	very seldom ... of it] have been working for many months in a musty museum
26	possible,' said Adela, 'that] possible that
27	evening. He] evening,' Adela said. 'He
31	At three] Well, about three
34	back), I] back). In that case I

93:36   letters. It seems] letters—letters of recommendation to some foreign scientists. He is the only man in this country who knows how much I know. It seems

43   done] had

94:1   I'll stay] I guess I'll remain

6   remain] stop-over

7   like] want

8   him.] Mr. Moore, don't you see?

9   own] om.

9   in my own home] at some place of my own

12–13   uncommonly pretty place] attractive country residence

16   said he] he remarked

16   view it is] little spot

17   to live before such a prospect] to have the beauties of nature always before your eyes

21   around] round

26   favour] benevolence

28   without] outside

29   broad] radiant

30   it was ... face] his was a nature very much alive

34   is not a simpleton] isn't a bore

35   frankly] freely

35   favour] benevolence

36   acutely] perfectly

37   pursued,] pursued, tacitly

94:41–95:4   favour? Why, I ... to match it] benevolence? Why, what does one want of any pleasant thing in life?' 'Dear me, if you never have anything pleasanter than that!' our heroine exclaimed. 'It will do very well for the present occasion,' said the young man, blushing, in a large masculine way, at his own quickness of repartee

95:1   mantle] chimney-piece

8   florid personalities] jokes so personal

15   broad] crude

16   have him go] see him depart

16   loth] very sorry

17   part] side

25   gracious impulses] mansuetude

25   were] was

28   bid him] give him leave to

35   Adela ... eyes] Adela shifted her eyes back to where they could see him

35:6   to have you remain] that you should stay

39   That's easily] That is very easily

41   and his collections] and collections

96:1–2   bidding you good-morning] separating from you

4–5   treasures as you prescribe] things as you recommend

96:6   Prescribe ... nothing] Recommend? I recommend nothing

12   magazines. Can] periodicals. There are ever so many scientific papers. Can

16   magazines,] scientific periodicals

26   The lattice ... the entry] There was a summer-door, composed of lattices painted green, like a shutter; it admitted into the hall

27–8   divided its wings] pushed its wings apart

29   veranda] porch

30   stick] cane

36   please,' she said.] please.'

37   about] round

41   What] After all, what

42   stay] stay with her

43   unadvisable] a criminal thing

97:4   It rests upon] It was produced by

9–10   to court mischance ... a petty] only to expose herself the more, for it would imply a gratuitous

11   fairly] om.

11   honesty] good intentions

12   gentleman. To this] gentleman; at this

13–16   made a swallow's ... 'I see no] arrived by a rapid diagonal, and now it served as a fresh starting-point. 'I have seen all the gentlemen can show me' (this was her syllogism): 'let us try something new! I see no

18   think,' cried Ludlow, 'it] think it

19   committed.'] committed!' cried the young man

20   be a] be rather a

20   said Adela, with a smile] Adela remarked

21   your] *your*

23   broad,] solid

28   mighty] genial

30–1   Your kindness ... I am passive] Look here, Miss Moore; your kindness makes me as gentle as a little child. I am passive

39   hotel piazza] piazza of the hotel

42   Adela] Adela, sententiously

98:6–8   I fancy ... like a walk] There is something in the air— I can't imagine what—which seems to say it is the last day of summer. We ought to commemorate it. How should you like to take a walk

8   favours] aforesaid benevolence

9   play] be

12   her novel] so rare an

14   classical] conventional

18   said Adela] Adela rejoined

98:19	shawl] jacket
20	veranda steps] steps of the veranda
21-2	this,' he said.] this.'
29	quite ... but I] quite in possession; that is, I put myself in his way, as it were, so that he had to speak to me : but I
31-2	confide ... table] ring for the servant
33	table] door-bell
36	tribute] tribute, if he would trust me with it
37	I think] It seems to me
41-2	that charming ... heroic] that sweet little cleric—isn't he a cleric, eh?—would have been the act of an angel
99:4	a good] at least
5-7	measured the ... the meadows] dawdled immensely over the interval, yet their arrival at a certain little rustic gate, beyond which the country grew vague and gently wild, struck Adela as sudden
8-11	adventure ... Nature] excursion so purely pastoral and no guile in a spirit so deeply sensitive to the influences of nature
14	generous] om.
15	simple] unsophisticated
15	common] casual
16-17	accepted by ... their esteem] regarded by the daughters of the scene as a person whose motives are pure
18-21	the echoes ... modest facts] the transparent airs and blue horizons of her adopted home; and she was reassured by Ludlow's appreciation of these modest phenomena
22	that] the
23-4	Summer in a ... a sensation] summer looking over dry specimens in a laboratory, and against an impediment
25	delightful girl] remarkably attractive woman
26:7	he celebrated ... within herself] he uttered his various satisfactions with abundant humour and point. Adela felt
32	barriers] resisting surfaces
32-4	crossed the ... successive meadows] passed through the little gate and wandered over empty pastures
39	pine] cedar
40	blue with ... woods] purple with mild masses of forest
42	pines] trees which had always reminded Adela of the stone-pines of the Villa Borghese
43	and] om.
99:43-100:2	a cluster of trees ... conversation] the murmuring cedars would give them a kind of human company
3-5	Before long ... phenomenon.] om.
6	me,' rejoined Ludlow, 'that] me that

100:7–8	pines expresses ... a change.'] trees is always the voice of coming changes,' Ludlow said.
9	does] is
9	said Adela] Adela replied
9	pines] trees
9	rustling] talking in this melancholy way
11	express it when] express the foreboding of coming events —that is what I mean—when
12	own] om.
12	going] about
16	feeling] inspiration
17	I do] Well, I rather think I do
18	a change ... life] some great change hanging over you
21	said] exclaimed
29	turned] directed
29	upon] into
36	young] om.
38	ingeniously provoked service;] accidental assistance:
39–40	the most ... land] a young woman who was evidently altogether superior
41	woman] person
41	fool] chit
42–3	not yet ... obtain it] never happened to suppose that he should find it open to him
101:1	final] brilliant
1–2	pleasing ... pleasing] what is called in the relation between the sexes success
3	a modest and discerning] an eminently discriminating
4	so speedily ... favour] fraternised with him at such a rate
6	back,' ... 'to my] back to my
9	regulation ... served me] regular way that saved me
10	discerned] detected
11	had] om.
16–17	success ... other] a triumph after all possibly superficial
17	Miss Moore,' he pursued, 'is] Miss Moore is
18–19	welcome. Assuredly,' he added] welcome,' he said to himself. 'Assuredly,' he added
19	gazed] glanced
22	strong] clever
24	truth ... he] truth that, as Ludlow continued to observe his companion, he
26	gaze] contemplation
29	glanced at] eyed
30	injury] impertinence
31	asked] inquired
39	rebuked] scolded
102:1	of years] of many years

102:4	Do I invite it] Do I seem to open to that sort of thing
9–10	blast of ... Ludlow's] puff of the actual conveyed in Mr. Ludlow's
11–12	such a name as he pleases] whatever name he chooses
14	vehemence] violence
14	had covered] many represent
19–20	introduce her ... company] thrust her injured heart into a company in which there was, as yet at least, no question of hearts
22	perfect young lady] youthful woman of the world, the perfect young lady
23–4	bewitching than ... circumstances] engaging than this civilised and disciplined personage under such circumstances
24–5	accomplished ... world] accomplished of coquettes
26	languid equanimity] judicious consideration
28	suffer] suffer in secret
29	companion with this injunction:] companion.
30	'Mr. Ludlow,' said she, 'tell me] 'By the way, Mr. Ludlow, tell me
34	delicious] very tempting
40	noisy and ugly] noisy, ugly
103:1	way] way of business
1	fancy] suspect
7–8	I'm plucky ... over-egotistical] I don't let go easily. If I strike you as very egotistical
9–16	that word is ... not nervous] that's a kind of metaphysical, sentimental, vapid word. But I know what I want to know, and I generally manage to find it out. I don't know much about my moral nature; I have no doubt I am beastly selfish. Still I don't like to hurt peoples' feelings, and I am rather fond of poetry and flowers. I don't believe I am very "high-toned", all the same
18	desperately hard to snub] remarkably hard to keep down
19–22	I should ... ungrateful] I shouldn't recommend anyone to count too much on my being of an amiable disposition. I am often very much bored with people who are fond of me—because some of them are, really; so I am afraid I am ungrateful
23	selfish] very low
23–5	such windy ... say that] things you can't prove. I have got very little "general culture", you know, but
26–7	God, I have a memory!] heaven, I remember things.
28	old] young
29–32	Is that ... common fellow] I know how to sit on a horse, and how to row a boat. Is that enough? I am conscious of a great inability to say anything to the point. To put

> myself in a nutshell, I am a greedy specialist—and not a
> bad fellow. Still, I am only what I am—a very common
> creature

103:33	fellow] creature
37	my] a
38	witty] embarrassing
39	a common fellow] second-rate
39	the] such an
104:1	patience] delicacy
2	I'm vulgar] I am very vulgar
3	strictest] literal
4	and then I walk ahead.] but it's my last concession!
5	Have you any sisters] Your concessions are smaller than they sound. Have you any sisters
10	possibly] om.
12	Study] Well, study
14	fancy] guess
15	reasonably] considerably
18	get letters] get some letters of introduction
20	Not I ... money] Not I, heaven forgive me! I am very poor. I have in hand a little money
26	will] shall
28	may be] will succeed in everything
29	Amen!] Thank you, awfully,
30	given] given here
32	substantially upon] in
43	importuned her so effectually,] pressed her so hard
43	had] om.
105:7	adventured] risked
8	humorous] comical
15–16	sober valedictory] leave-taking speech
16	felt] sincere
17	nobly bare of flimsy compliments] in very good taste
18	fellow] creature
22–3	his hat and overcoat] his usual hat and overcoat, his silver-headed stick was not in the corner
23	it displayed] that struck her
24	Adela] she
26–7	Finally ... return] She looked for Mr. Moore in his study, but it was empty
28	back thence] back from her quest
32–33	the repose of ... break with it] her old dignities and forms, but she was to break with them
105:42–106:4	But inasmuch ... maintain it.] om.
7	and looked him full in the eyes] without meeting his eyes
8	said she] she said, rather casually
14	That's what] That's exactly what

105:16	I mean ... difficult] Difficult for me—yes
17	difficult] easy
18	I don't know ... but I am] Let me hear what you call easy
19	stay] remain
23–4	pleasures and pleasures] attractions on both sides
25	the former] on one
26	invite me to accept it] request me to give it up—to renounce Berlin
27	say] do
28	invite] request
29	makes] *does* make
33	It means ... to mean] A great deal of absurdity
36	"fascinating"] irresistible
40	command] order
42	and they ... frankly] and now they were looking watchfully
107:13	cried] murmured
17	fancy] mere guess
19	She is an ... for me.] She's a different sort from any I have met, and just to have seen her like this—that is enough for me!
22	The day was ended.] om.

POOR RICHARD

Notes:

1. The variants recorded below are based on a collation of the original serial text of the tale (*Atlantic Monthly*, 1867) and its revised version in *Stories Revived* (1885).

2. In the revised text, the tale is divided into seven sections. Section i begins at 128:1; section ii at 133:4; section iii at 138:9; section iv at 142:33; section v at 146:15; section vi at 161:1; section vii at 169:7.

3. The following are the revised forms of proper names. Only the first occurrence of these forms is recorded.

> Richard Clare] Richard Maule
> James Luttrel] Robert Luttrel

> A Story in Three Parts] om.
> Part I] 1

128:3	narrow meadow] large pasture
10	had] would have
11	broad] om.
11	loveliness] a charm
12	plebian] undistinguished
15–16	massive ... good looks] both robust and rich. The good looks of her companion
17	cut] made
18–19	passionate] headstrong
19–20	her own ... attention] she had the air of a person a good deal bored but determined to be patient
26	foolish] horrid
28	foolish] horrid
129:3–4	leave,' ... 'to] leave to
4	that] om.
5	Of course.] Oh dear!
5	I listen,' added Gertrude] I wait for your words,' Gertrude added
7–8	one who ... rage] a young fellow who sees that he is in the wrong, whatever line he takes
11–12	That ... enough] I am quite satisfied with that
12	add something more] pile it up
13–14	flagrantly ... seconds] darting a vicious glance at her
16	position,' she said, 'if it] position if it
18	fancy] believe
20	Oh, of course] Oh, you think me a baby, I know
25	please you] make you like me
26	can] could

129:27   please ... any one] be liked by you or by anyone else

34   a thing ... tempted] a poor thing you seem

35–6   had ... heart] care for you in another way

38   may] will

39   a heavenly] an excellent

130:1   Gertrude] Gertrude Whittaker

1   not of] not one of

3   the heart] some, at least, of the faculties

4–5   devoutly ... lovable] honestly believe I should repay anyone who would bear with me

5   that] om.

5   thought] persisted

6   turned a penny] earned a cent

6–7   a woman] any woman

8–9   and be *pleased* ... intoxicate.] to simple liking—to friendship. The devil! Be friends with men whom you don't
make mad! You do me!

12   point] contention

14   grown vocal;] ringing in the air,

14   Of course I do] You have named it

16   contented] content

16   my friendship] what I have offered you

18–19   my ... sure] the kind of interest I take in you I am very
sure

21   dismiss you,—] turn away from you altogether—

24   Indeed] You don't mean it

29–30   intoxicating you] making you mad

31   like a ... her] learn to live on rational terms with a
woman than to fancy one adores her

31   intoxication] madness

32–3   break with ... idleness,] leave off your idle life

35   mistress.] 'adored'.

39   counsellor] care-taker

42   noble] capable

131:2   and of your heart] and even of your nature

5–7   'but'—... to end] 'but it's humbug—humbug from beginning to end

9   drive one mad] make one curse

11   But] Ah,

11   wife.] *wife!*

12   an awful] a deadly

13   order ... loving you] order—I began to live properly
when I began to love you

14   broken with] sworn off

15   of liquor] om.

19   no beauty ... now?)] none of the airs and graces of the
girls that are called pretty;

131:21–2	That ... inflamed it] Those clever things you just said were meant for a dash of cold water, but you can't drown me by holding me under a spout
23	it was] it's
24	very] om.
26	He spoke ... calmness] There was something now so calmly resolute in his tone
27	Here she] She
29	Richard Clare] Richard Maule
31	invaded ... breast] took possession of the young man
34	Oho] Oh, softly
42	head] diplomacy
132:1	head] diplomacy
2	heart] good-nature
2	a good heart] my good nature
5	am so explicit.] go into all this;
6	Listen, then] Therefore listen to me once again
27	resumed] went on
133:7	great] large
12	and homely-featured] with rather thick features
12–13	arriving at maturity] reaching her majority
13–14	Of ... make] Of a vigorous, active constitution
16	chief ... neighbourhood] principal persons of the country-side
22–3	compromise ... distinctions] shirk her implied obligations
25–6	moderation ... bespoke] kind of genial discretion which attracted
27–8	and yet discreet ... discerning] yet circumspect; thrifty, yet open-handed; literal, yet addicted to joking; keenly observant
29	and] om.
29	a prodigious] an immense
31	broadly] preponderantly
33	insensible of it] sensible of them
34	detect] elicit
35	watchful of] and inhale
36	deliciously] delightfully
38	sweet ... perfume,] desultory aroma
40	Miss Whittaker] Gertrude Whittaker
43	acknowledged] been conscious of
134:2	and had] and
6–7	impatience in equal proportions] eagerness in equal, contradictory proportions
8	his boyhood] jackets
10	farm] acres
11	it] them

134:12	farm] property
13	almost forcibly abducted] taken bodily possession of
20–1	to common ... averse] he was very slow in acquiring the arts which help a man to live happily with others
22	live] get on
23–6	resumed ... purpose] entered upon the enjoyment of the old place on which his boyhood had been passed, and to which he appeared to cling the more perversely as it was known to be very thin land
27–8	rejected ... counsel] seemed to take pleasure in braving their disapproval of his queer proceedings
31	ungrateful ... arrogant] ungrateful and conceited
32	conceit] vanity
33–5	which ... third year,] who had tried some clever experiments on the thankless soil. At the end of three years people spoke of him as cracked;
36	almost] really
37	them himself] this view of his condition
42	drinks] boozes
135:1	resumed ... with] began again to see something of
3	his rural compeers] the local swains
4	bitter] extreme
4	possible] om.
6	death; but when at last] death. When, however, at last
7	had] om.
12	Gertrude's junior] younger than the heiress
14	a vague ... repute] an impression of the poor figure he cut in the world
15	and to his] and his
17	of compassion] of easy compassion
17–18	a heavy ... from] all the back-news of
20	admonition] recommendation
24	defence, as ... virtue] defence—his exposure seemed so delightful
25–6	that he ... reproof] he could be scolded like that every day or two; nothing had ever touched him so softly
28–9	with ... opens] I have set before the reader
34–6	Miss Whittaker's ... comforts] this young lady's quick wits and good-humour, her liberal way of life and active charity
37	almost ... one] a regular luxury
38	repose,—] success—
40	own] om.
40	errors,—] bad habits—
41	varying glance] kind, clear eye
43	changing willow] murmuring apple-tree
136:3	had] om.

136:3–4	given ... pain] had not been at all to her taste
4	Richard Clare ... world!)] this blundering youth
8	that ... her] that—strange as it might seem—she was going to change her name for his
9	esteemed] regarded as
14–16	It is ... upon] It must be declared without delay that this assumption was precipitate and unfair
17	to be mercenary was] a mercenary habit was
21	declared] tried to make her believe
22	the ... affection] his disinterestedness
23	out of ... indifference] because she was not in love with him
24	for] on account of
27	relations] acquaintance
28–9	sentimental ... concern.] dangerous complications. She had regarded him as one more helpless human being to 'look after'.
34	sober] comparatively pacific
37–8	fancy ... bravado] believe it could take its time
137:5	hero, but] hero, certainly, but
6	no fool] not an ass
8	slender brains] limited understanding
10–11	of having ... by] of there having been such a question between himself and
12–14	he could ... bare] he would have a right to insist on something
15–18	an immense ... his struggle] a great deal of crude intention, but he cursed the ignorance which was such an obstacle to his doing anything in particular
21	farmer] cultivator
23	breaking with] renouncing
27	think] live
28	think] live
28	muscle] valour
30–1	dared ... add.] dared!
32	revolving] turning over
33	ideal schemes] little plans
34	for the ... enthusiasm] for making the stream of his passion turn some other mill
34–42	Yet whatever ... hospitality)] Yet, with however much of the same firmness and mildness she might still meet him, she could not feel secure against repeated intrusion
138:2	about only] only about
3	however] unfortunately
3	very] om.
4	own] om.
5	now] om.

138:5–6 sadly ... instrument] to ask herself whether it mightn't be helped in its work

10–11 friendship ... unexceptionable] acquaintance of a person so clever, so superior

12 one, she ... herself, who] one who

16 To ... like] To beg him to try to like

17 like ... ridiculous] care for *him* was absurd

18–21 the work were ... creature himself,] the matter would take care of itself—he would take a fancy to him in spite of every prejudice. But to begin to praise any object to her young friend was just the way to make him hate it. He himself was such a subject for pity

21–2 appeal ... compassion] recommend anyone to his benevolence

23 consequently at odds] therefore out of sorts

23–4 If some ... less] If she could put her hand on some creature less

25–8 to such a ... nevertheless] he might feel some sympathy for such a being. Captain Severn had, to her knowledge, not been a darling of destiny, but

29 with it] with his lot

30–1 something ... equanimity] a tacit rebuke in his resignation

32 estimate] opinion

33 fail ... situation,] throw away such a chance

35–6 But a ... she loves] But women have been known to show their affection for a man by sending him as a missionary to the cannibals

41 second-rate] om.

42 valour] abilities

42–3 His ... Richmond] The regiment of volunteers to which he belonged, and which was now part of the army of the Potomac

139:1–2 beneath ... encouragement] she had given almost every man in it—as a rich woman could do—some sign that her thoughts were with him

3–4 leave his regiment] be lifted out of regimental work

5 an excellentally useful man] a very useful officer

7 sister domiciled] sister who was domiciled

13 selection ... of] collection of specimens from

15 great] om.

18 confounded] taken aback

18 real] om.

19 assured him] protested

20 such as ... her] the suffering brave was

20–2 Never, thought ... grace] The Captain liked her on the spot, and thought of nothing else as he drove home

139:24	felt that] perceived
25	ever] om.
25	lover] real aspirant
27–37	Whatever might be ... allurements] He liked to see where he was going, and never went far simply because the country was pretty; he wanted to know where he should arrive
34–5	habit, or ... programme,] tradition
36–7	logical ... heroine] consequences of falling in love with our young lady
37–8	determined] taken a vow
39–40	evoked ... place] an income to point to, no great change had come to pass
42–3	doubted ... affections:] thought it wrong to draw a woman on;
140:1	making a widow] converting some fresh girl into a figure of mourning
1	was one in five thousand] pleased him as he had never been pleased, but that seemed to him no reason for recanting his principles
1–4	Before ... reason?] om.
6	earned ... then] earned enough money for two to live upon, then
12	should ... from] could seem to him a reason for not
13–14	this fact ... origin] the sentiment in question didn't dare —or hadn't as yet dared—to lift its head
14	most stoical] deep
15	certain] probable
15–16	made a ... his wife] accepted obligations gracefully enough from a person with certain rights
18	sentimentally distasteful] odious
19–20	this frigid instinct was] these logical ice-blocks were
21	whether ... away] gradually to evaporate and flood the position
22–3	it could ... possessor] he could keep up his consistency only at the cost of a considerable moral strain
25–6	be sternly ... impressions] walk very straight
31	constantly] om.
32–3	of one ... to love] a gentleman who would perhaps some day take to wife some woman, who, however nice she might be, couldn't be as nice as he
33	she] *she*
40–2	her common ... its effect] her taking her loss for granted. This left nothing between them but her casual hospitality, and the effect of that method, as yet,
141:1–4	kindliest ... little daisy] best form. They talked and fraternised, and moreover they watched each other, but

they breathed not a word of what each was thinking about most

141:6–7   as yet ... good-nature] only another of her social pensioners

15   courtesy] consideration

16–17   Gertrude, on her ... replied] Gertrude had replied to her venerable friend

24   accordingly presented] introduced

26–7   almost picturesque] really dramatic

28   pale face] pale, handsome face

28   and] om.

30   disagreeable] insufferable

32–3   scheme ... miscarry] plan would have no fruit

33   defiant silence] defiant, conscious silence

34   decidedly ridiculous] very pretentious

35   toward ... half-avowed] that half-confessed

39   was] were

39–40   whether they ... snobs] they were only a pair of grimacing comedians

41–2   consummate] extreme

43–142:1   added ... dignity] was only another proof of her tremendous cleverness

142:2–3   his sweetheart's sake] the sake of the woman he loved

7–8   mettlesome ... conversation] richness of resource of their hostess

9–15   her tenderness ... integrity] she ought to spare him an exhibition by which he could only be mortified—for didn't she know his thoughts, she who was the cause of them all? But the next instant he asked himself, with a great revulsion of feeling, whether he was afraid to see the proof of how superior she was to himself

20–1   and ... silence] by certain little calculated silences

23   of rage] om.

27   lapsed] sunk

28   profound] helpless

31   discerned] discovered

39   served ... villa] constituted Miss Whittaker's residence

41   short] smooth

42   anticipated] gone to meet

42   longing] desire

143:3–4   marked the reserve] noticed the taciturnity

6   had] om.

6   repair] make up for

8   happy juxtaposition] conjunction

10   man] fellow

15   rascal] scoundrel

143:17–18	I should ... face] He seems to me a very pleasant member of society
22	hater] reviler
22	lover] adorer
23	mistrust of his old] scepticism in regard to his old
26	he asked.] om.
28	some dozen] a good many
19–30	being kind,' ... shrewdness] being kind to people who are in trouble,' Richard remarked, with a shrewdness which he thought superior
31	face] appearance
33	cunningly] with calculation
37–8	a face ... forgotten] the sort of face you don't forget
39–43	expressions. Her face ... herself.'] expressions.'
144:3	sacred] cherished
8	fervid] significant
10	mouth] lips
11	it] *they*
11	itself] themselves
12	it was] they were
12	mouth] lips
13	an] om.
17	scrutinize] probe a little
22	he] *he*
22	a mannerless] an underbred
24	prove] turn out
25	sigh? It] sigh like the wind in the chimney? It
29	favoured] gratified
31	obvious infelicity] probable ill-luck
36	declared] mused
37–8	that this ... Major] there was some comfort in that. He didn't fancy the Major so very much
40	arrested ... of her] made her companion pause, turned round to await her
41	that] om.
145:3	most heroically] very high
4	anguish] bad feelings
4	intoxication] exaltation
4	surveyed] looked at
5	a kindling fancy] all sorts of remarkable ideas
5–6	tongue-tied ... fortune] tongue-tied, sulking at opportunity
8	sweet] the admirable
11	talk,—] express himself—
11	and] om.
13	course] character

145:14   upon his own place] in that part of its course which
            traversed his own property
16–17   in fair ... his head] with sufficient volubility, but with a
            kind of angry shyness, his head
26   resolved] determined
27   brave resolve] enlightened resolution
30   this touch at present] this puncture
40   again. He felt that] again, and at that instant
146:3   there ... bow] then show them how well he could dis-
            pense with their company
13   most generously] very characteristically
15   Richard got ... how] Richard hardly knew how he got
            through the following week
16–17   was actually aware of] suspected
17   and yet heroic] yet at the same time heroic
19   strictly] very
22–3   and more ... habits] than the exhilaration of liquor
23–5   adding ... austerity] keeping the score of his abstinence
26   he raised ... abstinence] nothing would suit him but not
            to drink at all
28   for the love of it] to splash about
29   we] I
32   in ... will,—] his own good intention—
33   premised] predicted
38   and swore] swearing
147:1   gross physical soberness] reform
3   ridiculous] comical
5–6   often outweather] recover from
6–7   through ... egotism] by the aid of the same egotism they
            were perhaps meant to chasten
7–8   as grim and sober] fasting as grimly
9–10   plunge ... idleness] stupefy himself with some drudgery
10   labour] task
11–12   the mechanical ... hours] mechanically getting rid of the
            time
13   squarely to face him] to be importunate
15–24   the results ... of life] this question of his own manhood
            it sometimes seemed not very important, after all, that
            Gertrude should listen to him. He tried later to build up
            a virtue by the most ruthless experiments and tests
33   lonely and black-windowed] dim and lonely
35–8   his love coming ... himself] his desire for Gertrude com-
            ing back to him, but bereft in the interval of a jealousy
            which now seemed to him to have been fantastic. One
            morning, at any rate, he leaped upon his horse and
            cantered back to Miss Whittaker's
42   steed stalled there] animal,

148:1–2　　horse ... the house] steed. On the steps of the house
　　3–5　　a generous ... just one] a nod which was intended to be
　　　　　very friendly, and Severn nodded back, but didn't speak
　　9　　　modest] om.
　　14　　young] poor
　　17　　and] om.
　　20　　cordial impatience] an invidious distinction
　　20　　of his hope] of all his hopes
　　31　　Poor Gertrude] Unfortunate creature
　　32–3　　You fool] You poor idiot
　　37　　You fool! you fool] You poor idiot! you poor idiot
　　39　　scene] incident
　　40　　at this juncture] om.
　　40　　a strong] a remarkably strong
　　40–1　　our purpose ... which] necessary to repeat here the words
　　42–149:2　a single step ... throats] an ace of a mutual understand-
　　　　　ing, and when a single movement of the hand of either
　　　　　would have jerked aside the curtain that hung between
　　　　　them, some malignant influence had paralysed them
　　　　　both
149:3　　this hypothesis] supposing so
　　3–4　　Severn, then ... mechanically] Severn had walked blindly
　　7　　was] were
　　8　　faced about] turned back
　　9　　there] om.
　　11　　violent] om.
　　13　　dreadful] om.
　　13–15　against her ... uncompromising] against her, and there
　　　　　even entered into her mind a certain element of dread
　　　　　of the man whose passion was so insistent
　　17–20　the splendid ... brutality] Severn's exaggerated respect,
　　　　　it gratified her, after a little, to remember that Richard
　　　　　had been brutal
　　23　　his sanity] conventional forms
　　28　　was missing] had deserted its post
　　38　　unwomanly] immodest
　　38　　can] shall ever
　　39　　can't] shall never
150:8　　Love gets ... gets none.] If you won't risk anything how
　　　　　can you demand of others that they shall?
　　11　　such ... Clare] an intemperate, uneducated boy, who
　　　　　would never grow older,
　　12　　was ... spinsterhood] seemed to convert her into a kind
　　　　　of maiden-aunt
　　12–24　'Am I, then,' ... gaping heart.] Yet her conscience smote
　　　　　her for her meditated falsity to to Richard, her momen-

tary readiness to succumb to the temptation to revert to
him out of pique.

150:25-6 Richard's heart ... than it] he any better suited to her
now than he

27-8 decent sorrows ... passion] vexation at losing Captain
Severn in a passion got up for the occasion

31 keenly] om.

38 yet] om.

38 heart] om.

40 soul] mind

40 of a real contempt;] that she really scorned him,

41 knew—or ... that] knew that

43 fatal and inconsiderate] reckless and ruinous

151:2-3 she rode ... his] took her way to his straggling

4 made her way to] rode round to

11 rich domain] wide fields,

12 deserted of its] abandoned by their

13 its abandonment] his absence

15 all too] om.

16 rumble, as of] rumble of

18 turn] bend

22-3 It was Richard.] om.

25 towards] to

25 silent Thank God!] sigh of really tender relief.

27 was duly represented] appeared to his advantage

41 Yes,' said Gertrude, 'I] Yes, I

152:3-4 An odd ... nor less] He was always wishing to produce
an effect upon her, and it seemed to him just then that
this was the way

5 An equally delicate instinct] It was a certain instinct of
calculation, too, that

8-9 busy,' she said, 'I] busy I

11 I don't know what all] doing a lot of chores

14 I'll] I mean to

23 a fool] an idiot

30 a fool] an idiot

31 stupid] nasty

31 fool] idiot

32-3 making love ... looked it] saying sweet things to you.
But if he had you wouldn't have objected—your face told
that

36-7 a fool] an awful ass

37 a fool] an ass

43-153:1 fail of justice] let me off far too easy

153:14 steep,] om.

15-16 horizontally] diagonally

29-30 returning his gaze] looking down at him

153:31–2	romance,' ... And] romance, it's reality,' thought Gertrude. And
33	romance] sentiment
35	a walking-pole] an alpenstock
37	at least,' smiled Gertrude, 'with] at least, with
154:1	prodigiously] tremendously
4	Dear me,] Oh, I say
8	in] on
10–11	revolved his speech] thought over what he had just said to her
19	prodigy] miracle
31	the good wife] Mrs. Catching
33	to a tête-à-tête over Richard's] face to face with her entertainer, over his
34	soberly] tenderly
35	augur] infer
36–7	had waxed ... sun] was higher in the heavens than ever
40–1	dewy ... importunities] quite surfaces to his crude unrest
42	to exhale ... sweetness] to have a kind of wine-like strength
155:2	figure,—] grace—
2–7	When she ... action.] om.
9	habitual ... repose,—] most frequent feeling when he was with her was a consciousness of the liberty to be still—
11–12	hot and vaporous] hot, vaporous
12	innocent, then, of] innocent of
15	dwelt upon] demanded
21	his mirror] his cheap mirror
23	Gertrude] Miss Whittaker
24	at peace] not in trouble
28	most] very
33–4	entourage] domestic arrangements
36	implied] inarticulate
40	'Richard,' she answered] 'My dear sir,' she said
156:1–2	as bravely ... before it] with renewed tenacity and felt like a hero
2–3	lifeless ... left him] with all his courage gone, and limpness and langour in its place
4	a prodigious] an extreme
11	read it out] done with it
13	Gertrude] She
13	those] all the
14	which] that were
17	difference,] differing opinion
18	great ... conservative] rabid Republican, and he in cool opposition
19	appearance] detachment

156:23-4   the thought of ... butchery] visions of carnage and suffer-
              ing,
     28   burden ... relief] bore, not a cure
     30   fain ... stay] like him to stay
     33   conflict between her desires] such undercurrent
     39   Captain Severn's features] the features of Captain Severn
     40   in courtesy to a brief] to exchange some
157:5   well enough] quite on your feet
     5   wound] hole in your side
     7   Major. I hope] Major; perhaps
     12   he thought ... excitement] thought he saw there a kind
              of agitation, of choked emotion
     13   And then] Hereupon
     15   a motion] a gesture
     16   sorrows] distress
     16-17   cried Richard] he cried to himself
     19   grip ... has] fist the young horse-breaker has
     23   Yes] Of course I am
     28   home. We] home. She is out for the evening. We
     29   defiance] a challenge
     33   Ah? I'm sorry] Dear me, I'm so sorry
     33   I'm sorry.] I'm so very sorry!
     38   felt like] was on the point of
     42-3   calmness ... weakness] urbanity, seemed to mock at re-
              traction
158:1   Captain] My dear Captain
     1   happy] glad
     2   your farewell] any message
     3-4   I was. Good-bye] I was. It was my last chance. Good-bye
     9   said that Major, at last] the Major remarked at last
     9   cleverly] brilliantly
     10   before,' said he.] before—never!'
     12   that] poor
     15-16   We'll ... said] We will take everything that's proper in
              the way of remorse for granted—consider that said
     16   very, very] really
     17-18   spoken, how ... might] stopped him off, how do you know
              but that I might have done so
     19   square] om.
     20   then, I] then, that I
     21   improvisation] invention
     22   make] have anything to do with
     24   a most unholy] his red-hot
     26   ugly,' he said, 'To] ugly. To
     27   and] om.
     28   the lie] my fault
     30   immensely] remarkably

158:33–4	Miss Whittaker's remaining unengaged] Miss Whittaker's not having other people running after her
35	don't love her] have no disinterested regard for her
40	shabby deed;] nasty thing,
43	apprehensions] little scruples
43	that] om.
159:1–2	retraction ... quarter] any fancied reparation
3	bosh. A lie is a lie] gammon. A fib is a fib
5	lie] fib
5	lie] fib
8	loving or not loving] having a disinterested regard for
11	rascal] cheat
16–17	Strike me ... your talk] Touch me and I'll kill you, but I propose not to notice your animadversions
19	with rage] with white rage
23	heart ... were but] heart, wishing Luttrel had been
25–6	confession! It] confession—it
27–8	drawing-room window] window of the drawing room
30	You, Richard] Mercy—you
32–3	conservatory. He fancied them] conservatory, and they seemed to him
36	that] om.
36	fancied] imagined
41	infinitesimal] indefinable
42–3	that that ... preoccupied] that this whispered invocation came from poor Richard. She had been following her own thoughts
160:3	her inference was] it was clear to her
4–6	She could ... such a visit?] Naturally he would come and bid her farewell, and still more naturally she had her vision of what might pass between them at such a crisis.
10	unnatural] strange
12	resentful impulse] rush of resentment
27–8	you're out] you are quite out
28	head] mind
30	Yes, a damnable fool of myself] I haven't made it better—I have made it worse
31	breathed freely] didn't quite understand, but he breathed more freely
32	going on at this rate] all these gyrations
37	pull] wriggle
161:1–2	incidents ... events] small accidents loom large
8	Perhaps he had not] Perhaps in the hurry of sudden preparation he had not
9	But] Still,
11–12	the object ... courtesy] indebted to her for considerable attentions

161:15–18   done more ... vulgar token] failed further than in appear-
             ing to forget what she had done for him—he had also
             lost all remembrance of the way she had done it.

19   accredit us with] give us credit for

22–6   borne it out ... had given] made it the occasion of all
             kinds of tacit vows; she had given

27   tenderness] charity

30   wrong herself] waste something that was now too precious

36–7   found herself ... apprehension] was haunted with the
             idea

162:1   civility] common decency

9   adieus] message of good-bye

9–11   had time ... companion] had a spare moment to come
             and see her. As Luttrel performed this office he watched
             his hostess

13   message] farewell

14–17   the assumption ... at all, which] to represent the absent
             office as alluding hastily and mechanically to Miss Whit-
             taker would be better than to represent him as not allud-
             ing at all, for that

22   those words] Captain Severn's excuse

23   had time] a spare moment

23   their] its

24   perfect] om.

25   broadening ... lively] deepening into a sign of lively

30   pre-eminently ... conscience] a person of fastidious
             delicacy

33   and delirious] delirious

34–5   the reverse of creditable] by no means akin to despair

38   Nature had] the doctors

39   condemned to] booked for

40   granting his recovery] even assuming that he should get
             well

41   within a month] for many weeks

42   nay,] om.

42   all] everything

163:1–2   secure ... moreover, so] possess himself of Miss Whit-
             taker's confidence, hand and fortune. He had no money
             and he had many needs, and he was so

3–4   his fortune by slow degrees] by slow degrees a career
             which had not yet taken the luxurious shape he desired

4   good breeding] refined tastes

6   luxurious] well-appointed

6   accordingly] therefore

7   most ... prosperity] spread the carpet of repose

8   a somewhat lighter calibre] rather a fainter outline

9   very generously] om.

163 : 10–11	a woman with a mind] a young lady with standards
13	sense] observation
13	obstacles] drawbacks
14–15	but an ... balance] and after all his arithmetic there was a balance in his favour
20	bravely] boldly
24–5	heart was preoccupied] affections were already engaged
26	brother officer] comrade in the Volunteers
27	his unaided ... deductions] simply watching and taking little notes
28	logical; for, on the whole,] numerous, and on the whole
31	simulated offense] apparent delinquency
35–6	attenuate ... fortune] spin it out, play upon it, and mould it into a clue which should lead him to the point he wanted to reach
38	solid] fine
38	too ... solid,] a little too stiff and solid
40	handsome in feature] a handsome fellow
41	younger ... women;] people who hadn't the beauty of cleverness:
164 : 1–3	his general ... the man] he looked like a man of action who was at the same time a man of culture and
5	own immaterial woes] selfish heart-ache
10	chamber] darkened room
10	wrapped in a heavy sleep,] immersed in sleep
12	thinly furnished room] bare bedroom
13	elaborate apartments] upholstered quarters
13	essential luxuries] objects indispensable
14	Not but that he had] Not that he had not
16	the old ... him was] old Mrs. Catching
20	excite him] work him up
22	said] remarked
23	the good-wife] Mrs. Catching
24	excite him] work him up
27	like you] with a tale to her own
27	the nurse] the goodwife,
38	as poor Richard,] om.
38	intimating] expressing
41	lay imaciated] lay there imaciated
42	and stupid. The issue was] stupid; the issue seemed very
43	forward to ... larger town] on to the county-town, which was larger
165 : 1–2	him to ... the farm] her to relieve Mrs. Catching
2	her vigilance] sitting-up
4–5	was assiduous ... successful] carried on his seige
8–9	resentment—if resentment] rancour—if rancour
9	utterly] om.

165:9–10   even to ... delicate tact] to any tactile process that he was master of

    15   owing ... force of] more indebted to the favour of

    20   whither his operation tended] what he was 'after', as they said in that part of the world

   22–4   It was not ... wife] She knew very well that she should never fall in love with him, but it was conceivable she might live with him happily

    25   sudden] sickening

    27   distaste] disgust

    32   that] this

    33   money] fortune

    35   would anticipate security] should make herself decently secure

    40   discharge] disembarrass

    41   which] om.

    42   been to] been over to

    43   decidedly] unexpectedly

166:1   linger over] dwell long on

   5–6   killed,' she said.] killed.'

   7–8   a guerilla] a beastly guerilla

  9–10   uncompromising] immitigable

    12   like] capable of

 15–16   give way to passion would] surrender herself to passion now would

 16–17   solemnity ... regrets] sincerety of what had already taken place in her mind

 17–19   pale, but ... presume] outwardly calm, though I must add that a single glance of her eye directed him not to presume upon it

    21   attitude,] position

  21–2   betrayal mattered less] revelations were of little moment

    24   I'm cold] I am very cold

    24   said] murmured

    29   I'm sure ... it all] It is always the best that are taken

    30   said Gertrude] Gertrude answered

    31   he] one

    31   his] one's

    39   and the sentimentalizing.] and the—the *missing*!

167:1   something] important issues

    3   theories and our] theories—our

    6   feelings] capacity to *feel*

    8   they are] that is

    9   them] that

    11   'Yes, if I understand you.'] 'To feel what?' Gertrude inquired.

167 : 12–13	'I mean ... I don't] 'Affection, admiration, hope!' said the Major. 'I don't
13	burning] burning, you know
15	feeling] sentiment
19	sober] significant
24	fancy myself an] regard myself as an
25	otherwise] remiss in that way
32	blushed] blushed, nor whimpered
35	Major Luttrel,' she said, 'I] Major Luttrel, I
168 : 6	James Luttrel] Robert Luttrel
17	insensible,' said Gertrude, 'if] insensible if
18	courtesy] politeness
18	upon me.'] upon me,' Gertrude said.
19	courtesy,] politeness!
25	Strictly ... love you] I don't love you—no, not at all
30–1	'I don't think ... If you] Gertrude was silent a moment. 'If you
40	You all. ... religious.'] You all.'
42	a delicate] an insinuating
169 : 2	and your advice, and your care] your advice, your support
13	out a brief] up a
19–20	I had ... of our] I should like him to hear nothing about our
23	of his good judgement] reasonable from him
29	Clare is ... everything] that gentleman is one of your suspicious kind
33	marriage] ceremony
38	fit] fit to be seen
38	*vice versa*] I should shock you
39	request by] request to herself by
170 : 11	the uncompromising ... bride] bright colours which those who knew her well must have regarded as a kind of self-defiance
13	amazingly] curiously
14	heavy] dull
26	mistrusted it] hung back from the next steps
27	resumed his visits at] made his way back to
29	feel] be
35–6	profound aversion to] kind of horror of
39–40	luminous ... seemed to] which seemed to shine with the idea of their possessor's taking a fresh start, it struck
171 : 1	you're engaged] you have got her
7	assumed] supposed
7	had] would have
12–13	confirm this ignorance] make this ignorance last a little longer; it was always so much gained
13–14	such terms ... correspond] writing terms

171:16	great, cushioned,] om.
19	Are you engaged yet] Have you got her yet
20–1	There was ... engaged now.'] The note of provocation in his tone was so strong that the Major ceased to temporise. 'Yes, I have "got" her, as you elegantly express it. We are engaged to be married.'
24	Yes, practically I am] Yes—so far as doing anything goes
25	What ... practically] What in the name of all that's conceited could you do
27	I feel about it] much I hate you
28	'You're a wise ... kindly] 'it will be very kind of you. And you will be a wise man,' the Major added
33–4	'Ah, if ... to say.'] 'Yes, but I thought hers was better.'
36	daily,] om.
37	defer] put off, in the same measure,
38	a bitter insult] an insult
39	would] should
39	he now found himself] he found himself now
172:3	in the ... landscapes] under the sky and among those natural things
5	great] om.
10–11	whose ... measure] who had used to seem to him above his measure altogether
13	heart] nature
17	an immense] a great
18	gate] gates
20	impassioned] excited
21	nervous] passionate
23	fancied] imagined
28	of Richard's presence] that he was in her house
32	Richard] the young man
34	you're at last] at last you are
40	ill] sick too
43–173:1	the dejection ... the misery] the blighted state of her person, the extreme misery
173:1–2	staggered back] moved backward
4	as if] om.
4	erratic] extravagant
6	through pity] through the most unexpected pity
30–1	resentment.] desolation!
32	a mighty rage against] a desire to throttle
43	foul things,—] odious things—
174:5	harassing] persecuting
8	entry] hall
28	I will speak,] Ah, you won't enjoy it,
28–9	'I've ... Gertrude] 'Gertrude, I have done you a vile wrong
31	was no wrong] didn't matter much

36	it] that
38	cried Gertrude] said Gertrude
42	Shut your infernal mouth] You're a precious one to talk
175:2	with a little bow] in a superior tone
3	and began] he began
5	nearer] near
8	said Richard] Richard went on
12	You idiot!] You eternal tormentor,
12	shouted] moaned
16	Luttrel] Major Luttrel
17	fancied] believed
23	away] absent from home
30	and] om.
43	opinions] inferences
176:6	deny] represent
6	visitor, seemed] visitor as absent seemed
18–19	in what] to something that
19	a serious grief] a very serious pain
20	profoundly] perfectly
24	thoroughly] om.
28	painful] distressing
177:2	to respect ... heart] not to protest against the inscrutable
6	honoured] was gratified by
8	colossal] om.
18	say simply] remark
20	utterly] horribly
23–4	an enormous] a tremendous
178:2	shocked] shocked at this piece of information
3–4	he was ... loved him] there was a gallantry in him, after all, and in this new phase he pleased her
6	and tardy] and poor tardy
15	with] against
16	our] my
16	our] my
23	on a captain's commission] with a commission in the Volunteers
24	some] much
28	had apparently become very] was now
29	now ... gentlemen] included even people who came from Boston to stay with her
34	most] om.
39–40	he found ... submission] he became reconciled
179:2	even ... St. Louis] the means to emigrate with advantage
12	happy] contented
13–14	twenty-seven ... account] nearly thirty years of age, some little romantic episode in the past is vaguely alluded to as accounting

THE ROMANCE OF CERTAIN OLD CLOTHES

Notes:

1. The variants recorded below are based on a collation of the original serial text of the tale (*Atlantic Monthly*, 1868) and its two revised versions in *A Passionate Pilgrim* (1875)—hereinafter mentioned as *APP*—and *Stories Revived* (1885)—hereinafter mentioned as *SR*.

2. In *SR*, the tale is divided into two sections. Section i begins at 210:1; and section ii at 212:41.

3. The following, in *SR*, are the revised forms of proper names. Only the first occurrence of these forms in that text is recorded.

> Mrs. Willoughby] Mrs. Veronica Wingrave
> Mr. Willoughby] Mr. William Wingrave
> Viola] Rosalind
> Bernard Willoughby] Bernard Wingrave

210:1	Toward] Towards SR
3–5	children ... respectable sound] children, by name Mrs. Veronica Wingrave SR
5–6	been left ... marriage] lost her husband early in life SR
7	children] progeny APP, SR
7	latter] young persons APP, SR
8	tender care] zeal APP; tenderness SR
8	fondest] highest SR
9	after] in remembrance of SR
11–12	these young persons] this youthful trio APP, SR
13	and of that] and that SR
13	mould] structure SR
14	genuine] good SR
15	blood,—] descent— SR
15–16	capital son and brother, and] deferential son, a patronising brother, APP, SR
17–18	Mr. Willoughby] The late Mr. William Wingrave SR
19	penetration of mind] liberality of taste APP; freedom of thought SR
22	record] call attention to SR
24	charming] romantic APP, SR
24	Viola] Rosalind SR
24–5	upon the ... one of] the younger he had called SR
27	Bernard Willoughby] Bernard Wingrave SR
29	request] injunction SR
29	an earnest entreaty] a formal command SR
30	there] om. SR
31–2	which ... studies] where he himself had acquired his taste for elegant literature SR

210:32–4   Mrs. Willoughby ... more. So she] Mrs. Willoughby
            fancied that the lad's equal was not to be found in the
            two hemispheres, but she had the antique wifely sub-
            missiveness. She   APP; It was Mrs. Wingrave's belief that
            the lad's equal was not to be found in the two hemi-
            spheres, but she had the old traditions of literal obedience.
            She   SR
211:1   was entered] presented himself   SR
4   twenty-third] twenty-fourth   SR
6–7   an utterly ... abode] a very dull, unfashionable residence
            SR
11   gentle *brusquerie*] originality   SR
14–16   England; whereupon ... daughters] England; whereupon
            poor Mrs. Willoughby, you may be sure, bade them hold
            up their heads   APP; the old country; whereupon poor
            Mrs. Wingrave, you may be sure, bade them hold up
            their heads   SR
17–18   This ... was] This gentleman was   SR
20   prepared] proposed   APP, SR
21   this country] the flourishing colony   SR
21   warm] sworn   SR
30   fair] white   SR
32   as] om.   SR
33   softest and finest emotions] softest, quickest impulses   SR
34   rich, fair skin] candid complexion   APP; slightly lym-
            phatic fairness   SR
34   and] om.   SR
37   it is ... wouldn't] she may have had reasons apart from
            her natural dignity   SR
40–1   was a ... animation] was a positive brunette, short of
            stature, light of foot, with a vivid dark brown eye   APP;
            had the cheek of a gipsy and the eye of an eager child,
            as well as the smallest waist and lightest foot in all the
            country of the Puritans   SR
41–3   She had ... as her] When you spoke to her she never
            made you wait, as her   SR
212:1   gazed] looked   SR
1–4   her somewhat ... end of it] a cold fine eye), but gave you
            your choice of a dozen answers before you had uttered
            half your thought   SR
6–7   maintain ... good-will] spare part of their attention   SR
7   young] om.   SR
13   respectful *empressement*] punctilious courtesy   APP, SR
15–16   an honest ... man] a capable, honourable, civil youth   SR
16   comfortable hopes,] complacency   SR
18   face] person   SR
19   on] om.   SR

212:21–2   forthwith ... acquaintance] have thought their other male
            acquaintance made but a poor figure before such a perfect
            man of the world SR
22–4   The imagination ... society] om. SR
23   women] woman APP
23   little] small APP
24   talk] anecdotes SR
25   vast] great SR
27–8   discourse upon] talk about SR
30–1   parlour,—quite ... and] parlour, and SR
31–2   the expense of] an outlay in APP
38   own movement] elders, SR
41   nice] fine APP, SR
42–3   satisfy ... charms] make up his mind whether he liked
            the big sister or the little sister best SR
43   balance] apportionment APP
213:2   marry one of them] stand up before the parson with one
            of them SR
4–6   indispensable ... in love] necessary, for Lloyd had too
            much young blood in his veins to make a choice by lot
            and be cheated of the satisfaction of falling in love SR
4–5   much of ... making] gallant a fellow to make APP
6   being] be APP
7   easily and] as they came— SR
10   hideous] odious APP; sharp SR
11   commit himself] come to the point SR
11   a] om. SR
12   but] om. SR
12–13   venerable dames] worldly matrons SR
14   take] treat SR
15   fair creatures] poor girls APP, SR
16–17   for the ... and modest] that their visitor should do or say
            something 'marked', they kept a very modest SR
19   sisterly friends betwixt] friends enough, and accom-
            modating bedfellows (they shared the same four-poster),
            betwixt SR
21   the young girls] they SR
25   love] ambition SR
25   great deal] large share SR
26   glory] selection, the distinction, SR
32   undertake] carry on SR
35   little] om. APP, SR
37–9   The young ... inspection] The two maidens were almost
            always together, and had plenty of chances to betray
            themselves SR
39   that] om. SR
40   those] the SR

213:41	which] om. SR
42	which] om. SR
214:5	coquetry] conquest SR
5–6	furbelows] kerchiefs SR
7	a little] an APP
7–8	a little agreement ... matters] a contract of fair play in this exciting game SR
22	alone before] alone—that was a rare accident—before SR
27	long] large SR
31	servant maid] servant-maid who had been having a tryst with her sweetheart SR
33	within] into SR
33	toward] which led to SR
215:1	and] om. SR
3	mamma] our mother APP, SR
5	young] om. SR
9	a couple of small rubies] a very small sapphire SR
29	shouldn't] wouldn't SR
30	said Perdita] Perdita answered SR
32	mamma] your mother APP, SR
32	conduct] intrigue SR
33	Mamma] My mother APP, SR
33	conduct] intrigue SR
34	asked my] asked for my SR
35	sister] dearest sister SR
36	sister] companion SR
39	But] However, SR
216:1	cursed] should curse SR
1	sister] Rosy SR
6	year, at least] year to live at least SR
10	proper] becoming APP, SR
18–19	dress, and upon] dress—on SR
36–7	sentiment uttered] love-making SR
38	she ... regard] he had dealt her a terrible blow SR
40–1	The lurid ... horizon] The great revolt of the Colonies was not yet in the air SR
217:1–2	Mrs. Willoughby] The good lady SR
3	most elegant] genteelest SR
4	county] Province SR
9	full and stately] stately and sweeping APP, SR
15	heavenly] celestial APP; heavenly SR
18–19	was quite ... should] could think of no form or fashion which would SR
18–19	pattern and trimmings] fashion APP
28	arm bare] arm, which was bare SR
31	Ah] Look, look SR
36–7	Yards ... laces] Innumerable yards of lustrous silk and

satin, of muslin, velvet and lace   APP, SR

217:38   word of envy] jealous word   SR

39   efforts] industry   APP, SR

41   challenged] received   SR

218:3   Lloyd] Arthur Lloyd   SR

3-4   an unmarried ... cooing] a bachelor; he declared he should be delighted to give up the place to the influence of Hymen   SR

6   priest] parson   APP; clergyman   SR

7   wedding gear] nuptial robes   SR

8   old] homely   SR

9   been fond sisters together] spent their undivided younger years   SR

11   Arthur impatient] Arthur was impatient   SR

16   heavy] full   SR

20   at] before   SR

21-2   shocked and pained] horrified   APP, SR

25   Viola] sweetheart   SR

27   in the] to the   SR

28   was ... comfort] appeared as elegant as it was commodious   SR

32   good] serious   APP, SR

33   her] Perdita's   SR

36-7   into ... restoration] into terribly low spirits and was not to be roused or cheered but by change of air and circumstances   APP; into terribly low spirits and was not to be roused or cheered but by change of air and company   SR

38   girl's] lady's   SR

40   purely physical one] mere bodily ill   SR

219:6   honest] bright   SR

9   shortly] very soon   SR

9   be confined] present him with an heir   APP, SR

12   solemn] important   SR

15   preoccupied ... condition] anxious about his wife and her coming ordeal   SR

16-17   and how ... effaced] and to note how she effaced   SR

19   certainly ... of it] turned it to prodigious account   APP; turned it to wonderful account   SR

29   and] she   SR

30   man swore at] man, at   APP, SR

32   wife] wife, uttered a passionate oath   APP, SR

40   about] away   SR

42   excess of diet] indiscretion in the way of died   APP, SR

42-3   of exposure] exposure   SR

220:1-2   the ... fatal] she was breathing her last   APP, SR

5   would ... night] should not get through the night   SR

12   to die] not to be warmed into life   SR

220:13–14	such ... veins] it SR
14	it all] all *my* fire SR
17	mistrust] suspicion SR
22	envy] be jealous of SR
24	fancied] coveted APP; simulated SR
25	do] attempt SR
27	melancholy] saddened SR
33	Viola] a one as Rosalind SR
34	dropped] lowered SR
221:23	lay] put SR
35	soberly] rationally SR
36	commerce] business SR
37–8	He ... sadness] He embraced it as a diversion from gloomy thoughts APP; He took advantage of it, to change the current of his thoughts SR
39	cherished] guarded SR
222:5	was ... health] would be full of danger for her health SR
6	the little creature's] his daughter's APP, SR
10	ride along with her] accompany her SR
13	gratitude] paternal joy SR
16	She ... moaned] That little person cried and choked SR
18	Viola] the aunt SR
19	little thing] poor child APP; little niece SR
21	for] to bring APP, SR
21	to be brought] om. APP, SR
23	fretted and fumed] shaken her head APP, SR
25	and] om. SR
25	town] whole country SR
26	young] om. SR
28–9	existed a bitter hostility] was as little love as you please SR
33	but the two] but of the two APP, SR
37	inasmuch as] in that APP, SR
37	old] early SR
38	conjectures] poignant mistrust APP; sharp suspicions SR
39	truth ... had been] truth. Viola's sentiment had been APP; truth. Rosalind's sentiment had been SR
42	said, was no paragon] hinted, was not a modern Petrarch APP, SR
223:7	great] big SR
12	prodigiously] exceedingly SR
15	little creature] young lady APP, SR
15	and she] and then she SR
16	Viola would then] Rosalind, at this, would SR
22–3	less obtrusive] more discreet APP, SR
24	be almost] almost be SR

223:26   that she] om.   SR
    28   and] om.   SR
    31–2   such ... *crescendo*] a *crescendo* so finely shaded   SR
    33   return] returns   SR
    37   ardent] pressing   SR
    37   out] to the end   SR
    39   should] would   SR
224:8   the three first] the first three   APP, SR
    11   great] fine   SR
    12–15   sustain ... repose] carry it like a woman of considerable
                fashion   SR
    16   immense] copious   SR
    19   glorious ... bidding] exquisite fabrics should await the
                commands   APP; exquisite fabrics should await the good
                pleasure   SR
    26   negative to ... that for] refusal that she saw, for   SR
    28   fancies] visions   SR
    32   desires] cupidity   SR
    37   slipper] shoe   SR
    40   bravely] boldly   SR
225:1   value at which] esteem in which   SR
    2   Great Heaven!] Gracious heaven,   SR
    2–3   a delightful] an agreeable   APP, SR
    13   counterpart] sequel   SR
    16   here ... ever] her temper, on that occasion, had taken an
                ineffaceable fold   APP, SR
    17   right,' ... 'had] right had   SR
    18   future? What] future?' she cried. 'What   SR
    21   very good passion.] very good as a 'scene'.   SR
    31   *Teneo* ... 'I hold.'] *Je garde,* said the motto—'I keep.'
                SR
    33   Keep it] Put it back   SR
    39   The child] Her little niece   SR
    41   little] small   SR
226:16   voice] tones   SR
    30   bloodless] blanched   SR

A MOST EXTRAORDINARY CASE

Notes:

1. The variants recorded below are based on a collation of the original serial text of the tale (*Atlantic Monthly*, 1868) and its revised version in *Stories Revived* (1885).

2. In the revised text, the tale is divided into nine sections. Section i begins at 227:1; section ii at 231:15; Section iii at 235:34; section iv at 239:22; section v at 242:28; section vi at 245:18; section vii at 250:21; section viii at 253:6; and section ix at 258:5.

3. The following are the revised forms of proper names. Only the first occurrence of these forms is recorded.

> Mrs. Samuel Mason] Mrs. Augustus Mason
> Mrs. Van Zandt] Mrs. Middlemas
> Dr. Van Zandt] Dr. Middlemas
> Mr. McCarthy] Mr. Masters
> Miss McCarthy] Miss Masters

227:2	a close] and end
5	*Mrs. Samuel Mason] Mrs. Augustus Mason*
7	here, ill] here, so ill
10	and feverish] very feverish
11	hotel chamber] bedroom
24	concluded] made up his mind
29–30	middle-aged ... fashion] middle-aged, fair, stout woman
228:1	still,' she answered. 'It's] still. It's
4	the wish] the simple wish
6–7	I've been living] I have remained
9–10	and your whereabouts] and of your being in this hole
16–17	wardrobe ... equipment] wardrobe, with strange military promiscuities
18	beautiful] om.
19	delicious] contented
22	her appearance] her neat, rich appearance
24	I mean ... dozen] I propose to be very feminine
29	actually] really
32	I've no ... circumstances.] Lord, do you call these circumstances—all these queer things?
33	Mrs. Van Zandt] Mrs. Middlemas
40	an excellent] a remarkable
229:1	Dr. Van Zandt] Dr. Middlemas
12	me] om.
12	to get well] to make me well
13	was meaning] intended
15	fancied] supposed
19–20	fancy you married] suppose that you were married

229:25   hole] *trou*
    29–30   river, and only ... rail] Hudson—only a matter of two hours by rail
    32–3   a dozen years] twenty years
    33   decent] excellent
    37–8   be very dearly cared for.] be 'done for'.
230:5–6   man-servant] servant
    6   an Englishman. He] a highly respectable Englishman, he
    19   in my hands] my property
    24–5   a subject capacity] an infinite opportunity
    27–8   perfume ... good-nature] fragrance of her good manners and good nature
    28   He felt like] He was on the point of
    30   bitter] so much more dismal
    35   to his] over his
    40   way] small
    43   wrappings] coverlets
231:2   cottage of liberal make] commodious villa
    5   considered himself presented] regarded himself as presented
    8   trunk] luggage
    12   kindled] lighted
    18   chamber] apartment
    20   the trouble ... strength] all struggles
    24   greensward] greenery
    26   unresisting] facile
    30   out] om.
    32   physician] man
    32   gentleman] practitioner
    34   a couple of] om.
232:2   young men] new generation
    4–5   an army surgeon] a surgeon in the army
    7   light-haired] fair-haired
    9   said Mrs. Mason] Mrs. Mason replied
    20   fancy] suspect
    29   push] seek
    29   fortune in] fortune—since evidently none was to come to him unsought—in
    31   leave] allow
    32   The adjacent country] This long-settled, almost legendary region
    35   to make ... physician] to feel their pulse and look at each other's tongues
233:1   fallible] quite out of his reckoning
    4   physician only as a good-humoured,] surgeon only as an amusing and
    7   case] condition

233:8	deeply seated] obstinate
9	unflinching] om.
12–13	I should ... constitution] you must have an excellent constitution
14	fallen] sunk
16	that] om.
18	Why, it's obvious] Oh, I know everything
22–4	in tangible ... a man] of what people are supposed to live for—of the motives and interests for the sake of which a man
26	books or ideas] work or play
31	it] this
33	I wish to ... of you] I wish very much I had known about you
36	around] round
36–7	I should ... hue] I never have seen anything so pink
39	from my heart] cordially
41	good-natured] philanthropic
43–234:2	resolute ... fine woman] practical and successful,' said Ferdinand, 'that it's quite a surprise to find her philanthropic. She's a dear woman
234:11–12	Mason's ... enforcement] Mason's impression that he was now very happy needed no enforcement
13	these were] these quiet, irresponsible days were
13	days] om.
14	resolved] determined
14–15	to his empressions,—utterly] to mere convalescence, utterly
15–17	a sufficient ... besides] excuse enough for his simply floating with the tide; but Mason had other reasons for idleness
17	the past] om.
21	I ever heard of] of Volunteers
24	innermost] secret
25	person] being
28	happen which] happen (some chance for distinction, some augmentation of honour), which
30	mortification,] regret
33–4	almost ... brass] for making a lasting mark
35–6	in the ... occupations] in the loathsome leisure of winter-quarters
38	fell sick] was laid up
41	worked] laboured
43	obstruction or diversion] hindrance or criticism
235:4–5	forms of ... or cousin] branches of science attached to being somebody's son, brother or cousin

235:9–10	was to ... he would] should extract some instruction from his idleness itself, and should probably
12–13	dawning of ... attachment] exercise of the domestic affections
16	vast] large
17	and of] and
22	happiness] that province
23	I take it that] om.
24–5	deliberately ... upon] regularly determined to be very fond of
27	rich] om.
27–8	liberal ... guest] liberal yet not exaggerated estimate of her guest
31–3	profoundly ... sphere] completely aware that he stopped thinking about it, as one ceases to think of an article of faith
35	evoked] produced
39–40	aggravation ... journey] fatigue and fever which inevitably followed his journey
236:2	gracious] conciliatory
2	conclusion] perception
4	neither ... beautiful] a lovely being
8	and] om.
10–11	she being ... property] her mother's property having been settled on the girl
14	no less than three] sundry
17	twenty-six] twenty-five
18–19	*au mieux* with her bankers] conscious of good investments
20–1	declared ... frankness] remarked
24	Caroline is no sentimentalist] Caroline isn't clinging or dependent
25	discerning] discriminating
29–34	A capital ... do with it] I never interfere with her life. She has it quite in her own hands. My position is little more than an affectionate curiosity as to what she will do with it
39	excellent] nice
41	loved] liked
42	She's ... conciliating] She has a very nice way of arranging such matters
43–237:1	half ... offence] so many admirers with so few scenes of violence
237:2	a world of] infinite
3	what not] her little fortune
4	suitors] *prétendants*
7	take for granted] suppose
8	a sentimentalist] one of the yearning sort

237:11	looks] family
13	close] end
16	charming girl. You] civilised woman; you
19	reassured] easy in your mind
22	It takes ... in love] To fall in love a man must be all there, and you see I am not
28	habitual] usual
30	a truly exquisite pleasure] an immense satisfaction
37–8	comfortable drives] passive wanderings
38	Mason] he
238:4	time] the summer
6	elegant] cultivated
9	contemplated] watched
11	provoke] encourage
13	be dressed] be charmingly dressed
13	in fresh crisp muslin] om.
14–15	felicitous ... things] felicitous: these things for her had long since become mechanical
19	the simple ... contours] the agreeable combination of colour and outline
21–2	beauty ... poetry] quality, and not a conventional, superficial perfection
23	and neither ... reverse] and had an appearance of activity
26–7	broad ... that] rather high and very clear, and her eyes were of that pure sea-green which
29	rising] crest
29	colour] hue
31	charms enough] items numerous enough
38	valued] delighted in
40	occupations] occupation
42	this] om.
43	of our] om.
239:1–2	I find you ... occasion] You don't tire me at all,' Miss Hofmann had been good enough to reply on this occasion
7–8	he was ... true] she continued to look after him. But she stuck
11	I'm] me
14	well-meaning] rather amiable
18–19	informal] easy to meet
20	easily] om.
21	confident] natural, familiar
22	Miss Hofmann] she
29–30	discourse infinite melody] wake up the echoes of Schubert and Mendelssohn
32	single] om.
38–9	Mason ... to sleep] Ferdinand fell into a doze
240:4–5	unnatural ... disagreeable] odd—almost unnatural

240:5–6	looked round ... Horace Knight] looking round, showed the face of Horace Knight
15	medicine] pathology
17	intelligence ... of it] handling of his ailments
19	affirm] say
19	felt more comfortable] had a much higher standard
20–3	push the ... was worse] inquire too closely, because he had a sickening apprehension that he should discover that in one or two important particulars he was not what he should be
25–6	sensible of ... I then] difficult. So long as I was in that beastly hotel I
32	a most ridiculous] a ridiculous
33	a good] om.
35	intend to spend] think of spending
37	I'm unable to answer you.] How can I tell you?
41	all thoughts] the very name
43	health ... pleasure] recuperation and enjoyment
241:1	pleasure, pleasure] enjoyment, enjoyment
2	pleasure,' said] enjoyment,' returned
2	she] it
3	her] it
4	she] it
12	O, nonsense] Ah, gammon
13	nonsense] gammon
15–17	you're ... mortals] you are fonder of being sick than of being sound, and that you're not fit company for reasonable mortals
19	step] peg
20	scruples and doubts] questions and considerations
21	the] a
21–2	to be perfectly indifferent] not trouble your head
27	physician] medical adviser
28	physician] medical adviser
29	burdening] bothering
30	fancies] whims
36	listen] will try
41	quite ... brow] more stern and a little fold appeared in his forehead
43–242:1	his companion's smile] his companion gave a vague, scarcely audible, rather foolish, laugh
242:3	smiling] laughing
4	you,' said Knight, half smiling too.] you; I shall think you did it on purpose.'
5	Mason broke into a laugh.] om.
6	that] your hating me
7	fellow] creature

242:9   obstinate patients] patients who are so mysterious
    10   burst ... which] began to laugh louder, and
    12   said Knight] Knight remarked
    13   Nay, laugh] Laugh
    13   cried] exclaimed
    22–3   his features ... good-looking] it, wondering considerably if there was anything in it
    23   conclude] say to himself
    33   descent] step
    33–4   an ... question] not encouraging
    36   being witness of] watching
    42   every inch] precisely
243:5–6   Miss Hofmann ... she said] 'I wish very much you might come,' the girl said
    12   Mason] Mason, not very brilliantly
    15   impression] suspicion
    17   asked Ferdinand] Ferdinand inquired
    20   Ferdinand shook his head.] 'The dance of death!' Mason murmured.
    23   said Mrs. Mason] Mrs. Mason rejoined
    25   and my roses] my artificial roses
    31   three buttons] a succession of buttons
    35   full white drapery] white cloak
244:16   I'm ill] I am very ill
    19   had] have
    21   had] have
    24   had] have
    28   I'm certainly] I certainly am
    30   effectually banished sleep] given me a fever
    34   danced] jumped about a little
    39   talking about it] crowding round her
    40   her,' ... went off.'] her before she went off,' Mason said.
    41   said Knight] Knight went on
    43   suppose,' said Ferdinand.] suppose.'
245:8   and] om.
    8   She's solid] She's a capital one to go
    8–9   as a physician] rather professionally
    11–12   frankly ... eloquence] himself, at this unexpected flight
    16   fancy,' he said.] fancy.'
    17   Of course I am] In my private capacity
    19   nor] or
    23   vigorous ... herself] swift and sure as she herself
    31   alone] without us fellows
    32   forty-five] fifty-five
    33   forty-five] fifty-five
    33   interesting women] sympathetic
    35   about] around

245:37   takes] will take
    39   In fine Mason was in love] In a word, Mason began to romance to himself exactly as if he had been in love, and there is no manner of doubt that he was
    40   patient] considerate
    41   and] om.
246:1   anything] everything
    9   high resolves] vigilance
    21   were] fell from their lips
    22   to a space] a tract
    23   ground] land
    25   rosy yellow] an exquisite tone
    33   said] exclaimed
247:3   Mr. McCarthy] Mr. Masters
    12   thither] there
    15   with] and there are
    21   members] extremities
    25   river] Hudson
    26   great] extreme
    29   seaward-shifting waters] noble river
    41   After ... moments] Presently
248:3   think,' said he, 'that that little] think that that dirty little
    9   you] om.
    15   Will] Shall
    18   some moment] a certain time
    32   extended] poked out
    34   graceless *brusquerie*] unexpected violence
    36   fancied] supposed
249:1   young] om.
    5   shawl] mantilla
    12   franker] richer
    14   slightly] a good deal
    16   temptation] temptations
    19   half] rather
    20   Half what] Rather what
    21   Half ungrateful] Rather ungrateful
    26   not] very far from being
    31   discerned] perceived
    35   stands in ... charity] tries to be human and charitable
    38   shawl] mantle
    40   might] sought to
250:3   great] superior
    5   The moments] Such moments as these
    8   chill ... consequence,] chill, or fit, or spasm, in consequence
    10   like children] like very small children
    12   delicate] refined

250:14–15   this ... taken] he had understood her
      19   surrendered at discretion] capitulated on his own terms
      24   adventure] effort the day before
      27   succumbed] let himself go
      29–30   delayed and broken projects] deferred and shattered
                visions
      33   attended] nursed
      41–2   ceased ... fallen] failed to bring him back to his old
                point: it stopped many degrees short of that
      42   twice] doubly
251:2   newly contracted] fresh
      5–6   In order ... house of] Ferdinand learned that, in order to
                make the house as quiet as possible, Miss Hofmann had
                gone to stay with
      12   said] exclaimed
      13   disagreeable] repugnant
      14   at the dinner hour] just in time for this repast
      15   was] happened then to be
      26   forbidden him] told him—in that inaudible way—not
      28–9   lost none ... ever] not become any less attractive
      30   they were bound] the ripe cluster of her charms was held
      32   observe ... assured] observe; and some reflections to which
                Mrs. Mason treated him in a day or two persuaded
      36   is feeling unwell. I've] was going to be ill. Pray, is your
                sickness catching? I have
      36   simple and gentle] mild and vague
      37   fright,—a fright] fright—but a fright
252:1–2   impression,' she said, 'George Stapleton] impression that
                George Stapleton
      8   unworthy] unlikely
      9   of Miss Hofmann] to be cared for by Miss Hofmann
      20   and] om.
      21   Would] Should
      22   work] measure his mind with something
      22–3   came in, radiant ... millinery] came home with that air
                of relief and reaction which people wear on emerging
                from their devotions
      25   led to] led on to
      27   all] om.
      29–253:5 Quickened by her ... a responsive passion.] Mason talked
                with her for half-an-hour, and told himself afterwards
                that he had 'swaggered' a good deal. But she appeared
                to take his swagger very seriously; she drew him out so!
253:12–13   principles, he ... of honour] meditation, he was a highly
                civilised being
      25   during Mason's fever] at the time of Mason's relapse
      29   as] om.

253:30   that she] she
   33   secret,' she said, 'if] secret. If
   35   peremptorily] with the least bit of irritation
   35   I give it up] I can't guess
   41   asked] inquired
254:1–2   with ... irony] trying to smile
   6–7   offers, to ... Dr. Knight.] offers to cast her lot at last with
          a country doctor!
   8   had] om.
   9–10   volition ... hammer-blow] he made a successful effort to
          recover it
   12   if struck] if she had been struck
   14   fancied] supposed
   17   soul] word
   18   his ... self-possession] the manner in which his friends
          had kept their secret
   23   Heaven] goodness
   24   Ferdinand said nothing.] om.
   25   ask,' ... 'whether] ask whether
   31   September] October
   35   eyes] face
   41   slackened] loosened
255:5–6   beautiful eyes. Now-a-days] a lovely figure. I had then!
          Nowadays
   10   Ferdinand, with the same laugh] Ferdinand
   12   a soldier for nothing. He] in the army for nothing; he
   13   a heavy blow] a blow as sharp as a sabre-cut
   13   man] soldier
   15–16 offered ... vocabulary] that occur to a man who finds he
          has been living in a fool's paradise
   18–19 esteemed but] esteemed and liked, but
   19   loath] reluctant
   25   been a genuine lover] come to the point
   28   stern] very tonic
   33   met] should meet
   39–40 skirts ... stopped] skirt, stopped
   42   weary] tired
256:1   Miss Hofmann ... head.] 'So they say.'
   4–5   smiling, and ... cake] patting her skirt softly with her
          whip
   10   pursued] went on
   19–20 thrown away, Miss Hofmann] wasted, sacrificed
   24–5   make his compliments] offer his felicitations
   28   it] my point
   29   the autumn] October
   34   cry out] call attention to it
   37   spirits. He] spirits—he

256:38	deferential languor as before] look of reluctant incapacity as before
257:5	would] should
9	she] her
10	supremely] exceedingly
16	magnificent] liberal
17	imagination] imagination and sympathy
18–19	with ... hyper-verities] with all the things people might do, as well as those they had already done or not done
20–3	the most ... nephew;] enthusiasm, almost with violence. Mrs. Mason planned out a residence in Europe for her nephew,
28	who should take] who, taking
28	and] should
29	accessible ... East] object of interest in the ancient and modern world
31	Continental] foreign
32	broad] om.
35	say twice] two or three times
38	the court attached] the court
39	quite] om.
39	sensible] enlightened
40	and] om.
42	grim] impudent
42	Nay, she] She
43	cleverest] most brilliant
43	young men] the new generation
258:2	very innocently] inadvertently
7–8	distinguished good grace] distinguished urbanity
11	going thither] being present
17	most] om.
21–2	pick and ... we might] confine itself to the essential. If I had had more room to turn round I should
32	Mason ... across.] om.
33–5	full-robed ... splendid] shining like a queen and fronted by a semicircle of half-a-dozen men
36	*bouillonnement*] vaporous surge
36	beautiful] white
38	half a dozen] om.
39–40	most gracious] friendliest
40	gracious] friendly
41	half] om.
41	itself] om.
41	around] round
259:1	a hundred ... women] all the company
2	upon] at
6	girls] persons

259:8–10   had him ... or wit] conducted him from room to room and presented to him the people of importance as if he had been a prince

11–12   others ... the best] others, doubtless, he made a sufficiently good

13–14   I am ... obliged] He was obliged, however,

14   that] om.

21   Miss McCarthy] Miss Masters

26   sternly] with much decision

27–8   horribly,' he added shrewdly] fearfully,' he added, candidly

29   You're *not* ... Mason] You are looking as fresh as a rose, Colonel Mason

31   madam,] om.

35–6   play at 'feeling well',] go through the forms of returning vitality

36–7   let disease have its way] broke down altogether

38   would] should

40   what he called] om.

41   heard him out] listened to him

260:2   altered his will] made certain alterations in his will

15   The poor woman felt] It seemed to the poor woman

16   and spent] and she spent

18   had said] had said to her

20   getting well.' On the] getting well. Everything was going on as it ought—up to that Sunday I dined at your aunt's. Then, suddenly, he went straight back. It's very puzzling.' On the

22   little] om.

33   said Mason ... eyes] Mason answered, looking at her steadily

34   Sit] Please sit

261:12   give] have given

12   have been] be

13–14   wedding ... September] nuptials were of course not deferred; they took place in October

15–16   thoughtful ... certainly] thoughtful; but this certainly was

A LIGHT MAN

Notes:

1. The variants recorded below are based on a collation of the original serial text of the tale (*Galaxy*, 1869) and its two revised versions in *Stories by American Authors* (1884)—hereinafter mentioned as *SBAA*—and *Stories Revived* (1885)—hereinafter mentioned as *SR*.

According to the *Bibliography* (p. 207), the *Galaxy* pages James used as his copy to revise the tale for *SBAA* have been preserved in the Scribner Archive. I had hoped to examine the manuscript revision but, unfortunately, the pages could not be located in the Scribner Collection at the Princeton University Library, the major repository of the Scribner papers. Apparently, the contents of the room at Scribner's, which contained a copy of every item published by the firm, were dispersed and are now not easy to locate.

2. The following, in *SR*, is the revised form of a proper name. Only the first occurrence of this form in that text is recorded.

        A. L.] Antoinette   SR

    A Light Woman.—Browning's Men and Women SBAA, SR

346:3	preserve] stick to SBAA, SR
4	break] drop SBAA, SR
5	is] *is* SR
13–14	set bravely to work] do something SBAA, SR
17	obstructions] impediments SR
27	we] I SBAA, SR
29	prettiness] charm SBAA, SR
347:1	and indeed] nor indeed SR
3	was never] never was SR
10	planted] deposited SBAA, SR
11–12	my heart ... ecstatic] I feel a kind of SBAA, SR
13	peccadilloes] little sins SBAA, SR
18	the old] an old SBAA, SR
21–2	grasp of my hand.] welcome you had a right to expect from me! SBAA, SR
22	to rap ... you like] as cordial as you please SBAA, SR
25–6	Mr. Fredrick Sloane ... subject] Mr. Sloane—we having taken the liberty of making you the topic SBAA, SR
27	Mr. Sloane] Frederick Sloane SBAA, SR
28	predestined] engaged SBAA, SR
29–30	esteem it a ... devoted head] like you very much to spend a month with him. He is an excellent host, or I shouldn't be here myself SBAA, SR
35–41	him—a perfect ... more than ever,] him. He is a very

strange old fellow, but you will like him. Whether or no you come for his sake, come for mine. Yours always, SBAA, SR

348:1   perfectly] remarkably SBAA, SR

2   regards] regard SBAA, SR

7–9   better can I do ... invoke the fates] can I do that is better? Speaking sordidly, I shall obtain food and lodging while I look about me SBAA, SR

9   basis] base SBAA, SR

10   delicious] enchanting SBAA, SR

11   a delicious] an enchanting SBAA, SR

11   a month's stay] to stay a month SBAA, SR

14–15   my incomparable] the virtuous SBAA, SR

20   affectionate soul] amiable disposition SBAA, SR

20–2   I made hardly ... his hands.] om. SBAA, SR

24–5   infuse a ... into the body] keep their bodies fair and fresh SBAA, SR

28   aspiring rectitude] straightness SBAA, SR

29   tower] spire SBAA, SR

30   formidable] alarming SBAA, SR

31–2   quite ... physiognomy.] altered me—*sehr!* SBAA, SR

32   was] were SBAA, SR

34   all answer] an answer SBAA, SR

36   trunk] luggage SBAA, SR

38   vast] big SBAA, SR

40–1   lake side] margin of this expanse SBAA, SR

43–349:1   unspotted beauty ... fraternal hills] shining vagueness, as if it were tired of making, all day, a million little eyes at the great stupid hills SBAA, SR

349:2–4   in which ... satisfaction] and in this interval Theodore made his position a little more clear SBAA, SR

4   old, widowed and rich] a rich old widower SBAA, SR

6–7   its numerical formula] anything definite about that SBAA, SR

7   a round million] about a million SBAA, SR

8   abroad ... things;] in Europe, and in the 'great world;' SBAA, SR

10   diplomat] diplomatist SBAA, SR

11   taken] lured SBAA, SR

12   serve as ... friend] mend his pens for him SBAA, SR

15   this ... existence] these *souvenirs intimes* SBAA, SR

16   boy] youth SBAA, SR

18   all] many other SBAA, SR

18   become ... immoral] have ceased to address themselves *virginibus puerisque* SBAA, SR

19–20   a jumble of ... excellent] a medley of gold and tinsel, of bad taste and SBAA, SR

349:24 room for] room arranged for SBAA, SR
29–30 landscape ... mellow glory] landscape, a fine Gains-borough, full of the complicated harmonies SBAA, SR
30–1 fantastic ... *chinoiseries*] row of bronzes of the Renais-sance and potteries of the Orient SBAA, SR
32 a vast] an immense SBAA, SR
37–8 the walls are] the place is SR
39 mutual] om. SBAA, SR
41 uses] makes use of SBAA, SR
350:1 the portentous soberness] certain pedantic tones SBAA, SR
2 and blacks,] blacks SBAA, SR
2–3 rooms of its class] libraries SBAA, SR
3 It's ... study] The apartment is of the feminine gender SBAA, SR
6 lightness, and unpedantic elegance] lightness, it expresses even a certain cynicism SBAA, SR
9 upon] at SBAA, SR
10–11 a worse-favoured human creature] an ugglier little person SBAA, SR
11 then] om. SBAA, SR
12 undersized] diminutive SBAA, SR
13 stature, bent] stature, and bent SBAA, SR
13–16 with years ... pallor] with his seventy years; lean and delicate, moreover, and very highly finished. He is curi-ously pale, with a kind of opaque yellow pallor SBAA, SR
19–20 thick-veined saffron-coloured] thick-veined, bloodless SBAA, SR
21–2 within their ... diamonds] in the battered little setting of their orbits they have the lustre of old sapphires SBAA, SR
24 like parchment] like a piece of parchment SBAA, SR
25 has kept ... hair by] has, apparently, all his teeth, but has muffled his cranium in SBAA, SR
25 has kept ... hair by] has, apparently, all his teeth, but has swathed his cranium in SR
32 lines]line SBAA, SR
32 are delicate] is pure SBAA, SR
33–4 eyes of a ... his lips] oldest eyes I ever saw, and yet they are wonderfully living. He has something remarkably in-sinuating SBAA, SR
36 upon] at SBAA, SR
37–8 the sombre ... 'Good heaven!'] a curiosity which he took no pains to conceal. 'God bless me,' SBAA, SR
40 home] America SBAA, SR
42 aged] weak SBAA, SR

350:42   uses it ... energy] makes it express everything   SBAA, SR

43   dotage, by a long shot.] dotage—oh no!   SBAA, SR

351:1   woefully old man] poor creature   SBAA, SR

1–2   inquiry ... health] inquiry of mine   SBAA, SR

3–4   had but ... left] was quite finished   SBAA, SR

5   live,' he said, 'out] live out   SBAA, SR

5   curiosity.'] curiosity,' he said.   SBAA, SR

6   dying,' I answered, 'from] dying from   SBAA, SR

7–8   was making ... statement] were laughing at him   SBAA, SR

9   know,' ... 'that] know that   SBAA, SR

10   life.'] life,' he remarked, blandly.   SBAA, SR

11   Poor Theodore! at these words he] At these words Theodore   SBAA, SR

15–16   Dear me, Mr. Sloane,' I said, 'don't ask] Don't ask   SBAA, SR

21   Christianism] Christianity   SBAA, SR

23   Catholic countries] pagan lands   SBAA, SR

24–32   'Good, good, good!' ... Mohammedan!'] 'What do you call pagan?' asked Theodore, smiling. I saw the old man, with his hands locked, eyeing me shrewdly, and waiting for my answer. I hesitated a moment, and then I said, 'Everything that makes life tolerable!'   SBAA, SR

33   broke out ... glee] began to laugh till he coughed   SBAA, SR

35–6   in the constitution ... an improvement] and this repast showed me that some of his curiosity is culinary   SBAA, SR

37   paralysis,] om.   SBAA, SR

39   Sweets, and spices,] Sauces and spices   SBAA, SR

42–3   a chamber ... possibly wish] a downy bedroom and a snug little *salon*   SBAA, SR

352:1   ourselves and of ... below] ourselves, of each other, and of the author of the memoirs, down stairs   SBAA, SR

3   told of] descanted upon   SBAA, SR

5   around] round   SBAA, SR

7–9   sagacity of virtue ... say nothing of] discriminations of a conscientious mind, in which criticism is tempered by   SBAA, SR

9   charity. At midnight] charity. Only, it may easily end by acting on one's nerves. At midnight   SBAA, SR

11   formally] rigidly   SBAA, SR

13   Good heaven] Bless my soul   SBAA, SR

16   supremely] remarkably   SBAA, SR

17   air] love   SBAA; air   SR

18   must be] is   SBAA, SR

352:19 hateful, delightful] relaxing SBAA, SR

  20 side, I honestly] side—standing there like a tall inter-rogation-point—I honestly SBAA, SR

  22 real] visible SBAA, SR

  23–7 if I had actually ... in cathedrals] whether I am really a materialist—whether I don't believe something? I told him I would believe anything he liked SBAA, SR

  28–9 know,' ... better.'] know whether you are not worse than Mr. Sloane,' he said. SBAA, SR

  33 bigger] larger SBAA, SR

  35–6 has ... of Voltaire] enjoys Voltaire, though he thinks him superficial SBAA, SR

  38 nicely] prettily SBAA, SR

  39 ministry] church SBAA, SR

  39–40 to lay the ... of science] with his mind full of theology and Tübingen SBAA, SR

  42–3 abortive doubts] sickly questions SBAA, SR

  43 sustenance] answers SBAA, SR

353:2 which] that SBAA, SR

  4 three] om. SBAA, SR

  4–5 whole ten years abroad] long residence in Europe SBAA, SR

  5–7 a little of ... indifference] some of his seriousness, and I just touched him with my profanity SBAA, SR

  9–10 returned to theology] searched the Scriptures once more SBAA, SR

  15 fragment] figment SBAA, SR

  20–1 which preceded ... devotion] that passed before he came to Mr. Sloane is really absolutely edifying SBAA, SR

  25 ill] to the bone SBAA, SR

  33 which] om. SBAA, SR

  36 and worldly dilettante] and dilettante—a worldling if there ever was one SBAA, SR

  39–40 perfectly ... have] can enter into it—his having, under the circumstances, SBAA, SR

  41 Just heaven] *Ce que c'est de nous* SBAA, SR

354:1 *totus, teres, atque rotundus*] on its own terms SBAA, SR

  3 like admonishing him] that I ought to notify him SBAA, SR

  5 Really, as I say, I] However, I SBAA, SR

  7 plain] ugly SR

  8–9 to compromise with his tendencies] not to be too much of a prig SBAA, SR

  11 forbearance] tact SBAA, SR

  15 reluctant] complicated SBAA, SR

  18–20 part; he plays ... flatters—] part; he has to simulate. He has to 'make believe' a little—a good deal; he has to put

	his pride in his pocket and send his conscience to the wash. He has to be accommodating—to listen and pretend and flatter; and he SBAA, SR
354:22–3	dominate ... worse] bully the old man, but I don't think I could humour him. After all, however, it is not a matter of comparative merit SBAA, SR
26	his brother] the other fellow SBAA, SR
26	Theodore is essentially] Theodore, at bottom, is only SBAA, SR
29–30	part then ... delicate fancy] part, therefore, artistically, with spirit, with originality, with all his native refinement SBAA, SR
31–2	as to misconceive ... *belle âme*] as not to appreciate a *nature distinguée* when it SBAA, SR
33	beautiful] charming SBAA, SR
37	understaying my month] going away SBAA, SR
355:7	slothful inaction] beastly laziness SBAA, SR
9	actually] really SBAA, SR
12–13	that I care ... comfort and I] to go in for nothing but present success; and I SBAA, SR
14	acute] om. SBAA, SR
16–17	intelligent ... strong] a clever, accomplished, capable, good-natured fellow, who can do anything if he would only try SBAA, SR
17–20	have a keen ... for Rossini] be rather cultivated, to have latent talents SBAA, SR
22	contemplation of men and women] spectacle of human affairs SBAA, SR
22	them] men and women SBAA, SR
27	hate] detest SBAA, SR
28	love] dote on SBAA, SR
28–30	a large portion ... care for him] it makes a difference to him, his idea that I *am* fond of him SBAA, SR
31	knowledge, my music] culture, my latent talents SBAA, SR
33–6	look me through ... healthy emotion] know me for what I am and let me see they had guessed it. Possibly such a fellow as that might get a 'rise' out of me SBAA, SR
37	bare ... what] bread and butter, what SBAA, SR
38	ten] fifty SBAA, SR
40	no less than twenty-five dollars] a trifling sum SBAA, SR
32	scheme.] plan: SBAA, SR
42–3	deliberately ... marrying money] made up my mind to take a wife—a rich one, *bien entendu* SBAA, SR
43	and utilize] om. SBAA, SR
356:1	superior] good SBAA, SR

356:3	superior] good SBAA, SR
3–4	myself ... gentle] myself kind SBAA, SR
4–5	doubt ... snub] don't think I should even contradict SBAA, SR
6	actually] even SBAA, SR
7–8	It's not ... my riddle] I really think this is my only way SBAA, SR
9	in a certain way] om. SBAA, SR
15	glorious destiny] noble fate SBAA, SR
16–17	past opulence] many dollars SBAA, SR
17	perfect] om. SBAA, SR
18	home] house SBAA, SR
18–19	absolutely ... old house] contact of the highest civilization I have known SBAA, SR
19–20	house *is* delicious] place is of velvet SBAA, SR
21	or I a] or a SBAA, SR
25–6	moonshine] silvery silence SBAA, SR
26–7	darkness ... orb] darkness rolls the brilliant ball SBAA, SR
28–9	around stand ... their glens] round about, the mountains, looking strange and blanched, seem to bare their heads and undrape their shoulders SBAA, SR
33–4	repeatedly explored ... of its shores] indulged in an immense deal of irregular navigation SBAA, SR
36–7	darkening ... greenness] making the water dark and quiet where they hang SBAA, SR
38	does the ... contemplation] looks after the boat and I after the scenery SBAA, SR
39	but] om. SBAA, SR
42–3	I doubt ... flattered man] *Je l'ai bien soigné,* as they say in Paris SBAA, SR
357:2–3	advises him ... deprave him.] dots his *i*'s, crosses his *t*'s, verifies his quotations; while I set traps for that famous 'curiosity'. SBAA, SR
3	is speaking] speaks SBAA, SR
4	power] powers SBAA, SR
5	*nil admirari*] of keeping his countenance SBAA, SR
6	clear outskipped his fancy] made him stare SBAA, SR
7	depravity, it's] corruption, which I spoke of above, it's SBAA, SR
9	downright] real SBAA; positive SR
10	over savoury] very tidy SBAA, SR
14	incurring] bringing on SBAA, SR
15	clearly, I think, as] clearly as SBAA, SR
16–17	round dozen of specimens] good many specimens of it SBAA, SR
19	jumble of virtues] list of foibles SBAA, SR

357:21–2　　generous, I ... charity] generous, and his rebellion against the ugliness of life frequently makes him do kind things SBAA, SR

24　　will] courage　SBAA, SR

26–7　　a human ... lodging for] a single brain to shelter　SBAA, SR

29–30　　went out of the world, and] took herself off and　SBAA, SR

32–3　　still be wearing ... on his sleeve] be able to recognize the touch of it　SBAA, SR

35　　wheels, as ... baby] wheels　SBAA, SR

36　　from his] from the time of his　SBAA, SR

36　　to within fifteen] till about ten　SBAA, SR

38　　hundreds] thousands　SBAA, SR

39　　thousands of dollars] a very large fortune　SBAA, SR

39–40　　a few thousands too many] considerably too much SBAA, SR

42　　but loudly admonished] yet audibly recommended SBAA, SR

358:1　　formed the rudiments] laid the basis　SBAA, SR ·

2　　literature; I can't call it] literature. I can't call him SBAA, SR

3–4　　magnificent, so ... ministrant] magnificent in this respect, so long as he must have his punctuation done by a *nature distinguée*　SBAA, SR

4–8　　become a rich ... Mr. Sloane's life] made up his losses. His turning the screw during those relatively impecunious years represents, I am pretty sure, the only act of resolution of his life　SBAA, SR

18　　regard] care　SBAA, SR

19　　fancied] liked　SBAA, SR

20　　twelve] nine　SBAA, SR

22　　regular] usual　SBAA, SR

23–4　　aggravation ... condition] increase of his ailments SBAA, SR

27　　largely] om.　SBAA, SR

29　　clipped ... intercourse] succeeded in quarrelling　SBAA, SR

30–1　　shown great ... of parasites] had capital fingers for plucking off parasites　SBAA, SR

32　　richly] much　SBAA, SR

33–4　　shrewdness and good sense ... happiness] sharpness and that instinct of self-defence which nature bestows even on the weak, that he has not been despoiled and exploité SBAA, SR

34–5　　they've been a sad lot of] they have all been　SBAA, SR

358:35–6	he's to be ... possessed] something is to be done with him still SBAA, SR
36	you] one SBAA, SR
39	and] om. SBAA, SR
40	fairly ... nose] spilled his pottage SBAA, SR
41–2	were, at ... set of] were mostly very common SBAA, SR
359:1	charmers] pensioners SBAA, SR
4–5	keep our noses ... shoulders] hold our porringers straight SBAA, SR
10	vapidly sentimental] superstitious SBAA, SR
11–13	a thinker ... Theodore's hand] and inquirer, a discoverer. He has not yet discovered that he is a humbug, that Theodore is a prig, and that I am an adventurer SBAA, SR
14	unvarying ... becoming] knowing a rule of conduct for every occasion in life SBAA, SR
15	cramped] skinny SBAA, SR
16	cunning] om. SBAA, SR
19	fancies] imagines SBAA, SR
19	weightiest] most solid SBAA, SR
20	lightest] hollowest SBAA, SR
20	deems] thinks SBAA, SR
23	pure,] om. SBAA, SR
23–4	taken ... step] done anything in time SBAA, SR
24	fancies] believes SBAA, SR
27	and] om. SBAA, SR
27	Stuff and nonsense] Mere vanity SBAA, SR
31	great] om. SBAA, SR
33	me] any one now SBAA, SR
34	timidity] pusillanimity SBAA, SR
36	or wondered, or] nor experimented nor SBAA, SR
38	and his poverty] his empty pockets SBAA, SR
360:5	any] om. SBAA, SR
6–7	is dying to ... and faith] would like very much to extract from me some intimation that there is something under the sun I should like to do SBAA, SR
8	half-malicious] half-malignant SBAA, SR
10	various ... malignity] giving him momentary glimpses of my latent wickedness SBAA, SR
11–12	a long row to hoe] a considerable job SBAA, SR
12–13	forswear his devotion—abjure his admiration] change his mind about me SBAA, SR
14–15	moral ... impart] low moral tone for an eccentricity of genius, and it only imparts SBAA, SR
15	richness of my charms] charm of my intercourse SBAA, SR
17	this lapse of] all these SBAA, SR

360: 18–19   an essential absurdity] a contradiction   SBAA, SR
19   honestly] om.   SBAA, SR
20   They are] It's   SBAA, SR
21–3   diversity, our ... tug of war.] agreeing to differ. for we haven't opposed interests. But if we should *really* clash, the situation would be warm!   SBAA, SR
28   Friend Theodore] My dear Theodore   SBAA; My good Theodore   SR
30   sacred] om.   SBAA, SR
31   common agony!] state of tension.   SBAA, SR
32   toward] towards   SR
34   condemns] disapproves of   SBAA, SR
38   man] reprobate   SBAA, SR
43   fool] ass   SR
361: 2   a fool] an ass   SR
8   a fool] an ass   SR
9   I'm—ah me, *what* am I?] I am simply a student of the art of life.   SBAA, SR
15–16   repaired to his bedside] went in to see him   SBAA, SR
18–19   non-attendance] absence   SBAA, SR
20–1   talked a ... hours more] talked for a while—a good while   SBAA, SR
23   fastidiously] superstitiously   SBAA, SR
25   roundly proclaimed] let him know   SBAA, SR
27   discreetly ... fiction] 'colouring' more or less   SBAA, SR
37   to understay] not to overstay   SBAA, SR
41   fairly] almost   SBAA, SR
43   Here] There   SBAA, SR
362: 1   ago, my ... hardly] ago I was not   SBAA, SR
2   knowing.'] knowing,' Max remarked.   SBAA, SR
6   I feel ... him] it's all I can do not to tell him   SR
8   poor sick old fellow] rotten old carcass   SBAA, SR
8   notion] intention   SBAA, SR
10–11   up some work] for some occupation   SBAA, SR
12   Work! Bah] Occupation? bother   SBAA, SR
12   work] occupation   SBAA, SR
13   afraid,' ... 'that] afraid that   SBAA, SR
16–17   much,' he said, 'that] much that   SBAA, SR
17   love me ... you do] be as fond of me as you are of   SBAA, SR
19   love] fondness   SBAA, SR
19   I'm no lover] I don't deal much in that article   SBAA, SR
20   love your friend] like my secretary   SBAA, SR
22   loves] likes   SBAA, SR
23   loves me, I'm afraid, far] likes me   SBAA, SR
32   amazed] greatly surprised   SBAA, SR

362 : 32	say] add SBAA, SR
32	I was moved] comparably moved SR
33	poor old heart] dilapidated organism SBAA, SR
33–4	horror and longing] sensibility SR
34	I take it ... afraid] He has evidently a mortal fear SBAA, SR
36	indisposition turned out] little turn proved SBAA, SR
39	'charming'] superior SR
41	the exhibition of his caprices] his humours and fancies SBAA; his humours and caprices SR
42–3	to deem it] to regard it as SBAA, SR
363 : 5–6	a ray ... virtues] the redeeming fidelity of the sex SBAA, SR
18–19	a number of delectable] certain long fantastic SBAA, SR
19	on] over SBAA, SR
20	fortunately] but fortunately SBAA, SR
22	the scantiest messages] a dry little message or two SBAA, SR
24–5	Mr. Sloane's disposal] the disposal of my host SBAA, SR
25	devours] clings to SR
27	stand] bear SBAA, SR
27–8	certain ... snubbing] sort of unexpected contradiction SBAA, SR
29–30	impart a flavour ... memoirs] give an unusual tone to our relations, remind him of certain historical characters whom he thinks he resembles SBAA, SR
30	fairly] om. SBAA, SR
31	vastly] very SBAA, SR
32	expounding,] om. SBAA, SR
35	and] om. SBAA, SR
35	and] om. SBAA, SR
38	confound his benevolence] put myself in a bad light SBAA, SR
39	vastly] om. SBAA, SR
40–1	seems actually to look] looks SBAA, SR
41	kind of romantic] om. SBAA, SR
42	Faugh ... it all is] Confound it all; it's a bore SBAA, SR
364 : 4	healthy, unerring,] better temper and better knowledge— his healthy SBAA, SR
5–6	pure ... over mine] well-regulated youth has over me SBAA, SR
8	alone for] is adapted for SBAA, SR
8	holds] has SBAA, SR
12	organism] composition SBAA, SR
12	best] rest SBAA, SR
15	morning] dewy SR
20	bended blue] warm blue air SR

364:22	young] om. SR
22	A. L.] Antoinette SR
23	very frank and fearless] lavish SBAA, SR
25	an out-and-out] a pure SBAA; a fearful SR
26	her eyes] the eyes SR
26–7	look as if ... their lustre] are quite articulate SBAA, SR
27–8	I had got ... of thought] I was growing too pensive SBAA, SR
29	What ... know not] There is something the matter with Theodore SBAA, SR
30	sombre reserve] silent stiffness SBAA, SR
34	darkness of his silence] immensity of his dumbness SBAA, SR
39	widow] Dora SR
40	minister] clergyman SBAA, SR
365:1	truth ... it was] truth, it was a charming epistle SBAA, SR
3	but with ... amplitude] much more than assented SBAA, SR
9	little] other SBAA, SR
10–11	her to ... brother-in-law] her and her little girl to live with the married pair SBAA, SR
11–12	declared ... gainsaid] remarked, as if it were quite settled SBAA, SR
12	It has come] Has it come SBAA, SR
13–14	house. Oh, the precious old fool] house? The shameless old villain SBAA, SR
15	boy] young man SBAA, SR
19	clever widow] young Dora SR
21	*bonhomme*] old man SR
22	poor ... sister)] the *belle capricieuse* SR
22	impolite] uncivil SBAA; exaggerated SR
26	remove ... jurisdiction] protect yourself SBAA, SR
28	rule] thing SBAA, SR
28	most] om. SBAA, SR
30	charming] always brilliant SBAA, SR
32	was] is SBAA, SR
32	perfectly uncalled for] quite too precipitate SR
34	aspect] look SBAA, SR
38–9	mentioned ... thanked] mentioned, thanked SBAA, SR
40	follies ... *haut faits*] bêtises as well as my happy strokes SR
41	keenly exasperated] a good deal vexed SBAA, SR
41–2	poor ... inscrutable] this angel of candour to deal in signs and portents, to look unutterable things SBAA, SR
366:2	boy] fellow SBAA, SR
4	cogitation!] cogitations. SBAA, SR

366 : 5–6	continued solemnity of demeanour] ominous behaviour SBAA, SR
8	any such ... vouchsafed to] the sort of notice that was served on SBAA, SR
10–11	seemed ... uncomfortable] seems to me impossible SBAA, SR
12	Nay] No SBAA, SR
12–13	should ... contrary,] should, on the contrary, feel SBAA, SR
20	that] om. SBAA, SR
20	notion] system SR
20	a favour] a particular favour SBAA, SR
21–3	occupation ... my duties] sort of work was odious to me; I had regularly to break myself in SBAA, SR
23	compromise with a dozen] trample on my SBAA, SR
25	labour is achieved] effort has been made SBAA, SR
26	thrown away] wasted SBAA, SR
31	too great ... my vanity] me too much. I am too conceited, if you like SBAA, SR
37	ugly] beastly SBAA, SR
42–3	listening ... physiognomy] visage as he listened to this, and, I suppose I may add the grimness of mine SBAA, SR
367 : 2	Here are] I will note down here SBAA, SR
3–4	jealous of me] jealous of Maximus Austin SBAA, SR
4	hates me] hates the said Maximus SBAA, SR
12	made his terms with] accommodated himself to SBAA, SR
14	Merciful powers!] Dear me, SBAA, SR
23–4	that it is ... some occupation] I should be obliged to leave him at once, and pick up a subsistence somehow SBAA, SR
28	this I, of course,] this, of course, I SR
30	supreme avowal] trump card SBAA, SR
35	any practical alleviation of it] doing anything for me SBAA, SR
38	into] to SBAA, SR
368 : 3–4	will,' he said, 'made] will, made SR
13–14	the will ... Theodore's favour] he had left everything to his saintly secretary SBAA, SR
14–15	sprang erect] popped up SBAA, SR
15	an ace] a hair's-breadth SBAA, SR
16	casting] stuffing SBAA, SR
18	replaced ... secretary] put the paper back into the bureau SBAA, SR
32	odd contingency] chance SBAA, SR
43	mend] rise SBAA, SR

369:1　　　　weighty] horrid　SBAA, SR
　　16　　　　removed it,] taken it out　SBAA, SR
　　24　　　　ruptured] violated　SBAA, SR
　　28　　　　you,' I said, 'to] you to　SBAA, SR
　　28　　　　papers.'] papers,' I said.　SBAA, SR
　　29　　　　Max] Maximus　SBAA, SR
　　30　　　　know, however, that] know that　SBAA, SR
　　31　　　　up some ... own making,] for some pages of notes which
　　　　　　　I have made myself and　SBAA, SR
　　33　　　　Theodore] *mon vieux*　SR
　　36　　　　a splendid furious] an extraordinary　SBAA, SR
　　40　　　　think,' he said, 'that I] think I　SBAA, SR
　　40　　　　thing.'] thing,' he said.　SBAA, SR
370:1　　　　simply in one] simply into one　SBAA, SR
　　2–3　　　papers ... taken it up.] papers.　SBAA, SR
　　4　　　　said] remarked　SBAA; said　SR
　　11　　　　said] exclaimed　SR
　　13–14　　a sombre paleness] plain white　SBAA, SR
　　15　　　　me. I wished] me, and I wished　SBAA, SR
　　15–16　　commission,' I rejoined, 'to] commission to　SBAA, SR
　　17　　　　superbly] very grandly　SBAA, SR
　　17　　　　said] remarked　SR
　　19–20　　the remote ... blue] his cold, detached　SBAA, SR
　　20–21　　property,' I cried. 'You're] property! You are　SBAA, SR
　　21　　　　up] om.　SBAA, SR
　　25　　　　refolded it] smoothed it together　SBAA, SR
　　26　　　　asked] inquired　SBAA, SR
　　30　　　　comply] do what he asked you　SBAA, SR
　　38　　　　No,' ... 'you'll] No, I have an idea you will　SR
　　39–371:1　'Upon my ... but indifference.] 'You are very bitter,' I
　　　　　　　said, sharply enough. 'No, I am perfectly indifferent.
　　　　　　　SBAA, SR
371:4　　　　Farewell] Good-bye　SBAA, SR
　　5　　　　Farewell] Good-bye　SBAA, SR
　　7–8　　　away ... into tears] away; his voice was trembling—there
　　　　　　　were tears in it　SBAA, SR
　　11　　　　see it] see what I feel　SBAA, SR
　　14–15　　These tears are tears] I could easily shed tears　SBAA,
　　　　　　　SR
　　17–18　　burying ... handkerchief] covering his face with his
　　　　　　　hands　SBAA, SR
　　19　　　　sake, Theodore,' I said, 'stick] sake, stick　SBAA, SR
　　19　　　　joy.'] joy!' I exclaimed.　SBAA, SR
　　23　　　　as far] so far　SR
　　26　　　　loved] cared for　SBAA, SR
　　27　　　　your incomparable gifts] something you have about you
　　　　　　　that always takes me so　SBAA, SR

28	prospects] prospect SBAA, SR
29	them] it SBAA, SR
30	they were] it was SBAA, SR
33	I loved you] you fascinated me SBAA, SR
35–6	and longing to ... in my heart] you would see that what you were doing was not fair. But if you have seen it, it has made no difference with you SBAA, SR
38	extraordinary foibles] nasty little nature SBAA, SR
372:2	that such] this SBAA, SR
5	off the track] beside the mark SBAA, SR
6	loved me. If ... me still] were such a friend of mine; if so, you ought to be one still SBAA, SR
6	for my virtue;] to my fine sentiments you attached yourself, SBAA, SR
9	love you] take one's friendship so seriously SBAA, SR
10	the feeling,] the feeling of affection SBAA, SR
10–11	me, love] me it SBAA, SR
14–15	silent; but ... frown] silent, but he looked quite sick SBAA, SR
15	actually seems] appears SBAA, SR
16–17	clearing ... be on] clearing-up oughtn't one to be on rather SR
17	you] you? SR
18	faculties] parts SBAA, SR
19	society, your talk] society SBAA, SR
20	them] it SBAA, SR
21	while,' said Theodore, 'understood] while understood SBAA, SR
22	little?'] little?' said Theodore. SBAA, SR
24	want of ... myself] my having kept anything back SBAA, SR
25	Well, Theodore, I] Well, I SBAA, SR
28–9	a vast distance.] the other world—if there be one! SBAA, SR
30	in his] out of his SR
31	believe gentlemen,' ... 'that poor] believe that poor SBAA, SR
32	bed.'] bed!' he cried. SBAA, SR
33–4	Theodore] old boy SBAA, SR
40	half-niece] niece SBAA, SR
43	can't say.] can't say. Yes, I shall wait for Miss Meredith. SBAA, SR

APPENDIX I
Note about the Text in *Stories Revived*

[The following unsigned note about the text—probably by James himself —appears in the first volume of all editions of *Stories Revived*.]

NOTICE

As the date of the original publication (for the most part in American magazines) is attached to each of the Tales comprised in these volumes, the reader will see that the greater number appeared for the first time many years ago—that the oldest, indeed, are of an almost venerable age; but it is proper to add that these earlier stories have been in every case minutely revised and corrected—many passages being wholly rewritten. In the matter of revision, in short, they have been very freely handled; some of the proper names have been altered, and in one instance the title of the story. The first and third Tales in the first volume are the only ones first presented in an English periodical (*The English Illustrated Magazine*), all the others (the latest of which is of 1878) saw the light on the other side of the Atlantic. It had come to the writer's knowledge that they were being to some extent 'hunted up', and there seemed to be good reasons for anticipating further research by re-introducing them. He is confident that they have gained, not lost, freshness by the process of re-touching to which they have been subjected.

February 1885.

APPENDIX II

Some Contemporary Notices of James's Early Tales.

[The *Nation* was the first to comment on James's work. The magazine carried a column in which it regularly reviewed selected writings appearing in other magazines of the day. Most of its selections were drawn from the *Atlantic*, the *Galaxy* and the *Review*. The notices in section A below first appeared in this column. Section B reprints excerpts from young William James's letters to young Henry James in which the former discusses the latter's early stories.]

(A) The *Nation* on the Early Tales

... 'A Landscape Painter' is a very charming love-story indeed, written with grace and spirit.

(Vol. ii, Feb. 1, 1866, p. 151.)

'My Friend Bingham' is by Henry James jr., who in this, as in others of the short stories which he writes so well, shows marked skill in analysis of character and a liking for dwelling upon fine shades of feeling. Particularly he seems to like to dwell upon the complexities of feeling which arise when women and men are thrown into relations with each other not of love simple and direct but of passional attraction, which for one or another reason cannot work freely. His stories are always finished works, and apparently the result of study, or, at any rate, of meditation.

(Vol. iv, Feb. 28, 1867, p. 168.)

In 'Poor Richard', as in his other love stories, Mr. Henry James, jr., shows his fondness for handling delicate threads of feelings and motives in the intricate web of character. We find a good example of his patience and perhaps over-refinement of thought in depicting his personages in the passage where the three men find themselves together with Miss Whittaker, and her rustic lover, a fierce and moody man, sits by while she converses with the others. Whether or not we admit it probable that Richard could have entertained a doubt as to his inferiority, we are at any rate ready to admit that in giving himself an answer to his question he reasoned closely:

> Richard sat by, wondering, in splenetic amazement, whether he was an ignorant boor or whether they were only a brace of ignorant snobs. He decided correctly enough, in substance, for the former hypothesis. For it seemed to him that Gertrude's consummate accommodation (for as such he viewed it) of her tone and her manner to theirs added prodigiously (so his lover's instinct taught him) to her loveliness and dignity. How magnanimous an impulse on Richard's part was this submission for his sweetheart's sake to a fact damning to his own vanity could have been determined only by one who knew the proportions of that vanity.

We may remark here, as we have named the two writers together [Oliver

Wendell Holmes's *The Guardian Angel* is discussed in the preceding paragraph], that in Mr. James's, as in Dr. Holmes's treatment of women, the influence, the physical influence, of sex is very perceptible; but in Mr. James's stories it is not only refined but subtle—an aroma, as it were; while the better known novelist deals with women, as if he were a materialist.

(Vol. iv, May 30, 1867, p. 432.)

The true poverty of 'Poor Richard' and his probable wretchedness begin to grow plain to the reader of Mr. James's elaborate study of character. But surely Richard, if not too subtle, does talk too lucidly in explication of subtleties. Evidently, however, plenty of a literary conscience and the consequent labour go into Mr. James's novel, and we dissent with diffidence.

(Vol. iv, June 27, 1867, p. 516.)

... Mr. Henry James, jr., writes 'The Romance of Some [sic.] Old Clothes', a tantalizing story which, when the end turns out trivial, is seen to be trivial altogether.

A story of a very different class is that one of Mr. James's which is finished in the February *Galaxy*. 'The Story of a Masterpiece' is very well thought out, and is, so far as we remember, the best of Mr. James's. Within the somewhat narrow limits to which he confines himself, Mr. James is, we think, the best writer of short stories in America. He is never commonplace, never writes without knowing what he wants to do, and never has an incident or a character that is not in some way necessary to the production of such effects as he aims at. By-and-by, no doubt, he will write of something besides love, will leave off subtly analyzing flirtations. In the tale of which we speak, a man in love with a woman, who is probably all she should be—to use a common phrase—but perhaps not all she might be, learns, on the sight of a portrait, painted with insight by an old lover of hers, the woman's essential worthlessness. It is a good idea and, as we have said, well worked out.

(Vol. vi, Jan. 30, 1868, p. 94.)

Mr. Henry James, jr., furnishes the good thing of this month's *Galaxy* in a little story which may be read with the satisfaction which one gets from any carefully finished work, slight work or weightier, of a thoughtful and clever writer. 'A Problem', he calls it, and the question proposed for consideration is the not unfamiliar but not easy one. How far do prophecies—prophecies of events in which human beings are actors— tend to fulfil themselves? The mode of presentation adopted is to relate some passages in the life of a young married couple who both have had dealings with fortune-tellers. One prediction partially fails; but it has had the effect of preparing the minds of Emma and David to pay a somewhat unusual attention to such matters and to think there may possibly be some power of prevision in predictors. Then come to light two prophecies of a sort quite capable of fascinating understandings not very solid, and of a sort, too, to breed troubles between man and wife. The case is well managed; but perhaps the picture, suggested rather than fully delineated, of the honeymoon happiness of a commonplace young pair is as skilfully done and as pleasant as anything else in the story. 'A Problem' may not be spoken of as showing, not so forcibly as some of Mr. James's other stories, but still very well, its author's principal powers as a story-maker and as showing them disjoined from a certain defect or fault that we, for our part, find in him. His subtlety in the dissection of motive is to be seen in it; and also there is present in its usual proportion his power to set before us, for inspection if not for action, a real person; but there is less of an enveloping atmosphere of what, for want of a more accurate term—in our inability to find a term nearly accurate —we call his voluptuousness. Women we have with us always in his stories; and almost always, we believe, his women appear in their strictly female aspect, in the aspect which they wear to the curious, somewhat puzzled, not very-much-admiring, much-interested young male of the species. It is, of course, easy to see how strong a temptation addresses itself to the artistic side of a story-maker's nature to deal with love and lovers.

(Vol. vi, May 28, 1868, p. 434.)

(B) William James on Henry James

Both stories ['The Story of a Masterpiece' and 'The Romance of Certain Old Clothes'] show a certain neatness and airy grace of touch which is characteristic of your productions (I suppose you want to hear in an unvarnished manner what is exactly the impression they make on me). And both show a greater suppleness and freedom of movement in the composition; although the first was unsympathetic to me from being one of those male *vs.* female subjects you have so often treated, and besides there was something cold about it, a want of heartiness or unction. It seems to me that a story must have rare picturesque elements of some sort, or much action, to compensate for the absence of heartiness, and the elements of yours were those of everyday life. It can also escape by the exceeding 'keen'ness of its analysis and thoroughness of its treatment, as in some of Balzac's (but even there the result is disagreeable, if valuable); but in yours the moral action was very lightly touched, and rather indicated than exhibited. I fancy this rather dainty and disdainful treatment of yours comes from a wholesome dread of being sloppy and gushing and over-abounding in power of expression, like the most of your rivals in the *Atlantic* ... and that is excellent, in fact it is the instinct of truth against humbug and twaddle, and when it governs the treatment of a rich material it produces first class works. But the material in your stories (except 'Poor Richard') has been *thin* (and even in P. R., relatively to its length), so that they give a certain impression of the author clinging to his gentlemanliness though all else be lost, and dying happy provided it be *sans déroger*. That, to be sure, is expressed rather violently, but ... I feel something of a ... want of blood in your stories, as if you did not fully fit them, and I tell you so because I think the same thing would strike you if you read them as the work of another.... If you see what I mean perhaps it may put you on the track of some useful discovery about yourself, which is my excuse for talking to you thus unreservedly. So far I think 'Poor Richard' the best of your stories because there is warmth in the material, and I should have read it and enjoyed it very much indeed had I met it anywhere. The story of 'Old Clothes' is in a different tone from any of yours, seems to have been written with the mind more unbent and careless, is very pleasantly done, but is, as the *Nation* said, 'trifling' for you....

I have uttered this long rigmarole in a dogmatical manner, as one speaks to himself, but of course you will use it merely as a mass to react against in your own way, so that it may serve you some good purpose. It must be almost impossible to get anyone's real, whole feeling about what one has written. I wish I could say it *viva voce*. If I were you I'd select some particular problem, literary or historical, to study on. There's no comfort to the mind like having some special task, and then you could write stories by the way for pleasure and profit. I don't suppose *your literarisches Selbstgefühl* suffers from what I have said; for I really think my taste is rather incompetent in these matters, and as beforesaid, only offer these remarks as the impressions of an individual for you to philosophize upon yourself.

*   *   *

I have got your last *Atlantic* story ('Extraordinary Case'), and read it with much satisfaction. It makes me think I may have partly misunderstood your aim heretofore, and that one of the objects you had had in view has been to give an impression like that we often get of people in life: Their orbits come out of space and lay themselves for a short time along ours, and then off they whirl again into the unknown, leaving us with little more than an impression of their reality and a feeling of baffled curiosity as to the mystery of the beginning and end of their being, and of the intimate character of that segment of it which we have seen. Am I right in guessing that you had a conscious intention of this sort here?... You seem to acknowledge that you can't exhaust any character's feelings or thoughts by an articulate displaying of them. You shrink from the attempt to drag them all reeking and dripping and raw upon the stage, which most writers make and fail in. You expressly restrict yourself, accordingly, to showing a few external acts and speeches, and by the magic of your art making the reader *feel* back of these the existence of a body of being of which these are casual features. You wish to suggest a mysterious fullness which you do not lead your reader through. It seems to me this is a very legitimate method, and has a great effect when it succeeds.... Only it must succeed. The gushing system is better to fail in, since that admits of a warmth of feeling and generosity of intention that may reconcile the reader.... Your style grows easier, firmer and more concise as you go on writing. The tendency to return on an idea and over-refine it, becomes obsolete,—you hit it the first lick now. The face of the whole story is bright and sparkling, no dead places, and on the whole the scepticism and, as some people would say, impudence implied in your giving a story which is no story at all, is not only a rather *gentlemanly* thing, but has a deep justification in nature, for we know the beginning and end of nothing. Still, while granting your success here, I must say that I think the thorough and passionate conception of a story is the highest, as of course you think yourself.

*MS. Letters in the Collection of
the James Family Papers*